Out of the turbulence of 11th century ~~~~
comes a magnificent heroine!

GREAT MARIA

The young daughter of a fifth-rate Norman baron, Maria is married by her powerless, futile father to a young knight, Richard. The unscrupulous, determined Richard wants Maria's father's castle—what he gets is an awakening woman, a passionate partner. From the start, their tumultuous feelings for each other match the dangerous, exciting, violent world they inhabit and hope to dominate. Together they make love and children, war and conquest, a marriage and a kingdom, yet . . .

GREAT MARIA

says *The Boston Globe*, is "as immediate as today's newspaper . . . a rousing adventure story, no dainty tale of bards and chivalry . . . it focuses so brilliantly on just a few central characters (that) they really live."

ABOUT THE AUTHOR

Cecelia Holland was born in Nevada on New Year's Eve, 1943, was raised in New Jersey, and now lives in California. Her earlier novels are *The Firedrake* (1966), *Rakóssy* (1967), *The Kings in Winter* (1968), *Until the Sun Falls* (1969), *Antichrist* (1970), *The Earl* (1971), and *The Death of Attila* (1973).

GREAT MARIA

Cecelia Holland

WARNER BOOKS

A Warner Communications Company

WARNER BOOKS EDITION
First Printing: December, 1975

Library of Congress Catalog Card Number: 74-8551

This Warner Books Edition is published by
arrangement with Alfred A. Knopf, Inc.

Cover illustration by Tom Hall

Warner Books, Inc., 75 Rockefeller Plaza, New York, N.Y. 10019

Ⓦ A Warner Communications Company

Printed in Canada.

Not associated with Warner Press, Inc. of Anderson, Indiana

For Roberta Pryor

GREAT
MARIA

PART I

VOCATION

I

❧

OTHER PILGRIMS OFFERED SILVER AT THE SHRINE;
Maria brought an armful of wildflowers. She laid the
vivid little blue blossoms down at the foot of the Virgin
and smiled into the statue's face. In the gloom of the
cave, her flowers were the only color. Kneeling, she began
the prayers she had come here to say.

She asked for the rescue of the Holy Sepulcher from
the Saracens, for her father's good health and salvation,
and for her own call into the holy life. The raw stone
floor was damp and uneven beneath her knees. The air
lay icy against her cheeks. She crossed herself. Down the
slot in the rock that led to this cave, her escort talked
and shuffled their feet. She closed her ears to the noise
and willed the womanly stone face above her to soften
and call her into a marriage with God.

The dank air raised gooseflesh on her arms. She started
to shiver. The moment of rapture faded. For a few more
prayers she struggled to bring it back, but the clammy
cold and the sounds of the men outside the cave distracted her. She genuflected to the Virgin and went out the
door into the cool spring sunlight.

The knights and their grazing horses were scattered
over the meadow and down the slope in the sun. Across
the little yard, beneath the beech trees, Elena was standing with the monk who served the shrine. All smiles, the
monk started toward her, and the maid with the heap of
Maria's cloak and hat followed after. She reached Maria's
side, digging into her basket for the gift of money. Maria
pushed the maid's hand with the offering toward the
monk. She hated giving money to God. Elena helped her

11

settle her wide hat on her head and tie the ribbons under her chin.

"God keep your highness," the monk said. His pale fingers counted the purse expertly through the leather and dropped it out of sight in his sleeve. "I hope your gracious and most mighty father is faring well, this spring?"

Maria mumbled some answer and went past him toward her horse. The monk hurried around to hold her bridle for her. She could not meet his eyes. She felt like a fool, shy and stupid. Behind her, Elena spoke smoothly to the monk, assuring him of Robert Strongarm's good health. Elena was no older than Maria but she was able to talk to men, even strangers. Maria gathered her reins.

This year her father had sent only six knights with her, keeping back the rest for some other purpose. They were lining up at the far end of the meadow, next to the road, and she nudged her horse toward them. She knew none of the knights' names; she saw them only in groups, all doing the same thing. While they arranged themselves around her, she looked up at the steep hillside above the cave. Hermits lived up there, safe from the world, close to God. On her mule Elena rode into their midst. The straw basket hooked on her arm was full of apples for their dinner. Side by side, the two girls rode out of the yard.

The shrine was in the hill country north of Maria's castle, and their way home led them over the steep little hills, half-covered with brush. Occasionally, in the west, the sunlight flashed on the sea. Elena got out the apples, gave two to Maria, and scrubbed one on her sleeve to a hot shine. The mailed coats of the knights around them jingled softly. No one talked.

Maria ate one apple and rolled the other up in her sleeve. Through the corner of her eye, she studied the young knight on her left. He looked hardly older than she —Maria was fourteen. He was tall and slender, his face pretty as a girl's. His helmet covered his head. She wondered what color his hair was. Beside her, Elena was munching through her second apple. Perhaps this boy was Elena's knight—she had hinted that someone highborn loved her. Maria thought Elena's ruddy cheeks and wide lips were coarse, but she did have nice hands. A ballad singer once had sung of a knight who fell in love with a glimpse of a maid's white hands.

The flinty road curled along the slope ahead of them, half-hidden in the hairy leaves of the overgrowth. When the bushes blossomed, all these ugly hills would be flooded with red and yellow. She liked to make her year's pilgrimage just at Easter, in hopes of riding through the bloom, but the winter had been dry and she was too early. Now the young knight rode slightly ahead of her. From this angle he was not so pretty. She waited for another glimpse of the sea.

Elena leaned toward her. "Did you see the lay brother at the shrine? He said he would give me his gold cross, the next time we come, if I sit with him in the orchard." She giggled. "Let's go again in the summer, he says there are lots more people there—foreigners, people from all over."

"Why would you want to sit with him?"

"If you had a lover you would understand."

"I will understand now. Tell me."

Elena giggled and turned her head away. Under the cloth of her bodice, her round breasts were like two apples. Maria knew that Elena stuffed her bodice with linen. Maria arched her back, to thrust out her own breasts, and sneaked a glance at her shadow on the ground; she could see no difference.

The warmth of the sun lulled her to sleep. In the early afternoon she woke and talked to Elena. The long day's riding had stiffened her legs and she let her feet dangle. They had climbed up into the hills. Short wind-driven trees curled in among the gray-green bushes and the rocks. Where the boy-knight had been was a man with gray eyes. Maria went back to sleep.

A yell brought her awake with a jolt so sharp she grabbed her horse's mane. The knights were surging up around her. Hoofs battered on the ground. All around her were the heavy mailed bodies of the men and their plunging horses. Somewhere people were screeching. Maria's horse reared, flailing out with its hoofs. An arrow jutted from its neck, fletched with red feathers. She jumped down to the ground. Iron rang on iron. The thrusting

13

flanks and shoulders of horses walled her in. Her mare sank to its knees. Elena's mule was gone. A stallion's wide rump swung toward her, and she dodged its heels. The horse's tail lashed her cheek.

"Elena!"

Ten feet away in the road, Elena lay sprawled on her back. She would be trampled. Maria went toward her. A knight bolted by her, and she heard a voice screaming in the Saracen tongue. The air was heavy with dust. She bent and seized Elena by the arms and heaved her up onto her feet. The girl slumped against her. Maria smelled blood and the crushed herbs in Elena's bodice. She closed her eyes. Prayers rushed through her mind. She opened her eyes again and drew a deep breath. She was Robert Strongarm's daughter and not a coward, to die with her eyes shut. A horse spun around before her. Hoofbeats pounded away. There was a ragged whoop of triumph in her own language. She lifted her head, dazed with being saved. The knights rode laughing around her, shaking each other by the hand.

Maria let Elena slide down to the ground. A knight rode up to her and dismounted. When she started to kneel down beside the maid, he took her arm and held her on her feet.

"Leave her lie, girl. She's dead."

Maria stared stupidly at Elena. Two knights lifted the maid up across her mule's saddle and covered it with her cloak. No one else had died, not even a Saracen. Maria wiped her eyes on her sleeve. The knight beside her took her by the arm to steady her.

The boy-knight was coming toward her. He had taken off his helmet; his hair was bright red. He led a roan stallion, a war horse, and the hand on her elbow tightened: they expected her to ride a war horse.

"No," she said.

The knight beside her said, "Come on—we have to go."

"No. Put Elena on this horse, I will ride the mule."

The redheaded boy and the knight exchanged glances. Their faces matched, and from that and the looks between them, Maria guessed they were brothers. Silently the boy led the roan horse around and put Elena's body

14

across its saddle. Maria bit her lips. Blood stained the worn leather of the mule's saddle and she wiped it away with her sleeve. The gray-eyed knight boosted her into the saddle. They rode away into the barren hills. The boy and the knight talked in low voices beside her. Elena's basket hung from the cantle of her saddle. Maria got out her crucifix and prayed over it.

The boy laughed, bright-voiced. Between her prayers she admired him. She remembered wondering if he were Elena's knight. She began to cry again, more from fright than grief. She realized that she herself would surely die, she felt death before her like a mouth that would swallow her. All the knights were staring at her, and she choked down her tears.

All afternoon they rode over the hills. Just before sundown they came at last to their home valley. For generations the villagers had plowed the fields, and the stretches of land along the river were cut into strips as intricate as needlework. In the middle of the valley, the serfs' round-roofed huts stood inside the hedge. Maria and her knights passed by at moonrise and continued on between the river and the fields toward the southern end of the valley, where the castle was.

Exhausted, Maria wound her fingers fitfully in her reins, her blank mind incapable of sleep. Once she swayed in her saddle and the knight beside her took her by the arm to brace her up. She thrust off his impersonal grip, angry for no reason she could think of. They left the river to skirt the bog at the foot of the castle's hill.

The two stone towers rose up against the sky. Maria's mule snorted with each stride. The knights slumped in their saddles and let their reins dangle. Maria twisted to look back at Elena's body, draped across the roan war horse. The redheaded boy caught her eye, riding behind her, and she jerked around straight again in the saddle.

They passed through the gate in the curtain wall and climbed the last of the road to the main gate. Nearly in tears again at being home, Maria rode past the porter into the open ward.

Her father came toward her from the foot of the New Tower. He wore his nightshirt, his fur cloak thrown across his shoulders, and his calves and feet bare below

15

the hem. Maria started to leap down from the mule, but a hand caught her arm and held her forcibly in the saddle.

"Roger."

The redheaded boy appeared on foot at her stirrup, to lift her down. Maria looked angrily over her shoulder at the other knight. She let herself slide decorously down into the boy's grip. She thrust him away and turned to her father.

He hugged her tight in his arms. She clung to the fur around his shoulders, her heart pounding. He said, over her head, "They attacked you."

"Saracens—we ran them off. But the maid was killed."

"Elena," the old man said. His grip loosened. Maria pressed herself against him, stunned. He said again, "Elena," in that same voice, and Maria stood back, furious, knowing now who had been Elena's lover.

IN THE MORNING the Saracens' attack was already blurred in her memory, like a dream, and Elena seemed long dead. When she went down to the hall, the other women treated her like a baby. No one seemed to care about Elena. "She's better off dead than taken alive," fat Adela said. The other women agreed with force. Maria turned her back on them, morose.

The cook sent for her; she went down the stairs and out to the ward. Several of the knights were grooming their horses along the wall. She trotted a wide half circle past them—all the knights' stallions kicked—and went on along the path toward the kitchen.

The stable door opened, down the wall, and the red-headed boy Roger led his black horse up into the sunlight. Maria pulled open the kitchen door. She stood a moment looking out at the young knight and went down into the kitchen.

On the table before the door, the day's bread was stacked to cool, beside it a tray of sweet buns still steaming from the oven. A scullion was stirring a pot over the fire. He shouted over his shoulder for the cook. Maria went forward into the kitchen.

Bald as a peeled garlic, the cook loomed up before her. A wooden spoon and a meat ax were jammed under the

16

sash of his filthy white apron. "You've let me run out of flour again," he told her. "Your mother always knew when I was going short of flour. If you'd give me the God-damned key—" he brushed past her, headed for the door, and she followed him. In passage she thieved a sweet bun.

"It's not bad enough I don't have ovens fit to bake in," the cook said. Behind his back she stuffed the hot bun in her apron. "I can't bake for fifty people in this kitchen—" His voice rose to a bellow. He opened the door and plunged out into the ward, Maria on his heels. "Now that he's letting any mounted trash take up the loafer's life here—"

Maria ran on ahead of him to the door into the storeroom. From the knights scattered across the ward there rose a general mocking answer, mostly oaths. The redheaded boy Roger paid no heed to any of it. She was careful not to look at him too long.

She kept all the keys in a ring on her belt. With the cook's help she opened the lock, and they went into the dark storeroom. The cook had to stoop to keep his head out of the strings of sausage and garlic and the sides of bacon hanging from the beams.

"Go in there," he said. "You're little and young—go back in there and find me a salt block."

Maria crawled in behind the kegs of meat. When she crept back out again, the kitchen knaves were lugging out wheat sacks into the ward. The cook stood beside the door presiding. He dragged her over beside him.

"If you'd give me the key, I could get things out when I need them."

Maria said nothing. She had no intention of giving him the key. Outside, someone shouted. The cook charged out the door. Maria rushed after him.

Three sacks of wheat stood in the ward just outside the storeroom door. The cook sprinted past them, moving fast for such a big man, and disappeared into the kitchen. Maria and the two kitchen knaves stood rapt, waiting.

Three knights burst up out of the kitchen. Their hands were piled with sweet buns. Laughing they wheeled to face the cook, who charged after them, swearing in a half-choked voice. The knights circled him. He struck at

17

one with his meat ax, and another darted in behind him and tripped him flat on his backside. The two kitchen knaves bleated with laughter.

The knights retreated; the honey buns were all eaten, anyway. Huffing, the cook strode up toward Maria. "Get that cart hitched—hop!" He smacked the nearer of the boys, and they raced away toward the stable.

"When your mother was alive," the cook said bitterly, "I was treated like a Christian in this damned robbers' den."

Maria stood behind him, so that he would not see the sweet bun in her apron. She was trying to gather the courage to talk to the redheaded boy—She would have to send some of the knights with the cook to the mill. She started across the ward to the stable door, in the base of the Knights' Tower, where the men were collecting. Roger was there but she could not make herself look at him. The gray-eyed knight was there, his brother; she went up to him.

"Please, will you take some men and go with the cook to the mill?"

He nodded, and she crossed the ward to the New Tower again like a rabbit back to its burrow. Inside the dark stairwell, she leaned against the wall and watched the knights, the redheaded boy in their midst. They all tramped away down into the stable, and she bounded up the stairs, buoyant.

ELENA'S GRAVE was in the burying ground just outside the castle wall. Maria let herself through the little door in the gate and walked around the foot of the wall, careful of the thorny shrubs sprouting in the sunlight. The ground pitched off steep as a waterfall, buried in pine. Far down there, the serpentine strips of the fields spread across the valley floor, slashed by the brown streak of the river. She went on around the foot of the wall, in and out of the shadows.

She said prayers for Elena and her mother, buried higher on the hill, and sat down in the sun with the castle wall at her back. The graveyard was thickly planted in herbs; certain things grew most potent there. Down in the valley, a boy rode a limping workhorse into the river to soak its legs. She wrapped her arms around her knees. Here nearly every day she and Elena had told each other stories of kings and wizards, enchanted weapons and horses and treasure, maidens despoiled and magic castles lost and won. Elena had despoiled the maidens. Maria had preferred the weapons and horses.

Abruptly she looked up above her. The redheaded boy was leaning against the top of the wall. Their eyes met. All over her body, her skin grew prickly and alive. He did not look away. After a moment she tore her gaze from his and pointed it elsewhere.

She could sit there no longer, not with him above her, and she raced along the foot of the wall toward the gate. He had looked at her so long, and with no reason to be doing it; she remembered his stare and held her breath. She dashed into the ward and ran across to the New Tower.

Just as she reached it, he reached it, jerking open the door for her. Now they were so close she could see his clear blue eyes. She went through the doorway, into the cool dark of the foot of the stair. He slid past her through the door and went up the stairs toward the hall. In passing, his arm brushed over her breast. She raced up the staircase two flights to her room.

That night, she could hardly sleep, and in the morning she lay late in bed, daydreaming. The other women clucked over her and tried to get her up but she ignored them. She could think of nothing but Roger.

When her father had the New Tower built, years before, he had ordered that a passage be made in the wall around the hall, on either side of the hearth, so that he could spy on his men. This passage opened under the stair. Now that Robert was aging he seldom went in there. Maria had found its entrance; now, loving the redheaded boy, she hid in the wall passage and listened for his voice among the arguments and stories and lies of the men.

During the days, whenever she saw him, he caught her eye in a searching look. They said nothing to one another. Maria could not imagine speaking to him—everything she felt for him would come out, and what if he refused her?

19

Adela and Flora, the women who helped her work, twitted her constantly and tried to convince her she was sick. At last, to quiet them, she made them swear an oath to keep the secret and told them about Roger. Flora agreed with her that Roger was wonderful but Adela only laughed, and later Maria heard them giggling in a corner and was embarrassed.

One morning in the early summer half the knights rode off on a raid. Old Robert stayed home, to help a mastiff bitch whelp her first litter, and when the puppies were dry and nursing, he went to the hall and sat down in front of the fire. Maria brought him a cup of wine. The hall was stifling hot, even with the fire banked. Maria and the other women hurried around the room, throwing all the knights' bits of gear out into the ward and spreading clean rushes on the floor.

"It's so hot," she said to her father. She came up beside him and put her hand on his shoulder. "How can you bear it? Come outside."

Old Robert grunted and heaved his bulk up straighter in his chair. In the bristled laps and folds of his face his eyes were bright as a young man's. He looked her over, set his cup down, and thumped his knee.

"Here, puss. Sit down."

Maria sat down on his knee. He muttered in his throat. "You are heavier than you were." He sighed and shook his head, fingering his chin, and looked her over once again.

"Now, see here," he said. "Adela tells me you are mooning over that calf Roger d'Alene."

Maria went hot as if she stood before an open oven. She would never talk to Adela again. Her father took her right hand and opened her fingers out of their fist.

"Maria," he said. "I think you should be married." He kissed her fingers.

"Married," she said, amazed, and leaped up. "Papa. To Roger? I can marry Roger?" She threw her arms around him.

The old man patted her back. "That isn't what I have in mind."

20

She stood up, cooling. "What?"

Her father smiled at her. "Not Roger." He pulled on his chin. "His brother—Richard, the middle brother."

"Richard!" Maria cried. That was the gray-eyed knight. "No. I want Roger. I'll go to a convent first."

"Now, Maria. Come here and listen to your old father."

"You want me to marry him? Why do you want me to marry him?"

"Come here." He beckoned to her. A deerhound lying under the window came over to him, and he slapped it away. "Maria. Do as I say."

She went reluctantly over to pull up a stool beside his chair and sit down. Robert took her by the hand.

"I have no son. All I have is you, puss. Therefore you have to marry and make me a few grandsons."

He went on a little about how in his old age a man's heart yearned for grandchildren to continue his line. Maria stopped heeding his rambling voice. She had never before thought of having children; she herself had been so recently a child.

"You aren't listening to me," her father said patiently.

"I'm sorry. What did you say?"

"I want you to marry Richard. He's older than Roger, he can take care of you. Roger's not much more than your age, he's just tilting with Richard over you."

"I'll wait for Roger." Her father made things more complex than necessary.

In the seams of her father's face the sweat lay glistening like jewels. Beneath his heavy eyebrows his small pale eyes were unblinking. At last he patted her hand.

"Listen to me. Richard is ambitious. I have to give him something to keep him satisfied a while. Trust me. I'll watch over you."

She sat with her hands clasped in her lap, staring at him, affronted. "Papa, don't you love me any more?"

"Of course I love you. Of course I love you." He took her hands again. "Puss, don't ever think I don't love you." He sighed. Still holding both her hands in his right hand, he wiped the sweat from his face on his other

21

sleeve. He looked her in the eyes. "Very well. Maybe he can convince you. Will you talk to him—when he comes back? Tomorrow."

"I won't marry him."

"Talk to him."

"All right." She would talk to Roger as well.

"Good girl." The deerhound still stood beside her father, who cupped its lean head in the palm of his hand. He nodded to her. "You'll come around to it, you'll see, one way or another."

He bent over the dog, talking to it. Maria went out of the hall to the stairway. She felt dizzy, as if she had drunk too much of something strong. If it was not her true love, at least someone wanted to marry her. Going downstairs, she broke into a run from sheer good feeling.

MARIA WENT into the end of the hall, where her father usually sat, and stood looking at the hanging on the wall. Her mother had made it. Once she had thought it beautiful but now since she herself had learned to weave she marked the twisted weft and the loose stitches. She turned away from the hanging, putting her back to the wall.

The gray-eyed knight was coming in the door. He shut it and put the bolt across it, which startled her, and walked slowly across the room toward her. He was stocky and broad-shouldered, his legs heavy-boned, but he was not tall: when he came up to her she had to lift her head only a little to meet his eyes.

"Your father says you won't marry me."

"I love another." She disliked having him stand so close to her. She backed away from him.

"Roger," he said. His eyes were the color of ice. He pulled a stool over next to her father's chair. "Sit down. No, girl. In the chair." With his hand on her arm he steered her from the stool to the chair.

Maria wrenched her arm out of his grasp. "You are a sorry lover."

"I know." He started to sit on the stool at her feet, but instead he propped his foot on it. "Roger's better at that than I. He dandles all the local maids."

Maria blinked at him. This new reflection of Roger unsettled her, but she could think of only one thing at a time. She said, "I will always love your brother."

"No. He just wants to play with you—I want to marry you."

His hands rose between them, palms up, begging her. She said, "Why?"

"Because . . ." his hands fell. "You wouldn't follow it."

"I will."

He straightened. She wondered how old he was—not so much older than Roger, after all: in the way he moved there was something of a boy's awkwardness. He sat down on the stool in front of her.

"Your father is a robber, he'll never be anything else. Roger just wants to be the King of the Robbers. But there's something else to be done here. This castle's at the throat of the whole region. The Saracens in the mountains have had no leader since Tib al-Malik was murdered. The King doesn't interfere here, the Duke of Santerois hasn't come south of the Roman Road in eight years. Someone is going to make himself great here, why should it not be me?"

His voice was quick and vehement. She took her eyes from his face. What he had said caught her imagination.

"Shall I court you?" Richard said. "What does Roger do, besides smile and be pretty?"

She lifted her head. "I'll marry you."

She saw that surprised him. She could not keep from smiling. She put her hand out to him. He took it; his fingers were rough with callus.

"Maybe I am a sorry lover," he said, "but I'll be a good husband, I swear it." He kissed her hand. She wondered if she ought to kiss him; she had never kissed a man other than her father. But the knight only got up and went out of the hall.

She turned to the window overlooking the ward. A dozen knights were gathered around the door. Among them, almost under her window, was Roger's red head. Richard walked out of the tower. The knights swarmed around him, their voices excited. He nodded, and they let out a yell. Below her Roger lifted his head. He met her eyes a moment and went to join the crowd around his brother.

II

✤

AT FIRST, MARIA'S FATHER TOOK CHARGE OF EVERYTHING
and wanted the wedding on Assumption Day, but on the
night before that, a caravan came down the road from the
Saracen port of Mana'a, and Richard and Roger went off
to attack it. They came back with three important prisoners. Arranging the ransoms kept the men's attention almost until the equinox. After that, it rained a while, until
Maria almost gave up thinking about the whole subject of
marriage.

On the first sunny day, they all rode down to the village
church, the serfs ran in from the fields, and Father Simon
married them. The inside of the church was painted with
round faces and sheep and the same hills she saw from
her window. She stood trembling before the priest, her
shoulders and breast drenched from the dew on the blue
and white flowers the women had given her. She knew she
could escape from this, if only she took heart. The gray-
eyed knight appeared beside her. His hand was cold and
clammy as a stone. Father Simon spoke of obedience and
chastity and kindness.

She and Richard knelt and received Communion. The
wafer clung to the roof of her mouth. She worked frantically with her tongue to pry it loose and then could hardly
swallow it. The knight put a gold ring on her finger. He
missed the first try, and she raised her eyes and saw him
worried and uncertain. Her heart lightened. It would not
be so bad after all. She put her hand on his arm and they
left the church.

In the yard, the peasants threw flowers at them and

shouted wicked jokes. Richard's older brother William led up a white mare, the saddle covered with rich red cloth, and Richard lifted Maria up onto its back. Their eyes met. The intensity of his look struck her like a blow. She gathered her reins. Her heart beat like a fist. It would not be so bad after all.

Newly rich from the ransoms, her father had hung the walls of the ward with Saracen cloth, blood red, silver, and white, and covered the banquet tables with roast meat, heaps of bread and cake, and fruit puddings and blancmange and wine. Maria, Richard, and Robert sat at a table hung with cloth of silver, and the knights and serfs mingled in the ward around them.

Laughing, Adela rushed up and threw a wreath of flowers around Maria's neck and kissed her. One by one, the knights were standing up before Richard and her father and offering to drink with them. Maria, who hated being drunk, mixed water with her wine, but the men and most of the women soon began drinking the wine whole.

Roger came before Richard and saluted him with his cup. His long red hair was bright in the sunlight, and he stood straight and slim as a birch tree. Richard by comparison was plain. He was watching her suspiciously. She realized she had been staring at Roger. The gray-eyed knight leaned toward her.

"Let's go."

Maria started. "Now? But it's—" She turned toward her father. He was drinking by turn with three of his knights. "Still daylight," she said; it was not yet noon. Her father threw his cup down with a clang and swung his head toward her.

"Are you still here?" He prodded her in the ribs with his forefinger. "Richard, don't you want my daughter?" He laughed and belched in a winy gust.

Maria got to her feet. The yell from the people around her boomed in the eaves of the towers. Adela and Flora rushed in around her and hurried her off. Half a dozen of the village women joined them. Halfway up the stairs, they began unlacing her bodice, and in her room they yanked off her clothes as if they were skinning her. Adela brushed out Maria's hair.

25

"Oh, what a beautiful bride you were! If only your mother could have seen you. I cried like a child."

They slid her nightgown on over her head. Washed and dried in magic herbs, the linen smelled like sweet grass. Adela's fat sister Alys brought her a cup of some potion that tasted like egg. While Maria drank it the women crowded around her, tying the ribbons at her wrists and throat. They lifted her up and carried her across the room to her bed. Alys said charms over her and touched her reverently on the bad places with a bit of wood. The bed was strewn with flowers. Maria lay on a mass of crushed blossoms.

The door banged open and the men flooded into the room, towing Richard along half-naked in their midst. A chair crashed over. The women screeched. They shooed out the men before them in a torrent down the stairs. The door slammed shut, and the shrilling voices and laughter dimmed. Maria sat up.

Richard came up beside the bed. His chest looked bigger without a shirt over it. Between the nipples grew a mat of brown hair, darker than the hair on his head. She wondered if the hair on Roger's chest were red. Her mouth was dry as a wad of fleece. He put on his nightshirt and sat down on the bed to take off his shoes. Turning modestly away from her, he stripped off his breeches and hose.

"Let me sleep on that side of the bed. I don't want to be against the wall."

Maria slid over into the middle of the bed. In the new nightshirt, covered with Adela's embroidery, he turned toward her, and there was a wild knocking on the door.

"Maria," her father shouted, his voice muffled by the oak door. "A toast. One more toast to my children." He laughed, drunk.

"Tomorrow," Richard called. "Later."

The door started to open. Richard said something under his breath; he crossed the room in three strides and slammed the door shut. Maria chewed her fingernail, willing her father to go away.

"This is my room now," Richard shouted. "Stay out of

here, it's mine." He bolted the door and came back toward her.

"Maria," her father shouted. "Come open this door!"

Richard climbed into the bed, kicking away the sheet and the blanket. Maria reached out her arms to him. He lay down on her, his breath in her face, his body warm under her hands. They struggled together in an awkward embrace, their nightclothes bunched in their way. He kissed her. Her father's shouts still sounded in her ears. She spread her legs apart. Richard pierced her body. She smothered down a cry, not of pain so much as surprise. He slid himself hard in and out of her. She wrapped her arms tight around his neck. In her ear his wild breathing whined, and suddenly he was soaked with sweat. After a moment he rolled off onto his back beside her.

Maria pushed herself up on her elbows. Her father was gone. Her mouth and her groin hurt. Richard sat up, throwing pieces of stem and flower petals out of the bed.

"Lift that pillow for me."

She turned the pillow behind him up to cushion his back.

"Did it hurt? What did it feel like?"

Maria busied herself with the flowers. She mumbled something. He drew his fingers through her hair.

"I've never seen your hair loose before."

"My mother's touched the floor, when she let it down."

He took her hair in both hands. There was a knock on the door. "Maria?" Adela called.

"Go let her in."

She climbed across him out of the bed and opened the door. Round with fat, Adela waddled in, carrying a dish of meat in one hand and a cup of wine in the other.

"I thought you'd be hungry." She kissed Maria on the cheek and left.

Maria put the dish on the chest beside the bed. Richard took the cup. She scrambled around him into the middle of the bed. Her nightgown was bloody. He drank the wine; his eyes probed at her.

"Where did you come from?" she asked.

"Normandy. Lac d'Alene, in the Avranchine. My father holds land there of the viscomte."

27

"Oh," she said. "We are Normans."

"I know." He put the cup down on the chest.

"Why did you leave?"

"You ask a lot of questions for a little girl. Come here."

"I'm not a little girl."

"Be quiet and come here."

She lay down beside him. He reached for her hips. She put her arms around him. This time when he mounted her the burning pain kept her rigid under him, and the thrusting of his body disgusted her. Once he kissed her but she turned her face away, impatient to get it done. Somewhere a distant woman screamed in pleasure. She thought of the feast in the ward.

Deep in her body, his body touched her into a brief, exquisite sensation. When she moved, following, it happened again. Her arms tightened around him. She twisted herself against him, trying to drive him deeper. In her arms he sobbed with lust and clutched her so hard she gasped.

This time when he moved away from her she could not look at him. She pressed her cheek into the pillow; she felt sore and used. He gave her the wine and she sat up and drank a little. His nightshirt was up around his waist. Like a snake, it was. Hastily she took her eyes away. He cupped his hand over her breast; he was her husband now and could do that.

"I thought you'd be frightened," he said. "Did you like it?"

Maria shook her head. "No. It hurts." Only bad women liked it. The warmth of his hand reached her through her nightgown. "Was your family great in Normandy?" she asked.

He laughed. "My father's fief is a short two hides. My eldest brother Stephen has driven each of us off as soon as we got to be his size."

"Why didn't your father protect you?"

Slowly he stroked his hand over her arm. "It's all the same, anyway. If we'd all stayed, there would have been nothing for anybody."

Maria lay still, drowsy. He touched her all over, fingering her, pressing his hands against her. She moved

28

so that he could pull up her nightgown, put her head down, and shut her eyes.

RICHARD'S BROTHER WILLIAM, older by several years, was a large, placid man, slow-moving, who smiled much. Maria liked him immediately. When she was two days' married, he went with her into the Knights' Tower to pack up Richard's possessions. She had not been there since the New Tower was built. The two towers were the same size, four stories high, each story forming a large square room, but the New Tower had a separate stairwell and the Knights' Tower only a steep wooden stair that went up through a hole in the center of each floor.

The knights stabled their horses in the bottom story and slept in the second and third, leaving the top floor for an armory. Their cots packed the rooms and the heaps of their gear took up all the flat surfaces. At the head of each cot stood a wooden cross where a mail shirt hung: like a scarecrow army. The windows were only arrow slots, so that the rooms were gloomy as barns.

Richard owned almost nothing. William stood beside his brother's mail shirt, watching her fold the few pieces of clothing and stack them on the single blanket. There were dogs wandering around the room looking for scraps; one came up and thrust its head under William's hand.

"We all left home with a horse, a sword, and a shield," he said. He rumbled with laughter. "Richard left home with my brother Stephen's mail shirt too, but that wasn't Stephen's idea."

Maria kicked a litter of candle stubs under the next bed. The floor was black with soot, puddled with dry wax. "Is this everything?"

William called over his shoulder, and one of the village boys who served the knights came across the room, weaving his path through the cots. Maria lifted the flat bundle of Richard's clothes. William and the boy took the hauberk by its frame and the boy hoisted Richard's long shield on his back.

"Here." William picked the helmet off the upright of the frame. "Carry this."

He dropped the helmet over her head. His voice faded

away, muffled by the packing around her ears. She stood frozen, the iron encasing her head; the nasal piece chopped her vision in half, the flared cheekpieces forced her eyes straight ahead. She dropped her bundle and snatched the helmet off. The two men were laughing at her. She tucked the helmet under her arm, bent to pick up her bundle, and followed them down into the stable.

SHE SAW LITTLE of her husband. Each dawn when she got out of bed, he lay asleep, and if she caught glimpses of him during the day, he always seemed busy. They ate supper together, with her father, but afterward, while she sat in the end of the hall at her spinning wheel, Richard and the other men argued and gambled at the far end of the room. Adela had taught her a charm to give him, to keep him faithful, which she made him every night in a cup of wine. In the darkness, in his arms, she sometimes pretended he was Roger.

Adela and Flora with their talk of dyes and village gossip irked her. She had no one to talk to and she missed Elena more now even than before. From the two older women, she gathered that what she and Richard did really ought to be a sin, but was not because men decided such things. Once, when she had tripped on the stair and bruised her leg, Adela asked her if Richard had struck her.

She mended William's clothes for him; Roger smiled at her once in the ward and blew a kiss to her. Her father poked her in the stomach. "Fill this," he said, and tweaked her breast. "Tell Richard to put the cork in." He guffawed. She imagined her mother and father doing what she and Richard did, and laughed, unbelieving.

A group of pilgrims traveled down the road from Agato in Santerois to the Cave of the Virgin, and Richard and her father went off to rob them. Maria woke when she heard them riding back up the road. She got out of bed and covering her nightgown with her cloak went down to the hall.

From the window overlooking the ward she watched them flood in through the gate. The creak of leather and the clopping of the horses' hoofs mixed with the grating

30

voices of the men. They had brought five knights back face down across their saddles. Her skin prickled up. Something had gone wrong. She leaned out across the deep window sill. Almost below her, William was helping Roger down from his horse. The young man held himself stiffly all through his left side. He leaned on his brother to walk away.

Maria's father was dismounting at the door into the New Tower. On foot Richard crossed the ward to him. They spoke. Her father flung up his head, angry. Richard shouldered past him into the stairway. The door crashed against the stone wall.

Maria slid off the window sill back into the hall. Adela with a blanket around her shoulders stood behind her.

"Shall I go wake up Cook?"

"Yes." The cook would surely be awake already; it was nearly dawn. Maria went out into the stairway and ran up the steps to her room.

Richard was already there, standing in the middle of the room pulling off his mail shirt over his head. She closed the door behind her. His sword and his helmet lay on the bed. She moved them off the clean sheet. Richard turned toward her. His helmet had left black smudges on his nose and cheekbones. His eyes glittered with bad temper.

"What happened to Roger?" she said.

"You stay away from Roger." He picked up his sword and took it to hang it on the wall. "Go get me something to eat—I'm starving."

She went down to the hall. The tables had been pulled out into the center of the room, and the knights were crowding around them. Her father roared in their midst. The table was stacked with bread. While she stood cutting a loaf in half, Adela and a kitchen knave came in with a great bubbling pot of stew.

The knights swarmed around it. Maria stood waiting for a chance with the ladle. Her father came up beside her. He draped his arm around her. He seemed the only man in high spirits. To someone beyond her he said, in a sleek voice, "Well, Richard's not far-famous for courage, you know." He hugged Maria against him. "Here, puss, give me a kiss. Go get me something to drink."

Maria drew away from him. He seemed pleased that Richard was upset. He wheeled toward someone else. She got hold of the ladle and piled meat on top of the bread in her hand. Her father looked around for her and called her name. She went upstairs to her room.

Richard was sitting on a stool on the hearth. He still wore the thick quilted shirt that went under his mail. She sank down next to him and put the food on the hearth.

"What happened?"

Richard wheeled on her. "Your father tried to get me killed. He put me and Roger on point and ran us right into the Saracens."

She cried, "That's not true—"

"He took the high road both ways, coming and going," he shouted in her face. "What does it look like to you?"

"You wouldn't dare say that to him!"

"Do you want me to?" He pushed her hard; she caught herself on her arm. "If I go down there again now, Maria, I'll kill him. I'll kill him."

Maria put her hand to her face. She got up and went off across the room. Richard put his back to her and ate. She stood watching his back. She could not believe him; she wanted everything to be peace. She said, "I think I'm going to have a baby."

His head swiveled toward her. Eventually he said, "A baby. When?"

"I'm not sure yet." She went over to the hearth and sat down beside him, her knees drawn up to her chest. She watched his face, curious. "Would you be glad?"

"Hunh." He scratched in the beard stubble on his jaw. His eyes veered toward her. "Yes. I suppose so. Yes."

Maria laid her head down on her knees. She said a prayer in her mind that the baby was there. Richard looked away again. They sat in the warmth of the fire, not talking, until the fire died and they got up and went to bed.

THE SAME SARACENS who had ambushed them burned a village just north of her valley, and Richard and her father raced off to their revenge. Maria and the other women spent the morning washing and spreading the laundry out on the grass to dry. Sick to her stomach, Maria ate only a piece of dry bread for dinner and went to the hall to spin the last of the flax.

The late autumn day was bright and crisp. She sat before the window, enjoying the faint breeze. She liked to spin. The even rhythm drew her into reveries and helped her think. The bells on her spinning wheel rang busily. She let the spindle draw the flax out between her fingers into a fine even thread. Lifting her eyes from the pale flax, she saw Roger coming through the door, his hair vivid in the late night.

There was no one else in the room. She went back to her spinning, alive to his approach.

"Little sister," he said, and stood before her. "How do you do, Maria?"

He dandles all the local maids, Richard had said. Maria stopped the wheel and wound up the tail of the thread. With the spindle in her hand, she faced Roger. "Thank you, very well. Are you in command, now?"

"I and William. But you command us all, I guess, don't you?" His blue eyes were clear as a child's. He bore his left side stiffly, favoring his wound. She tightened her fingers around the spindle.

"I wish I did," she said.

"Do you?" He sat down at her feet. "What would you command of me? Tell me anything you want me to do."

Maria laughed. She wished Richard were as handsome as Roger, with his fine mouth and brilliant coloring. Richard's jaw was too wide, he looked as if he were always biting down. Roger took the deep cuff of her sleeve between his fingers.

"I could make you so happy, Maria." He kissed the hem of her sleeve.

"No," she said. "I am married now."

"Maria." He took her hand, and she yanked it away from him. When he reached for her again, she raised the spindle between them. He got up onto his feet.

"You're just like Richard. That's Richard's kind of excuse: *Because I am married.*" He went off across the hall.

Maria stared after him. She thrust the spindle into her work basket. But he had only gone to the table against the wall, where he poured himself a cup of the wine. He came smiling toward her again, saluted her with the cup, and drank.

"Why did you marry him?"

"Ask him," she said.

"I know why he married you. That was not my question." He seemed amused. Even wounded he was full of grace. "Well?"

She shook her head. "Stop asking me that."

"If you want." He sat down neatly on the floor beside her.

"Did he have lots of women—Richard? Before."

"Richard? By the Cross." He leaned against her knee. "Don't you know him yet? He has no way with women, Richard." He drank again. "Or with men, either, I guess." His eyes moved over her; he smiled. "What's his way with you?"

"Roger." She got up hastily, moving away from him into the hall. The other women came in, and she helped them drag out the tables so that they could bring the supper.

Roger came up to her. "I'm sorry—I didn't mean to be free with you."

She tried to ignore him, her eyes downcast; she was dusting the top of the table. He went off. When she thought he must have gone she looked around at the door. He stood there, watching her. She looked quickly down, her face hot. He laughed and went out the door.

III

❧

IT WAS WINTER, WHEN HER FATHER SELDOM RAIDED. The dank, icy days kept most of them indoors. The knights gathered in the hall and drank and talked and cheated each other at games. Maria, her tasks done, sat in the window at the end of the hall sewing new shirts for Richard. She was sure now that she was with child. Her stomach and her temper had become very uneven. The cook seemed to guess: ruthlessly he served them meals she could barely stomach, until finally one day at dinner she took a bite of beef and left the hall, ran down to the ward and was sick.

The cook was shouting in the kitchen across the way. Adela called her from the stairs; Maria answered that she was well. She wiped her mouth on her arm and tramped off across the ward. The cook's voice drew her down into the kitchen.

He was beating a scullion over the head with his wooden spoon. She stood to one side, hot with anger. The cook let the scullion go.

"Well? What do you want?"

"Why did you even cook that meat?" she cried. "That beef is so sweet I can't eat it."

The cook rammed his spoon under the sash of his apron. "That isn't my fault. I cook what you give me out of that storeroom. If you'd let me have the key—"

"My father is very angry about it," she said.

"If your mother were alive—"

"Even Richard is complaining."

The cook's mouth shut, his lower lip jutting like a ledge. She stared at him; her heart thumped. He turned away from her.

"Well, what should I do—throw it all out?"

"Whatever you want." She wondered what else he could do with it. Feed it to the dogs. Sell it in the village. "Just don't serve it to us." She started toward the door. A scullion came in and the cook set on him with a roar. She went across the ward again to the New Tower. It was cold and she ran up the stairs toward the heat of the hall.

Even out on the stairs, she heard Roger shout. She dashed up to the hall. In the middle of the room, between the two tables, he and another knight stood yelling face to face. Just as she came in, the other knight hit Roger in the mouth.

Roger yelled. He jumped on the other knight and knocked him down and they rolled on the floor, fighting.

Richard grabbed his brother and her father grabbed the other knight and they dragged them apart, up onto their feet.

Over Richard's shoulder, Roger cried, "Odo, I'll kill you—"

"You can try," Odo shouted.

His arms around his brother, Richard shoved him back almost to the wall. Her father and another knight held Odo. The rest of the men watched keenly, enjoying it.

"No fights," her father called. "We are all Christians here—get your hands together like friends."

Roger and Odo glared at each other. Maria stood in the doorway, just behind Roger; she heard him say softly, "I'll kill him."

"Hide it," Richard whispered.

Her father cuffed Odo in the head. "Accept each other, or you both leave."

Roger's mouth was bloody. He went sullenly forward. Odo met him in the middle of the room and they clasped their hands in a short limp handshake. The other knights cheered.

Maria went around the room to her place at the table. Her father sat down beside her. "Where did you go? You missed a good fight."

"I went to talk to the cook about the meat," she said. Richard climbed over the bench on her right.

"What's wrong with the meat?" her father asked. He reached with both hands for the beef bone in front of him. Chewing, he swung his head toward her, but his eyes went like daggers beyond her, toward Richard.

Maria looked down at her plate. Her appetite was gone. She sat between the two men, none of them speaking, until they had finished their meal. With the other women, she cleared off the tables. The knights wandered out to their afternoon doings; Richard disappeared. Now that all the food was taken away, Maria was perversely hungry again and she went with Adela to the kitchen for something to eat.

When she came back up the stairs to the hall, her father and Odo were standing at the end of the room, in the middle of her woman's gear, deep in talk. No one saw her in the doorway. She turned and slid through the narrow crevice between the stairs and the wall, into the passage-way.

It was black as a mine, except where the peepholes let in threads of light from the hall, but she knew every foot of the passage and could hurry through it, sliding her fingers over the stone to keep oriented. Halfway down the passage, nearly running, she turned the corner and crashed into somebody else.

Hands clutched her. Panicked, she struggled in silence. Her elbow scraped painfully on the wall. Abruptly she realized whom she fought.

"Richard?"

The grip on her arms eased. He took her by the wrist and twisted slightly, to tell her he would hurt her if she did anything. They stood together in the utter darkness. At first Maria could hear only her blood beating, but then she picked out a heavy voice on the far side of the wall: Odo's voice. Her father answered him.

"You shouldn't have hit young Roger. They are like snakes, the d'Alene brothers, when one hates they all hate."

Odo grunted. "I can handle them." He sounded confident.

"Oh, you can," old Robert said. "I'll nurse my doubts about that. Anyway I don't allow feuds between my men, especially when one is my daughter's husband." His voice smoothed out. "If they give you any more trouble, come to me. There's ways to scorch snakes. If you know what I mean."

Maria moved her wrist, testing Richard's grip, and he squeezed her hard. Her father said, pleasantly, "Is there something else you want to say?" and Odo muttered a leavetaking. The man beside her pushed her. She started off ahead of him along the wall passage, back toward the stairs. Groping in the dark, he relaxed his grasp, and she tore loose and bolted away toward the stairwell.

Behind her there was a soft sound like something striking the wall. She squeezed out the crevice and raced up the stairs two steps at a jump.

There was nobody in her room. Through the window she saw the gloomy sky, the sun lowering. Adela and Flora would be in the kitchen helping the cook. She

37

wheeled to go back down to the safety of the crowded hall. Richard was running up the stairs. She slammed the door and bolted it in his face.

His weight crashed against it; the bolt held. Maria leaned against the inside of the door. In an even voice, Richard said, "Let me in."

She did not want to, but he would reach her eventually. She opened the door. He came in and shut it behind him.

"What were you doing in there?" he said.

"I go back there, sometimes."

"Not any more."

She stood her ground, saying nothing; she did not trust her voice.

"Do you hear me?"

"Yes," she said. "If I want to go in there, I will."

From the foot of the stairs, Adela called, "Maria? Cook wants you."

She started toward the door. Richard caught her arm. "Are you going to obey me or not?"

"I have to go to the kitchen."

He let go of her arm. She ran away down the stairs.

The cook needed onions. She let him into the storeroom and while he stood in the middle complaining, climbed up on a keg to get a net of onions from the ceiling. They went out to the ward and she locked the door.

"If you'd give me the key—"

She went off across the ward to sit in the sun with Adela and Flora. No one seemed to know how the fight had started between Odo and Roger. While Adela's voice ran aimlessly in her ear Maria sat staring across the ward, cluttered with chickens, dogs, and people. What she had overheard in the passageway unnerved her. Richard and her father hated each other. She was caught between them. Richard came out of the New Tower. He gave her an expressionless stare and walked across the ward to the Knights' Tower.

She saw nothing more of him until supper. She sat between him and her father and no one said a single word throughout the meal. Her appetite was coming back; she ate to glut. The sun was setting. The kitchen boys went around lighting the torches on the walls. Richard left the hall. Maria stayed a while longer, beside her father. She

38

could not talk to him. She realized, frightened, that she could not trust him. He got up and crossed the hall, toward Odo. Maria went up the stairs.

Richard was already in their room, standing in front of the fire, a poker in his hand. That surprised her. She had been sure he was in the wall passage. She went to the cupboard for his wine and the herbs of the charm. Standing in the lee of the bed, she shook the herbs from the box but finally put them back in again: it seemed unfair to give him a love potion when she was fighting with him. She went back to the hearth and put the wine into a pan to warm.

Richard said, pleasantly, "You're going to do as I say."

"Only if I want to."

He jabbed the poker into the fire, throwing the logs back, and put on wood from the heap beside him. On her knees on the hearth next to him, she braced herself against his next shout.

His hand closed on her shoulder and dragged her up onto her feet. She threw one arm up between them to ward off his fist, but he struck her arm aside and hit her on the cheek, caught her when she staggered, and knocked her again in the face.

Her eyes failed. Blindly she thrust her hands out, her fingers clawed, and her nails snagged his cheek. He pushed her away. She sat down hard, sick to her stomach, and wrapped her arms around her waist. Her eyes were still bleary. Richard was coming for her.

"Richard. The baby."

He hauled himself up short. Maria got her breath back, nausea sweet in her throat, and her eyes cleared. Roughly he lifted her up onto her feet. She clung to him to steady herself. He thrust her hard away from him.

Maria wiped her eyes dry. No one had ever struck her before with a closed hand. Her mouth was bleeding, and the whole side of her face hurt. Tears welled into her eyes.

Richard was poking savagely at the fire. On his cheek three long scratches showed in beads of blood. His head swung toward her. "Are you going to let this wine burn?"

She went up slowly beside him. The wine was bubbling. She poured it into a cup and mixed in more wine from the cupboard. Her mouth was swollen. On the back of her tongue she tasted something bitter.

"I hate you," she said.

"You'll do as I tell you."

She said nothing, exhausted. The warmth of the fire drew her irresistibly.

"Aren't you?"

"Yes," she said.

He muttered something in his throat and drank the wine. The red scratches ran down his cheek. She put her hand to her swelling eye. He pulled her arm down. He took her face between his hands, and she winced.

"You'll have a black eye tomorrow," he said. "What will you tell your father?"

She shook her head. "Anything. That I fell."

"Tell him I beat you. I want to see what he'll do."

Maria backed away from him. In the fire's warmth, she began to take off her clothes. He went around the room, putting out the candles and the torch. The heat of the fire licked her arms. Richard undressed in the darkness behind her. In her shift, she crouched before the fire, dying in its bed, a heap of throbbing coals and ash. The side of her head ached in the heat. She said her prayers.

"What are you doing over there?"

"I am praying," she said. She crossed herself. The fire was veiled in a layer of ash. Richard in the bed behind her was muttering discontent. She asked God to help her endure him and rose and got into the bed with him, into his burning embrace.

WHEN SHE SAT DOWN to breakfast the next morning, her father swore, wiped his hand on his chest, and turned her face to the light. Maria pulled away from him.

"I fell out of bed."

"He hit you, did he?"

She said nothing. Her left eye was swollen almost shut. Her father pulled on his chin. "He's a dog to hit a woman, even his wife. Why did he do it?"

"I told you," she said. "I fell."

She went off to her chores. Everybody stared at her. Flora and Adela whispered behind her back. The cook laughed at her. "It's a long way from your heart." When she went up to the hall again in the forenoon, Richard was sitting on the hearth playing bones with Roger. The scratches striped his cheek like a flag. She went up to her spinning wheel and got out the shirt she was making for him. She glanced at him once, while she was threading the needle, but he was watching her and she looked quickly away.

A short dark knight came in. When he saw Richard's face, he crowed derisively. "Who won?" Maria bent over the seam she was sewing. The men all laughed, even Richard. The seam was coming out crooked, and in a fury she ripped it apart.

Her father came in the door. Odo followed on his heels, along with several dogs. Old Robert threw his cloak aside. She could smell the wet wool of the lining. He strode into the middle of the hall.

Maria sat poised over her needlework. Her father put his hands on his hips. He was staring at Richard; the talk died. Richard got to his feet. Her heart began to beat painfully fast. She didn't care who won, so long as they fought. They faced each other a long moment in silence.

Her father broke into an unconvincing laugh. "I suppose she can take care for herself. You're not really married until you've drawn blood, they say, although not usually about the wife." He went up to the hearth, chuckling, the only man in the room even with a smile on his face. He put his hands out to the fire.

Richard said, "Is that all you want to tell me?"

"Well, you could try hitting the other end." Her father glanced at him over his shoulder. "It doesn't show." Odo came up beside him. They talked.

Maria let out her pent breath. They weren't going to fight. She went back to the mess she had made of her work; her face hurt, her stomach was sour again, she wanted to cry. She concentrated on sewing the seam down flat.

Richard came up beside her. She put her hands and the shirt in her lap. "Get away from me," she said.

"Obey me, the next time, and I won't hit you." He leaned up against the wall.

Maria clenched her fist. All the men by the hearth were

41

watching them, all but her father, all grinning. She hated Richard for hitting her and her father for not fighting him over it. She gave Richard a hard look.

"Now you're asking for it, you stubborn little slut."

She knew if she said anything her voice would tremble. He sank down on his heels. He hadn't shaved in two days; the scratches on his cheek were crusted with dry blood. "Have you told him yet?" He glanced over his shoulder toward her father. "About the baby."

She shook her head, wary. "I wanted to be sure."

"Are you sure now?"

She nodded. His eyes widened; he rubbed the back of his hand absently over his cheek. "When will it be born?"

"In the summer. The midsummer."

He took hold of her hand. She pulled against his grip. "Let me go. I have to do my work."

"You don't mind me so much in the dark." He clenched her fingers hard. When she stiffened at the pain he released her. "That's for talking back to me." He went down the room. Her father was watching her. She picked up her needle again and stabbed it into the shirt.

IV

❧

MARIA'S FATHER GOT HER A SADDLE OF WHITE LEATHER for her little mare. He gave it to her the morning of the first hunt of the spring, with much show of stripping off the old saddle and putting on the new one with his own hands. Beside Richard in the doorway, Maria laughed and clapped her hands, but Richard kept to a surly silence. Her father led up the white mare, and her husband lifted her up into the new saddle.

"You shouldn't even ride any more," Richard said,

giving her the reins. "And if you need presents, I will get them for you." He walked around the mare's rump toward his horse.

There were five of them to go hunting—Richard and Maria, her father, Roger, and William—and while the men got their horses mounted, Maria trotted her mare in circles in and out of the crowd in the ward, to show off. She liked to ride, even with the baby swelling out her body round as a cushion, and the mare bent neatly to her hand, backed up, reared, and went into a lope around Richard. He was in a foul mood; she rode to her father's side.

Loose-limbed on his old bay stallion, he leaned over her. "Do you like it, my dear one?"

"Oh, yes." She put her hand on the carved leather swell of the saddle. Long-faced, Flora and Adela stood on the step watching her, and Adela scowled at her. They thought she should stay in her room, even in her bed, and let no one see her with child. She had needed most of a month to convince Richard to take her with them. Her father shouted, the gate opened, and they rode double file onto the hillside.

Adela and Flora were wrong, Richard was wrong, and there was nothing to be unhappy about. Ever since her father had learned she was pregnant, he had treated Richard pleasantly, and now here they all were, going out together to hunt. She could not understand why Richard was so sullen.

They rode across the valley to the west. His brothers carried the hawks, hooded in leather. The dogs scattered around them sniffing at everything. In the deep, furrowed ground of the valley floor, the serfs were bent over planting seed. Even the littlest children went about to pick up stones. The hunting party crossed into fields plowed but not yet planted and from there into the oak wood.

Maria went up beside Richard. He was a good horseman; she was proud of the way he rode. For a while he pretended not to notice her next to him. Eventually he looked down at her from the back of his gray horse.

"You should not ride."

"I won't. Not after this." But she loved the spring hawking after cranes. Their horses swung into a canter, shoulder to shoulder. Two swine ran squealing into the wood away from them. The trees closed over their heads. Birds shrilled at them. In the distance the sunlight poured in through a gap in the roof of the wood.

The slope flattened into the sunlight of an open meadow. Maria's father led them out onto a point of dry ground that ran above the marsh to the beach. The horses dropped to a jog trot. Richard reined in to let her go in front of him.

"There are boats out there." He pointed toward the glittering water in the distance.

Maria shaded her eyes. The low surf rolled in along the beach. Beyond, the water danced green to the horizon. Near the sky, two white dots moved over the sea. One dot lengthened into a line and showed its curved sail.

Roger said, indifferent, "The villagers must fish there."

"The villagers have no boats," Richard said. "They are Saracens from Mana'a."

Maria drew her mare to a halt. The sudden bright sun was hurting her head. Instantly Richard brought his horse up beside her.

"I warned you," he said. "I'll take you home."

"Maria?" her father called, from down the beach, and she rode away from Richard, nudging her mare into a canter across the pale firm sand.

They hunted the rest of the morning along the edge of the marsh. Maria shook off her headache. Dragonflies swooped around her, hung whirring in the light, and zigged away. The broad golden marsh smelled of rot. Once, while she stopped to rest, a little deer came up through a stand of evergreens across the cattails from her. When she moved, the deer wheeled and lumbered out of sight, its barrel round with fawn.

Exhilarated, she rode on after the men. They had reined up along the bank of a stream. Out over the marsh, a crane unfolded its great wings and gathered itself into the air. The red falcon stooped above it. The crane's curved flight broke. Like a white feather it hung long in the pitch of the sky.

"Beautiful killing," Roger murmured, and her father muttered in agreement, his eyes fixed on the hawk.

Richard lured it back, and William raced off after the

44

dogs to retrieve the crane. Maria's mare splashed across the stream. No longer hunting, the riders spread out over the beach. Richard turned his horse down to the slow breakers and sat watching the Saracen boats. At the edge of the marsh, Maria's father was whistling to his dogs. She rode into the surf, up beside Richard. The curling waves broke around their horses' knees. She sniffed the brisk salty wind. On the sea before them, the Saracen boats were crawling north.

Richard reined his horse around her. "Let's go. You are getting sunburned." She followed him up the beach.

By late afternoon, they were riding into the foothills, where the beach disappeared and the sea came in to the rocks and the cliff. They cut across the wooded hills, reached the road, and swung north along it. Soon after they left the trees, the evening fell over them. They rode into the deepening twilight. The tired horses walked with their necks stretched and their heads down. Richard laid his rein slack on his gray's withers. Roger sang; the others joined in the refrain. Maria ate some blancmange she had brought wrapped in a napkin. She felt pleasantly sleepy, rocked by the white mare's easy stride.

Beside her, Richard said quietly, "Hold. Someone is coming."

They all drew rein. William called to the dogs. Maria's father rode up on her other side. The men shifted around her, their horses suddenly restless. A little band of men was riding toward them.

"Well met," Odo called, and he and four men came up around them. Odo was smiling but his face was graven with harsh lines. "The darkness fell, and we decided to see what had become of you."

Maria's father reached for her reins. She pulled the mare away from him, warned. Richard said, "Odo, you lie," and his hand went to his sword.

"Get him!" Odo roared.

Maria's mare reared up. A horse burst up past Roger, between her and Richard, and the man on its back hit Richard over the head with a club. Maria screamed. The horses fought and kicked in a tangle. Richard was doubled over his saddlebows. Beyond him the man with the club wheeled his horse to strike him again.

45

"Maria," Roger shouted. "Run! Run!"

She reined her mare around hard. All around her men were fighting. Her father was gone. She caught hold of the bridle of Richard's horse. Two hands taller than her mare, the stallion half-pulled her from the saddle. Richard was slack across its neck. She dragged him forward, between horses, toward the open road.

A knight loomed before her. He raised his sword but she was between him and Richard and he did not strike. She galloped past him, one hand in her mare's thick mane and the other on Richard's bridle. Iron rang behind her. She looked back: two riders were chasing her.

"Richard," she screamed. "Richard!"

He heard her. He heaved himself upright in the saddle. Blood streamed from the side of his face. He wrenched his horse's head out of her grasp. Wheeling, he charged back along the road.

Maria reined in. The full moon was rising, and the evening grew bright as twilight. The fighting ranged along the road. Two men already fought on foot. A loose horse cantered away from her. Roger's voice came to her, shouting something. The gray horse wheeled in a knot of darker bodies. Maria urged her horse forward. She wanted to throw herself barehanded into the fighting. Someone was crying for mercy. She would give no mercy. She galloped around the fighting, looking for her father.

His bay stallion stood in the middle of the road. The old man lay on the ground a hundred strides behind it. The dogs surrounded him. She rode up and started to dismount but the dogs leaped at her horse, barking, and the mare began to shy and fight. Maria struggled with the horse. In the middle of the dogs her father lay motionless on his back, his head turned away from her.

"Jonah! Lightning!" William rode up among the dogs, and they calmed down, their tails wagging. Maria made her horse stand. Two men on foot hobbled after William. They were roped together by the ankles. She dismounted and went up through the dog pack to her father.

"Papa."

When she put her hands on him a dog snapped at her. William shouted to it. Her father moved under her hands. She remembered how he had reached for her rein, before

Odo attacked them. He had known what was coming. The old man raised his head, groggy.

"Papa."

She sat back heavily. Other horses were cantering toward them. She stared at her father, wondering who had felled him, Odo or Richard. The old man sat up, his head in his hands.

Horses pushed up around them. Richard said, "Maria, get away from him." She climbed slowly to her feet. Richard braced his hands on the pommel of his saddle. He was still breathing hard. Roger caught her mare and brought it over to her. Dismounting, he came to help her into the saddle.

"You were very brave, Maria. They would have killed him if it hadn't been for you." He lifted her up on the mare's back.

She took hold of her saddle, dizzy. William and Roger got her father onto his horse. The two prisoners waited in the road, tied foot to foot. The ride back to the castle seemed long as a pilgrimage. She closed her eyes.

"Why didn't you take Odo alive?" William called.

"He wouldn't let me," Richard said. She started at the close sound of his voice, opening her eyes; he had come up right beside her.

"A pity," William said.

They started along the road again, the two prisoners striding awkwardly along ahead of them. William led her father's horse. The old man sagged in his saddle. The wind rose. Richard kept glancing at Maria's father.

"Damned dirty old pig, you couldn't even do this well."

Maria was still holding onto her horse's mane. She stared straight up the road. She imagined what would have happened to her and her baby, if Odo had killed Richard.

"How many were there?" Richard asked.

"Five," Roger said. "Not counting—" he nodded toward her father. His horse trotted a few steps to catch up with Richard's. "You think he was in it with Odo?"

Richard said nothing. They rode up around the shoulder of the hill. Above them was the castle. She held onto her saddle with both hands. The two men they had taken prisoner lagged on the steep slope, and Richard's horse trod on one of them. They skipped quickly out into the open road again.

The ward of the castle was crowded with men: the rest of the knights, standing around in the dark. "Look at this," William said. His voice rang in the silence. "All out to see which side came back riding."

Maria stopped her mare. Two of the men waiting in the dark came up to hold her bridle and she backed the horse away from them. Richard was giving orders. No one paid any more heed to her. She slipped down from her saddle. Her legs trembled and she held onto her stirrup.

"William," Richard said; he rode up beside her. "Lock the old pig up—find a good strong lock." He dismounted. His arm went around her waist. "Come on—are you nailed to that saddle?"

They went into the tower and up the stairs. Richard's teeth were set. Once he put his hand to his head. In their room, he sat down on the bed; Roger went to stir up the fire.

"Are you all right?" she said. "Let me see." She made him turn his head so that she could see the lump swelling up fat above his temple. His scalp had split open and his face was covered with blood.

"You're very lucky," Roger said. "You're a damned lucky man." He brought him a cup of wine.

"Oh," Richard said. "I move fast when something is aimed at my head."

There was water beside the bed. Maria got linen and washed his face off. Roger talked cheerfully of the fighting. Richard answered him in monosyllables. There was a knock on the door.

"Whoever that is," Richard said, "I don't want to see him."

Roger went over to the door, opened it a crack, and spoke through it. Maria washed out the linen. The water in the basin was stained with blood.

"What will you do to my father?"

He looked at her over his shoulder. "Now you believe me, don't you? You stupid sow. It's amazing to me you still have the baby."

She wrung out the linen and scrubbed ungently at his matted hair. Roger came over to them. "For God's love, Richard, let her alone."

"Who was that at the door?"

"Somebody swearing he loves us."

"Who?"

"Do you really want to know?"

Richard laughed. Maria dried his head off. She took the basin over to the window and emptied it into the ditch. Roger left. She put the basin down on the chest again and started to take off her dress. Richard turned her around, her back to him, and undid the laces.

"What will you do to my father?"

He pushed her dress open and down over her shoulders. His hands rested a moment flat on her skin. She turned to face him.

"It was Odo who tried to kill him," he said, eventually. "Not me. He betrayed me, but Odo betrayed him, that's why it didn't work." He smiled at her. "All right. I won't let him go. But I'll let him live. For your sake."

"Thank you," she said.

BEGINNING IN THE MORNING, Richard had the two prisoners whipped in the yard. Their screams awoke Maria, asleep late into the day, and she sent Flora down to make him stop, but Flora came back, looking sour, and said that he had only moved the prisoners to the other side of the ward. Although Maria could scarcely hear them, she could not fall asleep. She got out of bed and dressed herself.

When she went down into the ward, in the afternoon, the whipping had stopped. The two prisoners hung by their wrists against the wall near the gate, their heads slack. Richard sat on a stool in the shade nearby, drinking. The blacksmith from the village was pacing up and down flexing his arm, his whip coiled over his shoulder. Maria went into the kitchen.

"I knew it would come to this," the cook said. "The old man's been downhill since your mother died. He

49

should never have let the knave in the gate." For the first time since she had known him, he burst out laughing. "By the knave I mean Odo, of course."

In the room at the top of the New Tower her father lay on his back, snoring. The whipping had started again. Through the window the screams of the two men reached her faintly. She set down the tray she had brought and poured one of the cups full of the cook's best posset.

"Papa," she said. She sat down on the bed next to him, his vast bulk spread out under the blankets like a mountain. The snore broke off and he opened his eyes.

"Here, Papa, drink this."

He grunted and shut his eyes again. "That bastard Odo." He put his hand to his face. "Is that him down there?"

"No," she said. "Richard killed him."

In a flat grinding voice he called Richard several names. She tried to give him the drink, and he struck it away. She sat on the bed staring at him.

"Papa, did you really—was it really your idea?"

His eyes opened, and the corners of his mouth curled down. "I am a stupid old man," he said, "out against a clever young one, who I have faith will be a stupid old man himself someday." He shut his eyes again. "Get out."

"Papa—"

"Get out." He turned his face to the wall.

She sat there a while longer. At last she went down the stairs. Six or eight of the knights were sitting around the hearth in the hall. When she came in they looked studiously away from her. She went to the wine ewers on the table and banged on each of them to see which needed filling.

A shriek came up from the ward. The men around her all moved suddenly.

"One thing about Richard," the small dark knight said. "He spares the sermon. He goes straight to the sacrifice."

One man laughed, unnecessarily loud. Maria remembered the ambush and the knight who had not struck at her. Probably he was hanging on the wall screaming. She went hunting some place in the castle free of the noise, but she could find none, and until sundown she paced from room to room, praying that they would die and leave her in peace.

V

❦

THE TWO PRISONERS DIED THE NEXT AFTERNOON. THEIR bodies hung from the gate pole on the curtain wall until the summer. Maria's father, lying in his bed, began to waste. Maria went to the kitchen herself to cook his food and mix his drinks of herbs and wine. When Richard found out, he laughed at her, and she stopped, since she had marked also that her father still sickened a little every day.

"I don't have to poison him," Richard said. "He poisons himself. Are you ever going to have this baby?"

She and Flora sewed pads of cloth to use when she was in childbed. The fetid heat of the summer closed down on them. She felt as if she could not breathe. One night Richard's coast guards came to tell him that Saracen boats were sailing up from Mana'a. He and Roger galloped off with all but a handful of the knights; William kept command of the castle.

Of course as soon as they were gone Maria felt the first undulating tension in her womb. The midwife came, and the overheated room filled with women being important. Through the deep summer night, she lay on her side, her legs drawn up. Once she slept and dreamed of Saracen boats, shining like gold, slipping through the water, and the knights galloping across the dark waves to attack them.

51

By dawn she could neither sleep nor daydream. The women held her hands and told her meaningless soothing things. She had thought she would bear the pain silently and nobly, but she could not keep from screaming. At last the baby was born. The women fussed over her, feeding her a rank potion of wine, and kneading her belly painfully hard. Suddenly Flora was holding the baby out to her.

"Is that mine?" she said blankly. She felt nothing for it at all, it was just a baby. They put it down next to her. They all expected her to love it. And it was a girl, not a boy.

"You'll call her Matilde, for your mother," Adela said. "Won't you?"

"I hate that name. I'll name her Cecily." She touched the baby's face. It was an awful slate color, but it opened its eyes, its mouth sucked at nothing. Alive. She kissed its forehead. "Cecily."

MARIA OPENED HER EYES. She had wakened at the noise the men had made, tramping into her room. Richard took a splinter from the hearth, blew the coal at the end into a full flame, and lit a candle. With his brothers he stood over the baby.

"Why Cecily, in Jesus' name?"

"After her mother." Roger stepped back. "I'm sorry. I know you wanted a boy."

"I don't mind."

"Her mother was named Matilde," William said. "Mark, it's a name from stories. Where is the fat wench? Nowhere." He lifted the baby. Maria pushed herself up on her elbows. "I saw you both this little once. Both you knaves."

Roger made a disbelieving noise. He crossed the room to a leather sack on the hearth: loot from their raid. "They will not bring their goods north again in boats," he said. The firelight shone on his face. "We shall be great from this night."

Richard said, "They'll sail—they'll just stand out to sea, where we can't reach them." He bent over the baby. William crooned to her. Like the piping of a bird, a little wail started up, and William put the tip of his finger into the baby's mouth; that quieted her immediately.

Richard said, "William, another of your many crafts."

"Good night," Roger called, and went out. William laid the baby in the cradle. Richard stood with one hand on his hip, talking to him of their raid on the Saracens, while William stooped to rock the cradle. At last he stood up straight.

"God keep her," he said, shaking Richard's hand. "God give her a happy life. She'll be as pretty as her mother."

"Oh, prettier," Richard said lightly, and went with William to the door. Maria lay down again, sinking back toward sleep. When she wakened again, a while later, Richard was still there, standing with a candle in his hand, looking down at his daughter.

THE BABY WAVED ONE FIST. Maria caught it and kissed it. Cecily's tiny perfections fascinated her. She sat up on the bed, her legs folded under her, and opened her nightdress and gave the baby her breast. The baby was nothing like she had expected: she woke at odd hours and howled, she was always soaking wet, she demanded everything and gave nothing back but more work. Maria smoothed the baby's fine brown hair down over her skull. Her color was much better, save that her hands and feet were dark. She cupped the head in her palm. With her thumb she held her breast down so that the baby could breathe while she nursed.

"Cow," Richard said. He was lying in the bed behind her.

Maria got up. The baby had finished nursing and lay peacefully in her mother's arms, her dark blue eyes open. Maria changed her napkin and put the baby into the cradle. She stood beside it, rocking it. Richard got out of bed. Down the stairs, Adela called her, but Maria pretended not to hear. At first every woman in the castle had spent the mornings in her room, making her listen to their detailed and contradictory advice, and passing the baby from lap to lap; at last she had driven them away. Richard came up beside her.

"I have something for you," he said.

She turned, surprised. He had never given her anything before. He was looking down at the baby. He took his left hand from behind his back.

"Oh," Maria said. "A looking glass." Her mother had once had a looking glass. She took it out of his hands. It was heavier than she expected, the frame worked in gold, with cameos set in the four corners. She could not bring herself to look at her own face. She turned and kissed Richard.

"We took it in the plunder, the night she was born," he said. "I told you I'd give you presents. Do you like it?"

Maria said, "It's beautiful." She searched his face. "She looks like you. Do you mark it?"

He laughed. His head tilted down toward the cradle. "She is me. Part of me." He took the looking glass from her and held it to show her her own face.

Maria clapped her hands over her eyes. "What is wrong with you now? Here, look." He grasped her by the wrist. Maria resisted his pull. She was afraid to see herself. She was afraid of being ugly. But between her fingers she saw the image in the glass, and slowly let her hands down, taking the glass away from him.

"Oh, well," she said, and turned her head a little. Her chin was pointed and her nose too short, and save for her dark blue eyes she had no color at all: white skin and black hair. It was better than being ugly.

"Now you'll neglect me," Richard said, "and spend all day long looking at your face."

She held the glass in front of him, to show him himself. He covered the mirror with his hand. "No, I'm not vain, like you."

Maria kissed him again, one hand on his forearm. "Thank you. You are very kind to me." Putting the looking glass down carefully in the cradle, she slid her arms around his neck. "Let me take Cecily up to show my father."

"Hunh." His whole face soured; his mouth went tight as a trap. "Go ahead. I suppose you ought to." He reached behind him, took her wrists, and pulled her arms away from him. He strode toward the door, but first he looked down at the baby.

54

Maria's father, dying in his room, saw the baby and wept. For a while he babbled disconsolately of the punishments inflicted on him, who deserved only peace in his old age. He called Richard a variety of names and cursed him for making Cecily a girl. Maria left him almost at once. It frightened her to see him there, his flesh sunken around his bones, and his eyes milky with disease. Six days after her churching, he died in the night.

When they buried him a great crowd of people came, from all over the area, men and women Maria had never seen before: shepherds and fishermen, serfs, and hilldwellers. Few of them were sorrowful. They told wild stories about her father that ran back forty years. With the baby in her arms she walked along the hillside away from the graveyard. Richard came up beside her.

She said, "I wish you had killed him. It would have been better than having him die like that."

"It was your idea," Richard said. He held the postern door open for her. They went into the castle.

VI

❀

MARIA'S CASTLE STOOD IN THE WILDERNESS NEAR THE sea. A day's ride to the south the wood-covered hills rose into mountains, which the Saracens controlled. Beyond the shield of the mountains was the ancient city of Mana'a, now like Jerusalem in the hands of the Saracens.

North and east of the wilderness was Santerois, ruled by a Norman duke. Maria's father had always kept his reach short in that direction, shy of Duke Louis, but soon after Robert Strongarm died, the Duke of Santerois died also. He left as his heir a baby named Henry. The child's powerful relatives took care of him and fought for him, but they could not keep the Duke's tenants from seizing his castles, chasing out his garrisons, and starting wars among themselves.

Between Santerois and the northern edge of the wilderness lay the March of Birnia, a stretch of hills and fen. After the old Duke died, Richard led a dozen raids there. When he had savaged the countryside and burned several villages, the town of Birnia gave up to him, and he took Maria and the baby north to join him while he rebuilt what he had seized.

On the hill above the half-destroyed town, the Tower of Birnia was close as a stable and smelled worse. For the first few days Maria complained steadily, in hopes that Richard would send her home. The baby—they called her Ceci—was awake more during the day, and Richard was very fond of her, playing with her in his lap, while Maria argued with him over the food and the wine and the lack of servants and the smell.

"Make it better," he said, "and stop your damned mouth," and she withdrew into a grim silence and wondered if she could escape.

After she had refused to speak to him for three days, he beat her. She realized he would not let her go home. She went to the kitchen and told the cook and his knaves what she wished of them, and finding women in the town to help her, cleaned the hall and swept out the stairs, where mice were living in the filth along the steps. From then on, she worked every day, and Richard spent the day gone, and they did not talk.

The winter blew itself out in a gust of storms. Just before Lent, a messenger came from Theobald, a Count whose holdings bordered on the north of Birnia; Maria took the messenger to the hall, fed him, gave him wine, and set a knight to watch him until Richard came back. During supper, with the messenger on his right hand, Richard made small talk and exchanged bits of general news.

Maria sat on his left, eating without appetite. Richard ignored her. She watched him through the corner of her eyes. The messenger flattered Richard in an unctuous voice. She could not remember that any lord like Theobald had ever paid such heed to her father.

After the two hall servants had helped her take off what was left of the supper, she went up the stairs to the top room of the Tower, where she and Richard slept, and found him sitting there with the messenger. When she came in, their conversation stopped abruptly. She went to the cradle to see the baby. The sun had gone down; the only light in the room came from the fire.

Richard said, "Maria, go downstairs."

She gave them a curious glance and went out the door onto the stair landing. Richard came after her. She let him see her go on down the stairs. After he had shut the door and bolted it she went back up onto the landing. Their voices reached her, but not the words. She squeezed in the narrow door on the back of the landing and climbed up the ladder onto the catwalk around the top of the Tower.

From here their voices were clear as if she sat beside them. She could even see a little through a hole where a slate was missing in the roof. She sat down with her arms curled around her knees, shivering from cold.

At first they talked of obvious things: the roads, the necessity of warning one another of raiders. Since Richard had contact with the Saracens, the messenger had many questions about them. She put her cheek down on her knees. She told herself that he could not be blamed that he was not handsome like Roger, or of a kinder disposition. Richard was clever, he had a shrewd understanding, and she should be glad of him as he was, and not wish he were otherwise.

The messenger talked about the King's brother, the Prince Arthur Fairhame, who from what the messenger said lived in Count Theobald's pockets. Whenever he spoke of the baby Duke Henry, the messenger laughed and slighted him—"Still in a short shirt," he said once, although Count Theobald was supposed to be the Duke's vassal. Maria began to wish the messenger would come to his point. Richard said nothing at all.

At last the man said, "To be candid, sir, my master the Count is counseling Prince Arthur to seize the duchy and make himself our Duke. Of course, since he has only a few knights of his own, the Prince will need our help."

There was a long silence. Maria bent and looked in through the hole in the roof. Richard sat with his chin in his hand, his face expressionless. She could not see the messenger.

Richard said, "Neither Theobald nor I is such a great man in this country that our help could make anybody Duke, even that baby up there in Agato. I understand Count Fitz-Michael is the baby's champion. If your master wants to bring Fitz-Michael down on him, that is his mistake."

"There are others—"

"I dislike being one of many."

Maria trembled all over with the cold; her teeth rattled together. She was almost glad that Richard was getting up, even though he was ending the talk just when the business was coming out. She put her feet under her.

"You would not be one of many," the messenger said sharply. "Count Theobald as a mark of his favor will give you the hand of his daughter in marriage."

"Holy Mother," Maria whispered.

Richard sat down again. "I am a married man."

"Yes, but a way out might be found," the messenger said. "A robber chieftain's wench, we understand, of no lineage. Your only child is a sickly girl. Possibly you are bound in kinship. You know how easily these things are arranged."

Maria bit her lips. He spoke of her as slightly as of the baby Duke. *A robber chieftain's wench*, as if she were a serf.

Richard did not move. Finally he pushed his chair back and got up. "Well, maybe. I'll talk to you again tomorrow. Good night."

Maria waited until the messenger had gone and went down to the stair landing. She opened the door to her room. Richard was sitting in front of the fire, a cup in his hand. She crossed the room to her bed and lifted the baby up, whispering to her. Before, she had been forcing herself to see Richard's virtues. Now the thought of losing him filled her with terror and rage. He would never dare desert her. She changed the baby's napkin. Richard was

58

watching her; between his eyebrows were two short vertical lines. He was thinking of it, the wretch, thinking of leaving her. She put the baby in the bed. When she went back across the room, he took hold of her arm and pulled her over next to him.

"Where have you been?" he asked. "You're freezing."

She sat down in the warmth of the hearth. "It's very cold tonight—I was in the ward." She could not meet his eyes. His brothers were back in her castle, two days to the south; the knights here were all strangers. She had no friends here, no one to help her. She turned to put her other side to the fire.

"Here," he said; he gave her the wine cup. "Get your insides warm."

She sipped the strong red wine. "What did this man say?"

"Nothing important." He slouched in his chair, his chin in his hand. "Stop sulking, will you? I know you hate this place, but it's much better now. I'm very happy with it, I wish everybody worked as hard as you do. I'd be King of Italy."

Maria gave him back the cup. In spite of what she knew, his voice comforted her. She turned her eyes toward the fire and wished she had not overheard them talking, so that she could trust him.

VII

❧

JUST AFTER DAWN, RICHARD LEFT WITH A DOZEN knights, and Maria sorted out the kitchen knaves and set them to cleaning out the ovens, on the hillside below the castle, and the kitchen itself, choked with the debris of years. Maria sat in the ward with Ceci, watching how they did. It was Lent, and most of the people were fasting, so she did not hurry them.

The town women had come up to work, and they brought out the linen of the castle to air. Maria set the baby down in the corner and went to help them. It was a beautiful warm day, like the late springtime, beneath a cloudless blue sky, and while they shook out the linen, the women laughed and gossiped. When Ceci began to cry, a big, pale townswoman went to get her, and brought her back laughing and poking her fingers into the woman's mouth.

Maria sat down to give the baby her breast. The other women gathered around her, admiring the baby. Beside her, the big woman got a loaf from her apron and broke it in half.

"What a beautiful day this is," another woman said. "Not usual at all. *Lenten weather helps prayer*, my father always said."

The others murmured in agreement. Their jaws munched steadily through their dinner loaves. The women of Maria's village wore their hair uncovered, in braids; these had linen coifs on their heads, starched stiff as wings over each ear.

The fat woman beside her smiled at her. "I am the ostler's daughter—my father is the spokesman for the town in some of our doings. We keep the inn here, of course. She is a pretty baby. What is her name?"

"Cecily. Do you have any children?"

The wide face was bland between the wings of her coifs. "My husband died in the fire, when Birnia was destroyed."

"Oh," Maria said; she felt stupid for asking. "I'm sorry."

"He deserved it. Maybe now when Birnia is calm again I will get another husband. Here comes yours."

Maria stood up to see through the open gate. Richard on his red bay horse with a couple of knights after him rode up the hill from the town. He passed through the gate and across the ward. If he saw her, in the ward among the women, he ignored her, and she sat down again. She popped the baby on her shoulder and patted her back.

"Come, now," said the ostler's daughter, and got enormously to her feet. "We have six more baskets to bring down." She touched Maria's shoulder and led the other women off toward the Tower.

Maria laid the sleeping baby on the grass at the foot of the wall. Some broken bales of flax stood before the doorway down into the kitchen. Two dogs were fighting over a bone on the threshold. She looked around to make sure the baby was safe and went down the steps.

The cook appeared from the darkness in the back; he was shorter than she was, bird-faced. He hurried up to her.

"Come tell them they do not have to brick up the wall again. They sit in there and loaf and pretend they are bricking up the wall."

"What wall?"

"In the back—the old pantry." When Maria brushed by him into the kitchen, he followed. "I told them not to brick it back up—what's the use of that, I said—"

Maria walked across the dark filthy kitchen into the back, where the pantry was. Here stacks and bales of goods had been piled up against the walls on either side, except for the narrow doorway to the pantry and the cellar. Now the trash was gone. The wall there had crumbled partly away, the bricks had fallen out, and the gap showed an old doorway, which breathed a draft of cold air into her face.

The three little knaves were briskly stacking brick on brick, and by the way they worked she guessed the cook was right: they had been loafing, or they would have finished long before. But she did not want to do as the cook said. "Unbrick it. What's in there? The old pantry, you said. Maybe you could use it."

The knaves twisted to watch her. With a glance at the cook they took to unstacking the bricks. Maria moved out of the draft. With the cook behind her she went back up into the daylight and looked to see that the baby was all right. The ostler's daughter was carrying her around, laughing.

The cook said bitterly, "As much work as those boys do, they could do on the Sabbath and not make enough of a sin to pray over."

61

"Keep watch on them—make them do it." She crossed the paving stones to the sunlight, where the women were drinking cups of water and saying how weak they felt, and the fasting hardly begun. Lying on the grass in their midst, the baby rolled onto her back and played with her fingers.

"My lady," the cook's reedy voice called. He was coming toward her at a fast walk. "Lady—"

Maria stood up; he bustled over to her. "Lady, there is something there. God willed it. God told us to open up the pantry again."

Maria headed toward the kitchen. "What do you mean?"

The cook shook his head. After walking across the ward and halfway back, he was out of breath. His face glowed importantly red. "This fellow Walter Bris," he said, his voice lowered, "the man who commanded here when my lord Richard came, you know, he was not the true lord of this castle. This used to be a thieves' nest, here, quite like—" He cleared his throat, suddenly embarrassed. She went after him into the kitchen and back toward the pantries.

They had lit another torch, casting light into every corner of the back of the kitchen, and through the unbricked wall into the old pantry. The light showed a huge old clothes chest, half-buried in dust in the corner.

Maria caught her breath. She climbed through the rubble of the bricks and knelt beside the chest. She could not move it, not with her whole weight pushing it, and the lid was rusted tight.

She went out to the kitchen. The three knaves and the cook stood out of the draft, their faces beaming. To the cook, she said, "Stay here. Let no one in. I'll be right back." She herded the knaves out of the kitchen and ran across the ward to the Tower.

Richard was not in the hall. She climbed the stairs toward the top room. Halfway up she heard a stranger's voice there. She missed the first few words of what he said, but drawing closer, she overheard enough to know what he was talking about. She stopped on the stair, just below the door.

"My lord," the stranger said, "what further worth is

62

she to you? You have what you wed her for, Strongarm's castle and his men. Count Theobald's daughter will make you a lord."

Richard laughed. Maria could make nothing of his laughter. She went in the door, to stop them talking. Both the men spun toward her, their faces taut. The other man she had seen before: one of the castle's knights. She said, "Richard, there is something down here you must attend to," and turned away before he could read her expression. The other stood on the hearth. Her hands were shaking. She went out again onto the stair landing.

"I'm coming," Richard said. "Good day, Walter."

Walter Bris, Maria thought. Richard behind her, she went down the stairs to the hall.

"What is this, anyway?" Richard asked. "I've got important things to do—"

"This is important," Maria said. She led him across the hall to the outer staircase and down into the ward. The women were all sitting in a knot, playing with Ceci. She and Richard walked past them to the heaps of garbage before the kitchen door.

The knaves loitered in the shade, their heads ducked together in some gossip. Maria took Richard down into the kitchen, where the cook was standing bolt upright before the gap in the wall, like a sentry.

Richard went on before her into the pantry. She stopped to send the cook outside again. When she reached her husband, he was kneeling by the chest, swearing in a soft monotone in the darkness. His hands ran over the leather straps and the lid.

"Give me a fire-box."

She handed him her tinderbox. He got the charred linen burning and used its feeble light to go quickly over the locks on the chains that held the chest to the wall. The light flickered out. He sat the tinderbox impatiently aside, tried to force the lid and could not, pulled and shoved at the chest without moving it at all, and sat back on his heels.

"Devil damn me," he murmured. In the dark she could not see his face.

"Whose is it?" Maria asked.

"Mine, now."

He took hold of the chest and strained to move it. "That knight who was with me, just now—he was master here when I came, but he had only been here a few months, and this has sat for years, this box, look at it." He put his hands lovingly on the chest. "He'll cry all night when he hears of this, will Walter Bris."

Maria put her lips together to keep from saying anything about Walter Bris. Richard stood up straight, to draw his sword. The light from the kitchen leaped along the blade. With its edge he burst open the lid. The hinges shrieked. Maria craned her neck to see.

"Well," Richard said. The chest was packed with dark cloth sacks. He lifted one, and the rotten fabric gave and chips of dull metal fell out, flooding over the edge of the chest into the dirt. Maria grabbed one and spat on it and rubbed it to a patchy shine on her skirt.

"Silver."

Richard got up. "Come on." He pushed her toward the door and they went out into the kitchen. The cook hung in the doorway. Richard pointed to him.

"Go get Ponce Rachet down here. He's in the hall."

The cook strode eagerly away. The three kitchen knaves crowded into the doorway; when the cook went up the steps they pressed him with questions. Richard held out his hand toward Maria.

"Give me that money you took."

She handed it to him. He went up into the doorway, to look at it in the sunlight. "Saracen. Somebody's treasure horde. Walter Bris is going to weep." He put the coin in his wallet. "Get those people away from there."

She herded the knaves and the little crowd that had gathered behind them back across the ward. Richard stood in the kitchen doorway, his eyes intently on nothing and his arms folded over his chest. Maria went over to the serving women to get the baby.

The women surrounded her, bursting with questions, and she shook her head. "I know nothing. It is all nothing to me." Ceci was playing on the ground among them. She looked up and beamed at her mother. Maria lifted the baby and settled her on her hip, smiled at the ostler's daughter, and went to the Tower.

On the steep outside stairs she passed Ponce Rachet, hurrying down from the hall. Richard was still in the kitchen doorway. Maria went up to her bedchamber on the top of the Tower.

There was no one in the room. She changed the baby's clothes and put her to bed for a nap. From the window she watched Ponce Rachet carry a heavy leather sack up from the kitchen, pause to ease his arms, and start across the ward. Maria rubbed her palms together. She wanted to kill Walter Bris, but she did not know how. She would have to get him alone, in a lonely place. He was strong, a grown man in his prime, so she would have to catch him by surprise. She could poison him, but someone else might die by mistake, and she put aside that idea.

The door downstairs banged open. Feet tramped up the stairs toward her. She went to the rack beside the cupboard where Richard kept his weapons, and got a dagger with a long thin blade. God expressly forbade murder, but she would think of that later, when it was done. What he had said about her was worse than murder. She knew how Richard's ambitions ran: If Theobald's daughter would bring him what he wanted, she and Ceci would only be in his way. She tucked the dagger in her sleeve, kissed the baby, and went out, past Ponce Rachet coming up the stairs with a sack of treasure on his shoulder.

The sun was high in the sky. The hall was empty, save for a few servants and a woman weaving. The dagger hidden in her sleeve, Maria went down into the ward.

Richard was carrying a sack of money up through the kitchen door. She waited until his back was to her and went through the edge of the ward toward the stables. In the cool subterranean vault, several knights sprawled on the straw, arguing. None of them was Walter Bris. She went through the stables without even nodding when they greeted her and walked up again into the sunlight.

She looked outside the gate and around the back of the ward but Walter Bris was nowhere. She went back up toward her room. Ponce Rachet stood on the stair landing outside the door. He stepped aside to let her go by. Two huge bags of money sat on the floor midway between the door and the bed. Maria took the baby into a corner to

65

nurse her. Feet pounded on the stairs, and Richard came in, lugging another sack on his shoulder. Ponce Rachet followed him inside.

"That's all of it."

The two men bent over the sacks. Richard found a chest and dumped the clothes in it out onto the floor. Maria watched him narrowly. When she thought that he might desert her her eyes stung with tears. At last the baby fell asleep. She put her in the bed, between two pillows to keep her from rolling off. Richard and his knight were stacking up the money on the chest. Outside the window, the sky turned softly pink and violet.

Abruptly she knew where Walter Bris was: in the town with the messenger from Count Theobald. Richard would not have mentioned the marriage proposal to a man he obviously disliked; Walter Bris would have heard it only from Theobald's messenger. The cook had said Walter Bris had commanded here before Richard came. Maybe he had been the Count's man even then.

The evening cool swept in from the river and chilled her face. She went down the stonework outer stair of the Tower and waited in the ward until she could sneak out the postern door unseen. Walter Bris would not stay away from the Tower much past sundown, or Richard would begin to suspect him. She walked down under the trees that lined one edge of the road toward the town.

A crow cawed in the fields. Ahead, the torches on the wall of the town rippled in the wind. The dark settled down over the world. The fragrance of the softening earth rose around her. The moon had not yet risen, and she kept her stride short, for fear of tripping. When she reached the foot of the hill, she sat beneath an oak tree, her eyes on the town half a mile on.

Ceci might wake up and cry for her. Murder was a terrible sin, but what they were trying to do to her was a sin, too. The dagger lay in her lap, cool to her hand, the hilt wrapped in leather, the edges honed white. Down the road, a horse was cantering up from the town.

She looked around carefully, to make sure she was unseen. The moon appeared over the edge of the hills in the east. The horseman trotted up the road toward her. She stood up and crossed the ditch.

"Please," she called. "Help me—please—"

Walter Bris rode up to her and reined in his horse. "What are you doing out here?" He dismounted.

Maria pretended to faint, collapsing on her side, with the dagger under her. The knight muttered an oath. He knelt beside her.

"She's witch-wild. Strongarm's brat: crazy as he was."

He gathered her up, one arm under her shoulders and the other under her knees. She raised the dagger and stabbed him in the throat.

The blood spattered across her. He staggered; he shouted wordlessly, and she struck him again, writhing out of his grip. He fell. She leaped on him, her knees on his chest, and drove the knife to its hilt in his neck. His eyes glared at her, reflecting the moon. His yawning mouth erupted blood. He sagged and was still.

Maria backed away from him toward the trees. His horse moved restlessly along the dirt road. Her surcoat and her overskirt were spotted with blood. She wiped the dagger on the grass and tore off the top layer of her skirt. If she hurried she could be there to eat supper with Richard. She would never be cruel to Richard again. The knight lay crooked in the road, one arm flung out. Now, at least, he would not suffer for the treasure he had missed. She caught his horse and rode it back across the fields toward the castle, left it under the wall, and went in again through the postern door.

In the morning, while Richard still lay in bed, she took her bloodstained clothes out and buried them in the briars at the foot of the castle wall. She brought Ceci with her. For a while she sat in the tall grass playing with the baby and making her laugh. The baby's hair was starting to grow in, soft as air, dark brown like Richard's, wisps of curls at her ears and neck. She reached for everything she saw, the grass, Maria's fingers, the shadows of birds. When she lifted her face up to her mother's, her smile was wide as her cheeks. Maria had never loved anyone else, not even her mother, as deeply as she loved Ceci. The ghost of Richard's face in the baby's made it easier to forgive him for listening to Walter Bris.

67

At last she went back up to the Tower. While she climbed across the steep slope, Ceci astride her hip, a party of horsemen galloped up the road toward the gate. They would have found the dead man. She ran the rest of the way to the Tower.

Richard was sitting on the bottom step of the staircase on the Tower, talking to Ponce Rachet. When he saw her, he called to her and took Ceci from her arms. "Go bring us some wine," he said, but before she could go, he caught her wrist.

"What's wrong?"

Maria pulled free and ran up the outer stair toward the hall. She guessed at how she looked: she felt sick and weak. When she was pouring the wine, she knocked over a cup, and the wine splashed on her skirt like drops of blood. At that, she began to cry and for a moment could not lift the ewer or clear her eyes.

Outside, a man shouted. She set down the ewer and rubbed the tears from her eyes, picked up the wine, and poured two cups full. Taking one in each hand, she went out and down the stair to where Richard sat, a little crowd gathered around him.

They had brought Walter Bris back with them across a horse. At the sight of the body she nearly stumbled. Richard took the wine from her, and she sank down on the step behind him. Ceci babbled and pulled on the laces of Richard's shirt. Absently he caught her hand.

"We found him on the road," Theobald's messenger was saying. "He has been sliced to death. Who would have done it? His sword is still in its scabbard."

Richard cradled Ceci in the curve of his arm. The baby reached for his cup; she burst into a long dreamy string of nonsense. Richard shrugged.

"Probably he had a lot of enemies. He was no particular friend of mine." He pointed to a knight at the foot of the stairs. "Take him and bury him. Maria—" he looked around behind him to find her and lifted Ceci toward her over his shoulder. Maria took the baby upstairs, her knees unsteady.

AT DINNER, she could not eat. She stayed in her room the rest of the afternoon, playing with Ceci and sewing with two of the castle women whom she trusted not to talk to her. Richard came in and out of the room a few times, and each time started to speak to her but broke off. When supper was ready, she had a servant bring her a dish of it—she had been feeling sick to her stomach all day, she thought she might be with child again. She ate a little and threw the scraps out the window while the women weren't looking.

While she was sitting by the window nursing Ceci, after sundown, Richard came in and sent away the women attending her. She heard the mattress crunch when he sat down on the bed. Sliding her thumb into the baby's mouth, she moved her around to the other breast. Richard kicked his heels a few times on the bedframe.

Abruptly he said, "Did you kill Walter Bris?"

Maria startled. His voice was edged with disbelief. She licked her lips. She had waited too long to deny it, so she said nothing. Ceci held her breast in her hands and suckled hungrily.

Richard said, "Why did you kill Walter Bris?"

She had to twist to see him. The baby in her arms gave her courage. "He wanted you to leave me. I heard him. He said such things about me—*a robber chief's wench*—you should have defended me, but you didn't, you listened to them."

He rubbed his palms together absently. The baby, finished with the breast, was nuzzling Maria. She got up to take her to the bed. Richard sat watching her. She laid the baby down between the pillows, kissed her, and drew the cover over her.

Richard took her by the wrist and turned her to face him. "That was a damned stupid thing to do. You might have been caught."

"I was careful."

"Not very. I saw last night before supper the dagger was gone." He twisted her arm, to make her stand closer to him, her hip against his knee. "You could have gotten me into a lot of trouble, doing that—I should take a belt to you. Why didn't you trust me? I wouldn't give you up for a Count's daughter, even if Theobald were serious, which I doubt."

Maria turned her arm against his hand, and he tightened his grip. Her wrist hurt. She said, "You heard how they talked about me. I didn't have to tell you. You should have done it."

To her surprise, he opened his fingers. She drew her arm free. "Maybe you are right," he said. "I should have done something." His mouth stretched into a smile. Amazed, she saw the thing amused him. He said, "You've been spying on me. What did I tell you about that?"

"I'm sorry," she said. "I won't do it again."

"No, not tonight, maybe."

He was staring at her, his eyes sharp. He said, "Thank you for putting the knife back last night. I was afraid you meant to use it on me. Nobody else even suspects you, nobody here knows you."

"I told you," she said, "I was careful."

He shook his head. "You were lucky. If you do it again—" He gave her another piercing look. "Don't do it again. I ought to break your neck. What if someone had seen you? What if you couldn't kill him?" His eyes were sharp. "You did it alone. All by yourself."

She went off across the room. "I don't want to talk about it." On the hearth, she knelt and took a log out of the box beside the fire. All afternoon she had tried to pray. She would have to go to the Cave of the Virgin, to pray there. He was still watching her. She dumped the log on top of the fire and got up to go to bed.

VIII

IN THE CAVE, TWO WOMEN WERE PRAYING IN LOUD competing voices. In spite of the hot summer sun outside, the cave was cold and damp. Maria knelt in the back of it, holding Ceci on her lap. The baby looked solemnly around her. Maria took Ceci's coat from her basket and wrestled the baby into it.

One woman rose, crossed herself, and left the shrine, and Maria took her place. She had brought the baby's christening gown, sewn with crosses; she laid it at the feet of the statue. Before her, the baby sat bundled in her coat, looking curiously at the strange woman beside them. While Maria prayed, she kept watch on the child, who was learning to crawl. The strange woman left and an old man, richly dressed, took her place.

Maria asked a blessing for the baby growing in her womb, and for Richard, his brothers, and the souls of her parents. She had forgotten how happy prayers in this place made her feel. She had asked the day before for absolution for killing Walter Bris. Now she offered a prayer for his soul. Probably he was in Hell anyway and the prayer wouldn't help him.

Ceci reached out toward the christening gown on the statue's feet. It was just beyond her grasp, and she strained as if her arm might suddenly sprout another inch. Maria crossed herself. There were more people outside, waiting to be allowed in. She gathered up the baby and her basket and went out through the narrow corridor in the rock. A boy on crutches hobbled past her.

A dozen pilgrims waited in the yard of the shrine. They talked among themselves, or stared at the knights who waited in the shade of the beech trees. Inside the cave, the dank cold had made Maria shiver. Outside, the bright sunshine glittered on the rocks and the heat flowed like a liquid over the ground. She crossed the yard to the trees.

Roger stood in the shade, talking to the English monk. While she took off the baby's coat and put her on the ground, he said, "There are some travelers here from the north. I want to talk to them—do you mind?"

Maria shook her head. She was hunting through her basket for the purse of money Richard had given her. Roger went off under the trees where the ground was soft with mast. The monk bent toward Maria.

"Lady, we were all distraught to hear of my lord Robert's death. Most untimely—we have included him in our prayers."

Maria handed him the purse. "Thank you. Richard wishes your prayers as well."

The monk took hold of the bottom of the purse, but she did not let go of the top. She looked him in the eyes. "He will guard the road and protect the shrine here," she said, and when his face lost its practiced smile, she let him take the purse.

Stiff, the monk tucked the purse away. "I will speak of it to the abbot in Agato."

Maria bowed to him. "Thank you." Richard had said they would have to accept him as their overlord, now that he held Birnia; the road from Agato to the shrine ran through Birnia. Ceci had hauled herself to her feet and was standing on her wide-spread legs, her fists balled up in Maria's skirt. Maria took her on one hip and the basket over her arm and crossed the yard to Roger.

She had never come to the shrine in the summer. The many pilgrims waiting to go in and pray made the yard seem much smaller. Roger was leaning up against a tree, near the steep hillside; a young man with a pilgrim's hat and staff stood talking to him. When Maria went up to them Roger took her by the hand.

"This is my brother's wife, Maria."

She and the young pilgrim murmured at each other. She tugged her hand out of Roger's. Ceci was demanding to be put down. She set the baby on the ground.

"You said you intended to fight the Saracens," the young pilgrim said.

Roger nodded. "The Saracens hold the whole south coast and the mountains. There will be hard fighting—my brothers and I have been fighting here for years, all over the area, we know the Saracens. And they know us, I can tell you. There will be honor and glory to be won. And it's work for Christ, too, naturally."

"Do you need men? What about plunder?"

Two more strangers came up behind the man in the pilgrim's hat: young men, of Roger's age. The first introduced them to her and Roger, who shook them each by the hand. The tallest of the three smiled.

"I heard mention made of plunder?"

Roger leaned his weight against the fat beech tree behind him. He set his hands on his belt. "My brother Richard is the lord of this land. We want to fight the Saracens. I was telling your companion here that we need knights—good fighters who don't mind a long hard war. There's plunder, yes. The Saracens are rich. We mean to take Mana'a, in time."

"Mana'a," the man in the pilgrim's hat said blankly. His face quickened. "The Saracen city? Do you mean Marna?"

The tall man pursed his lips. Roger shrugged, his face schooled to innocence. "Marna. They call it Mana'a, and we've fallen into the name, I suppose." He gestured toward Maria. "Her father was Roger Strongarm, you will have heard of him."

They talked about wars. Ceci had gotten up on her feet again, clinging to Maria's skirt.

"You said your brother is lord here," the tall pilgrim said. "But I've heard this is lordless ground, since the old Duke of Santerois died."

Roger smiled. "Anybody who thinks it is lordless can try to take it."

The other men laughed. The one with the hat had a long staff, and Ceci leaned out and clutched it. Maria stooped to pick her up. The little girl hung on to the staff, refusing to let go.

"By God's holy book," the man in the hat said, "if your brother has a grip like this little knave's, you might be right about that."

Everybody laughed again. Maria detached her daughter

from the pilgrim's staff. In a high humor, the young men all shook Roger's hand again, bowed to her, chucked Ceci under the chin, and went off promising to come back in the spring. Roger swung toward her, his face bright with amusement.

"What if they knew the little knave is a girl?"

Their knights came up around them, bringing their horses. Maria put the baby in her saddle.

"Do you think they will come back—those knights?"

"They'll come back," Roger said.

THEY WENT SOUTH to her own castle. One day in August, Richard and his friends took over the village common to break a string of four-year-old colts. When she had done all her work in the castle, Maria took the baby down the hill, Adela coming with her to carry the basket with their dinner in it.

The common lay between the village and the river. The grass was browning in the summer heat. In the middle of it the men had put up a short strong post, to tie the colts. A strapping black with a white face was lunging and rearing around it. Maria set the baby down in the grass under an oak tree and helped Adela lay out the cloth and the food: bread, two cold roast chickens, cheese, and a leather flask of wine. Ceci crawled in the flowering grass.

"Hold him, Ponce!" Roger shouted.

Ponce Rachet was wrestling a bridle onto the black colt's head. Three other knights stood around helping. Richard came over to the oak tree, and Maria gave him the wine and a piece of the chicken.

"How are they?" she asked.

He sat down, his mouth already full and his jaws grinding. He said something unintelligible about the two colts they had already broken. Adela went off to the village, to see her sister.

Maria settled herself comfortably and ate a simnel cake. She licked the crumbs off her fingers. The new baby rode high in her belly, which made it hard to sit up straight. They were trying to sling a saddle onto the black colt's back. It lunged from the men's grip and knocked Ponce Rachet sprawling. Roger came up.

"Sit down and eat something," Richard said.

"Is there enough?" Roger sat down. He picked up the other bird. Maria looked around for Ceci. The little girl was crawling up the little slope behind her, toward the castle.

"Keep watch on her, will you?" Richard said. "What if a horse gets loose?"

Maria chewed on a piece of bread. The pounding of the hoofs and the dust were making her head ache. Now they were trying to chase the black colt around the snubbing post. Richard shouted obscene advice to them, his voice ringing in her ear. She threw the bones of the two chickens into the meadow. Richard lay back on his elbow, his head almost in her lap. She gave him the wine flask. He drank; with his free hand he rubbed the bulge of her body. She pushed his hand away.

"Where is she now?"

She looked over her shoulder. A hundred feet away, in the grass, the little girl sat surrounded by orange butterflies. Richard poked Maria in the side.

"Go get her. Why are you so careless with her? One of those horses could break loose—"

"Then she would be safer up there than here. If I ran after her all day, I would be dead. You spoil her."

He laid his fingers on her body again. Maria moved away. Roger was watching them, it made her uncomfortable when Richard touched her in front of him. Roger got up and went to join the men around the post. They had saddled the black colt. Ponce Rachet was swinging onto its back.

"When are you raiding?" she asked. All summer he had been forcing the villages around them to pay his new taxes.

He grunted. Picking up her knife, he cut himself a piece of the cheese.

"I haven't spied on you," she said. "Not once, since I promised."

"Therefore I should tell you everything."

"You will drive me to it."

The men leaped away from the black colt. On its back Ponce Rachet let out a yell. The colt doubled up into a buck. Roger cheered and laughed among the other men.

Richard was picking his teeth. He said, "Go get Ceci."

Maria got up and walked out into the sunlight. She scooped her daughter up at arm's length. The little girl laughed at her. Maria tossed her up and caught her, and she giggled. Maria carried her back to Richard.

Ponce trotted the black colt out until it broke into a gallop and turned it in circles to slow it down. Ceci immediately crawled away up the slope again. Maria sat beside the tree and leaned her back on it.

"I haven't made up my mind yet—about my war," Richard said eventually. He stuck the toothpick in the corner of his mouth. "It's not like raiding a couple of chance pilgrims which is all your father ever did."

Maria said nothing. She had seen him and Roger and his friends making plans in the evenings after supper.

"When I decide, I'll tell you," he said. "I suppose there's no harm in it."

"Thank you."

She let him touch her body. In the meadow, Roger and a dark-haired knight started away to the pen to bring another colt. Maria ate cheese. In the heat she felt even fatter than she was.

Ponce led the black colt away. Its head drooped; it walked trustingly beside the man who had broken it. Roger and the dark knight, Welf, were leading up a long-legged bay. Ceci was asleep in the sweet grass just behind Maria. She pulled the child into her lap, feeling sluggish and discontent, although he had given her what she wanted.

Richard went down to the meadow again. The bay hardly bucked at all, and the next after him was mild enough, but the third, a golden chestnut, fought the men like the devil. They had to throw it twice before they could bridle it. The dark knight saddled it and climbed up and was instantly pitched off into the grass. The men whooped and laughed. Maria braced her hands on her lower back. She decided to take Ceci up to the castle. When she looked, Richard was mounting the chestnut colt.

The horse flung itself into the air. In mid-flight it screwed its body around and swapped ends. Maria cried

76

out. She got clumsily up onto her feet. The colt squealed. Richard clung to its back. The other men were scattered around, silent for once, watching. Roger came up to her. He was smiling.

"He can't pass by a mettlesome horse. A quirk of Richard's."

The colt's mouth was bleeding; its golden color was lost under a dark sweat, but it fought tirelessly. It bounded off the ground, coiled in the air, and came down again hard. Richard had the sweat-soaked reins wrapped around his hands. The colt spun in a dizzying circle and reared straight up. Richard hit it between the ears with his fist. The colt flipped over backwards.

Maria's mouth filled with blood. She had bitten through her lips. She put Ceci down and lumbered heavily out onto the meadow. The colt lay still in the dust. Richard was hidden beneath it. The knights clustered around it. All along the riverbank, the serfs were running up to see. Roger raced past her and elbowed a path through the knights.

"Dead, by God."

Her knees weakened. She went around the sprawled body of the colt. Propped up on his arms, Richard was lying on the ground, his face streaked with sweat and black dirt, and his chest heaving. The colt lay across his right leg. Maria sank down heavily beside him. She knew she should pray but she was too relieved to think of a suitable prayer.

"You can't ride everything, you know," she said. Roger was calling to somebody to bring a horse over from the village.

"Don't bother with that, drag it off," Richard shouted to his brother. "I don't want to lie here all day, damn you." He looked at her. "When that horse went down, I was still on him."

"It looks the other way around to me," she said. She went back to the oak tree, picked up Ceci and the flask of wine, and walked back down again to the little crowd around Richard. Ponce and another man had gotten long-handled hoes from the serfs and were forcing them under the carcass, one on either side of Richard's pinned

77

leg. Ceci tugged at Maria's arm; she wanted to be let down, and Maria thrust her into the arms of the knight beside her. The man and the baby clutched each other, startled. Maria knelt down beside Richard.

"Open your mouth."

"Roger," he said. "Wait." He opened his mouth like a nestling, and she poured wine into it. Red dribbled down his chin.

"Heave!"

The men gave one long shout and threw themselves against the poles. They levered the colt's body slightly up off the ground. Richard scrambled backwards on his elbows. His face went suddenly gray, and he caught his breath.

"Harder," Roger called. He vaulted the colt and knelt down behind his brother, sliding his arms under Richard's. "Push, you knaves—by Saint Christopher: now!"

Straining, the men pried the corpse farther off the ground, rolling the body onto its belly, the long legs bending under the weight. Roger dragged Richard backwards out of the way, and the colt thudded back to the ground.

Squatting beside him, Maria fed Richard more wine. He braced himself up on his elbows again. His lips were white as the dust that covered his clothes. He reeked of sweat; his leather jacket was sodden with it.

"Well," Roger said, "you won't trouble the Saracens for a while."

Richard lay back and put his forearm over his eyes.

THEY GOT THE VILLAGERS' CART and took him up to the castle, where the bald cook pulled at his leg, declared it was broken, and tied planks against it to hold it rigid from hip to ankle. The flesh of Richard's leg was blackened and swollen fat as a young tree. He lost consciousness twice while the cook was setting the ends of the bone together. Finally the cook bound the planks tight.

The sun was setting. Everybody save Maria went down to the hall for supper. Adela took Ceci to feed her. Maria got Richard out of the rest of his clothes and washed the dust and sweat off his body.

He was awake again, but he said nothing; he stared at the ceiling as if he saw nothing, and around his lips the pain drew a white line. She put his nightshirt on him. Feet sounded on the stairs, and a kitchen knave brought in a tray of meat, cups, and a ewer.

Maria brought him a cup of the wine. The boy raced off downstairs again. She sniffed the wine in the cup; it reeked of herbs. "This will help you sleep better."

"I don't want it."

"Richard—"

"I don't want it, God damn you, let me alone."

Maria went up beside the bed. He was stiff to his fingertips. She took hold of his hand. His skin was hot and scaly to her touch. She thought of the pain of childbed. She reminded herself that no one died of a broken leg. He sank toward a fitful, painful sleep, and she sat beside him in the darkness, holding his hand, until Adela brought Ceci upstairs to bed.

IX

❧

RICHARD LAY IN BED FOR THREE DAYS, STARING AT THE ceiling, his eyes filmed and his mouth caked with fever. Maria and Adela fed him, gave him wine and milk mixed with herbs, put cushions under him, brought the chamberpot for him, and tried to talk cheerfully to him, although he did not seem to hear. Adela, who loved anything helpless, spent most of the day nursing him, and Maria had to do all her chores as well. At last Roger took most of the knights away on a raid, and she could rest.

On the fourth day, at last, she convinced the cook that Richard should be bled. They got some leeches from the village and the cook drew blood from Richard's left arm.

"I set a broken leg for your father once," the cook said. "He was up in two days." He salted the last leech and it fell off into the jar.

She slept on the floor, since her back throbbed with pain if she slept in the bed. That night, she woke a dozen times, when he gasped or whined in a dream. But in the morning, he was wide awake, and he ate everything she gave him for breakfast and sent her for more. On her way back with the second breakfast, she stopped in the hall. She was sitting there talking nonsense to Ceci when Adela rushed down the stairs, flung the hall door closed, and burst into tears.

Flora gave a piercing scream of sympathy. Maria set her daughter down and went upstairs. Richard was sitting up in bed. When she came in, he shouted, "Where is Roger?"

The shout whispered at the end. He was still indifferently strong, but she hung back, not caring to go within his reach. "I don't know. What did you do to Adela?"

"That fat psalm-singing whore." He weaved, unsteady. He flung back the covers and started to drag himself out of bed. "Where is my brother?"

"He took some of the knights and rode away," she said. She had been relieved at the time. She went up beside the bed and pushed him down again and pulled the blanket up over him. "He said he knew what you meant to do. I didn't think—"

"Think!"

"You were so sick—I couldn't do everything." Her throat filled uncomfortably tight. After all her tender ministrations he was shouting at her. He sat up again. She brought him the dish of meat.

"God-damned stupid silly sheep-hearted cow," he said. "Get out of here." With both hands he picked over the food on the dish, hunting for tidbits.

Maria stood still. She would not go downstairs like a servant, like Adela. In her womb the baby stirred and seemed to turn over. She hauled the pillows out from under him and stacked them between his back and the headboard of the bed.

"Where did he go?" Richard said, without looking up from the plate.

"Across the wilderness, toward Iste." The town of Iste lay in the southeastern hills, several days' ride away. Saracens ruled it.

He let out another string of bad names. Maria could not tell if he meant her or Roger. "Why did you let him? You'll do anything for him—"

"What was I supposed to do? He's your brother. Who would listen to me?"

"He's trying to steal my war." He chewed steadily. "Who is left here—Ponce? Welf?"

"Ponce," Maria said. "I'll get him." She ran down the stairs, glad to be away from him.

He and Ponce talked, and Ponce went down into the ward and sent a messenger to Roger. Maria took Ceci up to Richard, who played with her until they both fell asleep in the rumpled bed. Maria sat in front of her window and leaned her arms on the sill. If she went downstairs again, Adela would complain to her about Richard. Down in the village, two men were putting a new thatch on their church. Beyond, the milk cows were coming along the road, she could even hear the ringing of their bells. The air was hazy and yellow with sunlight: August sky. The sense in it all comforted her, that they were doing things that they had done before and would again, in a time that would come again, turning circles like the stars. She went downstairs and swept the hall and got the wood in.

In the afternoon she went upstairs to feed Ceci. Richard lay on his side, throwing hazelnuts into a cup on the mantelpiece. Adela and Flora came in and out with questions about supper. Whenever he talked to Ceci, Richard's voice was tender as a dove's, but the second time Adela came in and glared at him, he said, "You sow, if you look at me like that again, I'll pop your eyes out."

Adela stalked out of the room, all her fat jouncing, and banged the door shut. Maria laughed. She shouldered her bodice up and fastened it across her breast. On the floor, Ceci pulled herself up onto her feet.

"Keep your teeth together," Richard said to Maria.

"Dada," Ceci said, and chuckled. She sat down with a thump.

"There. Did you hear her?" Maria asked. "I told you she was learning to talk."

81

Ceci said, "Dadadadadadada." She thrust her arm out and opened and closed her hand. Richard waved back to her.

"Bring her here."

Maria scooped the child up by the arms and dropped her on the bed. Ceci climbed on him, laughing. He kissed the baby's face. Maria sat down on the bed beside him, her hands folded over her swollen body. She stroked his hair back.

"You should have told me Roger was going," he said.

"I did."

He glanced at her, surprised. Ceci took hold of his hand and put his thumb in her mouth. "I don't remember," he said.

"Do you remember how long you were sick?"

He tugged gently against the baby's grip on his hand. Ceci braced herself, her face frantic. At last, he said, "How long?"

Maria combed his hair through her fingers. "Four days."

"Dada," Ceci said.

IN THE MORNING there was still no word from Roger. It was Michaelmas, the feast day of the Archangel, the fall quarterday. A stream of local people came up the road to pay their dues to Richard. Most of them owed service as well, and Maria arranged for them to wait in the ward for their tasks. Toward noon, the cook took her place with the tallies and she went up the stairs to give Ceci her dinner.

Richard stood in front of the window, his splinted leg propped elaborately against a chair. He had gotten soap and water and was shaving himself in her looking glass by the light through the window. Maria sat down on the floor with Ceci. Richard straightened, stropping the razor.

"Nothing from Roger?"

"No. Not yet."

He said, "God gave dogs fleas and me brothers." Cocking his head before the looking glass, he scraped at his soaped face. Maria gave Ceci her cup. The baby turned it over carefully. Maria sopped up the spilled milk with the edge of her skirt.

"You should stay in bed, Richard. You won't get well."

He swore at her. She gave the little girl a piece of bread and honey. Going up beside him, she leaned against the wall next to the window.

"Don't forget," she said. "I can outrun you now."

He swiped at her with the razor.

"It's the quarterday," she said. "Is there anything you want them to do—the villagers?"

He washed off the razor. His eyes turned on her. "What did you have in mind?"

"The cook says we need new bread ovens. He has said it for years, my father never remembered. If we built them outside, the villagers could use them too."

He twisted his neck to present a different angle to the looking glass. The razor scratched against his beard. Maria glanced at Ceci, who was licking the palms of her hands, sticky with honey. Richard cut himself; he swore at the razor a while, inspected the damage, and washed his face off. Maria gave him a towel.

"Now will you go back to bed?"

"Bed," he said. He hobbled across the room toward the door, shouting for Ponce. When Maria went down again to the ward, he was out beyond the wall on the hillside with the serfs, explaining where he wanted the ovens built.

It took them three days to gather stones enough. Richard got his knights down to help, and when one refused because the task was base, Richard cursed him and threatened him until the young man, speechless, staggered back to work. As Richard got stronger, his temper got worse. Maria was glad that the constant steady stream of shepherds and outliving people with their goods and dues kept her busy. He struck at everyone. His leg in its coffin of splints immobilized him, but great with child she was slower than the other people, and once he managed to hit her. In front of everybody else she screamed at him, and he shouted back, calling her filthy names until she ran upstairs and buried herself in bed and sobbed with rage. All night long, lying beside him in the dark, she plotted to kill him. Just before dawn, Ceci woke, and she got up to quiet her. When she went back to bed, she began to cry. At once he touched her face. She turned and went clumsily into his arms, and they kissed.

Still Roger did not come back. Everybody went around the castle in terror of Richard. The moon had come into its full face, when Adela liked to find dyestuffs, and Maria leaped at the chance to leave the castle. With Ceci, she went down the road, Adela beside her, toward the village. In the fields on either side, the serfs harvested their wheat and barley. Their high-sided carts leaned in the ditch beside the road. Maria hitched Ceci up on her hip.

"Not in the next new moon, but the one after," Adela said, and laid her hand on Maria's bulging body. "It will be cool, then. Not like the last time."

Maria snorted at her. She was in good spirits at getting away from Richard. "It wasn't so bad, the last time." They walked through the thorn hedge.

The village was a circle of two-room huts, with the church the biggest building. Alys had planted herbs in the garden beside her house, in the shade of an oak tree. There the village women often sat spinning and weaving and gossiping. They were all cousins of Adela and her sister Alys. Cooing, they clustered around Maria and Ceci.

"Ah, Maria," Alys said. "She blooms when she carries her babies, doesn't she?"

"I sprout, too," Maria said. She gave each of the women a kiss, and they all made the Cross over her. They were great-breasted women, brown from their lives in the sun, wearing clothes of the same cut, the same cloth, as if they were one woman seen in half a dozen looking glasses. They rubbed their faces together with Adela's and sat down.

"And Master Richard?" Alys said. "Is he mending?"

Maria shot a warning look at Adela. "He is very well, God be good."

"God be good." Everybody crossed herself.

"But no word yet from Master Roger?"

Maria shook her head. "Nothing."

"Master Richard is none too glad of young Roger, I'll

tell you that," Adela said. "He's been cursing him since the day the red knave left."

"Adela," Maria said.

Alys gripped her knee. "We had it they were fighting. They are bad spawn, those two, mark." She squeezed hard. "You have your burden there, young woman. The Saracens are right, he is a dragon."

Maria braced her hands on her back. The women were passing Ceci from lap to lap and feeding her honey cakes. Adela and Alys carried on a long esoteric conversation about the virtues of two different dyestuffs. When they had agreed, Maria said, "What about a dragon?"

"The Saracens call Master Richard that, says the miller."

Maria made a face. "There is truth in it," she said.

The women tittered. Alys picked up her wool cards and began to comb a mat of fleece. Her right elbow pumped vigorously. "He is a good lord, he does not rob us, and now he is building ovens for us. We are pleased enough with him, although God have mercy on us poor Christians there's little we could do if we were not." She and the other village women crossed themselves. She rolled the wool from the left-hand card and folded it carefully. "He is not a dragon to us."

The villagers had no dyewoods to spare. Maria and Adela went off to the wood. The village dogs leaped and barked around them until they were halfway across the common to the river. Adela led the way, cutting across a fallow strip of ground and down into a meadow waist-high in uncut hay. They waded the river where it ran shallowest, and walked down the waste between two stands of wheat.

Maria shifted Ceci to the other hip. The child had fallen asleep, comfortably slouched against her mother's body. Adela was three or four steps ahead of her. Suddenly they walked into a hollow in the ground and nearly trod on two people coupling in the grass.

Adela shrieked. The boy scrambled to his feet, yanked his hose up, and raced off into the wheat. The girl followed him, leaving one of her wooden-heeled shoes behind. In tandem, the two ran off through the wheat, the

85

boy clutching his hose up around his thighs, and the girl limping and calling to him to wait.

Maria laughed so hard her sides hurt. Adela gave shriek after shriek of outrage, whirled, and snatched Ceci from her. Jarred awake, the little girl let out a scream. "Poor baby," Adela cried, pressing Ceci's face down against her enormous breast. "Poor innocent lamb."

"Oh, God," Maria gasped, and sat down, still laughing. She remembered the girl's white legs waving in the air and the boy riding between them, and she grew lecherous. She had not lain with Richard since he broke his leg. Restless, she got to her feet.

"Are you coming?"

They went on toward the wood. In the margin between the meadow and the trees, where the strawberries grew, midges hung in clouds. Maria took Ceci in her arms and covered her head with her apron. Her eyes shut, she plunged through the mist of insects into the deep fragrant shade of the trees. Adela was still muttering about lechery and sin. Apparently the freckled boy was one of Alys's children. They walked through a stand of pines and birches and down a little rocky slope to the boggy ground. Bright green swamp cabbage sprouted in the black mud. Maria stepped from rock to rock. Adela reached the far side of the swamp much ahead of her.

She set the baby down on dry ground. Ceci crawled to a sapling nearby, took hold of a little branch, and tried to draw herself to her feet, but the branch bent, and as hard as she pulled she could not get her backside off the ground. Maria, picking berries, burst out laughing. The baby let the branch go and stared suspiciously at the sapling.

Maria kept close by. Adela was hunting for mushrooms, crashing around in the underbrush, her voice continually raised. A woodpecker hammered on a tree above her head. Maria sat down to rest her legs and tied the berries into a square of cloth. Ceci squatted on her hams, picking with her forefinger at something on the ground. Her mouth was smeared with dirt and sap. She went down on all fours with a thump and crawled toward Maria. Her napkin, black with dirt, dragged around her knees, and Maria made her lie down and took her breeches off entirely.

In the late afternoon they started back toward the village. Adela chattered on about the girl and boy in the meadow, and how she would tell Alys so they would be punished. The sun was turning red and fat, down by the horizon. When they stepped out of the woods a trickle of an evening breeze cooled their faces. Maria lifted her cheek to it.

"Maria!" Adela caught her arm. "Look!"

For a moment, when she saw the white-robed riders galloping up the valley, she could not even draw breath. A faint ululation of voices reached her, like the howling of dogs.

"Saracens," Adela cried. "Saracens!" She ran toward the village, all her fat quaking, and her bags of dyes dropping from her apron into the grass. "Saracens! Help —Help—"

Fixed in her place, Maria clutched her daughter tight in her arms. The Saracens were galloping up between the village and the river. They had seen Adela. They veered toward her, toward Maria. Adela staggered toward the river. Her cap flew off and her lank hair hung down her back. She would not reach the village before the Saracens reached her. Already the white riders were splashing across the river. Maria dashed back into the wood.

The setting sun turned the Saracens' robes pink, like bloody water. Shrill-voiced, they raced down through the fields toward Adela. From the thorn hedge around the village a screech went up. Maria stopped in the gloom of the wood and caught her breath.

From here she could not see the castle. She scrambled into a thorny thicket, burrowing into the shelter of the entangled branches. Ceci began to cry. Maria whispered to her, put her fingers in the baby's mouth, bounced her frantically, and finally quieted her.

Adela had seen the Saracens coming, she had realized she would not reach the village, and she wheeled. Her skirts sailed around her. Stumbling in weariness she ran back toward the woods.

"Maria," she cried. "Maria—"

Maria put her hand over the baby's face. Adela was

leading the Saracens straight toward her. They loomed behind her, their white teeth like jewels in their beards. Panting, the fat woman labored three more strides to the edge of the wood, and the leading Saracen dived from his horse and brought her down.

Their horses swept through the edge of the trees. Maria sat rigid while they crashed into the underbrush around her. Her face stung from thorn scratches. She prayed for rescue, or for the horses to trample her and Ceci before they could be taken alive. Adela was screaming. The Saracens carried her out into the meadow and threw her down, star-shaped, a man at each of her wrists and ankles. Pulling back her robes, the leader dropped full length on her and began to rape her.

Maria bit her lips. Adela screeched and the baby started to cry. Frantic, Maria clamped her hand tight over the baby's mouth. Ceci clawed at her fingers. The first Saracen stood up, and another climbed onto Adela, his hands working in her breasts. She had stopped screaming. One Saracen drew his dagger and jabbed her in the ribs to make her jump.

Against Maria's hand, Ceci was howling. Maria crawled back into the deep brush. The thorns snagged her clothes and needled her arms and face. A tall Saracen turned and looked straight at her. He had heard her. He was wheeling toward her. Another man let out a yell.

The raiders scrambled into their saddles and spun their horses around. The leader straddled Adela, who lay slack on the ground, and cut her throat in a sheet of blood. Maria lunged back into the safety and darkness of the wood. When she looked around again, the Saracens were racing away, and a stream of knights was galloping up between the village and the river.

Ceci was shrieking. Maria carried her out of the wood into the last of the sunlight, to Adela. The knights charged past her, unheeding. Adela lay spreadeagled in the grass, blood pooled under her shoulders and her head. Maria began to cry.

The Saracens were already far down the valley. They were outrunning the knights, they would escape. From the thorn hedge, peasants raced toward her. Maria knelt and pulled Adela's clothes over her bleeding breasts and poor bruised cleft. Sinking down beside the body, the child in her lap, she covered her face with her hands.

CAREFULLY SHE SET the smith's punch at the top of the coin, struck it hard with the mallet, and worried the tool out of the hole. Richard was letting her make ornaments for his new clothes out of twenty Saracen coins. Another clap of thunder rattled the shutters of the window behind her. The rain had forced most of the knights indoors. Now that Roger had come back, the castle was packed with people. She put another coin before her on the table and picked up the punch.

His hair soaked with the rain, Richard came in, Roger a step behind him, and limped on his crutch up to her end of the hall. Roger thrust his head forward belligerently at his brother.

"Why is it my fault? I followed your plans, I did exactly what you would have done—"

Richard made an unpleasant noise. He lowered himself carefully down onto a stool and propped his crutch against the table. "What about her?" He nodded toward Maria, down the table from him. "Ceci was with her— what if they'd been caught?" But he did not seem particularly angry.

"I want to go after them," Roger said. He sat down across the table from Richard. "I'll ride them down if I must give up my life to it."

"Don't bother. We'll come on them again, sometime, in the course of things."

Maria bent over the coat, arranging the Saracen coins down the front. When she remembered the man rooting over Adela, sticking his knife in her to make her jump, she tasted gall in her throat. Richard hated Adela, and when the villagers asked if they could bury her in their own churchyard, he had let them take her body away without a word. Flora was upstairs crying. Maria lifted the mallet and struck a hole in another Saracen coin.

X

❦

FROM EVERYONE BUT MARIA, RICHARD HID HIS DELIGHT
that Roger's raid had failed. He gave Roger careful orders and sent him out on forays to chase back the Saracens, who were riding all over the foothills looking for
something to steal. Maria asked him to give no quarter,
so that Adela would be avenged, but the Saracens would
not stop and fight, and Roger had no skill at running
them to a standstill. That also pleased Richard.

The rape gnawed in her memory. Richard, with his
crutch, his friends, and his new high spirits, needed little
help from her, and Ceci was intent on learning to walk.
Maria sat in the window, spinning, and tried to think
about what had happened.

Together with the rape, she remembered the two serfs
humping in the grass, and the whole day began to find a
single form. She remembered the girl running after the
boy, calling to him, her overskirts still hauled up above
her hips; she remembered how Adela had run from the
Saracens, her skirts lying out like wings. Slowly it became
as formal as a dance. Placated by a sense of order in it,
she shook off the brooding humor, and discovered that
Richard had gotten her a new maid.

This was a girl named Eleanor, of Maria's years,
smooth and pretty in looks—his cousin, Richard said, but
two days after she arrived, Maria came on her and Roger
on the stairs, kissing.

Maria burst out laughing. They sprang apart and Roger
yanked his hands out of Eleanor's dress. He stammered
something. Maria did not stay to listen. Still giggling, she
went up the rest of the stair to her father's old room, on

the top floor of the tower—Roger slept there, now obviously not alone. She remembered Adela's preachery about lust and laughed.

"What is it?" Flora said crossly; she was gathering up Roger's litter of clothes and arms and tack.

"Oh, I am thinking of a joke Richard told me, it's nothing."

Maria picked up the broom and swept vigorously. Flora said sharply, "Well, don't tell it to me, if it's sinful."

Eleanor came quickly in the door. She glanced at Flora and marched across the room to Maria's side. In a voice like a priest's, she said, "It isn't what you think."

Maria straightened up. She was nearly nine months with child, and when she stood, a sharp pain daggered down the backs of her legs. "What do I think?" she said, and turned away, smiling.

Flora called, "What's the matter? Why are you whispering?"

"I am telling the joke to Eleanor," Maria said. She finished cleaning the room.

Later, in the kitchen, while she and Eleanor were wrapping up cheeses to ripen, Maria said, "You may do as you wish, but when he goes to someone else, don't kill yourself and leave me without help."

Eleanor lifted her chin. "I beg your pardon," she said, and went off into another part of the kitchen. Later, she and Roger were talking together in the ward, and he had his arm around her shoulders, his cheek close to hers.

Maria waited a few days to see if Richard would tell her what was between them. He never seemed to notice Eleanor; for cousins they were distant. The moon waxed. The heat of the summer lingered on. The climb up the two flights of steps from the ward to her room exhausted her. With Eleanor's and Flora's help, she contrived to spend most of the day in the hall.

She sat in her bedchamber one night, after Ceçi was asleep, while Eleanor brushed her hair. Through the window she could see the full moon rising. Eleanor's face showed in the looking glass, intent on her hands and the brush. She shook out Maria's hair, spreading it across her shoulders.

"When the baby is born," Maria said, "I want Richard there."

"Mary Mother. You will not say that when we put the knife under your bed." Eleanor stroked her hands through Maria's hair. "Men are not interested in childbearing. Ah, you're full of mad whims." She gave Maria a hug. "You'll be happy, when your baby's in your arms."

"I am happy now. Or would be, if you promised to bring Richard to me, when the baby is coming."

Eleanor laughed indulgently. "Ah, well." Maria scowled at her over her shoulder.

"Don't I suffer what you do with Roger?— Now you chuckle at me as if I were a baby."

"You are full of envy for me, because I have Roger."

"You have not got Roger," Maria said.

Eleanor's pretty face sharpened to a blade. She threw down the brush with a crack, her shoulders squared, and stalked out of the room. In the bed, Ceci murmured in her sleep. The wooden back of the brush had split up the middle. Maria put it on the mantelpiece, to use the bristles over.

From the thunking and clatter and voices on the stairs, she knew Richard's friends were helping him and his leg up to bed. Sitting on the pillow, she braided her hair for the night and coiled the thick black rope up on her head, like a crown. The looking glass was lying on the coverlet. She picked it up and turned to put the light of the candles on it.

Ponce and the dark knight Welf half-carried Richard into the room. They were drunk enough to sing, their faces high-colored, bending over Richard in imitation of the angels bearing up Christ. He steered them across the room, careful that they did not run his bad leg into the furniture, and made them leave him leaning against the bed, rather than in it. Ponce and the German knight sang their way out the door.

"Vanity," Richard said. "I should never have given you that glass." He took off his jacket.

"I love it." Maria wound her hair around her neck. "I thought you said Eleanor is your cousin."

"She is."

"Then she's Roger's cousin, too."

92

Richard threw his shirt aside. "Get me a nightshirt."

Maria went around to the cupboard and got out a fresh nightshirt. Putting it on the bed beside him, she knelt to help him roll the hose off his good leg. "Is she your first cousin?"

"Stop, will you?"

"Oh, you know, I am curious sometimes."

She watched him take his breeches off. When he noticed her eyes on him he cupped his hands quickly over his male parts. "Give me that nightshirt—I'm cold."

"It's right there next to you. Everybody is certainly modest around here. I suppose it's the humor of the season."

"Don't you like Eleanor?" He pulled on the nightshirt.

"Yes, I suppose so."

"Then why do you care what she does? Get into bed."

Maria crawled past him into the bed, and he swung his splinted leg up onto the mattress, like a gate shutting behind her. He thrashed around getting comfortable. She moved Ceci over out of his way. Richard blew out the candle.

"Will they marry?" she said.

"Why do you ask me all these questions? Ask them." In the dark his hands came at her like claws. She thought vividly of the Saracens with Adela. She lay stiffly in his arms, wishing he would leave her alone. Her vast body and his splinted leg kept them apart.

"Roll over," he said, his mouth against her ear.

"Please, Richard—"

She ducked her head away from him. The memory of the Saracens burned in her mind. He touched her, drawing his fingertips over her body through her nightgown. After a while, lulled, she lifted her head and kissed him.

"Roll over," he said.

She turned on her other side, putting her back to him. His arms slid around her. "That's better." He ran his hands under her nightgown.

"Be quiet," she said, "you will wake up Ceci."

THREE DAYS LATER, in the waning moon, in the morning, she lay down in childbed. At first, none of the women

93

would even send for Richard, but Maria made some threats to Eleanor, and at last the girl went after him. When he came she was deep in labor. The women screeched at him like magpies. On his crutch he hobbled over to the bed. Maria was lying on her side. She bit her lips to keep from groaning. He said, "What do you want?"

"Stay with me," she said.

Flora rushed up between them. "Here," she said, "you are uncomfortable, you will tire yourself." She rearranged all the pillows and made Maria lie down on her back. Going, she gave Richard a glare.

He bent to talk to Maria. "I'll just be downstairs. If anything happens, I can—"

"Stay," she said. "Please stay." Her body clenched tight like a knot. She gasped.

Richard said, "Somebody bring me a chair." He backed away. Flora rushed up and moved all the pillows around again.

Maria sank into a pain-ridden daze. Richard sat beside her; once or twice she saw him on his crutch pacing up and down through the women. At first she fought against screaming but when the baby butted out she screeched her throat raw. Richard came up beside her. His face shone with sweat. Near the fire the baby cried furiously.

"It's a boy," he said. "I want to call him Stephen."

Maria moved her head on the pillow. Emptied and exhausted, she had no real interest in the baby. "Robert," she said. "For my father." She put her hand out to him. "I was not brave."

He caught hold of her hand. Bending, he kissed her mouth.

MARIA STOOPED OVER the vat and stirred the fleece briskly in its bath of dye. The aroma of the hot steeped barks made her nose itch, as if she were about to sneeze. Over near the kitchen door, the baby let out a yell. The women had told her that the second baby was always an angel, but Robert made them all liars. Her wooden heels clacking on the floor, Eleanor scurried across the kitchen to pick him up.

"He only cries because he knows you will come to him," Maria called. She pulled a clump of the fleece up out of the dye. The deep green's depth and clarity kept her gaze; she knew it would dry to a disappointing off-color. With a twist of the stick she dunked the fleece back in again. Eleanor walked up and down across the kitchen, singing to Robert. On her shoulder a mat of black hair showed above the baby's blanket.

Maria sank down on her heels and looked for Ceci, who was playing under the table. With the little girl sitting on her hip, she crossed the kitchen after Eleanor. The old ovens had been torn out and the place seemed enormous. In the pantry door, the cook stood talking to Eleanor, a brace of plucked chickens dangling from his hand.

"I think you are justified," Eleanor was saying. "They shouldn't treat you like that."

The cook grunted something. He and Eleanor got along well together. "When the old man was alive—"

"Eleanor," Maria called. "Let's go." She carried Ceci over to the door. Eleanor followed her out into the ward.

"That poor man suffers so. I don't see why you dislike him."

"I don't," Maria said, surprised. "What is he telling you?"

"It isn't what he tells me," Eleanor said. They walked across the ward. The first snow had fallen the night before. Swept into piles along the foot of the wall, it lay in a thin white crust on the tops of the walls and the towers. The wind shook the clothes of the two men keeping watch on the gate. The sky was gray beyond the dark-gray walls of the castle. Shivering, Maria hurried to the door into the New Tower.

"And you shouldn't let everybody steal from the kitchen," Eleanor said. "I'm amazed you don't keep better order among your household, Maria."

"So am I," Maria said. She went fast up the stairs, to get away from Eleanor's sermon, and went into the hall. Richard and Roger were sitting before the fire, their shoes off and their feet up on the hearth. Maria went to her end of the hall.

Robert let out a raucous yell. His dark head bobbed from side to side above Eleanor's shoulder. Maria low-

95

ered Ceci to the floor behind her spinning wheel. The men seemed to take no notice of them. Eleanor gave Robert up to her and she sat down to nurse him.

The two women were weaving a tapestry. The fleece soaking in the kitchen was to make the border. Eleanor stood staring fixedly at the wall beside the loom, where they had drawn the design with charcoal. Maria glanced down the hall at Roger. He was ignoring Eleanor as intensely as Eleanor was ignoring him.

"It is so confused," Eleanor said, in a strained voice. She moved her head this way and that, to see the design from other angles. "There is no purity in it."

Maria thumbed up her nipple and poked it into the baby's mouth. "I like lots of things happening in the picture. I get tired of simple work."

"But look how crowded it is," Eleanor said. She turned her back to the men and sat down heavily on the little stool beside Maria.

"Are you fighting with Roger?" Maria said, and Eleanor made a little open-handed gesture of despair. Robert strained in Maria's arms, voracious. She looked around the hall for Ceci. The child was leaning against Richard's knee, her head on his thigh, smiling up at him, her long brown hair across her breast. While Richard talked to Roger he stroked her cheeks.

"See," Eleanor said; she was frowning at the design on the wall, and she covered the two dancing couples with her hands. "If we left this out, and let the rest of the celebration take up the room—nobody ever dances here, anyway."

"The villagers dance, on May Day," Maria said. "At weddings and Christmas." She laid Robert against her shoulder to make him burp. Fiercely he held his wobbling head up on his shoulders. "I like them there. They are the only happy people in the whole design."

Eleanor's eyes flicked toward Richard and Roger. "Everyone is happy." Her face was pinched and long.

Suddenly Roger bolted out of the room. Maria started. She said, "Besides, something has to happen in that corner of the work. Robert is asleep, will you take him up to bed?"

Eleanor snatched the baby from her and raced away. The door sighed shut behind her. Maria began to tie the ends of the warp threads down to the bottom roller of the loom, careful to spread them evenly. When she had knotted down half the warp, Richard came over to her, Ceci clinging to his hand.

"What are they fighting about?" she asked.

"I don't know." He stooped a little to see the design on the wall. "Sweet kiss of Jesus. What are these people here doing?"

"Dancing."

"That isn't what it looks like to me."

Ceci leaned over the basket of mending, trying to reach something, and fell in headfirst. He lifted her out by the ankles. She came up startled, her hands groping in the air. Richard lowered her to the floor.

"Is Eleanor pregnant?"

Maria scratched her nose. Naturally she had considered that. She shook her head. "No. She would have told me. I would know."

Ceci pulled herself to her feet, her arms around his knee. He winced away from her. "Ah, sweeting, not that leg."

Maria drew the child away from him. Richard eased all his weight onto his good leg. His eyes fell to the sketch on the wall. "Those people are not dancing. When does anybody ever dance around here?" Limping, he walked quickly down to the hearth again.

•   •   •

RICHARD WENT OUT RAIDING and left Roger to command the castle. Eleanor had taken to sleeping in a truckle bed in Maria's room, to help, she said, if Robert woke in the night. After months of broken sleep, Maria was glad of the chance to stay in bed when the baby fretted. But sometimes in the dark, Eleanor groaned and sobbed loud enough to waken her.

Three nights after Richard left, snow began to fall, at first only a thin shower of flakes drifting through the torchlight in the ward, but mounting to a hammering storm. In the middle of the night, Maria woke up stifling in the heat. Eleanor had built the fire as full as the hearth allowed and it was blazing bright enough to turn the whole room twilit. Maria slid out of the bed.

She thought she could hear hunting horns, somewhere far off, the cattle lowing. Eleanor was not in her bed. The covers were thrown back over the foot and her fur-lined slippers were still on the floor. The draft from the window was fanning the fire in the hearth. Ceci called out, "Mama?" from the bed behind her, and was asleep again when Maria went back to her. Robert was fast asleep in the cradle, overlaid with the flickering saffron light.

When she leaned into the window, the snow blew stinging in her face: the wind had torn the shutter off. She put a cloak over her nightgown and went out onto the stair landing.

The stair below was dark as a well. Above her beside the door to Roger's room a torch still blazed. She went up the stairs two at a time and knocked. The stone floor chilled her feet.

Eleanor pulled the door open. Her face was slick with tears. "What is it? Why can't you leave us alone?"

Maria said, "There is a fire in the village, I have heard the horns twice."

The girl swallowed. On her cheekbones high color showed. She called, "Roger?"

"Come in," Roger said. "I heard her."

Maria thrust the door open and walked past Eleanor into the room. The blaze of candles filled it, and Roger was dressed, so they had not been in bed after all. He went to the window and reached across the deep sill to open the shutter. The edge of the wall hid his face.

"I can't see anything. Are you sure, Maria?—Ah, I hear them." He stood back from the window. "Get me my fur cloak. We can't put out the fire. I'll bring them here, if they need shelter." His voice was unemotional, but when he turned toward them his pallor and the hollows of his eyes startled Maria: all his beauty was gone. He cared for Eleanor after all. He burst between the two women and ran down the stairs.

"I'm sorry," Eleanor said to Maria. She rubbed the tears from her eyes. "I am sorry."

"Come down and go to sleep, there is little we can do."

98

But it rankled that Eleanor should have thought she was spying.

Three houses burned in the village. Roger was out all night finding shelter for the homeless people. Through the next day, the snow fell steadily. With Eleanor carrying Robert after her and Ceci running before searching for places where the snow had blown in, she swept and cleaned and put the whole of the New Tower in order.

At noon, missing Eleanor and the baby, she went up the stairs after them. Eleanor stood in the doorway to the hall, the baby clutched in her arms, her shining unhappy eyes aimed into the room at Roger. When she saw Maria, the girl wheeled and ran away.

Maria caught up with her on the landing to their room and took the baby. "See if you can make Ceci eat her porridge. She eats much better for you than for me."

Eleanor's face sagged like an old man's. "I want to have my own babies."

"Good," Maria said. "Practice with mine." She put Ceci's hand into Eleanor's and went down to the hall again.

The few knights who had not gone out with Richard were massed at one end of the hall, cheering on a wrestling bout. As she came in, one of the wrestlers hit the floor with a thud. Maria went up to her end of the hall and sat down. She turned away from the room and put the baby to her breast. While he nursed she looked at the design on the wall and tried to imagine it filled in with colors. The two dancing couples were to have red clothes, and she decided to put a red bird in the corner diagonally across from them. Abruptly Roger came between her and the sketch.

"Do you think we should send a messenger to Richard?" he said.

"What—to tell him it's snowing?"

He sank down on his heels beside her. The day-old fuzz of beard on his cheeks was more blond than red; unshaven, he looked older. He scratched at his chin.

"I cannot bring myself to send Eleanor away," he said.

"Don't. She is my friend, and she will stay until I want her to go."

"But there is nothing between us," Roger cried, and

99

jerked his voice down. "Not any more. Why should she be here, if she will not lie with me?—" His hands rose between them. "Why did Richard leave me here?"

"You should marry her."

"No." His eyes were brilliant blue. "No."

"Do you love her?"

"Eleanor? I love fame, not Eleanor. I love valor, and outdoing other men." He lowered his gaze. His face had lost the marks of strain; he looked fresh again. "I suppose that's arrogant, isn't it?"

"No," she said. She put her hand on his thick red hair. Catching her hand between his fingers and his cheek, he turned and kissed her palm.

"My little sister, I will always love you best."

Maria laughed. When she tried to pull her hand free, he clung to her. Their eyes met. She wondered what it would be like to lie with him. She wrenched her hand free and lowered the baby into her lap. Hitching up her shoulder, she brought her bodice closed across her breast.

"If she stays," he said bitterly, "I will have to see her every day."

"You won't care, after a while," Maria said.

RICHARD CAME BACK, his horses loaded with plunder and Saracen captives. Eleanor and Roger fought and moped less and less. Once Maria came on them kissing on the stair, but they were not lovers again after that. Eleanor kept her arms full of Robert, even while she sat in the window with Maria and worked on the tapestry.

On Candlemas, all the mothers of the region went to Mass, even the women of the shepherds, and Maria went with them. Afterwards they took salt and bread into the new houses in the village, and the people gathered in the church and danced and argued and got drunk.

Leading their horses, Maria and Eleanor walked back up to the castle, Robert in Eleanor's arms, and Ceci riding on Maria's mare. Eleanor tossed Robert in her arms. The wintry air had brightened her face.

"Are you done with Roger?" Maria asked.

"No," Eleanor said. She held herself straight, like a

100

church image. "Although he is done with me. In God's sight, I am his wife. Someday he may see that it is so."

Maria eyed her skeptically. It sounded like a verse: a pledge to keep faith at great cost. She had meant to ask if Eleanor would not marry someone else. She knew Richard could have arranged it with no trouble at all.

"There," Eleanor said. "Someone is coming."

Maria shaded her eyes to see. The sky was a flat gray; the snow-covered valley stretched colorless beneath it. A rider was coming up the road from the north. She turned to her mare. There was no reason to offer Eleanor another marriage if she would not accept it. Stabbing her foot into the stirrup, she pulled herself up behind Ceci on the saddle.

XI

THE RIDER CAME FROM WILLIAM, DOWN IN THE TOWER of Birnia. Maria could make no sense of what little she overheard of his messages, but before the servants had led away his steaming horse, Richard and Roger had gotten all but five of their men into their saddles and off to the north.

In the black night before dawn, Maria woke and heard the dogs barking in the village. She leaned out her window. Richard and his men were galloping up the road. He shouted to the porter; his voice was harsh with excitement, and Maria went to the cupboard to get out her cloak.

"Mama?"

"Sssh—Eleanor is here." She made sure that Eleanor was in her truckle bed and ran down the stairs.

The racket of the knights streaming into the ward had brought out their servants and some of the castle women, looking for their lovers. Maria, the unfastened throat-latch of her cloak clutched in one hand, stood in the doorway. Roger made his horse rear and prance in the middle of the ward, to charm the women. Maria went out into the open.

Suddenly Richard loomed up before her on his bay horse. "Here," he said, throwing back his cloak. "Take this."

Maria reached her arms up, and Richard with a father's practiced grip lowered a little boy into her arms. Maria braced herself against his weight. Rigidly the child resisted her embrace and turned his head away.

"Who is he?" she called.

"Take him upstairs." Richard rode off. The child was sliding down out of her arms. Maria hitched him up again and carried him back up to her room.

On the stairs she could hear Robert's screams of rage and pain. Eleanor, her face smudged with sleep, was walking him up and down the room. Maria shut the door with her heel. The false dawn was blooming. The room was gloomy with its treacherous light. She took the strange child over to the bed.

Ceci sat up, her thumb in her mouth. "Mama."

Maria kissed her. "Eleanor, so long as we are all up, will you send down for our breakfast? And bring me some of the cider."

Robert was howling. His belly was fat with colic. Eleanor took him away with her to get the breakfast. Maria poured water into a basin, found a cloth, and washed off the strange child's face.

"What's your name?" Maria said.

The boy said nothing. He was stocky and robust, dark as a winter apple; his face was old with suspicion. Beyond him, on the pillow, Ceci looked frail by contrast. Heralded by Robert's shrieks, Eleanor came in the door with a steaming wooden cup.

"It's hot," Eleanor said.

Maria took the cider and blew on it to cool it. The strange boy was watching her, scowling, with a face like an enemy. She said, "God's eyes, don't look at me as if

102

I'm going to eat you." She drank off some of the cider and filled the cup again with water from the pitcher. "Drink this, like a good boy."

He took the cup in both hands and gulped down the cider. Maria tried to take it away from him, saying, "Slower, you'll be sick," and was surprised when he fought. She tore the cup out of his grasp and set it down, and went across the room to find him something to wear: the clothes he had on were filthy. When she went back to the bed, he had gotten hold of the cup again and was draining the cider.

"Bad," Maria said sharply, and slapped his hands. That had no effect at all. His face stony, the boy stared past her. She took off his clothes.

"Tell me your name," she said firmly.

"Bunny," the boy said.

The door opened. Flora came in with a tray, Eleanor behind her, Robert at last asleep in her arms. They had brought a bowl of porridge for the strange boy. Maria dipped up a spoonful of it, her mouth open to coax his appetite, but he was already leaning toward her, his mouth open and his hand reaching for the spoon. Maria brushed his hand aside and dumped porridge into his mouth.

Bunny was a common name, a mother's pet name for her baby. Richard sometimes called Robert that, when he was wrapped in his fur bunting. This bunny reached for the spoon every time she raised it. She dodged his hand patiently and fed him herself. He was not a soft or pretty child, and the unfitting name amused her. She scraped the bowl for him, and when he still seemed hungry, got him a piece of fruitcake from the cupboard.

"Mo' drink," Bunny said.

Maria got him another cup of the cider. The dawn light was bursting through the window. Robert slept in the cradle, sucking the air. She put Ceci's largest shirt on Bunny and tied the laces across his chest.

"Are you tired?"

Bunny put the cup on the bed; it fell over. Maria caught it. He said, "Piss."

"Come along." She lifted him down from the bed, led him across the room, and got out the chamberpot. "Do you know your real name?" she said. "Or who your father is?"

He rubbed his fists into his eyes. She gave up trying to talk to him. When he was finished, she put him into the bed beside Ceci.

"Mama," Ceci said, holding out her hands. "Good-night me."

Maria caught each hand and kissed it and kissed Ceci on the nose. "Go back to sleep. When you wake up again you can come downstairs." She kissed Bunny's cheek. "Good night, Bunny."

She went down the stairs. Most of the knights were warming themselves at the fire in the hall. Eleanor and Flora and the other women were bringing up a breakfast for them. Richard and Roger stood in one corner, talking. Maria went out onto the landing and behind the stairs into the wall passage.

It was cold, inside the wall. She went as quietly as she could, so that Richard would not hear her, and knelt down to peek through the hole.

The two brothers were standing between the wall and her spinning wheel. Roger had his back to her. He gestured persuasively with his hands.

"Think what we may gain. To control the duchy for a dozen years, perhaps, keep the justice and issue the taxes —who wouldn't give his hand for the chance!"

"Don't be stupid." Richard sat down on her stool. When he faced Roger again he seemed to meet her gaze. The shag of his new beard gaunted his face; he looked sleepy.

"How am I stupid?" Roger whirled hot toward him. "Are you afraid, Richard?"

Richard gave a quick glance down the room. "Because we would need the help of men who will never deal with us. Fitz-Michael, for instance, and the other counts. The Archbishop."

Maria pressed her lips together and smiled. The little boy was Duke Henry.

"You are such a slug sometimes—" Roger said. The cords of his neck stood out, and his hand cupped the air. "See what we might gain by a little risk."

In his most insulting voice, Richard said, "I see you are

104

all mouth as usual. I'll tell you what I decide to do." He started away down the hall.

Roger lunged after him. "Wait—is there no argument I can use? For our Crusade—for your son's sake?"

Richard laughed. He went on toward the door. Maria sprinted down the wall passage, squeezed through the narrow corner, and dashed out onto the stair landing. Richard stood in the middle of the hall listening to Roger argue. She galloped up the stairs.

Eleanor was gone; Robert and the strange child slept; Ceci in her nightgown stood before the window pushing everything she could carry across the sloping three-foot sill and down into the ditch below. Maria lifted one of Richard's shoes out of her daughter's hands and tossed it under the bed. The shoe's mate, two shirts, the metal basin, and Maria's pillow were scattered over the snow in the ditch four stories below the window. She slapped Ceci on the hand.

"No. Bad girl. Now someone will have to go pick all those things up again."

Ceci thrust out her lower lip and threatened to cry. Maria knelt to undo the little girl's nightdress. "You must go with Flora and help pick up." She looked into Ceci's face and her moon-gray eyes.

Richard came in, shedding his quilted armor padding, which he dropped on the floor. Ceci gave a glad cry. Naked in the morning light, she ran toward him, her skin blue-white, every curved bone showing. Richard caught her up.

"She just threw half your clothes out the window into the ditch," Maria said. She pulled the curtains shut on the bed, so that the little boy could sleep. Seldom used, the thick folds of wool gave off an odor of must and an old mouse nest.

Richard stood Ceci on the chest at the foot of the bed, so that they were at eye level. While he peeled off his clothes, she talked earnestly to him, whole long sentences, full of rhetoric, here and there even a word in French. Maria brought over her clothes and dressed her.

Richard opened the curtain and looked in at the sleeping child. "Is he all right?"

"He seems perfectly well. Hungry."

He put on his nightshirt. "What do you think I should do with him?"

She faced him, bland. "Who is he?"

"I saw you go into the passageway. Don't try to lie to me, you know who he is."

She took a step back from him, wary. But he wasn't angry. He went around the bed to the cupboard for some wine, and she followed him.

"How did you come by him?"

"Theobald had him. He thieved him from Fitz-Michael a couple of days ago in Agato and had to cross the border between here and Birnia to escape. Fitz-Michael's all over the hills looking for him." He brushed past her out into the middle of the room again. "Fetch me something to eat. Since Robert was born you never think of me any more—"

She went over to the stairs. She remembered telling Eleanor to get them breakfast, but if it had come, there was certainly nothing left of it. Richard stood in front of the hearth warming his hands.

A servant was coming out of the hall, one flight down the stairs. She sent him to the kitchen for a dish of meat. She shut the door and bolted it. Gathering up his discarded clothes on the way she went back to Richard. Ceci was gone, probably with Flora.

"Roger wants you to keep him and use him. The Duke."

He gave her the look he saved for her mentions of his brother. "I've heard the Gospel according to Roger." He put the wine cup on the mantel and turned his back to the fire. She went up in front of him and laid her hands on his chest.

"Did you stay up for me?" he asked.

"I slept a little." The shirt was embroidered with love charms. Adela had made it.

"I can't do what Roger wants. As soon as Fitz-Michael finds out I have him—" He rubbed his hand over his face. "I can see but two choices. I can give the child back to Fitz-Michael, and get some nithing reward, or I can give him to Theobald and Prince Arthur, and get some nithing reward." His voice rasped close to a whine. "It

106

wasn't such a deed to steal him, no matter what Roger says."

"Will Theobald fight us?"

Richard thrust out his lower lip. "Theobald is of no consequence. He has more men and more castles than I do but he's soft."

She glanced at the bed. Richard moved away from her. He kicked the stool around onto the hearth and sat down on it, his legs stretched out before him, slab-boned, stippled with dark hair. She sank down on her hams beside him.

"If you give him to Theobald, they'll set him aside and make Prince Arthur the Duke."

Richard snorted. "Prince Arthur will kill him."

Maria twitched. There was a knock on the door. She went to it, expecting to find a servant with Richard's breakfast, but Ceci and Flora came in, carrying all the things Ceci had pushed out the window.

"Oh, Flora," Maria said. "Thank you. Ceci must help you put them away." She kissed the top of her daughter's head and went back to Richard.

"Do you think you could manage to feed me sometime during the next week?" Richard said.

As if he were Robert, Maria crooned to him and brought him another cup of wine. She knelt on the hearth and poked vigorously at the fire. A kitchen boy came in with his breakfast. Maria brought over another stool and set the plates out for him: bread, cheese, some baked fish. While he ate she helped Flora and Ceci put away their goods. They went out. She drew the bed-curtain aside to look at the sleeping child. He sucked his fingers in his sleep, his black hair and dark skin dwarfish or Saracen. His parents were dead, the country was fallen into wars and disorder; perhaps he should die and let some capable man—Arthur—rule. They might not kill him, they might only put him in a monastery. She pulled the cover up over his arm and let the curtain close.

Richard was still eating, lounging in the heat of the fire, and she sat down on the hearth beside his stool. His bare feet were thrust toward the warmth. She put her hand on his ankle.

107

"What do you want to do?"

"Me? I want to give him to Fitz-Michael. Do you think I enjoy killing children? But I'm not losing an advantage for the sake of mere pity."

"If you can't have pity," she said, "how can God ever have pity on you?"

He snorted. His jaws moved steadily. "I don't want pity. I want justice, and I've never seen God dispensing much of that."

"I think you should give him to Fitz-Michael."

"Why?"

"Because—" She took her lower lip between her teeth, hunting a man's reason. "I would liefer have Fitz-Michael in my debt than Prince Arthur. Fitz-Michael is an honorable man, but Prince Arthur is probably more like Theobald." She knew he disliked Theobald.

Richard threw the fish bones into the fire, so the dogs would not get them. "You make about as much sense as Roger." He moved his leg slightly, so that her hand stroked his ankle.

"I'm just a woman," she said.

RICHARD WENT TO BED and slept until noon, with the little Duke curled up beside him. When they woke Maria gave them all dinner in the hall. It was a fair, fierce day. In the window an arched patch of blue sky streamed with clouds, and the wind banged the shutters on the wall. Maria let Bunny feed himself, putting a few bites of meat on the plate at a time. Ceci chattered nonsense between her spoonfuls of soup.

While he ate, Richard stared continually at the little boy. Maria saw that he was still trying to decide what to do. All the rest of the day, wherever she went, she took Bunny and Ceci with her. If they decided to kill him, she knew she could not stop them. The day trickled through, achingly slow. Even the cook knew who the child was and joked of stealing him away from her.

In the late afternoon, she brought all three children to the hall and sat in the space before the window, weaving. One of the knights had made Ceci a little wooden doll.

She squatted in the middle of the floor and carefully pulled out all its hair. Bunny climbed on the chairs and the table. The serving people and the knights wandered in and out of the room, each on some errand, their talk idle and plausible.

Roger appeared, his face high-colored, wearing a shirt much decorated with thread. Maria suspected it was lover's work and wondered who she was. Robert lay in the basket beside the spinning wheel. Roger bent over him and chucked him under the chin. Maria grew wary. Usually he paid no heed to children. She made two mistakes together and stopped weaving to keep from betraying herself. With the scissors on her key ring, she clipped the loose threads of the weft.

Sweeping up the scraps on the floor, she moved around Roger. Although he feigned to play with the baby, he watched the little Duke steadily. Bunny ran along the top of the table to its end and jumped down. Ceci was walking her doll around on the floor.

Roger's gaze was sharp as a bird's, full of thievery. Bent over the basket, his eyes intent on the little boy across the room, he had forgotten even to play with the baby, who let out a yell. Maria called to Ceci and Bunny and stooped to pick up Robert. She grabbed Bunny by the hand and towed him after her to the door.

That night, she and Eleanor and the children ate in her bedroom; she kept the door locked. When she went to bed, she held the little boy in her arms, so that no one could take him without her knowledge. The children slept. Eleanor snuffed the candles and went out again, leaving the door unlocked for Richard. The boy Bunny asleep against her breast, Maria lay in the dark and watched the dying fire. The logs fell into the shape of a lean head, like a wolf's or a snake's. It was hard to think someone might kill a little boy, but it could be done, and to some people would be worth the guilt, perhaps even to good people; hadn't she killed Walter Bris? And she felt no guilt for that at all, only satisfaction. The fire sank lower, the beast drowning in a soft bed of coals; she dozed.

A sound woke her. Richard stood beside the bed,

shedding his clothes. He climbed into the bed and his hands reached under the blankets for her and touched Bunny instead.

"Get him out of here. How can you be such a sheep?— He isn't even ours."

Wakening, Ceci called to him. Maria bundled the other child awkwardly across the bed, out of Richard's way, and murmured him to sleep again. She stroked Ceci's cheek and kissed her until she closed her eyes. Impatiently Richard dragged her back toward him.

"I'm afraid—I'm afraid—"

He smacked her. "Be quiet." Her head jangled. For a moment, her disarranged vision saw a monster's face above her in the darkness where his face was. With the children in the same bed, she could not enjoy him. She turned her head to one side and pretended nothing was happening.

RICHARD SWUNG UP into his saddle. Maria followed him out into the ward. The bay stallion's hoofs clattered on the frozen ground. Twenty knights were already waiting at the gate. She lifted Bunny up to him.

"If I don't come back," he said, "Roger's to follow me." He settled the little Duke in the saddle before him. Bundled up in makeshift clothes against the cold, the child took hold of the high square pommel with both hands. Abruptly he let go to wave good-bye to Maria. Richard wheeled his horse and rode toward the gate.

Maria walked across the ward after him. Standing in the gateway, she watched him and his knights trot down the hill through the curtain wall and out onto the road to the north. It would take them three days at least to find Fitz-Michael: more if they had to dodge Theobald.

Richard had worried a day over what reward to demand for returning the child to Fitz-Michael. Finally he had decided to take nothing at all. When Theobald heard of it, he would be dumbstruck. She hoped every man in Christendom heard of it. Turning, she went across the ward toward the kitchen, her arms wrapped around her body against the cold.

XII

❦

IN THE LATE SPRING, WHILE RICHARD WITH MOST OF HIS men was off fighting the Saracens below Iste, Maria fell sick and miscarried. She could not grieve for the lost baby, because Ceci also sickened. For three days Maria scarcely slept, although she knew from the beginning there was nothing she could do. The child lay on her back in the bed, hardly opening her eyes. Her hand in Maria's was icy cold. At last, on the morning of the third day, she died.

Eleanor let out a moan. Drained of her strength, Maria sat motionless beside the bed. Finally she raised her hand and gently closed the child's slack mouth. Eleanor flung her arms around Maria. At the sound of their weeping, Robert began to cry too. Maria let the other girl urge her onto her feet and help her to the truckle bed.

All day, she slept in snatches. Roger came in and spoke to her and kissed her. She heard them talking, later, about bearing off Ceci's body, and she propped herself up on one elbow and called to them not to wait until she slept, to take the child off while she was watching. They misunderstood; they thought to make it easier for her. After that, Father Simon arrived from the village and said many things to her, none of them important.

While she slept, she dreamed of the burial—she dreamed of telling Richard his daughter was dead and woke up with her teeth chattering. Looking toward the bed she saw that the child was gone, and she fell into a fit of weeping.

Eleanor brought her a cup of hot broth. "Here. You do yourself a disservice with this kind of grief." One arm

111

around Maria's shoulder, the girl fed her mouthfuls of soup.

Robert played on the floor, his black hair stuck together with conserves, putting everything he found into his mouth. Maria was stupid with misery. She pushed the bowl of soup away and ran her hand over her face.

"You must eat," Eleanor said, sensibly. "This is unseemly in you. Wait. Here." She picked Robert off the floor. "Here." She thrust him into Maria's arms.

Heavy and warm, he sank comfortably into her lap. He lifted his wide blue eyes to her. Maria kissed him. Holding him in her arms she lay down. She thought of the baby she had lost. She had scarcely realized she was with child before it was gone. Beside her, Eleanor picked up her mending and spoke of the ordinary things of the day. Maria shut her eyes. Robert slept curled in her arms. She would have more babies, more than could possibly die, each one a triumph over death. When she dozed again, she did not dream.

In the evening, Roger woke her up. He took her hands in his. "I would not trouble you, if there were some other way—"

"What's wrong?" Maria sat up. "Is it Richard?" If anything happened to Richard there would be no more babies.

"No—the crossroads in Birnia. William needs help, he wants me to meet him there with all our men. That's all I know. But there are only fifteen knights here now."

Maria grunted. Swinging her legs over the side of the truckle bed, she stood up. Her nightgown was soaked with blood. In the hollow her body had left in the bed, Robert yawned. She sat down again and dragged him into her lap.

"Where is Richard?"

"I don't know, somewhere below Iste—I sent a rider to him, when the—when—before."

Eleanor came in the door and hurried up to Maria's side. "Can you not let her sleep?" She hugged Maria tight as a mother.

"Sssh." Maria put her hand on Eleanor's arm. "Roger, you must take every knight to Birnia, in case it is Theobald attacking us." She gave Robert to Eleanor.

"That leaves you with no one to protect you," he said.

"Richard will come back." Rising, she got her cloak from the bedpost and shrugged it around her.

Roger sprang to his feet. "God's blood, you are valiant, I love you for it." He turned toward the door. Going out, he wheeled toward her. "I swear to you, Theobald won't slip past us, however great his army." He rushed off down the stairs.

Eleanor came up to her. "He could have decided that himself, he did not have to wake you."

"Oh, well. Now that I am up—" She went to the cupboard for fresh clothes. She did not look at the empty bed.

Before moonrise, Roger led all the men north. Maria went to the gate to make sure it was closed and barred. The night air was stagnant, full of unpleasant smells. Clouds obscured great patches of the sky. The people she saw peered at her, curious, and when she looked at them jerked their faces into false masks of sympathy. She looked away, unreasonably angry. She got the six knights' boys out of their tower and set them on watch and went back to the hall.

She caught herself listening for the dead child's voice. Her eyes burned. She fled upstairs to her room, and crumpled on the bed she wept painfully until her eyes were dry. Eleanor was feeding Robert before the hearth. He burst into tears, refusing to drink. Eleanor threw down the little wooden cup. She set Robert on the floor and paced around the room.

"Where is she?" Maria called. "Where did they take her?"

Eleanor came over and sat down on the bed. She stroked Maria's hair away from her face. "In the village. They will see to everything."

"When Richard comes back, we will bury her."

"Don't think of it. Put your mind elsewhere."

"Where?" Maria masked her face in her arms.

In the morning, another messenger came from William: Theobald was attacking Birnia with a great force of men. William had garrisoned the Tower, but needed more

113

help at once. Maria fed the messenger and sent him to the Knights' Tower to sleep. With Eleanor and Robert she leaned out the window, looking anxiously south. She had gotten no word from Richard since before she fell sick. If the Tower of Birnia fell, nothing would lie between Theobald and Maria's castle but fields and open roads.

"Richard will be here at noon," she said. "Meanwhile we must get ready for a siege."

She left Eleanor to take charge of the castle, the cook to help her, and brought the villagers up behind the curtain wall and set them to gathering stones. With Robert, she sat on the slope and kept watch; she cast about for some shrewd lie to use when noon arrived and Richard did not. To her surprise, however, he appeared in the mid-morning, leading a double column of his knights up the road, a train of eight mules in their midst.

Maria left Robert on the ground. She walked quickly across the steep slope toward the road. Richard reined his horse around to meet her and dismounted. Maria stretched her arms out blindly toward him. He pulled her against him, pressing her so tight against him that she could scarcely breathe. The doubled rings of his hauberk bit into her arms.

"Are you all right?" he said. He pushed her away from him, holding her away from him at arm's length. "What's all this, here?"

Maria told him about Theobald. "Until you came there wasn't a single knight here—The only weapons we have are the stones on the hillside."

Richard pushed back the hood of his mail. He used three or four of his favorite obscenities against Theobald. Abruptly he cursed God, with a vehemence that made her flinch. His voice shook. She turned away from him, cold.

"Get me a fresh horse," he said. "And my fur cloak, I damned nearly froze to death at Iste." He bellowed to his knights, still waiting in their columns along the road.

Maria led his horse on up toward the castle. In the gateway, she stopped to look behind her. Down on the hillside, Richard was sitting with Robert in his lap, searching through her basket. While she watched, he found the cheese and meat she had brought for her dinner. She took the horse into the ward.

Eleanor helped her find his fur cloak. They packed a roast hen and a leather bottle of wine for him and brought the bundle out into the ward. The knights wandered in and out, feeding themselves, getting new gear and horses, and carrying the full baskets of stones onto the top of the wall. Richard stayed outside on the hill.

Maria took the fresh horse down to him. He sat staring north, his jaws working steadily through the last mouthful of cheese. He was sun-darkened like a plowman, his eyes were pale as quartz. Robert crawled around him tearing up clumps of grass to eat. Dirt covered the little boy's face. He beamed up at Maria when she approached him. Richard did not move.

Maria sat down beside him. He said nothing and hardly glanced at her. His knights were already spilling down the road, their voices quiet. They would know, by now, everybody would know that Ceci was dead.

Richard turned to Robert and kissed him, a loud smack on the side of the head. With the little boy in his arms, he rose, and when Maria stood thrust the child toward her.

"Richard," she said. She did not know how to ask him for comfort.

He took a step away from her. "Don't speak of it," he said. "Please, Maria. Please." His hands out, pleading, he backed away from her, went to his horse, and mounted. Without waving, without calling to her, he rode away down the valley with his knights. She let Robert slide out of her arms. Until the columns of riders had vanished in the trees and hills of the distance, she stood watching him go, amazed that he had left her alone.

SHE HAD WANTED Richard there when Ceci was buried, but obviously he meant not to be, and they could wait no longer. In the evening, after they had made the castle as strong as they could, everyone except one sentry went down to the village to hear the funeral Mass. The people of the village joined them. Many people wept openly. The rumor went among them that it was a bad omen the little girl should die, that evil was about to fall on them.

Carrying torches to make their way, they climbed back

up the hill to the castle burying ground. The porter and a servant had dug a hole that afternoon, and the village carpenter had made a cross. All the mourners knelt around the flower-filled grave, and Father Simon began the prayers for the newly dead.

Maria closed her ears to the words. Wrapped in linen, the child's body lay on the ground beside the grave. The flowers tucked in her shroud were already wilting. Maria fell to crying, and Eleanor slid her arm around her waist. Father Simon spoke of the redeeming love of God. Maria knew she was not weeping for her daughter, who was safe in Heaven, but for herself, who had lost the dearest thing in her life.

They lowered the body into the earth and closed up the grave like a mouth. Maria throttled herself silent. If there was a virtue in it anywhere it was to endure it well. She let Eleanor lead her through the bleak torchlight back to the castle.

RICHARD CAME BACK with Count Theobald's son as a hostage and Theobald's sworn oath not to cross their common boundary for six months. Maria had no idea what to do with the hostage and to her relief Richard gave him into Roger's keeping. Roger led the boy off. Richard took the stool over to the hearth in their bedroom and sat down before the fire.

Maria could not tell if the firelight alone made his face so gaunt. Sitting down beside him, she pulled out her braids so that she could brush her hair. It was late: everyone else was asleep.

"How did you do? Did you fight him? Was Prince Arthur with him?"

"Yes—no." He hunched his shoulders. "We fought and we talked. Theobald is very good at talking. Of course Arthur was with him, he is Theobald's thing. I may have given them too much." He milled the air with his hand. "I can't do everything at once."

"What is he like?"

"Who, Theobald? Very good at talking." Getting up, he took off his shirt. His left side was mottled with yellowing bruises.

116

"You didn't give him a hostage, did you?"

"No. But I think we could have gotten more from them—I didn't know how weak he was. He'd been separated from some of his men. We could have gotten more. I didn't use the advantage."

They looked at each other a moment. Wordless, she saw how he cast desperately around for something else to speak of—she realized he would not talk of Ceci. She buried her hands in her lap. "Oh, well," she said, and knew of nothing to tell him. The silence wore on. Heavily she turned away from him and stared into the fire.

XIII

❧

AFTER CECI'S DEATH, MARIA LONGED FOR ANOTHER baby. Robert was too old and active: whenever she tried to coddle him, he pushed her away. Each month while the moon waxed she prayed she was with child, but each month after the full moon she gave off blood. She had never understood before why the village women called the blood the curse of Eve.

In the fall, when she had been barren several months, she spoke roundabout to Father Simon, and something he said suggested to her that she was being punished for murdering Walter Bris, more than two years before. The old priest told her that for the punishment to cease she would have to repent sincerely of her sins, and she prayed every day for the grace to be sorry. She never asked Richard what he thought. The one time she mentioned Ceci to him, he put his back to her and furiously did something else.

As a proof that she was truly sorry, she swore to build a chapel at the Cave of the Virgin. Whenever she grieved for Ceci, she thought of the chapel and her heart lightened. Richard at first would not listen to her. All winter long he and Roger fought the Saracens in the foothills; he was in and out of the castle every few days, arriving usually late at night, turning the whole place over, and leaving the next day before noon, to everybody's great relief. Then in the spring, after more than a hundred knights had come south to join his army, he seized the last two Saracen fortresses in the lowlands, and on Midsummer's Day he stormed Iste itself. Exhilarated with this victory, he gave her all the money he had in plunder and let her take the local serfs who had worked on the New Tower for her father.

There were ten of these men. She took them to the Cave of the Virgin, collected a dozen more from the village there, and talked the English monk into sending to the chapterhouse in Agato for a mason. A passionate energy captured her. She went over the countryside talking people into making bricks and cutting lumber. A French pilgrim at the cave knew how to plan for building, and he helped her devise the scheme for the chapel. The pilgrim drew it out on vellum, lingering on at the shrine long past the time when he would have gone on his way to France. He was an interesting man. At night sometimes Maria dreamed lasciviously of him although in the flesh she was always stiff with him and hardly ever spoke to him alone.

The English monk knew everyone in the region. He found other craftsmen to help her, and many of the local serfs came when they could to work on the chapel. Until the harvests were in, she had only her own men to dig and rake and smooth the ground she had chosen, but once the peasants had their grains and vegetables shored up and their meat salted, they walked with their families to the shrine and fell to work.

All this made her happy as she had ever been since her marriage. But sometimes when she thought of Ceci, she could not help but cry.

The master mason and his apprentices arrived in the balmy warmth of Saint Martin's summer. The mason, Brother Nicholas, was a large, foul-smelling man, muscular as a knight. The taut skin of his tonsure was bright

118

red from the sun. He prayed overnight in the cave, came out the next morning, tucked up his cassock between his knees, and told Maria she was doing everything wrong. Trailed at a good distance by his helpers, all expert at staying upwind of him, he went around making everything right. When she saw that he could do as well without her, she went back to her castle, which she had left in Eleanor's keeping.

Richard had just come back from Iste. While with Eleanor's help Maria took off her traveling clothes and re-introduced herself to Robert, her husband kept off to a corner of their room. Maria could tell he was angry. Eleanor took Robert downstairs, and Richard turned on her.

"I didn't marry you to live by myself."

"You married me to get this castle," Maria said.

He tramped up to her and stood over her. She thrust her chin out at him. "You married me to get around my father."

Richard knocked her down. "Don't talk back to me. I never did anything to your father." He pushed her with his foot. "Get up."

Maria lay back on the floor. "I think I'll stay here, so I will not fall as far when you decide to do it again."

Richard hauled her up onto her feet. "Shut the door. Everybody for leagues can hear you. You scream like an old gate sometimes."

Maria slammed the door shut. It rebounded inward. She thrust it closed. Her head throbbed. She went to the window and stood, her heart pounding, her eyes directed out the shuttered window. Richard stamped around the room swearing.

She said, "Why should I have to stay here—you were gone most of the—"

"I came back three times in July and twice in August and you could have managed to be here once. I couldn't even get my clothes mended." He threw something violently into the fire.

"If you had told me you were—"

"I shouldn't have to tell you," he shouted. "You should be here."

119

Maria stared at the wooden shutter. Her cheeks burned from fighting with him. She laid her hand on the cold stone sill.

"Are you finished now?" he said.

She turned toward him. "What?"

"Your church. Did you finish it?"

"No. It's hardly begun."

He flung his arms out. "Why now? Why can't you wait until I don't have a thousand things to do and a thousand people waiting for me to do one thing wrong? Jesus in Heaven—This place was chaos when you were gone. Can't you help me even a little? And I never touched your father."

"If you say so."

"Are you trying to make me hit you?"

They stared at each other across the room. Maria said, stiff-lipped, "I'm sorry."

"You're staying here, now. You're not going back down there. Do you understand me?"

Maria clenched her teeth. She started toward the door. Eleanor knew little of keeping the castle. There was much to be done before winter struck. Richard followed her across the room. When she opened the door, he put his hand on it and slammed it shut again in her face before she could go out.

"Where are you going?"

She made him a deep bow. "I beg your pardon, my most gracious lord, have I your grace's permission to leave you now?"

He sputtered at her. She pulled his hand off the door, opened it, and went downstairs. In the hall, Eleanor said, in a disapproving voice, "You are scarcely back from the holy place and you are already fighting."

Roger was in Iste, William in Birnia, and Eleanor did not like to ride. Maria and Richard hunted alone in the snowfields and the wood, after the wolves and foxes that preyed on the herds. Richard set a breakneck pace. Maria had to strain to keep up with him. Their dogs ran one trail due south into the mid-morning, lost it, and cut another almost at once. They galloped through the snow-filled stony woods. The hard exercise filled her with energy. Just after noon, at the foot of a steep boulder, the wolf turned. Maria wheeled her snorting mare away. The dogs barked and lunged at the wolf's throat and flanks. Blood splattered the snow and streaked the coarse fur of the wolf. Richard called the pack away. Crouched against the boulder, the wolf snarled breathlessly. Richard put an arrow to his bow and shot. The wolf's growl ended in a yelp.

The wolfhounds jumped and fought over the body. Dismounting, Richard waded in among them to retrieve his arrow. Maria looked away into the wood. The trees were stark against the snow and the flat gray sky. Her skin still glowed from the excitement of the hard ride. The whining and barking of the dogs made her horse restless, and she started back the way they had come.

Richard followed her. Unspeaking, they quartered through the wood, cutting toward the sea, looking for the wolf's mate. The empty woods rang with the horses' hoofs on the rocks. The wind was icy. In the mid-afternoon, the dogs without running a scent suddenly brought something to bay in a cleft of the hills ahead of them.

Richard was behind her. Maria galloped up through the trees, hanging onto her saddle in case the mare stumbled. The horse skidded to a stop in the mouth of a brush-choked ravine.

She cried out in surprise. The dogs were holding a man pinned down in the back of the ravine: a Saracen. He fended off the dogs with a long branch. Behind him in the snowy winddrift, another man lay, white as his clothes. Richard drew rein beside her.

Maria called the dogs back. They clustered around her, their eyes and their noses aimed at the Saracens. One or two of the big hounds lay down in the snow. She said, "That man is hurt, or sick."

Richard and the Saracen with the branch were staring at each other. The wind chilled Maria's face. The sick man heaved up a cough. She saw blood on his sleeve where he had muffled himself. Richard reached over his shoulder for his bow.

"Richard." She put her cold hands on the mare's neck. "They can't fight back."

"If that were you and me, they wouldn't hesitate."

"They are Saracens. They know no better."

Richard looked at her and back to the Saracens. He pulled the case off the arrows on his saddle. Maria whistled to the dogs. Bending her mare around, she started up the snowy hillside. The mare carried her clambering up over the rocks. One of the Saracens gasped. She reined in her mare on the steep slope above the ravine. The bow sang again. When she looked, Richard was walking into the ravine to get his arrows.

He rode up beside her. They walked their horses on along the strange, silent hillside. Brown and dun, the dogs scattered around them through the colorless trees. She glanced at Richard. His eyes were vague, as if he looked inward.

They let their horses pick their way down the slope. Ahead, the beach spread its pale sand at the foot of the gray rolling surf. The wind tasted salt. She nudged her mare forward into the open.

They rode down onto the beach. The sea jumped and tossed off to the gray horizon. He led her through the wind toward a fisherman's lean-to. They dismounted and brought their horses into the fragile two-sided shelter. The wind battered the thin boards over their heads. The surf boomed on the shore. They pulled off their clothes and coupled in the back of the lean-to, while the horses stamped and snorted and the dogs prowled around them. Wrapped in his heavy fur cloak, they lay still in one another's arms. The night was coming. They got up and put their clothes on and rode home.

IN THE SPRING, after the planting, Richard took his men into the mountains and Maria went back to the Cave of the Virgin, where her roofless chapel stood carpeted in new grass. Eleanor and Robert came with her. Every now and again Richard rode down from the mountains, and she had to go back to her castle to meet him, but he never stayed above a day and a night, and she left for the shrine again as soon as he was gone.

The summer pilgrims swelled the crowd of men and women working on the building. The chapterhouse had sent two brothers to help the English monk serve the shrine, and in a single day, all working together, the

122

monks, the pilgrims, and the serfs threw up a sleeping house in the village, a mile from the cave. There, before Michaelmas, in September, Maria bore a son.

That put her out of humor. She had taken for granted that the baby would be another girl, another Ceci. From Richard in the mountains a messenger came to instruct her to name the baby Stephen. Robert hated him at once.

Brother Nicholas baptized the child. The master mason was carving the mullions in the chapel windows, twisting stone vines and trees around them, and in the branches of the trees putting birds and snakes. After every day of work, the people would come up to admire what he had done. Everybody loved him, in spite of his stench. At the end of his year with them, when he had to go back to his monastery in Agato, many of the people wept.

On the day he was to leave, they gathered on the roadside in front of the chapel, the men in their stained tunics, with their work-hardened hands and faces, and the women in their shawls, and he went from one to the next blessing them by name and kissing them. Since he was a monk, they could give him no gift. Maria especially felt it sorely. She knelt before him with her two sons and he blessed them.

"Lady," he said. "Keep faith with God."

Maria kissed his hand. He took his staff and with his apprentices to windward of him walked away down the road. All the rest of the morning the men worked in a frenzy, but the women lagged and shook their heads and sighed.

At noon, Maria sat down under the trees in the yard of the shrine; opening her dress she gave her breast to the baby. Eleanor was calling to Robert on the stony hillside. Maria sang a ballad the French pilgrim had sung her.

Two horses were dragging a sled loaded with stone up the road. Behind them a few riders came, but she paid them no heed. The workmen were hammering inside the chapel. She fit her song to that.

A horse stopped in front of her. Startled, she looked up. Richard swung down from the saddle. She had not seen him since the midsummer. The sun had faded his hair to a light brown. She scrambled to her feet. The baby, losing the nipple, let out an angry cry.

123

"You look like a serf." Richard kissed her. "I'll take you into the woods, like a serf. Where is Robert?"

Maria shouted to Eleanor to bring him. Richard took the baby and juggled it. Over his mail, he wore a long white tunic, to keep the sun off. Maria put her hand on his back. He kissed her again. His mouth was softer than she remembered. Between them, Stephen cried, and Richard stood away from her.

"Here. Put this where it belongs." He touched her breast. She cradled the baby in her arms. She leaned against him.

"Show me your God-gift," Richard said. "Is it done?"

Maria sat down to finish nursing Stephen. "Why are you here? It isn't winter yet. Have you taken Mana'a already?"

He shook his head. The reins trailing from his hands, he sank down on his heels before her. His horse cropped the grass below the tree. "Why, are you unhappy to see me?"

She leaned forward and kissed him. He had come all the way down from the mountains just for her sake. She felt guilty she had not missed him more.

"Where have you been fighting?"

He gestured offhand. "Up there with the lizards and the rocks and the arrows."

"Papa," Robert screamed. He ran up the road toward them. Reaching his father he turned him by the arm away from the baby and Maria. "Papa!" He flung himself into Richard's arms.

Maria closed her dress. Eleanor, smiling, was walking up the road toward them. Richard wrapped his son in his arms. "Jesus, you're big. Here, give me a kiss." Robert screwed his face up and pursed his lips, and Richard kissed him. The little boy laughed and hugged him.

"Here," Maria said. She tucked Stephen into his blanket and stood up. Eleanor was standing under the trees watching them, her face wearing her blandest, sweetest smile. Robert preferred her to Maria, and now he was laughing and hanging on Richard. She gave the baby to Eleanor.

"Don't you want to see the chapel? Eleanor, take the

children down to the village." She got up, shaking the grass seeds from her skirt.

Richard lifted Robert up by the arms and settled him on his shoulder. Crowing, the little boy fastened his hands in his father's thick hair. Maria started off ahead of them, but Richard got her by the hand and held her beside him. His fingers were ridged with callus from the summer's fighting. While they walked across the yard to the chapel, she marked that he still stepped short in his right leg. Robert was bouncing up and down on his shoulders. Maria said, "Don't let him pound you like that."

"I would liefer pound you."

Her face grew hot. She squeezed his hand, and he put his arm around her shoulders.

The outside of the chapel was finished, save for the roof and the door. The brick rectangle had three windows on each long side, a wooden porch, and a space for a double door in front. Most of the workmen were inside laying down the planks for the floor. Maria took Richard all the way around the outside, to show him the windows Brother Nicholas had carved. He looked closer at the walls themselves, how the bricks and stone were fit together, and the building laid out and leveled on the hillside.

"Your workmen made all this?"

Maria nodded, proud. They were coming around to the front door again. "The master mason taught them, that monk I told you of—he even showed a boy from the village here how to make the drawings and measurements. Arnalto."

"Good." Richard lifted Robert down from his shoulders and set him on the ground. "I am taking all these men up to the mountains to build me a new castle."

For a moment, she stood still, to collect her jumbled thoughts. Robert ran shouting into the chapel, calling to everyone that his father had come.

Maria said, "When they are finished here."

"No. It will snow up there soon. If I can't shelter my men up in the pass, I'll lose it. You can have the workmen again when I'm done with them."

Maria walked several steps away from him, through the

125

dry grass of the hillside. The chapel was nearly finished. She had talked with the monks of consecrating it on Epiphany. It was hers, her God-gift. He had not come to see her, he had just come to steal away her workmen. Richard stood in front of the chapel, one hand braced on the wall, his eyes on her. She knew she could not stop him from taking every workman away.

Before her the steep slope fell off down toward the village. Eleanor was walking along the path, Stephen in her arms. Maria picked up her skirt in her hands. "Wait," she cried. "Eleanor, wait for me." She ran down the stony slope, through the thorny wildflowers. Out of breath, her legs stinging with scratches, she stumbled out onto the path a few steps ahead of Eleanor.

"What's wrong?" Eleanor said. "Oh, Maria, you've torn your skirt."

"I hate him," Maria said. She looked back at the chapel, but Richard was gone. She sat down on the path to take the thorns from her feet and began to cry.

WITH THE SUMMER OVER, and the tide of pilgrims dammed, the monks' guesthouse was empty except for Maria, Eleanor, and the two children, whose beds took up one corner of the long room. Maria changed Stephen's clothes and put him to sleep in his cradle. Eleanor was mending Maria's torn skirt, the needle whipping back and forth through the heavy blue cloth.

"Have you seen Robert?" Maria asked. She went to the window.

"You must bow to him, Maria," Eleanor said. "He is your husband."

"Let him bow to me for once. He's a dog to use me like this."

She reached out the window to close the shutters. In the evening a cool wind blew up from the sea, across the harvested fields and the sweep of brown pasture that lay between the village and the hillside where the cave was. She had chosen this bed because of its view of the chapel. She banged the shutters closed.

"This is more important than his work—this is for God."

"So is the Crusade." Eleanor shook out the skirt. "It's too great a tear to mend well, but you can use it for everyday. I don't understand you, Maria. What will people think? You should love Richard, no matter how he treats you."

"I hate Richard. You take him, he wouldn't care, Robert already loves you better than me, and Stephen could learn to. You be their mother, and when you lose them, you can suffer."

"You are overwrought." Eleanor sat down beside her and hugged her. "It is this sickly wind of late. They will ring for Vespers soon. Put yourself in a better mood for prayer."

Maria wiped her eyes. She sat staring at the floor, morose. The bell rang for Vespers, and Eleanor brought her cloak. They went out of the guesthouse toward the monks' little church, built by pilgrims' offerings.

In the clear autumn air the tolling of the bell rang like drops of water on a gold dish. From the village, spread along the narrow valley, people came walking up toward the little church. Maria with Stephen in her arms stood in front of the church, waiting for Robert. The last person went by her, and she had not found her son.

The voice of the English monk reached her, chanting the first phrase of the prayer, and the chorus of the villagers took it up. Usually with the workmen from the chapel, the congregation overflowed into the dooryard and stood looking in through the windows, but now the church was half-empty. Maria stood outside, in the deepening blue twilight, waiting for Richard to come. The night-singing birds began to call in the fields around her. From the chapel the voices of the villagers measured out their prayers. Stephen slept against her shoulder, smelling of sour milk.

Through the village came a train of mounted men and men on foot—her workmen, Arnalto leading them, their belongings in bundles on their shoulders. Richard spurred his bay horse over to her and reined in. Robert sat before him on his saddle.

"Come home," he said. "I will put these people to work and be back for Christmas."

"No," she said. She did not look at Robert.

127

Richard made a sound in his throat. He shifted in his saddle, creaking the leather. He met her eyes.

"I am sorry to do this. I know why you are angry. But it must be done. Can't you understand me?"

Maria said nothing. Robert was looking down from his perch in front of his father's saddle. "Stephen is little."

"Yes," Richard said. "As little as his mother." He wheeled his horse and rode away toward his parade of knights and workmen. Maria went up the hill to pray in the deserted chapel.

At moonrise, she came back to go to bed. She dreamed of riding a horse bareback over a wide yellow meadow. Noises broke into the dream. She woke with a start. In the darkness, men were rushing into the guesthouse.

Eleanor shrieked. Maria rolled out of her bed, lunging toward the cradle where her baby lay, and Stephen started his thin-voiced shrilling cry. Someone caught her from behind, his arms wrapped around her pinning down her elbows. She thrashed in his grip, grunted with effort, and kicked back, but her bare feet could not hurt him. Vast and dark, a cloth fell over her head and shoulders.

"Stephen," she screamed. "Don't hurt my baby—don't hurt—"

They were dragging her out of doors, wrapped in a thick cloak. She twisted, struggling to free her arms, to kick, and screamed again. Stephen was crying. Someone would hear, someone would help her. Horizontal, she was borne swiftly along, and the folds of the cloak lay against her mouth and nose. For an instant she could not breathe. She turned her head frantically until she found air. She landed on her side on something hard. An instant later, another body rolled up against hers.

"Eleanor," Maria called. "Eleanor."

"Yes—I'm here," Eleanor wailed. "Don't fight, don't give them reason to hurt us."

Whatever they were lying on began to jounce and squeal along. A wagon. The baby had stopped his wails. Panicking, Maria flung herself from side to side until she lay exhausted and half-smothered against the wagon's wall. She started to cry.

Eleanor was crying, too. Maria ran out of tears and lay still, trying to hear what was going on around them. It

128

must be Theobald, stealing them to use against Richard. But the longer she thought about that, the less likely it seemed. She lifted her head, straining to hear.

She could make out the sounds of the wagon and the team, the two men in the wagon seat, and three other horses. No one thieving her away would send only five men to do it. She lay back, brimming with anger, and squirmed over toward Eleanor.

"Eleanor," she said softly. "These are Richard's men."

Eleanor fell silent in mid-sob. Maria lay still, patiently listening; at last, Eleanor murmured, "Do you really think so?"

"Yes." Maria strained her arms against the ropes. They had bound the cloak around her above her elbows, like a wrapped cheese. She worked her arms back and forth to slide the blanket up.

Eleanor began to pray in a voice still choked from crying. Maria rested a little. The edge of the cloth around her was free of the ropes, and a trickle of cold air dribbled in. She took hold of the material in her teeth and tugged it loose.

The ropes fell slack over her elbows. Still half-bruised in the heavy cloth, she lay on her side thinking that perhaps she ought to let them take her to Richard, to apologize to him and to accept his apology, before something happened that could not be mended. She yanked her arms free, sat up, flung aside the cloak, and stood in the wagon bed.

They were rolling down the moonlit road, over the bare hills; three knights ranged alongside the wagon. One cried, "Wait!" and jigged his horse toward her. She braced herself to keep her balance when the wagon stopped.

"Don't touch me," she cried. She pulled the cloak up over her nightdress and struggled with the unfamiliar shoulder clasp. "If you touch me, my husband will kill you."

The three knights reined in their horses. Maria scrambled across Eleanor's prone body to the wagon seat and snatched Stephen from the arms of the man beside the driver.

"Hold her, damn it," a knight called, but his voice wa-

129

vered. The two men in the wagon sat motionless—they were serfs. "Stop her—grab her, pick her up, are you afraid of her?"

Maria stepped over Eleanor and jumped down from the back of the wagon to the road. A big blond knight wheeled his horse across her path. She did not recognize him. Richard would have chosen men she did not know.

"If you stop me," she said softly, "I will tell him that you handled me." Ducking under his horse's neck, she started down the road, back toward the shrine.

"Maria!" Eleanor screamed.

The knights galloped up around her, hemming her in with their horses. She cradled Stephen tightly in her arms. The moonlight shone on their mail and their shining, sweating faces.

"God's wounds, are you all afraid of a woman?"

Maria slid between two horses and went on along the road. The ground was rough under her bare feet. The talkative knight swore, and the other knights laughed.

"You go put your hands on Gripe's wife."

Eleanor was still calling to her, but she ignored that: it was not Eleanor's fight. Hoofs clattered behind her and a lone knight rode up around her.

"Now, come along," he said. He reached for her with both hands.

"If you touch me," she said, "you'll have to hurt me. Get out of my way."

"Now, listen—"

"Get out of my way."

The knight sat up straight. He reined his horse aside, and she walked off along the road toward the shrine.

XIV

❧

IN THE MORNING, WITH THE MONKS, SHE WENT AROUND the chapel to see what work they could do alone. The carpenter had hewn and shaped the planks for the rest of the floor, and the pegs were all cut. Brother Anthony had helped the workmen set down that part they had finished. He showed Maria and the other monk how to slide the grooved and tongued boards together and how to bore the holes. Twice they cut the holes through and missed the stud underneath, and when Brother Anthony finally pounded in the first peg, it broke off halfway down and they had to drill it out. At noon they were still working on the first plank.

She had left the baby with a woman in the village, who brought him up the hill to be fed at noon. Another woman had come with the monks' dinner. They talked on the porch while Maria nursed Stephen. The baby did not like the blustering cold wind, and Maria took him under the shelter of the trees. Brother Anthony had gone into the cave to pray. He came out again through the slot in the rock and put one hand up to shield his face from the sun.

Other women were climbing the road from the village. Stephen was asleep. Maria fastened her dress and went back to the chapel porch. The monks shared their dinner with her, while the village women and half a dozen of their grown children gathered. When they had all eaten, the women and their children fell to work beside them in the chapel. Brother Anthony rushed about trying to show them all what to do. Mostly they got in each other's way.

131

"Maria," a woman called, from the front of the chapel. "Here comes someone on a big horse."

She straightened up. She was helping to slide a plank into the floor, and the woman beside her inched toward her to take up the weight. Maria scrambled across the frame to the finished floor and went out onto the porch.

Richard was riding his bay horse up the road. Maria stood in the sunlight, watching him. Behind her the women hushed, and the children fell silent. Richard reined up in front of the porch.

"I've come to take you home."

"I'm not going home. Not until my chapel is finished."

He twisted sideways in his saddle to face her; he slung one leg around the pommel of his saddle. "Who is going to finish it? You? Do you know what you look like? You're grubby as a serf." He jumped down from his saddle in front of her. "Leave it. In the spring the men can come back to work on it. If you try to finish it whatever you do will carry away in the first high wind."

Maria bit her lips. Under the trees, Stephen gave a cranky cry. "Probably," she said. She crossed the yard to the trees, where a villager's half-grown daughter was trying to quiet the baby. Richard followed her, leading his horse after her through the beech trees.

"Are you coming home?"

"Not until my chapel is finished." She lifted Stephen in her arms. His blanket, his swaddlings, and his clothes were sodden. The girl held out her arms.

"I can do it, mistress. Let me do it."

The girl took the baby away. Maria stood in the middle of the winter-naked beech trees, facing Richard. He stared at her, unfriendly. Her hands were sticky from handling the lumber and she rubbed them on her skirt.

"One more time," he said. "Come home."

"No."

He turned to his horse and threw the stirrup up across the saddle. Yanking the girth loose, he reached across his horse's withers to unhook the breastplate from the far side of the saddle.

"I thought you were going up to the mountains," she said.

132

"Welf can do that. I would much rather stay here and watch you make a fool of yourself." He dragged the saddle off the horse's back.

Maria clenched her teeth. She marched out of the trees toward the chapel. All the work had stopped. When she went inside, the women were standing in groups. Their eyes turned bright on her. She crossed to the edge of the floor and stooped to help lift another plank.

Every day she went up to the chapel to work. Sometimes the local women and their children helped her. Sometimes even the few men left in the village joined them, but the serfs had their own tasks, and usually she and the monks were the only workmen. Once Brother Anthony fell sick, and since Brother Paul had to care for him Maria worked alone for three days in a row. Richard lived with her in the guesthouse. They slept in two beds tied together by the legs. When he was not going around the countryside on his own business, he came up to the chapel and watched Stephen for her, but he never helped her, even when no one else was there.

Christmas came. The villagers brought them a roast goose, which they shared with the monks. Afterward Brother Anthony and Brother Paul went up to pray in the shrine. Richard gave Maria tenpence to gamble with and taught her how to play dice. They were the only people staying in the guesthouse, and no one else came by all day long. Hardly speaking, they sat on the lumpy bed and threw the dice back and forth. At sundown she paid him back the original tenpence and arranged the rest of her winnings in twenty little stacks. While she took off her clothes and put her nightgown on, he counted them.

"You've won half my money."

Maria lit two candles and put the holders on the window sill above the bed. While she nursed the baby they threw the dice a few more times. Richard counted her money again. He swore. She changed the baby's clothes.

"Come to bed," she said. "I'm tired and I have to get up early tomorrow again."

"All or nothing," Richard said. "One more throw." He shook the dice in his fist.

Maria laid the baby down in the cradle. The candlelight

133

filled this part of the guesthouse with a murky yellow glow. They threw the dice again; she won again. Pleased, she piled up her money.

"One more throw," Richard said. He picked up the dice. "All or nothing."

"You don't have any more money."

"I'll owe it to you. One more throw."

She won again.

"Once more," Richard said.

"No."

"All or nothing."

"No."

"I gave you the money to start with."

Maria stared at him. "You must think I'm a fool."

"One more throw." He held out the dice to her. "Are you afraid?"

This time he won. Maria watched him sweep all the money over to his side, across the ridge in the middle where the two beds joined.

"If you were a Saracen," he said, "I'd have Mana'a."

He dropped the money into his wallet. She glanced down at the baby in his cradle beside the bed. Richard pinched out the candles. The darkness fell around her. She sat on her side of the bed, her head turned away from him, saying her prayers in her mind. He was right; she was a fool. His hand grazed the back of her neck.

"Stay down here tomorrow," he said.

Maria laughed. She lay down on the bed. The air was stuffy from the smoke of the snuffed candles.

"Just for the morning, then." He pulled on her night-gown. She moved closer so that he could reach her easily. "Care about me for once," he said.

She laughed again. Arching her back, she helped him pull the nightgown up and off over her head. She lifted her face to his kiss. The guesthouse stretched vast and open around them in the dark. His hand pressed up hard between her legs.

"Just until noon."

She wrapped her arms around his waist; she laughed.

THE WINTER STORMS BROKE. Half the roof blew away. She went all over the area begging straw for a new thatch, and in the constant drilling rain the two monks bound it on again. Every time the wind blew she expected to see it sail away. They built the altar. The work was hard; worse, it was dull, and several times she would have given up, but the rain had driven Richard inside and he was always at the far end of the chapel, staring at her. Brother Anthony fell sick again. Maria and Brother Paul hung the doors up three times before they opened and closed.

On Ladymas, they sanctified the church. The next sunny morning she and Richard started south toward their home. Stephen slept in a basket on Maria's saddle. They kept their horses to a walk for the baby's sake. Around them the low hills were bleak and patched with snow. The road was gutted; beds of pebbles showed where the rains had washed the dirt away. In the mid-morning they stopped beside the road. The sea flashed in the distance through a gap in the hills.

The baby fed hungrily. Maria shifted his weight in her arms. Richard sat down beside her on the grass. The horses grazed behind them, crunching the twigs of the brush. Maria laid the baby down on her lap and wiped his mouth on the edge of her sleeve. Richard put his arm around her shoulders. The baby was asleep; they mounted their horses and rode on into the morning.

XV

NOT IN THE NEXT SPRING, BUT THE SPRING AFTER, Richard went from Maria's castle to the hill town of Iste. To prove that the roads were safe now for travelers he brought Maria, her sons, and Eleanor after him in wagons, guarded only by the drovers and two knights.

Maria rode her mare. She would not sit in the wagon. The road wound through the rolling hilly countryside. The lower valleys were already planted in the spring crop. Sighting them, the serfs ran out of their fields to greet them. Maria could hardly understand their patois. For the first time, she heard Richard called Dragon.

On the fourth day they climbed into the steeper hills. The forest closed in around the road. Maria jogged her mare along beside the lead wagon, until Stephen began to shriek and she had to go back to the next to last wagon and pull Robert off him.

"Thief," Robert shouted. He wiggled out of her arms. "Eleanor, make him give it back."

Eleanor ran up the road from the last wagon, where she had been sewing with another woman. Maria held Robert away from Stephen by the back of his shirt. He turned and struck at her with his fists.

"Eleanor!"

"I'm sorry, Maria," Eleanor said. She climbed up the moving cartwheel into the wagon. "Robert, what a bad boy. What have you done?"

Maria picked up Stephen, who pushed his face against her shoulder and sobbed. His face and hands were covered with crumbs. He smelled of fruit pudding. Maria quieted him with a kiss and set him down.

"Now, Robert," she said. "He is only a baby. You can't hit him." She picked up a bit of greasy linen from the deck of the wagon. "Did he eat your pudding?"

Robert gulped at her. He glared at Stephen. "I was saving it. Papa says—I was saving it, I didn't even have any."

Eleanor soothed him, whispering in his ears. Maria nudged her aside. She picked up Robert's hands. "There is more pudding in the front wagon. You must not hit your brother."

Robert yanked his hands free. "Papa says I should guard what's mine. I didn't even have any!"

His blue eyes blazed at her from his grimy brown face. She shook her head at him. "You have to guard your brother, too. Don't you want to be a good knight? Like

Papa? A good knight never strikes someone who can't fight back."

"Mama." He chewed the inside of his cheek. "Why does being good have to be hard?"

Maria laughed. "If it were easy, it would be worthless." Eleanor had run up to the front wagon to fetch him some pudding. Maria stroked his black hair away from his forehead.

"Come ride with me. You can hold the reins."

He jumped up, his eyes snapping. An instant later he stiffened. "Knights don't ride palfreys."

Maria snorted. "Then stay here and ride the wagon." She pulled her mare by the reins up to the wheel and stepped awkwardly across the gap into the saddle. Eleanor was coming back to them, a chunk of fruit pudding in her hand.

"Mama," Robert called. He stretched his arms toward her. "Mama, I didn't mean it—let me ride—I'll hold the reins—"

Maria rode back to him and lifted him up before her. "Eleanor, watch Stephen." Giving the reins to Robert she took hold of the saddle pommel with both hands and let him steer the mare in and out of the trees alongside the road.

ISTE STOOD at the head of a mountain valley. From the window of the tower where she stayed, Maria could look out over half the green country she had passed in coming here. The sharp dialect the people spoke, heavy with Saracen words, confused her as much as the rapid tempo of their lives and the close quarters they lived in. Richard had given the little city and its valley to Roger. In his hall, musicians played for every meal, and the tumblers and dancers performed half the night. People from all over the area came to dine and be entertained. He even kept a lion in a pit in the courtyard and threw raw meat to it every evening. Maria quickly had the smith build an iron grille to keep the lion in and Robert out.

They went to Mass in Iste's old cathedral. The priest told stories from the Book of Judges, finding in each detail some ingenious likeness to Richard's war against the

Saracens. Maria admired the cathedral's painted dome and the tall statues of the saints and prophets, crusted with silverwork and enamels. The sermon dragged on. Her eyes went elsewhere. Two of the men in the row of people across the aisle from her wore coats of the same dark green. Their fat wives were watching her keenly. She straightened her gaze away from them, back toward the pulpit. The priest was still talking. She thought of the green coats; symbols of some secret bond, some conspiracy. She entertained herself a while devising an elaborate plot from which she could save Richard. He stood beside her, his eyes fixed on a point beyond the altar, his hands rammed down under his belt. He was thinking. He was always thinking. She went back to her green-coat conspiracy.

When the Mass ended, they went out onto the open porch. Roger came after them. "What did you think of my priest?" he said.

"Well," Maria said, "his sermon was very long."

Roger gave her a quizzical look. Richard laughed. "She didn't listen to three words of it in a row. I could have told you that." He stopped in the sun at the foot of the steps. Above him, halfway up the porch, Maria put her crucifix away in her sleeve.

"What did he say?" She looked from Richard to Roger. "Was it a good sermon?"

"You should have listened," Roger said. Richard went on laughing.

"I heard him. Nothing sings like a greased wheel. Except a well-praised priest."

"I don't have to pay him. He knows where the good works come from. Maybe you should offer him something." Smiling, he nudged his brother with his elbow. "I'd rather be a second Samson than some desiccated judge in a gold cloak."

"It must have been an interesting sermon," Maria said. "I'm sorry I missed it."

"So is Roger," Richard said. He knocked his brother's arm.

Roger stood beside him on the step. He was taller than Richard, and he went down another stride to make them

138

the same height. "Come hunting with us. Since you came to Iste I have not talked with you above half an hour at a stretch."

Richard shook his head. "I don't have a horse fit to hunt on. You've missed the best of it, anyway—it's nearly noon."

"You'd better find something fit to fight on. That bay won't take you another season." He struck Richard in the chest and went out across the broad paved square before them. A groom came up to meet him, leading his horse.

Richard watched him go. Maria stood on the step above him. She knew she should not grudge Richard his brother's love. The rest of the congregation was wandering down along the porch, standing in little groups to talk, and waiting for their horses and litters. Many of them were watching her. A servant led up her mare and Richard's big gray horse. Roger rode off with a group of other men, local people, still in their Sabbath clothes: not Normans. She started to get on her mare, but Richard stopped her.

"Damn you, can't you wait? Sometimes I think I married a boy in skirts."

He lifted her up into her saddle. While she gathered her reins, she watched Roger and his friends meet other men and ride out the gate.

"The first time I ever noticed you," she said to Richard, "was once when you kept me from getting off my own horse by myself."

Richard mounted his gray stallion. "It would be different if you looked decent doing it."

She brewed a nasty answer; he turned the back of his head to her. "I'm not going to fight with you."

Side by side, they rode across the wide, crowded square. Most of the townspeople were going home on foot. The older people all wore sober clothes, but their children were dressed in brilliant colors, their shoes trimmed with gilt. Richard leaned forward, his eyes directed down over his horse's shoulder.

"There he goes with that damned lumpy chicken leg of his." He dismounted. Maria slid down from her horse.

"I told you not to take this horse."

On foot, he led the horse by the bridle up the street.

139

She walked beside him. Richard glanced fretfully down at the horse's bad leg. "I've personally soaked that leg for three days."

They went up the street. Iste was plastered across the side of the mountain, decks of white stone houses rising from the foot of its vast valley, and most of the streets climbed hills. Their horses' heads bobbed between them, the gray stallion's long, veined head dipping with each stride. The street narrowed, the walls on either side rising high over their heads. Richard walked ahead of her into a narrow archway. A man on horseback was trying to come through from the other direction, but the way was too narrow.

"Hey, you there, move aside," the stranger called. "Let us pass here."

Richard said, "Get the hell out of my way." Maria followed him into the black resounding arch. Beyond, in the widened street, a man in a feathered hat stood to one side, his face splashed over with a nasty smile.

"My lord, I did not see it was you."

Richard snarled something at him. He led his horse past the other man. Behind the feathered hat, two litters waited, carrying women in wonderful dresses, their faces tinted rosy as a sunburst. Lounging in their cushions, these women eyed Maria with amusement. She walked up the street after Richard.

"A typical drab little Norman," one woman said.

Richard stopped to look at his horse's foreleg again. Its knee was puffed up soft as a rising loaf. Maria caught up with him. Here on the edge of the street the slope pitched away sheer to the roofs below. She could see over the whole lower town and out across the green valley, checked in vineyards and pasture. She glanced toward the archway. The elegant man and his women were gone. Drab. She touched her cheeks.

"More of Roger's people," she said.

"Yes."

She smoothed her fingers over her cheekbones. "I could paint my face up like that."

"I'd wash it off with lye soap." He picked up the horse's hoof and flexed its leg; the horse snorted in pain. "Jesus God, it's sore all the way up to his shoulder."

"Why do you suffer these people?" She sat down in the street, looking across the valley into the blue distance. "Do they honor you? Do they help you? All I ever see them doing is feeding themselves in our hall and ordering our servants around."

"Roger is a good lure. You'll see what I mean. Speaking of food, when are you going to find us a cook?"

He started on again up the street. She followed, one arm across her white mare's withers. Roger's present cook even burned the bread. Yet Roger's present friends kept on coming to supper and staying to watch the tumblers and the wrestlers and the men who sang and spoke poems.

"You should go among these people more," Richard said. "Talk to them. You might make friends of the women."

"Pah."

Throughout the spring, while Roger hunted and hawked and lay with the wives of his friends, and Richard went off talking to the town elders, Maria put Roger's citadel in order. She found carpenters to make furniture for him, she brought in several women to keep the place up, and she got another cook. The hot, dry air of the hill town was invigorating. Roger's servants came to her with their disputes over duties and their charges of theft and backbiting and laziness. It amused her to judge them, and she and Eleanor laughed over some of the cases, when they sat in her room at night sewing.

On a market day, with Stephen and Robert, she went to the square to buy cloth. Most of the vendors brought their trade first to the citadel, and until now she had been too busy to go at her leisure. The market place stood before the town's main gate, in the cathedral square. The merchants had set up their stalls beneath the city wall. A crowd of buyers flooded past their striped and painted awnings. Maria and Eleanor walked along in their midst, staring at the Saracen women in their heavy black veils and the Jewish men whose ringlets hung down over their ears. Maria carried Stephen on her hip. Robert ran on before them and pointed everything out as if he ruled it all.

Maria stopped before a stall that displayed woolen

141

cloth. She stroked her hand over the nearest bolt, admiring the smooth feel of the stuff, as fine as any she had ever woven herself, and the excellent red color. It was hard to make good red dye. The vendor hustled over behind his counter.

"Lady, you give me such honor I cannot think how to repay you, save to sell you some of this splendid cloth, fit for such a fine lady." Bending below the level of the counter, he lifted up three bolts of deep blue and purple wool.

"Oh," Maria said softly. She slid her hand under a fold of the blue cloth. "Eleanor, feel this."

Eleanor fingered the cloth. "I've seen better."

"What a surcoat this would make—see how smoothly it drapes."

"My sweet ladies," the vendor said, "this stuff will make you rivals of those few angels you do not already surpass."

Maria laughed. On her hip, Stephen was reaching down for the cloth. The vendor asked his price. Maria haggled with him a few moments—she had never bought cloth before, either she had woven it herself or the men had stolen it. She had no idea of its worth in money. At last she had him accepting half of what he had originally demanded.

"Eleanor," she said. "Is that a good price?"

"A very good price, lady," the vendor said. "You beggar me. If it were not you, my lady, I would refuse the offer, but I would rather have my cloth keep you warm at that price than become rich dressing sluts."

"Watch your tongue," Eleanor said sharply.

Maria counted out money to him. "Don't heed her, she is very proud. Will you bring this to my lord Roger's tower?"

The vendor bowed over his cloth. "For you, my lady, I would crawl to Jerusalem." He seized her hand and put a fat kiss on her fingers.

Stephen had gotten hold of a coin, and while Maria was taking it out of his mouth and drying it, Eleanor said, "Where is Robert?"

Maria looked quickly around them. The crowd surged

142

past, many-legged, full of donkeys and dogs. She thrust the coin into the vendor's hand. "He must be close by."

They walked across the thrusting, jostling crowd toward the cathedral. The air was gritty with dust. A knight in a red cloak rode past them, a belled hawk on his fist. Children raced around them with their hoops, and other children played between stalls and on the fence around the cathedral yard, but none of them was Robert.

Eleanor called a few times. A boy shouted back, mocking her, and she bit her lips. Maria could see how tired she was, how near tears. Someone touched her arm, and she wheeled, expecting her son.

It was only the cloth vendor. "You gave me too much, lady," he said, reproving, as if she had cheated him. "You gave me tuppence too much." He put the chipped coin into her hand. Before he had stopped bowing he was racing off again into the crowd, back to his stall.

Maria took Eleanor by the hand. "Come along. He must be somewhere. He can find his way back to the tower, if we miss him." She bounced Stephen higher on her hip and led Eleanor with the flow of the crowd toward the other side of the market place.

Abruptly, she saw Richard in the shade of the oak tree between the churchyard and the wall. On his left, a scribe scribbled in a tablet, and on his right, sitting on two long benches, was a little crowd of men. Most of them were old, many were Saracens. In front of them all, Robert squatted in the dust watching.

Eleanor let out a hoarse cry and rushed forward. Maria held her back. "No." She gave Stephen to Eleanor. "Wait here."

Eleanor withdrew into the lee of the wall. Robert with his chin on his fists was staring up at Richard, who pretended not to see him. Maria came up to Robert.

"Take Eleanor home for me," she said, "like a good knight."

He jerked his gaze up to her, ready to protest, and she nodded to him. He bounded up and raced off across the market place. Maria stood a moment where he had been. Richard sat sprawled in his chair with his legs stretched out in front of him crossed at the ankles, ignoring her.

143

Casually she circled around the oak tree and moved up through the shade to his shoulder.

An old man was talking about murders. When she stopped beside her husband's chair, he ran out of words, his mouth dropping open, and his eyes on her. Richard glanced around at her and back at the old man.

"Go on."

The elder stammered: he had forgotten what he had been saying. The other people stirred and leaned their heads together to whisper. Richard turned to the scribe. "Read the last."

The scribe sat up straight. On the crown of his head his dark hair grew in a short thick brush: he was a ruined monk. He read, *"but sometimes, if a man of the town killed a foreigner, he—"*

The old man cleared his throat. "He would be accused by two men of the town and if he was found guilty he paid a fine to the Emir. If two men of Iste couldn't be found to accuse anyone, of course, the murderer would go free. But if the dead one was a Saracen, we had to give up the murderer to the Emir, and if the murderer himself was a Saracen, you see, and the dead one a Christian or a Jew, usually nothing was done."

Richard propped his chin in his hand. "Yes. I can see why that was so, when the Saracens ruled here, but now I rule here. I like the custom without any decoration. If a man is murdered here, my brother will summon such people to his court as he thinks might have knowledge of the crime, and if he finds anyone guilty, that one shall pay a fine to me." He looked at the scribe. "Do you have that?"

The scribe's quill jigged furiously over the sheet of parchment on his desk. He dipped the pen into the inkwell and turned the page and wrote on. At last he bobbed his head and sat up straight.

Maria stood with one hand on the back of Richard's chair and listened to three more such exchanges. She had never heard of anyone doing anything like this before. Her father had paid no heed to the customs of any village, never learned them, and certainly never changed them. She did not wonder that Richard was having what he said written down. No one would bother to remember

144

customs if they were changed at whim. He never even looked at her again; he went on listening to what the old men said, and telling the scribe to leave most of it out— the customs of generations of the same people in the same place. Presently, thoughtful, she went away from the tree and walked home.

Horses and hounds packed the yard inside the citadel. The lion was roaring fitfully in its pit. Three or four young men walked around before the door into the tower, dressed brightly as tumblers. She ducked under the neck of a tall chestnut horse to reach the door. A stocky young man in a red coat caught her by the arm.

"Now, here's the meat. Roger!" Over his shoulder, he called, "I have found fine game right here—" He slid his arm around Maria's waist. She pulled away, and he bent over her. "Oh, she wants to fight." He tried to kiss her.

Maria slapped him. A man nearby gave a roar of laughter. "Pandolfo, use your spurs."

Pandolfo recoiled. On his cheek the mark of her hand showed red as paint, and to make him match, she slapped him as hard as she could on the other cheek.

"Ho." He snatched at her. She dodged toward the door. Another man seized her and thrust her stumbling toward Pandolfo, penning her between them. She put her back to the wall, looking wildly around for something to hit them with.

Roger on a black horse loomed up behind the two men. "Stop. Holy Cross, that is Richard's wife."

Pandolfo had hold of Maria's arm. Twisting, he looked at Roger, and his face blanched. He let go of her as if she were burning hot. Maria went up to the shoulder of Roger's horse.

"Roger," she said. Her lips were stiff. "Are these people your friends?"

Roger made a pleasant face. He dismounted. At his nod the young men went quietly away. "Don't be angry. They thought you were a serving girl, you go about with such a lack of ceremony. I never see you—they have never met you. Do I bore you? Come downstairs tonight, we're going to dance."

"Oh," Maria said. "I don't think you'll want me there —with all those pretty women."

His face brightened with amusement, his blue eyes snapping. "You know you are my only true love." Arm in arm with her, he led her into the tower. "How do you like my town?"

Maria made some uncondemning comment. They climbed the stairs to the hall, where the servants were arranging the tables for supper. Through the windows long sheets of sunlight came, lighting the Saracen carpets. She looked around the room to see that everything was done well.

"Maria," Roger said. He walked two steps into the hall and wheeled to face her. She felt bedraggled beside his easy grace; he might have lived all his life in palaces. "I'm bored to death here. There's nothing to do. Go hunting, chase women, dance—I'm not like Richard, I can't busy myself listening to old men search their years." He threw his hands up over his head. "Richard is turning me into a monk."

Maria laughed at him. "That isn't what I have heard."

"Well," he said, "maybe not entirely. But if he doesn't make a war for me soon, I will run out of women, too, and then I just may start in on his." He came back toward her.

"Oh," she said, "so I am your last choice."

Standing beside her, he touched her cheek with his forefinger. "Richard's jealous of you and me, isn't he?"

"Yes," she said. Softly she pushed away his hand.

"Does he have reason?"

She crowed with laughter. "Roger. No wonder all these women love you." She gave him a warm look over her shoulder and went out again onto the stairs. He followed close after her. On the landing, out of sight of the servants in the hall, she turned to face him.

"Dandle me. I like it."

Roger said, "Give me a kiss for encouragement."

She tilted her face up to him. The door below them slammed. They sprang apart. Robert raced up the stairs and darted between them. Over the boy's black hair she and Roger exchanged a look. Robert leaned on his uncle, and the red knight hoisted him up by the arms.

"Holy Cross, Sir Robert, what does your mother feed you, stones?"

146

Maria started up the stairs. Robert pulled on Roger, trying to take him off somewhere.

"Maria," Roger called, in a light voice. "Promise me you won't tell Richard about that dog that tried to nip you."

She looked down the stairs at him. The memory of Pandolfo unsettled her. "If you wish," she said, grudging.

He lifted his free hand to her and went with Robert into the hall. Maria climbed the stairs. She was relieved that Roger did not like this life. The brush with Pandolfo rankled, and she should not have offered to kiss Roger: that was a sin. Uneasily she set herself to doing something else.

XVI

❧

WILLIAM ARRIVED FROM BIRNIA THE NEXT AFTERNOON. In the crush of people that came out to greet him in the ward, Maria saw Pandolfo again, and he saw her as well. He turned swiftly away to hide in the crowd.

She began thinking of some way to get her revenge on him. Of course telling Richard, the easier way, meant breaking her promise to Roger. William walked through the crowd toward her, and she came up smiling to him and kissed his cheek. He was fat, his deep-jowled face belonged to an older man than he was. She took him into the hall to give him some refreshment.

William settled himself in a low-backed chair before the three big windows. "Where is Richard? Ah. I hear my nephew."

Eleanor came in the door, Stephen howling in her arms. William took the little boy, laughing down at him, and Stephen brightened and stopped crying and pulled on William's nose and ears. Eleanor went off on some errand. Maria sat down in the chair William had left.

"Richard is in the town. You should have seen him in the market place. He'll be home when they ring for Vespers—you know he won't miss supper."

William tossed Stephen into the air. The child shrieked with pleasure. "No," the big knight said. "We all have that in common, my family—big appetites." He looked around the hall, paneled in wood, with its large airy windows. "I'd give him two Birnias for this."

Maria smiled at him. "You must do well enough, William, your belts keep getting longer."

"Big appetites." He set Stephen down on the floor and brought a chair over beside her. He slapped his hands on his vast stomach. "This comes from fighting Theobald. It's all jaw-work. The other little knave looks like you, but this one here is Richard's."

"Robert," she said, surprised.

Robert himself ran in the door, Roger in tow behind him. William boosted himself back onto his feet. He and Roger embraced, William giving off loud wordless roars and clapping his brother on the back.

"William," Roger said. "Now I see why you have not come sooner. Who is the father?" He slapped William's wide belly.

William shouted, elbowed him, and shook his head. "The Saracens will run me thin again. Let me see you. I swore to your mother I would take care of you, let me see if I do my work well." He groped down Roger's lower leg as if he were a horse, looked in his ears, and hugged him again.

"Come sit down," Roger said. "How do you like my palace?"

"Oh, a palace, is it? You are a prince, now. Well enough. I like it well enough. It must be hard to keep it all, though, the town and the valley too."

"Richard does that. And Maria masters my household, leaving me to more important things."

A serving man had come in with a ewer of wine. Maria took Robert to help her fill cups for the two men. Robert ran across the hall to give William his wine. He leaned on the big man's shoulder, while the brothers talked of Theobald, their problems with horses, and the things happening in Santerois. Maria went to the window over the street and looked out.

"How is Richard?" William said. "Maria, come back, let me see you."

She stood beside him and put her hand on his shoulder. Roger said, "Richard's mad as ever. We should show him in a cage."

"What is it now?"

"Oh, you know. If he turns left, and the whole of Christendom turns right, everyone's wrong but Richard."

Maria and William laughed. The fat man laid his hand on hers, patting her like a favorite dog. Maria sank down beside him. The brothers talked about the Saracens. If she told William about Pandolfo, he would help her get her vengeance. She sat watching them talk together, her ears cocked toward the windows, waiting for the Vespers bell that would bring Richard home.

SHE HAD NO CHANCE to talk to William alone for the rest of the day. The three brothers ate supper in her chamber, with Eleanor and Maria serving them, so that they could talk over Richard's plans for attacking the Saracens in the mountains. Before they had half-finished they were deep in an argument, Roger and Richard nose to nose, and William sitting with his eyes moving from one to the other.

"The easiest way to take Mana'a is to take the mountains first," Richard said. He thrust his plate aside. "At the end, the city will fall into our hands. Now, look——"

"That's like chopping down the tree to get the apple," Roger said. "No one will care if we take a mountain village—all the glory's at Mana'a."

William pulled Richard's half-eaten dinner toward him. "You think of nothing else."

Roger was staring across the table at Richard. Maria went around behind him to take his wine cup away. Roger said, "The Emir of Mana'a alone has thousands of soldiers. We have a few hundred knights. Who will not fight unless you give them plunder."

"You're using my arguments."

149

"You can't seriously hope that we can take the mountains and Mana'a and actually rule them?"

"Why not?"

Maria crossed the room to the table where the ewers stood and filled Roger's cup with the sweet red wine of Iste. When she took it back to him, the three men had pushed their dishes to the end of the table so they could draw with their fingers on the tabletop. She piled the dishes up on a tray and brought a loaf and a cheese and set them down at Richard's elbow. With Eleanor and the bolt of blue cloth, she went into the back of the room, behind the bed, and draped the wool around her in different ways.

"Robert's got a headstrong way about him since we've been in Iste," Eleanor said, and sighed. "He never does what I say any more. You spoil him."

William said, "You're talking about every fighting man who'll follow us up into those mountains. As soon as we do, these people here will sink their teeth in our backs."

Maria held the cloth against her side. She liked the soft folds of the wool. "Cut it off here, Eleanor." Richard said something about taking hostages. She raised her head, wondering whom he meant, and a remark of Roger's told her they were talking of his friends here, the Lombard barons.

That meant Pandolfo. Eleanor said, "I wish you would—" and Maria jabbed her with her elbow to quiet her.

"What will we do with a dozen hostages?" William said. "Richard, you are asking for trouble."

"Take them back to Birnia with you and teach them to wait on us," Roger said. "They've all got perfect manners, it won't take much."

Richard said, "He's not going back to Birnia. I like this cheese."

Roger got up. "We can't very well leave Birnia open to Theobald. Who's commanding there? Ponce?"

"No," Richard said. "I just told you, I want him at the East Tower to keep our supplies moving. Maria is going to hold Birnia."

Maria stiffened. The cloth slid to a soft heap at her

feet. Stooping, she helped Eleanor fold it up again. Eleanor whispered, "What was that?"

Maria said, "This is the first time I have heard of it." She loaded the heavy cloth onto Eleanor's arms and went back into the room, to stand beside William, across the table from Richard.

"Who else is there?" Richard said. "I need both of you."

William folded his arms on the table, glanced up at Maria, and reached over to pat her heavily on the arm. Roger was standing across the room, near the window, filling his cup again. He said, over his shoulder, "That is not a woman's duty." He strode back toward the table.

Richard stuck his knife in the cheese. "She will do it better than you could. Anyway, Fitz-Michael and the young Duke are raising an army. Theobald will have to deal with them, he'll leave us alone. I'll give her some men—the old ones will follow her as well as me, for her father's sake."

"What about Welf?" Roger asked. "Let him command Birnia."

"No. I want him where I can watch him, he is ambitious. Let her do it." He lifted his eyes to her. "She's not as stupid as she looks."

Roger came up beside her. "She is a woman. She should not have to take up arms."

Richard grunted. "I told you, I don't think she'll have to do any fighting. She's one of us, she won't turn on us, she won't sell us if Theobald offers her a bribe. Let it be. Ponce will get here tomorrow. Welf and the others will be in tomorrow or the next day. We will have the oath-taking on the Sabbath. Your priest knows what to say. I have a piece of holy bone, it should keep your friends from spitting out the oath."

Roger gave him a long stare. He turned to Maria. "My sister," he said, "if you ever need me, send for me." Without a word to either of his brothers, he walked out of the room.

Maria started to clear off the table; Eleanor came to help her. William said good night to them and left. A scullion came in and took the tray away, and Eleanor followed him. The door closed.

"I hate Birnia," she said.

"There is no one else who can do it."

"But it's so far away. I thought we could stay in Iste—that way when you come back here we could see you."

"I'll come down there when I can." He was still sitting in his chair. He tilted it back on its hindlegs to reach her and drew her over beside him. "You won't have any trouble with Theobald. He's all jaw."

"You could have asked me." She stroked her fingers through his hair. If she could get Pandolfo somehow to Birnia, she could make his life miserable. Richard's hair was soft as Stephen's. She curled her fingers through it, plotting against Pandolfo.

Richard said, "What are you thinking about, witch?"

She stepped back, rattled, and made her face innocent. "Nothing."

That was a mistake. He dropped his chair on all fours, took hold of her wrist, and made her kneel beside him, her arm doubled by his grip. "Tell me," he said, in a pleasant voice.

"I can't," she said. "I promised not to."

His fingers tightened painfully around her wrist. "Whom did you promise?"

"Richard, let me go."

He twisted her arm, hard, and she whined. She said, "Roger."

His head bobbed up. Everything he thought showed in his face. She said, "No, it is not that." He fastened his eyes on her, his jaw rigid.

"You and Roger."

"It is not that."

"What is it?"

"I promised Roger not to tell you."

Fast in his grip, her forearm had gone numb to the elbow. Her shoulder ached with a steady throb. He said, "Swear to me that it is not—that you have not—" He cocked up his free hand to strike her. She could not move against his hold. She looked him in the eyes, her heart galloping.

He lowered his hand, and opened his fingers, letting go of her wrist. He said, "Swear to me that you have kept faith with me."

"I swear," she said, and crossed herself. Her other arm was numbed its whole length. She could not move her fingers. Slowly the flesh prickled alive again. His face eased. She saw that he believed her. She said, "If you don't trust me, why give me Birnia? Theobald might turn me fickle."

"I haven't trusted you since the day you murdered Walter Bris."

Maria started violently. His face was brimming with malice. She stood up, turning away from him. She had long forgotten Walter Bris.

He grabbed hold of her skirt. "Wait. Come here, I'm sorry I said that." He made her stand before him. "I haven't forgotten what we were talking about, either. What did you promise Roger?"

"I said I wouldn't tell you about something that happened to me."

"Between you and Roger?"

"No. Roger had nothing to do with it."

"Good." He stood up, her face between his hands, and kissed her. "Then don't think about it any more. I'll beat you the next time I see you with Roger."

Maria put both hands on his chest and pushed him away, angry. "You told me that I should make friends of Roger's friends—now you won't let me go down to watch the dancing." She went into the middle of the room, her back to him. She hated Birnia.

"Oh," he said. "You'll do with Theobald."

ON THE NEXT SUNDAY, with all the people of Roger's court, and all the chief men of Richard's demesne, they went to Mass. After they had received God, everyone gathered on the porch of the cathedral. There, one at a time, Roger and William, Ponce Rachet and Welf Blackjacket and the others of Richard's men knelt in front of him and swore themselves into his service. In return for their homage, Richard swore to protect them and to listen to their advice.

Afterward, Roger's friends did homage as well, some of them smiling, others less pleased. In the sack of Iste, Richard had found a crystal with a bit of bone in it, which he claimed was a fingerbone of Saint John, and he

153

made them take the oath on that. He had not required the oath on the relic of his own barons, and many of Roger's friends swore it in angry voices.

Finally Richard had them accept Robert as his heir. Standing beside Maria in his new blue coat, the little boy shone like a star.

They followed the oath-taking with a feast that began at dinner. When the sun went down they were still eating. The cook was producing a new dish every few moments. Ponce had brought a wagonload of wine from the low valleys, and everyone was getting visibly drunk, even Richard. Maria sat beside him, passing tidbits from her plate to Eleanor, behind her holding Stephen on her lap. The uproar of the people at the feast drowned the two lutes and the little trumpet playing in the alcove to her left.

She thought of Pandolfo, and looked curiously around for him. In the excitement of the oath-taking, she had not thought for some time of her revenge. He was not in the hall, and when she thought back she was sure he had not sworn an oath to Richard. Her curiosity pricked her, Robert and Roger were on her left, bent together over a handful of filberts scattered on the tabletop before them.

Roger said to Robert, "Now, watch." He threw one nut straight up in the air. With the same hand he scooped up two or three of the filberts on the table, one at a time, and caught the falling nut before it hit.

"Let me try," Robert said.

Roger smiled at her across Robert's bent head. She said, "Where is your friend Pandolfo, Roger?"

Robert tossed the nut into the air, grabbed one from the table, and knocked over his cup lunging after the first as it fell. A servant came over to clean up after him. Roger's face was suddenly bland. He said, "Oh—Pandolfo? I don't know—ask Richard."

Maria sat back, her eyes on Richard. He was drinking, the carved wooden cup raised into the sunlight. She knew he had overheard them. She brushed a crumb from his sleeve and looked back at Roger.

"You told him."

Roger shrugged one shoulder, gathering the hazelnuts from Robert. He dropped the nuts with a rattle onto the

154

tabletop, threw one high over his head, and picked up three more. Turning his palm up, he let the falling nut plop into his hand. When he did it, it seemed nothing. "I never promised not to tell him."

Maria sat back. The tumblers and dancers had gathered in the doorway. She nodded to the servant in charge of the hall, who waved out his men to roll up the carpets and sweep the floors.

The people along the tables let out a cheer. In a burst of music, the tumblers ran out to the middle of the floor and began their nimble leaps and somersaults. Richard's left hand rested on the table, heavy with rings. Maria wondered what he had done to Pandolfo. She twisted the Saracen ring on his little finger.

"I like this. Will you give it to me?"

Impassive, he studied her face a moment, pulled the ring off, and taking hold of her left hand put it on her forefinger. The tumblers were making a pyramid. He turned back to watch, but he kept hold of her hand. Maria laid her fingers over his, pleased.

PART II

ARROWS
OF GOD

XVII

❧

WILLIAM'S LONG RESIDENCE HAD IMPROVED THE TOWER of Birnia very little. His bachelor passions were hawking and dogs, and the whole Tower reeked of beasts. Maria and Eleanor lived two days in the inn in the town while the Tower was cleaned. When that was done, and all the linen washed and dried in the sun, they moved into the top floor.

Richard had sent twenty knights with her to garrison Birnia. All but one were old, and most were sick or halt. The young man was a green knight named Ralf who had lost his place in the army at dice. The others had served her father before she was even born. The oldest, Jean, whose fading hair hung down to his shoulders in the old style, she made the commander of the rest.

Her knights went out on regular patrols, kept watchmen at the crossroads and the bridges, and hunted down an occasional robber. The hot, stormy summer made a good crop. The serfs worked steadily over their fields. Pilgrims came along the road to the Shrine of the Virgin, and in the middle of the summer, Maria herself went there to receive the formal homage of the monks and to attend to her chapel. Now five monks served the shrine, and they had added a wing to the guesthouse. Maria lingered there until the end of the summer.

In the last of August, the young knight Ralf appeared with a message from Jean. Robert ran up to Maria where she sat under the beech trees near the chapel and hauled her out by the hand toward the road. The young knight dismounted and bowed, like a priest.

"My lady, Jean has ordered me to report that Count Theobald, with a mighty band of men, is coming along the road. He has sent to ask a hearing of you, that he might come across our border."

Maria stood in the sunlight, her eyes squinted. Ralf's manner set her teeth on edge. *"What is a mighty band of men?"*

"Forty men, my lady."

"I have never heard forty men reckoned such an enormous number."

Ralf gave her a patient smile. "May I remind my lady that we number eighteen—"

"Twenty."

"Eighteen. Two of the hacks in Birnia are ailing, they cannot ride. In view of our circumstances, forty men is a mighty band."

"Leave, if you are frightened."

"My lady, I did not intend to imply—"

"Then stop."

He clamped his mouth shut. Maria went down the road a little way. Stephen was scrambling up the hill, Eleanor in pursuit. Maria thought of Theobald and his forty men.

"Well," she said, "I suppose I will have to do something."

"My lady." Ralf came around in front of her again. "Jean suggests, and I agree, that we should make him leave his escort and come to the Tower itself if he wishes a hearing with you. He cannot know how weak we are, he will think himself in danger, that will put him at a disadvantage."

"You want him to see for himself that he's in no danger at all?"

"He could hardly lay siege to the Tower of Birnia with forty men, my lady."

He sounded confident, or perhaps bored. Suddenly she guessed that he was trying to raise his own green courage, not irritate her. Cooler, she thought Jean's plan over again.

"No," she said. "He'll expect something like that. Is he coming by the main road?" If God helped her, it would not matter if Theobald led a thousand men. The thing to do was to stop Theobald at the border and find out what he wanted, before he got any hint of her real strength.

160

"Yes, my lady. He left Occel yesterday by the King's Road."

Maria called to Robert. The King's Road crossed into Birnia more than ten leagues from the Tower, but only half a day from the shrine: a sign of grace. Eleanor hurried toward her with Stephen.

"I will meet Theobald at the Rood Oak," she said to Ralf. "There are six knights here with me, I will take them to escort me."

Ralf's face fell. "But—my lady—this is—"

"Perhaps you want to come with me?"

She meant it for a threat, but he drew himself up as tall as he could and said, "I shall. You will need a real knight with you."

Maria held her mouth straight against a smile. Before she could answer, Robert rushed up to her. Eleanor was close behind him, trying to keep hold of Stephen. Maria brushed Robert's hair back off his forehead.

"Count Theobald is coming and I have to go talk to him. You are going to have to go back to the Tower by yourself. Will you do it?"

"Mama! I want to go with you to meet Theobald."

"Do as I ask. You will have to save me if I do anything foolish. Find Waleran and take him with you."

Robert ran off down the hill toward the village, where Maria's six aged knights spent the days drinking and trying to seduce the girls. Ralf planted himself in front of Maria, his feet widespread.

"I must insist again that this is the course of folly. You should harken to Jean—he was left to command here. He knows best."

"Yes," Maria said. "I know." She started down after Robert, to make things ready for the journey.

AT NOON, they stopped beside the road in a field, to walk, eat dinner, and water the horses. Eleanor came up to Maria and asked, "Why did you send Robert home but not us?"

"Oh," Maria said. "Do you think Theobald will take us hostage, when he sees we are defenseless?"

Eleanor's face sharpened to a point. "Such a thought

161

came to me. Obviously to you as well. Theobald must know that Richard is far away."

Maria took her coif down from her hair. She had borrowed the fashion from the women in Birnia, but she wound the extra cloth around her head, instead of starching it into stiff little wings. Carefully she stuck the hairpins into her belt. She said, "Theobald knows what Richard would do to him if he hurt me." If she seemed afraid of him, Theobald would certainly take advantage of her. Perhaps if she acted unafraid, he would think her strong. Shaking out the coif, she hung it on a bush and smoothed back her hair.

Eleanor went off calling for Stephen. Maria took down her braids from the crown of her head. Eleanor in her red shawl stopped in the high yellowing grass to pick up the little boy. Beyond her, Ralf was leading the carthorses up from the river, his hands on their bridles. The other knights lounged along the side of the road.

Probably Ralf was right, and she should have listened to Jean. Maria did not believe it. Anything she did was better than waiting for Theobald to act at his will. She folded the white linen in half and wrapped it around her hair. She tucked the loose ends of the coif in at the back and went up to the road, to help Eleanor get into the cart.

THEY REACHED the meadows of the Rood Oak in the late afternoon. Early pilgrims had built a well there, beside the road. Travelers often spent the night in the open grass around the big stone cross. Maria had heard that the name remembered an old tree of whose branches the first pilgrims had made crosses to take to the shrine, but now there was no oak tree within leagues of the place.

While her escort and the two servants made a camp in the meadow, she took Stephen for a walk. He darted ahead of her into the fading light of the day, his fat legs milling, and his napkin down around his knees. Between spurts of chatter, he dug up stones and chased a green snake into a hummock of grass. When he tired, she carried him, walking slowly back toward the campfire, and thought over everything she had ever heard about Theobald.

162

In the twilight, with the fireflies rising and flickering in the meadow around their camp, the knights sat slouched before the flames. Eleanor and the other girl hurried around making supper. The wide meadows around them made them seem tiny and exposed, and Maria cast about for some way to protect them.

"Ralf," she called, and the young knight strode toward her. She gestured into the darkness nearby them, where some recent travelers had left a dead firebed and a frame for a cooking pot. "Perhaps we could make that seem to be part of our camp."

"I beg my lady's pardon," he said blankly.

"As if—" she lifted her hand toward the road, "—some fifteen or twenty men have just gone off. So that we will not seem so small a band."

He swallowed; he gave the meadows a distracted glance. "My lady, I don't really think—"

"I don't care what you think," Maria told him, between her teeth. She turned her shoulder to him and carried Stephen over to the fire.

Ralf and three other knights built a fire in the meadow, put some gear about, and moved the tethered horses over between the two camps. Maria sat by the fire and toasted bread on a stick. An old knight sank down beside her. He took Stephen into his lap and the little boy fell asleep. The knight rubbed his bald, freckled head.

"This tadpole Ralf is troubling you, isn't he?" the knight said abruptly.

"What?"

"Well. The others of us will know what to do, when the thing comes to it."

In the meadow, the bonfire blaze crackled and snapped embers up into the night sky. Ralf and the other knights were trudging back to their supper. Maria clasped her arms around her knees. What the old knight said only made her more uneasy. If Theobald took her prisoner here, she would kill herself. She would kill Theobald, too, somehow; seduce him and kill him.

"You know," the knight said, "in his great days, girl, your father was a mighty man. Richard d'Alene would not have done that to him, not in Strongarm's prime age."

"Richard did nothing to him," Maria said sharply.

163

The old knight patted her knee. Rising, he went to join his friends.

When the campfires had sunk down to heaps of coals, Theobald and his men appeared on the road. In the darkness the other army seemed to cover the meadows like a flood. Maria reminded herself that in her own demesne, new come from worship at her own shrine, she was right and Theobald was wrong. She called up Ralf again.

"Go over to Count Theobald," she said, "and tell him I am here and will see him now."

Ralf squared off his shoulders. "My lady, I must unfortunately once again suggest—"

"No," Maria said. She stared at him. After a moment, in a show of courtesy, he looked away. "Go get him," she said. "Now."

Ralf bowed elaborately to her and went off to do her orders. Maria sat down again. When Eleanor spoke, behind her, she jumped.

"I certainly hope God is remembering us," Eleanor said. She reached up to undo Maria's coif, and Maria pushed her aside.

"No. Count Theobald is coming, do I meet him half-dressed?"

"Tonight?" Eleanor said. "Here? I would liefer have the Grand Mahound into a convent."

"God will help me."

Eleanor said, "You ask too much of God," and got up and went away.

Maria did not call after her. She asked the other maid to bring her cloak and sat listening to the wind comb through the dry meadow grass. The knight Ralf returned and stood to one side, on her left like an honor guard, his hands folded on the buckle of his sword belt. Maria wished she had some work, to keep busy, but the firelight was too dim for sewing.

A slender man, late in middle age, came up into the light of her fire. "My lady Maria, he said. "I cannot tell you how delighted I am at this meeting." A servant came after him, carrying a little stool, and Theobald waved to him. The servant put the stool down behind him.

"Sit, my lord," Maria said. He was a small man, neatly turned out down to his hair and shoes, his smile fixed as a star. "We were at the Cave of Our Lady, when your message came, or I would have invited you to Birnia."

She met his gaze. Richard had said that Theobald outtalked him, and he did seem serpent-like, slender and quick as the green snake Stephen had chased. He had wanted to marry his daughter to Richard and set her and Ceci aside. She smiled at him, hating him, and he bowed again, the firelight catching on all the little ornaments of his coat.

"I am here, actually, for the sake of your shrine," Theobald said. "Since God took my Countess from me—" he crossed himself—"I have come now and then to that pleasant place to refresh my soul." His meaningless smile danced on his face. His quick eyes took in every detail of her camp. "You travel very lightly, my dear, if I may give tongue to my opinions."

"Our roads are safe," she said. "We are the only robbers in Birnia."

Theobald's smile stuck an instant. Maria gestured to Ralf, where he stood in the background, and said, "Will you serve us some wine? It's cold, in this wind."

Theobald nodded. "A crisp wind, this one, very unusual for the season."

"You are going to the shrine, then," Maria said.

"Yes. Of course, I may not require so great an escort as I have, since you say your roads are safe."

Maria tucked her hands in her lap. "Take them, if you wish—it is a Godly place, all men should see it." She looked guilelessly at him. "My lord and I are happy in the service of God, he in his way, and I in mine."

A crease appeared across Theobald's forehead. His fingers played with the gold brooch at the shoulder of his cloak. Ralf brought him a cup, which he took.

"Do you require a hostage of me, perhaps?"

Maria sipped her wine, cool from the night wind. Ralf had mixed it liberally with water; at least he remembered her tastes. She was tempted to accept Theobald's hostage but when she thought it through, she realized he would spy on her. She put the cup down.

"I trust you, my lord. I ask only that you keep to the road and treat my people kindly."

Theobald smiled at her. "You are as gracious as your

lord. How does his fighting go? We have heard, of course, of the oaths taken in Iste. Fitz-Michael is angry over it, you know—some of the men who swore forced oaths to your lord are barons of the Duke."

Maria shrugged her shoulders. "I will tell him you mentioned it." She remembered the little boy Richard had stolen away from Theobald.

"He is a cunning man, your husband." Theobald drank his wine. Ralf took his cup away. "But I think he overreaches himself, attacking the Saracens in the mountains. He should be content with Iste."

Maria drank another sip of her wine. "I know nothing of it, my lord, except it is our Christian duty to fight the Saracens."

"Yes. Ah, yes. Crusades are the pilgrimages of the young. If I myself were young—" He puffed a little, spoke of the time when to ride from Occel to the Cave of the Virgin was a dangerous penance. His fingers moved without pausing, pleating his sleeve, rubbing over the chased surface of the cup. He made a joke, and she caught herself laughing. His face smoothed out. Maria smiled at him, trying to charm him.

"Your lord's brother, Roger," Theobald said sleekly. "The finest knight in the south, some men say—men who should know. I have never had the honor to encounter him, either at parley or in the field."

"Roger is a hero," Maria said, with pride. "He is an arrow of God."

"And the older brother, William—quite another sort, we had some dealings, he and I—he too has taken the Cross?"

"Ye—"

Maria bit off the word. Ruffled, she saw she had told him what he wanted to know, and she said, "William told me somewhat of his talks with you."

Theobald smiled at her. He rubbed his upper lip with his forefinger. In the cart, Stephen woke and called out, and Eleanor quieted him. Maria looked Theobald in the face.

"I wonder you should be going off to the shrine, though, so near to the fall quarterday."

166

Theobald shifted on his stool, still favoring her with his sleek smile. "Earlier in the summer I was busy elsewhere. Had I the leisure I should have come at once, child."

"I wish you could stay on, then," she said, "but you will want to be back in your own demesne before the quarterday, won't you?"

Theobald's smile broadened. "I understand you." He got to his feet. "You have been most courteous to me, I shall not forget your favor."

He bowed to her; she gave him her hand, and he kissed it. He said, "Let me hope, child, that while you are mistress of Birnia, you will think of me as a dependable friend."

"I shall, my lord, with many thanks."

He made another bow to her, and with his servant carrying his stool started away. He swung wide off his track to look over the other campsite and its dying fire. Maria sat down again, angry. She felt like a fool for letting him know where all three brothers were.

"Ralf," she said. "We shall go home tomorrow."

"Yes, my lady."

"Send a message to Jean, tell him that we are coming. Put a watch on Theobald's camp."

"Yes, my lady."

Maria walked up and down between the cart and the fire. She wondered how much Theobald could know of the garrison in Birnia—if her pretense of strength might not trick her more than him. He took her lightly; she had marked it in his tone of voice. Creeping into the back of the cart, she lay down next to Eleanor, pulled the blankets over her, and tried to settle into sleep.

FROM THE ROOD OAK, she traveled south toward the Tower of Birnia, while Theobald and his forty men took the high road toward the shrine. Of the knights in her escort, Maria sent all but Ralf to keep on Theobald's heels and watch him. Ralf she took with her.

For most of the day, the cart crossed the fens, yellow and stinking in the late summer heat, the stretches of tall, stalky grass broken here and there by a scummed pool

167

ringed in cattails. Twice they had to stop, unload the cart, and use Maria's mare and Ralf's horse to help drag the wheels up out of the mire. Eleanor prayed loudly all day long. Stephen, tired of the cart and tired of traveling, cried or nagged or fretted. No one else spoke. They saw no sign of other people through the whole day.

Maria finally took Stephen in front of her on her horse to keep him quiet. Not a breath of the wind moved the air. The fen stretched flat and unchanging around them, as if they made no progress at all. The sun climbed to the zenith of the sky and dropped down into the west. At last they reached the river, winding thick with weed, and forded it.

Here the fields stood shoulder-high in ripening grain and beans. Marigold studded them to keep away bugs. In the last of the twilight, the serfs were walking home from their fields. Maria and her people camped beside the road at the crossroads.

The following noon, they reached the town of Birnia and drove past it to the Tower. Jean was on the wall, his face running with sweat in the afternoon heat, and when they rolled into the ward, Robert raced down the outer stair of the Tower to meet them.

"Mama," he said, before she could speak. "I am in command here, now, you must obey me in all things."

"Oh," Maria said. "Another one of you." She slid down from her mare; a groom led it away.

"And you must tell Eleanor," Robert said. "And make her obey me."

Maria patted his cheek. In the cart, Eleanor was giving everyone orders. Stephen had gotten away from her and was lowering himself carefully down the high cart wheel to the ground. His long arms swinging at his sides, Jean came across the ward.

"Is there any word from Richard?" she asked him.

"Nothing, my lady. Will you come in—the sun is so bright out here."

Maria followed him toward the stair. Eleanor was directing the serving girls here and there with their baggage.

"I sent out all the other men but one to ride the road while Theobald is here," Jean said. "I thought it best to

168

let him see as many armed men as possible, so that he may think we are strong."

Stephen on his round legs raced across the ward toward her. His aim was off, and he ran headlong into Robert instead. His brother thrust him aside so hard the little boy sat down with a thump. Wheeling back to Maria, Robert grabbed hold of her arm.

"Mama, you must—"

Stephen let out a howl. Maria bent to pick him up. To Robert, she said, "I will not obey you unless you are worthy. See how you made your brother cry." She kissed Stephen's grimy face. With Jean just behind her, she went up the stair to the doorway into the hall.

"Mama!" Robert shrieked, but she ignored him.

In the hall the air was cool. A serving girl was sweeping the ashes back into the hearth. Maria sent her for water and linen, so that she could wash her face. Jean came up before her, his expression bland. She sank down into a chair.

"You think I was rash to meet him there," she said.

"No, so long as you are here again," he said, in a mild voice. "What passed between you?"

The maid came back with a basin of water, and Maria splashed her face and dried it. Robert raced in to hold the linen for her.

"Mama, I am your knight now."

"Yes," she said, and patted his head. "Sit, Jean. Robert—"

The boy had already gone down the hall for a stool. When Jean was sitting, Robert leaned on his shoulder, and the old knight put his arm around the boy and smiled at him.

Maria repeated her interview with Theobald to Jean. "So he knows that Richard and his brothers are all in the mountains, far from here. I was stupid."

Jean grunted. "Yet he must be unsure of us. He would not have passed the chance to take you prisoner unless he thought we could do him some damage." He scratched his jaw, eying her. "That was clever, that with the campfire. That may serve, against a cautious man like this Count."

"We must have spies in his county, to tell us if he calls up his army."

Jean nodded at her. "I have arranged that, my girl, you do not have to tell me my work. But if he decides to attack us, there is nothing we can do."

"Something will happen."

Jean regarded her a moment. Deep pleasant lines marked the corners of his mouth; his eyes were clear pale blue. "Something never happens."

Maria gestured irritably at him to go. "I will talk to you later. Robert, go—"

"You can't give me orders. I am the commander here. Jean, tell her."

A hot answer sizzled in her throat, but he stood so straight, as if he were trying to be taller, that she had to smile. "Well, then," she said, "if it please you, would you ask Eleanor to see to our dinner? Thank you."

Robert made a salute to her and ran off. She sat alone in the hall, her mind on Theobald, his clothes and his restless hands. Two pages came in, boys of Robert's size, carrying a sling full of firewood: hostages from Iste. There were twelve hostages, ranging from a boy no older than Stephen to a young man. Richard had given her everything in Birnia except what she needed. She knew that was unjust. She got up and went to her room to change her travel-stained clothes.

XVIII

THEOBALD LINGERED AT THE SHRINE, BRIBING ALL THE monks. Maria began to worry that to challenge her he would stay past the quarterday, but at last he went back to his city of Occel. The quarterday passed. For many days thereafter she worked constantly, getting the goods stored away in the cramped spaces of the Tower. One morning, while she was overseeing the kitchen knaves stack up kegs of salted meat, a page ran into the storeroom to tell her a messenger had come.

Maria sent the knaves away to their dinner and the page for a cup of wine, and she went out to the ward. The messenger stood beside his steaming horse in the shade of the wall, just below the gate. His grimy face belonged to one of Ponce Rachet's men.

"Joscelyn," she said. "What news from the East Tower?" The page dashed up to her with the cup of wine, and she gave it to the messenger.

He did not drink. He said, "Lady, the news is bad. My lord Richard has been captured by the Saracens in the mountains."

"Captured."

The page was standing a little way off, watching her. Heavily she gestured to him to go. She lifted her face toward the messenger's.

"Where? What happened? Is he alive?"

"I don't know, lady."

"Drink," she said.

The messenger lifted the cup to salute her and gulped down the wine. She clasped her hands together. She struggled to make herself think calmly.

"Have they asked for ransom?"

The messenger held out the cup to her. Around his mouth the dirt was washed away, leaving a circle of clean skin.

"Lady, I know nothing of it. If I knew anything—" he spread his big hands. "He was taken alive. That's all we know. Ponce Rachet says if you are attacked you shall come to the East Tower. Don't try to stand here."

Maria licked her lips. Obviously he believed, and Ponce Rachet believed, that Richard was dead. When Theobald heard of it he would certainly attack her. She said, "Go get something to eat, in the kitchen. Please, for my favor, say nothing of this to anybody."

"I wish I had not had to say it to you." He led his horse away. The oldest of her hostages from Iste was loitering near the stable door. He came up to take the knight's mount. Maria went up to the hall.

Robert had gone off somewhere with Jean. By the

171

hearth, a serving girl was teaching a page to lay out the fire. Maria sat down at her spinning wheel, but she could not spin. Her hands shook like an old woman's. While she sat trying to calm herself down, Eleanor walked in.

"The purple yarn is dry," she called, "and I think there is enough of it to do the border of the new tapestry." She came up beside Maria, ready to talk of the design. Maria made herself speak normally and listen to what Eleanor said.

Jean came into the hall, Robert on his heel with a string of questions about horses. The old knight answered him absently. Coming up behind Eleanor, he said, "The messenger says he has already spoken to you."

Maria nodded. "Yes, there was—there has been a battle." She got up, searching for a good lie. "They have lost ground—they were beaten back."

The gray knight squinted. "A battle. Where?"

"Mama," Robert said, before she had to answer. "Is Papa well?"

"Yes," she said. "Papa is safe."

Robert leaned on her knees. "Is Uncle Roger safe?"

"Yes," Maria said. Jean was watching her steadily. She sent Eleanor away with a word. She held her voice even. "Jean, will you talk to the messenger tomorrow, before he goes back—Ponce Rachet should know we caught that thief." They had run down a robber on the road to the East Tower.

"And Uncle William," Robert asked. "Is he well?"

"Yes."

"Good. I like Uncle William but I like Uncle Roger best."

Jean fingered his stubbled chin. "Robo," he said. "Go bring me something wet. And your lady mother, too."

Robert ran off down the room. Jean dropped his voice. "What is this, about a battle? What is wrong?"

Maria stood up. "The Saracens have taken Richard prisoner."

Jean's face seemed to close up. At the other end of the room, Robert lifted the ewer, intent on what he was doing. The old knight took hold of Maria's hand.

"I'm sorry. Have they asked any ransom?"

Maria shook her head. Robert brought a cup carefully across the room to Jean. He had filled it overfull; the wine trembled on the brim. Jean backed away from it, letting go of Maria's hand. "No. Serve your lady mother first, who loved you first."

Maria took the cup. She had to force herself to drink the swallow of wine. Robert went back for the other cup.

"If Theobald attacks us," Jean said, "we cannot fight him. If he strikes we must retreat, he would take Birnia at once."

The wine was whole. She drank another long taste of it. "I will not lose Birnia."

Jean's pale eyes were steady. "It's all to no use anyway if he's dead."

Maria lifted the cup and sipped the strong red wine.

JEAN TOOK all the knights to the border, to watch for Theobald. Maria put her pages out to stand guard on the walls. They had less work to do, anyway, since the knights were gone. Robert made them all into an army and tirelessly ordered them around. Maria could not sleep. She took to drinking down a full cup of wine before she went to bed. When Eleanor saw it she gave her a look acid with disapproval.

"I need something," Maria said sharply. "If I must go to bed alone."

"You have ever been so temperate." Eleanor bent over the looking glass, plucking the stray dark hair on her upper lip. "Yet you are so shrewish now, I cannot help but be disappointed in you."

"God's blood."

"You ought not to take oaths before children."

Maria prayed for Richard. She had heard all her life what Saracens did to their prisoners. Thinking about him made her want to cry. For some diversion, she went down into the town. Before she had seen Iste, she had not understood towns, but now she made use of the market place and the craftsmen's shops. The people there knew her, pointing her out as if she were a talking dog. She was gay as a new bride, until Eleanor rushed up to her, her face glowing from the sprint down the street, and said, "The priest just told me that talk has it Richard is dead."

Maria's stomach shrank to a knot. "Where? Who told you that?"

"The priest, I said. Father Gibertetto. He says everyone is talking about it, all over town."

"Ah." Maria hitched up her basket on her arm and called to Stephen, who was watching the drunken men stagger out of the wineshop. "Let's go find out what they actually know."

The old priest begged her forgiveness. "I never meant you to hear it," he said, with an evil look at Eleanor. "I would speak nothing to your hurt, my dear lady." His watering eyes probed at her. "We shall say Masses for his soul."

"Don't," Maria said, "he is not dead yet." She went out onto the porch of the church, where she had left Stephen. Taking him up in her arms, she went across the market place and down the street toward the inn, where she had left her horse. Eleanor walked beside her.

"Maria—"

"Don't talk."

They went into the innyard. When he saw them, the ostler climbed down off the fence and went to get their horses. His widowed daughter came out of the door of the inn.

"Good morning," she said. "Come inside and have a mug of cider."

Maria shook her head. "I will, the next time I am here."

Large and soft-fleshed as a sweet cake, the ostler's daughter crossed the yard to her side. "Oh," she said, "they are talking it all over town, I suppose, about Dragon dying. Come inside, it's cool out here."

"Don't go in there," Eleanor whispered. "She is the worst gossip in the town."

Maria stepped away from her, rubbed by her tone of voice. "Go back, if you will—take Stephen, see that he takes a nap." She walked across the yard toward the inn.

The ostler's daughter caught up with her at the door.

174

She said, "This girl was not with you, when you were in Birnia the other time."

"She is my husband's cousin."

They crossed the inn's plank-walled common room and went down into the kitchen. It was above ground, with windows, so that the sunlight poured in and turned the steams and smoke in the air yellow as butter. A knave was kneading bread dough at the table. The room smelled of yeast. The ostler's daughter took Maria into the corner near the ovens and brought her a cup of warm cider and a dish of clotted cream.

"If you tell me it is not true," the ostler's daughter said, "I will believe you. These people put me by, they love rumor."

Maria ate a spoonful of the cream. The fat woman picked up a basket from the floor and took out a great piece of needlework.

"I won't lie to you," Maria said. "It may be true, but I am—I—we have heard nothing for certain, either way. It is just a rumor to me, too."

The ostler's daughter crossed herself. "God have mercy on you. I went for three days not knowing if my husband was dead or alive." Her fingers stitched the long green stem of a flower. "But if you know so little, how have these tongues come to busy themselves with it? Have you thought of that?"

Maria frowned at her. "What do you mean?"

"I heard this tale of Dragon dying from Ramkin, the charcoal burner. How would Ramkin know such a thing —a man who lives all but two days of the month in the forest? *Fen people keep secrets*. He heard it here, in Birnia town, from someone who wishes you ill."

Maria put down the empty bowl, her eyes intent on the woman's face. "Who?"

The woman smiled placidly down at her needlework. "Fulbert, the butcher. He sells hides to the tanneries in Occel, he is in Theobald's pay."

Maria said nothing, amazed. The ostler's daughter stitched the outline of a leaping lion.

"I know every secret in Birnia." Her voice was sweet with pride.

"Even mine," Maria said. "What are you making?"

175

"A vestment for old Gibertetto." She held it up. Among flowers and leafy stalks, the signs of the Evangelists stood at the four tips of a cross. "The secret I do not know is who told Fulbert, when there has been no one into Birnia from the south in more than a month."

She took the work in hand again and stitched yellow curls for the lion's mane. Maria folded her own hands in her lap, trying to find sense in it: the charcoal burner, the butcher, the tanneries at Occel, and the rumor that linked them all. She said, "Someone in my castle is betraying me."

The needle tacked down one end of a curl. "Perhaps."

"You would not have told me this," Maria said, "if you did not intend to help me."

The ostler's daughter lifted her round face. "I will do what I can."

THEOBALD MARCHED an army up to the border near the Rood Oak, but Ponce Rachet sent eighteen knights from the East Tower, and one night with their help Jean set fire to the meadows where Theobald was camped and in the panic and excitement ran off most of the Count's horses and killed several of his men. Theobald retreated. Jean and his old knights fell back to the King's Road. When Theobald pursued, they wheeled around behind him and shadowed him down the fen, picking off his sentries and scouts. But then Ponce Rachet's men had to go back to the East Tower, to meet some emergency there.

Maria heard all this from three of the old knights, who staggered back to the castle suffering a variety of ailments. She and Eleanor bandaged their wounds and dosed them for their arthritis and their bad backs. Outside on the wall, Robert marched the boys around, waving the wooden sword Jean had made for him, while Stephen hurried along behind. Maria watched them from the third-story window. The three knights were asleep in the bed behind her. Eleanor came up beside her.

"Maria," she said. "You heard them. You must send the children away."

"I heard. Jean's crafty, he is beating Theobald."

"You are mad, Maria—Theobald will shrug him off

176

like a fly, these three cannot fight any more, two are dead —they say Ponce Rachet's men are gone. There are only fifteen men left. Theobald has scores of men, he can get more when they die. He—"

"Stop, Eleanor."

Eleanor turned to look out the window. The boys' voices piped in the yard below. Robert's shout overrode them all.

"Is Richard dead?" Eleanor asked.

Maria put her hand on the warm stone of the window sill. "Don't you think I would know, if my husband were dead?" She turned into the room. "Mind these men. I am going to the town again."

She took Robert with her to the inn, left him to play in the common room, and joined the ostler's daughter in the kitchen, where the widow was sewing the horns on Saint Luke's ox. The two women greeted each other like old friends. The ostler's daughter made a place for Maria on her bench. Maria smoothed her skirts over her knees.

"Let me see. You are nearly done, you work hard—what is this stitch here?"

The other woman wove her needle through the loops of thread, gathering them into a tight round blossom against the linen. Maria could not follow it. The ostler's daughter said, "I have shown half the women in Birnia my stitches, and they try and try but turn out ugly scraggly work, and in the end come to me to make them their pretties."

Maria set her teeth together, determined to learn it. She watched how the other woman stretched the linen in her fingers while she sewed, to keep it straight.

"Who has visited the butcher?"

The needle flashed through the cloth. "Several people. Two men from Occel came here, but they stayed with us, and seemed to be no more than merchants. There was a small man, with a limp, who spent most of the day with Fulbert yesterday."

Maria shook her head. "I know no small man with a limp."

"Also, there were two men, father and son, very like—the older much the taller? No. And a needle-nosed young man, on foot, but wearing a short coat, like a knight. He came yesterday. Fulbert—"

"Yes," Maria said. She nodded once. "Haimo. He is one of my hostages from Iste." She had wondered when she marked him leaving: such a one would have no innocent business outside the castle.

The two women smiled at each other. Turning back to her work, the ostler's daughter took stitches along the ox's horn. Maria sat still. The warmth and light of the kitchen soothed her.

"And Fulbert has been sending our smith—Galga is his name—sending Galga off into the countryside, now and then. I think he may be taking messages to Count Theobald, up on the fen."

Maria grunted. "I will deal with Haimo." She got to her feet; now that she had an enemy within reach, she felt charged with strength.

"Have you heard any new word of your husband?" the ostler's daughter said.

"No. Nothing."

The woman looked quickly away from her. Maria pulled her cloak over her shoulders. "Thank you. I will remember what you have done for me."

"Such things as I do. Bring me some needlework, when you come again, and I will show you that stitch."

Maria went out to the common room. Half a dozen men sat around a table below the window, wine flagons scattered around them. They turned owlishly toward her. Robert raced to her side.

"Mama, come meet my new friends. I told them all about you."

Maria took his hand. The men at the table were making her uncomfortable with their stares. "No—we must go home." She led him to the door and out the wide plank steps into the yard.

A wagon blocked the gate. Two oxen stood steaming in their traces before it, their split feet half-buried in the mud. Maria held Robert back on the steps.

"Robert," she said. "You must help me. I need a knight's help."

The boy spun toward her. "Tell me. Oh, Mama, oh, I swear I'll do good."

She laughed. She crossed the yard toward her horse,

walking carefully to keep from muddying her shoes. Robert leaped around her.

"Mama! Tell me—"

"Ssssh. It is a secret matter."

He pressed his lips together. Maria gave him a strong hug and kissed his forehead. The ostler led up her mare by the bridle. She climbed up into her saddle, smoothing her skirts under her.

"Here you go, little prince," the ostler said. He boosted Robert up behind the mare's saddle, and Maria rode around the wagon toward the gate. The drover got back into his seat, shook out his whip, and shouted. The oxen shouldered into the harness. The ostler cried out, dismayed, and with a crunch the wagon smashed into the steps of the inn. Maria rode out to the street.

"Mama, now can you tell me?"

"When we are home again." Of the three knights in the Tower, only one could walk. She wished the bald cook from her home castle were here: him she could have relied on. Birnia's cook, the only sound man in the castle save Haimo himself, wheezed when he walked and spoke endlessly of spiritual matters.

They rode out the gate of the town. Maria nudged the mare into a long canter. She thought of waiting until Jean or Ralf returned, but Haimo might do other mischief, or he could escape. She could not endure it if he escaped.

Robert held onto her waist, and she urged the mare into a full gallop up the hill. The wind streamed in her face. They raced up the hard, rutted road, past the dead fields and the oak trees finally turned red. While they climbed, the air cooled to a wintry chill. Before them on the knob of the hill the Tower stood up dark gray against the sky. The gate was open. She jogged the mare through it and dismounted.

There was no one in the ward. Robert leaped down from the horse and went to take the reins. Maria said, "The secret is that Haimo is a traitor, and we must take him prisoner."

"A traitor!"

"Go up to the knights' room," Maria said, "and wait for me." She struck him lightly on the shoulder to hurry him off. Haimo was coming out of the stable to get her horse. While he walked he pulled on his short coat. Her heart knocked on her ribs. Robert disappeared into the Tower. The young man came up and took Maria's reins.

"Good afternoon, Haimo." She looked him in the face.

"My lady."

He led the mare off toward the stable. She locked her fisted hands together and hurried over to the Tower steps.

The knights' room stank of liniment and myrrh. Half the castle's dogs lay in the rushes on the floor in front of the hearth. Two of the sick knights snored in chorus. The other stood at the foot of the bed, stiffly trying to get his crippled arm into his shirt. Robert was helping him. The old knight pushed his head through the neck of the shirt and tugged it down with his left hand. He had been a huge man once. Now his muscles hung wasting from his rack of bones.

"My lady," he said, "what is this my knave here tells me?"

Maria went up to him. "Haimo—a hostage, he is the groom—he has been spying on us for Theobald's sake. Can you help us? There's nobody else."

The old knight grunted. "Get me my sword," he said to Robert. His right arm dangled from his sprained shoulder. "I'll never get this into mail. Where is Haimo now?"

"In the stable."

Robert brought the sword in its scabbard. The old knight took it by the hilt in his left hand. He threw off the scabbard in a coiling stroke of his good shoulder. "Let's go." He strode off toward the door.

They went down the stairs single file, Robert just ahead of Maria, and the old knight leading them. Maria said, "Robert, you must go to the stable and ask Haimo to come into the ward. Be careful. Don't warn him that we are waiting for him."

The knight opened the door out onto the stairs. The sunlight poured in past him. "Robo, look the bastard in the eye and say, *My mother wants her mare again.* No more. Go on."

Robert dashed past him and down the outside stair to the ward. The old knight let Maria out before him. They followed the boy toward the stable door, walking in the rut the hoofs of horses had worn into the path. Just before they reached the stable door, it burst open, and Haimo came flying out.

He skidded to a stop and flung himself straight at Maria. The old knight bawled, "Run, you dog!" Maria raised her arms between them to shield herself and the young man seized her by the wrists.

"I've got her. I'll kill her, if you—don't—I've—"

Maria kicked him, struggling against his grip. She rushed toward him and bowled him over. They fell together into the dirt of the ward. Haimo whined, his breath hot in her face. He struck her nose hard with his fist. An instant later he was torn away from her. She sat up, dazed.

"Mama," Robert screamed. He dropped his bloody dagger and flung his arms around her. "Mama, are you hurt?"

"No." She patted his back. Her eyes were watering. Her nose hurt with a pulsing sharp pain. Haimo lay in the rut before the door, his mouth open. The old knight planted one foot on his chest and drew the sword out of the young man's body.

"You damned dog," the old man murmured. He came toward them. His face was green with pain and he held his bad shoulder stiffly hunched against his neck. His fingers were slimed with Haimo's blood. He daubed Robert's cheeks and forehead with it.

"Your grandfather would have been proud of you, boy. I do not mean old Stephen d'Alene, either."

Maria's nose hurt. She said, "Robert, you warned him."

"Maria," Eleanor called, from across the ward.

"Mama, I didn't do anything. I just did what you said."

"He guessed." The old knight sagged down weakly to sit on the ground. "It was not the cleanest kill I have ever seen."

Maria got to her feet. "Can you walk? Let me help you."

"I can walk. Just let me sit here a while, and I will come up by myself." He lowered his head.

The steps to the Tower door were clogged with people staring at them. Eleanor called her again. Maria put her hand on Robert's shoulder. The boy was staring at Haimo's body. He twisted his blood-streaked face up toward her.

"Are you all right, Mama? He didn't hurt you, did he?"

She touched her nose gently. "No. I am fine." She had not meant Haimo to die. Now there was only Fulbert. Her knees quivered, and she laid her hand on Robert's shoulder. "Go tell Eleanor what happened. I have something to do now, back in the town."

FULBERT WAS A LARGE, handsome man. His face pebbled with sweat, he kept his eyes pinned to the floor. Twice he tried to speak, and she raised her voice and rode over him and forced him silent again—if he spoke, she knew, she would forget the speech she had made up on the way back to Birnia. Her hands trembled. She tucked them in her skirt and said, "I am not vengeful, but how am I to know you will not do it again?"

He cleared his throat. Abruptly he tilted his head up to meet her eyes. "By what right do you rule over us here? You are nothing but robbers. A man can defend himself against robbers?"

Maria said, "I will defend myself against you, if I have to. We killed Haimo."

His face yielded a little, the rusty color fading from his cheeks. In the stock pens outside, a sheep baaed. Fulbert's hand jerked toward the hilltop. "Whoever sits in that Tower brings me only misery."

"You are a man of consequence in the town," Maria said. "I am much loath to lose your service. Give me your promise you won't work against me. I swear I will be just to you."

"Justice," Fulbert said, contemptuous. Gracelessly he went down on one knee. "I swear." Taking her hand he put a dry kiss on her knuckle.

"God keep you," Maria said. She pulled her hand out of his grip and left the shed. He followed her, she heard his footsteps behind her but did not wait for him. So late in the autumn most of the stockpens were empty. She walked between them to the gate, where her mare stood with her reins tied to a post. Three of the butcher's boys squatted there against the wall and gawked at her while she mounted.

"Good-bye, Master Fulbert."

The butcher mumbled some farewell. Maria rode off across the town toward the gate.

On her way back to the Tower, a band of horsemen appeared, riding toward her from the east. Maria drew a deep breath to steady herself. She reined up to wait for them, wishing Eleanor were there with her long sight to tell who they were. One of the riders raised his arm and called to her.

It was William. She galloped off the road toward him.

He and his horsemen cantered toward her across the slope. The frosts had killed the green of the hillside. The sky was a smoky autumn color, like wool in the fleece. Maria reined up. She was afraid to ask him about Richard. He trotted his tall stallion over to her and leaned out of his saddle to kiss her.

"William," she said. "What is it?"

He took her by the hand. "I've come to do the Devil's work," he said, "but it can't be helped."

Confused, she swung her mare around to trot along shoulder to shoulder with his horse. "What do you mean? Richard—is he alive? Are they holding him to ransom?"

In the creased map of his face, William's bright colorless eyes narrowed. "Ransom? Oh. You mean the Saracens." He smiled. "Richard talked his way out of it. They have made a peace with us, those people. They are helping us now. No one told you?"

Maria's voice failed. William laughed at her. "He never sent you any word that he was set free?"

"Mother of God." She lifted her reins. The mare picked up speed and William's big Roman-nosed roan stallion moved out into a canter to keep up. "I thought he was dead," Maria said. "The wretch. He doesn't care about me at all. I thought he was dead. Where is he? Why did you come, and not him?"

"They are both fighting. Some of the Iste barons have rebelled against us—I have to deal with their hostages. How have you fared with Theobald?"

"Pah. He has taken up residence in the fen." She

glanced at the score of knights galloping behind them. "He has lots of men, many more than we do, and one of the hostages was bearing tales to a man in the town who is in touch with Occel. We had to kill him."

William coughed. He banged himself in the chest. He sat heavy and loose in his saddle, the slate-red stallion lumbering along beside her. "Theobald's still in the fen? I'll take care of him." He faced her, amused. "Richard never told you he was let free, and you thought he was dead."

"Do not laugh at me, William."

William laughed at her.

STOPPING ONLY long enough to eat his supper, William took his men out after Theobald. For two days Robert haunted the Tower gate for words of the fighting. Theobald and William maneuvered up and down the fen; abruptly Theobald marched away north. William and Jean hurried him over the border and fell back to the Tower. Robert pouted, robbed of his war.

News came from Agato that the friends of the young Duke had managed to get one of their allies elected Archbishop. Hearing that, William grunted and settled his vast shoulders into the back of his chair.

"That's why Theobald retreated, you see," he told Maria. "Now that the Archbishop is their man, Fitz-Michael and his friends can strike at Theobald whenever he leaves himself open." He locked his fingers over his enormous belly. A mastiff came up to him and laid its wrinkled head on his knee, and he stroked it.

"Maria," he said, "you have changed my castle all around."

"Take Mana'a and you can have it back." She was weaving a scene into the new tapestry: two hunting dogs standing up against their leashes.

"When we take Mana'a," William said, "Richard will think of something else he wants. He is cursed; he cannot be content." He gave a page his cup to fill. "Tomorrow I shall kill the three guilty hostages. I am glad none of them is very young. I love children."

"Why don't you marry?"

"I don't much like women." He chuckled, his belly rolling under his shirt.

"Neither does Richard." She threaded the bobbin with red yarn to weave the hounds' collar. "Don't you have any sisters?"

"Five of them. None would teach a man to like women. Richard has a twin sister. Or was that Drogo who had the twin? You were an only child, Maria, you cannot know what it's like to have fifteen brothers and sisters around you constantly, and another one coming every year."

"What is her name? Richard's twin."

William chewed his lip until she thought he had forgotten the question. She changed bobbins again, smiling, and cleared her throat.

"I am thinking," William said. "I think it was Judith. It must have been Judith." He shook his head, wistful. "She was the Devil's own shrew, Judith," he said, and sighed.

Maria watched her hands weave the hounds' white throats. She tried to imagine having so many brothers and sisters. Always someone to play with, or talk to. That reminded her of the little Duke, in Santerois, who was also a lone child; she said, "So Fitz-Michael is master in Santerois now."

"No. Oh, no. No one masters Santerois, just parts of it. Now he has the power of the Cross, but all the other barons are doing what we are doing—grabbing as much as they can."

"We aren't vassals of the Duke of Santerois."

"For Birnia, we are." William dug in his ear with his forefinger. "For your castle, we owe him some ancient service."

Maria stepped on the pedal of her loom and drew the bobbin through the warp. What Fulbert had said returned to her: they ruled in Birnia by robbery. The Duke ruled here by right. She broke off the yarn and let the end dangle.

"Who is the priest in Birnia?"

"Gibertetto," she answered. "He is a horrible old gossip. Have you never talked to him?"

William shook his head. "I avoid priests." He propped

185

his cheek on his fist. "When I tell him of this new Archbishop, Richard will ask me a lot of questions I don't know the answers to. Does the Archbishop rule our priest?"

"I suppose so. Who else is there?" The fire in the hearth shot up a shower of embers. It was the first bitter cold night of the late fall, when something always caught fire. She said, "Then you are leaving tomorrow?"

"Richard told me to be back in Iste for the beginning of Advent."

Maria giggled. "That was yesterday."

"Yes. I don't think he minds. He has learned about me, he always calls for me sooner than he really needs me. So you see, there is a way to manage Richard. One need only be patient with him." He erupted into muffled laughter. It ended in a leisurely yawn. Setting his head comfortably on the back of his chair, he went to sleep.

Maria glanced down at the end of the hall, where Jean and the other knights had gathered for the evening. Robert was among them, Stephen beside him, listening to stories. The warmth of the hall softened her; picking out another bobbin, she nearly yawned herself.

●　　●　　●

WILLIAM HAD the dead hostages buried in the town graveyard. For days afterward, when William had left, Robert followed her around asking about them, why they had been killed, who they were, and why their kinsmen had rebelled knowing the hostages would die.

"If you should ever give a hostage to someone, you would give Stephen and not me, wouldn't you," Robert asked.

Maria hung a string of garlic sausage from the storeroom ceiling. "We have never given anyone a hostage." She reached down from the ladder, and Eleanor handed her another string.

"But if you did—"

"Be quiet," Eleanor said. She put her hands on his shoulders. Stooping, she whispered in his ear, and he went reluctantly off, his face turned back over his shoulder.

186

"Is Papa coming back for Christmas?" He stopped in the doorway.

Maria tied sausages to the rafter over her head. Her arms ached from reaching up all day. "No. He is fighting the Saracens. As usual." She climbed down the ladder. A serving woman brought in a basket of onions and took it over to be hung in nets. "I'd get more heed from him if I were a Saracen."

"When will he come back?"

"Robert," Eleanor said sharply.

"Oh, shut up, you rotten old horse." He ran out of the storeroom.

"You spoil him," Eleanor said bitterly. "How unruly he is grown."

XIX

JEAN WAS TEACHING ROBERT AND THE OTHER BOYS TO shoot a bow. Every morning, they went out into the snowy fields below the Tower and shot arrows, while Maria watched them from the wall. Stephen had fallen into an evil humor. Left alone he made up games for himself and sang or dreamed, but when the winter storms shut all the people into the Tower, Stephen drove everyone wild with his crying.

Messengers came from Richard, sometimes directly, sometimes through Ponce Rachet. The news of fighting meant nothing to her, she had no idea if they were losing or gaining. Lammas passed. Richard stayed in the mountains. She did not ask him to come. The messengers told her about him only in the barest way: that he was well, that he was the same, an expression the messengers used often. Sometimes in the mornings she woke up lusty as a mare in heat. Once she dreamed she was lying with Roger.

Lent ended in a burst of heavy rain. The sun came out, the serfs planted their fields, and the rains fell again and rotted the seed in the ground. Maria rode through the fields near the Tower of Birnia, and the sight of the serfs weeping over their ruined crop unnerved her. She did what she could, she fetched new seed from other parts of the demesne and had it blessed, and her own people worked in the field around the Tower.

The crop was cursed, all the people said: when the second planting sprouted, blight struck it. At the same time, Stephen and several other children in the castle took fevers. The Tower was full of the wailing of sick children and the smell of angelica tea and myrrh. Every time Maria went up or down the stair she met some woman going in the opposite direction with a steaming poultice or a plate of mushed food. One child died of the fever, but Stephen bore it lightly. He was turning thin, with pale brown hair, and eyes as clear and gray as Richard's. The fever seemed to break his mood. When he got up from his bed he was quiet and sweet as a girl.

All through Whitsun, everyone went about with a long look, saying that the failure of the wheat and the children's fever was a sign of God's wrath, and something worse would happen. Midsummer's Day passed. In the grueling heat after it, the crops of peas and beans throve. The ostler's daughter told Maria that the local witch was claiming credit for turning aside the scourge.

Theobald had spent the spring in a border dispute with another neighbor, but in the end of the summer, he raided Birnia again. Jean, following William's example, harassed Theobald's camps and outriders, but they could not stop him from marching deep into Birnia and looting everything in his path. Ponce Rachet's knights hurried down to help them. Maria went into the town. The ostler's daughter talked with her most of the morning about stitchery and mint sauce for lamb. In the warm, sunny kitchen Maria composed a new speech for Fulbert.

The butcher was in his yard, dickering with a shepherd for a flock of ewes. When he saw her coming, he waved

188

impatiently to the other man to move away. Maria went up to him. Fulbert's handsome, fleshy face was set against her like a closed door. He said, "I have kept my promise," in a voice edged with anger.

"I know," Maria said. "I thank you for it. But now Theobald has attacked us again—" She put out one hand, pleading with him; she had seen children do it. "I am at the end of my wits—If I give him money, will he go away?"

Fulbert's expression softened. He gestured the shepherd farther off across the yard. Pigs and sheep packed the stockpens. The smell of beasts made Maria want to sneeze.

"A bribe, is it?" the butcher said. He came closer to her. "Yes, Theobald will take money. So will I. What will you give me to go between you?"

She swallowed. It had not occurred to her that he would have to be bribed as well. "Whatever you want—I have this with me—" She took her purse from her belt. Fulbert held out his hand. The purse sank into his palm. "Help me," she said, "and I will give you anything you want."

He tossed the leather purse in his hand, his face smooth. He actually smiled at her. "I will need something for my courier."

"Give him what you think fair, I will repay you." It was as easy as buying cloth. She cast her eyes down. "I cannot tell you how this eases my mind—I know you will help me."

"I will do my best, my lady."

Maria went back to the Tower. Robert's army of children was ranged around the gate. Flourishing his wooden sword, Robert himself blocked her way and made her dismount and ask him humbly for the leave to enter. Inside the gate, Stephen was screaming, and she left her mare and went quickly over to him. He had been tied to the little tree near the wall with several pieces of rope. Already he was wiggling free. His face was dark red with rage. Maria held back and let him untie himself.

"Mama, I'm not a hostage!"

Robert was running up and down before the open gate,

yelling orders. Stephen untied his feet. He had lost one shoe, and tears streaked his dirty cheeks. Maria picked him up.

"No, you're not a hostage."

"He isn't the King, either," Stephen said. He pushed at her impatiently until she put him down. "Tell him he isn't the King, Mama."

"He can play at being king, if he wishes." She gathered up the rope from the foot of the tree. "Come upstairs with me. You need not play at being his knight, either."

Stephen climbed slowly up the steep steps after her. "Tell him he isn't the King."

Maria opened the hall door. In the dim afternoon light, she saw a man standing before the hearth. Blinking, she saw that it was Ralf.

"My lady." The knight came toward her. Maria went into the hall and shut the door.

"Ralf, I thought you would go to join the Crusade."

"My lady, I felt more required here."

That made her smile. "Well, I'm glad you're here now. Have you got messages from Jean?"

"Aye, my lady. Theobald has made a permanent camp in the valley west of the Roman bridge, he must mean to stay there a while. From there he can hold the west part of the March. The shrine, and the village of Saint-Mary."

She sent Stephen off to play and sat down before the hearth. "We must get him out of there."

"I don't see how, my lady. Ponce Rachet's men are leaving in four days for the East Tower."

"We may not need them. Sit down, I have something for Jean to do, it will be hard to explain."

"I will listen attentively, my lady."

Maria began to tell him about the ostler's daughter and Fulbert. At first Ralf listened on his feet, but after a few moments he sat down on his heels on the hearth. When she mentioned offering the bribe to Theobald, he frowned, and when she repeated Fulbert's own demand, he shook his head.

"This is foul business," he said. "I cannot see why the master and the man both require payment, or why you allow this fellow here at all. In any case, my lady, my advice is that you eschew this matter entirely. Jean and I can deal with Theobald. We have a plan to destroy the supplies in the area."

"I don't want your advice," Maria said.

"But—giving him money—"

"Do you think I mean to pay him any money? I have no money." Exasperated, she flung her hands up. "All I wish is that Jean keep watch for the courier—I think it may be the smith from the town, a man named Galga. Stop him and make him tell what he knows. Bribe him, threaten him, beat him—anything, just force him to convince Theobald that if he bargains with me he'll get everything without having to fight."

Ralf stared into the fire. A page came into the hall with a ewer of wine. Maria tapped her foot impatiently on the floor. One of the dogs came up to her and tried to lure her into patting it. At last, the young knight said, "I will do as you say, lady."

"Thank you," Maria said, angry.

THEOBALD SENT TO HER through Fulbert that he would leave Birnia for 30,000 silver pence; this Maria said was too much. Theobald seized the village at the Shrine of the Virgin, but Maria went to Fulbert and wept and begged him to help her and said she would give no one any money until Theobald had let the village go. Theobald held on a little longer. He was calling himself lord of Birnia and made the churches under his control publish charters naming Richard and his brothers outlaws, but in the late summer they won a tremendous battle in the mountains, and Theobald at last gave up the village and demanded 20,000 pence.

Now another army marched down the road from Santerois. Maria held up her answer to Theobald. The newcomers sent two heralds to her, dressed in fancy tabards, to announce that this new power followed the Count Fitz-Michael and Duke Henry, who had heard of Maria's distress and were coming to her aid, since she was their vassal.

With Robert and Jean, who had returned to the Tower for orders, she went out to meet the oncoming army. The day was overcast. The land east of the Tower was rolling and open. They rode up through a stand of oak trees at the crest of a hill and looked out over Fitz-Michael's men, drawn up in three long columns under the lowering sky.

"They are greater than Theobald," Jean said. "If we can catch him in that valley where he is now, we can pay him back for all the trouble he has given us."

Maria grimaced. Richard would not like this talk that they were the Duke's vassals. She had gotten no useful word from Richard since Theobald invaded Birnia. Even the great news of the battle had come from Ponce Rachet. Robert, on his fat gelding between her and Jean, cried, "Here someone comes!"

Half a dozen men were galloping up the long treeless slope toward them. Maria let her reins slide through her fingers. "Jean, we will be safe here. Will you go back and warn Eleanor and the cook that we shall have several guests? Tell Eleanor to make the top room ready for them."

Jean leaned toward her. "Lady, don't let them stop—have them strike hard, before Theobald can escape."

Maria made a noncommittal sound in her throat. Jean galloped away through the oak trees. Robert was standing in his stirrups, his mouth open, his eyes fastened on the knights before them in their long, wavering lines. The six men approaching them reined their horses to a walk. Maria began to smile. She nudged her mare forward.

"Well met, my lord," she said; she did not have to ask which was Fitz-Michael, and she turned her smile on him, an older man, tall and slender. "You are a welcome traveler here."

Fitz-Michael rode up beside her. His dark hair was half gone to gray, and his hand when it took hers was cold as age. His sober clothes were magnificent. "So you are Strongarm's daughter," he said. He did not let go of her hand when he had kissed it. "You are as pretty as your welcome, mistress."

Four other horses shouldered up around them. Fitz-Michael gestured toward them. "My sons, Peter, Philip, and John, and my nephew, Henry, the Duke of Santerois, my ward."

Maria raised her eyes to the young Duke, curious. The

boy sat on his horse just behind his uncle. In his dark eyes no recognition showed. He said nothing to her. He was big for his age, swarthy as a serf. Another horse was coming.

"And my lord the Archbishop of Agato, Robert of Sio."

She said proper greetings to them, and the Archbishop blessed her. Maria detached herself from Fitz-Michael's clammy grip on her hand. "This is Robert, my son. My lord, I cannot tell you how your coming pleases me. Will you ride with me to my castle? I will make you welcome better there than here."

The tall man warped his mouth into a smile. "I must accept such a pretty company." He waved to his sons, who rode back toward the disorderly columns of knights on the slope below them. The young Duke turned his horse to follow.

"Your place is here, Henry," Fitz-Michael said.

The boy silently came up on Maria's left. She started off, her eyes on Fitz-Michael, beside her. Even his fingernails were clean and shapely.

"We shall treat you better than Theobald has done," he said. "Or Richard d'Alene, for that matter. I am told you have only a handful of a garrison, and Theobald is riding at will over the country."

"I have God's help, my lord."

The Archbishop, beyond him, said something in Latin too rapid for her to understand: an old man, white-haired. She glanced back at Fitz-Michael, who was smiling at her. "And now ours, lady, if you will accept it."

"I am your servant, my lord, in all things."

"Well said." He nodded to her. "We shall get on well together."

They went up the hill toward the castle. The people of Birnia ran from their town and cheered them all the way to the gate. Fitz-Michael's sons were settling their armies in the fields. Robert hung back, watching, and Maria called to him. The young Duke did not take his eyes from the road.

When they went through the gate into the ward, the castle women swarmed out, dressed in their best clothes, to welcome them, and Jean appeared on the staircase, still wearing his mail and his sword. Someone gave a cheer. Fitz-Michael waved and bowed and with many flourishes came to hold Maria's horse. The young Duke's mount carried him up beside her. He was looking sharply around the ward. Facing her, he said, "It was not here that I was housed, when Dragon rescued me from Count Theobald."

"No," Maria said, surprised. "That was my own castle, south of here."

His gaze swept out across the walls. Beyond him, Robert leaned forward and called "When was that, Mama?"

"When I was a weanling," the Duke answered him. "This Tower you hold by my grace; is your other castle in my rights too?"

Maria smiled at him. "I do not know the custom. Long ago, I think, before the castle was built, the Duke claimed the rights of justice there. But it was long ago."

"The older the better," the Duke said. He looked at Robert. "You will show me this place."

Fitz-Michael was getting impatient to help her dismount. She took his hands and slid down to the ground. Robert was still sorting out an answer. She gestured to him to get down and hold the Duke's bridle.

"Is he my master?" Robert said, when he had jumped down out of his saddle.

"Be courteous to him, whether he is or not."

Fitz-Michael said her name. She turned to him and let him take her arm. Together they walked across the ward toward the Tower.

His attendants arrived, with a carload of goods. A steady stream of servants marched up and down the stairs, installing Fitz-Michael and his horde in the top room. Maria moved her quarters down to the room directly below that one. When she had settled herself there, she went to the hall.

Fitz-Michael had brought a ballad singer with him. She sat on the side of the hearth and talked him into singing a long piece from the Song of Saint George. The singer was young; he played well, although his voice was shaky. When he had done with Saint George, he sang her a ballad called "The Great Deeds of Roger the Norman," a long, tortuous song full of thievings from other stories. Delighted, she made him sing it again.

Fitz-Michael came into the hall, even more elegantly dressed than before. He came up beside her. The singer was just finishing the refrain of the song about Roger. Fitz-Michael signed to him to stop.

"Don't sing her that fish-gut piece." He raised his eyebrows at her. "Surely you don't find such things enjoyable?"

Maria stood up beside him, smiling. "Roger is my brother, my lord."

The Archbishop approached them. A page brought them all chairs. Fitz-Michael got himself arranged so that he would not crease his fancy coat. He looked up at her, his eyes sharp.

"Yes—your brother, as you say, is becoming a man of some remark although, of course, the songs exaggerate. But no one's singing songs about your husband, my dear. They say other things about Richard Dragon, that he is treacherous, and cruel, and makes sworn bonds with Saracens—"

Maria straightened up. "My lord, my husband is an honest Christian knight, in whose castle you are sitting." Her voice quavered, but she stared him in the eyes.

The Archbishop muttered, "Well spoken," and Fitz-Michael twisted to glare at him. But when he looked at Maria the Count's face was pleasant; he even laughed. "You are loyal, I like that." He took hold of her hand. "Don't be in a temper, although you're pretty when you're angry."

"My lord, I did not mean to be sharp with you." She took her hand out of his grip. "I will bring you some wine, if you wish." Jean was coming in the door. She went across the room to get them cups.

XX

❧

FITZ-MICHAEL'S KNIGHTS RODE TO TRAP THEOBALD IN HIS narrow valley, but through Fulbert Maria warned him of their coming, and he escaped into the fens. Fitz-Michael complained of ill-luck. He and the Archbishop were loath to give up quickly the comforts and pleasures Maria made sure they had in Birnia. She drew all her own knights back to the Tower, since Fitz-Michael's men were there to do their work, and set them to keeping these people busy.

The Archbishop visited the Shrine of the Virgin and blessed the last of the summer's pilgrims. Fitz-Michael hunted William's packs of hounds and mastiffs and William's hawks. Mouse-shy, Theobald marched around in the fens killing woodcutters and an occasional traveler. Now and again Fitz-Michael stalked him along the road, but they never caught Theobald.

One afternoon, on the stairs, she overheard the Archbishop and Fitz-Michael talking, in the top-story room, where the strangers all slept. She took off her shoes and sneaked up behind the door. Through the crack between the hinges she could see into the room. Fitz-Michael's servant was shaving him. The Archbishop sat down with a grunt in a big chair by the hearth.

"It just seems strange to me that whenever we move, Theobald moves ahead of us," the Archbishop said. "After all, these people here don't want to give us any more reason to claim rights over them. If we saved her from Theobald—"

"We are saving her from Theobald," Fitz-Michael

said. "You saw how she greeted us. She's a pretty little wench, and very properly grateful."

"I don't think she's guileless, my lord. Nor do I think the way to impress her is to tell her that her husband's treacherous and cruel. You know my opinion of Dragon, but she hasn't seen him in two years."

The young Duke was running up the steps. Maria hid behind the door, and without seeing her he darted past her into the room. On his heels a wolfhound snuffled briefly at the foot of the door and went on.

"You are an old fool," Fitz-Michael was saying. He stroked his cheeks. She wondered if all men did that after they had been shaved. "She knows her betters when she sees us. And I mean to rescue her, depend on it—I want a short rein and a good bit on Dragon, and this is one means to it. When we beat Theobald, Birnia will be as much ours as his."

The Archbishop grunted. "You may find the mare's more bridlewise than the stallion."

Someone else was coming up the stairs. Maria slid out from behind the door and went away, and she heard nothing else.

They chased Theobald across the fens. The Archbishop and a small escort went back to Agato. Maria knelt in the ward before the old churchman to get his blessing, relieved that he would be out of her way. The young Duke and Robert were fighting with stick swords in a corner of the ward. In their shouting she missed the words of the blessing. The Archbishop made the Cross over her and kissed the crown of her head.

"Mark me, girl," he said, lifting her up onto her feet. "You cannot toy with Fitz-Michael too long, he is less foolish than you think."

"I, my lord?" She gave him a blank look. "No one knows better than I how wise my lord Fitz-Michael is."

The Archbishop snorted with laughter. He mounted his white horse. His escort was waiting for him in the road. The two boys, their game stopped, were watching him, and he waved. Robert waved back but the young Duke pointedly turned away.

The Archbishop shook his head. He picked up his reins in his ringed hands.

"We shall all suffer someday for that young man's bad breeding," he said. "God keep you, girl." At a trot, he rode out the gate and went on down the hill.

Maria had to ask her own castle, in the south, for some of their grain to keep her storeroom stocked. Although the harvest was coming, many of the fields around the town of Birnia lay untended and deep in weeds. Theobald still hunted the fen. One day while she was in the town, Fulbert sought her out to demand money of her, and she laughed at him. He slunk away, and many people turned to look at him.

Fitz-Michael and his sons hawked for gamebirds and hare. They held a feast in the ward of the Tower and gave presents to everyone. Most of the townspeople came up the road to eat and have a piece of silver from Fitz-Michael's own hand.

On the day after the feast, Maria sat in one end of the hall fitting a new coat on Stephen. The young Duke came in, with Robert on his heels, and they stood in front of the fire shouting a rhyming game. Maria looked over Stephen's head at them.

"Go outside, if you must be so loud."

Her son rushed over to her. The Duke followed him, his hands behind his back. Robert leaned on her knee. "We can't. It's raining. We went to the kitchen but Cook threw us out, and we went to the stables but Jean says we get in the way."

His face was quick and merry; she stroked back his thick wavy hair to see his eyes. He rubbed his head affectionately against her hand. The young Duke stood rigidly to one side, his face turned away.

"My lord," she said, "come here," and when he stood before her she straightened his shirt and his hair, but he did not soften under her touch. Baffled, she sent them down the room to build the fire.

Stephen watched the older boys, his face solemn. She took the basted coat carefully off over his head. He walked down the hall, drawing his hand absently over the stone wall, until he reached a place near Robert and the young Duke. Maria threaded a needle and began to sew the sleeve of the coat. Outside, the rain drove down rattling into the ward.

With a crash, the door swung open, and Fitz-Michael with his three sons strode in. They fanned out toward the fire, bringing a stench of wet clothes into the room. Half a dozen of William's dogs padded after them. A tall brindle wolfhound bitch trotted across the hall to the young Duke and the boy turned and patted her.

One of the sons took his father's cloak; Fitz-Michael warmed his hands a moment at the fire. He came smiling to Maria and sank down on one knee.

"Lady, we shall keep your table groaning with game as long as you have us here."

Maria put the needle in her pincushion. "You had good hunting again. Did the rain catch you far away?"

Fitz-Michael took her hand between his palms. "The other side of your hall is too far from you, my dear," he said, and mouthed her fingers. Over his shoulder he called for a stool. Maria tried to free her hand, and he tightened his grip on it and gave her a little quizzical smile.

"My lord," she said. She felt herself blushing, and she got to her feet.

"No," he said. "Stay. Keep me company for a while."

"Please, my lord," she said. She stood still, uncertain, and before she could move or speak, the young Duke was there before them, the wolfhound at his heels.

"Uncle," he said to Fitz-Michael, "let me speak to you."

Fitz-Michael pulled Maria by the hand until she sat down again on the stool. "Speak," he said to the Duke.

"My lord," Maria said, "if it pleases you," and pulled her hand out of his grip and went away before he could hold her. Eleanor had come in, and the servants were arranging the table for supper. She went among them to help.

"I warned you to close the shutters," Eleanor said. "It's rained in through the window upstairs, Robert's bed is soaked."

Maria put her hand on Eleanor's arm and looked over her shoulder at Fitz-Michael. The people between them hid him from her sight. "The old dog has a bone yet," she said, and laughed, her voice quaking.

"What?"

"Fitz-Michael wants to lie with me."

199

Eleanor gasped. "Holy Mother." She clutched Maria's arm. "What did you say?"

Maria put her free hand over her mouth, giggling. "I don't know. What should I say?"

"Maria!" Eleanor shook her. "And your husband gone to fight the wars of God."

Maria turned her back on the other woman. "You must be made of snow." She crossed the hall to the door, to send down for their supper.

That led her past the corner where her spinning wheel stood, and the look on the young Duke's face stopped her between steps. Fitz-Michael was bending over him, poking his forefinger into the boy's chest. "Keep your mouth shut," he said. "I'll feed you whip again, God save me." He struck the boy on the side of the head with his open hand.

The boy looked impassively up at him and said, "I will remember how you repay loyal men by stealing their wives, Uncle."

Fitz-Michael raised his fist, and the wolfhound bitch slid between them, her narrow head raised. Maria went up to Fitz-Michael; she took hold of the dog by the collar. "My lord," she said, "your coat is wet, and supper will come soon."

Stiff as paper, his cheeks folded into wrinkles when he smiled. "Thank you, my dear." He went away. The young Duke rushed toward the hearth, but Maria hooked her hand under his arm and whirled him around to face her.

"In my castle," she said softly, "I will fight my own fights."

His face went expressionless. With his other hand he pried her fingers from his arm and walked away. The wolfhound whined in her throat; straightening, Maria let her go after him.

WORD CAME the next morning that Theobald was moving north. The rain had stopped. Leaving the young Duke behind for punishment, Fitz-Michael rode off to chase the Count home. The Duke wandered listlessly around the castle, driving Robert away whenever he came up, until Jean saw it and took all the boys out to shoot their bows.

After they had cleaned the Tower, Maria and Eleanor went to the hall to work on the new tapestry. It was of Charlemagne riding to the hunt, and they had finished nearly half. Sitting down, Maria looked it over and said, "You have a better eye for the horses than I do."

Eleanor sniffed. She had not ceased sermonizing about Maria and Fitz-Michael. Maria struck her on the shoulder. "Why do you treat me like this? I will not lie with him—do you think I am a complete whore? Besides, he beats the Duke and probably he would beat me."

"He who has lain with her in his heart—" Eleanor could not remember what followed. Lamely, she said, "You encouraged him. I saw you at supper, how you fawned on him."

"If he comes near me, I'll stab him," Maria said. She picked up a bobbin and threaded it with the pale thread for Charlemagne's face. She did faces better than Eleanor.

Eleanor sniffed again. Leaning forward to weave in the next row, Maria said, "Perhaps you should go to a convent. You would be happier there, with the other saints."

"You are wicked to me."

"Don't be silly."

Out the window, a voice called. Someone was coming in the gate. Maria stood up and went to the hall door to see who it was. Several of the boys were in the yard below, with Jean, cleaning saddles in front of the stable. She went out onto the stair landing. Fitz-Michael himself came riding through the open gate.

Maria could hardly believe he was back. Furious, she went down the stairs to meet him in the ward. "My lord," she said, "have you beaten Count Theobald so soon?"

Fitz-Michael put his hand casually on her arm and led her toward the stairs. "He is well north of us, my lady, and my guess is that he will not stop until he is safe in his own country. I have no wish to ride around in the rain."

Maria shook off his hand. The rainclouds were crowding into the sky from the north. He took her arm again, and she pushed at him. "Please do not hold me, my lord, I mislike it. I should think you would want to stay with your men, if they are going to have to be uncomfortable."

He gave her a look as if she were witless. They went up the stairs toward the hall. The young Duke and Robert were there. When she came in the door with Fitz-Michael after her, the Duke's face stiffened and he wheeled away from them.

At supper, Fitz-Michael was full of good humor and conversation. Jean as usual stuffed himself, and Eleanor seemed to have taken a vow of silence; even the children were quiet. Maria had to speak to Fitz-Michael, although she was in a cold rage that he had come back when she had thought him gone for good, with his clammy hands. He sighed over the rain, lashing at the shutters again, and she claimed to love it. He sent a roast dove back to the kitchen because it was overdone, and she ordered it brought back up again and carved a leg for herself. While she was scraping the char off it, a servant came into the hall and around the table to her.

"My lady, there are messengers in the ward."

"Send them up," Fitz-Michael said.

"No, I'll go." Maria slid off the bench. "Robert, will you fetch me my cloak?" Whatever the messengers had to say, she did not want Fitz-Michael overhearing.

"Let me attend you," he said, rising in his place.

"My lord, please, stay at your supper—there will be no one to keep order over the children." She went between Jean's back and the wall and walked swiftly out onto the open landing at the top of the stonework stair.

The streaming rain turned the whole ward gray. Near the foot of the stair, two messengers waited, still in their saddles, side by side talking. In their cloaks, with the hoods up, they looked like two monks. She went down to the foot of the stair. The rain fell in her face. One knight was Ponce Rachet's messenger; the bearded man behind him she did not know.

"Joscelyn," she said. "My greeting to Ponce Rachet." She looked back at the bearded man, started. "Richard?"

He dismounted. She flung herself into his arms. He was soaking wet. The beard grazed her cheek and her lip. He held her so tight she could hardly breathe.

"Upstairs," he said in her ear.

"Duke Henry and Fitz-Michael are in the hall."

"They are still here?" He looked her over, his arm around her waist. The other knight went away. The rain was streaming down their faces. She wiped her eyes on her sleeve.

"You look thinner," he said. "What did you do to your hair? You look different."

She laughed; she leaned on him, his mail solid under her hand. The door above them slammed. Robert came down the steps, her cloak piled in his arms. He slowed.

"Papa—"

He flung the cloak aside and ran down the steps to Richard. Maria picked up her cloak. Robert wept in his father's arms. She climbed the stairs to the hall door. When she opened it, Fitz-Michael came toward her. She stepped into the half-lit warmth of the hall.

"Maria," he said. "You are soaking wet, girl. You should have waited for your cloak."

Richard barged in roughly between them. He gave Fitz-Michael a jagged look. Maria went over toward the table. She stood with her hands on the back of her chair.

"By Saint Charity," Fitz-Michael said, "it's Richard d'Alene, with a beard like a Saracen!"

Among the children sitting at the table, the young Duke leaped up onto his feet, and Stephen dropped his cup. Robert hurried into the hall after Richard, who tramped to the hearth, threw his cloak off, and put his back to the fire.

"Still here, my lord?" he said to Fitz-Michael. "Maria, I'm cold, bring me some wine."

"I'll do it." Robert raced toward the table.

Fitz-Michael stood in the middle of the hall, facing Richard; the young Duke had come up around the table. Before his uncle could speak, he said, "My lord, I must thank you for your kindness which we have so much insulted." His voice rang childishly high; he gave Fitz-Michael a harsh look. "I would treat no vassal so, especially one who has been loyal to me."

Richard took the cup of wine from Robert. "I'm sure you would not," he said to the Duke, "for all I remember being neither your vassal nor loyal."

Fitz-Michael said. "My nephew's manner is sometimes coarse and unworthy of his rank." He set his hands on his belt. "He says only the truth. Your wife has been very gracious to us indeed."

"She has a weakness for strays. I don't. I understand your army's already left Birnia. You follow them." Richard drank; his eyes never left Fitz-Michael. "Tomorrow."

The other man bristled up. In his magnificent dark coat he looked easily Richard's size even though Richard wore mail. He said, "You left Birnia unprotected, Master Dragon. Theobald was heavily oppressing your wife. We came here to defend her against him."

Richard threw the empty cup down. "From what I'm told, you certainly didn't help her much against Theobald."

"I'm not going to indulge you in an unseemly—"

"In fact, if you really were after Theobald, you'd have attacked Occel while he was gone," Richard said. "You didn't come here after Theobald, Master Cheek, you came here to take advantage of a woman."

Fitz-Michael's face was blazing red; he turned on his heel and strode out of the hall. Maria got a ewer from the table. No one in the hall spoke. The children were staring owlishly at Richard. She crossed the hall, picked up his cup, and filled it from the ewer. He took it from her, his eyes still on the door.

Stephen came up beside her, shy, his eyes on his father. Richard put the cup on the mantelpiece and grabbed hold of him. "Ah." He boosted the little boy up in his arms, laughing. "Look at this. The last time I saw this—"

Stephen glowed. He threw his arms around Richard's neck and hugged him. Robert hurried up to lean against his father. Maria stood to one side watching them. It was a shock to see him here, when he had been away so long. "Come upstairs," she said. "You can get out of your mail." She put her hand on his arm.

He put Stephen down. His hand closed over hers, and her skin went to gooseflesh. She went with him to the door.

"Papa," Robert cried. He and Stephen crowded after them. "Come see my horse."

Richard opened the door. "Later. In a while."

Robert's expression drooped. Maria went out onto the stair landing. He shut the hall door. They were alone on the staircase. She lifted her face and kissed him. His arms went hard around her. The soft crisp beard brushed her chin. He pulled her surcoat open in front and cupped her breast in his hand. Through the cloth of her dress her nipple grew taut and hard against his palm. Her thighs trembled. She slid her arms around his waist and drew him hip to hip with her.

The door opened loudly. They split apart. The young Duke, his head down, raced past them and up the stairs. Halfway to the next landing, he threw them a strange look. He bolted up toward his room. "God's wounds," Richard said. They climbed the stairs after him. They came to the landing, and he would have gone up another flight, but she held back.

"No—I sleep here, now, so that Fitz-Michael and the Duke could have the best room."

"Did you want them to stay?" He pushed open the door and went through it into the room. Maria stood in the doorway, watching him. He shed his mail coat. The beard, trimmed to a point and darker brown than his hair, made him exotic, like a strange beast. He dumped the shirt over the foot rail on the bed, and she went hotly forward into his arms.

XXI

❧

THE BED SMELLED OF SEX. THEY HAD DRAWN THE HEAVY draperies around it the night before, when Eleanor brought the boys in to bed. The dawn was coming. The confined space around her was twilit. She raised herself cautiously on her outstretched arm. Her husband lay asleep on his stomach next to her.

She put her head down. He had thrown off the blanket. His face and arms were suntanned dark as a barrel but on his back the skin was soft and pale. Outside the curtains, Eleanor spoke, and the boys answered in sleepy voices. The man beside her moved, coming awake; his head turned toward her.

"Maria," Eleanor whispered, just outside the curtain. The cloth shook and her face appeared in the middle. Her eyes widened when she saw Richard was naked and she withdrew her head and snapped the curtains shut.

Richard stirred. All night long they had gone at each other like plunderers, waking and sleeping and waking again. He opened his eyes on her.

"That was a good ride, little girl," he said. He pulled her over against him. "That was worth coming all the way down here in the rain for."

Outside the curtain, Robert shouted, "Papa is home!"

"Sssh—you'll wake them up," Eleanor said. "Go down and get your breakfast."

Feet trampled away. Maria shut her eyes. She lay with Richard's arms around her, wishing she could go back to sleep. She kissed his shoulder. Across his chest there was a long scar. She drew her fingertip along it.

"What happened to you?"

"It looks worse than it was."

"Did they hurt you—the Saracens? When they took you prisoner."

He propped himself up on his elbow. "They dragged me around a little. I broke my hand, but that wasn't their fault."

"I prayed for you."

"Oh," he said, a fine sarcastic edge in his voice. "That must have been what saved me."

She turned her back on him and scrambled out of the bed. She went to the cupboard for her clothes. The room was full of drafts, and the floor chilled her feet. Shivering, she pulled on her shift and a gown and reached up behind her to free her hair. Richard shouted down the stairs for their breakfast. Half-dressed, he tramped around the room. She brought him a clean shirt.

"I've been making you shirts and coats all since Michaelmas."

"Good. That's one reason I'm here, all my clothes are falling apart." He pulled the shirt on over his head.

"You promised me you'd come," she said, "but I suppose that's a small thing in your mind."

"I could not come before. I said I would come when I could."

The door slammed open. Robert raced in laughing, Stephen behind him, and they leaped on Richard. He scooped them up, one under each arm. Maria opened the curtains on the bed and threw the covers back to air.

"Go on," Richard said to the boys. "Pester me after I have eaten. Go play with Bunny."

"Who is Bunny?" Robert asked blankly.

Richard chased him out. Maria went around the room picking up her sons' litter of clothes and stones and dirt. Richard put his coat on. She could not stay away from him. In spite of herself, she drifted over and stood with her hand on his arm. He kissed her forehead. The kitchen boy came in with their breakfast; they sat down to eat.

"I WOKE UP in the middle of the night and couldn't breathe," the cook said. He wheezed a little, to prove he was sick. "I thought the end had surely come. I have not slept the sleep of grace these past three nights, for fear of dying."

"Lobelia for that," Eleanor cried, without looking up from the pot she was stirring. "A good lobelia pack, and something after to get the phlegm up."

The cook sniffed. "God sent me this for my sins. I welcome it for my sins' sake."

Maria poured a measure of chopped nuts into the fruit boiling over the fire and took a wooden spoon to mix them in. Eleanor said. "All the same, a good pack of lobelia would do you no harm." She straightened, brushing her hair back with her forearm. Now that the rain had stopped, the kitchen was perceptibly brighter.

"Do you need help, Maria?"

"No—it has to cook a while." Maria hung up the spoon on the hearth. Sticky walnut syrup clung to her fingers. She yawned.

"My, you are sleepy, aren't you," Eleanor said sweetly. "I shouldn't wonder, I heard you tossing and turning all last night."

Maria gave her a black look, and Eleanor simpered. Stiff, Maria went across the kitchen to the door. Richard had brought his horse out into the ward. While he curried it and brushed it, a cluster of boys gathered to watch. Even the young Duke was there.

"Don't let the conserves burn," Eleanor called.

There was a pile of little cakes on the bench beside the door. Maria stuffed a dozen of them into her apron pockets and went out to the ward. The air was sweet from the rain. Puddles still shone clear on the ground around the gate. Eleanor called to her again. She shut the door between them with her heel.

Richard had the gray stallion's forehoof up on his thigh and was scraping caked mud and dung out of it with a hoofpick. The boys stood around him watching. The young Duke strained his neck to see. He leaned up against the wall near the horse's head, the wolfhound bitch sprawled comfortably in the sun a few feet away.

Maria gave out the sweet cakes. The children's hands thrust at her, dirty and grasping. The last grubby brown hand was Richard's. She went up to the gray stallion's head and patted its face.

Robert had the hoofpick. He was wrestling the horse's off-hind foot up into his lap. Richard came up beside her.

"What are you making? It smells good."

She said, "Conserves. This is a beautiful horse."

Robert stooped over the stallion's raised hoof. The horse turned its beautiful head to look and carefully straightened out its leg. Robert tumbled headlong. Richard laughed; the other boys laughed too. The horse snorted. Maria thought it looked pleased with itself.

"I can do it," the young Duke said. He pushed himself away from the wall and went around behind the horse. Taking the hoofpick from Robert, he bent over the horse's hindleg.

"Here," Richard said. "It's easier like this." While he showed the boy how to hold the stallion's hoof between his knees, Maria watched him closely. It was strange to find herself suddenly equipped with a husband. She had forgotten him; he was a stranger to her, more a stranger even than Fitz-Michael. The stallion turned its head to look back. She took hold of its halter. The horse snorted softly and lipped her hand, and she fed it half a sweet cake. Its face was wide between the large intelligent eyes. Its kindness amazed her, that it let the green boys handle it.

"The Saracens gave him to me," Richard said. He came up beside her again, patting the horse's shoulder. "He's too light to fight on, but he's a hell of a riding horse."

"The men who took you prisoner? Will they give you another?"

He rested his arm on the wall and let his weight slack against it. She put her hand flat on his chest. The young Duke set the stallion's hoof down and moved around to the other side.

"Maria," Eleanor cried, from the kitchen, "the conserves are burning."

Maria called "Take the pot off the fire."

"What are you doing?" Fitz-Michael shouted, and she jumped, but he was yelling at the young Duke. He strode into the midst of the children, took the boy by the ear, and dragged him off. "You stupid lout, are you a groom, now? Will you not learn who you are?"

The young Duke tore free. The wolfhound had come to her feet. She loped after him across the ward. Fitz-Michael marched stiff-necked toward the Tower. His servants were upstairs packing his baggage. As soon as his back was turned, the other boys knocked each other in the ribs and laughed and made faces at him. Richard spat.

"Tuppence all his horses have thrush, he's too high-born to pick their feet out."

Maria turned back to the gray stallion. "Will you get me a horse like this?"

"After I take Mana'a."

"When will that be?"

He shook his head. He leaned his back against the wall, his eyes on the door where Fitz-Michael had gone in. "Maybe never."

From the kitchen, Eleanor shrieked, "Maria!"

"I thought when I had the mountains I could cut off

Mana'a and starve them out," he said. "But they are bringing their supplies in through the harbor, and I can't stop them, I have no ships."

Maria scratched the stallion's forehead. She knew nothing about ships. She tried to imagine Mana'a's famous bay. "Blue as the bay of Marna," a song had said once. She thought of her own seacoast, the green water dancing with whitecaps, the breakers striped with foam; it seemed distant as another life, gone forever. Her mood darkened. Heavily she went down to the kitchen to help Eleanor.

FITZ-MICHAEL'S ESCORT waited on the road outside the gate. Pages led two saddled horses to the foot of the steps. Maria picked up Stephen to get him out of the way. Robert and the other children were upstairs, saying good-bye to the Duke. At the foot of the stair, Fitz-Michael and Richard stood side by side, ignoring each other.

Maria went up between them. "It's a fair day, my lord," she said to Fitz-Michael. "God willing, you'll have an easy journey."

"Away from you, my dear, is no easy journey." He smiled at her, standing overclose to her. Across her shoulder he and Richard exchanged needled looks. Maria murmured something. She enjoyed the friction between them; while she smiled at Fitz-Michael she leaned against Richard. Her husband growled in his throat and stepped away from her.

Fitz-Michael turned to his crop-eared bay horse. "If you will summon my nephew—"

Maria put Stephen on the steps and sent him up to fetch the young Duke. Richard walked around Fitz-Michael's horse, one hand on its black mane. "Remember what I told you touching the Archbishop."

Fitz-Michael's long upper lip drew back from his teeth. "I am not your emissary. Treat with him through your own means." Lifting his reins, he backed the horse rapidly away from Richard, who spat precisely between its forehoofs and stalked off. Maria followed him. While she crossed Fitz-Michael's path, she caught his eye, and he smiled at her.

The young Duke ran down the steps, half a dozen other boys yelling at his heels. Richard boosted him up into his saddle. The wolfhound bitch had followed the boy up to his horse. She whined, and the Duke slapped his thigh and leaned down. Standing on her hindlegs, she laid her forepaws and her head against his knee. He scratched behind her ears.

"Good-bye, Lupa," he said softly. "Good-bye."

Richard spoke to the dog, which sat down beside him. He moved the Duke's leg forward in the stirrup and yanked his girths tight.

"Take her with you," he said. He slapped the Duke's gelding on the rump and walked off. His eyes went to Fitz-Michael. "You need all the friends you can make."

Fitz-Michael's face darkened, but he said nothing. The young Duke twisted in his saddle to watch Richard go off across the courtyard. Fitz-Michael shouted to him, and he lifted his reins. The wolfhound lay down next to Maria. Her ears drooped. The Duke whistled to her. Fitz-Michael rode out the gate, and the boy followed, but in the gateway he stopped and called, "Lupa! Come!"

The wolfhound bolted after him. Richard had disappeared. Maria went to the gate and stood watching the train of Fitz-Michael's servants and horses go on down the road, the wolfhound loping after them. She called to the porter to shut the gate and went up into the Tower.

Eleanor was sitting before the loom, threading bobbins. Maria moved her stool closer. Picking up the basket onto her lap, she sorted through it for the color she needed. "Thank God they are finally gone," Eleanor said. "That dreadful man and that sullen little boy. The cook told me he does not know how we will live through Christmas, we have so little store."

Maria leaned forward to do the next row of Charlemagne's crown. They had used up most of the wheat she had begged from her home castle. They had no meat left but salted pork. "We shall fast. I've always wanted to make a good fast." She changed the thread to weave a jewel.

"There is nothing to be had in the town. No one in the whole of Birnia has any grain. I foresee a hard winter for us all." Eleanor crossed herself.

"Telling the future is a sin, Eleanor. Shame. Have you decided yet about the trees?"

Eleanor had spoken of making the leaves of the trees silver and gold. She canted her head to squint at the tapestry. "I don't know. We have such a scarcity of gold thread."

Richard came into the hall. Maria watched him cross the room. She remembered lying with him and quickly turned her eyes back to the tapestry. "I doubt if it would add enough to justify using it."

Richard came up behind them. "I want to see this friend of yours," he said. "This ostler."

Maria stood up. "Now? Do you want to go to the town? Eleanor, bring me my cloak."

Eleanor climbed around the loom, the spinning wheel, and the baskets of mending. Planting his foot on her stool, Richard stared at the tapestry.

"You are getting better at it—which is your work?"

"I do the people, and Eleanor does the animals and the trees. See Roland?" She had made Roland full-face, in the space below Charlemagne, his milk-white cheeks framed in symmetrical golden curls. "And there is Oliver."

"When you were in Iste, did you see the inside of the Jewish temple?"

Maria crossed herself. "Holy Mother. What would I do there?"

"They have pictures on the walls of the meeting room. This is good, Maria, for you, but the people on the walls of the Jews' place might be alive."

A flood of hot shame took her. She threw the bobbins down from her lap and stamped out into the middle of the hall. Eleanor came in, and their eyes met; without a word spoken, their feelings passed between them. Maria turned so that Eleanor could put the cloak around her shoulders. She went out the door and down the steps into the ward.

Their horses were already being brought up. Her black mare, a hand shorter than the dark gray stallion, waited in the shade of the wall. The children were building a snow fort in the corner. Robert scrambled over the wall of packed snow and raced toward her.

"Mama—Mama—can I go, too? Let me go, Mama."

212

Maria caught his hands and swung him around. "Get your horse."

He dashed across the ward toward the stable. The other children still scrambled and tumbled over the snow fort. Stephen had a board in his hands and was hacking furiously at the wall. His scarf hung down to his knees, and his coat was ripped.

Richard came up to Maria's elbow. "What's the matter with you? I said I liked your work, but if you saw the pictures at Iste you would do better."

"I don't want to do better." She went away from him, toward her horse. "I want to do what I am doing."

"You certainly do that."

Maria whirled toward him; he dodged between the two horses, laughing at her. She snatched her reins up and mounted without help, throwing her heavy skirts across the cantle of the saddle. Richard led the gray stallion away from her. He vaulted up onto its back, kicked his feet into the stirrups, and calling for a groom sent him up into the Tower for his sword.

Maria rode to the gate, simmering. She knew she should not be in such a humor simply because he had spoken carelessly of her tapestry—he had even admitted it was good. He had attacked her for the sake of Jews. Her mare danced sideways, mouthing the bit. The groom brought Richard his sword, Robert rode out of the stable, and they trotted out the gate.

For late autumn, the day was warm. The wind from the river blew into their faces. In the distance, the thatched roofs of the town of Birnia rose above its log wall. Lined with oak trees, the road curved across the easiest slope, but Richard led them straight down the hillside and across the fields, his horse at a driving gallop. The hard pace chased away Maria's anger at him. Chirping to her mare, she raced up beside him, the wind rushing in her face.

When they came again to the road, they drew rein to wait for Robert, whose palfrey could not keep up with his parents' horses. Maria ran her eyes over the dark gray stallion. It scarcely seemed to breathe hard after the stiff gallop; she was struck again by its kind disposition and its look of intelligence.

"That's the finest horse I've ever seen."

Richard leaned down and patted the horse's dappled neck. Robert reached them, breathless from kicking on his gelding, and they started along the road, the boy between them. The gate was open. It was the market day: the street was dusty with the passage of many people. They cut down the main street of the town, going toward the inn. Around them, people turned and stared at Richard. A rustle of excited talk started up. A woman called a greeting to Maria; she waved. They came to the inn gate.

Before she saw Fulbert, she was almost on top of him, and he was grabbing for her bridle. His face was set with fury. She realized he had been boiling since she laughed at him in front of everybody. He seized her mare by the rein and Maria by the skirt and said, "Woman, you owe me money," and looked past her and saw Richard.

Fulbert's handsome face turned gray. Richard said, "Butcher, you take your hands off my wife," and he sprang away from her. Maria laughed. She watched Fulbert race off through the small crowd gathering to gawk at Richard. With her heel she urged the mare into the inn yard.

Richard came hot after her. 'What was that about?" ⁻

Maria dismounted. The broad inn yard was empty. The ostler's daughter had come out on the porch. The ostler himself was hurrying out to take their horses. Richard jumped down from his saddle.

"What did he mean, you owe him money?"

"It's a very long story, Richard, I'll tell you when we get home."

She met his gray eyes; his stare was intense with curiosity. The ostler reached them. She turned to him.

"Ermio, my lord husband wants to talk to you."

The ostler took her reins. "My lord, I am your servant."

Richard came hos after her. "What was that about?" the ostler, thrust his reins into the man's hand, and said, "I'll be inside, when you put them up." He started across the yard toward the porch. Robert leaped around him, laughing. Maria glanced at the gate. It was packed with

214

townsfolk straining to look over the heads of the people in front of them, to see Richard. She went on toward the inn, after him. Thinking of Fulbert, she laughed.

EVERY DAY, as he had done in Iste, Richard went into Birnia and talked with the ostler and the several elders of the town, having the customs written out and changing them when it pleased him. That made the townspeople angry. Many came and told Maria so at length whenever she went into Birnia. Every few days messengers came from the army laying siege to Mana'a, from Iste, from the East Tower and the Black Tower and her own castle, which now they had taken to calling that: Castelmaria. He listened to trials of justice and sent men here and there to do his business; Maria had never seen a knight work so hard.

She sat with the ostler's daughter one day in the kitchen. Richard had said that the ostler was of more use to him than any other man in Birnia. She told his daughter so.

"Oh, well," the woman said. She ate a morsel of bread and conserves. "You know what men will do—they cannot tend themselves, but they must tend to everybody else's doings. Spread the sweet thick, dear, we are very short of bread these days."

Maria dipped the knife into the jar of conserves. The ostler's daughter was kneading bread. Her arms were white as the dough. "My father talks much of your husband. In fact, no one talks anything else, he has vexed nearly everybody in the town, now, and is starting on his second round." She shrugged. "I like his look well, myself. I like a sober look in a man."

Halfway down, the bread and conserves stuck in Maria's throat and choked her when she laughed. She gulped it down. "Richard? Sober?"

"I was married to one of the other sort—the saints witness me, no wife was ever more tried than I, and thankful he went young to Hell."

Maria crossed herself. The ostler's daughter slugged at the lump of dough with both hands. Maria said, "God save his soul."

215

"God save his soul. I prayed to Saint Anne to make me a widow. The day I stood at his graveside was the happiest of my life."

"God send you a saint for your second husband."

"A saint! God send me a young husband, and a lively, that's what I want." The corners of her mouth tucked under plump cheeks. "But sober in his looks."

After the blight and the plundering of Count Theobald's men, the harvest had been sparse all over Birnia. Advent began. Maria put the cook to mixing bean flour half and half with the wheat flour, which was already half rye. Everyone was starving, and winter hardly upon them. People even went to Richard and complained, and to her surprise he summoned Father Gibertetto and got the old priest to give away all the grain and peas the parish had taken in revenues.

He did not ask her again about Fulbert. She thought he had forgotten, until one day just before Christmas, while they were sitting at the table after dinner, he said, "Give me one reason why I should not kill that damned butcher."

She looked off down the hall. It was snowing and the children were all out playing in it. Save for a few servants, the hall was empty. She wondered how much he had found out, whom he had asked. She faced him again.

"Are you going back to Mana'a?"

He nodded.

"Then I will keep Fulbert. I may need him."

He smiled at her. His face was unreadable. "Fulbert doesn't like you now, Maria. He thinks you cheated on him."

Maria grunted. "He asked to be cheated. When are you going?"

"After Christmas."

She put her hand to her face. Christmas was only days away. She had gotten used to having him there. Beside her, he drew an open loop with his finger on the tabletop. Slowly he traced a line across its mouth. He said, "I'm taking Robert with me."

She stared at him. She said, tautly, "Richard."

He shook his head at her. "Don't argue with me."

Maria turned her face away.

XXII

❧

THREE DAYS AFTER CHRISTMAS, RICHARD AND ROBERT rode off. Maria was certain now she was with child, so she felt easier about giving up her elder son, but the days after they left seemed empty and endlessly long. Eleanor wept quietly in the hall; Maria did not work at all on the tapestry.

Several wagonloads of grain came from Iste, heavily guarded. The grain belonged to five merchants of Iste, who came up to the Tower to meet her and present to her an ornate charter, sealed in red wax, which Maria could not read. The merchants' leader, a large smooth man named Manofredo, read it to her. It was a charter permitting the merchants to hold a market place in Birnia to sell their grain.

Maria took the charter into her hands and looked at it. She fingered the seal, which made the piece of vellum look important, and wondered what they had given Richard in payment for it. They filled her storeroom up with grain—grandly they waved away her offer of money for it, so clearly that was part of the price. She did not think it was all. The rest of their store they took to Birnia.

Maria went down to watch the market place. The noise of the crowd hurt her ears, and the crush in the streets and the square made her uneasy. While she was there, the merchants of Iste sold the grain at reasonable cost, but when she left, her spies told her, they began to demand as much as 50 pence a measure. Many people, especially the strangers from the forest and the fen country, were breaking into houses and robbing and building fires in dangerous places. Maria sent Jean with ten knights to keep order in town, and the next morning, Eleanor and Stephen following in the cart, she went down herself.

All around the town, outside the wall, serfs from outlying places had made their camps. They had no beasts and most of them wore only shirts and crouched over their fires to keep warm. The day was bitter cold. Clouds gray as iron filled the sky. Even in her fur-lined cloak Maria was shivering. The colorless faces of the serfs frightened her: even the children looked as if they might kill for a bite of bread.

She passed through the gate and came into the street, the cart rumbling along after her. Talking, packed together to keep warm, the people lined each side of the street, and some had clubs in their hands, and some had scythes and hoes. No one let out a cheer when they saw her, most of them watched her in a cold silence.

Just before the market place, she met Jean in the street, riding his old black horse and carrying a lance. He had spread his knights all around the town. Even a mob of townspeople would hardly attack a mounted knight. He rode his horse up shoulder to shoulder with hers.

"Manofredo has locked up the grain," he said. "He's saying he'll take it back to Iste unless he can sell it in safety."

Maria rubbed her nose with her forefinger. "Maybe we should let them go. How many men do they have?"

"Well, I count eighteen men-at-arms, and four knights, but that's not saying there's no more."

Maria frowned. There was no way to steal the grain, either here or on its way back to Iste. "Go bid them meet me in the market place—the merchants. Manofredo. Father Gibertetto!"

She rode forward, waving to the priest. He came half-running up the street, his elbows at an awkward angle, and his black gown fluttering. The street lay in silence, but as the priest reached her stirrup, a man somewhere behind her shouted, "Take her! Hold her hostage!"

Maria glanced around. Jean was gone. She bent down over her knee to hear the old priest. He clutched her saddle for support; his breath blew in a plume before his lips. "The butcher—Fulbert—" He gasped for breath, swal-

218

lowed, and went on. "He has told them Dragon means to bleed them white. They are even accusing him of spoiling the harvest. They want to call Theobald in—they say he is our rightful lord."

"Seize Maria," the voice behind her yelled. "They'll give us bread if we take her hostage."

There was a rumble from the crowd, and glancing over her shoulder she saw, here and there, a man with a weapon step forward toward her. In the cart Eleanor let out a low wail. Stephen stood and put his arm around the woman's shoulders. Maria spun her mare.

"Wait," she shouted. "Listen to me before you do anything. I am your lady—I am here to help you. If you lay hands on me, you'll get nothing at all." She rode her horse at a fast walk around the cart, past Eleanor's white face and Stephen's eyes. All around them were the mobbed faces of the crowd and the scythes sharp as sawgrass. "I'm starving, too, I and my children. Besides, if you touch me, Dragon will never sleep until he spikes your heads on the walls of your own town. Trust me—I'll take care of you, I have before."

Their bulled shoulders loosened, and the crowd stirred, here and there a man nodding. "Save us, Maria," a woman called, and a feeble cheer went up.

In the back of the crowd, a woman climbed up on a barrel and shouted, "Don't listen to her—she's Dragon's wife, she lies, the witch!"

Maria kept her mare walking swiftly around before the crowd. Among the brown faces of strangers she saw people she knew. In a voice pitched to reach them, she said, "You people from Birnia town—you know me. Why are you letting these people come here from all the wild places and stir up trouble for me? You know who will suffer for it in the end."

"Maria," a man called, and the cheer came back, stronger now. The woman who had shouted against her climbed down off the barrel and disappeared in the crowd.

"I'm going to talk to the merchants," Maria called. "Go home—stay here—do what you will, but let me talk to them. I promise you will eat as soon and as well as I

219

do." She turned her mare, and with the carthorse loping on before her she followed Stephen and Eleanor at a fast trot down the street to the market place.

Jean rode up to join her. In the wide treeless square, people roamed about by threes and fours. The merchants and their soldiers were gathered in a clump before the church. Maria's knights rode in a single file out of another street and came to follow her. Before the north gate, across the square from the church, another mob was swarming restlessly along the foot of the wall. With Jean half a length behind her, Maria rode up to the merchants, who were all on foot.

Manofredo in a splendid marten's fur cloak held up both hands toward her. "My lady, I absolve you of all blame for the way we have been—"

"Who are you to come in here and make trouble with my people?" she said, and when he started, his eyes round as balls, she bound her face into a terrific frown. "You've made a fine mess here for me—what will you do to help me clean it up?"

"My lady! I assure you, we had nothing to do—there is treason here! What these people are saying about our most excellent prince—"

Maria said, "They are starving. And if there is treason here, it's against me, and I will deal with it, not you. I'll buy all your grain at a penny a measure."

Manofredo's voice failed in his throat. He gobbled at her, horrified. Maria looked around her. The other merchants were staring at her, their mouths slack. "How much grain do you have?"

"My lady!"

Maria crooked her finger at the knights. "Surround these men. This one must have the keys to the storeroom, get them and give them to me."

"My lady!"

The knights wheeled their horses up around the merchants. Most of them carried their lances on their saddles. The merchants' men-at-arms stood fast by the townsmen, but their four knights, all Normans, obeyed Maria.

"How much grain do you have?"

"My lady, at a penny a measure we will lose money. We could sell at that price in Iste."

"Then go back to Iste," she said. "I will keep the grain and send you whatever my counting comes to."

The merchants' frightened, angry faces tilted up toward her. She looked steadily at each of them; she made her expression like a wall, to cow them. One by one, they turned to Manofredo.

"We have no choice, then," the merchant said. "But you may be sure we will take this to my lord Roger's court in Iste."

Maria shrugged. "Do as you please." Relaxing, she stretched her neck to look around the market place. "Jean," she called, "get these people out of the streets. Tell them if they are not indoors or outside the gates by noon, you will chase them out."

Jean shouted orders, and the knights reined their horses around and galloped off. Manofredo folded his arms over his elegant fur-covered stomach.

"We have Christian justice now in Iste," he said. "You will see that we are people of consequence."

Maria wheeled her mare away. Jean came up to her; the wind lifted his long gray hair. "My lord Dragon isn't going to like this."

"That's not your concern." She looked around the market place for Father Gibertetto. Stephen was trying to climb out of the cart, and she went over and took him up before her on the mare.

"Maria," Eleanor said. "Maria, what's going to happen to us?"

The ostler was coming, followed by his servants, all in arms. Maria called him over. While he crossed the market place toward her, she thought of Fulbert.

"Jean," she called.

The knight pressed his horse sideways toward her. "My lady."

"The butcher. He's behind this, most of it. Will you do something about him?"

Jean smiled at her. "My lady." Drawing his sword, he rode off toward Fulbert's shambles. The ostler was at her stirrup. Maria dismounted to arrange with him the distribution of grain to the crowd.

IN SPITE OF THAT, most people went hungry that winter. Maria had to give away much of her own store. Being with child, she suffered the famine badly, lost two teeth from the back of her lower jaw, and spent many days in bed.

They heard in the middle of Lent that Richard had forged a great chain in Iste and borne it by eighteen wagons over the mountains to Mana'a. This chain he stretched across the mouth of the bay to seal it off against ships. The serfs of Birnia got in their winter crop, and the famine eased. Many had died, especially old people. Clouds blanketed the sky at Easter, an evil omen.

Fattening on the spring honey and the blancmange she always craved when she was pregnant, Maria grew stronger and happier. In the summer, together with a large company from the town of Birnia, she made a pilgrimage to the Shrine of the Virgin, walking most of the way, although she was great-bellied with child. On the way back, she met a messenger galloping along the road from Birnia.

Before he even reined up his horse, he was shouting his news. Mana'a had surrendered. The Emir of the city had done homage to Richard. The news was to be announced in every church in the demesne, and everyone was to celebrate the rescue of the city from the hands of the Saracens, the victory of the Crusade, the triumph of Christ. As soon after the baby was born as she could safely travel, Maria was to come to Mana'a.

She sent the messenger on to the shrine and went herself to the church of Birnia, prayed, and helped Father Gibertetto with the proclamation and the sermon. The people of the town were still simmering over the incident of the grain merchants of Iste, and to put them in a good humor for celebrating, Maria gave the ostler enough wine to get the whole country drunk. That night, while bonfires glowed all over the countryside, and the people of the castle drank and danced and fornicated in the ward, she bore a baby girl.

That she took for a sign, that God should have finally given her another daughter. She made several presents to the Shrine of the Virgin and named the baby Judith. But everybody instantly called her Jilly.

Eleanor carried the baby all over the castle, showing her off and letting the other women make much of her. Maria had forgotten how tiny babies were. With Stephen beside her she sat in her bed watching the creature twitch her wrinkled hands and struggle her head up off the coverlet.

"Ugh," Stephen said, at last.

"Yes. I know." She gathered the baby up. "But she will be beautiful, someday." She kissed Stephen's forehead. "You looked just as bad, and now see how handsome you are."

Stephen squirmed over to lean against her shoulder. "Did Robert look like that?"

"Yes. And Ceci, too."

Eleanor came in with a stack of clean swaddlings. She sailed around the room straightening up the mess. "Stephen, you are a big boy now, you must not sit on Mama's bed."

"Stay," Maria said.

"You are babying him," Eleanor said, in a nerve-jangling singsong. "His father will not like that. Come, Stephen. Leave Mama alone with the new baby."

Stephen stuck out his tongue at her. Eleanor grunted and carried a pail of dirty napkins down the stairs.

"Who was that?" Stephen said. "Who you said before. Ceci."

Maria gave the baby her breast, Inexpert, the little girl fumbled away the nipple and let out a squall. "Ceci was your first sister, whom God took to Heaven, before you were born." She held her breast in the baby's mouth. Soft as air, the baby's lips sucked, and deep in her body something tightened pleasantly.

"Why?" Stephen asked.

"I don't know."

"Were you sad?" He lay down with his back across her legs, his arms stretched out, and played with Jilly's foot.

"Yes. I'm still sad, in fact."

"God won't take me, will he?"

The baby was sucking hard now. Maria smoothed down the tendrils of waxy hair clinging to her skull. Patches of fur grew almost invisibly on the baby's back and shoulders. She said, "I hope he doesn't, because I

223

would miss you so much, but if God should take you, it would be to Heaven, where God rules, which is better than any place in the world."

"Even Mana'a?"

Maria laughed. "Even Mana'a." Her laughter had startled the baby; she cried. The tiny piping made Maria laugh again, fascinated. Stephen said, "Do you love Jilly as well as you love Robert?"

Maria nodded. There was a long pause.

"Do you love her as well as you love me?"

"I love you all."

"Exactly the same?"

"Not in the same way." She touched his hair. "I love Robert because he is Robert, and you because you are you, Stephen Fitz-Richard. And Jilly because she is Judith."

"Judith," Stephen said. He rolled onto his stomach and smiled up at her. "I love the baby too. When I grow up I'm going to marry her."

"I thought you were going to marry me."

"You already have a knight." He took the baby's foot in his hand. "Jilly. Judith. Jilly. Jilly."

XXIII

AFTER THE NEXT QUARTERDAY, WHICH WAS MICHAELMAS, she put Eleanor and her children in the cart and started off to Mana'a. First she went to Castelmaria, her home, where she met William on his way back to Birnia. For two days she lingered there, talking to him about Birnia. To be back in the place where she had been born and grown up made her content.

"Tell me about Richard," she said to William. "Was he angry with me for robbing the merchants of Iste?"

William's face altered subtly. His eyes buried themselves in wrinkles. "I will leave him to tell you that. I think you did right—I know those people, especially Fulbert, and of course you had only a few knights."

"Then he was angry."

"Oh, he said a lot of remarkable things. You know how Richard talks. Did you do something about Fulbert?"

"He is dead."

William smiled a slow, wide smile. "I told him you would."

At dawn, after Eleanor swaddled herself and the baby in acres of coats and Maria put Stephen twice into the cart, William himself led her black mare from the stable. He was taking 120 knights back with him to Birnia and did not grudge her the six men of her escort, now lined up in a column on the road. He helped her into the saddle. With one hand on her mare's withers, he looked up at her, his jowly face earnest.

"Maria, my darling, whatever happens to you in Mana'a, you can always depend on me—I was like Roger, I never believed you would hold Birnia, but you did." He took her hand, turned her palm up, and kissed it. Standing back, he lifted his arm in a salute and walked away. Maria with a surge of affection watched him go to the gate. She folded her fingers over his awkward tender kiss. When they rode out the gate, he waved to her.

Their way led across the rounded, pine-covered foothills to the south. Stephen made Maria let him ride in front of her on her horse. The steaming heat of the early autumn raised a putrid, insect-ridden miasma from the marshes that lay in the pockets between the hills. Eleanor covered the baby's face with her blanket. Once, halfway to the high road, they passed a train of serfs and their donkeys, carrying earth in baskets to the swamp. Maria could not guess why they chose to settle here. She slapped at the insects that hung whirring around her ears and eyes. Half-wild with bites, her mare lunged and bucked and pawed at her underside.

They reached the high road. Now, massed shoulder to

225

shoulder, the mountains heaved up before them, their lower slopes still summer-green. Eagles floated in the air above the naked black crags. On the third day, after they had left Castelmaria, they reached the Black Tower, built on a peak above a narrow pass, where the German knight Welf Blackjacket had already taken command.

From a window on the staircase, Maria looked out across the heartland of the mountains. Vast and cold, the toothed ridges rolled off one beyond another into the opaline horizon.

"Do you like our mountains?" Welf Blackjacket said, behind her.

Maria turned toward him. She had not heard him come up the stairs. "Yes. I have never been here before." She followed him up to the hall of the castle. "Did Richard build this place?"

The German knight looked over his shoulder at her. "Part of it. I built some. Saracens built some. Come here." He went to the window opposite them. The hall was bleak as a cave; she wondered why he kept it here, on the top story of the castle, until she came up to the window.

He made room for her so that she could see. The sun was dropping down behind the mountains. The sky streamed with oblique light. Before them, the peak rose into a spur of rock and fell away in a sweeping curve across the distance, sheltering the pass below. The sundown light began to blaze on the peaks. The lower slopes darkened and disappeared into the night. While the dark crept upward, the light on the rock spur passed from gold to fading red to purple, until at last the black night swallowed it all.

"The Saracens call the mountains *The Stepmother*," Welf Blackjacket said. "Because they are so beautiful and so cruel."

Behind him, a knight was lighting the torches on the walls. Welf stood staring out the window, a slight dark man in a black leather coat studded with silver. Maria hugged her arms against the sudden icy temper in the air. The tone of his voice piqued her. She said, "Were there mountains where you came from?"

"Not like these." He faced her, smiling. "Everyone thinks I am mad, because I love these mountains—he wanted me to stay in Mana'a but I could not." A man brought him a long pole with a hook on the end, and the German knight reached out the window and drew the shutter closed. "Come sit down, girl."

Maria went after him toward the hearth. Her muscles ached; all day long they had chased Stephen up and down the slopes of the highway. She said, "Even William says how wonderful Mana'a is."

"Yes, as I told you, everybody thinks I am mad."

She laughed. They sat down at the table, their backs to the fire. Eleanor's complaining voice reached them from the stairs, where she had stopped to rest her legs. Welf leaned his forearms on the table.

"This is the castle he was trying to repair when you were building that church." He clasped his hands together before him; his eyes poked at her. "That was very interesting—I had never seen Richard d'Alene successfully withstood before."

"He knew I was right," she said.

"Gripe doesn't care very much about right and wrong."

"Gripe?"

Welf smiled at her. "That's what we used to call him—before he got the other name. Gripe. Because he never lets go."

Eleanor sank down beside Maria. "God keep me, my legs are broken." She settled herself on the uncushioned wooden bench.

"You knew him when he first came here, didn't you?" Maria said to Welf.

"I came south with him. Ponce Rachet and his brother and I and Richard d'Alene, we came all together to join your father, back the year the village burned down." He fingered his chin. Around his neck on a chain hung a black wooden cross. "No one would have chosen Gripe out of us. He is not the bravest of us, or the most high-born, and God knows his piety is very lean."

"No," Maria said. "Richard will not go to Heaven."

His men brought their supper in on wooden platters: a fat roast, bread, an apple pudding studded with raisins. Maria kept her eyes on the slight dark man beside her. She said, "My lord, why did you come back here?"

227

The German knight took his dagger from his belt to cut his meat. The men who had served them sat down at the table, side by side with him. Many bowed their heads to pray before they ate.

"I have no wish to dance in an orbit around anybody," Welf said at last. "I want an epicycle of my own, however small." He started to eat; his knife clattered on the plate. Outside, a high wind had sprung up. Maria ate greedily, her appetite whetted by the cold. The German knight said nothing more. After supper, she went to bed.

THE NEXT MORNING, the road bore them steadily higher, running along the spine of the mountains. Here it was already winter. The raw wind snapped at them and chilled their faces, and snow covered the slopes. Maria began to mark how hard Richard and his knights had fought here. Twice in one day, she rode under the ruins of strongholds raised on peaks of rock so barren only eagles nested there now. Beneath one of them lay a valley charred black from end to end, like a burned-out Hell.

Along the road, in the trees, skeletons hung in chains. Once they passed a huge flat mound of dirt beside the road, with a great cross standing at one end, and a fence of Norman swords thrust into the ground around it. Stephen, standing in the cart, counted forty-three.

Maria knew it was a grave. It moved her almost to tears; she could not tell why. Eleanor muttered of Devil's work. After that, the road traveled steadily downward. Often they saw riders in the distance, up on the slopes, watching them. At last they came out of the mountains. They had gone from fall to winter to summer again, all in eleven days: in these low foothills, flowers bloomed, trees were green, and even the air smelled sweet.

In the far distance the sea ran white along the shore. Laughing with excitement, they hurried toward it. On either side of the road, there were orchards full of trees. A delicious fragrance came from them, and the trees were heavy with golden fruit. Even Eleanor murmured at the odor, and Maria made them stop and bring her some of the fruit, but the hard little yellow globes were too sour to eat.

In the late afternoon they reached the sea. The road ran along the foot of a tall dirt cliff, combed and rutted by the weather. Saracen trees cluttered the top: scaly stalks topped with clumps of leaves like huge green feathers.

On their right the bay spread out before them. Stephen bounded out of the wagon and ran through the salt grass toward the beach, ignoring Eleanor's angry hail. Maria had just finished feeding Jilly. She laid the baby against her shoulder and patted her back. Inland on the road, the cliff rose like a wall. People walked on top of it. She stood on the wagon seat, looking for her son. Birds dipped and sailed over the dark blue water of the bay. Smaller birds ran back and forth along the beach after the waves.

Stephen was only a speck racing along the sand. Beyond him, on the shore, lay a mass of wreckage. Maria put her face to the wind and breathed of the salt-charged air.

"Maria," Eleanor said. She tugged at Maria's skirt. "You'll fall. You'll drop the baby."

Maria thrust Jilly into the other woman's hands. Sitting down, she pulled off her shoes. "Stephen! Stephen, wait for me." She leaped down from the wagon and ran through the jagged grass onto the beach.

Screaming with pleasure, Stephen was chasing the breakers. Tiny brown birds raced away from him over the wet sand. He had lost one of his shoes in the ruck of sea-weed and shells at the high-tide line. Maria stopped to get it.

"Stephen!"

Far out on the bay, there were Saracen boats, their triangular sails full with the wind, pretty as birds. Maria followed her son down the beach. Tendrils of her hair escaped from her coif and stuck to her cheeks. Her lips tasted salt. She strode out, stretching her limbs, her hair flying out behind her.

"Mama," Stephen shouted. He had reached the heap of wreckage and was climbing on it. "Look at this. It's some kind of boat."

Maria ran after him, walked to catch her breath, and broke into a run again. Drawn up on the sand was a rank of wooden barges, crusted with dead weed and scale.

When she climbed up onto the first, she saw that there were fifty or more of them, pulled up on the sand, joined by a chain whose links were as wide as her waist.

"What is it?" Stephen leaped toward her along the wrecked barges.

"The chain for the mouth of the harbor." She bent to put her hands on the link nearest her. Hot from the sun, it would not budge even when she threw her whole strength against it. She stood up, wiping the rust from the palms of her hands.

"Someone is coming," Stephen said.

Maria straightened. A line of horsemen filed down the cliff. Two of the riders had left the road and were galloping toward her through the stalky grass. Even from here, she could see the leader's flamboyant hair. She flung up her arm.

"Roger!"

He saluted her, reined his horse in, and jumped down from his saddle. "My sister." With his hands on her waist, he lifted her down from the barge. His smile flashed; his handsome face was vivid. "Sweetness," he said, "how pretty you are now." He hugged her. When she innocently raised her head he kissed her mouth hard. His tongue stabbed into her throat. She stepped back, unnerved, and he turned to Stephen.

Rubbing her mouth, Maria looked at the other rider, who was just reining up. It was Robert. She ran to meet him. He dismounted and stood before his horse, and from the stiff way he stood she knew she should not kiss him. He stood almost to her shoulder. "Robert. You're so tall."

In his tanned face his eyes were blue as the bay of Marna. He said formally, "Mother, I am very glad to see you again—and my brother—" He broke, he rushed into her arms, and she hugged him and they both wept. She kissed his hair.

"Richard sent us to meet you," Roger called. He stood behind Stephen, his hands on the boy's shoulders. "He has important work to do. Something with the old Emir." Lifting his arm, he called out in the sharp-edged tongue of the Saracens. "Robert, go get your mother's horse."

Robert leaped back into his saddle and galloped away.

Roger came up beside Maria. He gave her a long oblique look, smiling. She moved a step off from him.

"Roger. You shouldn't have done that." She touched her mouth.

"Maria," he said, "you have owed me that kiss since Iste."

"I suppose I should be flattered. You are a hero now, I guess—even in Birnia they talk about you."

"Oh, as far away as all that? We are great men now, sweetheart. We have already had a spokesman from the Pope to visit."

Maria's mouth fell open. "From the Pope? From Rome?"

A Saracen was riding up from the road, leading her mare by the reins. Robert rode to meet him, and they galloped toward her. Roger said, "Yes. From Rome. You cannot tell, these days, but I think we got the honest Pope."

"What did he say?"

Robert and the Saracen reached her. She took her mare's reins. Roger lifted her up into the saddle. The Saracen was watching her. Roger said, "Ismael, this is my brother's wife."

The Saracen did not bow. Under his headcloth, his face was dark and lean; he was young enough to be beardless. Uncertain, she smiled at him and he smiled back enormously, his teeth white as a cat's. Roger spoke to him in a clatter of Saracen.

"Stephen, you ride with Ismael. He is your father's friend."

Stephen had been standing behind Roger. He went forward, up between his mother's horse and the Saracen's. He gave her a quick worried glance. The Saracen boy helped him climb up behind him on his sock-footed chestnut mare. Maria's eyes caught on the tassels and jewels of the Saracen bridle. She reined her horse around.

They cantered across the sandy grass to the road. Maria waved to Eleanor, in the wagon. The baby would not mind if she saw Richard now or later. She turned her mare toward the city and urged her into a gallop. Roger came up beside her. Beyond him, supple as a birch, Robert rode his horse along the edge of the sand.

"He rides like Richard," she said.

Robert puffed himself up. Roger smiled. "We have been teaching him. He goes all over with us. When we stormed the citadel of Mana'a, he was there."

Maria's stomach contracted. "I thought the place surrendered—did you have to storm it?"

"Just the one citadel. That convinced the others to give up." He pointed ahead of them. "Look."

They were riding up the steep road to the top of the cliff. As she reached the height, Mana'a appeared before her. Blazing white in the sunlight, the spires and walls of the city spread across the far edge of the bay and back toward the mountains. Its sprawling outskirts covered the entire end of the plain. Its towers soared up above the thick fringe of Saracen trees, making dwarves of the people who hurried along the road at the foot of the wall.

Maria glanced at Stephen. One hand tight on the cantle of the saddle, he was leaning around Ismael to see ahead. Her eyes fastened again on the Saracen. Against her will she remembered the men who had raped and murdered Adela. Of course he would have been only a baby then. Ismael. She looked ahead toward the city again.

Roger veered toward her. "It took us ten days to sack it, Maria. There was even a harem. It was a feast."

Ismael had overheard. She caught the resentful flash of his black eyes. So he was not Roger's friend. She said, "Is the Pope's man still here?"

"No. Richard tired of feeding him," he said. "You must teach Richard manners, he still acts like a robber." Looking beyond her, he spoke to Ismael. His glance shortened again to meet hers. "I told him you can teach Richard anything." He smiled seraphically.

Maria made a noncommittal sound in her throat. The city gate loomed before them, three stories high. Richard's white dragon banner flew from the peak, rustling in the breeze off the bay. She and Eleanor had made the banner for him in Iste. They trotted through the arch of the gate. The horses' hoofs clattered in the narrow way.

Robert thrust his horse up between Maria and Roger. "There are six gates," he said. "I've ridden both ways through every one. This one is called the Gate of the

Mosque. That's because there's a mosque over there. A mosque is a Saracen church."

They rode at a jog through a paved square, past a fountain and a little market. Robert supplied a stream of information about this and other wonders that they passed. Stephen, his cheeks apple-red, looked all around. He rode straight as a little king behind Ismael's saddle. Ismael turned his deer-eyes on her.

"Good boy," he said, pointing to Robert, and nodded, and jerked his thumb over his shoulder at Stephen. "Good boy."

"Yes," she said. "Thank you." She had never talked to a Saracen before; it confused her to try. The bay mare jogged forward into the noise and smells and traffic of the street.

She had thought it would be like Iste, like her village at Castelmaria, only bigger. Now she saw that this place was utterly different, and she grew frightened. The voices that struck her ears spoke a language that had always belonged to her enemies, their faces were enemies to her. The men wore sweeping white robes like Ismael's. Even the beggars went armed. The few women she noticed were veiled in black shawls. She began to feel exposed. They all seemed to be staring at her, but when she forced herself to look calmly around they were hurrying incuriously along on their own business.

"Mama!"

She admired the things they pointed out to her, spoke, and pretended not to be frightened; it was silly to be frightened, here Richard was the master. The city's beauty itself unnerved her, the sweep of white walls and towers, the streets wide and paved with stone, and everywhere, flowers and trees, vivid color against the white, and the high shrill voices of Saracens.

They came at last to a high wall with a double gate. A Saracen porter came to raise the iron grid to let them pass through. Two knights sat dicing in the space between the two gates. They called to Roger, who waved.

They rode on through gardens massed with blooming trees. Ahead, on a rise, three round towers stood. Roger led them to the right, up a short slope covered with fir trees, and between two of the towers into a ward. They reined in their horses. Maria braced her hands on her saddle pommel. Around her, covered with green vines, a low wall ran, connecting the three towers. She dismounted; instantly a Saracen servant came to take her horse.

"Come with me," Roger said. He took her by the hand. "You will find nothing if you look for it in the proper place." He led her through a small door. Her sons had disappeared. She hung back a little, uncertain.

Roger took her into the middle tower. The floors were made of tiles. Heavy carpets covered them, even here, where many people walked. The rooms were wide and bare of furniture. The walls were pierced with vast windows that cast patterns of light across the floor. A veiled woman padded by her, eyes downcast. Roger had spoken of a harem. The whole place was damned. They went up three steps and into a wide room, sun-filled, longer than it was wide. Roger said, "Wait here," and left her totally alone.

She walked once around the room. Her palms were greasy with sweat. She wanted to go back to Castelmaria, to Birnia, anywhere she knew. The walls of this room were painted a glossy blue; over them, in slashes and loops and dots, ran some abstract yellow decoration. A screen cut off one part of the room. Behind it, on a low lacquered table, several dishes stood, as if waiting for someone to come have dinner. In the middle of it was a bowl of fruit. She took the top piece, not knowing what it was. Crossing to the nearer window, into the light, she broke the hard pod open with her hands and picked out one of the plump red fruits inside. It was sweet; she ate six.

The window opened out over the tops of trees; somehow, without climbing stairs, she had gotten into the second story of the tower. She leaned out to look into the gardens below her. Even the bright colors of the flowers were foreign to her. Two men were walking along the gravel terrace at the foot of the tower, almost beneath her. One wore a Saracen headcloth, but the other she knew. She picked one of the fruits from the pod in her hand and dropped it on him.

Richard wheeled, looking up. "Maria."

"Roger said I could not find you," she said.

"Roger should know you by now. Wait there." He started off at a run; the Saracen hurried after him.

Maria leaned in the window. The air was perfumed from the garden below. The sun was going down, and the white walls of the towers were turning pink. She went back into the room. Under the other window, on a table with a checked top, were two troops of chessmen. Afraid to touch them, she stood restlessly beside the table.

Richard came in. Taking her chin in his hand he gave her a quick, bearded kiss. "I was beginning to think you were staying in Birnia until the baby learned to walk. Where is she?"

"Eleanor has her, back in the cart."

The Saracen had come into the doorway behind him. She met the man's eyes, and he looked at her coolly down his arched brown nose.

"Stay, Rahman," Richard said. "We've been talking all day, you must be hungry."

The Saracen lifted his head. His black beard streaked with gray, his djellabah heavy-hemmed with gold thread and little jewels, he reminded Maria of a statue of Moses. "You are gracious, lord, but I will leave you, the night is coming." He spoke perfect French.

"Stay," Richard said. "I insist." He turned and spoke, and a servant came silently from nowhere and went out the door. "Come sit down."

He towed Maria by the hand behind the latticework screen. Sitting down, he dragged her into the chair beside him. "Just be quiet," he said softly, and lifted his voice. "Emir."

The Saracen appeared in the space between the screen and the wall. "Lord, I fear to intrude upon you and your lady."

"Sit. I mean your company to please her as it does me."

Another servant came around the screen, and Richard spoke to him in Saracen. The Emir, gathering his robes around him in his beautiful brown hands, moved a chair aside and settled himself in its place on the carpet. His eyes brushed Maria's and turned pointedly away. Her back muscles tightened; she did not like him.

Richard leaned back in the chair. Servants brought in

235

trays of cut and candied fruit, bread, cake, and little cups of something thick and sweet. One carried off the unused chair They went about entirely with their eyes downcast. She began to wonder how they found their way.

Richard said, "All the slaves here speak—"

"Slaves?" Maria said.

"Yes. They are all slaves."

Maria glanced at the Emir and said nothing. She took a slice of fruit from the tray.

"They speak Saracen, which you will have to learn. I have found some women to help you who speak a little French." He tipped the chair back on its hindlegs. "Eat, Rahman."

The Saracen bowed. His long fingers, coated with jewels, closed on a piece of bread. Richard watched him steadily.

"Who is Ismael?" Maria said.

The Emir's head rose sharply. Richard brought his chair down on all fours. "A mountaineer—a good boy, the son of a friend of mine. You've met him?"

Maria swallowed a mouthful of sweet fruit. "Yes. He came with Roger."

The Saracen cleared his throat, and she spun toward him. "What is wrong, my lord?"

He looked at Richard; the jewels on his hands flashed. "Among my people, lord, we do not share our food with women."

Maria clenched her teeth. Her body burned with the insult. Richard said, "My wife is my counsellor, Emir. She's as close to me as my brothers. I won't disparage her for your sake."

The Emir started a phrase in his own language. Richard said, "Speak French."

The two men stared at one another. Maria rubbed her hands on her thighs. At first she was pleased that Richard should defend her, but when she saw how they watched each other she knew this was an old fight, and nothing to do with her. She ate more fruit and drank from one of the tiny cups. The sweet liquor did not quench her thirst. The Emir reached out for another cake, and his eyes moved from Richard's.

"I am your servant, lady," he said.

Maria kept her mouth shut, afraid of saying the wrong thing. In the hall, footsteps sounded, and Roger's voice called, "Richard?"

Richard stood up and went out from behind the screen. His attention turned inward, the Emir glanced idly at Maria. She gave him such a look that he stiffened, his hand rising to his beard.

Robert and Stephen rushed in, their faces smudged with dirt, and surrounded her. "Mama," Robert said. "Papa says I'm to show you everything here—"

"Sssh," Maria said. "Don't be so loud, the Emir Rahman will think us country people." She stood up; the Saracen turned his head away from her. "Show me where we are to live."

RICHARD STAYED with his Saracen. Robert took her and Stephen on a bewildering course through the tower, first to a room in the ground story, where three fat men in trousers came out and bowed unctuously. Stephen drew back beside Maria, his hand sliding into her grasp, but Robert went straight up and spoke to the men in Saracen. The three men smiled and nodded and whacked each other gleefully in the ribs with their elbows. The boy strutted back to Maria.

"Mama, I've told them who you are, and about Stephen, and they will obey you now." He nudged Stephen. "But not you as much as me, because I am Papa's heir. We sleep here. Mama will sleep upstairs."

Stephen swung toward her. "Mama—"

"Don't be afraid. Robert will be with you."

"And Uncle Roger," Robert said. "He lives here, too. Come on." He ran up the corridor.

The three men bowed rapidly three or four times to her and hurried back into the room. One of them said, mimicking him, "Mama," and they all laughed. Maria and Stephen trotted after the other boy. People—slaves, she knew, like the three fat men—were walking slowly along the walls lighting the lamps set in niches in the stone. The yellow light threw a pattern of curved shadows over the black and white tiles of the floor. Catching up with Robert, Maria laid her hand on his shoulder.

"You fought, your uncle said."

"Oh, Mama. Not really. I was in the back, with Uncle William—we never even got through the gate until the citadel surrendered." His voice brightened. "But I have a sword now."

Stephen looked around her at him. "A real sword?"

"Yes."

"Aaah—not a real sword. You couldn't even pick up a real sword."

"Sssh," Maria said. She held them apart—she had forgotten they did not like each other. They walked up a wide staircase covered with carpets. Passing a window, she saw to her astonishment that they were in another tower altogether.

"It is a real sword," Robert cried. "It even killed somebody."

"Ants," Stephen cried. "You squished some ants with it."

Maria grabbed Robert by the upper arm. "Be a good knight—don't give in to temptation." She turned Stephen dexterously around backside to her and spanked him hard. "Don't pick fights." She swung him face forward again. They went through a double door into a small room, lined with cupboards. Richard's mail shirt hung on its frame in one corner, and when she came in, a knight got up off the couch in the corner, saluted her, and went to stand guard outside the door. Robert ran off to find Eleanor and the baby.

"He lies," Stephen said. "He doesn't have a real sword."

Maria stooped to face him. "Shall I spank you again?"

He squeezed his lips together; his gray eyes were stony with rage. She turned him and slapped him on the bottom.

Eleanor hurried in. "Oh, Maria. You have to do something. There are Saracens everywhere here, all the women are Saracens. Half of them don't even speak French!"

"Richard said—" Maria opened the door before her. "Holy Mother Mary."

She walked into a room as big as a church. Eleanor jabbered behind her. Maria went on into the middle of the room. Pieces of saddle gear cluttered the floor. No one had cleaned the place in weeks, and the furniture was coated with dust. She was halfway across the room before she noticed the bed, curtained in blue silk, against the far wall. Screens of white filigree hung across the three arched windows. The last gray light of the day lingered in the room. She looked up at the ceiling and clapped her hands together. On the deep blue ceiling, stars twinkled, set in the constellations of her own sky.

Still rattling on, Eleanor came after her, Jilly in her arms. "I wish you would not run off and leave me—when she cries, I can't feed her, poor child."

Maria reached for the baby. Eleanor looked past her, and her expression stretched into a false smile. "Here is Richard," she said, eluded Maria's grasp, and took the baby across the room toward the door.

Richard came into the room. "Let me have her." He got the baby from Eleanor. Maria sat on the bed, watching him. He took the baby over to the window, into the light; he murmured something too soft for Maria to hear. Eleanor went around the room lighting the lamps in the niches on the walls. Maria pushed off her shoes. She rubbed her bare feet on the carpet. With the lamps on, the stars in the ceiling sparkled like little fires.

"Give her to me now," Eleanor said, and got the baby back. She went out of the room. Richard watched her go. Slowly he crossed the room toward Maria.

"Isn't she awfully little? The baby? Nothing's wrong with her, is there?"

"You should have seen her when she was born."

"What do you think of Rahman?"

At the Saracen's name, she stood, her temper up, and he shook his head at her. "You don't like him because he slighted you. I mean other than that."

"Was he master here?"

"The Emir of Mana'a. If he'd been a better man, he would rule here still."

Eleanor came in again and hurried around the room, picking things up and putting them down again in other places. Maria tilted a pitcher on the chest beside the bed. It was full of water; she poured some into the basin next to it so that she could wash her face and hands.

"What is he now?" she asked.

"Croesus of Lydia."

"Who?"

"Yes, that's what I said. Some pagan king in a fable." He turned his head. "Eleanor, go away."

Maria dried her face. The towel was made of some soft cloth she did not know. Eleanor came up beside her, ignoring Richard. "Maria, do you—"

"Get out of here," Richard said; his voice rose toward a nasty whine. "How often do I have to tell you?"

Eleanor turned square toward him. "These Saracens may think you are great now, Cousin, but to me you are still the little boy in the hat."

Richard wheeled on her; he thrust his head forward. "Well, to me you are still my brother's whilom whore."

Eleanor gasped. Ten feet separated them. She crossed it in three strides and slapped him across the face with a crack like a rock splitting.

"Richard," Maria cried. Before she could get between them, he fastened his hand in the front of Eleanor's dress and tore her clothes open down to her waist.

Eleanor screamed. She shrank away from him, her body folding, and her arms crossed over her breasts. Maria with one arm around her shoulders turned away from Richard. Eleanor shook in her embrace. Maria looked over the woman's bowed head at Richard. He turned and strode out of the room; when he slammed the door a lamp fell off a nearby shelf.

Maria drew Eleanor over to the bed and made her lie down. The gown was ripped open down to her belly. Her small breasts were pink-tipped and firm, like unpicked apples. She sobbed into the pillow.

"You shouldn't have hit him," Maria said. She removed Eleanor's clothes and got her between the fine camlet sheets. "Lie still now, go to sleep a while. You'll feel better."

"You heard—" Eleanor gulped. "What he called me."

"He wasn't really angry until you hit him."

Jilly cried, outside the door in the anteroom. Maria straightened. She knew by her voice the baby was hungry. Eleanor tried to sit up, but Maria pushed her down again.

"Go to sleep. Sssh—lie still." She rose and went across the room. When she reached the door, the baby stopped crying. Her breasts, full of milk, hurt sensuously. She was afraid to open the door. Beyond, in the anteroom, Richard's voice crooned in a strange endearment. She pushed the door open and went through.

Richard was sitting on the couch, holding the baby up before him, her face to his face. He turned away from Maria, but the baby began to cry again, and he had to give her to her mother. Maria sat down and put the baby to her breast.

He did not look at her; she did not speak to him. After a moment, he went out. She heard him talking to the knight outside the door. She put her hand over the baby's head. In the morning she would sort everything out. Everything would make sense in the morning. Uncertain, she stared at the wall.

XXIV

❧

RICHARD TOOK HER TO SEE THE ANCIENT CATHEDRAL OF Saint Joseph of Marna, which faced the harbor across a huge cobbled square. The Saracens had turned it into a mosque. There was an Archbishop of Marna, but he lived in Rome. Richard said he was an old man, unfit for travel, and showed no interest in coming to his rescued church.

The cathedral had been built long before the Saracens came to Mana'a. Its walls were of dark stone. The recessed front porch was set with three pointed archways. Inside, the Saracens had raised dozens of thin columns to chop the area into aisles, and they had plastered the walls over with their flowing, cryptic designs. Richard said it was writing.

They went out onto the cathedral porch. The bay faced them, bounded by the headlands at its mouth. The market place swarmed with Saracens. A groom brought their horses, and their escort grouped around them. Halfway down the dusty street, Maria turned to look at the cathedral's flattened dome and the bell tower. She liked it; she had felt safe there.

"That will be our cathedral," she said. "When it is Christian again."

Richard nodded. "I want William to take charge of it."

"William." He was in Marna now, content with his dogs and hawks. She reined her horse closer to Richard's. The knights of their escort encased them like a husk. The crowded street led them up a short steep hill. "Why should he do it?"

"You mean, why not you? No. Women are not bishops. When this bishop in Rome dies, I want someone of us to succeed him. William is the only one, Roger's not fit, Stephen will probably not be of a decent age."

Maria studied him through the tail of her eye. Off to their left, on the far side of a little square, another mosque appeared. Its porch was crowded with Saracens.

"What will you do with that one?" She pointed to it.

"That's one of their important mosques. We'll have enough churches without taking away their mosques."

Maria reined in. Behind her, a knight called out, and the others stopped around her. Richard turned back toward her. The short, trimmed beard made him look like a Saracen himself.

"Richard," she said. "These people are heathen. Their mosques are idolatrous."

"Come on—I'm not going to argue with you in the middle of the street."

He rode away from her; their knights clattered off around him, and she trotted her mare a few steps to catch up. The Mana'ans flooded along the street around her. Surely now they would all have to be Christians. There was no reason in it unless they were all made safe for Christ. Roger had told her that when Mana'a fell, the native Christians ran into the streets killing Saracens and Jews. They would all be Christians now, when God had triumphed here. They rode up a steep hill and through a little gate in the wall that wound around the palace.

The knights left them. Richard and Maria rode through a desolate part of the green park. Trees hid the three towers on the crown of the hill. A hare raced away from them into the underbrush.

Maria said, "There will be Christian churches and Saracen churches—will you let the Jews have their own churches too?"

He held his horse even with hers. "Yes."

Maria shook her head. "While they are God's enemies they are our enemies."

"They are not against us any more—you must think differently now. They are our people now, like the people at Castelmaria—"

"The people at Castelmaria are like me," she cried. "They worship God, they know me."

"Come on."

He lifted his horse into a canter. She followed him around the base of a steep, rocky hill, and he led her up the slope toward the sunlight. The trees grew thick around them. The branches overhead shaded them. At the crest of the hill stood a small round tower made of brick. Richard's horse clattered across the pavingstones around it. He dismounted and let his reins trail. When she caught up with him, he was knocking on the tower door.

It opened, and a young knight came out, blinking at the sunlight. "My lord." He threw the door open.

"Go watch our horses." Richard brushed past him into the half-lit room beyond.

The young knight took her reins and led her mare out into the little ward. Maria stood on the threshold, looking into the small square anteroom.

"Bring that lamp over here." Richard stood in front of the inner door.

She picked up the oil lamp on the table at the other end of the room. The smoke smelled of grease. Richard turned so that the light fell on the padlock of the inner door. The lock clicked open. He put his shoulder to the door and thrust it wider, growling on its hinges.

"What does Roger think about this—to let the Saracens alone?"

"Roger is going back to Iste." He leaned against the

243

door frame. "He's just getting in my way here. The people here hate him, they call him *The Christian*. He doesn't care much for them."

"They still call you Dragon. That's an insult, too."

"Yes, but they like me. And I like them, even Rahman. I like what they have. I like the kind of men they are. Even Rahman."

The blank doorway drew her eyes. She wondered what was in there, in the darkness like a lair.

"Rahman hates me," she said. "And I see how you are with him, you don't like him."

"He doesn't know you. They make no use of their women, except to bear children and such things. But then I've never met a Saracen woman who wasn't silly and stupid. Roger loves them. He keeps them, like dogs."

She took a step forward toward the door. "What is in there?"

"Go in and see."

The lamplight crept over the threshold and across an unswept stone floor. She stretched her neck, trying to make out the room within. Richard laughed at her; from deep in the darkness, a misshapen echo answered him.

"Here."

He took the lamp from her and walked ahead of her through the doorway. The weak light surrounded him like a little room. She stayed so close behind him that she trod on his heel. The air smelled of must and stone and something alien. They walked across emptiness to a wall of wooden casks stacked higher than her head.

Richard gave her the lamp again, grasped one of the kegs on the top row, and pulled it down with a crash. The wood split. Gold money flooded over the stone, winking like eyes in the light of the lamp.

He pulled her by the arm deeper into the vast room. Taking the lamp, he held it so that the light showed her carpets rolled and heaped by the dozen along the wall, the boxes and kegs in piles all around them, chests with locks as big as skulls. He scooped up a handful of black seeds from a tall jar and held it under her nose. "Pepper. There are cloves, too. Cinnamon." Stooping, he groped under a chest, got out a long key, and opened the chest's fat lock. When he tipped up the lid, the lamplight shimmered on the bolts of golden cloth inside. They went on through the dark, past more chests, more kegs and boxes and jars, everything an inch deep in dust. At the wall, at the foot of a wooden stair, he turned and faced her, the lamp's flame light between them.

"This was Rahman's treasure," he said.

Maria stood looking around her. The casks and jars were only shapes in the black room. The lamplight sparkled here and there on a hasp or lock.

"Rahman had all this," Richard said. "But he lost Mana'a to five hundred knights. He mistreated his people. He gave no justice, and he punished the Christians and the Jews for not being Saracens. When we came, not even the Saracens would fight for him."

Maria said, "We took Mana'a because God willed it."

"So all the Saracens tell me."

She twisted her hands together. The lamplight winked on the rings on his hands. The treasure around her was like a weight pressing against her. It was Saracen, it was wicked, the goods of the Devil: the Golden Calf. Richard's face, masked in the short dark beard, was expressionless.

"Why can we not simply do what we are supposed to do?" she asked. "We are Christian, they are not. Why do you make everything so complicated?"

"Just think about it," he said. "Listen to me and turn it over in your mind." His mouth twisted. "What little you've got."

"No."

"I will proclaim this in a charter—that we will suffer the Jews and the Saracens to practice their errors."

"No."

"You'll witness it. You and Roger."

"No."

"Will you use another word?" he shouted; his voice roared in the dark. Maria took a step backward. He thrust his head toward her. "You have no choice. You will witness the charter if I must tie you up and carry you there. If you witness it, you can't act against it later, you know—that's a sin. You pig-brained little sneaking crooked bitch—what you did to me with the merchants of Iste was a sin, too, and if you make me lose my temper

245

I'll smack you for that the way I should have when I first saw you!"

Maria wheeled and plunged into the darkness toward the door. Behind her he swore in a ragged voice. She stumbled past a row of kegs and barked her shin on something metal.

"Maria!"

Her breath caught in her throat. She could make out nothing in the darkness; she groped frantically before her in the empty air. At last a thin rectangle of daylight showed her the doorway. She slid through it into the warmth of the anteroom.

On the threshold of the door into the open, she stopped and tried to master herself. Across the ward, at the edge of the green lawn, the young knight stood with his back to her, holding their horses' reins while they grazed. She struck the tears from her eyes. She would never find her way out of the city and across the mountains to her home.

The door to the treasure room grunted closed behind her. She turned and faced him across the anteroom. He locked the padlock and put the key into his wallet. She could not meet his eyes.

"I will do whatever you say," she said. She despised herself for a coward. She went out into the sunshine, toward her horse.

EVERYTHING IN MANA'A was strange. After the snug, crowded towers of Castelmaria and Birnia, the palace rooms stretched on and on, empty of people. It amazed her that every day they were fed, they were cared for, by these strange attendants she could hardly speak to. In the middle of such a city, she could not find supplies for them —she did not know how to get grain, where to have it milled, or even who the cook was; yet every day she ate fresh bread.

Richard told her they had all of Rahman's slaves now, who would work for them as well as for Rahman. He did not tell her how to rule them. They had strange names she could not pronounce and did not come to her for their instructions, they went to Rahman. When she had to talk to them, Robert spoke for her, and Richard taught her a

246

few words of Saracen—bread, meat, water, wine—but the sense of the language eluded her.

Eleanor, sunk in prayer, crossed herself whenever she saw a Saracen. Maria walked from room to room, carrying Jilly, wondering if God would even listen to them here. It was all work of the Devil.

From a window, she watched Stephen and Robert gallop around in the meadow below the palace, striking with sticks at something on the ground. Ismael rode up to them and they played together. Ismael baffled her. She thought he was a hostage; he fawned on Richard like a woman. But he spoke to her and the boys with no deference at all, and he hated Roger and Rahman and did not care who knew it. She stood in the sunlight, one hand on the window frame, and watched the three riders turning and turning in the meadow, like an enchantment. Nothing obeyed her sense of order. If she knew it was not true, perhaps it would all disappear, and she would be safe in Castelmaria again. In her arms, Jilly stirred, and she sat down with the baby in her lap.

She was in the room where she had first met Rahman. When she leaned sideways, she could see out the window to the new wall that Richard was building around the palace. The workmen climbed on the unfinished end, dragging stones up into place. They were sealing her in. A yellow butterfly swooped in the window and fluttered around the room, trying to light on the colors of the walls. The baby turned her head to watch it.

Richard and Roger came into the room. While a slave went for wine, Roger came up and spoke to Maria. Richard called him and he went back across the room. Maria shifted away from them. They stood at the other window, looking out at the new wall.

"Cut the ward in half," Roger said. "Run a wall from this tower to that, and we will have a good crossfire on anyone who breaks in any gate."

Jilly was asleep. Maria put her against her shoulder and stroked the baby's back. Richard made no sign he knew she was there. They talked about fortifications and she lost their line of thought. The slave brought wine. While they drank, Richard said, "I have finished the charter, do you want to hear it?"

"You are mad," Roger said. "If you let them keep their faith, they will revolt. They hate us. Maria, tell him he's mad."

Maria ignored him. Robert and Stephen and Ismael were racing their horses in among the pine trees. Ismael's white robes flashed over the green grass.

"You said something about patrolling the Ridge Highway," Roger said. "I can help you more in Iste than here. Let me go back home."

"After I've published my charter," Richard said. They talked of horses, roads, supplies, and bad weather. Rahman came into the room. Maria stared out the window. The three men spoke together. Rahman's crisp, accented voice put her on edge. Richard said something, and Roger laughed. In an oiled voice Rahman paid her husband some small flattery.

Maria stood up. Down in the trees below her window, Ismael and Robert on foot attacked Stephen. The smaller boy got his back to a tree, drove them off, and ran toward his palfrey where it grazed in the meadow. Robert's shriek of derision came faintly to her. Ismael held him back. Maria took the baby away to the room of the star ceiling.

In the narrow antechamber, her three Saracen maids were sitting idle, all giggles, their veils dangling ready to cover their faces if a man appeared: they even veiled themselves before Robert. Eleanor sat alone in the enormous room beyond. Her lips moved in a low buzz of prayers. Maria put the baby in the cradle. She walked around the room, longing for some work to do. All her life she had always worked and now, here, there was nothing someone else could not do better, or would not want done differently than her way.

"Maria," Eleanor said, "I must talk to you."

Maria came over beside the cradle. Eleanor took her hand. Her cheeks were pale and dry as parchment, but her eyes were red as if she had been crying. She held Maria's hand against her cheek.

"I want to go back to Castelmaria. I don't want to stay here. I feel as if the ground here is breaking up under my feet. I'm sorry, I'm sorry. Please let me go home."

Maria jerked her hand free. "But what about me? Are you going to leave me here alone?"

Eleanor put her face in her hands and sobbed. Maria licked her lips. Through the corner of her eye, she caught a motion at the door; the three Saracen women were looking in, avid.

"Go," she said to Eleanor. "Go to Castelmaria."

Eleanor put her arms around Maria. "I know you feel as I do. Come with me. You don't have to stay here."

Maria thrust her away. "I said you could leave. Let me alone. Where is my looking glass? I know I put it on that chest."

Taking a piece of linen from her sleeve, Eleanor wiped her eyes and blew her nose. Slowly her eyes wandered over the room. She got to her feet. "It's here, somewhere. I saw it this morning. I'll help you look."

The door was empty, the Saracen women gone. Maria opened the cupboard and searched through the combs, belts, and shoes on the bottom shelf. They went twice over the room, feeling behind the furniture and in all the chests and cupboard—Maria found a pin she had lost.

"It isn't here," Eleanor said. "Maria, do you think—?"

"I must have left it in the little hall."

Eleanor's eyes squinted. Her mouth looked pinched at the corners. "I think someone stole it."

"No. I left it in the hall." Her hands were trembling. "If you are going, pack your clothes—I will talk to Richard tonight about sending you home."

"Maria, don't be angry with me."

"I'm not angry with you. It's just that I left my looking glass in the hall. Go pack, Eleanor. Leave me alone."

"What a temper you are in of late." Eleanor bustled out of the room. Maria sat down on the wide bed. If they could steal her looking glass they could take everything she had. She searched through the room again, knowing it was gone, and lay down across the bed and cried.

ONCE A DAY, on Richard's orders, a priest came from the city to instruct Robert and Stephen and the three or four Saracens who wanted to know Christ. For the first few days of this—Eleanor had left, there was nothing to do—

249

Maria sat in the back of the little hall and listened to the catechism. The priest walked up and down along the windows, past Rahman's chessmen, and the boys and Saracens sat on mats before him.

"Who made me?" the priest asked, pacing.

"God made me," the class answered, in a chorus.

"Why did God make me?"

"God made me to know Him, to love Him, to serve Him, now and forever, on earth and in Heaven."

Maria stitched a rising sun on the shirt she was embroidering for Jilly. The priest went on through the lesson of the day, ten new questions and answers, and told them stories from the Gospels. The priest at home had taught her in the same way before she received Christ for the first time. Then she had thought the questions silly and obvious, but now they were like a kind of mail, all the little questions linked together with answers, proof against sin. She could pick out Robert's voice; he learned everything quickly.

On the fourth day, after they had recited all the questions and answers they had learned, Stephen asked, "Who made the Saracens?"

Maria lifted her head. The priest wheeled. His black gown swung against his ankles. He clasped his hands behind his back.

"God made the Saracens," he said firmly. "But the Saracens have harkened to the Devil Mahmud and turned their backs on God."

Stephen said, "That isn't what the Saracens say."

Robert pounced on him, knocked him down, and struck him in the face. "Renegade!"

Stephen covered his head with his arms. The Saracens jumped up, excited. "Robert," Maria cried. She threw down her work and rushed over to them. On his back like a beetle, Stephen kicked and clawed at his brother, who hit him again in the head. Maria pulled Robert away by the arm.

"Do you disobey me?" She shook him. "Shall I tell your father you disobey me?"

"Mother!" Robert gawked at her. He backed a step away from her. Stephen sat up on the carpet. "You heard what he said—" He kicked Stephen in the leg.

"Stop," Maria said. She lifted her eyes to the priest. "I heard what he said, but he isn't—you must not—"

The priest said, "My lady, I advise prayer for this fellow. Let him come back tomorrow, when he has asked God's forgiveness."

Stephen cried, "I won't—" Maria hoisted him to his feet and shoved him on before her out the door to the next room.

"Stephen," she said. She took him by the shoulders. "What are you doing? Why are you saying these things?" She knelt before him and hugged him tight. "Do you want to go to Hell?"

"Mama," Stephen said. "I was just asking—" His voice dribbled away. "Mama?" He threw his arms around her neck. "I'm sorry, Mama, I didn't mean to."

Maria held him against her. In the hall behind them, the class recited, Robert's voice the strongest. She wondered where Ismael was.

"Stephen," she said. "Come with me."

He followed her to the room of the star ceiling. Two of her Saracen women were working there, chattering in their own tongue while they put away clean clothes. Maria wondered which had taken her looking glass. The baby slept in her cradle. Maria went to her clothes chest and got out her mother's crucifix.

"Here, Stephen." She knelt before him and put the crucifix into his hands. "Take this. Look at it when you think of such questions."

"Rahman said—"

Maria clenched her teeth. "So it's Rahman. I should have known it. What is he telling you? Why do you listen to him?"

"He just said to ask the priest something." Stephen folded his hands around the crucifix; his thumb rubbed nervously over the little painted Christ.

"So he tells you questions to ask? How is that different from asking the questions the priest tells you to ask? See how Christ hangs on the Cross, Stephen? Remember, every sin—" she thought with guilt of her own sins— "every sin is like hanging God on the Cross again." She crossed herself; the thought of Walter Bris lay like a stone in her mind.

"Rahman says Jesus was just a prophet, like Ibrahim, and not God at all."

A door slammed. The Saracen women burst into giggles and put up their veils. Maria called out to them to go. They darted out the door, and Richard came in. Behind him followed two slaves, who helped him get out of his mail and took it off to be oiled. He hung his sword in its scabbard on the wall. Maria went to get a fresh shirt.

She said, holding the shirt out for him, "Rahman has been teaching heresy to Stephen."

"What?"

Stephen stood like a wooden man in the middle of the room. Richard put his arms through the sleeves and Maria tugged the shirt down to his waist. His sun-streaked hair hung in his face. He gave her a sharp look and turned his eyes toward Stephen.

"Come here."

Stephen said, "Will you hit me?"

"Yes," Richard said. "Come here anyway." He shook down his sleeves. "This shirt doesn't fit me. Why suddenly does every shirt I put on bind me across the back?"

"It's one of the new ones," Maria said. "The Saracens made it."

Stephen came slowly toward them. Richard pulled the shirt off over his head and stuffed it into Maria's hands. He smelled strongly of sweat; the thick brown hair clung damply to his chest. Stephen crept up to stand before him. Richard put his hands on his hips.

"What heresy?"

Stephen mumbled unintelligibly. Richard shoved Maria with his elbow. "Bring me a decent shirt."

Maria went to the cupboard. Behind her, Richard said, "I'm not going to hit you. I would have, if you hadn't come. What happened?"

"I was just asking—Rahman said to ask Father Peter who made the Saracens. Rahman is teaching me how to play chess. He told me a lot of things I didn't know."

Richard coughed. "Oh. I see. What's that?"

Maria brought him an old shirt she had made herself. Stephen was showing him the crucifix. "Mama says that every time I sin it's like hanging God on the Cross."

Richard held his arms out, and Maria put him into the shirt. "Ah. Better. Don't let anybody else make my shirts." He drew up the laces on the front of the shirt. "Stephen, keep the crucifix. You can listen to Rahman if you want, but he knows no more than the priest, which is nothing, so don't believe him. Run get me a belt." He turned his back to Maria. "Scratch my back."

Maria raked her nails methodically up and down his back. "That isn't what I wanted you to tell him."

Richard laughed. He moved his shoulder, and she scratched his shoulderblades. "What did you want?"

"Tell him not to talk like that—Robert beat him, the priest will tell everyone we are heretics—"

"Stephen," Richard called. She lowered her hands, and he kissed her absent-mindedly. The boy dashed up, Richard's belt coiled in his hand. His brown hair stuck up on the crown of his head; his short straight nose was scratched. Richard sank down on his heels, eye-level with him.

"Mark me. Say what people want to hear, and do as you please. No one will ever notice the difference."

Stephen blinked at him. "What?"

"Rahman is a liar." Richard pushed him away. "God is a Christian, Muhammed served the Devil. Go away."

"Say your prayers," Maria called. Stephen went out the door with a skip. Richard was putting on his belt. "What did you say?"

"The prime lesson. He's too young to understand, you taught it to me. Rahman is a liar. He spies on you, did you know that?"

"No." She hunched her shoulders. "Tell him to stop."

"I don't think he will. Rahman spies on everybody, he takes bribes, he lies, he bears false witness—"

"Kill him."

"Oh, Maria. Another God hung. I need him, I can't do much here without him, at least for now."

"What has he said about me?"

"What have you done wrong lately?" He tapped her on the jaw. "He tells me so many lies I never believe him."

The door opened, and Robert ran in, Ismael right behind him. "Papa," he cried. His clear blue eyes flew to Maria. "Mother, did you tell him?"

"Yes. She told me. Do you remember what I said about bearing tales?"

Robert jittered before him, his fists clenched. "But, Papa, this is important!"

"If it's important I can find it out for myself." Richard smacked him. "Go tell the cook I want to eat."

Maria went over to the cupboard and got out the ill-fitting shirt. All the old shirts were woolen, too hot for Mana'a; the new shirts were made of fine camlet, soft and cool. She got out her scissors and clipped the threads that held the sleeves into the armhole.

Rahman stood in the doorway. She watched him covertly, morose. She wondered if he had stolen her looking glass. If Richard found out she had not caught the thief, he would probably beat her. He hardly noticed her—any more, except to lie with her or punish her. He called to Rahman, calling the Saracen into her own room, as if he were not preying on Stephen and spying on her. Rahman was stealing her son from her—Stephen would never listen to Richard. She let her hands fall idle in her lap, exhausted.

TWO DAYS LATER, in a crowded ceremony in the middle ward of the palace, Richard had his charter read permitting the Saracens and the Jews to practice their errors. Besides Maria and Roger, Rahman witnessed the charter, and several other Saracens and four Jews of varying ages in long black coats. Maria used the little Saracen ring Richard had given her in Iste to seal the charter. Afterward, the Saracens and the Jews surrounded Richard. Left to themselves, she and Roger walked away together out of the crowd.

"Now I can go back to Iste," Roger said. They went out through the unfinished wall to the garden. He tossed his seal ring up into the air and caught it. "I'll be glad to get out of here, believe me."

"What will you do?"

"Hunt. Gamble. I've got some claims along the border I can fight over." He drew her arm through his and laced their fingers together. "Poor Maria. You look so downcast lately."

"Yes," she said. She stopped; they stood facing each other in the middle of the garden. "I am not pretty any more."

"You are always pretty. You're much too fine for Richard." His fingertips brushed her cheek. Bending down, he kissed her. She shut her eyes. His mouth moved hard over hers, his chin raspy with beard stubble. She leaned against him. Her heart began to pound. His hand slipped down over her hip.

"Roger." She pushed herself out of his arms. Her mouth was dry. All over her body her skin tingled vibrantly. "I think you'd better go back to Iste."

He smiled at her. "Come with me."

"Roger." She eluded his reaching hand. "No."

"Are you afraid of him? I'll take care of you."

She looked up the slope, toward the wall at the top of the garden, and the towers rising beyond it. Quickly she went back along the path. At the gap in the wall she glanced back over her shoulder. Roger was still there, watching her. She ran the rest of the way.

XXV

"SEE?" STEPHEN SAID, AND HELD UP THE NARROW BOARD to show her. "That says—*Stephen.*" He chalked the last mark. "*Stephen.*"

Maria cut the thread and took the sleeve out of another shirt. "Rahman taught you this?"

"Yes. And this—says—*Maria.*"

She put her hands in her lap. They were sitting in the little hall, with the sunlight streaming across them. Stephen's hair looked almost red. On his board, her marks were like bird tracks, with only one round place. His had more curves in it. "He taught you to make my name?"

"Yes. Papa's is longer and I don't remember it. Rahman says one who cannot read is unfit to rule. Robert can't read at all."

Maria was threading a needle. She held it up to the light to find the eye. "You should not heed Rahman. Your father said that he lies. Your father cannot read, is he unfit to rule?" She could not read.

"Papa is older than Robert."

Maria drew the thread through the needle. There had been no more trouble with the catechism. Now the priest was teaching them music and numbers, also, which Stephen liked. She set the sleeves properly into the shirt and Stephen chalked intently on the board. The priest was a fool, anyway—at supper she had asked him if her witness of the charter permitting errors required some penance, and he had stammered like an idiot. Sitting beside her, Richard had laughed out loud at it.

"Stephen," Rahman called, from the next room.

Maria sewed small, tight stitches, ignoring him. Stephen walked out of her range of sight. Maria hoped they would go. The voice of the Saracen rubbed on her nerves.

"Maria," Stephen said. "Rahman wants to talk to you."

Maria stabbed the needle into her thumb. She put the shirt down on her lap. A drop of blood fell on it. "Let him talk." She licked off her thumb and sank her hands into the shirt; it was ruined now anyway.

Rahman in a silken voice sent the boy out of the hall. His djellabah draped in snowy folds, his immaculate hands with their armor of rings dark against the cloth, he stood before her, his eyes aimed over her head.

"There is a document I wish. It is of no importance to my lord. I will tell you where it is, and you will bring it to me."

Maria stood up, face to face with him. He was just her height; he stared loftily over her shoulder. The whites of his eyes were tinged with brown. He smelled of flowers like a woman. She said, "What do you mean?"

256

He shut his eyes and opened them again languidly. "My lord would not like to know how you kiss your younger brother when my lord's back is turned."

Maria stiffened. A cold calm filled her. For an instant she hated him so hard she could not bring herself to speak to him. Roger had left that morning; she was alone against Rahman. Evenly, she said, "Tell him, Rahman. I will deny it, and we will see whom he believes."

Rahman's smug expression slipped. His eyes moved toward her. "I have witnesses," he said. "We will let my lord judge." He turned and walked out of the room, his shoulders square as a board.

Maria sat down. "Son of God, have mercy on me." She crossed herself. She folded the shirt and stuffed it into the basket at her feet, wondering when Rahman would tell Richard. She could tell him herself, but he would believe her. He had said he believed nothing Rahman said. It was hard to be righteous when she was guilty. Surely Rahman would wait, half a day at least, to let her change her mind and submit to him, so that he could get the document. She ran up the stairs to the room of the star ceiling.

Richard was still in bed. Jilly lay curled up asleep against the small of his back. Maria fished her out of the bed and took her across the room to change her clothes. Richard murmured in his sleep and rolled over.

The Saracen women were loitering in the antechamber. Maria gave them the baby, to divert them, and crowing with pleasure they carried her off. Maria locked the outer door after them and shut the inner door dast. She went back to the bed.

"Richard." She walked her fingers up his back.

"Ummm."

"I just talked to Rahman. He wanted me to get some document for him."

Richard rolled onto his back and sat bolt upright. His beard was scruffy from sleeping on it. "What document?"

"I don't know. He said it wasn't important to you."

He swung his legs over the side of the bed. "Why did he think you would rob me?" He took a fistful of the front of her dress.

Maria met his eyes. "He said something about me and Roger."

He slapped her so hard her head rang. "What about you and Roger?"

"Let go of me."

His eyes were dark with bad temper. "You did nothing with Roger?"

"No. Let go of me."

He kept hold of her a moment longer, let go, and got out of bed. "What document? Where did he say it was? Get me some clothes." With a twist of his arms, he pulled off his nightshirt. But before she could go, he caught her by the wrist. "Didn't I warn you about him? Now will you pay heed to me?" He tried to kiss her. She thrust him off; her head hurt where he had struck her. She went to bring him some clothes. He knelt and rummaged through the big chest where he kept his charters.

She went out of the palace toward the garden, looking for Robert and Ismael. They were riding up from the park. She stopped and waved to them, and they galloped over to her, single file down the lane through the banks of roses. Robert bounded down from his saddle and ran to her.

"Mother. Come into the city with us."

On his chestnut mare, Ismael smiled at her, all teeth. Maria put her arm around Robert and hugged him.

"Maybe tomorrow. You can show me how to find my way around. Robert, I need your help."

He pulled himself taller. "Of course I will. I promise. Like the other time, in Birnia." He crossed himself.

Maria said, "I want you to spy on Rahman for me."

"Rahman," Ismael said. He jumped down from his mare, his dark eyes brilliant with curiosity. He and Robert cackled at each other in Saracen. Robert threw his arm around Ismael's neck.

"We will both help you. We will do whatever you command."

"Come here, where it's quiet." She nodded down the path. "I'll tell you what you must do."

BY WHAT HER SON and Ismael told her, she realized that Rahman had set the household slaves to spying on her and on Richard wherever they went. The next morning she summoned the slaves into the middle ward and told them that they were free. Robert translated for her. At the apex of his speech, he flung his arms wide, like a sermoner. After scarcely three weeks of catechism he was talking about becoming a monk.

The slaves did not look happy. Many burst into tears and cried out that they were to be sold. Maria waved them quiet again. Through Robert, she told them that nothing had really changed, they would live and work in the palace as before, and they stood easier, their faces relaxing into smiles. She gave them all new titles in French and put them to doing the jobs she was used to having done. If anything necessary was left out, she would learn about it soon enough. The three men who bought and sold supplies she kept to that task, since she had no way of buying in kind any more, and all the money looked the same to her.

Later, she hunted out Stephen where he was playing with Rahman's chessmen in the little hall. He had lined the green men up on the checked board and was moving them in various ways down toward the other side. She stood in the window, warming herself in the sunshine, and let him finish what he was doing.

Over his shoulder, he said, "I can write Papa's name now—shall I do it for you?"

Maria sat on the window sill. "Yes, if you want. I have a friend's favor to ask of you."

He frowned at her, a chessman in his hand. "What is it?"

"You are as suspicious as your father," Maria said. "Promise me you will do as I ask."

"Mama, how can I promise when I don't know what it is?"

Maria rumpled up his hair. "What a rogue you are, not to promise it—am I not your mother?"

"It's about Rahman, isn't it?" He leaned on his knee, half-lying in her lap. "He's my friend—Robert has Ismael, why can't I play with Rahman?"

Maria said, "I want you to stay away from Rahman. Just for a few days. If you do, I'll never bother you about him again."

Stephen threw the chessman down. "Everybody is mean to me."

Maria turned away from him, toward the window, trying to find the right persuasion. In the garden below her, something moved. She leaned out to see. It was Rahman, sneaking up the path in the shrubbery toward the palace. In the far end of the garden, Ismael and Robert were searching up and down the aisles of hedges. Maria put her head out the window.

"Robert!" Emphatically she pointed down at Rahman below her. Rahman broke into an undignified run for the palace. In the depths of the garden, Ismael whooped, and the two boys raced like hounds up through the roses. Maria turned back into the hall.

Stephen was trying to see around her; he danced up and down before her. "What is going on? Is it a game? Nobody lets me play but Rahman."

"You can play with me," Maria said.

"You're just a woman."

"You're just a little boy. Come on. We can ride in the park."

In the afternoon, she took Jilly out to the garden. While she was sitting with the baby on the cropped grass in the sunshine, the oldest of her Saracen maids came up to her and sat down beside her.

"My lady," the woman said. She had a long, plain face like a horse. "I have something for you." From her cloak she took Maria's looking glass.

Maria cried out. She took the glass in both hands. The Saracen woman looked away across the wide lawn, bounded in shrubbery.

"We all stole from the Emir Abd-al-Rahman," she said.

For a moment, neither of them spoke. Maria rubbed the silver surface on her skirt. The baby put her hand out toward the bright object.

"Will you punish me?" the Saracen woman asked.

"No. I'm glad you gave it back." Maria cast about for something harmless to speak of, to seal the peace between them. "How did you learn to speak French so well?"

260

The woman smiled, her dark eyes downcast. "My mother was of your people. She was taken in a raid, when she was a young woman. She belonged to the Emir al-Simmah." She turned. "I have come here also, lady, to warn you that the Emir Abd-al-Rahman has told your lord that you kissed the Christian knight."

Maria started. "Did Rahman send you?"

"No." The older woman's mouth twisted. "I understand why you might think that. But I am not his slave any more."

The baby had rolled onto her back. She stuck her feet in the air and reached for her toes. Down the slope, in the fir trees, the wind sang a long mourning note.

"Does everybody know I kissed Roger?"

The Saracen woman lowered her eyes again. She touched the baby's hand. "The men do it. Why shouldn't you?" Her voice turned bitter. "All the men do it."

Maria hunched her shoulders. She thought of running away. She had known this would come. The Saracen woman lifted Jilly in her arms and bent over her, murmuring in the alien tongue. Maria stared at the pine trees. The wind ruffled through the layers of their green branches. Someone was walking down the slope behind her. Without raising her head, the Saracen woman fastened her veil across her face. She stopped her soft whispers. Maria picked up the looking glass. In it she saw Richard, standing just behind her.

He spoke in Saracen to the other woman, telling her to go, but the woman disobeyed him. She held the baby tight against her. Maria saw how frightened she was. She asked, "Lady, do you wish me to stay?"

"No," Maria said. "Thank you. Please take Jilly to bed."

The woman hurried off, stoop-shouldered. Maria put the looking glass down beside her. Her hands were shaking.

"You dirty whore," Richard said, behind her.

She stared down into the pine wood. His hand closed on her shoulder, and she stood up before he could use force against her, facing him. She pushed his hand away.

"Deny it," he said. He stood close over her. "Tell me it was a lie."

"What did he say?"

"That you are a dirty whore."

"That is a lie."

He jerked his head back and spat into her face. Maria stood rigid. Waves of heat beat up into her cheeks. At last she lifted her hand and wiped her cheek.

"I thought you were better than that, Maria. Another one of Roger's ditch-wives—"

"Stop," she said. She put her hands over her face.

Richard's mouth was an inch from her ear. "You're just another common, willing, filthy female thing—"

"Stop!" She dropped her hands and stared at him. "I just kissed him—"

"Do you think he loves you?" Richard shouted at her. "Do you think he cares about you? If you'd ever heard him talking about women—the things he says about women—"

She sat down again on the slope, her hands trembling. "I'm sorry."

He stood looking down at her, his hands on his hips. "I don't believe you." He walked away up the slope. Maria sat with her eyes turned toward the pine wood. The wind rose, its voice cooing through the branches. He was right: if Roger wanted her it was just because he did not have her. She wished she had never let him touch her. She put her chin on her fist and stared into the pine wood, eaten with remorse.

XXVI

❧

"YOU SAID YOU'D GIVE ME A RIDING HORSE."

"What do you need a horse for?" Richard asked. "Where are you thinking to go?"

"You promised me a horse," Maria said. She went down the hillside ahead of him, skirting the edge of the rose garden. While she walked she pushed her hair back and tied the ribbon around it again. Richard steered her by the arm through the gap in the hedge. They came out on the green grass in front of the stable.

Three Saracen grooms were arguing together in the doorway. Seeing Richard, they fell silent and backed quickly off the threshold. Maria went past them into the stable. The smells of straw and horse made her wrinkle up her nose. A horse nickered.

Her eyes grew used to the half-light. The long low building stretched out before her. On her right, the horses moved around in their boxes, their heads reaching over the doors into the aisle. The first head belonged to Richard's gray stallion. She patted its face.

Richard walked on past her. He called out in Saracen, and the grooms leaped away down the stable aisle. Richard sat down on a wooden saddle rack against the wall opposite the stalls.

"Where are you going, that you need a horse?"

She scratched under the gray stallion's jaw. "Is there any place I can't go?"

He grunted. "Where do I start?"

A groom led a tall mare up between them. Maria turned toward the horse. It was a deep blood bay, its mane and tail shining black. Richard slid down from the saddle rack. He bent to feel the mare's legs. He and the Saracen groom talked in the other tongue. Maria went off along the row of stalls, looking at each horse. She took her surcoat off and hung it on her arm. The stable smelled and sounded the same as any Christian stable. If anything it was cleaner. In the middle of the barn she came on a small white mare.

She leaned on the outside of the stall. The mare snorted suspiciously at her.

"Maria." The groom was brushing off the bay mare. Richard came up toward her. "Ride this horse, so that I can see if you can handle her."

"I don't want that horse," Maria said. She looked back at the white mare, which took one step cautiously toward her. "I want this horse." She held out her hand to the mare.

Richard stood beside her, looking into the stall. "Where have you seen this horse before?"

"Nowhere. I just like her."

The mare licked Maria's palm. Richard said, "On sight. Without even riding her."

"She's pretty."

The mare stuck her nose into Maria's face and sniffed, and she laughed. Richard tramped off down the stable, calling to the groom. He sounded angry. He had been angry for three days. They put the bay mare away and saddled the white mare, and they all went out to the park.

Here the ground fell off in a long gentle slope toward the wall, green in the bright sunlight, although it was still winter. The mare came out of the stable snorting with every step. She shied at the wind and danced on her toes around a bare spot in the grass. The groom talked to her in Saracen baby talk. Maria put her coat on the ground.

"Maybe you'd better let me ride her first," Richard said. "She hasn't been out of the barn in a while."

Maria took the reins from the groom. "She's a good girl." She waved the groom out of the way. Richard lifted her up into the saddle.

The horse snorted, but did not move. She was so excited at being out in the open meadow that she was already breaking into a dark sweat, but she waited until Maria signaled her before she started off at a quick walk. Maria jogged her and cantered her in circles around the meadow. The white mare was soft-gaited as a cat. Maria backed her and spun her around. She galloped up beside Richard.

Right in front of him the mare neatly bucked her off. She landed on her back in the soft grass. The mare galloped away down the green meadow toward the gate, her tail like a flag. The groom ran after her. Maria sat up.

Richard held out his hand to her. "See—you're not as good a rider as you think you are." He pulled her up onto her feet.

Maria looked down after the mare. "Isn't she beautiful? Can I have her?"

"You think you can handle her?" He started back up toward the stable. Maria followed him. He glanced at her, and in spite of himself he smiled.

"I wonder what her name is."

She stopped to watch the white mare, trotting along beside the groom up the meadow. Richard went into the stable. His voice sounded hollow in the roof. She followed him into the dark horse-smelling barn. He let himself into the stall with a lanky black colt. Maria went up to the door.

"Thank you," she said.

He turned his back to her. The groom led in the white mare, her flanks steaming. Maria leaned against the stall door and watched Richard groom the black colt, talking to it in French and Saracen.

"I hope you're not waiting for me to go up to the tower with you," he said over his shoulder. "I've got a lot to do down here."

"I'll help you." She reached over the stall door and patted the colt's neck.

Richard's head swiveled toward her, his eyebrows drawn together over his nose. He stared at her a moment. "Go get me a sponge."

She brought him a wet sponge. He wiped the colt's eyes and mouth and nostrils. The groom left. Maria opened the door, backing up. When Richard came out of the stall she put her arms around him.

"Is this what you did with Roger?" he said.

"No." She kissed him.

265

His arm went around her waist. She pushed the door shut. The groom came back into the barn, saw them, and left at speed. She pressed herself against Richard, stroking her body against him.

His arm tightened around her. With his free hand he fumbled the latch on the stall closed. Maria rubbed her face against his shoulder.

"What did you have in mind?" he said. "The floor?" His kiss was softer than Roger's. She opened her mouth and he slid his tongue over her lip.

"Come on."

The last stall was empty. Clean sand covered the floor, deep and soft. They didn't even take their clothes off. The strange place and the chance of being seen stirred her up. She rocked him, gasping, until he stabbed her into an intense sweet pleasure.

He lay still on her, his face against her hair. "That mouth doesn't lie."

"Richard, you talk too much." She locked her arms around him. It was the first time she had enjoyed lying with him since she had come to Mana'a. Her skirts were rucked up around her waist. She moved her leg against his thigh. His face was running with sweat. His arms tightened around her.

"Papa?"

"Shit." Richard lifted his head.

Footsteps ran toward them through the stable. They pulled quickly away from each other. Maria yanked her skirts down.

"Papa, where are you?"

Richard stood up. "I'm here." Maria handed him his belt. Her hair was loose and she pushed it away from her face. Robert hung over the door.

"Mama! What are you doing in there?"

She looked up at Richard; she burst out laughing.

Robert and Ismael had found a huge old feather parasol somewhere in the palace. When she went out to the city with them, a servant carried it over her head to keep the sun off. In the streets outside the palace, streams of people surged noisily through the markets, haggling over chickens and goats, and swarmed thick around the water vendors on the corners. Maria rode the white mare along between Ismael and Robert. Ahmed, the black servant, came after them with the parasol.

They followed the wide street out across the city, riding from one market to another, each with its own crowd and sound and smell. She had never seen a place so thick with people. The boys shouted to her, each one trying to pull her attention in the opposite direction. She peered down the side streets, running off between the white walls of buildings. On her right the ground fell away steeply. Beyond the rooftops and the plumed trees, in the distance the bay was a dark blue ribbon.

The mare shied halfway across the street. Maria reined her around. An enormous shell was lying in the dirt, like the armor of a monstrous beetle. Ismael said it was a dead leaf from one of the Saracen trees. Maria tried to make her horse go up to it, but the mare flattened her ears back and refused. They rode on.

"There, Mother, see?" Robert pulled patiently on her arm. "See?"

She stood in her stirrups. Where he was pointing, there was a big stall offering fruit for sale. In the back of the stall there was a naked hairy man, three feet high: a monkey.

The crowd shoved her on. On the corner of the street, a man stood on the back of a cart, talking passionately in Saracen, with many eloquent gestures. Nobody listened to him at all. They passed a stall selling ribbons, thousands of ribbons fluttering in the breeze. Maria turned to look back. Ahmed, the parasol staff braced in his stirrup, was reading a book, his horse plodding along after hers.

"Mother," Robert cried. "I'll buy you a songbird."

Maria turned forward again. They had stopped in front of a stall alive with birds, sitting by the dozens on long perches, and hanging in little wooden cages from the uprights. Ismael was already reaching into his purse.

The bird-woman smiled. Her front teeth were missing. With a bow and several gestures, she invited Maria to choose one of the birds. The boys scrambled out of their saddles and shouldered each other out of the way, fighting for the right to pay for it. Maria pointed to a sparrow on the left upright of the stall. The woman gave her the cage and grandly refused the boys' money. Maria thanked her, the woman bowed and smiled, and they rode on.

They came to a wide square. Suddenly three Saracens approached her, all on horseback, their eyes fixed on her. Her spine prickled up. Robert and Ismael closed around her.

"Stop," Robert shouted. "What do you want?"

The Saracens drew rein. The leader spoke in his language. His eyes never left Maria's. He bowed several times. His clothes were rich and in his sash he carried a sword in a jeweled scabbard. Ismael and Robert talked.

"Mama," Robert said. His voice was high-pitched. "I think he wants to bribe you."

Maria went hot all over with embarrassment. The Saracen watched her expectantly. She turned the mare and rode away, back up the street. Wheeling to follow her, Ahmed nearly dropped his book. The boys rushed up on either side of her.

"Mother, we should find out who they are and tell Papa."

Maria shook her head. "I don't want to talk to people like that. I have to go home anyway, Jilly will be hungry."

"Oh, Mama—but there's so much—"

"You go on by yourselves." She was still carrying the sparrow cage in her hand. Reining down, she hooked it to her saddle pommel.

"Mama, how will you find your way without us?"

"The palace is right over there." She pointed up the hill. "And Ahmed will go with me." The black man, deep in his book, sat with the parasol tipped uselessly against his shoulder. She waved to the boys. "Good-bye. Be home before dark."

"Good-bye, Mother."

The boys rode off, waving to her. Ahmed's gelding turned to follow. Maria swung the mare around in front of him and plucked the book out of the servant's hands. She gave him a weighted look. Hastily he gathered his reins and his parasol and rode after her.

On the way back to the palace, she passed a leather worker's shop, and saw on display a tasseled bridle like Ismael's. The leather worker understood a little French.

268

While he was measuring the white mare's head and showing Maria a choice of snaffle bits, a commotion started in the street.

Richard on his gray stallion, a dozen knights behind him, was plowing toward her through the crowd. Maria went around in front of the white mare. Richard saw her. He reined in. The knights trotted up around him. The people in the street crowded together to stare at him. Maria climbed into her saddle. She waved to the leather worker.

"Red—make the tassels red." She called Ahmed and went out into the street.

"I'm getting a bridle like Ismael's," she said to Richard.

He looked around them. "Did you come out here by yourself?"

"Ahmed is with me. Where have you been?"

They rode together up the street. All the people around them were looking at them. He gestured vaguely out toward the city. The wall of the palace appeared ahead of them, and they turned toward the gate.

"Out letting people give me a lot of gratuitous advice," he said. "King Jesus Christ, all these people here think I'm a halfwit." He pressed his stallion over toward her and bent down to tap the cage. "What's that?"

"Oh." She unfastened the cage from her saddle. His horse shouldered hers around the turn into the gate. He raised his hand and pointed. The knights rode off along the foot of the wall. Maria held the cage up to see the bird inside. It crouched against the bars, its feathers fluffed, its eyes brimming with terror.

"A woman in the market gave it to me—I didn't really want it, but she was so kind, how could I refuse it? I'll let it go." She opened up the door of the cage. The bird clutched the bars in its claws. It would not come out, even when she turned the cage over and shook it.

Richard was staring at her. Their horses carried them up the meadow toward the stable. Ahmed was holding the parasol over them both. She looked into the cage. The bird flattened itself against the bars. Its eye slowly shut. She held the cage out to Richard.

"You do it."

He took the cage and broke the door off with his fingers. Leaning down from his saddle, he dropped it into the grass. Maria twisted around and tossed Ahmed his book. She nodded to him to go. Richard straightened up again; Ahmed left them and they rode on across the meadow.

Maria turned to look behind them in the grass for the bird. "Are you sure it can get out?"

Richard laughed. "If it recovers from being shaken half to pieces." He put his hand on his hip, still staring at her. "You shouldn't go around alone in the city, you know."

"I had the boys with me. Are you telling me not to go there again?"

"Do what you want. You will anyway."

FOR THE NEXT FEW DAYS, she and the Saracen women went about the palace, changing all the furniture around. Maria got several of the magnificent carpets out of the treasurehouse and had them hung on the walls. She took the lattice screens down from the windows to let the sunlight in. The wide, airy rooms were bright as the garden, so she had fresh flowers put around the whole palace every day. For the first time, she felt as if she belonged in Mana'a.

She played with Jilly in the garden. She brought the little girl up the stairs to the room of the star ceiling and found Richard there, lying on his side across the bed, talking to Rahman.

Maria carried the baby over and dumped her on the bed. She scrambled on all fours into her father's arms. Rahman was sitting cross-legged on the floor. Maria stood beside the bed, her eyes on the Saracen, who feigned interest in the far wall.

"Richard," she said, "this is my bedroom. I don't want him in my bedroom."

Rahman gave a gratifying start. Richard said, "King Jesus Christ. Stop, will you?" He held Jilly at arm's length above him; she kicked her fat legs and screeched.

"I don't want him in my bedroom." Maria stared at Rahman. Grim, the Emir turned his head to meet her gaze.

Richard muttered something under his breath. Rahman got carefully up onto his feet. He shook out his immaculate robes.

"I should not have lowered myself to entering a woman's quarters, lord, save you wished it of me. I will go to my castle." Richard had given one of the three towers over to the Saracens.

Richard said, "Stay here."

Maria clenched her fist against her skirt. "If he can come here, then I won't."

"Lord." Rahman bowed his head. "I wish you a good day." He looked at Maria down his Mohammedan nose and went out of the room. The door shut with a thud behind him.

"Your mother's a shrew," Richard told Jilly.

Maria sat down on the bed. Although it was still morning, the heat was already uncomfortable. The Saracen women had told her of the blazing summers in Mana'a, when everyone with somewhere else to go went. She took her hair down and brushed it.

"Aren't you supposed to forgive your enemies?" Richard said.

"Not Rahman."

"You're such a good Christian."

Jilly climbed on him, pulling on his beard and chewing his fingers. Her voice rose in a babble of excited talk. Richard tossed her up in the air, caught her, and rolling suddenly to his feet set her on the floor.

"I have some work in Iste." He walked off around the room. Jilly on her hands and knees pursued him at top speed. He turned to face Maria again. "Well? Aren't you going to say anything?"

Maria shook her hair back. She brushed it down thick and black, so long now she could sit on it. "What should I say? I want to go with you."

"I'm sure you do," he said. He came up beside her and took a tress of her hair between his fingers. "I'm sure Roger does, too."

"You get a lot of righteous indignation out of one kiss, Richard."

He sat down behind her on the bed. In the middle of the floor, Jilly got carefully up onto her feet. The sunlight gilded the ends of her light brown hair. Maria laid the brush down. Richard buried his hands in her hair. He put his arms around her. She closed her eyes.

XXVII

❧

"THERE MAY BE BEGGARS AND THIEVES LIVING HERE," Robert said. Maria jumped down from the top of the wall and landed next to him in the deep drift of leaves. "So we have to stay together. Ismael!"

Ismael appeared on the top of the wall. He bounded to the ground a few feet away. Maria followed the two boys across the paved ward. Grass and weeds sprouted up through the cracks in the stones. The dark building before her was an empty hulk, its roof gone, sunshine streaming out through its top windows, and the main door hanging on one hinge. Maria stopped to look around.

"This is the citadel you stormed."

Ismael caught her arm. "I come here—me many many brothers—" His free hand swooped through the air. "The Emir like a—like a—" he raised his hands—"great wind! We crash in, we—" his arms described their charge; in his search for words he panted—"bury everything. Floods and oceans. We—"

Robert dragged her on toward the citadel. "Mother, come on, we can't stay very long or we'll get into trouble with the watch. Don't listen to him, he was in the rear-guard with me."

They went through the broken door into a hall. Their footsteps resounded hollow from the walls. Leaves had blown through the door and collected in long trails across the tiled floor. Maria blinked in the gloomy light. The hall smelled of dust.

Ismael ran across the hall before them. "We rush on. Many many brothers after the Emir."

"Rahman?" Maria asked, uncertainly.

"Papa," Robert said.

She went to a side door. Beyond it was a little room whose walls were covered with pictures. There was no furniture. Even the walls were cracked, as if someone had tried to loot them too, but she could still make out scenes of hunting, gardens and fountains, all peopled with little Saracens no taller than her thumb.

"What is this?"

Robert came up beside her. "What? Come upstairs—wait until you see up there."

Maria drew one finger across the figured wall, striping the dust. She stood back to see the painting higher on the wall. Ismael said coldly, "Bad work here. Pah."

She looked around, intrigued, and the boys pulled her toward the stairs. Ismael hurried on ahead of her. Maria said, "Why is it bad work? The pictures are beautiful."

They climbed a long staircase. The bare metal struts of the railing hung from the wall. Most of the stone steps were broken and two were gone entirely. Ismael said, "Bad Mana'an work." When they reached the head of the stairs, he turned earnestly to her. His hands threshed the air.

"These people Mana'an folk. I is Majlas al-Kerak. I is brother, Emir is brother, Robert brother." He took hold of her hand. "Maria brother as well. We no—" he veiled the lower half of her face with his hands. "No wine, no sell brother to slave." He nodded profoundly. "All such Mana'an by course."

Maria stared at him. His beautiful eyes searched her face anxiously. Abruptly he smiled. "Maria brother?"

"Yes," she said. "If you wish. Not if I must give up drinking wine. What about the pictures?"

"Pictures." He tasted the word. "Pictures. We no pictures." He shook his head. His long forefinger pointed to the sky. "God make—" His hands shaped the space before him. "Men only thank God. No make. Man no God."

Robert said, "Mother, come on, we can't stay very long."

Maria went after him, Ismael beside her. That was why

273

the walls of the palace were decorated with prayers instead of pictures; the Saracens thought pictures were sinful. She shrugged. Little they did made sense to her. She went after Robert up the stairs.

The upper stories of the citadel were full of debris and broken furniture and trash. Thieves and beggars had built fires there to warm themselves. Mice lived in the dust and owls in the rafters. The boys hunted busily for treasure. From their talk, she gathered that Robert had found a knife buried in the rubble the last time they came here.

She sat in a window and looked out. The hill dropped away sheer below her. She could see out over the cathedral's busy market place and its awnings, across the bay to the headlands in the distance, where the sea dashed white over the rocks. The red-tiled roofs of Mana'a swept in an ample curve off down the beach. The palace was behind her. Richard had gone out early that morning to another of his incessant councils and would be away all day.

What Ismael had said clung to her thoughts. It had never occurred to her that Saracens had heretics, too. She wondered which were orthodox, Ismael's mountain folk or the Mana'ans. But of course it made no difference, if they were not Christian. Ismael's people sounded strict: she wondered how they could accept Richard, a Norman.

"Mama." Robert slid his arm around her and leaned his head on her shoulder. "Aren't you glad we came?"

She stroked his hair with her fingers. He was turning handsome. She smiled at him, trying to imagine him a young man. "Robert," she said, "will you stay true to me?"

"I will." He hugged her. "You are my lady. I want to wear your favor, you must give me something fine."

Maria laughed at him. "Ah, you will break every woman's heart in Marna."

"Oh, Mama."

She kissed his forehead. "We have to go back home—see how low the sun has fallen."

They had left their horses with the black slave. When they climbed over the wall again, he was gone, and the horses were gone. Maria drew back against the wall, her eyes worried on the sky. The sun was setting. Jilly would be hungry. Ismael and Robert conferred in Saracen. Robert licked his lips, his face sharp with concern. Ismael ran off down the street to look around the corner. In the distance, the Saracen priests began the sundown call to prayer.

"Mama," Robert said. "I think we are in trouble."

Maria's arms were cold. She moved into the last of the sunlight. "What happened? Do you think the watch came by and chased him away? Ahmed wouldn't have run away."

Ismael was hurrying down the steep narrow street. The high walls on either side of him made his footsteps boom. Robert walked up and down in front of her.

"Don't be afraid, Mother. I'll take care of you. I'll tell Papa it was my fault."

"Jilly always gets hungry at sundown." She had been trying to feed the child with a cup, but the little girl still loved her breast. She would cry. "Where could he have gone to?"

Ismael was racing back toward them. She started down the street toward the cathedral. The evening breeze swept out toward the bay. Overhead, the first stars began to show. Robert strode along beside her. The street was cut into wide shallow steps down the steep pitch of the slope. A man passed them, riding on a little donkey, his wife walking behind him with a sack over her shoulder.

"Mama, maybe we ought to go home."

"On foot?" The palace was miles away. "Besides, we have to get our horses back. And we can't leave Ahmed —maybe he's gotten lost."

"If he has, it's his fault."

Ismael jogged up beside him. He shook his head sadly. "Ahmed go. Ay ay." He leaned forward, saw that Robert held her by the right arm, and threaded her left arm through his. "Cry not. The Emir much no see us."

"What?"

Ismael fluttered his fingers. "No fear."

They went to the end of the street and turned left into the wide cobbled thoroughfare. A woman passed them, a Christian, unveiled. Between the buildings, in the distance, the bay rolled its dark water.

Maria could not decide what to do. The watch was sent

out from a tower in another quarter entirely—the meanest area of Mana'a, she had been told: the two hundred men-at-arms who patrolled the city were based there to help keep order. She wondered if the black servant had run away.

Twilight deepened around them. The swarm of people in the streets thinned to nothing. When they came at last to the cathedral, the square was empty. Night had fallen. Dogs fought and snuffed through the heaps of garbage behind the deserted bazaar. A filthy one-armed beggar bustled up to them.

"Alms, alms—"

Maria dug a coin from her wallet and threw it to him. The stump of his right arm thrust horribly through his ragged coat, and she stepped away from him, repulsed. She started up the steps to the cathedral porch. Robert lingered, talking to the beggar in Saracen.

The cripple answered him, his hair flopping in his eyes, and put his hands out for money. Maria started down the steps again. Ismael thrust Robert aside. He held up a coin and clasped the beggar by the hand, the money between their palms. The beggar smirked at him. Throwing back his rags and the grotesque stump, he produced a perfectly sound right arm and pointed across the market place.

Ismael whirled and ran across the square, his djellabah flapping; he lost his headcloth and did not stop to pick it up. Robert ran out onto the cobblestones to get it. The beggar adjusted his stump. Darkness covered them. In the bay, lights bobbed up and down: anchored ships. The cold wind from the mountains chased leaves across the porch of the cathedral. Maria stood on the steps, gnawing on her knuckle. Her breasts were tight with milk. Jilly would be crying for her. Robert raced up the steps toward her, Ismael's headcloth in his hand.

The beggar whined something at him. Robert drove the man impatiently away. He strode along the steps, his eyes on the city where Ismael had gone. The beggar scurried up the steps toward Maria.

"Mah-eee-ya," he said; he grinned at her. His tongue lapped at his lips. He dug in his rags and pulled out a little wooden cross. "Mah-eee-ya."

Robert charged up the steps after him. "Stay away from my mother!"

He shoved the beggar roughly away from her. The man wheeled. Maria reached nervously for the dagger in her belt, but the beggar only pushed Robert backwards. The boy fell sprawling across the stairs. Hoofbeats sounded in the dark market place. A shuttered lamp bounced toward them. The beggar scuttled like a crab up the steps and vanished onto the cathedral porch.

"Come," Ismael was crying. His voice hurried toward them with the hoofbeats across the square. "Come—Lord Maria lost! Lost!"

"I can't understand one word he says," a voice said, in French. Maria stumbled down the steps, spent with relief. "By God's eyes, it's a Christian woman."

"Lord Maria," Ismael said, with emphasis. Their lantern raised, the two watchmen rode behind him toward her.

"You, there, woman, you can't stay here after sundown, do you have a place to go?"

Maria began to laugh. Her legs quivered, and she sat down hard on the step. She could not stop laughing; she buried her face in her hands.

THE WATCH KNEW nothing of the black slave Ahmed and the four horses. Borrowing mounts from a nearby hostel, they took Maria and the boys back to the palace. Robert and Ismael argued in Saracen the whole while. Robert explained to her that he thought Ahmed had run off to be a robber, but Ismael believed the servant had taken their horses to sell for passage back to Africa.

Jilly was fast asleep. The Saracen woman had fed her from a cup. She said that the child had gorged herself and never missed her mother. Maria paced across the darkened room. Her taut breasts were leaking into her clothes. Richard had not yet come back. There was no way to tell him that she had lost four horses and a servant without making him angry.

"Mama?"

Robert peered in the door. When she waved he slipped into the room.

"Ahmed isn't here. I told you he wouldn't come back."

Maria shook her head. "Maybe the watch will catch him." It would be hard to smuggle four horses and a feather parasol out of Mana'a, even at night. She picked up an orange from the bowl of fruit on the table and bit into the skin so that she could peel it. Restless, she moved around the room, leaving bits of peel on top of the furniture. "It is all so very strange."

A pebble rattled on the floor below the nearest window. Robert said, "Ismael." He leaned across the window sill into the night.

"Mama! Come look!"

His voice startled her; she jumped, and her skin went to gooseflesh. "God's blood, Robert, be easy with me." She went up behind him and looked out the window.

His teeth bright as the moon, Ismael stood in the garden three stories below the window. On his shoulder he had the feather parasol.

Maria gasped. She leaned out the window. "Stay there," she called to Ismael. She had not eaten, and her stomach was knotted with hunger. She stuck the orange into her sleeve. The Saracen women, tittering, watched her and Robert rush away. Maria went down the staircase two steps at a time. Two servants coming upstairs flattened themselves against the wall to let her go by.

All the doors but one on the other side of the palace were locked at sundown. They pried open the shutter in the boys' room and climbed out through the window into the ward. Ismael trotted toward them, spinning the parasol at arm's length over his head.

"Horses, too," he said; his face was sleek with pride. "All crook in Emir fort."

Maria looked where he was pointing. He meant the half-built gatehouse on the new wall.

"What were they doing in there?" Robert cried.

"Ssssh." A pellucid calm took her over. She met Ismael's eyes. He spread his toothy smile across his face. "Rahman," Maria said.

"Rahman," Ismael murmured.

Maria stamped her foot. She tried to think of one of Richard's long obscenities.

278

"If we tell Papa," Robert said slowly, "do you think he would mind?"

"I would liefer he didn't know." She turned back to the window, hauled herself up onto the stone sill, and swung her legs and skirts inside. The two boys followed her. They struggled with the feather parasol, which was too large to fit through the window. Maria stood away, brushing her hair back off her cheeks, and Ismael worried the parasol at an angle through the window casement.

Robert had gone out of the room. Now he raced back through the doorway, skidded on the smooth carpetless floor, grabbed her to keep from falling, and almost brought her down too.

"Mama," he cried. "Papa is coming back—I saw him riding up from the main gate."

"Mother Mary." The parasol was jammed in the window casement. "Ismael. Can you get our horses out of the gatehouse and take them to the stable? Hurry. Robert, go to the kitchen and bid them send our supper up to our room." She pulled off her coif, stroked the stray wisps of her hair back, and jammed the dirty linen down on her head. Lifting her skirts in her fists, she ran through the next room to the staircase, up to the little hall, and out the door into the torchlit middle ward.

Richard was just dismounting from his horse. Rahman and Stephen stood before him, and she withdrew quietly behind the vines hanging from the porch eave. Richard picked up Stephen, who clung to him with both arms around his neck. A groom led off the horse. Rahman was talking in a voice syrupy with concern.

"They have not come back, lord. You see that it is deepest night. Your dear lady is . . . sometimes naïve. We fear some wickedness has befallen them in the city."

Richard stared at him, his face perfectly blank. At last he shook his head. "Rahman, you are no match for my wife." He strode past the Saracen, Stephen hugged in his arms. "Maria, what is going on?"

Maria walked out of the porch toward him. "You must be hungry," she said. "I've waited so that we could sup together."

"Mama!" Stephen tore himself out of Richard's grasp. "Where did you go? I looked and looked for you—"

"Sssh," Maria said. "You should be in bed." She lifted her cheek for Richard's kiss. Over his shoulder, Rahman's eyes met hers; he looked as if he'd drunk vinegar.

"Rahman, please send Ahmed to me, when you have no further need for him."

Rahman walked stiffly away. Richard said, "You had better tell me what this is all about."

Maria followed him into the palace. Stephen held her fast by the hand. "Mama, I was afraid. Rahman said—" Maria bent and kissed him and patted his cheek.

"You should not listen to Rahman."

"Why didn't you let me go, too?" One hand holding her skirt, he ran along beside her while she caught up with Richard. He did not slacken his pace for them, and they had to trot to keep up.

"What have you done now?" he said.

"Nothing."

They went through the antechamber and into the room with the star ceiling. She sent Stephen to light the lamps and helped Richard take off his leather jacket.

"Did you get what you wanted, today?" she asked.

"Jesus." His eyes moved slowly over her. "Look at your clothes. What have you been doing, climbing trees?"

"Robert and Ismael and I went riding." There was a knock on the door. She crossed the room to let in the servants with their supper. While they laid out the dishes and made the table ready, she washed her face and hands. Her skirt was filthy from the citadel floor and the half-peeled orange had soaked her right sleeve with its sticky fragrant juice. Stephen sat on the bed before her.

"Mama, you should tell me where you are going. Rahman says—"

"Sssh. Have you eaten supper? Good. Go downstairs to bed. Robert will be there now."

Stephen made a face. "You always play with Robert and not me." He ran out of the room.

The servants had brought out the little table and set it up before the windows. Richard was sitting down to eat. "Maria, are you coming?" She took the carved backless chair beside him. The aroma of lamb and apricots made her mouth water.

"What is the Majlas al-Kerak?"

280

Richard chewed down what he had in his mouth. "Ismael's people." He broke a loaf of bread and sponged up the sauce on his plate. "The Brotherhood. Those are their strongholds on the tops of the mountains." He lifted his hand, and a servant brought up another platter of meat.

Maria remembered Ismael's talk of brothers. The lamb was delicious; the fruit sweetened the delicate meat. She let another man put more food on her plate. In the shadows, the master server, Dawud, stood keeping the service orderly.

"Ismael's father is the chief judge," Richard said. "The headman of the Brotherhood. There was a rival, but we killed him."

Maria indicated the bread. A servant cut her a piece and spread butter on it. She said, "Who was it that captured you, that time?"

"Ismael's father." He stopped long enough to taste from two platters, waved one away, and watched the man put slices of meat on his plate and spoon sauce over them. "They are like monks, the Brotherhood, save they marry —no one keeps anything for himself, they are all slaves to their Order."

Maria finished the food on her plate. When she sat back, a servant brought her a clean dish and poured another wine for her. She called to an idle man to light more of the lamps.

"Are you one of the Brotherhood?"

Richard threw her a sharp glance. "I am the Emir of the Brotherhood."

Maria laughed. The master server put a silver tray on the table and with a flourish lifted off the cover to reveal a boned stuffed fowl decorated with vegetable flowers. Deftly he sliced the bird into thick pieces. Richard wiped his hands on a cloth.

"What are you laughing at?"

She shook her head. "Whom did you meet with today?"

"The Sanhedrin of Mana'a. In full plumage." He ate with great energy. "What were you laughing at?"

"God's blood, Richard, you are persistent. Ismael and I had a talk today about heresy, that's all. What did the Jews want?"

281

"What everybody wants. To rule me." He licked his fingers and reached across the table for another slice of the chicken. The master server moved the platter out of his reach before he could help himself.

"He has Christian manners," Maria said. "Doesn't he, Dawud?"

The master server cleared his throat. His knife slipped, and he nearly dropped the piece of meat onto Richard's plate. Maria pushed her cup around the table, thinking over what he had told her.

Richard said, "Everybody tells me to get rid of Rahman."

Maria took a knife and spread butter on a piece of bread. Along the walls, in the half-dark, the servants stood suddenly motionless; their eyes shone with interest. Richard drank his wine. He got up and strolled around the room, waiting for Maria to finish so they could start on the next course.

"Stephen likes him," she said. She pushed her plate away. "You have said he is useful to you."

"I don't need him," Richard said. "Not any more."

The servants came forward to clear the table, their eyes shining. Before the meat was cold, Rahman would know everything they had said here. Obviously that was what Richard intended. She said, "Keep him. Who knows but the next man might be just as wicked and twice as clever?" They were bringing in a tray of cheeses, and she reached for the wine to take the taste of the meat from her tongue. "Do what you will."

Richard smiled at her. "I was thinking of it."

IN THE MORNING, when she went into the little hall, Rahman's chessmen were scattered over the carpet, all the heads lopped off. She stooped and picked up the little white Sultan. When she looked up, Rahman stood in the doorway.

"Who did this?" She held the chessman out toward him.

Rahman's eyes lanced at her. "No. Not you." He took the pieces from her hands. "It was that barbarian mountaineer."

Maria did not speak. He fit the little Sultan's head to its

282

body, as if the break might suddenly heal. If Ismael had broken it, Robert had helped. Rahman went past her, toward the window and the sunlight.

She picked up the other pieces, carried them in her skirt to the table, and spilled them out on the checkered board. From this part of the room she could see through the window along Rahman's line of sight. Outside, on the new wall, Richard was overseeing some work of measurement. Rahman put the broken Sultan almost apologetically down on the table.

"Do you play chess, lady?"

"I?" Startled, she blinked at him; she had never known him friendly before. "No—how would I learn that?"

"You would play good chess," he said. "Someone should teach you." His voice turned suddenly bitter. "It might keep you from men's affairs."

"Does it keep you from horse-stealing?"

Rahman sniffed at her. He turned again toward the window.

"Why don't you teach Richard?"

The Saracen's head swiveled toward her. He let out an explosive snort. "He would ruin me. He already has." He looked down his nose at her. "What will you tell him of this?" His hand indicated the chessmen.

Maria grunted. "Nothing. Why should I tell him?" Richard was short-tempered enough. The Saracen woman came slowly through the door, bent double so that Jilly could cling to her hands and walk before her. When she saw Maria, the baby went down on all fours and raced across the floor toward her.

Rahman left the room. Maria sat down on the floor to play with Jilly. Richard had refused to tell her what he was going to do with Rahman; obviously Rahman did not know yet either. She wondered if the Emir would dare show him the broken chess set. She knew the boys had done it because the little figures represented men. Jilly climbed on her, pulling off her coif and poking her fingers into Maria's mouth.

"Mamama."

"Mama," Maria said. She pretended to bite the little girl's thin fingers. She remembered Ceci doing this. Now when she thought of Ceci, the dead child had Jilly's face, her soft brown hair and pale eyes. She bounced the baby into a high-pitched hicketing laughter.

"Mamamamama."

Ismael had to be punished. All her tapestries were pictures. She clapped her hands with Jilly, fighting down her will to spite Rahman. A servant came in to clean away the broken chessmen, and she told him to leave them there.

"Mama," she said to the little girl. "Say Mama."

MARIA SAID GOOD-BYE to Ismael and Robert at the Emir's Gate and rode back alone through the city. It was a bright, hot day. In the streets the people of Mana'a conducted their affairs and arguments at the top of their lungs. She rode toward the harbor, between the low hills like ruined mountains where the rich Saracens had their palaces. A chant of voices trailed her: "Mah-eee-ya!"

She stopped on a street corner to watch a sword swallower delight a crowd of children. Already she missed Robert and Ismael. Richard had sent them up to the mountains as a punishment, but they took it for a treat: they could not wait to go.

She moved off down the street again. She took her feet from the stirrups and let them dangle. On either side, the stalls of the astrologers and magic-makers were packed with people. The white mare stepped out into her cushioned jogtrot. A stream of merchants' knaves raced up across her path, shrieking their seductions at her. When they did not draw her, they ran off to the next rich passer-by.

The huge square before the cathedral was jammed. The people haggled across the counters of the merchants' stalls and fought to get up through the crowd. Towering over the Mana'an folk, the mailed knights of William's escort waded up to the stalls that sold marchpane and sherbet. A groom sitting on the cathedral steps took the white mare. The one-armed beggar scurried toward her, but she waved him off and went past him into the porch: Richard would have given him something.

The iron-bound doors were open. Through them she could hear William's voice complaining. She walked down the center aisle. Workmen were pulling down the Saracenic columns and the false walls. The air was foggy with dust.

Jilly on his shoulders, William appeared before her, saying, "Richard, I am too stupid to be a churchman."

"Mama," Jilly said, and stretched out her arms.

William lifted her down. "Maria, my sister." Giving the child to her, he stooped and planted a wet kiss on her forehead. Maria put Jilly down on the floor. "I cannot understand it," William said. "Roger gave me to think you were wasting away here."

Richard grunted, behind her. "Roger indulges himself. Maria, she is eating the dirt."

Maria took the stone from Jilly before she could stick it in her mouth and gave her a big ring of keys to play with. Richard said, "You'll do very well, William. I'll tell you what to do."

"That's what I'm afraid of." William clasped his hands over his vast belly and heaved it up above his belt. "I know you too well, Richard, I don't want to be your cat's paw."

Maria looked over her shoulder at her husband. He was sitting on a chunk of the stone altar rail, his hands on his knees. He said, "I am trying to remember once when I've used you as a cat's paw."

"You would, if I let you."

Maria measured the altar with her eyes, trying to imagine furnishings for it. Richard said. "Maria, have I ever used him for a cat's paw?"

"Don't pull me into it." Jilly stood up, holding onto her skirt, and stared uncertainly off across the cathedral.

William said, "You practically tell Roger which hand to wipe his bottom with. Now you are trying to take Birnia away from me—"

"You can rule Birnia. I told you that. William, that old man will die soon. Do you want someone who does not love us—"

"You could find some clerk loyal to us. Besides, the Archbishop of Mana'a would have no might—every church save this one is in the diocese of Agato. Are you going to name their Archbishop, too?"

"—Somebody who does not love us come in here and lose Mana'a again to the Saracens?"

William's mouth drooped, pensively. He scraped one foot over the dusty floor.

"We are here," Richard said, "because they suffer us here—the Saracens and the Jews. It's a balancing act to make an Egyptian tumbler weep. Let some man rule who does not understand that, we will not keep power here."

Over near the sanctuary, Jilly fell down hard and let out a wail. Maria went to pick her up. In the depths of the cathedral, workmen were hammering, and something crunched and collapsed in a shower of noise. When she carried Jilly back over by the men, the sour look on William's face told her he was about to give in.

"I can keep Birnia, you said. I like it there, it's my home now."

Richard was twisting the ring on his forefinger. "I have told you twice now you have done well in Birnia."

"One more condition. You might not tell me what to do. I'll do what I think is right."

"You can do anything you want. You can turn every Christian in Mana'a into a monophysite. Just keep counsel with me."

Jilly on her hip, Maria turned to William. "I will keep you company. You won't be lonely. Where is Stephen?"

William sighed. "I like Birnia—he'll want me here for the best of the spring hunting, too." He patted her cheek. Wide-legged, he started toward the vestibule door.

Richard took Jilly in his arms. When they went out into the cathedral garden, the heat struck them like a wave. Stephen was climbing in the mulberry trees at the far end, along the wall. Calling to him, they went to the gate to get their horses and go home.

XXVIII

❧

"PROMISE ME YOU WILL NOT TALK OF IT TO ROGER."

Richard gave her a suspicious look. The road ahead of them dropped abruptly five feet to a gravel wash, and he spurred his horse ahead of her down the steep slide. Maria's mare scambled down the embankment, snorting, and trotted up beside him again.

"You mean, that I know he kissed you? Why? Would it make it better if I didn't know?"

"Infinitely," Maria said.

They stopped to wait for the wagons to find some way across the washed-out road. The Ridge Highway wound across the shoulders of the mountains. The slopes on either side of them were buried in the thorny gray-green brush of the high zone. In all directions, she could see into the limitless distance, as if she looked across the whole world. The sun was already lowered past nightfall in the valley beneath them, although the rock peaks still blazed in daylight. Richard turned toward her again.

"Why? Tell me the truth, for once, and I'll promise."

"I just don't want to bring it up again."

"That's unconvincing."

"That is the truth."

They rode on down the slope into the mountain night. After moonrise, they came to the gate of Iste. The torches clustered on it shone like jewels in the darkness. A crowd of people waited to greet them. Roger was among them. Maria turned to Richard again.

"Swear you will not speak of it."

For a moment he was silent. Maria stared at him. Behind her, Robert was talking to Ismael. Stephen had gone back to the wagons. At last, Richard said, "I promise."

"Thank you." She faced forward again. "Mary Mother," she said. "Eleanor is here." She lifted her reins. They hurried their pace along the uneven road.

Eleanor ran forward to greet her, stretching out her arms. The two women wept and hugged each other. Maria found herself laughing for no reason. "Where is Jilly?" Eleanor asked, and sniffed. She patted her eyes. "You cannot think how I have chafed this day, waiting to see you again. Where is Jilly?"

Maria pointed behind her to the wagons. The boys had vanished. Eleanor clapped her hands together. She strained toward the carts slowly rolling up the road toward them. Maria climbed into her saddle again. On either side of the road, a dark mass of people waited, calling out in excitement. Eleanor was edging forward, cocking her head from side to side, trying to make out the people in the oncoming train. Maria rode toward the city.

Richard and Roger were talking directly under the gate, their horses blocking the way, as if they were angels. Maria rode her mare up through the orange torchlight. Roger turned toward her. Before he could speak to her, Richard jammed his horse in between them wedging them apart. He struck Roger's hand down.

"Don't touch her. If you ever kiss her again, Roger, I'll kill her."

He pressed his horse sideways through the gate toward her. In the covered archway the hoofbeats rang out sharp as hammerstrokes. Maria's mare scurried into the dark city ahead of him. The ratttle of their hoofs boomed across the empty market place. She reined the mare to a halt. Richard came up beside her.

"You promised me—"

"You swore me an oath when you married me," he said.

They crossed the market place. The torches and people spilled through the gate after them, and Roger trotted up alongside Richard. In the dark Maria could not see his face. Three abreast, they went up the street, silent. Behind them, Eleanor called her name. Maria waved.

"If you have a pretty wife, you should take care of her," Roger said. They were coming into a steep, narrow

288

street; he wheeled his horse across the way, to make Richard hold up. The torchlight from down the hill shone on his face. He thrust his hand out. "Richard, she refused me," he said. "And it wasn't the first time. Why get angry about it now?" Irresistibly, he smiled.

Richard muttered in his throat. Their servants were approaching them. The torchlight glowed higher on the brick walls on either side. Gracelessly Richard shook his brother's hand. Roger turned his horse. With Richard between him and Maria, they rode up the steep street toward the citadel.

Maria held her horse back and let them go on. The parade of torchbearers marched along the street around her. Richard and Roger went on toward the blunt shape of the tower above them; they were talking. He had forgiven Roger immediately. Jealous, she watched among the nosiy band of people in the street for Eleanor.

"WE DO NOT worship idols," the Jew said. He stepped back so that she and Eleanor could precede him through the door. "But when we acquired this building for our temple, the pictures were here, and we love beauty. Here, my lady." He came up beside her and showed her the way across the darkened room, striped with low benches. Going off to one side, he lit his tinderbox.

Eleanor leaned against Maria's side. "This place smells bad."

"Sssh." Maria had thought of asking the priests if coming here was a sin, but she had not wanted to hear them say yes. All around this room, in the dim light of the lamp, people appeared on the walls. The Jew lit another wall lamp, and its yellow glow spread across two faces and part of a horse.

Maria turned to study the pictures. The caretaker walked with his taper from lamp to lamp, and the rich light spread like a dawn, revealing dozens of figures on the walls, dogs and horses, fantastic curled petals of flowers and trees.

"They are very beautiful," Eleanor said stiffly.

Maria put her hand lightly on the wall. The pictures were made of chips of colored tile. After Richard had made so much of them, she tried to find them ugly, but their gestures drew her eyes, their faces made her like them. The Jew came up beside her.

"We think that these are Roman work, perhaps even of the time before Augustus. Our scholars have come from as far as Rome to see them."

"My husband told me of them."

The Jew bowed his head. "God be kind to the Dragon of Marna."

Maria stared into the face of a young man on the wall. A lock of his hair hung over his eyes, and she thought of Robert. The caretaker directed her gaze elsewhere. "Here, you see," he said, "this was once plastered over. We were fortunate in having the help of a man from Antioch, who removed the plaster without damaging the work." He went on about how that was done, including the many prayers the congregation had devoted to it, but Maria did not listen. She stared at him a moment, to see how his face was shaped, and looked carefully back at the faces on the wall: she saw how the artisans had exaggerated here and there to give them their expressions. The large black eyes of a middle-aged woman met hers, candid as a friend, and she laughed.

"Of course," the Jew said, "we cover them during divine worship."

Maria walked away from him, intent on the pictures. Eleanor cleared her throat in a guttural bark. "My lady, you told the lord Robert that you would dine with him."

"The lord Robert can feed himself." But she turned, remembering what she had yet to do before supper. Richard had complained of the fleas in the bed—she had never minded fleas, but they attacked Richard like beasts of prey. And Roger's servants had some problems to be sorted out. She smiled at the caretaker.

"Thank you." She knew what Eleanor and the priests would say if she gave him a present of money. "I shall speak of you and your pictures to my husband."

The Jew inclined his head slightly. "The favor of the prince is life."

Maria digested that. Eleanor leading the way, they went into the outer room of the temple. The maid brought

Maria her cloak. Walking to the gate, they spoke idly of the building of Iste. The Jew urged her to visit the Greek monastery in the old quarter of the city.

"Well," she said. "Perhaps." They went out to the street. The sun was bright but the wind had an edge to it. "Thank you. We will come again, perhaps." In her faltering Saracen, she asked the groom to lead their horses after them. Her stomach was queasy, and riding made it worse. They walked up the steep hill toward the citadel, visible above the roofs and trees that covered the slope.

"That man thinks very much of himself," Eleanor said. "They are arrogant, the Jews. God despises them."

They went along a side street and through a narrow bazaar. The women of the Jewish quarter hurried up and down past them. Maria began to wonder how they lived —they could not hold land or keep beasts, their homes all belonged to the Lombards, who took a money-rent from them. Their looks at her were more curious than arrogant. Eleanor babbled emptily on beside her. She crossed a tree-shaded square, where a dozen boys sat listening to an old man recite, and went up another long street to Roger's gate.

When they came into the ward, Roger's lion was roaring so that the sound echoed off the castle wall. Maria's mare snorted and flung up its head. She gave the horse a quick pat and walked toward the lion pit.

Robert and Ismael were kneeling beside it, jabbing with a stick down at the lion. The iron grille that was supposed to cover the pit stood propped against the wall behind them. Two pages, one carrying an armload of candles, lingered to watch. When they saw Maria coming they raced away. The lion snarled and bounded into sight up the wall of the pit. Ismael struck it in the face, and the beast recoiled from him. Maria came up behind Robert.

"Both of you ought to be spanked," she said. "Put the grille back."

Ismael squatted on his haunches. Cheerfully he smiled up at her. "Maria fear not. I fight lion much often." Robert stood up, but he made no move toward the grille.

"Maria fear for lion," she said. "Robert, this is your

291

uncle's beast, and not yours to poke at and tease. The poor thing—isn't it sorry enough that it must live in a hole in the ground?"

Robert nudged Ismael with his toe. He said something in Saracen, and they bubbled with muffled laughter. Ismael threw the stick casually aside. Straining, they slid the heavy grille across the paving stones and dropped it clanging into place. Maria went closer. The lion prowled around the pit, looking quizzically up at them. Its straw-colored hide was lined down the back with red-brown. Roger had gotten it as a cub; now, full grown, it looked half as long as the pit. Robert came up to her.

"Where did you go? You promised to be here for dinner." He was almost as tall as Ismael now. His blue eyes were just below hers. "Am I still your good knight?"

"Yes. When you aren't in trouble." She hugged him. Swaggering, Ismael came up on her free side, holding the long stick like a lance under his arm.

"I much well fighting at lions often."

"There are no lions in Mana'a," Maria said. "Roger says this one came all the way from Africa."

Ismael leveled a contemptuous stare at her. "Is many lions here. Roger iggorant." He made a gesture with his hand.

"Don't believe him, Mother," Robert murmured.

"I don't. Ismael, put down that stick." She started toward the door into the tower. Ismael flung the stick end over end into the air. It fell beyond the wall; someone in the street bellowed in rage. The boys sprang off toward the stable, crowing.

Maria went up to the hall. The musicians were practicing in one corner. Sunlight streamed in through the open tops of the windows. She unpinned her cloak and gave it to a servant. Two maids came into the hall, one carrying a baby in her arms. Maria paused, interested. She had marked the baby the day before, when they first came to Iste; his hair was bright, clear red. She pretended to look for something on the table beside the two maids.

"What is your baby's name?"

The girls bobbed their bows to her. "Jordan, my lady,"

said the girl who held the baby. "But he isn't mine. His mother's married and gone away."

"Ay," Maria said. "I thought something of the sort. Take good care of him."

"Oh, yes, my lady."

Eleanor reappeared, her face set with purpose. "Maria. The cook is very eager to see you. Can you not hurry?"

"I am," Maria said, and followed her.

THE KITCHEN was in an uproar; when she had spoken to the cook and cleared up the confusion about supper, she and Eleanor went back up to the top room of the tower, stripped the beds, and hung the linen out in the sun to chase away the fleas. Maria returned to the hall. As she came in, the musicians began a quick, light song. Roger was there, with Louise, an older woman of his household, practicing a dance.

Roger and Louise stood facing each other, their hands clasped between them. Maria advanced into the room. They had not seen her. Intent on the music, they stood bobbing their heads in time to it.

Louise said, "Now. One, two, three—"

They skipped forward, whirled around, caught each other's hands, and skipped forward again. Louise laughed. Maria stood in the middle of the room. Roger's hair was vivid as a fire. He and Louise tried a complicated twist, entangled their arms, and burst out laughing.

"Maria." He signed to the musicians. The pipes and the mellow horn fell silent. "Come dance with me."

Maria smiled at him. "I'll watch."

Louise backed away from him, her face smooth and cheerful, yielding her place with him. Roger walked over to Maria.

"It's just a dance. I'll teach you. You'll like it." He reached for her hand, and she tucked her arms behind her back.

"Dance with Louise," she said. "I'll watch you."

He shrugged. "Coward," he said, under his breath. His handsome delighted smile flashed; he went off to join Louise again.

Maria circled them, going to stand next to the musicians, between the sunlit windows. Roger and Louise walked slowly through the complicated turn. The red knight watched his feet. Maria saw the loving glances Louise gave him and hid her smile with her hand.

The musicians began their song again. Roger and Louise turned and stepped and turned across the hall, the woman a shadow to the man's brilliance. Maria wondered what he looked like without his clothes on. He was taller than Richard, long-legged, his shoulders wide and his chest flat. She imaged lying with him. Her groin grew sensuously taut. The door opened, and Richard walked in.

She pulled her face expressionless. Roger called, "Did you find him?" He and Louise swung in a series of half-turns back toward Maria.

Richard threw himself into a chair on the hearth. "He wasn't there. I talked to his son." He stared unsmiling at Maria. She went around the dancers to the table and got him a cup of the strong local wine.

"I went to the Jews' temple this morning." She handed him the cup. Sweat soaked the armpits and the back of his shirt. He refused to look at her. He lifted the cup to drink. He smelled rank.

"Roger," she said. The music had stopped. "I'll dance with you." She went over to him, holding out her hands.

Louise backed away. Roger glanced past Maria toward his brother. His wide mouth warped into a smile; he shook his head slightly. Maria took his hands in hers. She looked down at her feet. "Show me what to do."

He taught her a simple step and turn, walking through it first without the music. The musicians picked up the song. Roger winked at her; his fingers tightened around hers. They danced across the hall and back again. Richard sat staring fixedly in the other direction, his shoulders hunched.

"Poor innocent brother," Roger said softly. "Caught fast." He raised his voice. "Richard. Come dance."

Richard let out an indefinite negative grunt. Maria had to laugh. The song ended. Roger showed her another step. He said, "Wait until we come to the part where I pick you up."

The door opened. Four men in long coats came into the hall. Maria stopped in mid-turn, recognizing them. She let go of Roger's hand. The four merchants walked forward, toward Richard.

"My lord, we come seeking justice."

Maria went up behind Richard's chair. He said, "What is this?"

Roger stood in the middle of the hall. "That I told you of. Those merchants whom Maria cheated, down in Birnia. Here, Manofredo, didn't I tell you not to bother my brother about this?"

The merchants stood in a clump, buttressing each other. Their clothes were long and draped in folds like curtains: townsmen's clothes, who did not ride. Manofredo said, "My lord, we have brought our case before my lord Roger's court—"

Richard shot a glance at Roger. "What did you say?"

"What do you think? I'm not going to hang my own sister in the stocks."

"If they want justice," Maria said, "give it to them. They sold the fruits of the earth for profit to starving people."

Manofredo spread his hands. "We seek no profit, only to have our case truly heard. We had your charter—" He produced a piece of sealed vellum.

Roger said, "Richard, this is yours—I'll watch."

Richard hitched himself up in his chair. Maria laid her hand on his shoulder. He reached up and pushed it away. He said, "Manofredo, she says she gave you money."

"My lord, it was hardly enough to—"

"Whose money do you think it was?"

The merchants' meaty faces sagged. None of them spoke.

"Mine, Manofredo. Therefore I find her not a thief, but a shrewd market wife. I supplied you with the charter, the wit to make a profit was your responsibility. Get out."

Silently the merchants bowed to him and left. Maria went around in front of Richard's chair. He glared at her.

"I think I prefer Solomon dividing the baby," Roger said. Louise and the musicians went out. He sauntered over beside his brother. "What did Luwigis' son tell you?"

Maria took Richard's cup away. When she came back, Richard was saying, "They don't like us very much, do

295

they?" He took the cup from her with one hand and closed the other around her wrist.

"I get along well with the Lombards," Roger said. "It's you they can't stomach. And the Saracens."

"You deal with them, then." Richard let go of her wrist and took hold of her hand. She laced their fingers together. He drank his wine; they talked of the affairs of Iste.

XXIX

❦

In the middle of the night, the dogs woke her up with their passionate barking, She opened her eyes. The barking came from far away, outside the citadel, as if someone were riding by the gate. But a shrill, hysterical note crept into the barks, and she sat up.

More dogs joined the racket. Beside her, Richard stirred, coming awake. Abruptly, right below their bed, the three dogs in the room with them burst into a thunderous barking.

In the next room, Eleanor woke up with a scream. Richard rolled over. "Those God-damned dogs." He pulled Maria sleepily into his arms. The three dogs had run from under the bed to the door, volleying barks. One whined and scratched at the door.

Richard sat up, suddenly alert. "What's that?"

"What?" she asked.

"That." He flung the bedclothes back and slid out of bed.

"Mama," Stephen called from the next room. "Robert and Ismael are gone."

Maria climbed out of bed. Eleanor was cooing to Jilly,

who had begun to cry. Now Maria could hear the distant throaty roar of the lion.

She snatched her cloak off the bedpost and started toward the door. Richard in his nightshirt grabbed his sword from its scabbard on the wall. The dogs hurled themselves madly at the door. When Maria pulled it open they nearly knocked her down pouring out into the stairwell. Richard bolted past her.

"Maria—" Eleanor cried.

"Stay here." Maria dodged her grasp. "Stephen, stay with Eleanor." Barefoot, she ran after Richard down the dark, narrow stairs, into the racket of the dogs.

The servants who slept in the hall were massed on the next landing and Roger with a torch and the cook's daughter stood on the one below that. He said, "The lion is out," and led them in a dash down to the door into the ward.

"I can hear him." Richard took the torch from Roger so that his brother could find the key. "We'll need a bow to kill it."

"I like him," Roger said. "He's never gotten out before —let's see if we can—" He opened the lock, and Richard thrust the door wide.

Six or eight knights stood in a clot on the threshold. They moved quickly to either side. Maria went hard after Richard, brushing past Roger. The cook's pretty daughter screamed. Stopping short in the moonlight, Richard said a soft, elaborate oath. Maria put her hand on his arm.

The lion was running at a loose trot back and forth across the far side of the ward, roaring and shaking its mane. The moonlight was bright enough to gleam on the gold collar around its neck. A pack of wolfhounds huddled in one corner of the yard, a mass of heads and shoulders that sounded all throat. The grille was propped up against the wall.

Halfway up the twenty-foot wooden gate, Robert was clinging with both hands to the crossbar; Ismael the lion-hunter was even higher up out of danger, his feet braced on an iron bolt on the top hinge.

Roger started to laugh. Rapidly the laughter spread

through the people watching. The lion made a short rush at the corner full of dogs, and madly the dogs hurled themselves back on top of one another, screaming.

"God's blood," Maria said, relieved. "Let them spend the night there."

Something brushed against her. Stephen leaned up on her side. She twitched the cloak to bring him under its warmth.

Richard gave Roger an evil look. "I don't think it's funny."

"No. You would not." Roger slid by him. "We will need a rope—a net, if we can find one." The red knight went calmly down one side of the ward toward the stable. The lion saw him. Its roar rumbled out. Cautiously it circled over to investigate him. Roger whirled and lunged toward it, shouting, and the lion recoiled away from him. The people watching cried out in one voice. Roger went down into the stable.

The cook's daughter had her knuckle in her mouth; when he disappeared, she clapped her hands. "Holy Mother," she murmured. Her eyes shone.

Richard said, "Get all these people out of here." While Maria marshaled the servants and women back into the tower, he stood watching the lion prowling up and down around the pit. Finally it lay down, its long tail drooping over the edge of the pit. Every few moments the tail tip flicked up.

"Emir," Ismael called, from the gate, and said something in Saracen about falling.

Richard answered him in some detail. At the sound of his voice, the dogs doubled their barking. Fastidious, the lion licked its shoulder. Maria folded the cloak closed around her and Stephen, standing on the threshold to watch.

"I told him not to," Stephen said softly.

Richard walked slowly out into the middle of the ward, carrying his sword in both hands across his body. The white nightshirt flapped around his shins. Over his shoulder he called out several names. Six knights jumped from the doorway behind Maria and rushed toward him. Roger came out of the stable, a coil of rope over his shoulder and a drover's whip in his right hand. The lion eyed them alertly, its circular ears erect.

Maria put her hand under Stephen's chin to turn his face up. "You should have told me, if you knew they meant to do this."

"He made me swear not to tell."

The knights formed a rank that stretched from Richard across the ward to Roger, who stood in the open, uncoiling his whip. The lion got to its feet. The dogs suddenly seemed to run out of breath. Their tongues flopped out of their mouths, they lay down on top of one another in the corner and watched. Maria took three or four steps forward, pushing Stephen on before her.

The lion paced across the ward to look the men over. Roger flipped the long drover's whip out across the paving stones. The lion watched it briefly, turned, and bounded down into its pit. Maria shut her eyes a moment. She wondered if they could bolt the grille fast to the ground.

Robert and Ismael dropped to the foot of the gate. Richard was standing ten feet from them, the sword in his hands. Roger came up to Maria. He slid his arm comfortably around her.

"Lean on me," he said. "Your mother's heart must be faint."

Maria peeled his hand away from her breast. Robert and Ismael were approaching Richard by tentative steps. Coiling the whip, Roger took a bit of rawhide from behind his ear and tied it. Gleefully, he shouted, "Richard, shall I hold them for you?"

Richard lifted his head. At his look, Ismael stopped cold. Roger went over to Richard's side; then spoke quietly.

Robert came up before them. "Papa," he said, in a grave voice, "if you will let me explain—"

Richard grabbed him by the nape of the neck, whirled him, and spanked him with the flat of the sword. Robert yelped. "Papa—no—please—not here—Papa"

Ismael was creeping backwards. Maria laughed. The cloak whirled open, and Stephen spun away from her and ran into the tower. Maria went up beside the men. Richard lowered the sword and turned Robert around to face him.

"Enough?"

Robert held his backside with both hands. He stared at Richard's bare feet. Maria touched his shoulder. "Go get your father his cloak." Robert broke into a stiff run toward the door. Maria glanced at Richard.

"The other villain is getting away."

"Ismael," Richard said.

Straight as a lance Ismael marched up to them. "Emir," he said, his voice lofty. "I is go."

Richard said to Roger, "I think he wants to go up into the mountains and meditate on the great Saracen art of bragging."

Roger smiled; his eyes narrowed. "Let him hang on the gate a while. I liked that."

"Emir," Ismael said, alarmed.

"It's my lion, after all." Roger spat. "You know it wasn't Robert's fault."

Richard struck his brother on the shoulder. "I don't know anything like that. Go on."

Roger went off toward the stable. Bright with malice, Ismael's eyes followed him. Richard spoke to him in Saracen and started toward the tower.

"Emir," Ismael called. He brushed between Maria and Richard, knocking into her in his haste. He prayed something of Richard.

"No," Richard said. "I am tired of this, you told me you'd keep him out of trouble." She knew he spoke French for her benefit, and when Ismael begged him again he denied him in Saracen. Maria went on to the door into the tower. The moon was setting. Before they got to sleep again it would be dawn. At least she had gotten the fleas out of the bed, and perhaps soon they would both enjoy a full night's sleep.

ISMAEL LEFT the next morning for the great Majlas stronghold of Simleh. He and Robert wept and embraced and swore terrible oaths of friendship. When they had

300

ridden out together to the gate, Maria went up to the hall to work with Eleanor on the embroidered pattern for a new tapestry.

Stephen came downstairs. He put his hand on the back of Maria's chair, bending to look at her work. "I am going to the baths," he said.

"Oh, you are. What are you going to do there?" She was putting in the outline of the tower. They had decided to picture a castle garrisoned with saints, under siege by the Devil and the Beasts of the World.

"Mama. What do you want me to do?"

"You can keep your clothes on like a Christian and not take baths." The Mana'an men had a passion for sitting around in pools of water, talking about books and music and indulging in the vilest pleasures. She stitched in the stones of the tower.

"Are you ordering me not to?" Stephen said. He hung on her chair, his breath warm on her cheek.

Robert came into the room, all downcast, two dogs on his heels. He sank down on a matrah beside the hearth. Maria watched him sympathetically. "Yes," she said to Stephen. "I am ordering you not to."

"Mama." He kissed her cheek. "I won't. I'm too little to get in, anyway." He sauntered off, elaborately nonchalant. Passing behind Robert, he murmured something she did not quite catch.

Robert leaped up and chased him. Stephen ran out of the room, his brother two steps behind him. The dogs gamboled around them, barking. The door slammed shut. Maria groped through her basket for the other pincushion. The door burst open and Stephen raced in. He dashed up to her and spun around toward Robert, snatching out his dagger.

Maria cried, "Stephen." She got up, spilling the basket across the floor. Before she could reach him, he slashed at Robert. Eleanor shrieked like a silver whistle. Maria lunged between the two boys and when Stephen stepped back she struck him hard across the face. Dropping the dagger, he burst into tears.

She wheeled toward Robert. He had one hand clamped

301

to his thigh. "Mama, he cut me." He reached around her toward Stephen, and she hooked her fingers in the neck of his shirt.

"Sit down. Eleanor, go find tabib. Holy Mother Mary." She knelt before Robert—blood was soaking through his hose. She took hold of the slashed cloth and tore it away. Thick as sauce, the blood rolled from the lips of the wound.

Roger came into the hall. "Who is that screaming?" He strode up beside her. "Holy Cross."

Maria sat back. Stephen and Eleanor had gone. Roger laughed. "A hand higher, Robert, and you'd never be making Richard any grandchildren."

"Roger," Maria said. She pressed the edges of the wound together with her fingers.

"What happened?" Before she could stop him, he went to the window over the ward. "Richard," he bellowed. "Your son's just nearly been gelded."

Maria said, "Roger, go away." Eleanor had come back with the cook, who bent over the boy's bleeding leg. Maria backed away. She looked around again for Stephen; he had disappeared. She picked up her basket and went around the room gathering the spilled needles, thread, and wax.

Richard came in the door. "What's going on in here?" When he saw Robert and the cook, he turned back to the door. "Stephen," he shouted.

Maria was feeling sick again. She sat down to rest. Richard came up behind Robert. The boy twisted to look at him.

"Papa, he drew a knife." His voice cracked with shock. "And he even started it."

Richard looked at Maria, who nodded. She took her embroidery in her hands, shifted the hoop, and stitched the face of Saint Jerome.

"I have to go," Richard said. "Maria, when I come back, I'll see to Stephen." He cuffed Robert across the jaw. "Next time, jump a little higher, will you?" He walked off toward the door.

Maria took small running stitches. She wanted to have

a lock on Saint Jerome's hair fall over his forehead, but on the embroidered design the scale was too small. The cook put a heavy plaster on her son's wound. Robert said, "The viper." The sound of that pleased him; he said, "The little viper bit me."

Maria kept silent. Stephen was probably somewhere out in Iste, but he would come back before sundown: he was afraid of the dark. She bent Saint Jerome over the rampart of the tower to throw a Bible at the Lion of Wrath. Richard should send Robert to the Majlas. He would be happier there, with Ismael. She bit off the thread with her teeth.

STEPHEN LAY SOBBING across his bed in the next room. Richard buckled on his belt again. He walked slowly across the bedchamber toward Maria. "When they get older, they'll be better," he said. "When they can go to war."

"If they don't kill each other first," Maria said.

Jilly sat on the bed beside her. Her face was wrinkled with worry. " 'Teben is crying."

" 'Teben was wicked," Maria said. She brushed the little girl's feathery brown hair. Richard had gone back to the door into the children's room and was watching Stephen through it, one hand on the wall.

"Papa hurt 'Teben."

" 'Teben hurt Robert." Who was away gambling or worse with Roger. "You must never hurt your brothers."

"Why?"

"Straight to the crux," Richard said. He lifted the little girl up in his arms. "She's logical as a Greek." He kissed her mouth. Jilly climbed energetically onto his shoulders. He sidled over and touched Maria's cheek with the back of his hand. "You're burning hot."

Maria shook her head. Her hands and feet were swelling, and the midwives had warned her to stay in bed as much as she could. Jilly settled herself on Richard's back and kicked.

"I'm finished with my work here," Richard said.

"There's a robber by the East Tower I have to run down —I'll take Robert with me." He swung Jilly down the arms to the floor. Stephen had stopped crying. Sitting down beside Maria, Richard took her hand and straightened the thickened fingers. "Try to make this one a girl, will you?"

Maria laughed.

TWO DAYS LATER she woke up feeling as if someone had struck her across the back with a hammer. Richard had been gone a day. She lay alone in her bed until the maids brought her some breakfast, when Stephen and Jilly came in. Stephen went off to write a letter to Rahman, and the little girl climbed up onto the bed and played with Maria. She was agile as a cat; Maria had to stop her twice from climbing up onto the bedposts.

The pains grew steadily stronger. She knew she was going to lose the baby. One of the girls had come in, the redheaded baby Jordan slung on her hip, and Maria gave her Jilly and asked her to find a midwife.

"Mama," Stephen said. "Is something wrong?" He hurried up to the side of the bed. Maria bit her lips at the pain.

"Stephen, go away."

"Mama," he cried, frightened.

"Go!" The pain eased slightly, and she sighed. Like a beast it gripped her again. She let her eyes close. Her body clenched, wringing her until she screamed. Stephen's footsteps pattered away.

Blood gushed from her body. Slowly the pain subsided into a tight, cramped squeeze. She was drenched with sweat; she felt clammy and cold and dizzy, and she was lying in a pool of blood. She could not move. God was punishing her. She wondered in a daze what it was for this time. The women came in, trailing Stephen, burst into soft murmurs, and scattered around the room.

Eleanor bent over her, kissing her. "Oh, Maria, Maria, my dear." She lifted her in her arms. "Louise, come help me."

"I'm . . . all right," Maria said. She was shuddering with weakness. "What a mess." Two of the women were pulling off the bedclothes. Even the pillows were splattered with blood. If they didn't hurry it would ruin the mattress too. Eleanor went to help them, and she lay back. No baby. The baby was gone. Like a ghost a faint pain stirred in her womb. The women brought warm water and washed her.

Someone was hammering on the door—she realized that the noise had beat unheeded on her ears, now and again, since the women came in. Stephen stood at the head of the bed, his face gray and his mouth working. She sat up.

"Stephen, go away. Eleanor—"

With Eleanor's help, she got up, took off her filthy nightdress, and put on a clean one. Her knees were trembling so hard they nearly dropped her to the floor. The women bundled up the ruined bedcovers. Maria's head floated lightly on her neck. The pounding on the door reached her ears again.

"Who is that?"

Eleanor hurried to the door and unbolted it, and Roger spilled in. "Maria—"

"She has lost the baby." Eleanor crossed herself. "Take her into the children's room—put her on the boys' bed. Jesus have mercy on her. See how pale she is."

Maria shut her eyes, jerked them open again, and saw them coming toward her in triple. Roger picked her up. "Maria," he said; he carried her across the room. Against her forehead, his cheek was cool, stubbled with beard.

"Here." He put her down on the bed in the little room beyond hers, whose window opened east. The room was dazzling with sunshine. "Maria. Look at me, sweetheart." He took her face between his hands.

Eleanor scurried up beside him. "Let her alone."

Maria was unbearably thirsty. She tried to swallow. Stephen came into the room. Tears stood on his cheeks. He crept toward her.

"Roger," she said. Her dry voice wheezed. "Take him away."

305

"No," Stephen screamed. He seized hold of the bed-post. "No. Let me stay here. Mama—" He struck at Roger, who lifted him effortlessly up. "Mama!" His fist bounced off his uncle's shoulder. Roger carried him out of the room and shut the door.

Eleanor brought Maria a cup. "Drink this. Oh, Maria, I'm sorry. I'm so sorry."

The wine in the cup stank of herbs and blood. She choked on it; her throat locked and would not swallow, but she gagged it down. She lay back. Eleanor knelt beside her, praying in a frantic voice. They had not made a pilgrimage to the Shrine of the Virgin since before Jilly was born. If she went to the shrine she would feel better. She stared at the sunlight on the stone wall, grieving for the baby.

SHE WOKE UP again after dark. Three or four candles burned on the chest beside the low bed. The doorway was outlined in light from the next room. Eleanor brought her a draught of herbs and wine and gave her some bread to eat.

"My lord is here." She fluffed up the pillows.

"Richard? He came back? Where is he?" Maria propped herself on one arm to drink the wine. She moistened the bread in it and devoured it.

"I'm right here." Richard's shape came in the door, from the light into the dark. Eleanor slipped out past him. He said, "You look hale as a horse to me. They gave me to think you were dying. You could at least look sick, if you got me all the way back here—"

"Richard—"

Flippant, he said, "I'm sorry you lost the baby, Maria, and I'm glad you're not dead." He turned his face away. Heavily he sat down on the side of the bed. In another voice, he said, "I'm sorry."

She put her hand on his forearm. He lay down beside her in the narrow bed, and they put their arms around each other. For an instant he held her so tight she clenched her teeth.

Eventually he said, "Let me up. You're supposed to be sleeping."

306

"Stay." She coiled her arms around his neck. Silent, they lay pressed together in the narrow bed.

"I'm getting up," he said at last, although he made no move.

"Stay here. Just until I fall asleep."

"God's death, you're such a baby."

His body was warm and heavy in her arms. She closed her eyes, comforted.

XXX

FATHER GILBERTETTO, THE PRIEST OF BIRNIÀ, DIED OF fever. Richard sent to the monks of Saint Mary, to ask them to name another priest. The monks refused, since by custom the church of Birnia was in the diocese of Agato. Richard charged the monks a special tax on their guesthouse, but still they would not help him.

In the spring after her miscarriage, Maria went with Jilly and Eleanor to the shrine to worship, and they stayed in the guesthouse and attended the pilgrims while the monks were busy. After the crowds and noise of the cities, the little village made her content. To remind herself that she was a sinner, she meditated often on the Passion, and she fasted several times between Sabbaths, enjoying the lightness of spirit it gave her.

Brother Nicholas, the monk who had helped her build the chapel, was now the abbot of the little band of monks who lived there. He still smelled like a charnelhouse, and they marked that he never gave them dirty clothing to wash. When he was not praying, he painted the interior walls of the chapel.

When she had been there for several weeks and heard Brother Nicholas's sermons, she went up to the chapel one morning to catch him alone. He was painting an angel in the back of the altar. She walked up slowly behind him, stopping when she caught the first whiff of his stench. Over his shoulder, he said, "Sit down, my sister, talk to me."

His paint-splotched hand loaded the brush and dabbed blue flowers beneath the angel's feet. Maria sat down. It amused her that he should call her what Roger and William called her. His work covered most of one side of the chapel: beasts played in the night forest along the wall before her.

"How does your lord, Maria?" Brother Nicholas asked. He painted the angel's robe in long ripples, more like water than cloth.

"Richard is well," she said. Dirt grimed the monk's neck and ears. He was filthy as a boy. "He is what I wanted to talk to you about."

Absently he dipped the brush into the pot and set the paint down. "What concerns you?"

"Sometimes—the way he talks—" Maria clasped her hands together in her lap. "He loves the Saracens and their works. He is turning into a Saracen."

The monk gave her a startled look over his shoulder. After a moment he took up a pot of darker blue, but he only toyed with the brush.

"Tell me what I must do," she said.

He painted the folds of the angel's robe. "You can see that I might not talk carelessly of such a matter, even to you, Maria. He must confess his sins alone, of his own will, and ask God for help. For your peace, keep in mind that God gave you charge of no soul save your own."

He stirred the dark blue with the brush. "If he is profane or violent toward you, of course, you must take care for yourself and your children.

Maria laughed. Before her on the wall was the golden lion, flowers strewn in its thick gilt mane, and its eyes bright as pomegranate seeds. "My children learn young to care for themselves."

He held his brush and pot on his knee; his curved mouth smiled. She saw how handsome he had been, as striking a man once as Roger, she guessed. He said, "Why

308

are you so concerned? I know you serve Christ—is it for God's sake? Or your husband's?"

"I pray," Maria said, uneasy. "I try to remember God's will."

"Who tempts you otherwise—your husband? Ah, my sister. Tell me what makes you blush so high." He turned to paint more blue into the robe.

"He tempts me," she said, "or I tempt him—sometimes when I—when he lies with me, it is—" She could not say this to a monk, and the thought of lying with Richard made her feel as if she were melting. She put her hands over her eyes. "It is nothing, you know—" She laughed a strained laugh and took her hands from her eyes.

Bent double to see, Brother Nicholas was painting the robe. Ahead of his brush, the paint lay flat against the wall. Behind him it curved into soft shadowed folds. He straightened.

"Go on."

"Sometimes I think I am possessed. I do such things with him—I want to do such things—I hardly know what I do. I should refuse. But—but—" She twisted her hands, all her secret places softening and moist.

Immediately she was stiff as a pipe reed, terrified that she had spoken of profane things in a church, and to a monk. He had led her to it, tempting her. But he was not watching her, he seemed unexcited, his hands steady with the brush and the pot of paint, his eyes intent on his work.

"Yes," he said. "Each child of Adam loves what delights the flesh." He blurred the dark blue with the edge of his sleeve. "I know your sin in mine. I suspect you are right. We are possessed, you and I."

Silence fell. Maria drew her hands slowly over her bare arms. It comforted her to talk to the monk. She felt he would not judge her, that he liked her anyway. Outside, the larks sang like flutes in the high grass around the chapel. Brother Nicholas folded the angel's hem with his brush.

"I have read that the true Creation itself is wholly spiritual," he said. "That this carnal world and our bodies are the Devil's gross counterfeits of God's work, and that is

309

why our bodies die and molder. I don't believe that myself, but it's an instructing figure."

Maria squirmed around to her right to bring another part of the wall before her: the silver Unicorn, eyed in daisies, against the black forested wall. "What shall we do? About our common sin." She had seen horses kick out precisely the way Brother Nicholas's unicorn kicked.

"Our sin." The monk's voice sharpened, amused. "You do not care much for philosophy, do you."

"I am too stupid," she said, to make him feel better, and in a flash of bad humor added, "So Richard tells me, that I am a stupid cow, or some such."

The brush handle rattled on the paint pot. "You're not stupid," the monk said. "But craft or lack of it makes no difference, really. We are possessed, you and I, by ourselves, until we yield to God. We know how we sin, but we can't let go. We have more faith in ourselves than in God."

Jilly rushed in the door and across the paved floor of the chapel. "Mama! E'nor says we must go back now."

"Sssh." Maria caught her by the arm. "This is God's house, be quiet."

Brother Nicholas said, "Why did you come here, my sister?"

Maria pulled Jilly's shirt straight. "Go outside and wait for me. Pick the daisies, we'll chain them." Jilly ran off. The walls of the chapel rang with her footsteps.

"I like it here," Maria said. "It's quiet and good, and there is much I can do, useful things—new linen, and the laundry, and the guesthouse mending."

"Is he pleased that you come here? Your lord?"

"He told me I should come. In Iste, after I lost the baby. He knows I'm happy here. I didn't mean to make him seem unkind to me."

Brother Nicholas smiled at her. "Now you regret talking to me. I will keep your confidences, if you will keep mine."

At first she wondered what he had confided, until she marked how lovingly he worked, the beasts in the forest decked out in flowers, and remembered what he had said

310

about the carnal world. Jilly called, and she put her feet under her and rose, reluctant to leave him.

"Thank you."

His head bobbed. "Come back. I am usually here." Bent over, he stroked color onto the wall, his nose almost touching the paint.

EVERY MORNING, she and Eleanor swept out the chapel, prayed until noon, and spent the afternoon in chores. After they had made the August cheese, Maria sat under the tree before the chapel door and sewed shirts for the monks. Jilly ran along the chapel wall, stalking butterflies. Two old people were climbing up from the village, bent together like two intergrowing trees.

The worst of the summer's heat was over. The sky was a hazy blue. Richard had told her to come to Castelmaria for the quarterday, and he would meet her there. She missed him.

"I cannot sew this seam," Eleanor said, fretful. "It won't lie flat."

"Let me see."

While Maria trimmed the seam properly, the older woman called to Jilly. The little girl was running down the hillside. "She never listens to me, the wicked child." At a stiff trot Eleanor followed Jilly through the weeds toward the village. Jilly laughed in the distance, buoyant.

"My lady," said a voice she did not know. A man in a flat cap was walking toward her, leading a gray palfrey.

Maria put her sewing down. He bowed to her, a satiny smile on his face. "You are the lady of Marna."

"I am the lord of Marna's wife," she said. By his clothes and horse, she guessed he was a churchman. Eleanor was coming back up the hillside. Jilly struggled captive in her arms. Maria stood.

"My lady, my name is Mauger, a deacon of the Archbishop Robert of Sio, who remembers you with affection."

"I know him," Maria said. "What do you want to say to me?"

311

Mauger spread his hands apart. "Perhaps in another place. In quiet."

Maria rubbed her arms. The man looked like a moneylender, fat across the jaw. His neck rolled over his collar. His easy townsman's manner hobbled her tongue. Eleanor came up to them.

"Come down to the monks' house, Master Mauger." Maria took Jilly from Eleanor's arms and started down the hill path, carrying the child on her hip.

The deacon mounted his horse and cantered away down the road. Eleanor hurried avidly up beside Maria. "What is it? You left your work behind. What has you so flighty?"

"He says he is from the Archbishop."

"Maria!"

Maria put Jilly down on the path. "Go to the guesthouse."

The child raced off, shouting. Eleanor picked at Maria's arm. "What can it be? Have you done something wrong?"

Maria did not answer her. They went through the village. A fresh group of pilgrims was gathered around the well drinking. A local woman waved at her. Maria cut between the monks' barn and a hut to reach the log guesthouse. Mauger was already there, his sleek gelding hipshot before the front door.

"Eleanor," Maria said, "feed Jilly, she must be hungry." Wary, she went through the front door into the long, sunlit dormitory.

The deacon was standing in front of her window, looking up at the chapel. He turned toward her. "My lady. Do sit down. I hope you are not wroth with me for disturbing your afternoon."

"No," Maria said, in a brittle voice. "What is it you wish to talk to me about? Have I done something wrong?"

"No. Not at all, my dear girl. Not at all." He looked out the window again. "We are told you built this chapel, my lady, with your own hands."

"It was a penance," she said. "Many people worked here."

312

"It was the act of a devout daughter of Holy Church. My lady, Mother Church needs your help again. We need you against one whom we cannot withstand. Only you can rescue us."

Maria said, "I will, if I can."

"Lady, it is Richard of Marna."

Maria looked away.

"He defies the customs of Mother Church. He and his men are trying to drive the priest of Birnia out of his church—an honest man, a good and willing servant of God."

"No." She shook her head. "Richard is an honest man, too. It's silly and dangerous that our churches should be guided from Santerois."

"Lady." His long surcoat, covered with discreet dark embroidery, rustled around his feet. "God's will be done. Is that not the bedrock of our faith? Your husband is even now in Birnia, doing the work of the Devil."

"In Birnia?" She stared at him, surprised: Richard was only a day's ride from the shrine and he had not sent word to her.

"Lady, if he continues in this course against the priest, the Archbishop will excommunicate him."

Maria turned away from him. The door opened, and a gust of noise heralded the new-arrived pilgrims, dirty from their travels, their voices thick with some accent. Brother Paul herded them past her down to the far end of the room.

"My lady, as one of the faithful you would be conjoined to have nothing to do with him. If he dies under the ban, his soul will be doomed to Hell."

"No," Maria said. She knew Richard wouldn't care if he were excommunicated. She stared at the rough log wall before her. Reaching out, she peeled a long shred of bark from it.

"What do you want me to do?"

"Intercede for us. He will not even hear our envoys. Tell him what will happen to him if he does not obey God."

She picked at the bark with her fingernail. "If I do—If I talk to him, you will not curse him."

313

"He must agree—"

"No. I won't talk to him at all, if you hold such a treaty over me. I'll do what I can, but you must swear to me that you won't curse Richard."

Mauger smiled at her. There was a medal of Saint Anthony in his cap. He said gently, "Lady, this love ought to be for your Redeemer."

"I love God," she said, and crossed herself. "Do you agree to my bargain?"

"Yes. God will help you. I agree." He bent over her hand. "I will pray for you, lady."

Maria knelt, and he blessed her. He went away. Eleanor came in with Jilly and made the child ready for bed. The Vespers bell began to ring. Maria sat on her bed and tried to sort out what the deacon had told her. The pilgrims rushed away to the chapel for prayers.

"Maria, aren't you coming?"

"What?"

"Why—Vespers is beginning, can't you hear the bell?"

Maria went to the door. "I have to go to Birnia. Keep care of Jilly for me. I will come back in a few days."

"To Birnia! Maria, are you mad?"

Maria crossed the guesthouse yard. In a double file, the people of the village, the monks and pilgrims were climbing the hillpath to the chapel. Their voices rose in a chanted prayer. The fading light of the sun lay on the chapel's gray stone, light pink, like blood in water. The evening wind blew down the hillside and cooled her cheeks. She went back for her cloak and walked across the village to the commons to catch her horse.

SHE WENT ALONE, keeping the white mare to a comfortable trot. The sun sank. She rode into the east, toward the evening. The road stretched on before her, empty of other travelers, a pale dirt strip through the meadowlands around her. She began to hope that bandits might attack her, so that she would not have to go to Birnia.

The moon rose. The road led her over low hills and into a wood. The mare's hoofs in their even beat sounded loud as a drum. The trees closed around her. A bat dived before her, squeaking. The mare shied. In the wood, brush crackled.

Weariness dragged at her. In the fringes of her vision, shapes moved and startled her, and she jumped out of a half-sleep. She knew she could go no farther. She dismounted, tied the mare to a tree, and slept wrapped in her cloak, facing east.

She woke up with a foul taste in her mouth, blinded by the early sun through the trees. The mare was eating the green buds off a sapling. Maria mounted and rode on. At a well in the forest, a family of serfs gave her a loaf of bread and a cheese.

She did not know what she would say to Richard when she reached Birnia. If she could not sway him, the Archbishop and the deacon Mauger would think she had broken her promise: they would damn him and probably her too. The road left the wood and followed along the southern bank of the river.

All through the day, travelers passed by. Many were pilgrims. They followed her with their eyes, a woman riding alone. In a newly built village, she begged some milk and smoked meat for her dinner, and ate it sitting beside the road above the river, which curled calmly brownbreasted through the golden hay on either side. The peace in Birnia was Richard's doing. She wished Mauger appreciated that. A while later it occurred to her that once her father and Richard had terrorized this highway, worse even than the Saracens.

She prayed to God to help her. In a short spurt of resentment, she prayed that Mauger would suffer a suitable plague for getting her into this. She was close to Birnia now, and she put off riding on. Around the curve of the river, three or four boats appeared, netting fish.

She stood to watch. The skeins bellied out behind them, like sails filled with the river. The boatmen rowed a dozen strokes, to keep the boats abreast. The current took them slowly on past her, their voices like tones of music in the distance.

The longer she waited, she knew, the harder it would be. Getting on her horse, she rode on at a short lope. The

315

sun lowered in the sky. God would know she had kept her oath. She prayed for help, she prayed to know who was right and who was wrong.

Before her, down the plain, the town of Birnia came into sight, a haze of smoke hanging above it. Even from here, she could make out a banner flying from the peak of the Tower, on the hill above the town.

The figure was Richard's white dragon. She did not want to go there. If he had wished her to come, he would have called for her.

Her temper rose. He was going behind her back, and he deserved whatever he got. But she did not want to go up to the Tower, and eventually she turned the mare and rode into the town itself.

She left her mare at the inn stable and walked back along the street. The sun had set and everyone had gone home for supper. She put up the hood of her cloak, though the day's heat still lingered in the town. She wanted no one to recognize her.

In the deepening twilight she reached the church and went inside. There was no one there. Two candles burned on the altar. As part of her service to the church, she provided its candles; she would have to rebuke the priest for wasting wax, lighting his candles before it was even dark. She went to the altar rail to pray.

When she had said a Credo and confessed her sins, the side door opened and a young priest came in. He crossed the nave, genuflected before the crucifix, and calmly looked Maria over from the far side of the altar. Taking up a taper, he lit more candles, filling the little church with flickering orange light.

Maria pretended to pray. Between her fingers she inspected the priest. He was her age, perhaps younger. The knobbed bones of his face showed as if the softer flesh were worn away. She sat back and caught his eye.

Instantly he was beside her. "May I help you?"

"Deacon Mauger sent me," she said. "I am Maria of the Castle."

"I'm sorry. Mauger is my kinsman, but I don't know you."

She said, "Dragon is my husband."

His smile vanished. He said, "If you came here to argue with me—"

"No. Mauger said I'm supposed to help you."

"I don't see how you can help me." He walked across the church, his hands clasped. "He says if I do not leave of my own will, he will burn my church. They have denied me food, clothes, even sleep some nights, shouting at my window."

"I can talk to him."

"No one can talk to him. He is flesh, and corrupt, given over to corruption, his ears are stopped to Christ."

Maria crossed herself. The young priest's vehemence made her uneasy. When he spoke he leaned eagerly forward; he would welcome a fight to prove his righteousness.

"He has brought Saracens here, into this very church," the priest said. "Men who worship the false prophet Mohammet have defiled God's most holy place."

Maria walked away from him into the side aisle of the church. On the walls were painted scenes from the Passion. She went along until she found Jesus being lashed, where she knelt to pray that the priest might turn milder. His profligate use of candles fretted her—candles were always scarce.

Hungry, she went to the inn and knocked on the back door. The ostler's daughter let her in. While she brought her a dish of bread and beans, the widow said nothing beyond greetings, but Maria could see how the woman itched to ask questions.

"Richard is here," Maria said, eating.

"Oh, yes. Every morning he comes down and threatens the priest."

"Is the priest holy? Do you like him?"

The ostler's daughter put her hands under her chin. "I like an older man, more settled."

"Does he preach well?"

"He makes much talk of corruption and filthiness. I suppose he is a good preacher, he is pious enough, everybody remarks on it, and very learned—he talks of places

317

and people no one has even heard of." She lowered her voice. "He is adamant against the Saracens."

"Richard has Saracens with him here?"

"Several of them. But he masters them, at least, no one has been murdered yet, although I know of some who are asking to be first."

Maria took a crust to wipe up the last of the juice. "I wish I knew what I should do."

"I think you should come sleep. I take it you are not staying at the Tower? I will give you my bed."

"No—I'll wait in the church."

The ostler's daughter took hold of her hand. "Don't get between them, my pet. They are stone against stone, those two."

"I wish I were back in Mana'a," Maria said, glumly.

"Stay with me—where will you sleep in the church?"

"On the floor."

Maria went back to the church and walked around looking at the pictures on the walls. In them all, Christ wore the same expression of thoughtful joy, while the Romans were whipping him, while he carried the Cross. When the priest came in again, she marked the same look on his face.

"I'm told my husband comes here in the morning," she said.

"Yes—he has said I may not preach another sermon, he comes every morning to bar folk from the church."

The priest drew himself up proudly. She said, "What do you do, then?"

"I offer the Mass."

"Alone?"

"With my sacristan." His face soured. "The people here are un-Godly, anyway—few heeded my words when they could hear them daily."

"Well," she said, "tomorrow I will hear you." She went into the back of the church. The priest lingered a while. She spread her cloak on the floor and lay down on it. Finally she heard him walk away, and shutting her eyes she waited uneasily for sleep to come.

XXXI

❧

IN THE HALF-LIGHT BEFORE DAWN, SHOUTS WOKE HER up. She sat, brushing her hair out of her eyes. Outside in the street a crowd was talking in a dozen excited voices. She heard her name spoken. She put her clothes in order and pushed her hair back with her hands. The bell overhead in the church tower began to toll.

Dawn was just breaking. The air was fresh and cold. She opened the church door and went out onto the porch. In the square, ranged along the fence around the churchyard, a dozen people stood. They peered at her curiously. The smith Galga was among them, who had been Fulbert's courier, a hoe over his shoulder.

The sacristan came out to the churchyard, from ringing the bell. Just behind him walked the priest. They opened out the church doors and went inside. But the people did not follow them.

Now those in the back of the crowd were leaned out to see down the street. Maria's heart stuck in her throat. Ismael and four of his brothers galloped up to the gate, scattering the folk in the square, and dismounted.

"Maria," Ismael said. He skidded to a stop. "Oh, wrong."

With four more of the Majlas, Richard rode up to the gate. He put his hand on his horse's withers, started to dismount, saw her, and settled back into his saddle. The look on his face cooled her temper.

"What are you doing here?" she said, and went up to the gate. She ran her eyes over the townspeople. "Go in. The Mass is beginning."

No one moved. She swung the gate open. In the

319

church, the priest's voice began the singsong of the Introit.

A townsman stepped forward. His foot crunched on the gravel of the street. Three others followed him toward the church.

"No," Richard said. "Ismael, get her out of here."

"Dirty pagan," someone called, in the crowd.

Ismael's teeth appeared against his scraggly black beard. "Emir," he called, and spoke in Saracen.

Richard dismounted. He scanned the crowd once. When he faced Maria again, she could read nothing in his expression. He said, "Let me talk to you."

"No."

"Come on." He took her by the elbow and moved her across the churchyard. The crowd suddenly quieted. Richard pushed her along up the steps and through the church door.

Just within the doors, he pulled her to one side, out of the crowd's sight. The sacristan and the priest, in the midst of the service, stammered to a silence. Richard swung her around to face him.

"Maria, I could kill you for this," he said, and hit her.

WHEN SHE WOKE, she opened her eyes on the soot-encrusted ceiling of the good bedchamber in the Tower of Birnia. By the length of the shadows she knew it was afternoon. There was no one else in the room, and she sat up. Her jaw ached on either hinge. He had hit her once, square on the chin. She had no clothes on, there was no garment within reach to cover her. She sat for a while, listening for sounds on the stairs. At last, convinced there was no sentry outside the door, she got naked out of bed and hunted for her clothes.

The cupboard next to the window was full of William's clothes, and before she could look elsewhere, footsteps sounded on the stairs. She got back into bed. William came into the room. When he saw her awake, his expression changed.

"Good evening, William."

"Eh, Maria." He fingered his ear. "It's all up now." He brought a stool over and sat down beside the bed. "Richard packed the priest off to Agato, and the Archbishop is going to excommunicate us."

"No," Maria said.

"I met a deacon of his on the road—I and the wagon with the priest. The deacon took the wagon and gave me his oath they will unchurch us next Sabbath."

"Mauger," she said.

"That was his name." He stood up, patting her knee under the covers. "I'll go tell him you are awake."

"William. No." She sat up, alarmed, the covers pulled up to her neck, "Give me my clothes first. William, please."

He shook his head. He was already on his way to the door. "No, Maria." He pulled the door shut, but it didn't latch. A moment later she heard him calling for Richard.

She lay down, pulled the covers over her, and feigned sleep. The door swung idly on its hinges. Far off, a cow mooed. The room stank of dogs. She would always think of Birnia whenever she smelled dogs. The door creaked again, and he came quietly into the room. She breathed evenly, shallowly, as if she were asleep.

"If you want your clothes back, you can sit up and look at me."

She sat up and looked at him, the bedclothes gathered around her. He was standing at the foot of the bed, his hands on the railing.

"You damned stupid little cunt," he said. His voice was raw. She stared at the blanket over her knees, unable to look at him; she knew she had betrayed him.

"Your clothes are in that cupboard. I'll have your horse saddled and in the ward tomorrow morning. I don't ever want to see you again. I don't want to hear your voice ever again. Just leave me alone."

He went out of the room. The door sighed closed and halfway open again. Maria laid her cheek down on her knees. Through the narrow window, the late afternoon streamed soft pink. She prayed that he would come back. Every sound she heard drew her eyes to the door. Once it really opened, but it was only William, bringing her a dish of meat for supper.

He was edgy as a deer, gnawing the inside of his mouth. He said, "He's calling the priest back, or I'm leaving. It's that simple." His voice was louder than necessary. "I'm not staying here under the ban."

He went away again. She could not eat. She put out most of the candles and lay down to sleep. A dozen times, she dreamed that Richard came in the door. Before dawn, she put on her clothes. While she waited for the light to break, she walked up and down across the room, twisting her Saracen ring. When the sky paled, she pulled the ring off and put it on the table beside the bed.

Her mare was saddled and hitched by the reins in the ward. The cook's knaves were just bringing the bread out of the ovens. The crusty aroma followed her out the gate. The morning was bright and crisp. She rode back to the shrine as hard as she had ridden in the other direction.

Brother Nicholas, sitting on a ladder, was painting a set of scales into his angel's hand. He listened to her without speaking, his body smell harsh and smothering, and his brush moving rhythmically to the pot of glistening gold paint and back to the wall. Maria told him everything from the deacon's first appearance at the shrine to the moment she left the Tower of Birnia.

"It's my fault," she said. "Mauger lied to me. If I hadn't gone, Richard wouldn't have beaten the priest. Now he is damned because of me."

Brother Nicholas put the paint down on the ladder step. "You're accusing Brother Mauger of something grave, but my knowledge of him fits what you say. I'll have to talk to your lord."

"He may not let you. But if you can reach William, he will get you a hearing with Richard."

The monk climbed down the ladder. Maria backed away from him to get clear of his odor. He said, "You stay here. Pray, walk—rest a little." He smiled down at her. "You seem to think you did something unforgivably wicked. But what you did was right-intended."

She knelt down, and he made the sign of the Cross over her. The monk went away. Maria prayed a little and walked down to the guesthouse, feeling less as if she had sold Richard to the Devil.

Jilly saw her coming, shrieked, and ran across the room to meet her. A pilgrim was lying on a bed at the far end of the guesthouse. Without raising his head from the pillow, he shouted, "Can no one control that child?"

Maria picked up the little girl and carried her back to their end of the room. Eleanor caught her arm. "I was so worried about you, Jilly cried and cried."

"I went to Birnia."

"You said that. Why? Oh, Maria, what you've done to your gown."

"Richard is there." She sat down, Jilly on her lap. The little girl rubbed affectionately against her. She had Richard's hair and eyes, like him she was always dark from the sun. Eleanor took the brush from their common chest, sat down, and worked over Maria's hair, untangling the knots and snarls. Jilly played clap-hands with Maria, singing in a high-pitched scream that got the pilgrim shouting again.

"You should not have gone alone," Eleanor said. "You might have been murdered. Or worse than murdered." She gave Maria a significant glance.

"The roads are very safe."

"Yet I wonder my lord let you come back alone."

Maria clapped her hands twice on her thighs and twice on Jilly's. The little girl sang with passion. The pilgrim roared an oath and stamped out of the guesthouse. Eleanor's hands stroked her hair.

"Is he coming here soon?"

"Who?"

"Richard, of course," Eleanor said. "He will be pleased with Jilly, she is so big now, and so pretty. I think he loves her best. It's odd that a man of his nature can be so tender with children."

Maria clenched her teeth. She felt Eleanor's voice like a needle; no matter how she turned, it would pierce her through. Jilly sang in a treble parody of the monks' chanting.

"Perhaps you will be with child again," Eleanor said.

"I did not lie with him, Eleanor, we fought. He sent me away."

The brush stopped in her hair. Jilly's singing wavered. She looked up into Maria's face, her forehead wrinkling. "Mama?"

"Oh, Maria," Eleanor said.

"Mama." Jilly reached up to her. Maria kissed her worried upturned face, murmuring nonsense to her until the child laughed again.

"If you want to know," Eleanor said, "I think you will be happier without him." The brush worked in Maria's hair again. "They are the Devil's men, those three, even William. Doing the Devil's work."

Maria frowned; she had heard the words before. Eleanor said, "We will stay here a while, won't we? Or we could go to Castelmaria. The people there love you and will support you."

Maria rounded on her, Jilly in her arms. "Please. Don't talk to me like this. I am unhappy, he has exiled me, why do you give me no consolation?"

Eleanor's narrow face tightened; she had plucked out her eyebrows to thin arcs, so that she always looked surprised. "Well," she said. "You don't need consolation, Maria. You need prayer." Stiffly she walked out of the guesthouse.

AFTER THE PILGRIMS, Maria walked up to the chapel for the Sabbath Mass, carrying Jilly on her hip. Eleanor came along behind her—whenever Maria saw her, Eleanor pinched her face to a blade and stared pointedly elsewhere. The sun was just rising. The dew on the grass drenched the hem of her skirts up to her knees.

Brother Martin and Brother Paul were standing in front of the chapel, talking in soft Latin. Paul was holding a piece of vellum in his hand, but Brother Martin, seeing Maria come, tapped the other monk on the arm and drew him away. Maria stopped short, so that Eleanor ran into her.

"I beg your pardon," Eleanor said coldly.

Maria went into the chapel. Eleanor insisted she had not talked to Mauger, the deacon, but Maria knew she was lying. She went up to the front of the chapel, where the pilgrims were gathered to admire the painting.

She had begun to be angry at Richard. When she thought over the incident at Birnia, she saw how she might have stood against him, instead of cringing under his temper like a beaten dog. The pilgrims crowded around her, and Brother Paul came up before the altar to begin the Mass.

"Dominus vobiscum.

"Et cum spiritu tuo."

"Oremus."

Maria set Jilly down on the ground before her and gave her a piece of bread to eat. The people around her prayed in loud boisterous voices. They said a Credo and a Paternoster. Brother Martin read from the Gospels.

Paul came up to the pulpit. "My children," he said, and coughed. He had a reedy voice and sometimes went up into the hills to exercise it with shouts. He took a charter from his sleeve.

Maria straightened up. It was the same charter he had been reading when she had come up the hill. He spread it out on the lectern and held it down with both hands.

"The Archbishop of Agato requires that this be read in all the churches of the diocese, and in the churches of the demesne of Richard d'Alene, the lord of Marna, and of his brother William, the lord of Birnia—"

Maria got Jilly by the hand. She heard the whole congregation turn to look at her. She fixed her eyes on the door and walked straight for it. Behind her, Paul read, "That this same Richard d'Alene and this same William d'Alene shall henceforth be cut off from the community of Christian men—"

She stumbled over something and went on. Brother Paul's voice pursued her. At the door, the bright sunlight washed over her. If Brother Nicholas had been here, Paul would not have read that before her. Behind her the hum of voices broke into an excited roar. She led Jilly swiftly down the path toward the village.

Halfway down the hillside, she heard Eleanor calling to her. Maria paused in mid-stride, but she set off again at the same speed. Jilly rushed on ahead of her. Still calling, Eleanor ran after her nearly all the way to the village before she caught up.

"Maria." Eleanor put her arms around her. "My dear."

325

"Let go of me," Maria said.

Eleanor fought for breath. "I have—misused you. I know. Please—forgive me."

Jilly ran up to them, and Maria stooped and lifted her. Eleanor put her arms around the child's waist, saying, "You're tired—let me take her." She tugged; Maria hung on, and Jilly yelped in pain.

Maria let go so suddenly that Eleanor sat down hard in the high grass. Jilly's cry struck her like an arrow. She longed to be back in Mana'a, with all her children there, her household, the things she loved to do.

Eleanor said, "Maria, come, have some breakfast, you have not eaten yet."

Maria allowed the other woman to steer her around to the monks' kitchen. They got some warm bread and honey and sat under the trees to eat. Jilly fell asleep in the grass at Maria's feet. A village girl brought two buckets of milk into the monks' porch. Maria ate without interest and threw the crumbs to the geese and chickens.

"We cannot stay here the rest of our lives," Eleanor said reasonably. "If not to Castelmaria, where? Will he let us go into a nunnery?"

"Oh, God—" Maria pressed her hands to her eyes. "I would die of boredom in a nunnery." She thrust her arms between her knees, bunching up her skirts. "I have thought of finding another place in Mana'a. I don't know if he will allow it." She rubbed her forehead on her wrist. "I suppose I shouldn't care what he will allow."

Eleanor leaned toward her. "Maria, make him give you your own castle. Castelmaria is yours. You can live in Mana'a, but don't let him take what is rightfully yours."

"I don't know what to do." Maria shook her head. "Don't talk to me now, I am still thinking about it." If she lived in her own house, she could take a lover. She knew how Richard would feel if she did; the idea grew steadily more attractive.

"Whatever you do," Eleanor said, "get everything you can from him."

Jilly lay asleep at her feet, her arms sprawled across the crisp autumn grass. Maria bent to pick the child up. The exhilaration of revenge was already fading away. She took Jilly into the guesthouse. The prospect of another day in this place, with Eleanor for her only adult company, stretched flavorless before her.

THAT GROUP of pilgrims prayed and left, and a few days later another group came down the road, drank from the well, and took the beds in the guesthouse. Maria and Eleanor washed their clothes and took them out to the meadows to dry. In the afternoon, carrying the laundry on their heads, they walked back through the village.

Eleanor had held off all day, for once, but now she said, "Have you given any more thought to where we will go when we leave here?"

"To Hell," Maria said. They came up to the door into the guesthouse, and she reached for the latch. Stench reached her nostrils; she made a face; an instant later she whirled to face Brother Nicholas.

"My sister," the monk said. "Please come talk to me in the common room."

"Yes. Eleanor, will you?—Thank you." She put the bundle of laundry inside the guesthouse door and followed the monk across the dusty yard.

It was past nones. When they went into the monks' house, all but Brother Paul were up at the shrine. Brother Nicholas signed to her that she should sit down on the wooden bench along the wall. Brother Paul sniffed, rose, and moved to the far side of the room.

"I have been to Agato," Nicholas said. "The Archbishop is heartily sorry for the disrespect with which his servant Mauger treated you. Of course he is more heartily sorry that Mauger was brainless enough to be caught at it. They've lifted the ban from your husband and his brother because Mauger promised you it would not fall on them. If your husband will allow the priest to return while the case is put before the Curia in Rome, the Archbishop has said he will take no further action."

She began to speak. He held up his hand. "Let me go on. I have talked with my superiors in Agato, and we are taking your lord's part in the issue and will speak for him before the Curia."

Maria stared at him, amazed. She said, "Nicholas, you have done a miracle. Has Richard agreed to it?"

327

Brother Nicholas scratched his armpit. "Yes. I had some trouble meeting him, as you said I would."

"What did he say about me?"

"Nothing. I told him that we were doing what we could because of the great love we owe you, but as far as I could see it made no mark on him." He rubbed his chin with his forefinger. "It was no miracle. He's a reasonable man. I expected another sort entirely, by what you said. I rather like him."

"You like everybody," she said. She hunched her shoulders. Richard would not take her back. She would not go begging him to be taken back. She would lie with Roger and let Richard know it. She said, "Thank you for what you have done. I still think it was miraculous."

"What have I done? For mistreating the priest, I've charged Richard to come here and fast three days and pray in the cave. I want you to stay here until he comes. That way, at least, you may heal one another."

"Heal," she said. "How can I forgive what he has done to me?"

The monk scratched himself idly, his eyes steady. "When I left, you thought you had mortally offended him. God will help you, my sister. I know you will do God's will." He rose and went out of the room.

THE RAIN FELL in a battering, drenching downpour. Occasionally the thunder muttered in the distance and an indefinite flash of lightning lit the air. The path up the hillside was a running waterfall, and Maria took the long way, by the road.

In the fog the sodden countryside was deep in mud and strange as another world. She had left her cloak behind, as a kind of penance. She went into the chapel. She knelt at the altar and prayed for help. Not even the monks had stayed up on the hillside during the storm. The crashing of the rain on the roof deafened her and made it easier to think. She went out the side door of the church and crossed the yard to the cave.

Two candles burned at the foot of the statue. The cave itself was dark. Maria stopped just inside it. Her mouth dried up. The thunder outside rolled a long sustained crash, like a barrel falling downstairs.

Richard took hold of her hand. He fumbled her Saracen ring back onto her forefinger. With her free hand, Maria scraped her wet hair back off her face. He pulled her into his arms, and she pressed her face against his chest, fast in the circle of his arms.

PART III

A FEW CHOICE WORDS

XXXII

WHEN THEY REACHED BIRNIA AGAIN, THE PRIEST WAS ALready back in his church. William instantly found an errand that took him off across country. Richard, shriven, his public penance done, sat all day long in front of the fire and drank.

After supper, Maria went up to him. "Come upstairs with me."

"No. Stay. I want to talk to you."

She had been expecting something like it all day. She said, "Well, come up here and let me spin, if you are going to keep me awake anyway." William's spinning woman had died, leaving half the season's wool piled in the storeroom.

Richard followed her, carrying his chair, and drove the two pages dozing in the corner away to the far end of the hall. "I talked to that monk about settling some of his Order in the valley of Iste." While Maria threaded the wheel, he sat down in his chair, tipped it back on its hindlegs, and balanced. In his left hand he held his cup. She had never seen him fall over. He said, "Not a big house. A dozen monks. What do you think?"

She took off her shoe to work the spinning wheel with her bare foot. "It might make up for some of the things we have done."

"I thought more of having a place to train clerks." He braced himself with one hand on the wall. "The garbage in the Roman streets turns out a Pope. I can't have my way over a village priest."

Maria watched the spinning wheel, drawing out the wool between her thumb and forefinger. She had apologized to him three times, and each time she thought he

333

gloated, behind his reassurances and kisses. He preened his moustache, staring at her. "You and your stinking monk. He made me swear not to persecute the priest—he preached me lots of the Gospel, too, I didn't tell you about that. I haven't suffered so much piety since the last time I heard Mass. Did he make you promise anything?"

"What do you mean?"

"I want you to spread a rumor in the town that the priest misused you."

"He never touched me."

"Maria," Richard said, "you did this to me. Now you must help me, damn you."

She took her foot off the pedal. "You want me to tell lies for you."

"That's right," he said. "You've told enough to me."

The wheel had stopped behind the treadle. She rolled it forward half a turn. Richard brought the chair down on all fours and leaned toward her. "I didn't ask you to get involved in this, you know."

"Do it yourself." She pressed her foot down on the treadle. "Brother Nicholas will never find out."

"Me—they won't listen to me—" His voice rose, whining with temper. "I am the man who hit his wife in the church during Mass." He tramped away down the hall. Maria could hear him swearing.

She spun three or four steps of the treadle. She remembered that Brother Nicholas had called him a *reasonable man*, and she laughed. A page came in the door from the outside. The shoulders of his rumpled coat were spotted with rain. He went over to Richard. Maria watched the wheel spin, devising a story to tell about the priest, in case he talked her into it.

Abruptly Richard was there beside her, and she startled. He sat down on the chair and stared alertly at the door.

"What is it?" she said.

"Theobald." Richard's eyes never wavered from the door. He rolled his cup between his palms. "Theobald is here."

Maria bent to pick up another roll of carded wool.

Fluffing one end of the wool with her fingers, she meshed it with the tail of the spun yarn. When the door opened, she looked up without raising her head.

Richly dressed, his cloak's wide hood lined with marten fur, Theobald strolled in, his eyes and hands moving. His sleek chestnut hair was sprinkled white. He wore a long coat like a townsman—Maria had never seen him in mail —and a belt with a long-sword in a gold-studded scab-bard. Behind him came two other men, one obviously his son.

Richard stood up. "I'm sure you have some good reason why I should not take you prisoner."

Theobald's neat, rat-chinned face only smiled. "You will want to hear what I have to say." He turned his gaze on Maria. "My lady, I am pleased to see you again."

Maria put her hands in her lap and did not try to spin. A knight had come in behind them, one of Richard's men; Richard signed to him to wait. Theobald's son brought him a chair. Composed, his eyes glinting, Theobald sat down.

"We have had our differences, Marna, but surely nothing that cannot be put aside in favor of some mutual profit?"

Richard smiled at him. He stood in front of his chair, the cup in his hand. "Go on."

"For some years now, we and the other main tenants of Santerois have been content to fight one another, dealing with Fitz-Michael one at a time. The duchy is completely overturned now, no one wins any more. We—other men and I—want to join together, overthrow this green Duke, get rid of Fitz-Michael and his pack, and see peace shine on our corner of the world again."

Maria looked from him to Richard. Richard's face was rigidly expressionless. He said, "What other men?"

"I cannot tell you that until we have your pledge of support."

"I cannot pledge you anything until I know who you are."

Theobald's hand twitched over his belt. Sitting down, he had to look steeply up to meet Richard's eyes. He seemed uncomfortable. He said, "Perhaps I can change your mind. We have the resources to give you what you most desire. Join us, and you will be the Duke of Marna."

For a moment Richard did not move, his eyes on Theobald. Against the wall by the door, the knight waited, intent on them. At last Richard lifted his cup.

"Get out," he said to Theobald. He drank.

Theobald's face fell still. He blinked once, looked at Maria, and stared up at Richard again. Slowly he got to his feet, and his son brought him his cloak. They went out the door in single file.

Maria stood up. The knight started after them. Calling him back, Richard sat down in his chair.

"Holy Cross," he said. "He must have been hatched out in a dunghill."

"You should have taken him," Maria said.

"Oh, no." Richard nodded to the knight. "Go to Agato. Keep to yourself, watch the Duke. You heard him, just now. Whatever happens, I want to know about it."

"My lord." The knight saluted him and left the hall.

Maria put away the spindle and the spun yarn and poked her feet back into her shoes. Under his breath, Richard said, "Duke of Marna," and laughed. She went up beside him.

"Come to bed."

He drank his cup empty. Drops of wine glistened in his beard. "Will you start the rumor for me? About the priest?"

"God's blood. Do you forget nothing?"

He smiled at her, sleek as Theobald. "Do it."

"I will. I suppose as long as the poor man's here you'll just make him miserable."

"That's right."

They went out the door and started up the stairs toward their room. Maria said, "You should warn Fitz-Michael and the Duke."

"Why should I help them?—It's their Archbishop who has been giving me all this trouble." He pushed her ahead of him through the door. "I thought you wanted to go to bed?"

THE OSTLER'S DAUGHTER looked relieved to see her. When they had settled in one corner of the sunlit kitchen, and the scullion had brought them a tray of jam tarts, she said, "So you let him back into your grace again. You are broad-minded."

Maria brushed crumbs from her dress. "Every husband beats his wife, now and then."

"Not necessarily before the holy altar during the elevation of the Host."

While the other woman sewed placidly beside her, Maria ate another of the tarts. Eventually, cautious, she said, "I am afraid that this priest really must go."

The woman lowered her hands and her work. "Oh? Everyone thought they had been reconciled, when Dragon sent the Saracens away."

Maria shook her head. "No, it is impossible."

"I'm not surprised." She stitched rapidly. "Especially after yesterday's sermon. You were not there, we all marked it."

Maria broke open a sweet cake and picked out the nuts. When the ostler's daughter did not go on, she said, "Well?"

"He spoke on that charter, the Saracen charter, that was sinful—corrupt, he called it, that word he likes." She nibbled a tart quickly away to nothing and licked jam from her fingers. "He is an unpleasant man. What were you thinking of doing?"

"Richard said to start a rumor. That he abused me, or something of that sort."

The ostler's daughter chewed steadily. "Ramkin will be here within the next few days. You know Ramkin, the charcoal vendor."

"The crier of Birnia," Maria said drily.

The other woman laughed. "If I tell him the priest winked at you, he will have it to the next dozen houses that you escaped his lust only by the personal intervention of Almighty God." She crossed herself. "It will take little enough. No one likes him here, that priest, all he ever talks about is our sins."

Her cook came through the back door of the kitchen, and the ostler's daughter called him over. They had a short, sharp dispute over the discreet use of garlic. The cook marched stiff-necked over to the hearth. The woman settled back again, soft and white as a Saracen dumpling.

"I thought you would be married again," Maria said. "Have you turned them all down?"

"Hah." The woman's eyes sparkled at her. "Your battle in the church reminded me of the evils of marriage. I have put on a nice cushion now——" She stroked her plump round arms. "I have no wish to run myself to a skeleton for a man's sake."

Maria laughed. They turned to talk of their sewing.

RAMKIN DROVE his charcoal cart out of the forest. Maria stayed out of the town, lest anyone ask her to deny the rumors. William had come back. His spies reported that the town was full of scandalous talk, the church ill-attended, and the priest more adamant than ever.

They all went hawking after rabbits in the fen beyond the river. Maria took Jilly in front of her on her mare. When the child fell asleep, she sat with Eleanor under a hedge and held the little girl in her lap, watching Richard and William ride out across the bleak sweep of the fen.

"Don't you want to come back to Castelmaria?" Eleanor asked. "Don't you miss us?"

"Of course I do. But——" Maria shrugged. "Perhaps it is the sunlight in Mana'a, so close to the sea——I like it there."

Eleanor nagged her a while longer, reminding her of all the wonderful things at Castelmaria. Far down the brown fen, the two brothers were racing their horses. The sky was full of light clouds, darkening along the western sky. Between the fen and the dun sky, there was no color anywhere. Jilly woke, yawning, and sat up.

"Well," Eleanor said, "there is a knight in Castelmaria, not a young man, but in the best of life——he says he wants to marry me."

Maria crowed. "Eleanor. Are you? Why didn't you tell me before?"

"I'm not certain I want him. I thought——if you came back to Castelmaria——" The woman's hand gave Maria's

338

arm a loving touch. "I would have stayed with you. But if you will not be with us so much any more—"

"What is he like? Who is he? Do I know him?"

Eleanor turned her profile to her. "He knows of Roger —he says he honors me that I have kept faith with him so many years. He has fought with Roger in the mountains."

"Why marry this man, if all you can think of still is Roger?"

Eleanor lowered her eyes. The fading light made her soft and pretty again, as she had been in her youth. "I don't love Roger. I never did. But he was so handsome, and he talked so well. . ."

She smiled, remembering. At last, Maria said, "What did you quarrel about, you and he?"

"He said he would marry me, if I came away with him, but when he had what he wanted—" Eleanor clasped her small, veined hands, white from the potions she used every night. "I could not lie with a man who thought me unworth marrying."

"Come to Mana'a. It's better now, you'll like it now."

"No. I can see that you must stay with Richard, but not I. He's a heretic and a blasphemer. He has no feelings."

Maria said, surprised, "That isn't true. His feelings run very deep, I think."

"Then he doesn't show it." Eleanor sat staring down the fen. Beyond, over her shoulder, the sun sinking through the clouds turned sickly yellow. "He doesn't care about you, Maria."

"You don't know him."

"Know him—he's my cousin! He's cold as a snake."

Maria stood Jilly on her feet and rose. Across the long fen, fading into dusk, the twilight wind ran. She could not see Richard or William. She went to her horse, Jilly trotting at her heels.

"Maria," Eleanor said.

Maria lifted Jilly up into the saddle. Eleanor came up behind her and took hold of her arm.

"Please."

"Take this knight," Maria said. "We will endower you, you won't marry like a serf." She put her foot in the stirrup and swung up behind the little girl. Eleanor clutched her skirt.

"I apologize. I meant nothing. You know how I talk."

Maria reined her mare away. Heavy as metal, the first few drops of rain struck her shoulders. Richard and William galloped out of the dusk.

"Come up on the high ground," Richard called. He leaned from his saddle to lift Eleanor up onto her horse's back. Three gray rabbits hung by their hindlegs from his saddle pommel. The hawk rode on William's fist.

Maria pulled her cloak around Jilly. The child took hold of the saddle's pommel.

"Mama? Will it be all right?"

"Oh, yes."

In the cave of the cloak Jilly leaned back against Maria's body. Down by the sulphurous horizon, lightning forked out of the sky. The thunder rolled across the fen. Richard came up beside her. They galloped through the rain down the hard-packed road.

Sweeping in from the sea, the storm fell upon them. They had to stop their horses. Maria closed her cloak over Jilly's head. Richard put his arm around her shoulders. They leaned together, their backs to the hammering rain.

The thunder crashed. Threads of lightning splintered across the sky. Clouds billowed huge as castles over the flat, barren fen, its hollows already flooded, the high cattails streaming doubled over by the wind. Rain ran down Maria's cheeks and into her eyes. Richard had his cloak over them. Jilly whimpered, and he spoke to her. The thunder broke hurtful in Maria's ears. She looked up into the battering rain and the clouds hustling like an army across the sky.

The rain was slackening. The lightning flickered, and the thunder grumbled off banging along the edge of the sky. The rain ceased. They lifted their heads. The thunder rambled away, mild as lamb's hoofs.

They straightened apart from each other. Richard's hair and beard were drenched. Drops of water clung to his eyelashes. Jilly called, "Papa," and Maria lifted her toward him. He took the child in front of him on his horse. Maria rubbed her cheeks dry on her arm.

340

The sky lightened. They moved off again down the road. Maria turned the sodden fur of her hood out to dry.

"Eleanor wants to marry," she said. "What did you say his name is, Eleanor?"

"William the German," she said. She and William d'Alene were riding along side by side behind them. Richard nodded.

"He's second-command at Castelmaria—he's something older than she is." He glanced back at Eleanor. Under his breath, he said, "Old enough to get into bed with anything." He curled his arm around Jilly.

"Were you frightened, kit?"

Jilly shook her head, solemn. She lounged in the curve of his body. Maria felt a pang of jealousy. Jilly with her gray eyes and soft, curling hair would be pretty someday. She was pretty now. Maria looked away.

MARIA AND ELEANOR went into the town of Birnia, to buy some lace for Eleanor's wedding dress. Richard had arranged for the dowry. They were talking of a Christmas wedding. Eleanor had forgotten their fighting, but Maria could scarcely hide her dislike from the other woman. To disguise it she let Eleanor take Jilly in the cart with her.

They came to the market place, half-empty in the late morning; many of the stalls were unstocked. The ostler's daughter was walking along the side of the square that fronted on the churchyard. Maria rode over to meet her. The priest came out onto the church porch. She stuck her chin in the air and ignored him.

The ostler's daughter leaned over the wheel of the cart. She and Eleanor discussed embroideries for the trousseau. Maria dismounted. The priest was coming across the churchyard. She put her back to him.

"I wish he would leave," the ostler's daughter said softly. "I have not heard Mass these past three Sundays, he is putting me in the way of sin."

Maria could not keep from laughing. Her mare snorted. Several other men were approaching her, their eyes fixed on her. She stepped back, alert to them. The priest grasped her upper arm.

Eleanor shrieked. Maria spun away, striking aside his

hand. The ostler's daughter turned a white, startled face toward her. Tall men stood between them, closing around Maria; she scanned their faces. The yellow-haired smith was among them.

"You are making a mistake," she said, her voice low. "I have been your friend in the past."

Behind them, Jilly screamed. Maria lunged at the men around her, trying to escape between them. The smith caught her around the waist. She flew into a panic; she drove her fingernails at his eyes, and when he flinched back struggled in his arms chest to chest with him and brought her knee up hard between his legs. He grunted and caved in at the waist, but someone had grabbed her by the hair.

"What are they doing?" a woman cried, somewhere, and other people called out. The smith and his men bundled Maria down the street. She screamed for Jilly. Her arm was twisted up between her shoulders. No use in fighting. She sobbed for breath, in the grip of many arms. They carried her in under low roof beams and put her down.

The smith gave quick orders in patois. He was a long, ropy-muscled man, his shoulders enormous from his work. His eyes shone in the darkness of the hovel. The five men who had taken her packed the room, stooping under the low roof. The air reeked of their bodies.

In the corner was a straw tick covered with a blanket. She sat down on it, her legs under her. Jilly was not there, nor Eleanor—she wondered if they had been taken elsewhere, or if they had escaped. The smith and the priest stood before her, the smith bent to clear the roof.

"You cannot mistreat her," the priest said. "She came to my help once—she stood between me and him." He cast a frightened look at her.

The smith shoved him. "You fool. Who do you think spread those tales about you?" He nodded toward her. "See? She's listening." He struck the priest in the chest again. "Go do as I said."

The priest's face was haggard. His eyes were buried in black hollows. She thought he looked guilty. The other men were leaving, and the priest followed them out the low door.

Maria looked around the place. In the opposite side of the room there was another tick of straw. Between them was a stone hearth and a bench. The floor was swept and the hearth laid out with a fresh fire. The pot hanging over it was soaped to make it easier to clean: she wondered if the smith had a wife.

The smith pulled the door closed. He sank down on his heels, talking to a stranger. Maria slumped her shoulders, her eyes on the fire, to eavesdrop on them.

"It worked," the smith said.

"Oh, ay, it worked. For now. Dragon will unwork it." The stranger spat.

"The priest thinks—"

"Hang the priest." The other man pulled a scornful face. "He's a fool. Could you have talked him into this otherwise? We are not here to get back the ancient customs of Birnia, we are here to keep Dragon busy. And maybe make a little for ourselves. Listen to me. Forget holding her here. Theobald will make us rich enough if we can get her to Occel."

The two men bent together and their voices dropped to whispers. A grunt exploded from the smith. He glanced at Maria. So they were Theobald's men, part of Theobald's conspiracy against the Duke.

She looked around the hovel again, searching for some weapon. Richard had still been asleep when she left the castle. He would not miss her for hours. If Eleanor had escaped—she wondered again about Jilly, gnawed with worry.

The two men were staring at her. The stranger tugged on his lower lip. "We have to cross the river. If we can get her out onto the fen he will never find us." He nudged the smith. "Go bring us some horses."

"Don't hurt her, for God's love," the smith said. He went out. The stranger came bent-legged toward Maria.

"Don't hurt her. Don't hurt her." He leaned toward her, face to face with her. His breath was rotten. "When we get out on the fen—"

Maria spat into his face. The gout of spittle struck him in the eye. He shrank back. He smacked her across the cheek, and falling sideways she caught the handle of the pot on the fire and turned it over on the stranger's head.

The man screeched. Boiling yellow soup streamed down over his head and face. Maria lunged for the door. Her skirts entangled her, and she went to her knees. She dived through the door into the street. The screams of the man in the hovel followed her away. The street was thronged with people, wheeling to look at her. She sprinted down the alley. A flock of chickens ran squawking ahead of her. The stench of manure reached her nose. Stopping to take off her shoes, she threw them over a fence. Behind her voices rose in a general chorus. She turned a corner and raced across an expanse of high grass. Dogs barked. She slid through a brush-choked passage between two fences.

Just as she reached the open street again, a pack of men rushed into sight. They screamed and pointed at her. She wheeled. She scrambled back down the overgrown alley and raced through someone's garden. The men were only a few yards behind her. Her lungs burned painfully. She stepped on something sharp and limped hard across a narrow street. Strange buildings surrounded her. The men were running after her. She circled behind a high fence. At the corner there was a rain barrel half full of water. She climbed into it and crouched down, and the rising water submerged her.

Through the water and the barrel she could hear the men trampling up around her, even their voices although not the words. When she had to breathe again she raised her head slowly up above the surface.

Above the rim of the barrel, the backs and heads of the men showed all around her. She drew a breath and quietly went under water again. Her heart was pounding. She bunched her skirts and sleeves in her hands to keep the cloth from floating. Her lungs began to burn. She looked up through the water. The men were gone.

She put her head up and got her breath. Her coif was gone. She shook the water out of her ears and tried to make out what was going on around her. Distantly she heard shouts. A cock crowed. She peeked over the rim of the barrel; the alley was deserted. She climbed up onto the barrel, hanging onto the high fence. Her clothes were weighted down with rain water. On the other side of the fence was a garden. She lowered herself down into it and

344

crept along through the orderly rows of beans and peas, her clothes squelching, looking for some safe place to hide.

SEVERAL TIMES she heard people in the alley and the street, even in the garden, looking for her. They never came into the back of the grape arbor, where she was lying in the sun drying her clothes. Her stomach growled with hunger and she ate some of the grapes, so sour her mouth puckered.

In the afternoon she went out to the street again. It was empty. Even the chickens and dogs seemed to have disappeared. Surely if Richard had come looking for her, the town would have been full of noise and people. She went down an alley, keeping to the shadows.

On the far side of the town, a crowd roared. Taking heart, she trotted down an empty street. She was tired to the bone, and her bare feet hurt.

The crowd gave up another roar, ahead of her—in the market place, she realized, and she stretched out her stride, limping. Her foot was cut. She stopped to rest and went on, trotting and walking and trotting again. At the end of the street, she came up behind a wall of people that hid the market place from her.

No one looked at her. They were all too interested in what was happening out in the square. She squeezed past the crowd and suddenly came on William, sitting on his roan stallion beneath a tree. Maria stood by his stirrup, glanced at him, and turned toward the market place.

A solid wall of people surrounded it. Knights studded the crowd. In the middle of the vast, empty square, Richard was riding up and down, dragging the smith Galga along behind him by a rope around his ankles.

"I don't know," the smith screamed. "In Jesus' name—"

The roan horse let its near hip slacken; it snapped at a fly on its breast. William said, "She's halfway to the border by now, poor thing."

Richard stopped his horse. On the ground, the smith moaned, curling up into a knot. His arms and legs were skinned to the bleeding meat. His shirt hung around his waist. Richard spurred his horse and dragged him halfway across the square. Here and there in the crowd, people groaned. The smith screamed.

A knight burst out of the crowd. "My lord, we've searched every house and hovel in the place—"

"Then start again," Richard said.

The ostler came forward, his arms out. "My lord, I beg you—"

Richard pointed to him. "You're next." He reined his horse around, and the smith gave a hoarse yell.

Maria moved up in front of William's horse, looking around the ring of people. Across from her, at the edge of the churchyard, the boiled, blistered face of Theobald's agent showed among his neighbors like a red dot.

"William," she said, and turned to him.

William blinked at her. The smith gave a shriek behind her.

"Maria," William said. "What are you doing here?"

She pointed. "That man with the red face is Theobald's man."

Grabbing his reins, he spurred his horse into a gallop across the market place. Richard wheeled out of his way. Maria went forward into the open. The boiled man raced away into the crowd, and William charged after him. The people scattered before him, screaming, and the noise spread through the rest of the crowd to an excited roar: they had seen her.

Richard rode up to her, the smith bouncing along behind him. The crowd surged uneasily around the market place. He threw his leg across his horse's withers and slid down to the ground in front of her. Knights rode past them on either side.

"Serlo, chase these people out of here." He put his hands on her arms. "Where did you come from? Are you all right?"

"Yes. Where is Jilly?"

He jerked his head in the direction of the Tower. "Your friend got her and Eleanor out of the way." He turned away from her, untying the rope from his saddle, and walked coiling it back to the smith. William rode up.

"He hid in the crowd. He won't be hard to find, with that sunburn, he shines."

346

Maria laughed. Her hands were shaking, and she remembered to cross herself. "He's from Occel—they were going to sell me to Theobald."

The ostler came up toward her. His forehead was beaded with sweat. He took her hand and kissed it.

"Thank God and Saint Michael you are safe, my lady. Thank God." Still clinging to her hand, the ostler gave Richard a brief, black look.

Richard slung the long coil of the rope into the ostler's hands. "Somebody from the town gave me this. Maria, where were they holding you? Why did they let you go?"

"I let myself go. Sunburn—I gave him the smith's dinner in his face, that one. Then I hid in a garden."

"If you'd stayed caught, I'd have found you right away." He picked up his trailing reins. To the ostler, he said, "I will talk to you tomorrow, when I am less in a bloody humor. You've let Theobald's men shelter here before, so don't think I'll be generous—"

The ostler wheeled toward her. "My lady, we did no harm—"

Maria nodded to him to go. Richard vaulted up into his saddle. He pulled her up on the crupper; her arms around his waist, she rode pillion behind him all the way up to the castle.

IN THE MORNING, he went to the town to judge them. Maria met him on the way back to the castle, opposite the oak tree where she had waited once for Walter Bris. She reined up, and Richard slowed his horse and approached her. The day was overhung with clouds. A wintry wind bent the dry grass. Maria nudged her mare around beside his horse.

"What did you do to them?"

Richard stopped his horse. He looked a moment down the Santerois road. The wind bellied out his cloak. Sitting down again in the saddle, he turned toward her.

"I have the priest and the man with the burned face. I left the townspeople unpunished—didn't I tell you I would? Why do you harass me?"

William was coming down toward them from the castle. Three of his men brought along his wolfhounds, and he carried a bow. He jogged his horse up, his face blank, and said, "Richard, I gave the smith fifty marks."

"William," Richard said.

"He wanted more, but I said—"

"William!"

Full of false surprise, William's jowly face peered at Maria. "Oh. Doesn't she know?" He pulled his horse away before Richard could move and galloped off across the fields, his men and his hounds loping after him in a long stream through the grass. Maria swiveled her head toward Richard.

"The smith is your man."

Richard looked steadily away from her.

"You arranged to have me carried off," she said, with rising anger. "You used me as bait to trap the priest."

"If you'd stayed where you belonged—"

"They might have killed me! What if they had raped me?"

"Nobody would have dared touch you until they got you out of Birnia, and I made sure—"

She turned the mare and galloped away up the road. Richard caught her in a dozen strides. He got the mare by the bridle and stopped her, facing her over their horses' heads.

"Why didn't you tell me?" Maria cried. "I should have guessed, by what the smith said—I should have known. Eleanor is right." She was half in tears with rage. "You don't care about me at all."

They stared at each other; the mare tossed her head, and Richard let her go. He said, "Are you finished?"

She wiped the tears from her eyes. He laughed at her. His eyes went past her, looking down the Santerois road. He said, "It worked, didn't it?"

"You damned dog." She backed her mare away from him and rode on up to the castle, furious.

XXXIII

❧

MARIA OPENED HER EYES. ALTHOUGH IT WAS DEEP IN THE night, the fire still burned high. Richard slouched in his chair, his feet crossed on the hearth. She propped herself up on one elbow.

"Come to bed."

He turned around to her, smiling wide as a child. "Can I put away the knives?"

She got up and went over to the hearth. She crouched down into the warmth of the fire. "What are you going to do to the priest?"

"I'm going to hang him." Richard's voice was round with satisfaction. "For abducting my wife."

She wrapped her arms around her knees and stared into the fire. His hand stroked roughly down over her hair.

"Eleanor is right—you don't care about me at all."

He pulled her hair. She tipped her head back, and he kissed her. "Eleanor is a goose," he said.

Maria straightened, taking his hand. She turned it palm up before her. It was impossible to fight with him when he was in such a high humor. He picked up his wine from the floor beside the chair and drank. She knew he was waiting for word from Agato.

"Why are you so interested in Theobald's plot?" she said. "Why can't you tend to Marna, and let those other people get themselves in trouble?"

"Do you remember what he said—about making me the Duke of Marna?"

She nodded. The fire was heating her nightgown un-

349

comfortably warm, and she moved sideways to it. Richard said, "That means the King is in it. Or the Emperor."

He jerked his head around; Maria strained to hear what he had heard. Slamming his chair down on all fours, he made for the door. She snatched her cloak from the chest at the foot of their bed. While she got it around her shoulders and latched, she ran down the stairs after him.

In the hall, darkness covered the rows of sleeping people. They crossed to the outer door. A dog barked in the ward. Richard pushed the door open. A sleepy voice called out. Maria and Richard went out onto the landing above the ward.

Moonlight frosted the castle wall. Richard jammed his hands under his belt. His face was rapt. Maria stood behind him. The porter was opening one half of the gate. On the walls, the sentries clustered to watch.

One rider trotted into the ward. He reined his horse up to the steps, and his head even with Richard's feet.

"I need your help," he said. The moonlight shone bright on his solemn upturned face: a young man, his dark hair cropped short in the new style of the north, not the knight Richard had sent to Agato.

Richard murmured, "Why, it's Bunny."

"Duke Henry," Maria said. "God keep you, my lord."

"My uncle Fitz-Michael has been murdered," the young man said. "The Archbishop, too, and Luys, and they nearly killed me. They are all in arms against me. You have to help me."

The door behind them banged open, and a servant brought out a burning torch. Maria took it from him. The door was full of curious people and she shooed them back into the hall again. She sent the knights off on errands and the castle servants to getting the young Duke a plate of supper and some drink. Richard and the young Duke went upstairs. When the servant brought the dish of food to the hall, Maria took it and followed them.

When she came into the room, the young Duke was saying, "You'll have to fight them eventually anyway. They hate you as much as they hate me." He saw her and stood up. Maria took a stool over to put the dish on, and sitting down again he fell on the meat like a starveling.

"Who besides Theobald?" Richard asked. He stood in front of the big cupboard, unlocking it. Maria sat down on the bed. The young Duke glanced at her. She could see he did not want to talk in front of her. His clothes were shabby as a sailor's and the soles were ripping off his boots; he was already taller than Richard.

"She hears everything anyway," Richard said. "One way or another." He took his knives out of the cupboard and hung them up again in the rack on the wall.

The young Duke chewed steadily. He said, "All I want is my rights. What my father ruled."

"The King is probably involved, you know," Richard said comfortably. A knife blade flashed in his hand.

"Do you think so?"

"If he isn't, he ought to be."

"You have to help me. You helped me before. I can't trust anybody else."

Richard fastened the bar across the rack of knives. "What makes you think you can trust me?"

"Oh." The Duke shrugged. He glanced at Maria. "Neither of your brothers is married. Fitz-Michael's daughter is a young widow—my cousin. Nothing binds like a blood knot."

"Is she pretty?" Maria asked. Richard closed the cupboard.

"Pretty." The Duke's harsh expression made his swarthy face look much older. "She is my cousin." He used bread to wipe up the last juices on his plate.

"I want Theobald's country," Richard said. "And you acknowledge my rights in Marna." He went over to the hearth, beside the young Duke.

Maria hunched her shoulders. She slid off the bed and went to take the young man's dish. When she came back upstairs again, they were deep in plans. She opened the shutter on the window. The sun was rising. She walked over between the two men.

"What do you think of this?" Richard asked.

Maria glanced at the young Duke, yawning behind his

351

hand. To Richard, she said, "Someday you'll reach for something and lose your arm."

Richard laughed. "Come with me. You know Theobald, it will be all talk." He palmed her backside.

Maria pulled his hand away. She said to the Duke, "My lord, you can sleep in the next room down—William's room."

He followed her down the stairs to the next room. She crossed the dark to open the window shutter. The young man gaped in another deep yawn. When she went back to the door he threw her a truculent look.

"Santerois is my birthright," he said.

Maria stopped in the doorway, "I'm not against you, my lord. I'll see no one wakes you. Good night."

"Good night," he said.

ISTE LAY under a rime of snow. When Roger thrust back his hood, his hair was bright as blood. "Well met," Richard said. They rode together stirrup to stirrup in the middle of the gate and embraced.

Maria searched the little mob of courtiers with Roger. She had expected Robert to meet them too. Richard and his brother burst out laughing.

"William is only half-blooded," Roger said. "What do you expect?" He pushed by Richard and leaned from his saddle to kiss Maria. "My sister."

Maria put her hand over his mouth. "Gently, Roger." She met his blue eyes. Like a flame lighting, her old feeling for him came back. Richard was watching them, no longer smiling. She turned to the Duke.

"My lord, let me make my brother Roger known to you."

Roger held out his hand. "We met once—you would not remember it. God help our common cause."

The Duke took his hand in a strong brief clasp. "God is my judge."

Roger crossed himself. He backed up his horse and turned to ride beside Richard. They started across the snowy market place. The Duke looked curiously around him. He was wearing a cloak of Richard's, the fox fur of the hood as black as his hair. Maria rode beside him.

They followed the two men up the street toward the citadel.

"I've never been to Agato," she said. "Is it larger than Iste?"

"I cannot tell," the Duke said. "They are so different."

"Agato is on a river. On a plain."

"Yes." His voice threatened to crack, and he pressed his lips together. The new growth of his beard blurred his cheeks. She shook her head. They had been weeks in Birnia, organizing an army. During it, she had not softened him to any kind of talk. She nudged her mare up beside Roger's horse.

"Where is my son? Richard said he would meet us here. Didn't the messenger come?"

"I let him go out to chase some bandits," Roger said.

"Robert? By himself?"

Roger laughed at her. "Richard, she needs another baby to coddle—have you gone monkish?"

Maria laid her hand on her stomach, swelling with the new baby. Richard pushed his hood back. He nodded from her to the young Duke, riding alone behind them. She held her mare back until he caught up with her.

"There is Roger's castle," she said.

The Duke glanced up ahead. The tower rose like a rock spur from the hillside. He twisted in his saddle to look out over the valley of Iste. Their horses climbed up the steep road. Behind the fences on either side, dogs barked them up the hill.

"You can see halfway to Agato from here," the Duke said.

Maria nodded. Snow-covered, stitched with trees and hedge, the valley rolled south to the keen blue of the sky. "We are the only people who have ever taken Iste by storm," she said.

"Were you here?"

She shook her head. "I mean Richard and Roger. I have never seen a battle, I don't want to."

"No," he said. He turned his eyes elsewhere. "You kept us from Theobald, that time. Until long after I little understood what a game you made of my uncle." He twisted his body, his shoulder to her, shutting her out.

353

They had reached the citadel. Maria rode in to one side of the ward. The young Duke dismounted and came to help her down out of her saddle. Before she could take his hand, Richard crowded him out of the way. She slid down into Richard's arms. They went into the tower.

LOUISE SAID, "So Eleanor is marrying. At her age." She tipped up the lid of the chest. "Oh, Maria." She held up the new embroidered surcoat, and the other women all sighed.

"Don't unpack it," Maria said. "You'll just have to put it back again—I'm taking everything with me to Agato."

The women gasped again. Maria had Jordan on her lap, Roger's redheaded bastard. She set him down on his unsteady legs. Louise said, "Maria! You're not going, too?"

"Yes, and all of you with me. If I'm to be miserable, I want company."

They shrieked. Maria laughed at them. In their midst, Jordan missed his footing and sat down hard. He pulled himself up onto his feet again.

"Maria! Why?"

"Because Roger is getting married," Maria said, "and I'm going to watch."

"Roger," Louise said. In unison, they all turned to look at a girl in their midst, Catherine, the prettiest of them. Her eyes widened. She looked stricken from one to the next of the women and rushed out of the room.

The other women broke into excited comment. Maria lowered her eyes. She wished she had been more careful. A looking glass lay on the bed beside her. She picked it up and put her face into the oval frame. Her eyes were darker blue than Roger's. "Well," she said. "Come along, there is much to do."

THE NEXT MORNING, she went down to the market place. Louise and the girl Catherine gave her company. On foot, they shopped among the bolts of cloth, the nuts and fruits and candy, and the silversmith's pieces of jewelry. Catherine was listless and hardly spoke; the rims of her pretty eyes were red. Maria bought her some marzipan in the stall of the sweet vendor. They sat in the sunshine before the big oak tree, where Richard heard his trials of law, and a page went off to bring them wine.

"Catherine," Louise said, "you are being silly. To pine over such a man." She laid her hand on Maria's thigh. "I beg your pardon, dear Maria, but you know that I always speak frankly."

"He loves me," Catherine said.

"Bosh."

"Of course he loves you," Maria said. She devoured her blancmange and was instantly hungry again.

Louise goggled at her. Catherine sniffed and smiled, half-dreaming, her head bent like a swan's. She was the most tearful girl Maria had ever seen. Louise whispered in Maria's ear.

"You must know Roger has had dozens of women." Her breath blew hot on Maria's neck.

"Yes, and he's loved every one of them." Maria smiled at Catherine, who sat idly breaking her marzipan into pieces. "I loved him once."

Catherine tossed her head up. Her eyes were brilliant green. Louise cried, "Oh, Maria!"

"I loved him madly. I wanted to marry him, but Richard and my father made me change my mind." She smiled at Catherine. "You see how things went best against my will. Maybe he'll still love you—she isn't as pretty as you are, the Duke says."

Catherine shut her eyes and sniffed. Maria ate the girl's marzipan. The sun was coming out from behind the clouds. The half-frozen, filthy snow heaped under the oak tree was running in a hundred driblets. They would march on Agato when the knights of the Saracen Brotherhood reached Iste. The Duke at first had balked at using Saracens against Christian men, even his enemies, but Richard had insisted. Maria held her hands out to the warmth of the sun.

The gate stood open, as always during the day, and people came in and out in a steady stream. She watched two old women in shawls carrying an enormous load of live chickens on their shoulders. She wondered where they all came from, who they were, what their lives were like. A balding man, his face caught up in a snarl, rode past her up the street. Richard was losing the hair on the crown of his head. She would have to tease him about it and see if he minded.

"Roger," Catherine whispered.

He was riding down the street, two of his friends on his heels, all three gaudy as pages in their velvet coats. Roger veered his horse toward the oak tree. Drawing rein, he dismounted before them.

Maria called to him, but he was looking down at Catherine, a calf-look on his face. Maria settled down again. Two Saracen knights rode in the gate. Neither of them was Ismael, but behind them came a young knight she knew.

"Robert!"

He wore his black hair long, in the old style. His face was brown as the Saracens' from the sun. He galloped over to her and leaped down from his saddle.

"Mother." He hugged her. "I knew you'd be here when I got back. Oh, Mother." His voice squeaked in dismay. "Are you going to have another baby? Catherine. See my mother? Isn't she beautiful?" He lifted Maria up off the ground.

A few yards away, Catherine was head to head with Roger, talking in a low voice. Robert whirled Maria around and set her down again.

"Where is Papa? Did the Duke come with him? Roger says there will be a war—"

"Yes. Walk back to the castle with me." She hooked her arm through his. "You won't know Henry, he is grown up."

"So am I." He threw out his chest.

"I am given to understand that."

They walked up the hillside, keeping to the edge of the street. Louise followed after; Robert led their horses. He draped the wide leather reins over his shoulder.

"I've been fighting bandits. Did Uncle Roger tell you?"

"Did you catch them?"

"Some. Some of them got away. They are no trouble."

Maria laughed. She leaned on him a little, to make him strut. She admired his blazing blue eyes. "So you like to fight"

"Oh, yes." He drew a deep breath.

356

"Is it fun?"

He shook his head. "It's better than fun. It's better than anything." He crossed himself quickly. "But I will never fight save for God. And Papa."

Maria hugged him against her. "Ah, you are a splendid son."

"Oh, Mama." He opened the postern door in the citadel gate and hung back to let her go before him. On the wall, a guard shouted his name, and he whooped an answer. "Is Ismael here yet?" he asked her.

Maria shook her head. She smiled at him, delighted with him. On his cheeks and upper lip fine dark hairs were sprouting. "Don't tell me you are growing a beard?"

"No." He fingered his chin. "Do you think I could?"

Maria laughed. She hugged him again.

"Robert!" Richard shouted, from across the ward. Robert put her down with a jolt. She turned to watch him charge his father. While the young Duke stood in the tower door, his eyes on them, they shouted and pummeled each other. Maria started across the ward. The sun was brilliant, in spite of the cold; she shaded her eyes with her hand.

XXXIV

❧

ISMAEL ARRIVED WITH FIVE HUNDRED OF THE MAJLAS al-Kerak. The army rode north again toward Agato. At the East Tower, Ponce Rachet had collected one hundred and fifty knights and two hundred men-at-arms. Traveling in three long columns, the army crossed the frontier of the duchy and struck over the high, rolling plain toward the Roman Road.

They reached the highway in a single day. Maria, riding with the wagons and servants and camp followers of the army, followed the road north into the gray-white distance. The few villages and farms they came upon were deserted: the people had all fled north before the army. Ponce Rachet's men-at-arms marched along before and behind the eighteen wagons, but for several days Maria saw no sign of the Saracens or the Christian knights, save for Richard and Robert, who came to sleep in her camp.

The snow was melting. The plain, shelving down toward the river bottomlands ahead, sprang with green life. Under the inch of slush, the road was hard and strong, but a stream ran thick with mud in the ditch. Maria rode at the head of the column of wagons, where the footing was best and she could keep her clothes fairly clean. The mud turned the white mare's legs black to the hocks and knees. The blank dripping plain and the white sky felt like a void around her.

One day, toward noon, horsemen appeared all over the plain to the north, west of the road. Hunting horns blasted in the distance. Maria gasped. The head drover bellowed to his oxen to stop. Before them the column of men-at-arms hurried to one side of the road, taking their pikes in their hands, their voices raised.

Hundreds of riders were galloping across the plain, half a league away, and coming down toward Maria at a dead run. They were fighting hand to hand. The distance blurred their voices and the clash of their weapons. In the wagons behind her the women screamed. Someone yanked on Maria's skirt.

"Maria!"

Her mare snorted and shied. Maria wheeled toward the other side of the road. Speeding up from the east, the Saracens raced toward her. Their wailing off-key war cries turned her arms to gooseflesh. They crossed the road through the train of wagons, scattering the men-at-arms.

Maria held her breath. A wedge of knights flew toward her across the muddy plain, coming like a club. Her mare was dancing sideways. She put one hand on the sweat-soaked neck. The Saracens darted through the narrowing space between her and the knights. Their lances dropped

358

level, the long slim blades white from honing, and they swerved to meet the knights like a scythe.

She tasted blood in her mouth. The Saracens engulfed the knights. Two of the Christians broke free and charged toward her. Behind them the Saracens shrieked their ululating yell. The hair on her head stirred and stood on end. Her mare reared up. Before her a Majlas lancer raced across the path of the two oncoming knights. His long blade struck the leading man in the belly and drove him off his horse. The last man galloped up between Maria and the regrouping men-at-arms and escaped away to the east.

Maria reined the white mare in a tight circle. The Saracens were taking prisoners of the knights they had caught alive. In the beaten, blackened snow a dozen bodies sprawled or screamed. Ismael on his sock-footed chestnut mare galloped up to Maria and cheerfully displayed his teeth. Clasped in the crook of his arm, his lance jabbed up at the sky. The blade and the next two feet of the wooden shaft were wet with blood.

"No stop," he called. The chestnut mare wheeled. The tassels of her bridle tossed. "Stop, never never leave much again." The mare spun and charged away.

From the wagons behind Maria, people vaulted to the ground. Even the women climbed eagerly down over the wheels to the road. Screaming in exultant voices, they rushed out to the fields. The Saracens were moving off with their prisoners. The camp followers and men-at-arms and Maria's own servants fell on the half dozen slain and wounded knights and fought over their shreds of clothes and armor.

Maria clicked to her mare. The head drover still sat with the reins drooping from his hands. He slapped the leathers against the rumps of his oxen and called out, and the team pushed forward again. Along the road behind them, the driverless oxen shouldered into their harness. All the men-at-arms had run off to loot in the bloody meadow. Even their commander was gone. She stood in her stirrups. All across the plain, by twos, in little groups of five or six, men were hacking at each other with swords and lances. Even Ismael, now, was only one of the white

359

robes that fluttered and dashed over the mud and the new grass. The baby quickened, a thread of feeling down her side. She put her hand on her belly over her womb.

In a straggling mob, the men-at-arms returned to march before her. No longer orderly, they carried sacks of booty on their shoulders. Their mood had changed: as if they and not the Saracens had fought the little battle, they swaggered triumphantly along shouting war cries and singing victory songs.

The sun was struggling to break through the clouds. High overhead, a flock of cranes flew north, their arrow-shaped flight pointing toward Agato. The fighting came and went like flames along the horizon. Maria rode between the wagon and the ditch. She thought she could smell blood in the air. The broad, featureless plain tricked her eyes; everything seemed much closer than it really was.

The men-at-arms ahead of her were pointing away. Their calling voices, excited as children, ran along the massed ranks and back into the wagons. Maria's servants got up to see. They were coming to ground where a battle had been fought, and bodies littered the meadow and clogged the ditch beside the road.

Maria crossed herself. Already bloated, the dead faces lay against the moist earth or bobbed in the ditch. Their eyes bulged froglike and monstrous. No one broke from the road to rob them. The women made loud disgusted noises. Maria turned her head away. If she attended such things it would mark the baby.

In a dank humor, she rode listlessly through the overcast afternoon. The fighting and the dead men, even the reactions of the women in the wagons, seemed gross and meaningless: she could not understand why anyone would risk dying like that. She might die like that, if his enemies defeated Richard. The men-at-arms before her were roaring a song whose words she hoped she did not hear right: something foul about women.

Late in the afternoon, a village appeared down the road, a clutter of thatches and walls in a dimple of the plain. A thin flag of smoke hung in the air above the rooftops, the first sign of local people she had seen in Santerois.

The men-at-arms beside her were calling to one another, jumping up to see over the heads of the soldiers in front of them. At once they broke into a trot. The white mare snorted, laying her ears back, and Maria reined her almost into the ditch to get out of the way of the column of men. They swarmed away down the road, lifting their voices.

Maria's horse leaped sideways. She turned it around. She struggled to think what to do. The road dipped into the hollow. The men-at-arms flooded along it and into the little village. Their voices turned to shouts.

"Maria," Louise was calling from the wagon. She waved to Maria to come back. There was a crash in the village. The men-at-arms were attacking it. Maria swung the white mare and galloped down the road after them.

The mare shortened stride on the little slope. Before her, the men-at-arms packed the road, shoulder to shoulder, their pikes jabbing toward her. In the middle of the village, an enormous old oak tree stood, its branches fuzzed with new green buds. Several people were sheltering in it.

Maria shouted. No one heard her. A man-at-arms climbed into the tree, and the people taking refuge there screamed.

On the far side of the village from Maria, a knight on a horse was watching it happen. She kicked the mare forward into the packed men, and reluctantly they shifted and stepped on one another to let her pass. The men-at-arms were climbing into the lower branches of the oak tree. The wretched villagers scrambled higher, screaming. A baby was crying. Maria kicked at the backs of the men in front of her. They parted and she forced the mare in among them.

The men in the tree were dragging a woman down out of the branches. She shrieked like a torn bellows. Maria whined under her breath. Frantically she wedged the mare through the mob. The knight opposite her was shouting orders no one heeded. The men-at-arms tore

361

the woman out of the tree, and Maria burst up behind them and leaped down from her horse. She charged in between the woman and the three men attacking her.

"Get back," she shouted; her heart was thumping, and she clenched her fists.

They blinked at her. One said, "Where did that come from?" and reached for her.

A pike struck his arm down. The keg-shaped man who commanded them strode up beside Maria. "That's enough," he said to the three. He tilted his pike up between them.

"I'm sorry, my lady," he said to her. "Just these pups after a little—" He nodded behind her, at the ground behind her.

She turned and sank down beside the village woman crouched against the trunk of the oak tree. The woman was shaking, too terrified even to cry. Her dress was torn open in front. Bloody bitemarks showed on her breast. Maria stood up.

"Borso," she said to the commander, "get these men out of the village and up where it's dry enough to camp." She pointed at the three young men. "Except them."

Borso glanced around him, in no hurry to obey her. She went up face to face with him. She was so angry her voice quavered. She said, "Did you hear me, Borso?"

"Yes, my lady." He turned briskly and bellowed orders. The thick press of bodies in the village began to ease. Maria stooped again beside the woman.

"It's all right now. Don't be afraid."

The woman closed her eyes. Maria touched her; she recoiled against the trunk of the tree. Maria straightened.

The strange knight was coming toward her, a boy scarcely older than Robert. His freckled face was dished and soft around the mouth, like a colt's. He said, "My lady, I was left in command here—"

"Who is your captain?"

"My lady, Ponce Rachet—"

The three young men-at-arms were shifting uneasily and looking around at their companions, slowly moving out of the village toward the high plain. Trailed by two other men, Borso came back. "My lady, it won't happen again. They didn't know who you were, they must have thought you were another villager."

Maria glared at him. "Put some guards around in here —men you can trust."

"Yes, my lady." He signed to the three young men. "Get back up there and see it doesn't—"

"Stop," Maria said. "I didn't tell you to dismiss them."

"Now, my lady—"

She peered up into the tree again. The people clinging to the high branches looked down at her like owls. "Come down," she called. They did not move. She raised her hand toward them. "Come down, I can't protect you if you stay up there."

One by one the eight people climbed out of the tree before her. Her men stared at them. When the young woman rose to go, clutching the remnants of her clothes about her bleeding breast, the men all cried out lewdly.

Maria spun around, close to tears. "Shut your dirty mouths." She marched up to Borso, who scrubbed his face with one hand and smiled down at her as if she were a child.

"Tie them to the tree." She jerked her chin toward the three bound men. "Let them spend the night there."

The men fell into a stunned silence. Borso said, "Hey, now, for the sake of that slut?"

"Do as I tell you."

The young knight dismounted, solemn-faced, and came forward. "My lady, we should really wait for my lord Marna's judgment on this."

A rush of hot words stuck in her throat. She started to stamp her foot but instead hit him in the face with her fist. At the sharp unexpected pain in her knuckles she cried out. The young knight gaped at her, hardly moved. She looked around at the men before her.

"God's blood," she said. "If Richard were here, he would hang these men, and you as well, if you argued with him." She stared at Borso. The toothmarks on the woman's breast returned to her mind. "Yes," she said. "Hang them."

A wordless sound exploded from the young knight. She cast a hard stare at him. She did not look at the three

363

young men-at-arms. Before her, Borso's face slumped. His mouth tightened, lipless, and he did not meet her eyes.

"Get a rope," he said.

The three young men gasped. Maria said, "See that they talk to a priest first."

She stood under the tree, while Borso and the young knight waited beside the three prisoners, and the other men went for rope and a monk. Her legs hurt but she did not move or sit down. Almost at once the other men-at-arms began to collect in the village to watch. When the rope came, the place was packed. No one spoke. Borso tied the knot, the priest shrived the three men, and one by one Borso hanged them. Maria stood there through it all, but she did not watch, she kept her eyes on the ground, for fear of marking the baby.

The men-at-arms filed away in a sudden babble of comment. One or two laughed, exulting in the sight of death. Borso came up before her and saluted her. "My lady, I will put sentries around, it will not happen again."

Maria lifted her head. "You are mad," she said, and went off behind the tree and was sick.

RICHARD DID NOT COME that night, or send a messenger. In the morning she felt as if she had not slept at all. The day was just breaking. The chill and the dense patches of fog that shrouded the plain drove her almost to weeping. When the oxen were hitched up and the march began, she stayed in the wagon with the other women, eating sweet bread.

"Maria," Louise said. "What happened in the village? We heard people shouting down there."

"Some of the men got after a woman."

A servant ran up beside the wagon, a platter in his hands, and laid it down at her feet in the wagon bed. "My lady. To break your fast." He stopped to bow and flourish, and the wagon carried her away from him.

Louise whipped aside the cover of the platter. A hot steam rose into Maria's face. The roasted hare crouched on the plate before her turned her stomach.

"Isn't that good of him," Louise said. She reached out

for a bite of the crisp skin. "These people care a great deal for you, Maria."

She mumbled something. She turned her eyes away. The wagon jolted out of a rut and back in again. Catherine said, "Don't you feel well?" She clutched Maria by the sleeve. "Look!"

Maria started up, cold. Through the mist that covered the plain, a widespread rank of horsemen was riding. She stood up. Her knees wobbled. The drover called to his oxen and stopped the wagon.

"It's Richard," she said. Her heart lightened. Robert came just behind him. The other knights veered away toward the back of the wagon train, where the spare horses were led.

Richard reined in beside Maria's wagon and swung down from his horse. His nose was red and peeling from the sun, and his hands were battered. He ignored the fluttering of the other women. Leaning over the side of the wagon, he grabbed the hare in both hands and tore off pieces and stuffed them into his mouth. High-spirited, Robert shouted to Maria.

She sat down in the wagon again, one arm along the side. Chewing steadily, Richard gave her a greasy kiss. "You look like Mother Hell. What's wrong?"

A groom jogged up two fresh horses toward them. Robert yanked his saddle girths loose. Maria said, "Some of the foot-soldiers tried to rape a woman in the village where we camped last night." She gestured toward it, just out of sight to the south. "I hanged them."

"You." He spat out something unchewable. "Where was Borso?"

"Borso was there. I nearly hanged him, too." She touched his shoulder. The heavy mail was wet with dew. Beyond, the groom was changing his saddle to a fresh horse. She felt suddenly much better.

"Are you fighting?"

He shot an evil look at her. "No. I'm going to church."

Maria laughed. He drank her cider and Louise's and Catherine's His fingers were swollen and stained with blood. The other women watched him owlishly. His pike across his shoulder, Borso was coming toward them at a lope.

"Papa," Robert called. He vaulted up into his saddle and reined his horse around into a half-rear. His skin was red with excitement. Maria waved to him.

"Have you seen Roger?" Richard asked.

"No. Ismael crossed the road yesterday. Where are you fighting?"

"Aw, Jesus. All the way from here down to the river and halfway to Birnia, and I've ridden every God-damned foot of it myself."

"Papa," Robert shouted. "Come on."

Maria took hold of Richard's beard and pulled his face down toward her. "Be careful."

"Papa!"

"I'm coming." Richard stepped back. "Roger should be somewhere around here—if you meet him send him up ahead." He turned to his horse. The groom was fastening the breastplate to the saddle, and Richard gathered up the reins. The horse pinned back its ears. It scuttled away from him, and he kicked it in the belly and swore at it until it stood still for him to mount. Borso trotted up to him, taking off his hat.

Richard waved in her direction. "Do as she says." He turned his horse. The sun was burning off the mist. The plain rolled beneath it, brown and green. Robert, wheeling to follow his father, called good-bye to her, but Richard only galloped away across the road toward the east. His men streamed after him, single file.

Catherine leaned on the wagon seat, her eyes dreaming after them. Louise picked up the wreckage of the hare. "That son of yours is a handsome one, Maria."

Maria stood up and beckoned to a groom. The women went on with their breakfast, talking about their fathers and husbands and brothers. Catherine wept quietly. The voices of the women fell to whispers. Maria tipped her ears to listen.

"He's a piece of a man."

"I wouldn't mind being alone in a soft place with him, mark you."

"Just the same," Louise whispered, "he has a foul temper, and I don't know why she puts up with it."

Maria glanced at them, and quickly they made themselves busy with their food, so she knew they meant

Richard. She sat down again, amused. Louise gave her another cup of the cider. The sun was butting through the clouds. After the miserable dawn the day was turning bright and warm. Her mare trotted toward her after the groom, and she climbed across the side of the wagon into her saddle.

XXXV

❦

IN THE MIDDLE OF THE FOLLOWING DAY, THE ROAD LED to a castle on a treeless bluff to the left of the road. Beyond, she saw the first distant glitter of the river. At the foot of the steep hill lay a town of some twenty or twenty-five buildings, ringed by a stone wall. Orchards of leafless trees covered the flat ground just beyond. On either side of the town were barren fields.

Borso stopped the men-at-arms and loped back toward the wagons for his orders. Maria reined in the white mare. On the slopes of the hill, below the castle, there seemed to be a camp, and men crawled over the steep rocky ground below the castle's curtain wall. Much of the hillside had been burned off.

"Whose camp is that?" she said to Borso. "Wait." Three horsemen were riding across the hillside toward her. Duke Henry led them. She settled down into her saddle again.

The young man rode up to her, the hood of his black mail shirt thrown back, and his dark face vivid. "I'll take these men," he said. "You can shelter in the town. I need supplies, these people have destroyed everything. Where is Richard?"

"I don't know—yesterday morning he was going east. I—"

"There is a messenger here from the Emperor."

"The Emperor!"

"He will talk only to Richard."

The corners of her mouth twitched. Few people called Richard by his given name. She said, "Well, then, it won't hurt to let him wait. Where is he now?"

"In the town. In the church. I made him leave the best house for you. He wouldn't talk to me." Reining his horse around, he drove the men-at-arms ahead of him up the steep path toward the castle. Halfway to the siege line, the men-at-arms broke into a trot under his harrying voice. Maria sent the supply wagons after him and rode into the town.

The wide, treeless square was crowded with palfreys, gorgeously harnessed, and grooms and baggage and the low courtly flutter of voices. Maria's servants went on before her, to locate the best house and make it ready. She let her mare amble through the square toward the church. A group of men lounged there, dressed in coats sleeved in the German style, fitted from wrist to elbow. Coarse shredded gold detailed the cuffs of their surcoats. Their hats sprouted feathers. She stared at them, awed: to her every Emperor was Charlemagne.

They had seen her. They leaned toward one another, and a graying man in a short spade beard motioned to a page to bring her. Maria rode quickly off.

The house the Duke had kept for her was two large pleasant rooms of whitewashed stone, on another side of the square from the church. Maria gave a groom her reins and he led her mare away. The wagon rolled up before the door of the house. Louise spoke with authority about what it meant to have three feathers in one's hat in Germany.

The little page ran up to them. "Madame," he cried, in a piping foreign voice. "Madame." His hair was white as an old man's. Maria pushed at him with her hands.

"Go tell your master if he will not talk to Duke Henry, I will not talk to him." She turned her back on him and helped Catherine down out of the wagon.

Her servants briskly unloaded the wagon of its goods. Maria went into the house to show them where to put everything. When she came out again, the little page was waiting for her. Behind him, in the square, was the man with the spade beard.

"Madame—"

A dozen Saracens trotted into the square. Their filthy white robes were splattered with blood. Maria shoved the page off. She went toward the Saracens, looking for Ismael. Ten feet from the German in his feathered hat, she stopped, and they exchanged a look. The man smiled smoothly at her, at his ease.

Richard and the young Duke rode past the Saracens into the square. Maria met them. A groom jogged out to take the horses. Richard dismounted.

"You look tired," she said. "You'd better come inside."

"Tired." He jammed his hands under his swordbelt. "I could sleep on a meat hook."

The young Duke drew up his horse behind him. "My lord Friedrich," he called. "This man is the lord of Marna."

The German advanced. His skin was fine and pink, as if he never worked. He fixed his eyes on Richard. "Richard of Marna," he said, "I bring you the greetings and requirements of your Emperor."

"If the Emperor wants to talk to me," Richard said, "and require things of me, let him come tell me himself."

The German spread his mouth in a humorless smile. "The Emperor is your overlord, God's minister on earth. I should not have to remind you, Richard d'Alene, that his will is the will of Christ, and as a Christian knight you owe him obedience, wherever he or you might be."

Maria took Richard's helmet from him. For a moment he did not move, his eyes on the German smoky with fatigue and bad temper. Abruptly he flung his arm out toward his Saracens.

"Do you see those men, Friedrich? To them, there is no Emperor." He went off toward the house. Maria smiled at the astonished look on the face of the Emperor's man. She raised her eyes to Duke Henry.

"Come in, my lord, and dine with us."

Duke Henry grunted; he was watching Friedrich. The German stood a moment longer. Maria thought he would speak. But he swung around and marched stiffly toward the church. She went inside.

While she helped lay out the dishes on the table, the Duke sat absorbed across from Richard, who was explaining something about castle gates. The two men plunged into the supper. For a space there was no sound but their steady chewing. Maria brought a stool over to Richard's chair and sat down. He moved his cup over in front of her so that she could drink.

"I'm beginning to think Roger is lost," Richard said abruptly.

"Nobody can get lost in Santerois," the Duke said.

"You don't know my brother."

"He's a great knight."

"He can take any three men in Italy. My son will be like that."

"Where is Robert?" Maria asked.

"East of here." He put the honey pot down in front of her. "I hope he's finally decided to sleep. Did Borso's men give you any more trouble?"

Maria shook her head. She picked among the bits of meat on his plate for the choice morsels.

"Those footsoldiers are good men," the Duke said. "They listen sharp to their commander, too."

Richard grunted. "Maria's been hanging the ones that don't all along the road from here to Marna."

"Richard," she said.

The young Duke fingered his empty cup. A servant came up behind him to take it. The young man said, "Why did you?—" and whirling, leaped up, his arms flying up to shield himself and to strike.

The servant cringed away. The Duke cried, "Don't do that!" He sat down again. His face was suddenly pale and much younger. The servant crouched moveless behind his chair. Maria signed to him to take the cup away to be filled.

"I'll teach my household to be more clumsy, my lord," she said.

Richard leaned one elbow on the table, pushing his plate over in front of her. "Eat, Maria, why are you starving yourself?"

Maria kicked him in the shin. She finished his meat and bread. The servant approached them cautiously, his footsteps loud on the plank floor, and set the cup down before the young Duke. He picked his teeth, his eyes on Richard's face.

Richard said, "I didn't think Theobald knew how to tell the truth, but by God, he did."

"Theobald." The Duke straightened. His dark face smoothed out, expressionless. "What truth did he tell you?"

"Last summer, when he was peddling his conspiracy to me, he gave me to think the Emperor was in it. He offered to make me Duke of Marna."

Maria spread honey on the last piece of bread. The Duke lifted his hand like a veil across his face. "You knew about the plot against me."

"Well, most of it."

They stared at each other. Maria put the bread and honey in her mouth. The young man shook his head. His hand dropped to the table again.

"You are a cold bastard, Richard. Why did you talk to the Emperor's man that way? He is still the Emperor, even if he is against us."

Richard laughed. He rubbed his eyes. "Go on, finish eating and get out of here, I'm sleepy. Are you going to start sapping under the wall tomorrow?"

The Duke was piling his hands full of bread and sweet cakes. "From that ditch. I'll send for you when we start."

Maria followed him to the door. Both his hands were loaded with bread; he needed help with the latch. When she turned back into the room, Richard had cradled his head in his arms and gone to sleep. She stood beside his chair. Sleep softened his face; he looked almost handsome. The servants quietly removed the supper dishes and padded away into the back room. The door closed.

"Richard."

He stirred. Waking, his face hardened and aged.

"Richard. Come to bed."

IN THE NIGHT there was a knock on the door. Maria climbed out of the bed, put her cloak over her nightgown, and went to answer. It was Roger, his hair black in the moonlight.

"Where is Richard?" He tried to push past her, and she

371

blocked his way. "Maria." He reached for her with both hands. She fended him off, and when he moved toward the door again pulled it closed.

"Roger, don't wake him up just because you aren't sleepy. Where have you been?—No one has seen you for days."

He lounged up against the wall of the house. "Oh, I had my own war for a while, down south. What's this about the Emperor?" He took her by the wrist. "Such soft skin." He started to kiss the inside of her wrist and she pulled her hand away.

"Roger."

He laughed at her, reaching for her hand again. She gave a quick glance around the darkened town square. On the roof gables the sentries all looked asleep. He squeezed her hand.

"Tell me about the Emperor."

"Oh. There is a man here from the Emperor, to tell us not to support Duke Henry, I suppose, but Richard won't talk to him."

"Oh." Roger smiled. "Does the German know what he's missing?"

"I'm worried. It seems like not talking to God."

"I don't think Richard does much of that, either. Here. Don't worry." He kissed her hair. "None of the talk makes any difference. Robert's with me. Go inside, you are cold." Smiling, he touched her face and strode to his horse.

"MARIA!"

Maria ignored her. Louise had been leading the servants in a general wail all morning, and no one was doing any work. Standing at the far end of the bed from Catherine, Maria straightened the bedcovers and tucked down the corners. From the other room came the delicious odors of the dinner cooking.

"Maria!"

She went up to the tight knot of people and made them give way, so that she could reach the threshold. Ismael had come during the night. His headcloth across his face, he squatted beside Richard's chair, out in front of the house, while the man in the gray spade beard paced up and down the church porch. Louise clutched Maria's sleeve with both hands.

"He won't even listen to them," Louise said, her voice a strident whisper even Richard must have heard. "He can't do that to the Emperor—"

Maria freed herself from the maid's grip. "Go find something quieter to do. All of you, go on, if you can't busy yourselves, I'll find work for you."

The women scattered across the house. Maria walked out into the sunlight. Her sleeves were rolled above her elbows, but she did not bother to tug them down again. Coming up behind Richard, she laid her hands on his shoulders. Pulling down his headcloth, Ismael smiled at her.

"Ismael," she said. She stroked the hair back over the balding crown of Richard's head. "Wouldn't he make a nice monk?"

Ismael's smile evaporated. Richard tilted his head back to look at her, upside down. She said, "You remind me of Brother Nicholas."

"Then I will stop washing."

She stood with her hands on his shoulders, glancing at the Germans on the porch. He rolled his head back comfortably against her breast. The Germans were staring. She felt the touch of their eyes on her, as if she were naked.

"Do you like that kind of sleeve?"

"I haven't marked their sleeves. You'd never get a hat on me like that one, though, with the feathers."

A rider cantered in the gate and slowed his horse to a walk. Maria said, "Well, you'll have to wear some kind of hat now, you don't want your head to get sunburned." Ismael backed away. She marked he was limping. On the porch of the church, the Emperor's man in his splendid hat advanced into the sunlight. The rider reined his horse toward Richard.

"My lord Santerois's greeting, my lord, we are going to start digging now."

Richard stood up, his back carefully to the Emperor's man. Ismael put the flap of his headcloth across his face again, and his eyes flickered toward the church porch.

373

"Ismael," Maria said. "Stay with me."

He reached her in one giant bound. Richard put his head back and laughed. A groom was leading up his horse. Maria hooked her arm through Ismael's.

"Will you come for supper?" she said to Richard.

"If we're done." He mounted and rode out of the square. Maria led Ismael back toward the house.

"What happened to your leg? Has the tabib seen it?"

Ismael shrugged one shoulder. "It is harmless." He glanced at her quickly to see if that were the right word. "Harmless. Al-Tabib—" He gestured indefinitely. They went into the house, full of bustling servants.

"Well, sit down." She led him toward the table. There was only one chair. Going back to the door, she watched the Germans on the church porch confer. She swung the door closed. Ismael sat in her chair. Self-consciously he took off his headcloth. Maria went up beside him and sat on her heels.

"What happened? Did Shai fall?" Shai was his chestnut mare.

"Oh, no. Shai never fall." He straightened up, indignant. "In high close place Shai always foot-foot." He shrugged. "I fall. I go very long—" He stretched one arm out, leaning into a lance stroke. "I go very bold," he said proudly.

She laughed, delighted with him. She put one hand on his arm. Behind them, Louise in a ringing whisper said, "Well, she doesn't have to have him in under the same roof with Christians."

Maria went cold to her heels. Ismael twisted his face away. Ashamed and humiliated, she could not make herself speak. Her hand still lay on his arm and she pressed her fingers against him. Lifting her head, she glanced over her shoulder at Louise, as usual talking, and the woman's voice cut off short.

"Bring me some water," Maria said. "And clean linen."

The servants withdrew to other areas of the house. A man brought her a pitcher of water and a basin, and a pile of linen. She poured the water over Ismael's hands so that he could wash.

"Did you say the tabib looked at your leg?"

"No hurt." He dried his face in the linen. "It is harm-

374

less. Just much wickedness." With his hand he indicated his entire leg. Bending close to her, he murmured, "Emir righten." Sitting up, he smiled triumphantly at her.

"Maria!" Louise shrieked, near the door.

Maria got up. She crossed the room and opened the door again. Brilliantly dressed, their little palfreys shining like ladies' dogs, the Emperor's man and his party were riding sedately out of the town.

"Ismael," Maria cried. "Come with me."

With Ismael on her heels she ran across the square to the gate. The Emperor's man and his little parade were just turning through the crossroads below the castle. Neat as their mounts, they trotted away to the north. Above them, on the hillside, the lines of men digging into the clay-colored earth stopped to watch.

Maria turned and started back toward their house. Ismael walked beside her. "Emperor now is made enemy?"

"Enemy," she said. "Yes, of course."

He threw his arm around her shoulders. "I save you, Maria."

"Oh, Ismael."

In the mid-afternoon, Richard, Roger, and the young Duke stamped into the house, shouting to be fed supper. Maria's servants helped her bring out the table. Richard told a filthy joke, and Roger laughed. The young Duke lowered his eyes.

"Look at sweet innocence," Roger said. He sauntered around the room, his eyes on the Duke. "What's the matter, knave, can't you find a girl to take it from you?"

The young man's gaze was pinned to the floor. He said, "My lady Maria—"

Maria herded the servants out again. Ismael gave the young Duke a look warm with sympathy and quietly left. "Don't worry, Bunny," Richard said. "I was a virgin when I married, and it worked as if I'd practiced for years."

The Duke raised his head. At his expression Roger whooped, derisive. Maria took him the ewer of wine to fill his cup.

"You are all in a fine humor," he said.

"They gave up." Roger drank. His face screwed up with distaste and he put the cup on the table. "The wine is off—you can't jounce wine around in wagons and serve it the next day, Maria, for God's love."

"Who gave up? What do you mean? The castle? Here?"

"They surrendered." He shrugged. "When the Emperor's man rode away, the garrison opened the gate to us."

Maria went across the room for the jug of cider. Richard was sitting on the bed, listening to the young Duke. While the young man talked he stabbed his knee with his forefinger. Maria took the cider back to Roger. She said, "It's a sign. You see God is with us."

Roger poured out the strong-smelling cider. His eyes shifted to look over her shoulder. "I think Richard wants your attention, sweet."

"Give me a drink of your cider."

Roger's eyes narrowed. He lifted the cup to her lips. She drank, and he turned the cup around and drank from the same place. Their eyes met. He winked at her.

Maria could not keep from laughing. She crossed the room toward the bed. "Roger says the wine is spoiled, do you want cider instead?"

"Yes, I would—" the Duke said, and Richard said, "No." He grabbed for her wrist. "Stay here."

Duke Henry went away to get himself cider. Taking Richard by the beard, Maria turned his face up toward hers. "Oh, I think bald men much finer than redheads." He still gripped her wrist. She pulled his scabbed fingers free. "You are hurting me."

Richard stood up. "Roger, are you sure you want to get married?" Ill-tempered, he swatted her on the backside. She slid out of his reach. Her flank stung painfully even through the thick layers of her skirts.

"Who but a wife would love you?"

The Duke was staring at her as if she had turned into a toad. Richard's chair had been put up to the table. He dragged it out and reversed it and sat down. He looked her over.

"Roger. What price do you think she would bring me at the auctions in Africa?"

Roger leaned against the wall, his face lively. "Strip her down, Richard, I'll give you a bid."

"Not if you saw her, you wouldn't."

376

Maria started toward him. He got up and dodged behind his chair, brushing by the Duke. "She kicks, too," he
told the young man. "Someday I'm going to take an awl
and sew a red ribbon on her tail."

She sat down in his chair. "My lord," she said to Duke
Henry, "you have witnessed him misusing me."

The young man frowned. His face was priestly with
disapproval. "A galled horse bucks, doesn't he?"

Roger roared with laughter. Richard shoved a cup of
cider into Maria's face, and she took it. "So does a galled
mare," she said. Richard stood over her, his feet wide
apart. She got up face to face with him, pushing her swollen body out between them.

"Do you want your stall back, my lord?"

Richard lowered himself into the chair. Taking hold of
her clothes he pulled her hand over hand into his lap.
"Pax." The servants had come to serve the food. Aromas
of meat reached her. Maria put her arm around Richard's
shoulders.

"What will the Emperor do to us?"

Richard looked sharply at her. "The Emperor's beyond
the Alps." He stroked her gown over her belly. "This will
be sitting up before he even remembers us." His arm went
around her waist. She put her hand on his hair, unsure.

XXXVI

❧

A HOT, FIERCE WIND BLEW IN GUSTS ACROSS THE PLAIN.
The white mare capered from hoof to hoof. On the castle above the town, a new banner flew from the peak of
the gate: Duke Henry's banner. The young Duke was re-
ceiving the sworn oaths of the garrison in the village
square before her.

Richard and Roger had already gone on. Borso's men-at-arms were staying in the castle as the Duke's garrison. The hot wind blasted in a sudden burst through the square, rattling shutters and carrying off people's hats. The white mare bounded sideways, snorting. On the far side of the square, Robert looked around toward her.

The homage taken, the Duke mounted his horse, and they rode out of the town to the high road, where the wagons were already lined up waiting for them. Maria went to the head of the wagons, to see her serving women. One musician was there, playing for them on his horn, and she stayed to listen to him. The Duke set his few dozen knights around them in a broken column. He and Robert rode along in front of the train.

Maria cantered up to them. The road swerved to travel east along the lower bank of the river: the same river that ran through Birnia, a passage of dark slow water between banks like bluffs. Here, a kind of beach lay below the southern bank, littered with rocks and dead branches graying in the sun. She swung her horse up beside Robert's.

"This is fat land." She waved to the broad fields and the river.

The Duke favored her with a cold stare. "Lady." Spurring his horse, he rode back along the column.

Maria turned to look after him. Her throat and ears burned. "Brat," she said, under her breath.

"Have you been fighting with Papa?" Robert asked.

"Is that what he thinks? Tell him that's how we make love."

Robert smiled at her, merry as a deer. "I told him when Papa roars, he's happy. Did you hear how I rescued that knight?"

"Yes. I understand you had to be rescued yourself immediately thereafter."

"Mama."

The knights behind them were singing. Robert joined in the chorus. Maria resisted the leaden mood pressing on the edge of her mind. Before them the plain swelled full as a breast along the river. She unclasped her cloak and laid it down in front of her on her saddle. The turned earth of the fields smelled moist and rich.

378

"Robert," she said. Several riders had come into sight on the road ahead of her. "Call Bunny."

Robert wheeled forward in his saddle. The four knights directly in front of them were closing ranks. One shouted an order. Maria reined in, and the whole column stopped. The Duke galloped up through the heavy plowed ground toward the head of the column.

On a curved road in the distance, the dozen strangers stopped in a clump. Half a league separated them from her. She could make out only that they were mailed knights. The high wind took away their shout. The white mare edged toward Robert's horse, laying her ears back. Far ahead of them, two of the horsemen broke away from the others and cantered along the road toward the Duke, waiting alone in front of his power. Overhead the strangers bore a white banner.

"Come on." Maria clicked her tongue. The mare trotted up through the ranks of knights. Robert trailed her. They reached the Duke's side. She glanced at him, and he turned the back of his shorn head to her.

Robert came up between them. "Who are they?"

The young Duke said names. "Theobald's friends. Their castle is much south of here. Richard must have taken it." Maria watched him through the corner of her eye. He scratched nervously at his chin, watching the strangers before him.

Under their white flag, the two rebels reined their horses down and within a few lengths of the Duke stopped together. The younger called, "My lord, I pray you, give us an ear. We wish you only peace."

Maria said, under her breath, "Make them come on foot."

Beyond Robert, the Duke spurred his horse two steps ahead of her. "Keep out of this." He raised his arm, and the knights behind them ranged up closer to them. In a ringing voice, he called, "What do you want?"

The two started to ride forward. The young Duke said, "Get off your horses."

Robert threw Maria a quick smile. The two rebels dismounted and walked toward the Duke. The massed knights behind Maria gave up a quiet, contemptuous murmur.

"My lord," the rebel said, "we have come to save our honor in your cause. If you will give us leave to follow you, we shall prove that Saracens are no more valiant than your own barons."

Maria covered her smile with her hand. Ismael would have to hear of that. The Duke answered at once, offering terms: harsh as winter. He took their oaths of loyalty, making them kneel down in the muddy road, and they mounted and joined the column when it moved on.

The two rebels and their followers had collected in the ranks just behind Maria. She heard the younger one say, "Look. I told you he brought his harem."

"Sssh—what if she speaks French?"

A harsher voice said, "Take your stable tongues off Dragon's wife."

The two Santerois men blurted out some hot words. Maria turned, and the men stilled.

Robert went off with the young Duke. Left alone, she thought against her will of the three soldiers she had hanged. She was glad that she had not watched. She was glad she did not remember their faces. Grimly she prayed for them the rest of the afternoon, until at sundown another of the rebels appeared on the road ahead of them and asked to be forgiven.

While the Duke was listening to the man's speeches, a white river of Saracens galloped up from the south. The knights around Maria, Richard's men, did not even look to mark it, but the rebels gaped, and the man speaking to the Duke lost his voice. Richard brought his big black horse smoothly to a stop before Maria.

"What is this?"

"Rebels," she said. "Changing sides. I don't understand it."

The Saracens rushed up around them like surf. She called to Ismael, in their midst. The young Duke mounted his horse.

"Marna!" He raised his fist in a greeting.

"Bunny, where are you camping?" Richard shouted.

The young Duke waved his arm down the road. He and Richard exchanged information at the tops of their lungs. On foot between them, the stout graying man who had just surrendered looked aghast. The Duke galloped off and the Saracens at Richard's shout raced after him.

Maria turned to follow. Darkness was coming. The wind had died suddenly. In the west the sky was dark red. When Richard came up on her right, she said, "Why are all these men deserting Theobald?"

He shrugged. "Either they don't trust the Emperor, or they don't trust Theobald. Probably both." He reached out his hand to her. "Come on."

He wheeled his horse and urged it into a lope. Maria cantered after him. They crossed the road into a fallow field and rode down the dark meadows toward the river. Behind them a voice called helplessly to them to stop.

The stars were pricking through the sky. Now the wind rose again. She felt it fresh against her cheek. The soft ground pitched away under them. They let their horses find their footing down the riverbank to the crisp sand along the water's edge. The river ran muttering in the darkness, smelling like moss.

"Bunny thinks you are a shrew," Richard said. He rubbed his face on his cloak. Their horses lowered their muzzles to sniff the stony sand. Richard dismounted. Maria slid down into his arms. She kissed him.

Their arms around one another, they walked to the shelter of the riverbank. Maria said, "Well, it's no Bunny I'm sitting on the cold ground with." They sat down side by side. The sand was still warm from the sun. "I don't think he likes that name."

"Yes, it's too bad, isn't it?"

She laughed. Their horses dragged their trailing reins down to the river to drink. She slipped her fingers under the wide cuff of his hauberk and stroked the inside of his elbow through his sleeve. For a moment neither of them spoke.

"What are you thinking about?" he said abruptly.

"What?"

"You have that slack-jawed look you get when you're thinking."

"I'm not going to tell you if you insult me."

"You were praying."

"I don't remember."

381

In the meadows beyond the river, an owl gave a low hunting call. Richard was watching her intently. "What do you think of, when you pray?"

"What do you mean?"

"Do you think of God? What does God look like, do you think? Like a man?"

Somewhere down toward the road, a voice was shouting for him. Maria moved her hand up his arm, inside the full heavy sleeve of his mail. "I used to think God probably looked like my father."

"Your father." He moved toward her suddenly. The sand ground under him. "You are the only good your father ever did."

"Emir," Ismael shouted, closer than before.

"He told me something once—after you killed Odo. He said, *I am a stupid old man out against a clever young one, who I have faith will be a stupid old man himself someday.*

Richard snorted. "Not as stupid as he was."

Something huge sailed over her head and landed in front of them on the beach. She shrank down against the ground. It was Ismael, on his horse. Richard stood up. Before he could speak, Ismael in a spray of sand jumped his horse back up the bank again and was gone.

Relieved, she laughed; she got up beside Richard. With her help he shed the heavy mail shirt. The pale linen padding he wore made it easier to see him. She touched him, and he leaned down on his elbow, his head almost in her lap.

"What do you think about now? About God?"

"Now?" She put one hand on his hair. "The sea. Music. Stars. Something like that. Or the spaces between things."

"What things?"

She shrugged. "What do you think God is?"

"God is an illusion."

She started. She said nothing, frightened and repulsed.

"Well? Aren't you going to argue with me?"

She stroked his hair down. He laid his head on her thigh. She said, "I'm going to miss your hair, when it's gone."

"Stupid cow." He rubbed his face against her body.

"Why are you so concerned about God, if it's just an illusion?"

"I don't know. Because it's easier to think about God than Theobald."

"When are you going to fight him?"

"'Fight what? If we could fight it would be easy. Theobald has no army—half his friends have come over to us, and the rest are going home to wait and see what happens. Even Prince Arthur has run away." He tugged on her hand, drawing her down above him. "Lie with me."

"I thought that was what you wanted. Wait until I get my cloak."

AGATO COVERED the riverbank for nearly a mile, far outreaching its wall. The streets were narrow and deep in mud. The huts of weavers and wool-carders stood almost in the same streets as the tall stone houses of the cloth merchants. The tower of the cathedral rose above the town like a watchman.

When they rode into the town the cathedral's bells were ringing. The Duke led them straight to the church, where they thanked God for their victory. When they came out again, through the middle archway, the square was crowded with townspeople. They cheered, and their voices echoed back from the two- and three-story buildings fronting on the square.

Robert brought Maria's horse and helped her mount. The roars of the crowd changed to gasps and hisses: Ismael and the Majlas were coming up the street. An old woman on the cathedral steps made the sign against the Evil Eye. Maria urged her mare forward.

In the middle of the square Richard and Duke Henry were waiting. Suddenly all around them a tremendous cheer went up. Robert screwed himself around in his saddle. "Uncle Roger," he said. "He sends men on ahead of him to tell folk who he is, and to start them cheering."

Richard and the Duke had overheard him. They looked at each other and laughed. Maria stared suspiciously at her son. "That isn't true."

Robert smiled at her, pleased. "I've heard it said."

The men who once had followed Theobald now gathered around the Duke, the dark center of a flower in the midst of their busy attentions. Gradually they were crowding him away from Richard. Maria drew her horse aside. They had decided the night before to garrison the three castles in Agato and in the morning leave to run Theobald down. She began to wish she had not agreed to stay in the town.

"Whore," a woman screamed, in the crowd. Maria paid no heed until Robert gripped her arm.

The woman was pushing up between people toward her. She held out a cross like a charm against Maria. "Whore. Saracen whore."

Robert thrust his horse up to shield her. His hand went to his sword. Maria caught his wrist. "No." She could not lift her eyes to see how many people heard. Already the onlookers were bundling the woman off. Maria's cheeks burned. The voice went on calling faintly, even though the woman was lost from sight in the crowd. The men rode off again. She pressed toward Richard, grateful to be moving.

MARIA WIPED SCENT on her wrists. She held her hands under her nose and sniffed the fragrance. Behind her, Louise lifted her hair up in coils on her head and fixed it there with heavy jeweled combs.

"What if they don't come?" Catherine asked. She leaned in the window, straining to see out to the city.

"They will be here." The army had been collecting on the plain all day long, coming in groups and columns from the north, where they had captured Theobald. Richard and Robert had not yet appeared. Raising her looking glass, she watched Louise mass her thick black hair on her head.

"I look as if I'm going to tip over."

"You look beautiful," Catherine said breathlessly. "Doesn't she? Doesn't she look splendid?"

The other women murmured in agreement. Maria stood up, careful not to dislodge her hair. Louise came smiling around in front of her.

"Here." She stood on her toes and changed a comb.

"Everything will come down as soon as I move."

"Sssh."

Louise took a brush and fiddled with the long curl over Maria's ear. The other women were dressing one another. A hum of excited talk filled up the room.

"They're here!" Catherine screamed. "They are coming!"

Maria leaped up and ran over behind the girl. The women piled up against the window. "On the bridge," Catherine wailed. "Oh, oh, he is so handsome—look at his hair—"

Maria leaned on the girl's back to see. "If you blubber all through my feast, Catherine, I'll smack you." On the bridge below the window, Robert and Roger were crossing side by side, bearing the white dragon banner over their heads.

"Who is that? Poor creature," Louise cried.

"Theobald." Maria climbed on a stool to see over their heads. Theobald rode along over the bridge, his hands bound behind him and a rope halter around his neck. A footsoldier led his horse by the reins. Richard came after him, and the Duke in his black mail.

The sun was setting. Maria drew back from the window. Catherine pressed herself against the window frame, sighing like a lovebird, her eyes on Roger. Maria made sure her hair was securely fastened and went down the stairs to the hall.

Fitz-Michael had had five children, three boys and two girls, but one daughter was a nun. The others were already in the hall, listening to Maria's musicians. She and her servants had hung embroidered silk on the walls and covered the floors with Saracen carpets. Instead of the battered furniture she had found here, they had brought in her own chairs and tables.

Stiff as icons, Fitz-Michael's brood sat in the candlelight, their hands folded in their laps. The girl was very fair, her dark blond hair smoothly coiled under her little lace-trimmed coif, her mouth artfully red: a young widow, the Duke had said. Roger had had enough virgins, he would not miss it now.

"The men are in the courtyard," Maria said. Her page ran up to her with a stool, and she sat next to the girl,

Anne of Demoges, who would marry Roger. "Do you enjoy the music?" She resisted the urge to eat from the plate of marzipan before her.

"It is quaint," Anne said. "A peculiar style, my lady." She aimed her gaze pointedly at Maria's bulging front. "When the ladies of Santerois are with child, we stay secluded from public looks."

Maria reached for the marzipan. "A good reason not to get with child. We weren't told you had children."

Anne pressed her fingertips to the base of her throat. Her jewels were beautiful: clusters of rubies and emeralds. "A way of speaking."

"Do you have children?"

Anne looked down her nose, exactly like Rahman, and Maria giggled. "No," Anne said coldly. "I am not blessed with children."

"I wasn't laughing at you—you reminded me of a friend of my husband's—the Emir of Mana'a."

"I," Anne said, "remind you of a Saracen?"

"Yes. We are enemies, he and I—I am very vindictive. It comes of being a robber's daughter, and not of your exalted place in life."

Anne froze, her cheeks suddenly blotchy. "We did not ask for this marriage."

"No. But you are fortunate to get it. We are fortunate, too. We will accept you, if you will accept us."

Anne put her profile to her and did not answer. Maria licked the taste of almond from her fingers. It was going to be a difficult courting. The door from the hall opened, and Robert came in. Duke Henry was just behind him.

Robert had cut all his hair off. A wilting wildflower bobbed above his right ear. He came straight across the hall to his mother and knelt down beside her.

"See? I am still alive."

"Don't make fun of me." She turned to introduce him to Anne, but the girl had gone to join her brothers, making much of the young Duke.

Richard walked in the door. He was still armed and in his mail. Maria stood up. The young Duke swung toward him, brushing off his male relatives. Anne he towed forward with him.

"This is my cousin Anne," the Duke said. "My lord Richard d'Alene the lord of Marna."

Maria put her hand on Robert's arm to quiet him. Richard said something in greeting. Maria could not hear Anne's reply, but Richard bridled up. He said three words to her and went off toward the door.

Anne gasped. Several people turned to look. Maria laughed. Robert was staring after Richard, his mouth open. She put her finger on his chin and pushed his lower jaw shut.

"You look like a cat catching flies." Richard had gone out of the room.

"Mama, what—"

"The bride's family seems to think we are baseborn." Robert's face twisted. Maria caught his hand. "No. Don't do anything. Nobody can deal with it better than Richard. Go rescue Bunny." The Duke's relatives had surrounded him again.

"I'm not a toady." Robert walked stiffly away.

Maria gestured to the musicians to play. Fitz-Michael's sons were of no consequence; she had never been able to remember their names. She went to the door, to go after Richard, and it opened and Roger came in.

"Maria. What happened—Richard just went by me looking like thunder." He laced his fingers through hers. His eyes swept the room. "Which one is mine?"

"Roger. We all are."

Roger chuckled. He chucked her under the chin and went over to the knot of strangers. He was taller than Anne's brothers, taller than any other man there save Duke Henry. His red hair was like a target for eyes. Robert came up to him, worshipful, and the red knight put his arm over the boy's shoulders. On Anne he turned his generous grace.

Off to one side, the Duke stared at them. Maria went across the room to start the servants around with the wine and cakes. She had seen the Duke look once or twice at Fitz-Michael in the same way. Richard came in, dressed in his blue coat. Ismael followed on his tracks. The Duke's expression altered. They stood together, talking.

Maria got two cups of wine and went up beside Richard. "My lord," she said, "let me serve you."

Richard said to the Duke, "We should hang Theobald before he gets away."

Maria held out the cup to him, but Ismael took it. "I drink," he said. He smiled, exuberant.

"Ismael," she said. "That's a sin."

The smile widened by several teeth. "I drink." He took a deep swallow of the wine. His face went suddenly green. Maria guessed he had been expecting something sweet, like sherbet. Richard got the cup from him.

"Go away."

The Duke drank his wine. "My lady, do you like my cousin?"

"Oh," Maria said thinly, "she is very beautiful, we shall have her often to Mana'a to visit."

Ismael lingered. Robert shot him a hard look, and he sidled off along the wall. Richard turned his back on him. Maria put her hand on his arm. She glanced over her shoulder at Roger and Anne.

The Duke said, "She's getting along with him, at least. I guess Roger could win anybody. When do you want to marry them?"

"After we hang Theobald."

The Duke gave him a bland stare and walked away. Richard said, under his breath, "Bunny, you can back like a crayfish."

"Threaten to leave," Maria said. "What can he do without you?"

"He'll do it." He drained his cup and tossed it to a hovering page. "They are all working on him, but they know him little. Who does this girl think she is, anyway, Christ among the angels?"

"She does now." Maria watched Anne and Roger talk. The fair girl's laughter rang out. She gave Roger an adoring look. Maria turned back to Richard.

"Did you miss me?" he said.

"Sometimes." She ran her fingers over his chest. "How do you like my hair?"

"Down." The page had returned with his cup. He lifted it to drink, his eyes on her hair. "It's all coming down anyway."

She gasped, her hands flying to her head. Richard

388

laughed. She felt carefully of her hair, still securely fastened above her ears in its elaborate loops and curls.

"Now that was a brat's trick," she said.

Richard shook his head. A platter appeared between them. He took a stuffed date from it and put it in his mouth. "Theobald asked about you."

"Theobald." She glanced beyond him at Ismael, who was taking a bite from every piece on a tray of cakes. "Did you tell him I am well? Ismael seems to think someone wants to poison you."

"Ismael," Richard called. "Go away now."

The server brought over the cakes. Richard started to send them away. "The Brotherhood poison each other in their feuds. He just wants to be important."

"Or have a sinless taste of wine." Maria took a cake.

Richard laughed.

Presently, the servants brought in the table and the food, and they sat down to eat. Roger and Anne sat side by side across the table from Maria and Richard. Anne fawned on Roger already, her eyes gluttonous on his face. Her brothers drank too much. The youngest slid quietly under the table during the game course, while the other two argued with anybody who would speak to them. The Duke cursed them, and one fell silent and the other cursed back, until the Duke threw a cup of wine in his face. Anne leaned forward to scold her brother silent. Maria, mixing water with her wine, watched it all, entertained. Roger's right hand and Anne's left were hidden under the table. She knew they touched each other.

"Henry," one brother said. "We should settle this issue of our cousin Theobald."

"It's all the same to me," Richard said. "You can hang him, or you can cut his head off."

"Sir, you'd have my sister marry in mourning," the brother said. He was striving to make his voice pleasant.

"They'd better marry soon, or I'll want blood sign before I pay a Morgengab."

Anne had heard him. Her cheeks went white, and her hand appeared above the level of the table. Her brother stood.

"Sir—"

A servant brought in another array of dishes. Richard leaned out to see. "Maria, you can start eating, they've brought in the blancmange."

The brother put his fists on the table. "Pay heed to me, you fatherless renegade."

Robert, on Maria's right, started up out of his place. She held him down. Richard leaned forward. His eyes glinted. He said, "Pigs have fathers, and dogs have faith. I don't pay heed to either of them."

The brother stood up. "That, sir, I take for an insult!"

"Why, puss, how did you think I meant it? What were you—born in a manger? Great Muhammed's horse, the whole family has its head up its backside. It must be the Lombard blood. Even your father knew when I was insulting him."

"Richard," Maria said. The Duke was smiling down at his plate. Several of the servants were listening, amused.

"My lord," the brother said. "I don't have to listen to that."

Richard was reaching for the bread, his eyes elsewhere. Across the table from Maria, Roger was smiling wide. He spoke softly to Anne, who turned to look up at him, still frowning. Roger flirted her back to good humor. The brother did not speak again. Maria turned to her husband.

"How did you catch Theobald?"

The Duke snorted. He put his elbows on the table while he chewed his meat. Roger said, "Maria, you and Theobald were fair matched, that time in Birnia." Anne's eyes never left his face.

Richard said, "We cut him off from Occel. You know how he is, he surrendered when he saw we outnumbered him." To the Duke, he said, "Kill him now. He'll start to make bargains, and Theobald can deal his way out of anything."

"Or perhaps your wife will help him escape," the Duke said.

Silence fell. Robert said, alone, "What?"

Richard thrust his plate away from him. "Bunny," he said, "stop your mouth."

"Richard," Maria said.

The Duke got to his feet. Everyone was watching him, still as the furniture.

"I don't like being called Bunny," the Duke said, "and you are in my city, in my castle, and sometimes, damn it, you talk too much."

Robert whispered, "What is this all about?"

"Sssh," Maria said.

Richard sat back. "You're probably right," he said, mild as milk.

Maria let her breath out. Under the other side of the table, she marked, Roger took Anne again by the hand. The Duke sat down in his chair beside Richard. The servers brought them the fish course. The young man's eyes were downcast.

"Maria," Roger called. "I'll be your champion, if Richard won't defend you."

Maria threw a piece of bread at him. "I am my own champion. As my lord Henry knows well."

The young man looked over at Richard. "I will hang Theobald on Sunday," he said in a low voice.

Richard struck him on the arm. "I'll keep watch on Maria in the meanwhile. Roger, when do you want to get married?"

They talked about that. Maria glanced behind Richard's back at the young Duke. He was watching her, unsmiling. She looked away.

XXXVII

THE MARKET PLACE OF AGATO, OPPOSITE THE CATHEDRAL, WAS clamorous with people. In the midst of the square stood the high scaffold where Theobald was to be hanged. Maria rode back to the shade of the cathedral wall. Roger was beside her. In spite of the wind she was sweating and the baby kicked her painfully every few moments. The crowd banged around her mare, their curious eyes on her. People stood in a solid pack on the porch and steps of the cathedral. A cutpurse ran through them so fast she could only sit and watch him go with a dozen purses in his bag.

Surrounded by Saracens, Richard plowed across the mob toward her. The boys of the city screamed and darted around him, and the big white dragon banner floated over his head. The townspeople crossed themselves as they passed. A few angry voices called, "Jerusalem, Jerusalem."

Maria wiped her face on her sleeve. Richard pulled up beside her. "You shouldn't have come. God's death, you're as red as an apple. A pregnant woman at a hanging."

She grunted at him; her heart hurt. The Duke appeared on the far side of the square. The people gave up one huge cry and rushed toward him. He called to his knights and they closed around him, sealing him off even from these people who loved him. Maria wished she had a cup of water. A drop of sweat trickled down her back.

It would be strange to see Theobald die today. For half her life he had been their enemy. Because of him, she had killed Walter Bris, and Robert had helped kill Haimo. She fell to thinking of Ceci. Her grief for her daughter had been bitter as aloes once. Now it was blunted and worn away, almost sweet. She was another person, now, from the girl who had watched Ceci die. Not as good a person, probably. She remembered fighting with Richard over the chapel. Like Theobald, she had never dared match him force against force. Now Theobald was coming through the crowd, his hands tied behind his back, to be hanged. She lifted her head, brought out of her memory.

Theobald came up to the front of the scaffold and mounted the steps. His face was ghastly white. His eyes like a vulture's were ringed in black. He walked short-strided, as if his feet were broken.

"Was he tortured?" she said to Richard.

"He wasn't my prisoner."

Maria bit her lip. There was no reason to torture him, a man without secrets to tell. The hangman brought the rope up to the scaffold. Theobald stood holding his head back, his fine clothes ripped to rags, his body crooked with pain. Something was whistling in the air, shrilling closer, shrieking in the air, and she screamed.

Her mare reared. Robert cried out. Richard fell off his horse. Maria swung herself awkwardly down from her plunging mare.

"Richard—"

He was conscious. He groaned and tried to sit up. The arrow had taken him through the forearm and into the right hip. She put her hands on his shoulders and pushed him flat again.

The Saracens had closed around them, stirrup to stirrup, walling them in with their bodies. She heard people screaming, and war cries, and the racket of fighting in the square. Robert dropped down beside her.

"We have to get him out of here," Robert said.

"Can you cut this arrow? Richard, for Jesus' sake, lie still."

Robert stooped, drawing his dagger. The mob screeched beyond the Saracens' white backs. Maria crept around so that Richard slumped against her. "Ismael," she said. "What is happening?"

"Many blood," Ismael said. "All Christian men. Roger kills, kills."

Robert straightened. He held two feet of bloody arrow in his hand. Richard was trying to sit up again. She put her arms around him.

"I can ride."

"No." Maria raised her voice. "Ismael, help me."

Ismael spoke in Saracen, and two brothers dismounted and helped Robert lift Richard in a chair of their arms. He groaned, and his eyes closed. His body sagged in their grip. Carefully they raised him up onto Robert's horse, and with his son behind him supporting him they rode in a flock of swirling robes to their tower.

RICHARD DID NOT wake up again. He lay on the bed in the top room of the tower, a bloody sheet across him. The Majlas tabib bandaged the wounds in his forearm and his hip with herbs. A steady stream of the Brotherhoood came

393

in and out the door. Maria drew back into the corner. Their urgent voices, saying nothing she understood, stabbed her with fear. The baby weighed her down. The close, hot stench of the room turned her stomach queasy. She put her hands to her face.

Robert came in, with Roger just behind him. The Saracens drew back, and the tabib spoke rapidly to Robert, his hands and nods indicating Richard. Another Saracen held up the long notched arrowhead. Roger, listening, shook his head once, and Maria's breath stopped in her throat.

He saw her; he strode around the bed to her. "Maria. Come out of there. Come sit down."

"What are they saying?" He had come between her and the bed, and she moved so that she could keep her eyes on Richard. "Is he dying?"

Roger lowered his voice. "The arrow was tainted. They are doing all they can. They are masters of leechcraft, these people. Come down to the hall."

Maria raised her eyes to his face. "Roger," she said, "What must I do?"

"There's nothing you can do, Maria. Except pray. There's nothing anybody can do." He looked over his shoulder. "Robert, bring me a cup of wine."

The tabib came up beside her and pushed a cup into her hand. His round face was framed in kinky graying whiskers. He gave her a cheerful smile and with gestures told her to drink. Robert stood beside her. She sipped the head-spinning potion in the cup.

"Take her away," Roger murmured.

Maria turned to him again. "Roger."

"Go on, Maria. There's nothing you can do."

She let her son maneuver her out of the room to the stair landing. The updraft of air from the stairs cooled her face and throat. Her head felt enormous and light as a dandelion from the Saracen drink.

"Robert." Her hand closed on his sleeve, holding him in front of her on the stairs. "What are they saying? Is he going to die?"

One step below her, her son turned toward her again. "They say—if he lives the night—" Like a child he held out his hands to her, and she put her arms around him.

"Robert," she said. "Wait here a moment." She went back into the room. The stink of blood and unguents loosened her knees. Sinking down beside the clothes chest, she felt along the wooden bottom. The tabib was talking in a high voice to the other Saracens. Roger, staring out the window, had not marked her coming in. She found the six-inch brass key and went out again to Robert.

"Come along," she said. "Where is Ismael?"

They went down the stairs to the hall. Beside the hearth, Ponce Rachet stood in a pack of men, their voices pitched in mutters. The women of her household were ranged around the room. When Maria came in, they rushed toward her, and she sent them off.

"Robert," she said. "Find Ismael." She went across the room to Ponce Rachet, who faced her, taking off his hat.

'He is still alive." She rubbed her eyes, wondering how much to tell him. His plain, seamed face softened. He dismissed the other men with a word. Maria said, low, "The arrow was poisoned. I am afraid—I am so frightened—"

Ponce's hand steadied her arm. She met his eyes. She said, "Swear to me you will support my son, if Richard dies."

"I will," he said. "There are many who will not, you know—the boy's very young, and there's Roger."

Maria gulped for air. Her head was foggy from the Saracen drink. Her hands were stained with blood. She said, "I will put the Saracens to guarding the tower. Someone might sneak in and try to . . . finish it."

Ponce nodded. "What do you wish of me?"

Robert and Ismael burst into the room. They strode over to her. She caught her son's arm. "Robert, you must go back to Mana'a."

"Mama!"

Ponce Rachet pursed his lips. Maria held out the key. "Take this. it's the key to the treasurehouse. The charters are all in the big chest under our bed, it isn't locked. Watch Rahman. Say nothing to anyone but Stephen."

"Mama, I'm staying here."

"No,'" Ponce said. "Your mother's right. If he dies, you have to be in Mana'a. Go on."

Robert stood a moment, poised, his eyes shifting from one to the other. Maria faced Ismael. She said, "No one gets into this tower without my word. No one."

Ismael saluted her with his hand and rushed off. Robert followed him. She looked at Ponce again. Her mind plodded stupidly. She put her hands to her face.

"What happened?" she said. "Who shot him?"

Ponce cleared his throat. "Theobald's friends. Trying to rescue him. William in Birnia should know of this."

"Tomorrow," she said heavily. She lowered her hands. "When we know more. What about Welf? In the Black Tower. Richard mistrusts him."

Ponce hooked his thumbs in his belt. "They are just cross-grained. Welf's sound."

"Then he should know, too. I—"

His hand on her arm stopped her. They turned around. Roger was coming in the door. She nodded to Ponce, and he left. Roger came up to her.

"Rest a little, Maria. You'll hurt your baby."

"Did you kill Theobald?"

"With my own hand. I'm going back to my fortress. I'll leave one of my men here, in case anything should happen.'" He kissed her cheek and went away. Maria climbed on up to the room full of Saracens and blood and the smell of herbs. She felt weak and unready against an enormous threat. Sitting in a corner, she gathered her strength, her eyes on the bloody man in the bed.

THE ASSASSINS had attacked the Duke also. Poisoned arrows had killed his horse and two men nearby him. A torch in one hand and a sword in the other, he rode from house to house, seizing Theobald's whilom friends. From the window, Maria saw these men led in chains across the bridge. The sun lowered at the end of the deserted street. Not a lamp burned in the whole of the city. No one moved. In the darkness the river droned over its mossy bed. A dog barked insistently in the distance.

At midnight the Duke rode up to the tower. The Saracens, surrounding it, held him until Ismael came, and Ismael, who liked him, brought him up to the candlelight

396

room where Richard lay. The tabib was asleep in a chair in one corner. Maria had just finished cleaning up the room for the third time.

"I have them all," the Duke said. "If he dies, you may name their death."

Maria's lips moved. She did not have enough breath to speak. Heavily she sat down beside the bed. The Duke came over to her. Ismael took a candle and went around to the far side of the bed.

"How did Anne and her brothers fare?" Maria asked.

"Philip's dead." The Duke's face worked. "Richard was right. We waited too long to finish Theobald. It was my fault—"

Maria turned away from him. "You talk like a fool." She kept still, hoarding her strength. The Duke sat down on the floor beside her. In the darkness beyond the bed, Ismael's face, painted in candlelight, looked old as the tabib's.

No one said anything. Louise brought them a tray of food. She did not eat. A candle went out. Ismael sat on the foot of the bed, his fingers knotted together.

Maria walked up and down around the room. She felt anchored by the baby that kicked and turned below her heart, holding fast in her gross mountainous flesh. The heat of the night soaked her with sweat. The young Duke dozed, his head cushioned on his arms. The tabib woke. He lit more candles, felt of Richard's face and arms and chest, and covered him up again snugly. Ismael spoke to him, but the tabib pushed him off. Above the crescent of gray whiskers the man's face was meaninglessly cheerful. He went down the stairs. Ismael sat down beside the bed and put his headcloth over his face.

The night dragged along. Maria got fresh candles and as the old ones guttered in their holders replaced them. The tabib came back, a cup in either hand, made her sit, and poured the contents of one cup down her throat. The potion turned her sleepy, but she held herself awake, afraid of sleep. The tabib left and did not return.

She crawled into the bed beside Richard and laid her head down. On his back, his face turned away from her into the darkness, he seemed already lapped in death. She thought of the three men she had hanged. She knew she had no right to beg for Richard's life. She picked up his hand and held it, too tired even to cry.

Sleep took her. She dreamed that she and Richard walked through a city of burning rubble, beneath a sky foul with smoke. All around her, in the ruins, babies screamed, but when she bent to pick them up, they died in her arms. "Don't," he said. "Don't. You can do nothing." The arch of the Emir's Gate appeared before them, and she realized that the blasted city was Mana'a.

Clammy with sweat, she woke up and lay still, clinging to his hand. The room was gloomy with dawn light. Beside her, Richard whispered her name.

She pushed herself up on one elbow. He was facing her, she saw the glitter of his eyes. His voice was feeble even in a whisper.

"Maria. I'm thirsty."

ROGER MET HER at the door into the hall. Beyond him, Anne and her brothers waited before the hearth. Roger said, "Sister, you look like a walking ghost. Are you sure we need talk of this now?"

"God's blood," she said. "I will go mad if I don't do something."

She went past him into the middle of the room. For the early summer, the day was dank, and the candles were all lit. Anne's pleasant brother came toward her, his hands out. She was mildly relieved to know he was not Philip. He took one of her hands in his.

"Lady," he said, "we are a fellowship of mourning."

"After his words to us, I would not be here otherwise," the other brother said, and Anne caught his arm to quiet him.

Roger came toward them from the door. "When he comes to Hellgate, Richard will have a few choice words for the Devil." He stopped beside Maria. Low-voiced, he said, "Is he any better? Is he awake?"

"He is the same," she said.

"Everyone else who took an arrow has died," the unpleasant brother said.

398

Maria turned toward him. "My lord, I have never harmed you, please don't torment me."

Anne came up to her. Her mouth was framed in deep lines. "This is his humor, when he grieves. Come with me into the sunlight. Let us leave the men to their deliberations."

Maria said, "I had in mind to listen to them. Roger—"

Roger pulled a chair up to the hearth. "Stay, both of you." He called to a page to bring the other chairs. "Anne, come sit with me."

Maria sank down on a little wooden stool. Richard had wakened only enough to drink. He was too weak to lift his head up. She had no idea what he wanted in the marriage contract. She had never heard of a written marriage contract before. They sat down around her. The young Duke came in, his face fretted, and they began to talk.

The brothers wanted to settle certain rights of the dead man on their sister for a dowry. While they went over the lands and the services, Anne left, obviously embarrassed at the dickering. The Duke sat with his elbows on his knees, picking his teeth. They came to the homage that Roger should swear him, and he agreed with a nod of his head.

Maria made them add the phrase *Saving his duty to the lord of Marna*, which the brothers accepted in a bad grace. She was not minded to give up on it and finally they let it in.

They convinced her that the brothers were hot to get Anne and Roger married, and she paid more heed to them. They argued over the Morgengab with Roger like people in a market place. But even here, they were slowly surrendering. Obviously they thought Anne would be marrying someone more than the lord of Iste.

Roger was looking at Maria. She raised her eyes to him, and he said, "What do you think of that? Is that fair?"

She had not heard his offer, but by the looks on the brothers' faces, they were consenting to it. She laid her hands in her lap. "How can she have a Morgengab? She is a widow, not a maiden. How often can you eat a piece of cake?"

The unpleasant brother was surprised into laughter. The pleasant brother leaned earnestly toward her. "Here we are accustomed to some Morgengab with every marriage."

Maria glanced at Roger. The young Duke was smiling, his eyes pinned on the floor. She said, "My Morgengab was a baby. You can give her that."

Roger said sharply, "Richard himself mentioned the Morgengab."

"Richard," she said, "may not live to pay it."

Already the two brothers were agreeing to leave out the Morgengab—Anne, it turned out, had holdings of her own, in the duchy. Maria sat back. She thought of the man in the bed above them. Her eyes burned. She felt sodden with fatigue. A page came over to take her cup and fill it again.

Anne and her brothers left, and the Duke immediately afterward. Maria took him down to the door to say goodbye to him. Ismael was sitting on the threshold, and she sent him off to bring the Duke's horse.

The young man stood beside her in the tiny airless room at the foot of the stairs. She tugged on his rumpled coat to straighten it.

"Thank you," she said. "For staying last night."

Taking her by the wrists he held her away from him. He stammered something and went out the door so fast he nearly knocked a Saracen sentry off his feet. Maria watched him from the doorway. She had thought he liked her better now. It rubbed her that she could not touch him.

Clouds lowered the sky. A thin patter of rain traveled across the courtyard. She went up the stairs again. Every few steps she paused to rest. Roger was waiting on the landing outside the hall. Before she could speak, he gripped her by the elbow.

"I did not like that insult you dealt me, Maria. You slighted me in front of them."

Maria gaped at him. Her throat filled painfully tight. Before she could reply, he pushed her on up the stairs. "Go on. I want to see my brother."

He did not wait for her. While she was still dragging herself from step to step, he went in the door to the bedchamber. What he had said burned in her mind. He had never spoken harshly to her before. She followed him into the room.

Richard lay asleep, his face once more toward the wall. Roger went up beside the bed. The tabib stood on the far side of it. They spoke in Saracen.

"You said he was the same." Roger wheeled toward her. "He seems worse, to me—" He drew her toward the doorway. "Has he wakened?"

"Once." She put her hand on his arm. "Roger," she said, suddenly almost in tears, "I did not mean to insult you."

"Oh, Maria." He held her hard against him, his arm around her neck. "Don't harken to me, we are all raw. But you shouldn't be jealous of Anne." He squeezed her again, her enormous body in their way. "You know I will always love you best. Tell me if anything happens. I want to know the moment anything happens." He went down the stairs again.

Maria went back to the bedside. Richard slept deeply, his breathing even. His skin was harsh with fever. She touched him, and he turned his head and opened his eyes.

"Maria." Before she could answer, his eyes closed and he slept again.

The tabib came up to her. His eyes were hooded like a hawk's. His smile was cherubic. He patted her arm, laid his folded hands against his cheek, and shut his eyes. She crept into the bed next to Richard and fell instantly asleep.

XXXVIII

IN VELVET, IN SATIN, FLECKED WITH JEWELS, THEY STOOD in Agato's cathedral and heard the new Archbishop turn Roger d'Alene into a married man. Maria, nine months with child, was cooking inside her heavy clothes. She leaned once on Robert, and the boy glanced at her and took her arm.

A choir of children sang marriage hymns in the background. Candles marched up and down the high altar, shining on the vessels of gold, the gold paint on the statues, the triptych, the crufifix, the six-foot Paschal candlestick opposite the pulpit blazing with light. Richard stood behind Roger at the altar. Anne's brothers were still sulk-faced from seeing him well, which delighted Maria.

They knelt to pray in a single thunderous voice. She thought of her wedding in the village church at Castlemaria. Whatever Roger believed, she was not jealous of Anne. She put her hand on Robert's shoulder, and he helped her rise. Up by the altar, Richard got stiffly to his feet. The sleeve of his black and gold coat was slit to the elbow to accommodate the bandages on his forearm.

The cathedral bells tolled. Anne and Roger came down the aisle, their attendants like a host behind them. When they passed Maria, she felt guilty at her thoughts: Anne beamed, leaning like a child on her new husband. Maria followed them out of the church.

On the porch, Robert next to her, she paused in the central archway to get her eyes used to the bright sunlight. A flock of beggars lurked in the shadows. Probably there would be sweets and money thrown to them, later.

Richard came up to her elbow. Their Saracens waited in the alley beside the cathedral, discreetly out of sight.

Grooms led up two horses harnessed in red and white leather. Roger helped Anne to mount. Maria pulled away from Richard and crossed the porch to the steps.

"Lady," she said, "God's grace to you on your wedding day." She stood by Anne's stirrup, smiling up at her.

"Thank you. Thank you, good sister." Anne leaned from her saddle to take Maria's hand, and Maria kissed her fingers.

The couple rode off. A dozen children in elaborate costumes raced after them to throw flowers and distribute cakes. Her brothers brought their horses along in their train. The crowd followed them out of the square, and the Saracens rode up in a rank across the front of the cathedral.

"You're so forgiving. Why did you kiss her, when she's spat on us?"

"She'll like us better, now that she is Roger's wife."

A groom was leading up their horses. Richard shifted his weight, resting his bad hip. Maria went up one step beside him, into the shade.

"Do you remember when we married?" he said suddenly.

"Yes," she said. She smiled at him.

"You're sentimental as a Jew." He went down the steps toward their horses. Maria followed him. He lifted her up into the saddle. The effort drained him and he nearly dropped her.

"Don't fall off."

Maria gathered her reins and spun the mare in a circle on her hocks. When he had mounted, the Saracens surrounded them, and they rode toward the Duke's castle, across the bridge garlanded with flowers, over the brown, slow-moving summery river.

MARIA SAT UP in bed. It was still early in the afternoon. Save for her, the room was empty. She swung her legs over the edge of the mattress and slid down to the floor. A wooden cup stood on the bench beside the bed, half full of the tabib's infusion. They had kept her in bed for three days with such drinks. In her nightgown, barefoot, she crossed the room to the new baby's cradle.

"Holy Mary."

The cradle was empty. Maria gave it an angry swing and went over to the cupboard for some clothes. Footsteps pounded on the stairs. The door burst open.

"Maria! Wake up!"

Drunk as an alewife, Richard lurched across the threshold. The new baby was tucked in the crook of his arm. Maria caught him by the sleeve and took the baby, unmindful of the young Duke wobbling along behind him. Richard hooked his arm around her neck. His breath stank of wine.

"Marita. My catkin. Give me a kiss." He pressed a loud kiss to the side of her face. Suddenly he swung her up off her feet, the baby against her breast, and spun her in a circle.

"Richard—"

"What's wrong?" He whirled her and the baby around again. Her head swam for a dizzy instant after he stopped. "Have I ever dropped you?"

"Put me down, or I'll vomit all over you."

He dropped her feet first to the floor and walked away. "My wife has a keen sense of weapons."

Maria climbed up to sit on the bed, her legs under her. The baby was asleep. She laid him carefully down on the covers beside her. "Where did you take him? Why are you so drunk in the middle of the day? Bring me something to put on—that robe, in the cupboard.'"

The young Duke was leaning unsteadily on the wall, his face set in a drunken frown. Richard sat down in the chair beside him. "Get it yourself. My leg hurts."

The young man pushed himself upright and sauntered across to the cupboard. Taking the robe from the hook, he flung it across the foot of the bed. He tilted himself up against the wall again at Richard's side.

"Bunny, don't do that," Richard said. "You will ruin my discipline."

"Don't call me Bunny."

Maria pulled the robe on over her nightgown. Picking up the girdle she knotted it around her waist and hitched the sleeves up above her elbows. "I'll call the baby Bunny, if you name him Henry."

The Duke began to speak. Richard slammed his elbow back into the young man's side. "What do you want to name him?"

"I told you," she said. She got clean napkins and changed the baby and swaddled him. "I want to call him Richard."

"Why?"

"I don't know why. But I do." They had gone all through this before.

"That's no reason. Besides, you named the others, but for Stephen."

Maria put the baby in the cradle and rocked it a few strokes. The young Duke refused to meet her eyes. He sank down unsteadily on his heels, his back to the wall. Suspicious, she said, "Richard, what have you done?"

"Bring me some wine. Cross of Christ, Maria, you are lazy—sleeping all day—"

Maria bent over the baby in the cradle. Now on his forehead she saw the faint gleam of christening oil. She put her fingertips against the baby's face. She did not want to call him Bunny.

"Richard, you are low."

"It was my idea," the Duke said.

Maria went past them across the room. "I don't believe you." When she opened the door, the page stationed out on the landing sprang to his feet, and she sent him for the wine. She slammed the door and turned back toward Richard.

"You had him christened behind my back."

"You needed your rest." He smiled at her. Reaching out, he caught hold of her wrist and pulled her over beside him. "The Brotherhood has given you a new name."

"Oh," she said. "What?"

He said a long Saracen word. "It means—*Mother of Many Sons.*"

"Tell them I reject it."

She sat down on the floor beside his chair. She rubbed her head against his arm, and he straightened and using both hands uncoiled and unbraided her hair. The page returned, lugging a ewer of wine, cups clustered under one arm. Richard combed her hair out through his fingers. Maria shut her eyes. She enjoyed his touch. She laid her head down on his thigh.

"I forgive you," she said.

"There, Bunny," Richard said softly. "I told you she was no shrew."

The Duke laughed. "You didn't see her cheat your brother out of Anne's Morgengab."

The baby let out a short, fierce wail. Maria crossed the room to the cradle. She lifted the baby in her arms. "Henry," she murmured, trying to like the name. Louise and Catherine whisked in the door. "Catherine, bring up the musicians, will you?" Opening her clothes, she sat on the bed and thumped her nipple erect. The Duke turned his eyes away. The two men got to talking. Maria looked down at the baby sucking on her breast. At least now he was a Christian. Louise went around the room picking up after Richard.

"Are you going to Occel?" the young Duke said.

Maria lifted her head. The three musicians filed in the door, carrrying their lutes and horns. Louise arranged them in one corner, near the window.

"I don't know," Richard said. "My brother there has a better way with those people than I do—my brother William."

The musicians, their heads bowed together, tuned their instruments to the leader's pipe. Maria laid the baby on her knees and shrugged back into her clothes. Fat as a slug, the baby emitted a faint hicket. Maria kissed him, laughing.

"The christening failed. We shall have to do it again."

She carried the baby over to Richard. The door opened, and Robert came in, Ponce Rachet just behind him. Richard cradled the baby along his forearms. It hicketed solemnly into his face.

"It must be a Christian demon." He stuck his thumb in the wine and rubbed a cross on the baby's forehead. "In nomine patris—"

Maria snatched the baby away from him. "Don't blaspheme over my son." She held out the baby to Louise, who took him off to change him. Robert came up beside Maria and put his arm around her waist.

"Mama, you're still fat."

Maria hugged him. Richard tilted his chair back on its hindlegs. "Fat. Is she ever thin? I run her halfway down again, and she's off swelling with another one of you."

Ponce laughed. Maria stooped to get Richard's empty cup. He and Ponce talked. Robert said, in horror, "Mama, he is drunk."

She thrust the cup into his hand. Her legs were already tiring. She sat down on the warm brick hearth just behind Richard.

"Go get him more, then, before he gets a headache."

Ponce Rachet hooked his thumbs in his belt. "I have some cases for you to try, at the East Tower. Nothing that can't wait, if you must go down to Occel."

In the sunlit corner, the musicians burst into a song for dancing. Richard turned his head toward Maria. "What do you want to do?"

"I don't want to go to Occel. It's too dangerous. Theobald's cursed us."

Robert brought Richard a cup of wine. "Papa, let me go. I can do it. Stay here until you are strong again. My lord Henry—"

Richard knocked him off his feet. Maria straightened up. She put one hand on Richard's shoulder as he sat before her in the chair. Robert sprawled across the floor in a shining puddle of wine. The Duke's cup clattered into a corner. Louise screamed. The musicians played merrily on.

Ponce Rachet's long, homely face tightened toward a smile. "Gripe," he said. "Give me an order."

Richard heaved himself upright in his chair. He twitched Maria's hand off his shoulder. Robert got to his feet.

"I'll go to Occel," Richard said. "Get ready to leave."

Ponce made a salute to him and went out the door. Robert stood still, his teeth clenched, his hands clasped behind his back. His fancy blue coat was stained with wine. He and Richard stared at each other. At last Richard said, "Get out."

Robert met Maria's eyes and left the room. The Duke stood up. "I wish you had been my father," he said to Richard, "but I'm glad you're not. I'm leaving. My own levies are joining me, so I will need your help only three or four days more."

"My lord," Maria said. "Come back and sup with us."

"I will." His black eyes stabbed toward Richard. "Look after my godson. Don't take him to Occel." He tramped away, shouldering a path through the men waiting in the doorway. "Robert?" he shouted, on the landing. "Wait for me!"

Richard reached for the cup on the floor beside him and knocked it over. He let out a burst of incoherent obscenity. Maria took the cup across the room. Two knights came toward him from the doorway.

"My lord Welf Blackjacket sent—"

"Go back there and wait."

The knights withdrew from the room. Through the open door she could see the many people crowded onto the landing, waiting to talk to him. The musicians were reaching the end of their song. She wondered if they had heard anything else through it all. Richard leaned on the arm of his chair, terrifically drunk.

"How soon can you travel?" he said.

"Whenever you decide.'" She gave him the wine. "The baby won't care.'"

"I thought you didn't want to go to Occel."

"I didn't want my baby named Henry, either.'"

"I have to go," he said. "They are all watching me now. You must see it's a test."

"Yes,'" she said. "Like having sons, and bearing wounds. But it is another kind of test for me."

He stared at her a moment. Lifting the cup he took a long sip of the wine. "Where would you rather go?"

"To Castelmaria," she said. "Jilly is there. And Stephen could meet us there."

"Then we will go to Castelmaria."

XXXIX

❧

FIRST THEY WENT TO THE EAST TOWER, WHERE AFTER the arrogance of Agato, Ponce Rachet and his wife were easy as old clothes. Richard summoned his court and heard pleas from all over the area. Like an oven, the summer heat closed down on them. Maria sat in the shade of a briar hedge and nursed her baby, while Ponce Rachet's wife talked of children and colic, and how her younger child sneezed whenever he had to do with dogs.

"He must be bewitched," Maria said. The boy tumbled in the grass of the meadow. He was robust for his age, fat as his mother. She tickled Henry's feet and the baby jerked his knees up to his chest. At the far end of the meadow, at the foot of the castle hill, a group of men stood beneath the big tree where Richard was trying his cases of law.

"I have taken him to the Shrine of Our Lady,'" Ponce Rachet's wife said. "Perhaps if I brought him to Marna, to the cathedral—are the relics there?"

"Yes, we have some relics,'" Maria said, "but what you must do is find a witch who can lift the enchantment. You need not come all the way over the mountains." She imagined the fat chatelaine, in her peaked white coif and wooden shoes, hunting through Mana'a for relics.

"God have mercy." Ponce Rachet's wife crossed herself. She bent toward the baby. "Lambkin. Little lambkin." Under her breath, as if the whole world listened, she murmured, "There is an old woman in the fen who is witchwise, they say. Naturally I stay away from such people." She crossed herself again. "They say she has philtres, and—"

"Love philtres," Maria said. She glanced again toward the tall green tree. "In the fen, you said?"

Ponce Rachet's wife blinked at her. "Yes, but— It's leagues from here. I have only heard—"

"Can we go there and back in a day? We'll take Ismael and some of the Brotherhood, they will be proof against witches." Maria lifted the baby up to her shoulder.

Ponce Rachet's wife's mouth opened like a flower. A sudden rush of color darkened her cheeks. "We must not tell the men," she said. She clapped her hands together. "We could go this very afternoon. But we cannot tell the men."

"We don't have to," Maria said. "Just let me think of something of Richard's I can take to her."

THE WOMAN in the fen was not old. She kept a cottage in a patch of trees on the high ground. Ponce Rachet's wife explained the enchantment on the child and let the woman look into the little boy's eyes and breathe once into his mouth. Maria held herself back, wary. Her hair had come down while they rode. She took off the linen coif and tied it around her waist.

The fenwoman's face was white as starch. She traced her beautiful oval eyes with black, so that her face had the arranged look of a picture.

"You must come back in the late summer," she told Ponce Rachet's wife. "I have not got the herbs now, they must be gathered under the Dog Star. He should have been to me when you first marked this, though, now you will have to be patient."

While she talked, Maria wandered along the little picket fence around the hut. The garden grew in a wild unordered profusion of rampion and fennel, blossoming vines, spears of onions and garlic, and patches of mint. A brown mastiff lay in the shade of the hut. When she touched the fence he growled, and she backed away.

From the top of the hill she could see across the broad fen all the way up to the road: leagues of featureless sunbrowned marsh grass. Her Saracens waited at the foot of the hill, with the baby. Ismael would come no nearer for fear of the Evil Eye. Ponce Rachet's wife was agreeing to give the fenwoman a white hen and a black cock, a feather-bed, and some silver money. The fenwomen lifted her eyes to Maria. "You are curious enough, my girl, what are you looking for?"

Maria dipped a little bow to her. "Lady, by your leave, I hoped you might make me a charm.'"

"A love charm.'" The fenwoman smiled. "For your husband or your lover?"

"My lover," Maria said.

The fenwoman stared her in the eyes, and Maria dropped her gaze. The woman laughed. "I will need something of his. Clothing, perhaps. Some of his hair."

Maria went down the hillside, through the close-growing fir trees. The Saracens were grouped in an uneasy knot, their headclothes drawn over their faces like women's veils. She groped in the basket on her saddle. The baby in his arms, Ismael rode over to her.

"Maria. No must she *see* us. No, no."

"Be quiet and stay here." She took the shirt from the basket. "What could she do to you?—She is a Christian witch." Henry was asleep. She tucked his large wrinkled feet under the blanket and ran up the hill.

The fenwoman had gone to the far side of her house. When Maria reached her again, she was in her garden picking herbs for Ponce Rachet's wife, who stood at the fence, saying, "And sometimes, around Lenten season, my husband is very hot of temper, days on end—"

The fenwoman gave her a handful of herbs. "Steep these in water, turn around three times, saying what I just told you, and drink it down. Do that three days at sunrise, but do not go to Mass between them. If you confess it to a priest the charm will fail." She came toward Maria and took the shirt. Before Maria could avoid her, the woman reached out with her scissors and snipped off a lock of Maria's long black hair.

"Wait." The hair and the shirt and the fenwoman vanished into her cottage.

Ponce Rachet's wife rolled the herbs carefully into her shawl. Her little boy threw rocks at the mastiff. Maria fingered the stumped tress of her hair. It frightened her to have some piece of her body in the hands of a woman like that. The door flew open, the fenwoman came out, carrying the shirt.

"Here. Burn this utterly, and keep the ash." She unfolded the shirt. Within it, tied with red thread, the long hank of hair was coiled into a lover's knot. "As long as you keep the ash you will hold his heart." From her apron she took a square leather packet. "Put a pinch of this in his drink, before you lie with him."

"Ah."

Maria put the packet into her sleeve. She tucked the folded shirt under her arm and reached into her wallet. The fenwoman shook her head. "No. I take nothing in barter for love charms." Her wide smile split her face, and her fine huge eyes tlited up at the corners. "So Dragon is your lover. Beware his wife, it was told to me that she is witchwise."

THEY RODE BACK across the fen toward the East Tower. Once they stopped in a meadow while Maria nursed the baby. Ponce Rachet's wife gathered an armful of larkspur and primrose. The Saracens let their pretty mares graze. At first the men roamed aimlessly, but one by one they sat down at the far end of the sweep of soft grass, all facing southeast, and Maria knew they prayed.

Ponce Rachet's wife was winding her flowers by their stems into garlands, one for her and one for Maria. She jiggled a flower in front of the baby's nose. He fixed his gaze on it. His arms and legs moved witlessly.

"Bunny," Maria said. She bent and nuzzled his face. "My bunny baby." When he smiled at her she had to laugh.

"I cannot say he favors either you or my lord."

"No. He looks like no one. He just looks like himself."

They went on along the road. The sun was setting, but the East Tower was visible before them, a square gray peak among the rounded summer-dry hilltops. Serf children herded cattle toward them, and the two women and the Saracens moved off into the ditch to let them pass.

Giggling, the children hid from the Saracens behind their cows.

Ismael cried, "Robert comes!" His horse catapulted forward down the road.

Maria lifted her head to see. Robert was galloping along down the road toward them. A thrill of panic ran down her spine. Something had happened. But when he drew rein before her, he was laughing.

"Mama! Papa has been looking all over for you. There is a messenger here from Rome."

"Rome!" Ponce Rachet's wife said.

Robert called to Ismael. His horse reared up, its hoofs almost over her head. Maria cried, "Wait—where are you going?"

"Papa has sent the Majlas back to the mountains. Don't worry—I'll meet you at Castelmaria." He waved and rode away. The Saracens galloped after him.

Maria jigged her mare on, cradling Henry in her arm. The little band of horsemen shrank away to a flutter of white robes under the trees. They broke the horizon and vanished into the darkening sky. Ponce Rachet's wife plucked at Maria's sleeve.

"A messenger from Rome—where will he sleep? I cannot take you out of the top room. I'll have to give him our bed."

"You can sleep with us." The love potion could wait until Castelmaria.

"No—no. We will sleep in the hall, with the servants. What am I going to have for the meat at tomorrow's dinner?—Thank God he did not come for dinner today!" Her eyes widened at the mere thought.

They cantered up the hill to the curtain wall and rode into the ward of the castle. The sun was setting. The servants were gathered at the door down into the kitchen, waiting to take the supper up the hall. Maria gave Henry to Ponce Rachet's wife. She jumped down from her saddle and turned to take him back.

Ponce strode up to them. "Where have you been?" He glowered at his wife.

She puffed up angrily. Maria said, "The fault was mine. If there is a fault. Where is Richard?"

"In the hall, girl."

413

His wife put out her arms. "You'd better give me that baby."

Maria went through the door into the stairwell. Her hair, full of wilting primroses, was hanging loose down her back, and her skirt was grass-stained. She would have to change her clothes before she met this messenger. She raced up the stairs. When she was halfway to the hall landing, the door opened and two pages led a strange man out onto the stair above her.

He was dressed so beautifully she needed a moment to realize he was a priest. She froze. Over the heads of the pages, he saw her, and he smiled.

"My lord," she said. Wreathed in dead wildflowers, a devilish potion in her sleeve, she went up the steps to him and knelt to kiss his ring.

He made the sign of the Cross over her. "God bless you, child." He lifted her up by the hand, like someone in a song. His fine-boned handsome face was as planned as the fenwoman's paint. "Were I her master, such a pretty lady would not wander alone after dark."

Richard had come into the doorway behind him. "Oh, she's very tidy tonight—sometimes she comes in looking as if she's been fighting with dogs." He took her by the arm. "Father Yvet, will you come down again to eat supper with us?"

"I will, my lord." The priest's eyes danced with good humor.

Richard pulled her toward the hall. Maria shook him off. "My lord, I must go upstairs and dress." She bolted up the stairs ahead of the monk.

None of her women was in her room. She splashed water on her face and put on a fresh gown, and she was sitting before the little corner hearth brushing her hair when the door opened and Richard came in.

"Where did you go? How do you talk Ismael into running off anywhere with you?" He sank down behind her stool and lifted her hair in his hands. "You looked like a hayfield tumble, and he loved it. I fear he is a worldly priest, Father Yvet, and I wish I knew why he is here."

"What does he say?"

He shook his head. "Nothing."

Maria twisted to look at him. "What do you say?"

414

"How can I talk to a priest? I know nothing of philosophy. I said we were leaving for Castelmaria—"

The door opened and Ponce Rachet's wife came in with the baby, crying at the screech. Maria got up to take him in her arms. She poked her little finger into his mouth, and he sucked hard, his eyes in a purposeful frown.

"My lord," Ponce Rachet's wife said, "I will not listen to any of this—we are not going to sleep here with you, we will sleep in the hall. That's what I told my man."

"Good," Richard said. "Tell him I agree with you."

"That's what I said to him." Ponce Rachet's wife left.

"I told her they could stay here," Maria said. The room was not large, but the wooden bed was certainly big enough for four people.

Richard walked across the room. A page came in with a ewer and filled the jug of wine she kept in the cupboard. She had put the love potion in her chest. Her imagination began to hurry through its possible effects.

"I told Father Yvet that he could come to Castelmaria with us," Richard said. He strolled up to the fire, his hands on his hips. Maria laid the baby down in the cradle.

"It must be about the Emperor," she said. "They have come to make us bow to him."

"No—why do you say that?"

"Isn't he from the Pope? And the Pope is the Emperor's man."

"Not this Pope." He came over toward her again. "Where did you go? Whom have you been betraying me with now? You looked like a May Day wench, your hair down like that."

"Father Yvet didn't mind." She put her hair up loosely on her head and dug into her sleeve for the combs and clips to keep it there.

He started away. "You've always been hot for churchmen. I'm hungry. Come down when you're ready."

"I'm ready." She raked the combs backwards into her hair and went after him down the stairs.

The evening meal was all laid out before the hearth, untouched, three courses already congealing on the table. The servants, who could not eat until Richard and Maria had done, grumbled loudly at either end of the hall. The pages served the wine. Richard pulled his chair back and sat down.

"You know I'll find out eventually where you went today," he said, when Maria had slid onto the bench at his left. "Why don't you just tell me?"

"We rode. We picked the flowers."

Father Yvet came in the door. She started to rise but Richard held her down. His servants brought the churchman ceremoniously up to his chair and seated him on Richard's right hand, facing the hearth. His spare, amused face gave her no sense of his age: she suspected he was no older than Richard, in spite of his smooth gray hair.

The priest rinsed his mouth with wine and ate a few bites. He would not let the servants give him more than a morsel or two from each dish, although Maria marked that he ate even of the spiced Saracen eggs that Ponce Rachet's cook was just learning to make well.

The churchman raised his head and smiled at her. "I have heard much spoken of the Shrine of Saint Mary. I understand it is a local place of pilgrimage."

Richard put his elbows on the table. "Yes. There's some old story of a miraculous well. Ask Maria, she goes there nearly every year."

"Yes." Father Yvet smiled at her, paternal. "You built the little church there. Tell me about your shrine, child."

"Oh," she said. "It's just a woman's place. A cave in the hillside. I've been told there is a hermit on the mountain, but no one has ever seen him." It embarrassed her to speak of it to so polished a man. "You must have made many pilgrimages, Father—to the great holy places."

"Yes—I am just now come from Ephesus, in fact, where Timothy was bishop." He spoke of Constantinople and Nicaea. Ponce Rachet came in and spoke, low-voiced, into Richard's ear. The churchman was describing a Byzantine court, and trying to hear both she caught neither.

Father Yvet was full of stories, and clearly he was in no hurry to get to the point of his visit. Maria leaned on the table to listen. Richard stroked his moustaches down with his thumb. Father Yvet mentioned Antioch and several other Bible places.

"Of course no pilgrimage really is worthy of the name,

416

not after one has made the pilgrimage to Jerusalem itself."

"You've gone to Jerusalem," Maria said. "But that is perilous, in these days, Father—you make too little of your courage."

"Lady." He bent his beaming smile on her. "Courage is the virtue of the Crusader, like your lord. The virtue of the pilgrim is humility."

"Perhaps." Maria folded her hands in front of her on the tabletop. "The knight at least can fight if he is attacked."

"Yes. But the pilgrim can run away."

Maria smiled, pleased with that. Suddenly she liked him, she felt a bond with him.

"No pilgrim can outrun a knight," Richard said. "The Christians of Jerusalem won't fare peacefully under this new Emir."

Father Yvet sat back to let a page serve him from a tray of cheeses. "We have exchanged messengers with the Sultan of Baghdad, to deal with that."

Richard said, "Which Baghdadi Sultan?"

Father Yvet's smile stuck forgotten on his face. "You are well informed."

"Not me. The Venetians. They put into my harbor in Mana'a. Excuse me." He pulled his chair around to talk again to Ponce Rachet. The churchman's lean face, no longer humorous, was aimed at him like an ax.

"Constantinople, Jerusalem, Ephesus, Antioch," Maria said. "Where else have you traveled, Father Yvet?"

He turned toward her, smiling again. "In truth God made me a wanderer in this world. I've been east as far as Mosul and west as far as Aachen."

"Aachen," Maria said. That was the Emperor's castle. She looked quickly at Richard. Ponce had gone away.

Richard put his hand on his beard. "Where is Mosul, Maria?"

She shrugged. It sounded like a Saracen name. "Africa?"

Now the two men were laughing at her. She stood up. "I would stay to entertain you more, since I do it so well, but you must have your own high-minded man's talk."

"No," Father Yvet said. "Stay, child. I did not wish to drive you away."

"You did not, my lord." She went out the door.

When her women had helped her take off her clothes and put on a nightgown, she dismissed them for the night. From her chest she got the little packet of the love potion. The women had banked the fire and lit most of the lamps. The room smelled of the fragrant burning oils. She went to the cupboard, between the bed and the wall, and poured out a cup of the wine.

She shook a little of the scaly brown powder from the leather packet into her palm. Probably it would not work until she burned the shirt and the hair. She sprinkled a pinch of the dust onto the surface of the wine. It did not look like very much and she put in another pinch.

"What are you doing?" Richard said, behind her.

She jumped straight in the air. Whirling to face him, she hid both hands behind her back. He reached around her, and she slid away along the wall, toward the cupboard.

"What are you doing? You are poisoning me." He grabbed her around the waist and snatched for the wine cup.

Maria held the cup away from him at arm's length. She tried to twist out of his grip, but he pinned her against the wall, leaning on her, and stretched his hand toward the cup. His fingertips brushed the chased surface. Behind his back, she flipped the leather packet onto the floor under the bed. Richard's full weight pressed on her, hard, and she let him have the cup.

"What is this?" He stood back a step, still holding her around the waist. Suspiciously he sniffed the wine.

"It isn't poison." To prove it, she drew the cup and his hand down, her fingers over his, and sipped the wine. "It's philtre." The wine tasted sweet of herbs.

"What?" He pried her hand away and when she reached for the cup again held it up beyond her grasp. "A love potion. To keep me faithful or to make me strong? Neither one's a compliment."

"A woman in the fen devised it." She leaned against him. "Drink it—what harm can it do?"

He lowered the cup and drank. Maria waited, keen with interest. He set the cup to her lips, and she drank three swallows. He finished the rest. They stared at each other. She searched his face.

"Do you feel anything happening?" he asked.

"No." Whole wine always made her head whirl. "Do you?"

"Well, not real—Yeeeow!" He sprang at her.

Maria shrieked. She dodged around the foot of the bed. Richard began to laugh. He sat down on the bed, his shoulders shaking, and laughed until tears ran down his cheeks into his beard.

The baby cried, and Maria went to quiet him. "I don't think that was funny."

Richard's laughter chuckled off. He wiped his face on his sleeve. Maria rocked the baby to sleep. Every few moments Richard laughed again. He lay down on his back across the bed. She sat beside him.

"Now the fenwoman knows my wife feeds me potions."

Maria shook her head. "I told her you are my lover."

"Sweet Baby Jesus."

He touched her. She lay down next to him, facing him. He propped his head up on his crooked arm. "What did you give her of mine?"

She cupped her palm over the crown of his head and brought his face down to be kissed. "Haven't you noticed something missing?"

The drink had warmed her and made her sleepy. She touched her bare foot to his. Their legs entwined. "Did you send the messenger to Mana'a?"

"Yes, I've told you twice, God's death, you are a nag. They will all be at Castelmaria, Stephen and Jilly and Robert." He drew her down against his chest. She felt warm and drowsy, as if nothing could ever possibly go wrong. Softly she moved her hands under his clothes to his body.

XL

❧

"MARIA?" PONCE RACHET'S WIFE CALLED, FROM THE foot of the stairs.

"I am here."

On her hands and knees, she poked her head under the bed. Rushes two fingers deep covered the floor, spotted with mousedung. On the far side of the room, Ponce Rachet's wife's wooden shoes and heavy brown hose walked into the doorway. Maria straightened up and got to her feet.

"Oh, that Father Yvet is such a charming man," the chatelaine said. "How sad I am that he must leave so quickly." She helped Maria pull back the bedcovers to air. Together they put the room in order, and Maria went down to her other chores.

In the afternoon, she burned the shirt and the lock of her hair in an iron pot, collected the ash, and sewed it into a piece of silk. Once again she hunted for the rest of the philtre, but it was gone. A dog had probably taken it. She put the silk into the bottom of her chest.

They left the next day for Castelmaria, riding over the hills and the high meadows where the shepherds grazed their flocks. In the afternoon, Richard went off hawking. Father Yvet rode with Maria in the column before the wagons. She had not seen Stephen or Jilly in almost a year, and she packed his ears with stories of her children. The churchman was gallant enough to pretend interest, but she marked how his gaze drifted away to the barren hillsides, flecked with rocks and an occasional spotted goat, and she fell silent.

"Your father was master of this region, wasn't he?" Father Yvet said, at last.

Maria glanced sharply at him. "My father was a robber."

"A robber!" Startled into laughter, he turned his handsome head toward her. "What do you mean?"

She lifted one shoulder. "He robbed the shepherds and the pilgrims and the Saracens. That's what Richard meant, last night, that knights could outrun pilgrims. This was all wood, here, and wasteland. There was no other way to live." It occurred to her that Richard might not want her to tell him that. "But we are honest folks now."

He said, "My child, you could not be otherwise."

Maria laughed. "You are very kind. After these mighty people you have met, we must seem very plain. I hope you will come to Mana'a."

"Perhaps I may." His face quickened with interest. "A robber. Of what race?"

"We are all Normans. Are you? Where were you born?"

"I am a Lombard by birth. The name of my home village you would not know."

She did not have to prod him more to get him talking about himself. His graceful speech and his fine, elegant face held her the rest of the afternoon. At nightfall, when they had stopped in a rocky meadow to make a camp, they rode together to the edge of the grass, where the grooms were tethering the horses. Father Yvet dismounted and came to help her from the saddle.

"Then your husband was a robber," he said, looking up at her, and she took his hand and let him lower her to the ground. "Of course. *Dragon.*" He took her arm in his. The meadow was already full dark, swarming with people bringing wood and taking horses. Fireflies glinted in the trees around them.

To himself, he muttered, "So the Emperor was humiliated by a common thief."

Maria kept silent. His tone rubbed. Here and there around them, a campfire crackled up in a burst of flame. Suddenly Richard on his dark stallion blocked their way, a hawk on his fist. He threw the churchman a vicious look, dismounted, and said to her, "Come walk with me a little."

"I will." She disengaged her arm from Father Yvet's, but up ahead, the baby cried. "There, you hear that," she said. "Go put your horse up."

He gave Father Yvet another prickly stare and led his horse away. The churchman watched him go, his face lively. "He is jealous of you."

"No. He's just taken the hawk's humor."

She went up to the fire and got Henry from the maid-servant's arms. Sitting down in the warmth, her back to the crowded meadow, she opened her dress and gave the baby her breast. Her women kept the other people away from her. While the baby tugged heartily on her breast, she thought over what the priest had said.

Richard sat down beside her. "You have a courtier now."

"I wonder at you sometimes. Even Father Yvet remarked you are jealous of him."

"Did he? Good. What did he say to you?"

She put her hand against the baby's fine hair. On the top of his head the pulse thrummed evenly. "I told him my father was a robber. He made much of that."

"God's death. Why did you tell him that?"

"Should I not? Perhaps you would tell me all the things I may say, as for example, *Good day*, or—"

"Stop," he said. "Tell him anything you want. You said he made much of it. How do you mean?"

She repeated what Father Yvet had said about the Emperor. Richard sat scratching his beard under his chin. The fire shining on his eyes turned them clear as light.

"Do you like him?" he asked.

"Yes," she said. "I suppose so. Yes, I like his voice."

"Which one?"

Gorged, the baby had fallen asleep. She said, "I like Father Yvet very well. He doesn't go off hawking and leave me to ride by myself." She pulled her dress closed.

"Now who is jealous? I think you are right, catkin. Father Yvet is here to make me bow. But not to the Emperor."

"To whom, then?"

"Father Yvet, to start."

422

Maria gave the baby to the maid. Behind her, in the trees, the wind clacked branches together. His hands to the heat, the churchman stood on the far side of the fire, charming the knights there. "His father was a weaver," she said.

"He told you that?"

"Yes."

Richard rubbed his hands on his thighs. "I will need your help."

"Oh," she said. "I have heard that before."

"LET ME SEE HIM," Eleanor cried. "Let me see—" She stretched her arms out for the baby. Maria stepped away from her horse. The ward at Castelmaria was dense with people. Everybody was talking and laughing at once. Richard's horse walked up before her. He shouted to someone on the wall. Maria went through the mob, searching for Jilly and Stephen.

"Maria!"

Flora ran up to her, sobbing, and they embraced. The old woman babbled nonsense, as if Maria were a baby. She reminded Maria of Adela, of her mother, of her childhood; she too began to cry.

Stephen was standing on the step into the New Tower. Beside him, there was a little girl with long brown hair. Maria, entangled in Flora's arms, called out to them, but if they heard her they made no sign of it, they did not smile or come toward her. Eleanor, behind her, had the baby. Flora's mouth was already pursed to coo at him. Maria crossed the ward to the New Tower door.

"Stephen,'" she said. She tried to put her arms around him, but he pulled sharply away from her.

"My lady, don't kiss me, I am too old for that now." He turned. "Jilly, come greet our lady mother."

The little girl came grudgingly around him, her eyes lowered. Except for her shining brown hair Maria would not have recognized her. When Maria reached out to touch her, the child recoiled from her. Eleanor was coming. Maria drew back from the two strange children before her.

"Jilly," Eleanor said, the baby in her arms, "have you

423

shown your lady mother what a well-mannered girl you are?"

Wooden, the little girl took hold of her skirt and flexed her knees in a rigid bow. Eleanor shooed them all on through the door and up the stairs.

"I have changed your room," Eleanor called. "I think you'll prefer this."

Maria said nothing. Stephen and Jilly climbed the stairs before her. She felt like a fool. She had longed so much to see them, and now they did not like her. They came to her old door and went in.

"Maria. When I heard Richard was shot, I prayed all night." Eleanor stabbed a kiss at her. "Oh, how you must have suffered. I prayed for you, I felt your pain. Oh, you precious, precious thing." She crowed over the baby. "Jilly, come see your precious baby brother."

Maria sat down on the bed. The old cupboard was gone: her mother's cupboard. The bed was turned against a different wall. Strange thick carpets covered the floor. Jilly was looking unwillingly down at the baby, her hands twisting murderously behind her back.

"Jilly," Maria called. "Come here."

Stephen hurried into the room. Two porters brought a chest after him. The maids were all clustered around the baby. Maria wondered if Jilly had even heard her. Stephen came by her side.

"Mama." He gave her a quick kiss on the cheek. "There."

"What are these, Rahman's manners?" She wrapped one arm around him. He struggled, and she hugged him hard against his will. He squawked, his hands thrusting against her.

"Oh, Mama."

"What else did Rahman teach you? Jilly, come here."

Eleanor said, "Judith? Do as you are bid." She looked over her shoulder at Maria. "She is a most biddable child."

Jilly dragged herself reluctantly over toward Maria, who turned her around and started to brush her hair. To Stephen, she said, "What else does Rahman teach you?"

"Oh." His eyes rounded. "About stars, and how to play chess, and geography—"

"I mean about me." She stroked her daughter's hair, thick and soft like Richard's.

"Rahman likes you, Mama," Stephen said earnestly. "He told me so. But you are just a woman." He sat on the bed next to her and put one arm around her shoulders. "So Papa and Robert and I must protect you, even when you don't want us to."

Maria fingered a tangle out of Jilly's hair. Under her touch the child was ungiving as a piece of wood. Richard came in, shouting something back down the stairs behind him. His voice boomed across the room. He strode over to Maria.

"Here." He caught her hand and clapped something into her palm.

Jilly flinched. He reached out to touch her and she slipped between him and Stephen and raced out the door. Richard stared after her.

"What's wrong?" Maria looked quickly down at the coin in her hand. Stephen cried, "Mama, I can read it." He plucked the silver away from her. She lifted her face toward Richard. He was still watching the door, puzzled.

"Why did she run away from me?"

"She has forgotten us, that's all."

Stephen held the coin out to her between his thumb and forefinger. "It says *Ricardus Dominus.*"

Maria took the money back. On one side was a mass of Saracen decoration, and on the other a man's head, wreathed in Christian marks. Richard tramped off across the room, pulling open the cupboard doors. He found the wine in the last place he looked. The cupboard doors stood wide open all around the room. Eleanor went around loudly shutting them. She and Richard paid each other thorny looks. Maria nearly laughed. At least something was the same. She turned to Stephen.

"Did Rahman teach you that, too? To read Latin?"

"Yes. That means *Richard, lord.* And that is Papa, there."

"It's very handsome," she said. "If only your father looked like that." She hugged Stephen again. The boy rubbed against her affectionately. "Richard, did you hear him? Stephen can read Latin now."

Richard mumbled something. He charged off down the

stairs. Her son followed him. Maria sat on the bed. She had forgotten what a year meant to children. She got up and began to change her clothes.

SITTING IN THE HALL with Eleanor, Maria helped her spin the season's flax. Eleanor seemed much different to her, as if when she became a wife she became another person. She sounded Maria about the Santerois war and Richard's wounding and Roger's wedding.

"What is she like, Roger's wife?" Eleanor asked. "Oh." She put her hand on Maria's. Richard and Father Yvet were coming in the door. "What a presence he has. Is he from the Archbishop?"

Maria drew the linen thread out between her fingers, her eyes on the wheel. "He is from the Pope."

Eleanor straightened and stared avidly toward the men, who were sitting down by the hearth. Two pages hustled over to be sure they were comfortable.

"Roger's wife is very haughty," Maria said. "She disapproves of all of us. Except for Roger, naturally."

"Will they be happy?"

Maria worked the treadle of the wheel. "They were happy when they married. She is fair, the girl. And young enough. You know Roger."

"He is frivolous," Eleanor said. Her face was smooth as wax, as if she had never loved Roger at all.

"Richard thinks she will make him give up his little boy."

"Jordan?" Eleanor pursed her lips. "I wouldn't wonder. I would."

"I wouldn't." She tried to imagine a bastard of Richard's living in her household. Someone coming to her: *I have your husband's child*. Midway down the room, he was trying to catch her eye. He waited until Father Yvet was looking elsewhere and gestured firmly with his head toward the wall.

"What's the matter with Richard?" Eleanor said.

Maria fumbled her foot into her shoe. "He is in a strange humor lately. Will you watch Henry for me?" She got a candle from her basket and went out the door and behind the stairs into the wall passage.

426

The black tunnel swallowed her. She groped her way through it, remembering the bumps and spines of rock only after she had banged her feet against them. When she rounded the corner, she heard Father Yvet's voice.

"My lord, my mission here is as pleasant as it is simple. I am to assure you that the Holy Father will accept you as his vassal and recognize your claims to all of Marna."

Maria clicked her tinderbox furiously until at last a little flame glowed in the fluff of tinder. On the other side of the wall, a chair grated on the floor. She blew on the tinder to make it burn and reached for her candle. Whatever the priest had come to Marna to do, it certainly was not what he was saying: the Pope did not have vassals.

Richard said, tentatively, "I'm honored by the recognition. I think the Emperor is my overlord."

"No—that is a usurped power, you see. Marna is part of Constantine's gift. In the course of events, that's been corrupted, but the true order of things here is obvious."

"Maybe you'd better tell me who Constantine is," Richard said.

Maria was pleased that he didn't know either. She sat down on the floor. The candle showed her the rough, blind walls of the passage.

Father Yvet went off into another of his stories. Old candle butts littered the floor. She lit them and set them in niches on the wall. Bending, she put her eye to the peephole.

Richard sat in his chair opposite her. The churchman between them had his back to the wall. Father Yvet's hands moved gracefully. He explained how the Emperor Constantine had given the whole world to the Pope to rule.

Richard said, "I had a man from Aachen say that I owe the Emperor obedience. Now you come tell me this. You are confusing me, and I don't like being confused."

Father Yvet straightened. The back of his chair dented the smooth wool of his robe. "Come," he said quietly. "You are shrewd enough to know that until you pay homage to your rightful overlord for Marna, you will be only an outlaw here, responsible to no one. The Emperor will never recognize you now, since you insulted him. He'll take his revenge on you at his pleasure. We are offering you a way to escape what could only be a mortal blow to your power here, perhaps your very life."

Richard said, "Thank you. I am very grateful to you."

Maria sat up straight. The burning candles turned the air stuffy, and she put most of them out. She wondered if Father Yvet knew Richard well enough to catch the whine of temper in his voice.

"We will expect something of you in return," the churchman was saying. "There is the matter of the priest you murdered—"

"I murdered no priest. Hold."

"Papa," Stephen called. Footsteps ran across the hall. "Excuse me, my lord, for interrupting you. Papa, Robert is coming."

Getting up, Maria pinched out the last of the candles. Beyond the wall, Richard said, "Go find your mother."

"But Papa, I can't—"

"I said, go find your mother."

Maria ran off down the passageway. When she reached the stair landing, Stephen was half a flight down. She called his name, and he wheeled.

"Mama." His eyes popped. "Where were you?"

Maria went down to him on the stairs. "Ah, Stephen, I have never seen you with your face clean." She spat on her thumb and rubbed away the smear on his cheek. "Has Robert brought Ismael with him?"

"Mama, how did you know?"

Maria went down into the ward, Stephen in her tracks. The day was brilliant with sunlight. She made a wide circle around the horses in the ward. Stephen ran ahead of her in the ward.

"Jilly," Eleanor's voice called, somewhere in the tower. Maria went out the gate onto the windy slope.

Robert and Ismael were riding through the curtain wall. They spurred to a hard gallop and raced up around her and Stephen. Robert leaped down before her.

"Mama. We stayed to hunt, up in the hills, did you miss me?" He flung his arms around her shoulders. His voice cooled. "Hello, Stephen."

"Hello," Stephen muttered.

"Mother, did the Pope's messenger come with you?" He

backed up onto the road, throwing his black cloak over his shoulder. Little blue wildflowers sprouted down the front of his coat and in his horse's black mane. Ismael came up smiling between them.

"Maria. No much witch, no?"

"Hah," she said. She took hold of his hand. "I am sad of you, Ismael. I thought you were bold. Yes, the Pope's man is still here."

Ismael turned back to his horse. "Then I very well go."

"Stay down by the beach, so the Emir will know where to find you." She went between their horses and down the road a few steps, to point over the green crest of the wood. "There are fishermen's shelters there, and Robert will bring you some food."

In the castle, Eleanor was still calling for Jilly. Maria put one arm around Ismael. "It won't be for very long."

Ismael swung up onto his red mare and galloped away. Maria frowned. Something moving on the hillside below her had caught her eye. It was Jilly, running through the waist-high green toward the curtain wall. The child disappeared in the brush.

"I have, you brat," Robert was saying hotly, behind her. "You can ask—"

"You're such a liar," Stephen said.

Robert cried out. He lunged toward Stephen, and his brother raced away through the gate. Robert chased him across the ward. Maria took his horse by the bridle and led it inside.

"My lady," a groom said, and she gave him the rein of Robert's horse. Muffled, Robert's voice shouted in the stable, and he pounded on the closed door. Maria went quickly toward the New Tower, pretending not to hear him.

XLI

❦

"DO YOU STILL LIKE YOUR WEAVER?" RICHARD SHOT A sideways look down the hall toward Father Yvet. "Christ witness. Every man with an ox tries to fatten it on me."

Father Yvet stood before the hearth, the center of a small worshipful crowd. Robert and Stephen were among them. The churchman's voice was answered by a general laugh. Robert leaned forward, his face vivid with some idea. The priest inclined his head gravely to listen. He had been listening all day, especially to Eleanor. Maria had seen them together three times.

"Do you think he meant all that?" she said to Richard. "It sounded to me as if he wanted to find out how much you would believe."

He took hazelnuts from the bowl beside his chair and cracked the shells between his thumb and forefinger. "Did Robert find Ismael?"

"He's down by Crane Beach."

Eleanor came in, carrying Henry. Jilly like a servant hung on her skirts. Maria's eyes followed them. Richard put another nutmeat to her lips, and obediently she opened her mouth to receive it.

"Now you're going to suffer for killing that priest."

"Don't let me yield to temptation and kill this one."

Maria went over to sit down with Eleanor, in the far end of the room. They talked of babies. Jilly lingered nearby them, her fingers turning in her hair, and her eyes listless. When Maria put out her hand to her, the child shrank away. On the back of her hand was a long scratch. Eleanor's babble unheeded in her ears, Maria sat watching her daughter steadily. That afternoon, when she had spied Jilly racing down the hill outside the castle, she would have sworn an oath the child was naked. The baby whimpered. She took him from Eleanor and went upstairs.

At dinner, she sat between Richard and Father Yvet. Richard was not talking; he stabbed his knife into the meat and drank hard. Blossoming into a profusion of stories, witticisms, and recollections from Scripture, the churchman dominated the rest of them. He was so sunny Maria could scarcely believe he meant them harm. Highspirited, Robert argued with him about faith. Eleanor leaned forward eagerly, her lips parted to speak as soon as they gave her enough quiet.

"Mother," Robert said. "Has Father Yvet made the trip to the shrine?" He turned his gaze on the churchman. "You should see my mother's holy place, Father, while you are visiting us."

"Yes. I should like to. Will you take me there?"

Robert leaped up, buoyant. Stephen cried, "Why can't I take him? I was born there, Mama—"

"You are too young," Robert said.

"I am not!"

Eleanor turned toward the churchman and spoke to him, but his eyes stayed on the boys, and he did not heed her. Robert was still on his feet. He said, "Papa, can we go? Tomorrow?"

"Maria," Eleanor said, "we could go too. Jilly, eat your fish."

Jilly reached out slowly and took a piece of the fish in her fingers. Eleanor turned toward Richard. "Please, my lord. We could all go. You make the pilgrimage so seldom." While her back was turned, Jilly dropped the fish under the table.

Amazed, Maria throttled down her laugh. Richard was agreeing to the journey and refusing to go himself. Eleanor clapped her hands together. Under the woman's eyes, Jilly carefully picked up another bite of fish and made as if to eat it.

"Well, I'm not going, if Papa doesn't," Stephen said sullenly.

Eleanor turned to cajole him, and Jilly tossed away the bit of food. Robert said, "Then, don't. In fact, I forbid you to come."

Richard said, drawling, "If you two want to fight, why don't you go upstairs, where you will not present an example to these other Christian children?"

"Papa, it was his fault—"

"God damn you," Richard shouted, "go upstairs!"

Stephen was already climbing over the bench, away from the table. He waited stiffly in his place, his eyes on Eleanor. When she nodded, he ran off across the hall to the door. Robert held his ground.

"Tomorrow, sir," he said to Father Yvet. "If you wish."

"I am very pleased to have your company," Father Yvet said, smiling. Robert left them. Richard was drinking again. The priest turned to Maria.

"Your sons are gentle-mannered young men."

Richard set his cup down hard. The wine sloshed onto the table. He walked off down the hall. Eleanor stared after him. "His temper is worse than ever, I see. All our prayers have availed nothing."

Maria turned her back to her. To Father Yvet, she said, "Robert likes you. Talk to him—ask him not to fight with Stephen."

"I will speak to him. But the younger boy is the culprit." He bent toward her, as if they spoke alone together, in a little room. "You will come with us tomorrow, won't you?—It's an easy journey, I'm told. A pleasant outing for you."

Maria smiled at him, pleased at his attentions to her. Face to face with him, she could not dislike him. "Thank you. I can't go, I have so much to do here." The shrine would be packed with the late-summer pilgrims.

Eleanor rose. "Jilly. Look at your dress. And you're commonly so tidy." She hoisted the little girl by one arm to her feet and swept the crumbs from her skirt. "Off to bed, now. Bow to your lady mother." Jilly performed her mechanical curtsey and was led away.

"But it's your shrine," Father Yvet was saying. "Who could show me better?"

She shook her head. "Richard won't let me go."

"You are wasted here," Father Yvet said. "On this bully."

"Father," she said, "I love my husband, and he is no bully."

"I'm sorry. I was overbold. Come, look at me." Like a lover he tipped her face up by the chin.

"Are you my friend, Maria?" he said gently.

Maria glanced around them. Eleanor had left the room. The servants were taking away the supper. Eleanor's huge fat husband, William the German, was making himself comfortable before the fire. The dogs swarmed around his knees and he fed them cheese. Richard was nowhere. She turned and gave Father Yvet her best smile.

"I am your friend, if you are mine," she said.

"Then perhaps you will help me understand your lord."

She searched the room again for Richard, and the churchman said, "He's gone. Don't be afraid of him. Ultimately, if you trust me, you are serving him better than he serves himself."

Maria looked down at her hands. "I trust you, Father."

"Do you know if your lord has had any communication with the Emperor since the incident in Santerois?"

"None," she said. "I am sure of it, I have been with him constantly since then.

He nodded, pleased. "I thought that."

Maria wet her lips, her eyes on his face. "Father, tell me the truth. Will the Emperor punish us? What will happen to us?"

He touched her hand; his fingers were cold and dry. "Don't look so worried, child. The Emperor is only a man."

"But he is Christ's man," Maria said.

Father Yvet shook his head. "The Holy Father is Christ's man—Christ's chief instrument on earth. The Emperor has stolen his rights, over the years, but the Holy Father is above the Emperor, as the soul is superior to the body. So the Emperor will learn, if you help me make your lord the sword in the hand of the Holy Father."

"My lord, I don't understand you."

"It's very simple, child. For many years the Emperor has used the disguise of reform to rob the Chair of Peter

433

of its rightful prerogatives. Now the moment has come to restore the preeminence of Christ."

Maria crossed herself. The round, rolling words reminded her a little of the Mass. She said, "My lord, I will help you if I can."

He touched her hand. She faced out into the room, her heart pounding. Eleanor had come in. She sat down next to her husband and began to talk to him. Maria saw that Eleanor talked rather more than William the German. She wondered what lying with so gross a man was like. Two pages were heating a poker in the fire, to mull cider, and she beckoned to them.

"I have heard much of this edict," Father Yvet said, "this Saracen charter allowing them to practice their idolatrous faith. I know you are a true Christian."

"I am, my lord, by Saint Mary."

"Yet I am told you witnessed the charter."

"I could not do otherwise," she said.

"He forced you?"

The eagerness in his voice embarrassed her. She looked away from him. "I am only a woman, my lord." Brother Nicholas would be at the shrine. She almost decided to go with them, to see how he liked Father Yvet. The page brought her a cup of the hot cider.

"Will you have some?" She put the cup down in front of the priest.

"Thank you, child, no." He smiled at her like a boy. Maria took the cup and sipped from it. The sweet apple liquor warmed her tongue.

"My brother William did not witness the charter," she said.

"No. So I am told."

"Richard does not rule William."

"And he is a Godly man? A friend of Holy Church?"

"William loves piety." She crossed herself to take the curse off the lie. Robert had come in again. Eleanor swiveled in her chair to speak to him, and he answered her and came around the end of the table to Maria's side.

"Mother," he said. "Come with us tomorrow. It would be like Mana'a. You could lower a rope out the window." He sank down on his heels next to her chair, smiling across her at the churchman. "I think we drive my father mad—he knows we deceive him constantly but he can never catch us at it." He elbowed Maria. "We'll leave before dawn—steal away, before Papa is up." He looked again at Father Yvet. "My father is a late sleeper, being a drinking man."

"Robert, don't poke me." She got quickly to her feet. "I cannot go, there is too much to do here—you've seen how Eleanor keeps the place. Father Yvet, I pray you, pay no heed to him."

"What will he say?" Father Yvet lean's face sleekened with amusement. "Here, Master Robert, tell me all your mother's secrets."

Robert stood up. "It's nothing, Father—our joke." He caught Maria's hand. "Come with us. Come on—you never do anything with me any more."

"You flirt, Robert." She escaped off across the room.

When she reached the doorway, she turned, her back to the stairs. Robert was sitting in the chair she had left. Father Yvet was talking to him. She stood on the threshold, where she could watch them.

After a moment, to her relief, Richard came out of the wall passage behind her.

"Did I do it well?" she said.

"You are a master. But you shut up Robert just when I was learning something."

They went up the stairs. She said, "Eleanor's husband is a very silent man. Jilly is only afraid of you because you shout. Play with her a little."

"Play with her? I'd sooner play with Eleanor. She is a brat now. Why didn't William witness my charter?"

Maria shut the door behind them. "It was the hunting season."

ELEANOR WRINKLED up her nose. "I can assure you, such foul stuff will never pass my teeth." She broke a little simnel cake and spread it with honey and butter.

"But they're good. Here, Jilly." Maria tried to give the child half her Saracen bun. Jilly shrank away from it, her face knotted up in distaste.

"Oooh."

"You see." Eleanor patted Jilly's shoulder. "Father

435

Yvet is a Godly man. He will have no taste for vile pagan food."

Maria gave up. She sat back in the chair, yawning. The candle light pooled on the table, shining on the hands and faces of the people around its edge. In the darkened hall behind them, many of the servants still slept. The door opened and Robert came in, trailing Stephen, and a moment after they had sat down, Father Yvet appeared. Maria went over to the north window.

"It will be a good day for your pilgrimage," she said. She folded her arms on the window sill. In the clear blue night before dawn, the smoke of the village chimneys rose straight as pine trees.

"Mother, is our dinner packed?" Robert jabbed at Stephen with his knife. "You can come, if you can talk her into it." To Father Yvet, he said, "Stephen is my mother's lamb." He glanced at Stephen. "Baabaa."

Stephen started up. Father Yvet pushed him back down on the bench. "Eat, Master Robert, so that we can leave. A good day's travel begins with a good breakfast."

Maria went down the stairs and across the frost-covered ward to the kitchen. The cook was packing two large baskets full of food. "They'll just have to take what they get," he said. "Coming in here and telling me they want a full meal to eat on the way."

He stuffed an enormous pudding into a basket already bursting with roast meat. Maria went into the pantry for a cheese. The kitchen door banged open; she heard Jilly's voice. She went out to the warmth of the kitchen again. Jilly was squirming into the narrow space behind the rear table. The cook went on with his packing.

The child saw Maria and froze. Maria smiled at her. She took the cheese over and put it into the second basket. Jilly disappeared into her hiding place.

"Did you like the chorek?" she asked.

The cook shrugged. "It was fair-tasting bread. That sweet spice and all. Fair." His bare skull shone. He gave her an oblique look. "Get it in Mana'a, do you?"

"In the harbor. I'll send you some."

His head bobbed. Robert opened the door and came

436

the three steps down into the light. "Mother? We are ready."

Maria fastened down the tops of the baskets. "Now, don't eat everything. Let other people get enough. Are you taking a page? Then take one. Josse, he has never been."

"Maria," Eleanor called, from the doorway. "Have you seen Jilly?"

"No, Eleanor, I thought she was with you."

Robert lifted the baskets, and Maria followed him up into the ward ahead of her. The sky was full of high blue clouds. In the ward, the horses stamped and snorted in the chilly air. Father Yvet marshaled his little party out into the open. William the German had backed out of the trip the night before, but Flora had suddenly decided to go in his place.

"This will teach Jilly not to go off by herself." Eleanor lapped the front of her cloak and fastened the brooch. "Still, I'm sorry she must miss it." She got into the cart with the baskets and the page and Flora. Robert mounted.

"Come join us, Master Stephen," Father Yvet said. The boy was standing just behind him. "Let me make a friend of you."

Stephen locked his hands behind his back. "I am my father's friend." He walked away toward the New Tower.

"Father," Maria called, and went up to the churchman. He stood staring after her son, his face pinched with anger. "Give my greetings to the abbot, Brother Nicholas."

"I will." Pleasant again, he kissed her forehead. He led the little train out the gate.

Maria went into the New Tower and up to the hall. In spite of the early hour, Richard was awake, standing beside the table eating breakfast, while William the German opposite him explained some business. Stephen waited nearby. Maria went upstairs to tend to the baby.

She nursed Henry and was sitting on the bed changing his clothes when Richard and William the German came into the room. They tramped across the carpets. Richard took his sword down from the wall and pulled the belt over his shoulder.

437

"We're going to the village. Something to do with this fair. And I may go to the mill afterward. When Stephen comes back, if I am not here, tell him to meet me at the mill."

"What are you going to do about Ismael?" She glanced at William the German's broad, shrewd face. He smiled at her. "He's probably freezing. You know how cold it gets down there at night."

"I sent Stephen down there with my fur cloak."

Richard went out. Maria followed him down the stairs, the baby on her hip. The ward was busy with the people of the castle at their work. Richard stopped in the middle of it, looking around him.

"Hugh! Bring me my horse!" He turned back to her. "Who taught that old onionhead in the kitchen to make chorek?"

"I did." She put the baby down on the ground at her feet. The geese were scattered across the ward, and she kept watch for them. His bay stallion trotted up from the stable, throwing its head against the groom's hold on the bridle. Richard mounted. She picked up the baby again and walked beside him toward the gate, one hand on his horse's shoulder.

"Poor Ismael. He's probably—"

"Don't worry about Ismael. If a messenger comes from Roger, tell me."

They went out the gate onto the hillside. Maria shaded her eyes against the early sun. The air was brilliantly clear; the valley lay brown and placid before them. A haywain was rolling down the road from the village.

"Now teach him to make Saracen eggs," Richard said, "and I will canonize you." He took his foot out of the stirrup and nudged her. She stood on her toes to reach him, and he kissed her. With William the German he galloped down the road toward the village.

Carrying the baby, Maria went off across the hillside toward the curtain wall. The early frost had killed the grass; it crackled under her feet and left burrs and hooked seeds all over her skirts. Henry slept with his head on her shoulder. Fifteen feet from the curtain wall, she stopped still.

Between her and the high wall, the hill dropped off steeply in a sandy bank. Naked except for her shoes, Jilly sat in the dirt, digging vigorously with a stick. Two cloth dolls lay beside her. There was no sign of her clothes.

Maria crouched in the tall dead grass. Jilly snatched up one of the dolls, a shapeless thing with black yarn hair. "No, no, Eleanor!" She pounded the doll on the head with her stick. "Eleanor was bad again, Judith," she told the other doll. "What shall we do?"

Maria backed away up the hillside. Henry sagged against her. She moved slowly to keep from rustling the dry brush. The doll Eleanor, apparently on counsel of the doll Judith, received a thorough beating. Maria went back toward the castle again. Halfway up the hill, she began to laugh.

SHE WENT OUT to meet Stephen. He would not tell her Richard's message to Ismael, but by the things he said, she gathered that Ismael was staying close by Castelmaria. They rode across the wood to the mill. She raced Stephen three times and beat him twice. In the deep oak wood the still air smelled of leaves and mold. Here and there patches of sumac glowed dark red in the sun. She jumped her mare over a windfall and turned to watch Stephen. His horse refused it, and grimly he turned and drove the brown mare at it again, and at the last step, when it was going to jump, his courage failed and he let the horse stop. He struck the mare spitefully with his reins.

"Don't," Maria called. "Come around it."

He rode through the brush around the barrier. They galloped on into the narrow trench of the valley where the mill stood. She saw how Stephen brooded on the jump he had not made. They reached the mill, at the end of the brush-choked valley, surrounded by a stand of cedars.

Around the mill there was a cleared meadow inside a split rail fence. When Maria and Stephen rode up to it, a cart and three of the villagers blocked the way through the gate. Maria waved to them, dismounted, and tied her horse to the fence. Eight of the dogs from the castle were sitting under the big tree at the gate, their eyes steady on the upper branches, where the miller's cats sat elaborately licking their paws.

"Piers," she said. She shaded her eyes with her hand. "Where is my husband, drowning the miller?"

The serfs all laughed, and Alys's son said, "We just took the stones inside, Madonna, nothing has happened yet."

Maria climbed through the fence and with Stephen walked across the meadow to the mill. She pushed the door open.

Inside, the round room resounded with the howling of the grindstones. The floor, the wooden gears, even the walls and the roof beams were caked with moldy flour. Maria circled around the trap door in the middle of the room, its lid cocked open.

The scales were at the far end of the room. "My father had the weights made," the miller was shouting. His voice carried over the roar of the grindstones. Richard was pacing up and down in front of the scales. The miller stood beside him, his face slack with apprehension. His boys were piling weights onto the scale platforms.

Maria went past the stacked bags of grain and stood where she could watch the scale. The miller's eyes never left Richard's face. The boys heaved the castle weight up onto the platform. Richard kicked out the chock.

The scale rocked and swayed and finally balanced evenly. Maria shook her head, frowning; she knew the miller cheated on his weights. The miller's face was dripping with sweat. Richard waved to the boys, who removed all the stones from the scale, and brought another set of weights.

"My lord," the miller shouted. "I never used those weights—I never even knew they were down there—I only used my good weights. You saw, you saw my weights balanced yours—"

The miller's boys swung the second set of stones up onto the left side of the scale. Stooping, they hoisted the castle weight and dropped it onto the right side. The scale crashed heavily down on the side of the castle stone.

"As I breathe, my lord," the miller was roaring. "As I love God—"

Richard seemed not to hear him. He gestured to the boys, who gathered up the false weights from the scale. Maria stayed to watch. She remembered how often this miller's father had cheated her. But Richard only led them all outside.

The boys carried the weights across the yard and threw them into the millpond. The three villagers jeered and shouted and made figs at the miller. Maria called to them to come load up the castle weights again.

The miller, by habit still bellowing, cried, "I've never cheated anyone—I never knew they were there—I never used those weights—"

Richard said, "Henceforth you will give me tenpence every quarterday. You can start Christmas. Tenpence. This next Christmas."

The miller's voice gave out. His face the color of flour, he stared into the empty air. Maria suspected that tenpence every quarter would beggar him, if he could not steal. Christmas was less than a full quarter away.

She turned around. Richard's horse grazed along the side of the mill. The water streamed over the mill dam, silver as fish. The serfs loaded the castle weights carefully into the cart and backed the ox through the gate into the road. Richard went around the mill to get his horse.

The miller wheeled toward Maria, his hands out. "Madonna, have some Christian mercy on me."

Maria smiled at him. "If I judged it, you'd be in the pond with your weights around your neck."

Richard led his horse over to her. "Did you see Ismael?"

"No. What are you—"

He turned his back on her and mounted his horse. The miller caught hold of the big iron stirrup.

"My lord—"

"If you stay honest, I will consider a remission."

He rode away. Maria ran across the yard to her mare. The oxcart was already halfway down the road through the valley, hidden in the trees and brush. Richard and Stephen rode up beside her. She mounted. Stephen whistled and called to the dogs.

"And people say only God can make something out of

441

nothing, Richard said. "Didn't I just make forty pence a year out of twenty pounds that wasn't there?"

"Yes," Maria said. "Which is nothing."

Stephen said, "What's a remission?"

"If he turns honest I'll lower the fine." Richard reined his horse around, his eyes on her. "Justice is profitable."

Maria laughed. They rode three abreast along the dirt path. The dogs snuffed busily around them. Stephen said, "Will he be honest now?"

"Do snakes fly? This one's father gave false weights when I was living in the Knights' Tower and your mother was still skipping rope."

"When did you live in the Knights' Tower?"

"I never skipped rope," Maria said.

"I remember you and a carrot-headed girl jumping rope and singing an indecent song about a bell."

"A bell," Maria said. An old tune sounded in her mind. "Oh."

> Good girls wait for blessing
> Bad girls ring the bell.
> Good girls go to Heaven
> Bad girls go to hey-nonny-nonny-o.

Richard laughed. They rode down the valley along the riverbank. Ahead of them the oxcart had nearly reached the bridge.

"What does that mean?" Stephen asked.

"It was a clapping game," Maria said. "Not skip-rope." She had not thought of the song in years. Richard was smiling broad as a sailor at her. She said, "You have an evil mind."

He held one hand up against his chest. "You were this high to me then. And flat as the top of a table. We bet on when you'd bud."

"You bet on anything."

The boy was looking from her face to his father's and back. Richard said, "We had nothing else to do. Except fight."

"Why were you living in the Knights' Tower?" Stephen asked.

"I was waiting for your mother to get old enough to marry."

Maria glanced at him. They came to the bridge. The cart rattled across and on down the road. Richard took his horse to drink. Maria dismounted and sat on a rock beside the river, kicked her shoes off, and stuck her feet in the cold water. Stephen waded along the bank hunting for crayfish.

Richard pulled her hair. "I remember once I caught you and that redheaded girl in the stable, cramming your faces with raspberry tarts you stole from the oven."

"Oh. Don't remind me. I was sick for days. I still can't eat raspberries." She leaned back against him. "Was that you?"

"You don't remember," he said.

"All I remember is running away from a very mean knight." She rubbed her cheek against him. Stephen was scrambling through the stalky brush along the riverbank. "Poor Elena. The Saracens killed her. She was my best friend."

"You weren't alone." He took hold of her hand and manipulated the fingers. "God's death. Half the tower got into Elena. She'd kick up her heels for a penny. Or a raspberry tart."

"You didn't. Did you?"

"She didn't like me."

"Poor Elena."

He kissed her. Stephen shouted in the distance, out of sight in the reeds along the riverbank. Most of the dogs had gone with him. Richard crooked his arm around her neck, her head fast in his grip. His free hand groped between her thighs.

She said, "Sooner or later Father Yvet is going to find out what a spider you really are."

He rubbed his face against her throat. "Oh, Maria. Haven't I been good to you?"

"Ever since Father Yvet started courting me."

He pulled her down onto the grass. The sun was warm on her face. She put her hand under his shirt. He lay on top of her, his knees between her legs.

The dogs barked close by. Stephen shouted. Maria

pushed Richard away; he was trying to kiss her, and for an instant he went on trying, pinning her down. She could not budge him. The dogs rushed up around them. Maria thrust at him hard, and he let her go. She sat up, her heart pounding.

Stephen bounded toward them. He was soaking wet to the hair. They got on their horses and went home.

XLII

MARIA TOOK HENRY DOWN TO THE VILLAGE IN THE EARLY afternoon. Richard and William the German had each given the fair a tun of wine, and the villagers were just tapping the second when she arrived.

Everybody for leagues had come: shepherders and woodcutters, even the people who left the hills otherwise only for Easter and Christmas. The meadow swarmed with them. They spilled over across the river and into the village itself. She took the baby over to see the woodcutters' trained bears dance.

Calling greetings to the people she knew, she stood watching the swarm of serfs. The shepherds' wives spread their finest blankets and shawls on the grass, to show off their patterns. Maria admired them. She got a sweet cake fresh from the oven and strolled around the meadow, enjoying the sudden variety of faces and sights.

Behind the wine wagon, the village boys and half a dozen knights from the castle had gathered to box. She stood trying to get Henry to watch them. Robert shouted to her. She went around the wagon and crossed a stretch of beaten grass toward him. Under an oak tree, he and several other men were standing around a double ox yoke, wound around and around with chains. Maria walked up.

"All right," Robert called. "Here goes." He bent, took hold of the yoke, and struggled to lift it. The yoke would not budge.

The other men laughed. Among them, William the German's broad face was scarlet with good humor. Robert stopped again and heaved. This time he hauled one end of the yoke a hand's breadth off the ground.

The men roared and beat their hands together. A cannikin of wine went quickly among them. Maria laughed; she pulled Robert toward her by the arm.

"Ah," she said, "your talents lie elsewhere.'" She hugged him.

"Papa," Robert cried, over her shoulder. "Come lift this thing."

Richard came up beside her. "What thing?"

The men around them shouted at him, challenging him to it. Maria settled the baby more comfortably on her hip. Richard put his foot on the yoke and pushed, without moving it at all.

A little crowd was gathering. The knights among them began to make bets. More cans of wine appeared and circulated from hand to hand. Richard peeled off his shirt. On his forearm dull purple ridges of scars rose under the dark hair. Maria took Henry's chin and tried to make him look. The baby pulled impatiently away from her. Richard bent over the yoke. He heaved; nothing happened.

"Go on, Dragon," someone yelled from the back of the crowd. "Breathe on it." The men all whooped.

"King Jesus Christ," Richard said. He grasped it again. The muscles of his back coiled. The chains clinked reluctantly. Maria murmured. All around her people yelled, their voices rising as the yoke rose slowly off the ground. Richard got it waist-high and dropped it.

A round cheer went up. "Try it again," Robert called, but Maria whacked him in the ribs with her fist, and Richard was already standing back, reaching for his shirt. He slapped William the German across his enormous belly.

"You do it."

445

The fat man smiled. He went up before the yoke, reached down, and raised the yoke up to his knee, brought it smoothly to his chest, and straightened his arms over his head. The crowd screeched. Even Henry crowed and pointed. William turned around once under the yoke and set it down again. Instantly other men rushed to try.

Richard started toward her. His eyes went beyond her, and he turned in the opposite direction. Maria looked over her shoulder. She heard her name called. Father Yvet sauntered up to her.

His habit was fine and soft as a prince's clothes. His brushed hair gave off a metallic sheen. "You should have come with us yesterday. It was a most pleasant journey."

Maria looked for Richard; he had gone. A serf woman, brown as the dirt, was kneeling before Father Yvet. Talking about the shrine, he did not notice her until she tugged on his habit. He blessed her. Maria boosted the baby up on her hip. They went together across the meadow.

"The cave is a holy place, don't you think?" she asked. "I have a feeling there. Like something listening."

"It was charming. Beautiful." They walked on together. She steered him toward the brown grass along the river, and he told her of the trip. "Your friend the abbot thanks you for the cheeses," he said.

"Brother Nicholas? How is he?"

"Well. Well-ripened," Father Yvet said. "I wonder at such people, sometimes—why they think offense to others redounds to their own piety."

"I think he was once a great sinner," she said. "Now he is humiliating himself as much as he glorified himself when he sinned. Did you talk to him very much?"

"No. Our interests are separate, aside from the dubious value of the penance he imposes on the folk around him. He is unworldly."

"Do you think so?" she asked, astonished.

"He is very fond of you, Maria."

The stream of people before them burst apart, and a giant pink sow, shining with grease, hurtled straight at Maria. She leaped sideways. Stephen clung with his arms around the sow's neck and his legs around her barrel.

Snorting in blasts the beast bolted away, hotly followed by a dozen screaming boys.

"That is your son," Father Yvet said, surprised.

"Yes—they try to ride everything." She put Henry on her other hip and crooked her free arm through the churchman's. "There," she said. "The jugglers are starting." She towed him in that direction.

Beyond the little knot of people at the jugglers' wagon, Eleanor stood scowling, her arms folded across her breast. "Father Yvet," she called. Her voice carried like a hunting horn. "Are you going to sanctify this sinfulness by your presence?"

"Lady, if my presence could sanctify sin, you would not find me wandering through the world."

"Oh, Father Yvet." Eleanor simpered at him. Maria went around them. Already in their red and yellow costumes, the jugglers were setting up their stage.

"I wonder where Jilly is," Eleanor said.

Maria turned. "Eleanor, will you do me a friend's favor? Can you take—"

"Henry to his cradle." Eleanor lifted the baby in her arms. "I will. Keep watch for Jilly, she is so easily frightened in crowds." Bent over the baby, she walked up the hill toward the castle.

Maria stood staring after her. The woman's dark green bodice showed vividly against the golden brown of the hillside. While she walked she hugged the baby.

"Your friend has no children of her own," Father Yvet said. "It seems a shame, she is so devoted to little ones."

To a burst of pipe music, the two jugglers tossed their knives and colored balls into the air. The children gasped. They pressed up close to the stage. Maria clapped her hands together. The jugglers' craft delighted her. She watched them spin up two of the children's hats into the stream of juggles.

Father Yvet was staring at her, a smile on his face. He said, "You are still a little girl, aren't you?"

Maria laughed, turning away. It rubbed her that he should take her for a child. They started off together around the edge of the meadow. The churchman paid her an assortment of flatteries. The knights were racing their horses up and down the road through the village. A roar went up from the mob around the oak tree and another man held the chained yoke up over his head. On the far bank of the river, a boy and girl sat dipping their bare feet in the water and holding hands. Maria looked for Richard. He disliked crowds; she thought he had gone up to the castle.

Two fiddles and a drum began to play in the middle of the meadow. "Oh," she said. "Come watch them dance." She lifted her skirts in her hands. "You don't think it's a sin to dance, do you?"

"No. I am not one of these people like your friend, who find sin in everything." He strolled along next to her. "These country folk have so few pleasures, I cannot grudge them their dancing."

Maria led him across the meadow. A bank of serfs and knights stood before her, clapping their hands in time. She slid through the packed crowd to see.

Shepherds and villagers kicked and bounced in a circle before her, alternating men and women. In the middle of their ring, Richard and Jilly whirled in their own strenuous dance. Her long hair flying, her hands in her father's raised over her head, the child flung herself from foot to foot. Richard threw one arm around her and spun around, lifting her against him off the ground. Her legs sailed out.

"Papa!"

Maria glanced at Father Yvet, but the churchman had gone. She shook her head, impatient with him, and joined the people clapping out the rhythm to the dance.

FATHER YVET SAID, "You told me you did not murder the priest, yet he is dead—despite, I am told, the intervention on his behalf of your gentle wife."

Maria had brought a cushion into the hall passage to sit on. She lit another candle, curious who had told him: Eleanor or Brother Nicholas.

"We shall have a complete explanation of it," the churchman said. "And assurances—"

"Father Yvet," Richard said, "stop tilting with me. I will support the Holy Father, provided he agrees to my conditions. One of my conditions is I hear nothing more about that damned priest."

Maria bent to look through the peephole. Beyond the wall, Father Yvet said, "We shall determine the conditions, not you.'"

"Oh, no,'" Richard said. He thumbed down his moustaches. "You are wrong there, weaver. I will tell you who gets what, and who does what, between me and the Holy Father. Do you think I am a lout, weaver? I know what my service would mean to the Emperor. No matter what happened in Santerois. He would give me anything I asked for the use of hundreds of the best knights in Europe, Norman-trained, Norman-led, and already here, south of the Alps."

Father Yvet, for once, did not speak.

Richard said, "I wonder if you realize what those men would mean to the Holy Father and Rome in the hands of the Emperor."

Maria could not see Father Yvet's face, and she straightened away from the peephole, her back creaking. Richard's voice was greasy with satisfaction. He said, "What's wrong, weaver? Haven't I let you mock me, all this time, and court my wife in front of me?"

Furniture rattled on the floor. Angrily the churchman said, "Don't force me to abandon you to your fate."

"My fate. If you leave here, weaver, I'll ruin you. I promise you, unless you do my work, you will never see another embassy."

"I do your work!"

Maria picked at a broken fingernail. The candle smoke got in her nose, and she waved her hand in front of her face to clear it away. Father Yvet said tautly, "My lord, I am in the service of his Holiness, and—"

"Go back to him, then. Someone else will do it, if you don't. Tell him to send me a Norman."

"My lord!"

"Go on. Get out of my demesne, and don't stop in Santerois, either, or you'll find out how far I can reach."

The fine wool rustled. Footsteps padded across the hall. The door shut. The other chair creaked. Richard's voice came through the peephole.

"Go get in his way—he will come to you next."

Maria stooped to whisper through the hole. "You were too harsh—he won't come back now, you ruined it."

"Do as I say, damn you."

She pinched out the candles and sidled down the wall passage. Her skirts were filthy and she shook them out. Going down the stairs, she opened up the door into the ward a crack.

Father Yvet was pacing up and down in the sunlight, his face grooved with thought. Maria stayed in the dark stairwell a moment. Richard was right, he was going to submit. Two servants, chattering, rushed in and up the stairs, and she went out to the ward.

The churchman came toward her, smiling. His handsome face was drawn with strain. He took her hand. "Maria, good morning to you."

"Good day, Father." She let him ease her over toward the far side of the ward, out of sight of the hall window. Robert and Stephen were sitting on top of the wall. She hoped Father Yvet did not realize they were talking to each other in Saracen.

"Yesterday," the priest said, "you said something to the lady Eleanor—you asked her for a friend's favor. Now I must ask such a favor of you."

They walked toward the gate. Maria edged out into the sunlight, away from the clammy stone wall.

"You know how jealous your husband is of our friendship," Father Yvet said. "Now he has tried to dismiss me. For his own sake, you must prevail on him to let me stay here." He swung toward her, his hands on her arms. "If the Holy Father withdraws his support, Marna will surely fall."

"What must I do?"

"He must let me talk to him again. I can smooth over the breach between us. But I cannot go back to Rome without some agreement."

That at least was true. Maria turned away from him, amused. She wondered if Richard were watching. "If I help you," she said, "you must keep faith with me. You will owe me a friend's favor, too."

He came up close to her side. "I swear it."

She faced him again, looking him straight in the eyes.

"I will do what I can. But he does not heed me over-much."

The churchman smiled down at her. "He listens to you, I suspect, more than either of you realizes." Stooping, he kissed her on the brow.

"THERE IS A TRICK," Stephen murmured.

Maria craned her neck to see. The serving people were taking away the litter of the meal. At the far end of the table, Father Yvet had laid out straws in three rows like a triangle. Robert and Stephen were stretched out across the table to watch. Robert took away some of the straws, Father Yvet took others, and again Robert was left with the last straw, losing. Maria glanced at Richard.

"Do you know it?"

Richard shook his head slightly, his eyes on the game. Eleanor and her husband were deep in some discussion, on Maria's left side. William the German contributed mostly grunts. Abruptly Richard straightened, and a moment later the porter shouted, out in the ward.

"Let me try," Stephen said.

Robert waved him off. His hand hovered over the rows of straws. Father Yvet caught Maria's eye and smiled at her. He and Richard had talked all afternoon. Now, suddenly, they loved each other. Maria had not listened; she had been trying to teach the cook to make Saracen eggs. A page ran in the door and danced impatiently, waiting to be summoned. Maria nodded, and he rushed up to Richard's side.

"My lord—"

Richard bent over the arm of his chair to listen to the little boy's message. Maria glanced at Eleanor. "You could have tasted the eggs, at least."

The other woman sat up stiff in her chair. "It is vile food, I cannot eat it."

"Father Yvet," Maria called. "Did you enjoy my cook's eggs, tonight?" Finally the bald cook had shouldered her aside and made the Saracen eggs his own way.

"My lady," the churchman said, "I have made only one inquiry of food since the day I found myself on a terrace in Athens, surrounded by hungry cats and eating whole baby squids. I ask only that the food be delicious. Your cook is a master."

Maria rewarded him with a smile. Beside her, William the German pinched his wife's lips shut. The page had left. Richard sat biting off the long hairs on his moustaches.

Ismael came in the door. He was rigid with fear. He fastened his eyes on Richard and came straight toward him. Father Yvet got at once to his feet.

"Ismael!" Robert vaulted the table. He strode up to the young Saracen and they embraced. Stephen instantly took his brother's place over the riddle.

Father Yvet did not hesitate. He advanced along the table toward them.

"Father Yvet," Richard said. "This is my foster son, Ismael."

Face to face with the priest, Ismael craned his neck to see for himself that the man was tonsured. Amused, Maria saw that he kept his mouth firmly shut. Father Yvet uneffusively withdrew to the game. Richard canted forward and asked something, teasing, and Ismael produced his smile. He beamed at Maria.

"You mark," he said. "I brave to witch."

Fortunately Father Yvet did not seem to hear. Maria said, "Yes, now we must find another lion."

A page came up to attend him, and he sat down and was served a meal. Maria folded her hands in her lap. A servant took away her cup and Richard's. Richard was watching the churchman. She said, "What happened between you?""

"Why," he said, "I've made a friend of him."

The churchman was absorbed in his game with Stephen. The boy's lips moved soundlessly. His fingers tapped on the table, counting. Maria set her chin on her fist. Stephen took away one of the straws.

"All right," he said.

The churchman's smile stiffened. Unspeaking, they lined up the game again, and again Stephen won. He called, "Papa, it's like an equation."

"Come show me," Richard said.

Stephen excused himself to Father Yvet and brought the straws up around the end of the table to Richard.

Robert beside him, Ismael ate steadily, his long brown fingers stripping a roast hen. Father Yvet watched him. A page brought a dish of sweets to each of them by turn. Beside her, Stephen taught Richard the game and beat him twice.

"What's the key?" Richard took something from his shirt.

"Play me again," Stephen said.

"Tell me the key first."

Maria tasted her wine. The page had left it whole and she set the cup aside. Richard took it.

"Just one more time." Stephen made his choice of the straws in the little design.

Richard slid Maria's cup back toward her. She said, "What did you put in my wine?" and took his hand; he clenched his fist. With her nails she pried up his little finger, revealing the edge of a leather packet.

"Drink it." He thrust her off. Swinging in his chair, he put his back to her and played the straw game.

"Papa," Stephen said, disappointed. "You figured it out."

Maria lifted her cup. The wine smelled sweetly of the love potion. Richard straightened, watching her intently. She took a long sip and held the cup out to him.

"Ricardus Dominus," she said.

XLIII

THEY WENT TO MANA'A. THERE JORDAN WAS WAITING for them, Roger's redheaded bastard, and the news like a counterweight that Anne was with child. Maria made Jordan her page, although he was still too small to go around the palace by himself. With the boys and Jilly, she

453

went to all her favorite places in Mana'a. Everybody remembered her. She loved to hear them call her name in the streets—"Mah-ee-yaa—" like a donkey braying, familiar as kinsmen.

William came from Birnia to talk to Richard about the county, where he had been keeping order. While he showed Father Yvet his plans for the new front doors of the cathedral, Maria bribed the deformed beggars to parade on the steps, and after Father Yvet had exercised his sympathies and horror, she made them wash off their running sores and show him their false humps and wooden limbs.

On Martinmas, they feasted on the beach, a hundred servants and a tun of wine and barrels of coals to keep the food hot. Everybody came who was of any consequence in Mana'a, and they covered the sand with their matrahs and little wooden tables. Richard kept wanting to leave, but everybody else, even Rahman, played or walked or napped in the sun. Jilly built a series of sandcastles. She carried Henry around and talked to him as if he were one of her dolls. Jordan crept into Maria's lap and went to sleep.

"Why can't I just go home?" Richard said. "No one seems to care that I'm here." He lay back on his elbow in the sand, his face turned into the sea breeze. Before them, the white beach ran off in a long curve toward the city.

"Stay. Whom would I talk to?"

The boys were galloping their horses along the beach. Father Yvet and Rahman walked side by side up from the road, deep in animated speech. Maria watched them, intrigued. They were similar men, not least in their attitude toward women. She wondered what they were talking about.

The tide was going out. Jilly had fallen asleep. Henry sat carefully dribbling sand in her hair. Ismael and Stephen on their African mares galloped along the edge of the surf, head to head; Robert lagged behind.

Richard nodded toward them. "Over a distance Robert would win."

Servants brought them wine. They talked about the cathedral. William had brought three men with him and

454

many plans. Richard disliked all of them. Maria was trying to soften him. She stroked Jordan's hair.

"How could she send him away? He is adorable."

"Not everybody mothers the world. Sweet Infant Jesus. They are doing it again." He got to his feet.

Robert and Stephen were fighting in the surf. Their horses stampeded away through the scattered servants and children. In the foaming water the two boys tumbled locked together. One—she knew it was Robert—came up alone, thrusting his brother down beneath him. A wave broke over them. Ismael hauled Robert off by the arms.

Maria rolled Jordan out of her lap and rose. "Where is he?" Suddenly Stephen's dark head bobbed up in the sea, just beyond the breakers, and while she slackened in relief he swam ashore. Jordan, banged awake, began to cry. Sitting down again she took him in her arms.

Ismael was holding Robert away from Stephen. The sharp crack of their voices came up the beach. The servants and guests had paused in their doings to watch. Even Father Yvet had stopped talking. Richard sat down again.

Robert threw off Ismael's hold. He jogged up toward his parents. Stephen followed him sullenly. Stopped before them, Robert looked at Richard's expression and cried, "Why are you angry with me? It was his fault." He thrust one arm out toward Stephen.

"I don't care," Richard said. "You've ruined your mother's feast. Go home."

Robert did not move. "But Papa, it isn't—"

Richard got to his feet, and the young man backed off a step. He was already Richard's height, although the slope made him shorter by a head. Richard nodded to Ismael. "Lock him in his room."

Robert's burning blue eyes turned to Maria. "I'm sorry, Mother." He strode away, Ismael behind him.

Drenched, Stephen waited on the sand slope below them. Richard sat down again.

"Go pack."

Maria said, "Richard."

His head swiveled toward her. "Shut your mouth."

"Papa, may I take my books?"

"Take whatever you want."

Stephen went off toward his horse, trailing its reins along the edge of the surf. In Maria's arms Jordan moved warmly; his head rested against Maria's shoulder.

"I'll give him one thing," Richard said. His eyes followed Stephen. "He fights like a girl, but he never makes excuses."

Robert and Ismael had gone. Stephen galloped his brown mare away down the beach toward the city. Jilly brought the baby to Maria. The little girl stood in the wind, her hair tangled around her shoulders. She took Richard by the hand.

"Where is Stephen going?"

"Castelmaria," Richard said. Standing up, he shouted in Saracen for his horse.

STEPHEN WAS HALF IN TEARS. He kissed Maria and Jilly a dozen times, until his sister began to cry as well. In the shadow of the wall, Rahman stood silent. Maria hugged Stephen tight. The sun had just set, but already cool darkness swept in from the bay.

A groom led Stephen's horse across the ward toward them. He was taking a little pack donkey as well, loaded with his books and clothes. He mounted.

"Mama," Stephen said. "Will he let me come home for Christmas? Mama, I don't know anybody at Castelmaria."

"Sssh." Maria gestured to the Saracen woman behind her. "You should go away for a while, I suppose, and be by yourself. Here." The Saracen woman handed her the sword, and she passed it up to him.

"Mama." He took the sword in both hands and drew the blade halfway out of the scaboard. "What am I to do with this?"

"If you are going to fight," she said, "you might learn to do it well. Good-bye."

He saluted her and rode off. The Saracen woman whispered to Jilly. The child followed her back into the palace, her head turned to watch her brother go. Stephen waved to Rahman, standing against the wall. He led the little donkey out the gate.

The full moon was rising. It would be cold, in the mountains. Probably he would sleep on the beach until morning. She hoped he did not ride all night. Rahman went into the palace. She stood in the dark, waiting a moment to calm herself, before she followed him.

Half the lamps in the corridor were lit. Servants padded back and forth on their slippered feet, carrying the remnants of various suppers. Rahman went into the little hall and sat down at his chess game. When Maria came up beside him he pretended not to notice her.

"Are you teaching my sons to hate each other?"

Rahman moved the chessmen around the checkered board. His hands were knobbed with arthritis. Gray streaked his impeccable beard. At last, he said, "Lady, you misjudge me."

Maria said nothing. She picked up one of the ivory pieces and passed it from hand to hand: she had given him this set after Ismael and Robert broke the other.

"I had no son," Rahman said. "I love Stephen as if he were my son. Would I encourage him to fight the other boy, who is already a hero to your people? No. Stephen came to me too late, he was already Christian.'"

Surprised into another line of thought, she put the chessman down on the board again, and he took it at once to another square. She said, "Robert is a hero to some of your people."

"Perhaps. But not to me. Not to me."

She stood there a while longer, thinking over what he had said, and at last went downstairs and through the corridor into the Tower of the Cross. There, the windows all stood open, letting in the night breeze, and the lamps were still dark. Richard's voice reached her when she was still on the stairs.

Robert answered, reasonable, "I know, Papa, but I can't help it, he's like a flea, he bites and bites and I have to scratch him out."

"He's your brother," Richard said; his voice was much wilder than Robert's. Maria went up to the door. Ismael

457

saw her first and smiled at her, and she went into the twilit room.

Robert was sitting on his bed. He caught her hand.
"Mother. Why is everybody so harsh with me? I didn't
hurt him."

Richard was sitting with his chair rocked up on its hind
legs, his hands fisted on his thighs. Maria faced him. "If
they go on like this, we might as well go back to robbery."

Richard snorted. "Stephen is a priest. You like him because he is soft."

She throttled down the hot words in her throat. Ismael,
in the back of the room, sudddenly got up and came past
her out the door. "Do as you please," she said to Richard,
and turned angrily to go after Ismael.

Richard caught hold of her skirt. He brought his chair
down square. "Robert, stay here tonight—I will leave the
door open, do me one courtesy at least and stay anyway."
He towed Maria out to the corridor.

They walked to the stairs. He took hold of her arm.

"They've always hated each other. When you were
building the chapel, down at Saint Mary's, I remember it
from then."

She said, "One day they'll hurt each other." They went
up the staircase and into the anteroom to their bedchamber. The Saracen woman was rocking Henry in her
lap. Jilly sprawled asleep on a cushion beside her. Maria
took the baby, and for a moment the two women stood
looking down at the child and talked of little, innocent
things.

"Good night," the Saracen woman said. She touched
Henry's cheek. "God keep us all." She went away.

Maria carried Henry into their bedchamber and across
the layers of carpet to the cradle. He trembled in his
sleep. For an instant his lips worked busily.

Richard put Jilly down on the bed. Maria put out two
or three of the lamps so that the stars in the ceiling began
to shine. Although it was November, the perfume of the
garden reached her, satisfying to her senses as wine.

"What are you thinking about?" he said.

"I feel different just for being in Mana'a. It's very
strange."

He kicked his clothes away, standing naked in front of her. His body was worked and thickened with muscle. Across his hip the scars lay like chains under the pale skin. "You are mad. You and Stephen."

"Let me call Lalla to take my clothes off, or help me yourself. You like Stephen."

"He is a priest. He thinks too much."

Maria laughed. He lifted off her heavy surcoat and pulled her gown up over her head. "I like the girls best," he said.

She brought him a cup of wine. "You might not, when she gets to Robert's age."

"I'll marry her to Bunny." He stood looking down at Jilly.

She sat down on the bed. A candle at the far end of the room guttered out. The dark crept toward them. "She's just a baby."

"It's you he loves."

"God's blood. You're the one who's mad."

They got into the bed together. "Whom can he compare you with?" Richard asked. "You and Anne are the only women he knows." He handed her the empty cup. "Even I prefer you to Anne."

PART IV

SARACEN
DEFENSE

XLIV

❧

MARIA HELD OUT THE COAT, AND RICHARD SLID HIS ARMS into it, settled it on his shoulders, and did the gold hooks up the front. "How do I look? The color is too bright." He twisted to admire himself while she brushed up the nap of the dark red velvet. "It's comfortable, at least."

Maria came around in front of him, pleased. The coat looked better than she had pictured it. The deep-cut sleeves reached just below his elbows, and the fitted sleeves of the undercoat were of the same gold satin as the wide cuffs. The jeweled hooks had come all the way from Africa. "Put on your belt." In his short brown beard and the velvet, he looked like a prince.

She went across the room, nodding to a page to bring her cloak. Through the window, she could see the green valley that lay before Iste. No one worked today in the fields: they were all celebrating the christening of Roger's son. When she turned back toward Richard, a strange knight stood in the doorway.

"My lord, my name is Walter, I served you—"

"In Santerois. I remember," Richard said. He was buckling on his belt. "Speak.'"

The knight crossed the room toward him. Maria turned away to let them talk alone. There was a looking glass on the chest below the window, and she stood it up.

"Maria," Richard said sharply. "Come here."

She went up to him. His voice alerted her, she signed to the page to wait in the doorway. To the knight, Richard said, "Say this once more."

The knight cleared his throat. "When you and my lady come from the church, after the christening, my lord

Roger intends to take you prisoner and make himself the lord of Marna."

Richard was watching her, his face settled in angles. "Do you believe this?"

Maria rubbed her sweating palms together. She wondered why the knight would lie. "Yes," she said. "That is why you are not the baby's godfather."

Richard lifted his head, his eyes on the knight. "How do you know of this?"

The knight said, "My lord, it is openly talked of here."

"Then it may be just a rumor," Maria said.

"We have to go through with the christening," Richard said. "Walter, you know where my escort is quartered. Tell Renald, he is the commander, tell him when we have gone to the church they should leave Iste and wait for us on the road to Castelmaria. Quietly."

Walter strode out. Maria beckoned to the page with her cloak. Richard walked in a circle. "It must be a lie. It cannot be true. Devil damn him. Do you believe this of him? Devil damn him." He snatched the cloak out of the page's arms. "Get away from me."

Maria sent the little boy downstairs to tell the others that she and Richard were coming. She put one hand on Richard's arm. "I will hold the baby over the font. When the ceremony's done, I shall keep hold of him, we can walk away. If nothing happens he will never know."

"I can't take a sword." He dropped the cloak in a heap and unhooked his coat. "Get me the long dagger." He stripped off the coat.

She brought the dagger and helped him strap it to his chest. When he had the coat on again, she shifted the long blade until the natural folds of the velvet hid its shape. Her heart was hammering. She took a deep breath to settle herself.

Richard said, "I don't like using babies."

"It must be done. Help me." She turned her back to him. He picked up the cloak and slung it around her shoulders.

The page rushed in. "My lady—"

"We are coming now."

She shook out her skirt. Richard shut his eyes and

smoothed the expression from his face. When he opened his eyes again, he smiled, bland as a monk. They went down the stairs. Maria thought of their own children, thankful they had left them in Mana'a. They walked into the open, sunlit hall.

Her hands were scummed with sweat. People came up to her, bowed, spoke to her, smiled into her face. Beside her, Richard made a joke, and there was laughter. Roger stood across the room. His hair was like a torch. Someone complimented her on Richard's coat. Slowly she made herself speak pleasantly to these people. She knew Anne and her family had brought Roger to this.

Before the christening, they heard Mass in the domed cathedral of Iste. Through the prayers and the rehearsal of the Passion, she wondered what Roger would do to them. He would have to kill them, sooner or later, Richard first. She could not believe he would kill Richard. She put her hand against his, and he took hold of her fingers and squeezed them. They knelt to pray.

She and Anne's brother received Christ. The congregation went to the side of the cathedral, to the green marble baptismal font. Drawn and pale, Anne stood opposite Maria, her brother at her elbow. Roger came up behind her. The baby in its long lace shirt lay first in the brother's arms, while the priest spoke, and the brother answered.

Maria took the baby, supporting his head expertly against the curve of her arm. To her satisfaction he was not as pretty as her babies and not redheaded. The priest anointed his forehead and made the sign of the Cross over him. Now the brother took him again, and the priest sprinkled the baby with blessed water and welcomed him into the community of God. Maria glanced behind her. Richard in his magnificent coat stood with his eyes on her. The priest rang a bell. The ceremony was over. The brother still held the baby. Anne, her arms crooked, was reaching for him. Maria slid between her and the font and plucked the baby from the brother's grip.

"Anne, my sister," she said. "How beautiful your baby is."

Anne's face went brittle as ice. Maria followed the

465

crowd toward the front doors of the cathedral. Anne pursued her.

"Give me back my baby."

Maria moved at speed up the nave, beneath the painted dome. Richard came up beside her, unhooking his coat with one hand. The baby cried. She put the tip of her finger into his mouth to quiet him. The congregation was spilling out across the porch into the sunlight. She and Richard went through the double doors.

The bright sunlight hurt her eyes, and she stopped. By twos and threes, on foot and on horses, the crowd scattered off through the town toward Roger's castle. Richard took her by the arm and propelled her down the steps and into the churchyard.

From either side, groups of men pushed swiftly up around them. They wore mail. They carried drawn swords. Richard pulled the dagger from his open coat.

"Wait," Anne cried. "Roger—"

A dark knight came from the men surrounding Maria and Richard. "My lord, you have no escape," he said, and saw the baby.

"Wait," Anne called, and sobbed once.

Richard went up to the dark knight and yanked the sword out of his hand. "Go fetch our horses."

The dark knight took a step to one side, confused, and from the mob of armed men an apprehensive murmur rose. Behind them, unseen, Roger called, "Do as he says. Get their horses." He walked up in front of Maria. The dark knight dashed back into the crowd.

"You are brave, to come so close to me," Richard said.

Roger turned away from them. He was unarmed, except for the short dagger even Maria carried. He put his hands on his belt. The band of knights broke in half. Through the gap the dark knight led their horses.

Maria gave Richard the baby. He laid it in the crook of his arm and put the dagger on its body. A woman moaned. Maria hoisted her skirts up and climbed into her saddle. The poised knights around them were watching Richard like a pack of hunting dogs; waiting only for Roger to give an order.

"Take him anyway," one man called. "Take him, for God's love."

With her rein and her heel she edged the white mare over to Richard. When she lifted the baby again the blade caught the sun in a flash that dazzled her. She cradled the baby against her shoulder and thrust the dagger into her sleeve.

Richard vaulted up onto his horse. The sword across his saddlebows, he circled the stallion around his brother.

"Roger," he said. "I will never forgive you this." Spurring his horse, he crowded Maria on before him across the churchyard.

Maria lifted the mare into a canter to cross the open market place. The baby was crying again, and she shifted his weight against her stomach. They galloped out the gate and veered to either side around a wagon.

"They are coming." He pressed his horse over beside the white mare and grabbed hold of her rein. Maria took the baby in both arms, careful of the dagger in her sleeve. They rode down the short slope and out across the valley. On either side the brown fields stretched toward the hills, speckled with new green. Richard glanced back. Ahead of them, their knights rode in a triple file up from the crossroads.

"Stop," Maria called. "The baby."

Richard sat back in his saddle and pulled the horses to a ragged halt. The baby was screaming with rage, its eyes squeezed tight into a hundred wrinkles and its mouth half the size of its face. Maria kissed its forehead. She swung her right leg over the pommel of her saddle and slid to the ground. A hundred yards up the road, the knights from Iste were drawing rein. Their dust hung brown in the air over them. She scrambled across the ditch to the field, put the baby on the ground, and pulled off her cloak.

"'You are a pretty baby," she said, "but you have wicked parents." She laid him on a double thickness of satin and ran back to her horse.

Their enemies shouted and charged after them. Maria hauled herself up into her saddle. Richard threw her reins to her and shooed her on ahead of him. Over his shoulder he called a long, taunting curse. Their escort trotted up around them.

"Where?"

"Castelmaria." Richard spurred his horse, and they galloped down the road into the valley.

●　　●　　●

DURING THE NIGHT, they stopped once to rest their horses. Three or four of the knights had been clever enough to bring skins of wine, and everybody sat around in the dark on a hillside, getting drunk in the cold. Since Roger and his men had been on their heels at sundown, they could not risk lighting a fire. Maria hugged her arms, shivering.

"Why did you leave your cloak?—You are witless sometimes." Richard stamped away from her into the darkness. A moment later he came back and sat down beside her, his arms on his knees. "How could he do this to me. What did I do to him to make him betray me?"

"It was Anne," Maria said. She brushed against him, and absently he slung his arm around her shoulders. She yawned. "If Roger had ordered it, they would have taken us, baby and all."

"Walter," Richard called. He turned to her. "If they had, would you have let me kill it?"

Maria said nothing. Footsteps crunched on the grass, and the knight from Iste came up between the trees. "My lord."

"How many knights does my brother have?"

"All the great men of Iste," Walter said. "Some of them are not so loyal to him as most, but they all—" he stopped.

"What?" Richard said.

"Well," Walter said. "You know. They all think you are—" his eyes flicked toward Maria, "a little too pleased with the Saracens."

Richard lifted his hand, and another knight came over to him. "Is this his excuse? At least no Saracens will help him. His wife's brothers will bring their powers, too. I judge his strength at one hundred and fifty knights and three or four hundred men on foot. He's not green at this,

468

he must start at Castelmaria, and I will go there." He nodded to the other knight. "Take my horse and the next two strongest and kill them getting to Mana'a. You can find fresh mounts at Simleh on the Ridge Highway. Tell my brother William to hold Mana'a. My son shall meet me at Castelmaria. Al-Kitab at Simleh is to hold until I call him. Walter. Ride to Agato. Tell Duke Henry to his face what has happened here. He will know what to do. Go."

The knights disappeared into the darkness. Richard went after them a little way and brought back a half-empty sack of wine. He sat down beside Maria in the grass. She reached for the wine skin, her teeth chattering. While she drank he took off his coat and draped it around her shoulders. She settled gratefully into the warmth his body had left.

"Are you coming with me?" he said.

"What do you mean? Where else would I go?"

"You've always had a certain tenderness for Roger."

"God's blood," she said, "I have a certain tenderness for you."

He threaded his fingers nervously through hers. "How could he do this to me?"

"I don't know."

Richard dragged her up onto her feet. "Come along. We can't stop now."

On foot, the knights came up around them, bringing their horses by the reins. The white mare moved like a ghost in the busy darkness. Renald led her up to Maria. "My lord," he said, "take my horse."

Richard boosted Maria up into her saddle. "I'll walk."

"My lord, you and your lady must get out of danger—we have twelve men and ten horses, two men will have to stay behind."

"Renald," Richard said, "I will do the thinking. Get on your horse." He walked off into the dark, and Maria reined her mare around and followed him.

JUST BEFORE DAWN, they reached a stream and stopped again to rest. Maria had slept in her saddle, and the fresh light brought her spirits up, but Richard was limping hard and leaned exhausted against her mare. She dismounted, made him sit, and took the horse down to drink.

This stream rumbled down a hillside into the meadowy floor of a valley. Streaks of mist lay on the dark green grass under the trees. The knights sank down on the ground around the stream and let their horses graze. The water was cold enough to numb her hands. She washed her face, took off the velvet coat, and turning her back on the men nearby she hiked up her skirts and ripped away the muslin underskirt. She buried the cloth in the water. While it soaked, she slipped the bit from her mare's galled mouth and knotted up the reins. Her hands were dead with cold. She took the dripping cloth back to Richard.

He was sitting with his back against a tree, taking his shoes off. The feet of his hose were sodden with blood.

"Here," she said. "Wash your face, you'll feel better."

He took the wet cloth and plunged his face into it. "Unh." He raised his head. "Get me something to drink." He scrubbed his face vigorously.

Maria ran down again to the stream. Her skirt was soaked through from the dewy grass, and even her sleeves were wet. From one of the knights she got an empty wine skin, flushed it out with water, and went upstream from the others to fill it.

Now the sun had burned away the mist. The sky showed pale blue above the hills. She lifted the heavy wine skin by its thong and started back up the slope. A knight was climbing a tree; she veered to watch him through the lower branches.

Richard was washing his feet with the wet linen. "Tell me why any sane man walks. Give me that." He seized the wine skin and drank thirstily. Maria, sitting down beside him, shook out the muslin. Blood stained it.

"Renald," Richard shouted. "Do you see anything?"

In the tree, branches shook furiously. "No," the knight called.

Richard made a sound in his throat. He drank again, slopping water down his front. All his clothes were ruined, especially the velvet coat. She took it in her hands and turned it over, looking for anything she could salvage.

"If we'd brought Jilly and Henry we would never have

470

gotten away," Richard said. He leaned his back against the tree and stretched his legs out in front of him and sighed.

"'Are you going to sleep?'" she said.

For a moment he said nothing, his eyes closed, and she thought he was already sleeping, but at last he moved and sat up. "Not yet." He took the torn and filthy velvet from her. "Poor Maria." He laughed. "I told you the color was wrong. Make the next one blue." He wrapped his arm around her neck, pulling her against him. "My talisman. You always bring me luck."

"It doesn't seem to work for me."

His arm tightened around her. After a moment, he got up on his bloody feet and walked stiffly down toward the stream. His men bunched around him to talk. Maria folded the ruined coat. She could use some of the cloth again; she would make a sleeveless coat for Jilly, when they got back to Mana'a.

XLV

❧

AT NOON THEY CAME OUT OF THE HILLS, STRIKING ACROSS plowed fields toward the road, and twenty of Roger's men attacked them. Richard was on foot. Two more of their horses had gone lame in the dark, so only eight of his men were mounted. Roger's men charged toward them across the fields from the road. A horn sounded. Maria swung the mare toward Richard. The horn whooped in her ears.

The sword in his right hand, Richard vaulted up behind her, tore the reins out of her hands, and shot the mare straight toward the leading rider of their enemies. "Follow me! Come on!"

At the jab of his spurs the mare stuck her nose out and

bolted. The enemy knights spun toward them, spreading out in a quarter moon before her. In the deep, plowed earth their horses strained to lift their feet. Maria clutched the pommel of her saddle with both hands. Richard was breathing hard in her ear. The white mare was already tiring in the heavy ground.

Richard's men surged up around him. Two or three of them charged in among the enemy knights and at a dead gallop fought hand to hand. "Dragon!" one shouted, and the other voices took it up savagely. Abruptly the mare's hoofs struck solid ground, and she lengthened her stride. Richard steered her down the fallow strip between two fields.

A knight on a black horse charged toward them, head to head. His horse's nostrils flared red-rimmed, its ears pinned flat to its poll. Maria gripped the mare with her legs. Richard shouted, and she shut her eyes, her teeth clenched. His arm whipped around her waist. The mare's shoulder struck something hard and bounced off and struck again. Iron clashed over her head. A strange voice whined in pain. The mare wheeled violently on her hocks. Richard's body twisted from shoulder to hip, stretching her with him. The mare spun again. Maria opened her eyes, saw nothing before them but the empty road, and cried out, exhilarated.

Richard lifted the reins, jerking the mare back on her hocks. The blade of his sword was dappled with blood. Maria relaxed her grip on the wooden saddle pommel. God was protecting them, they were right and their enemies were wrong. That was how God did. The fighting men behind them ranged across the fields, their cries echoing. Richard spurred the mare into a hard canter—used to stallions, he handled the little mare too roughly.

"Are you all right?" he said.

"Yes."

Flat fields stretched before them, dark brown from the plow, divided by strips of greening trees. "Maybe someone here will have horses."

"Here come more." Laying his sword across the mare's withers, he wiped his face on his sleeve. "I wish to God I had a shield."

Down the road a band of men was riding, their horses

shoulder to shoulder. Maria caught her breath. There were five of them, they wore mail, they carried shields. God would help her. If she lost faith, God would do nothing at all. Richard touched her shoulder.

"Get down—go through the fields, get beyond them. Hurry!"

She jumped down to the road. The knights before them were spreading out to encircle Richard.

"Take him alive—we can throw him—"

Maria pulled off her shoes. She ran out into the dark rank-smelling earth of the field. Fifteen steps from the edge of the road, she looked back. Her heart jumped in her breast. They were afraid of him—outnumbering him so much, yet they held back, wary, and he gathered the mare between his spurs and the bit and launched the little horse straight at them.

"Get the hell out of my way!"

Maria ran on, stumbling over the furrows and sinking to her knees in the loose ground. Her skirts tangled in her legs and she fell headlong, tasted blood in with the dirt in her mouth, heaved herself up, and went on. They were fighting, back there: she could not see Richard. Her lungs burned. She made herself breathe deep with each breath, but her legs grew heavy and hard to move.

Two knights pulled away from the fighting and galloped down toward her. The man leading thrust his sword into its scabbard. She staggered on across the fields. She was beyond the knot of fighting men now, and she cut back toward the road.

The knight reined up before her. Behind the nosepiece of his helmet was a face she knew. He reached down for her. The other knight drew rein behind her.

"Lady, come with me."

"Judas," she cried. "Go help your lord!"

The knight's arm stretched toward her, but he stiffened, and his expression changed. Without a word he straightened into his saddle. Wheeling his horse he galloped back toward the road. The knight behind her swore. She turned, but before she could see his face he was charging after the other man, drawing his sword.

"Dragon—Dragon—"

A black horse bolted along the road away from the

fighting. A body bounced and flopped beneath its hind hoofs, one foot locked in a stirrup. The two knights who had come for Maria threw themselves back into the melee. Their swords rose like scythes. Someone shouted in rage.

"Dragon!"

Maria leaped forward toward the road. The black horse kicked the battered body free. Shaking its head, it trotted along the side of the road. When she approached, it shied from her. She stumbled on the edge of the ditch and landed on her hands and knees. The black horse was wandering down the road, jogging a few steps, walking a few steps.

"Ah, boy," she whispered, holding out her hand. "Good boy." Her knees hurt where she had fallen on them, and she could not bend her legs. She shuffled toward the horse. "Whoa, boy." It blew snorting through its nostrils and stretched its head out, and she took hold of the rein just behind its bit and scratched beneath its jaw.

Somebody screeched. The horse shied, dragging her along the edge of the ditch. She gathered the reins and mane and climbed up into the saddle. The stirrups dangled far below her bare feet. The horse sidled nervously along the edge of the ditch. She gathered the reins and turned it toward the fighting. Her mare, riderless, limped heavily toward her. Behind it a tall bay horse charged clear of the pack, its rider clawing frantically behind him.

The bay horse stumbled and caught its balance. Up behind the knight, Richard hung on with one arm around the man's throat, a dagger in the other hand stabbing down and down and down into the armpit of the knight's hauberk. Each time he struck, the bay horse staggered. It bolted past Maria, lengthening stride. Richard flung the knight sideways out of the saddle and grabbed for the reins.

Maria turned her horse after him. A hunting horn blasted, behind them, and their enemies galloped after them. Without spurs she could not make the black horse catch up with Richard. She kicked it savagely in the ribs and doubled up the reins for a whip. Reluctantly the horse stretched out.

474

"Richard," she shouted. "Richard, wait—"

He held back until she caught up with him and sliced the black horse across the flank with his dagger. It flattened into a dead run, snorting in fear. Maria looked back. Their enemies were coming on—none of them now shouted Richard's war cry. Her knees hurt, and the palms of her hands were bleeding. She took hold of the reins and drew the black down to save him for the rest of the ride.

BY MIDAFTERNOON they had outdistanced the knights behind them. They cut across the hills toward the high wilderness. Following a narrow track through a bog, they came to a village of skin huts like a ring of toadstools below the treeless slopes of a pass, and the shepherds there gave them bread and milk and honey. They rode on across a desolate moor. The sky was turning gray with clouds.

Richard said, "Roger's men must be all over these hills. I wish I'd held onto that sword. Anyone could come up to me now and hit me over the head with a rock."

Single file, they rode into the oncoming night. There were no trees, only the bleak windy moor. Maria's muscles were stiff and cramped. She dozed in her saddle. Richard kept them to the lower ground, so that they would not show up against the sky. Rain began to fall.

Just after the night reached them, they rode into the woods again. She followed him blindly through the dark and the rain. A branch sliced across her cheek. Her horse stumbled, and she clenched her teeth to keep from crying out. Now and then they stopped while Richard studied the way before them. Each time when they went on, her body was stabbed with pain. The rain crashed through the branches and leaves of the wood. Everything smelled of dank earth. They had stopped again. Richard drew her down out of her saddle.

"Marita. Maria."

He carried her across an open space. Rain splashed in her eyes and mouth. Heavily he sank down on one knee, got up again, and took her into a tight, closed place,

475

shelter from the rain. He put her down on something soft, and even before her head touched the ground she was asleep.

THE WOVEN BRUSH of the ceiling was pocked with sunlight. She lifted her head. They lay side by side in a low round hut made of branches and thatch, drifted full of old leaves. Out the little door, she saw their horses grazing in the green meadow. Richard slept, a dollop of sunshine in his hair.

She got up, loath to wake him, and crawled out the door. The sun stood halfway up the sky. Washed in the rain, the whole green meadow shone like a jewel. She walked after the horses through the tall grass, looking for water.

Behind the hut, someone had butted stones together to catch rainfall. The mossy brown hollow was full of water. She stripped off her filthy surcoat and gown and washed her face and hands. At first she thought of airing out her clothes, but she was afraid that Roger's men might see the bright colors through the trees. She folded the cloth, unwilling to put it on again. Peeling off her shift, she sank down naked in the grass and washed her body.

She looked down at herself, at her belly pleated from bearing babies, and her veined, sagging breasts. Suddenly she felt time and age attacking her, all of them, Roger and Richard as well, killing her and them by pieces, as if Roger betraying them had torn out the parts of her that loved him, their common past, and made her suddenly old. She put on her shift again. With her other clothes under her arm, she went back into the hut, back to Richard.

He lay on his side, watching her. She sat down to fix her hair. He put his head down on his arms, his gray eyes following her hands.

"Are you hungry?" she said. "I still have half a loaf in my saddle pouch." She combed her hair through her fingers.

He shook his head. She fussed a knot out of her hair with her fingers. She wanted to lie with him, and she

476

moved her leg so that as if by chance her thigh brushed his arm.

"What are you doing?" He rolled over; his arms snaked around her waist. "Marita. Tell me where it itches." He tumbled her over on her back on the ground.

"Richard." She snatched at his fingers.

"Is it here? Ah. Do you like that?"

She kissed him. They lay down together in the leaves. He took her wrist and put her hand on his crotch. She reached under his clothes. His member stiffened against her palm, harder than flesh, softer than bone. Jacquot, the men called it, Johnny Cock, the Hammer and the Anvil. She stroked him, and his arms tightened around her. She wanted him hot, she wanted him to need her. They pulled off her shift and his clothes, unhurried. A daddy longlegs dashed away into the wall of the hut. Against her bare side the leaves were slippery. Richard's hand tightened in her hair, drawing her head down. She put her mouth obediently on his erection. He caught his breath. She kissed him and sucked on him; in her mouth the head of his stick was sweet and ripe. She lay down beside him again, and they coupled.

"What if Roger's men come?"

"They'll wait." He rolled onto his back, dragging her with him, her hair wrapped around his wrists. "Do it." He bucked against her.

She rode him like a man. She put her arms around him and worked, at first for his sake, but the deep, powerful caress made her burn, her breath came short, she twisted and thrust herself against him, her fingers digging into his shoulders. He stroked her hips and thighs, talking to her. Sometimes she listened to him and sometimes she didn't. She pressed her face against his neck. Her body brimmed deliciously full and alive.

"Aaaah."

"Marita. Do you like that?"

She sighed; she stretched herself along him and lay still. The damp, stall brush around her made her nose itch, and she sneezed.

Richard murmured. Painfully hard, his arms closed around her, and his body moved up under her. They were

477

tangled in her hair. He put her down on her back and doubled her legs up between them. Maria took his face between her hands and kissed him. His body worked smooth as a river back and forth through her. She ran her arms down over his back, greedy for his strength. Something was falling into her eyes.

"We are breaking the hut."

Richard straightened up onto his knees. They had rocked up against the brush wall. She slid on her back after him into the middle of the hut. He bent over her again, he fumbled between them, trying to reconnect them.

"I know there's a hole here someplace."

At the first thrust she cried out. She clung to him, arching her back. He packed her full. She shut her eyes, bursting with him. "Maria," he whispered. His arms gripped her. "My angel. My baby. My star. Love me. Love me." Under her hands his back sprang with sweat. Sweat dripped from his beard. They kissed. Her hair around them like a web, she locked her arms around him, and he shuddered and gasped and drove once more into her and lay still.

After a moment he said, "Am I too heavy?"

"No." She did not want him to move.

He did anyway, sliding down beside her, and braced himself upon one elbow. He drew his fingertip in a line from her breastbone to her navel. "We shouldn't have done that, we have a long way to go, and they're probably ahead of us again."

Sunshine flooded in through the broken roof, streaming with dust motes, and Maria sneezed again. Her body felt voluptuous from lying with him.

"Now I'm hungry," he said. "Where is the bread?"

"In my saddle pouch."

He got the loaf, found his knife in the litter of leaves and clothes, and cut the bread in half. "You think Anne poisoned Roger."

"In Agato, mark, when they thought you were dying, they were very keen Roger should have Marna."

He ate. His eyes were smoky. "You never told me that before."

She shrugged. She ate some of the bread. Richard said,

478

"I don't believe it. He has never liked any woman enough to listen to her."

"He is faithless."

"But not to me. He was never faithless to me." He put on his ruined hose. "God damn him, he is my brother."

She got up and groped around the half-destroyed hut for her shift. The breeze through the broken roof touched her breast like a hand. She put her clothes on. He said, "Rahman is always telling me you are frail. You're strong as a horse." His smile broadened with malice. "The strong end of the horse, too.'"

Maria snapped her fingers in his face. He snatched for her and she stuffed his shirt into his hands.

"I have never betrayed you," he said. He pulled the shirt on over his head. "Even when you were gone so long in Birnia. I have never fucked another woman."

"Who else would let you?"

He grunted. "You'd be surprised." He found his belt.

Maria gathered up her hair and plaited it in a thick rope. They went out of the hut. Their horses were grazing at the far end of the sweep of grass, near the edge of the wood. Maria and Richard went toward them. Halfway across the meadow, he reached out his hand, and she took it.

"Now I know why I prefer you to Anne," he said.

THEY RODE ON across the hills all the rest of the day and half the night, working their way west along the defiles above the green valleys where the shepherds summered their flocks. Clogged with rocks and thickets, the thorny wood resisted their passage like an enemy. The rain started again. They stopped to rest until dawn and went on again.

Twice the next day they saw riders in the distance. Once they heard a horn blasting, far off in the direction they had come. Richard's horse went lame. When it could no longer keep up with the black horse, he killed it and cut out its heart, and they ate the blood-soaked raw meat. They climbed down a series of steep hillsides into the lowland wood. In the afternoon, while they were leading the black horse to save its strength, an arrow came from nowhere and whapped into the ground between them, but they never saw the bowman. At last, late at night, they came to Castelmaria.

Richard banged on the gate. There was no answer. Maria got down from the horse and tried the postern door, which was latched on the inside. Richard swore. He pounded on the gate with his fist.

"Who's there?"

"Marna!"

A head popped over the wall, startled. "My lord. I didn't see you—"

"Well, you do now," Richard shouted. "Get this gate open before I—"

The head disappeared. Ropes squeaked beyond the gate, and the latch rattled. The gate swung inward. "My lord, I—"

Richard thrust past him. "Get William the German."

Maria started across the ward toward the kitchen. She heard the porter say, "My lord, they've gone to the shrine —"

"Who's in command here?"

She broke into a trot down the little path into the kitchen. The door was shut fast, and she opened the little window in it, reached through, and undid the latch. Her stomach was knotted up with hunger. Wrenching the door open, she went down into the darkness and warmth of the kitchen.

When Richard came in she was sitting on the pantry floor, eating bread and cheese. He sank down beside her and she handed him the jug of milk. Silent, they finished the rest of the cheese between them.

"My lord?" someone called, in the kitchen. The voice was uncertain.

"In here," Richard said, around a mouthful. He shoved the milk at her. "Can't you find me something to drink besides baby food?"

Maria tore a loaf of bread in half. A knight tramped into the pantry door. Richard turned to him.

"I want double sentries on the walls. Rouse out the Knights' Tower. Forty men to patrol the road and the wilderness back toward Iste and bring in anybody they

480

find." He swallowed with difficulty and crammed bread into his mouth. "Shut the gate in the curtain wall."

"My lord." The knight saluted briskly. He took a step toward the door, his face turned toward them. "My lord, who is our enemy?"

"My brother Roger."

The knight went out. Maria followed him into the kitchen for a lamp. His voice rose, excited, in the ward. Other voices called out. The kitchen door banged open, and two scullions came in, yawning. She sent one for wine and went back into the pantry.

"Do you think he'll attack us here?"

He shook his head. "He had only one chance, to catch us in Iste or on the way here. Now he has no chance at all. He's stupid, you know." His voice was bitter. "He's a very stupid man."

"Mama?" Stephen looked in the door.

Maria got up; he came to her, and she hugged him. He turned so he could see his father. "Why did you come here? I thought you were in Iste. Can I go home now?"

Maria sat down again. She wrapped her arms around her knees. "We were in Iste—we—"

"Roger betrayed me," Richard said. "Roger tried to kill me." The scullion brought in a big pitcher of wine, and he drank from the edge. He wiped his mouth on his sleeve.

Stephen stared at him a moment. "Mama?" he said, unsure, and turned to Maria. The scullion hung in the doorway, intent.

Maria took the pitcher of wine. She watched Richard pack another chunk of bread and cheese into his mouth. She said, "He'll escape, won't he? To Anne's country."

"Maybe. If he does, Bunny will help me hunt him down."

"What will you do to him then, Gripe?"

His head swiveled toward her. He gulped down the food. "Why, I'll kill him, Maria. What did you think?" He got up and went out of the pantry.

She got up, shaking the crumbs off her skirts. "Mary Mother, I'm tired." Her voice trembled.

Stephen caught her arm. "Mama. What happened?"

"What he said. Roger tried to seize us, to take Marna, and we held the baby hostage and they let us go." She hobbled out into the kitchen. Stephen clung to her like a child. The kitchen was full of people. In the darkness she saw only eyes and wet mouths. She said, "They hounded us here all the way across the wilderness—if they had caught us, they would have killed us." She went out into the ward.

He took her arm and helped her across to the door. The ward was swarming with knights and servants and horses. The gate banged open. Men rode out in a double column. The noise made her head pound. Her son opened the door for her. Gratefully she went into the cool quiet of the stairwell. Stephen helped her up to the top room.

"Mama, are you all right?"

"I'm just tired." She sank down on the bed. When she thought of it, the incident in Iste seemed to have taken place in another life. She spread out her arms across the bed, forgetting that Stephen was still there.

"I hate him," Stephen said, in a choked voice. "I hate him. I hate Roger. I hate him." He banged out the door; she heard him running down the stairs.

IN THE MORNING she went to Mass in the village, to thank God for preserving them from Roger. Afterward, with her two maids beside her, she rode up toward the castle again. The fallow meadows on either side of the road were a flood of yellow wildflowers, belly-high to the horses. Clouds of butterflies hovered over them. The sun lay warm on her arms, and she pulled her sleeves up to her elbows.

A pack of horsemen waited before the gate in the curtain wall. They split apart to let her pass through their midst. Most were Christian knights, but in the gateway itself, Ismael stood with his mare's hoof braced up on his knee. When she dismounted, he turned and flung his arms around her in a flamboyant embrace.

"Maria." He stood back, his face glowing. "We come much fast."

"You must have. Is Robert with you?" She pulled her

482

reins over the mare's head. "Come up to the castle with me."

"No, no. I go. Robert make horse for me. I go many place of brother." He flung his arm up to shade his face. "Much more on, I come back."

The women called to her; they were halfway up the road. She waved to Ismael and walked after them. In the middle of the ward, surrounded by people, Robert was stripping the saddle from an exhausted horse. She came in the gate, and he brushed past the knights and servants around him and hurried over to her.

"Mother." He kissed her cheek. "How could Uncle Roger do this to us?"

Maria put her arm around his waist. "I don't know. God must be punishing us. Or him." She looked up at him; his blue eyes were vivid in his Saracen-dark face.

Over his shoulder, he called, "Joseph, take that horse to Ismael-Malik, at the curtain wall." He lowered his voice to her. "Mother, what happened? What did you fight over?"

She stepped back. Stephen was walking across the ward toward them. Robert saw him, and she got out of their way.

"Robert," Stephen said, and stuck out his hand. Robert clasped it. In his mail he looked much the older. Abruptly they embraced each other.

"Ah, Stephen—"

Maria left them alone. She went up into the New Tower. Richard had gone off to ride the road to Iste, to harry back the men who had harried him. She climbed the stairs to the hall, which the servants were just sweeping, and went to the window overlooking the ward.

Robert and Stephen were still standing in the middle of the ward, talking. She sat down in the narrow shaft of sunlight cutting through the window. The serving women brought in fresh rushes and opened them over the floor. The rushes smelled of the rosemary dried with them.

The two young men came into the hall, and the girls all paused. The older women swatted them giggling back to work. Maria laughed. She was glad the girls thought her sons worth looking at. She watched Robert cross the room, wondering if he were still a virgin. Stephen came up beside her, but Robert stoppped at the table to pour himself a cup of wine.

"Mother," he called. "What started them fighting?"

Stephen raised his voice to send the servants out of the hall. Maria glanced at him, intrigued. Robert came up to her, a cup of wine in either hand. He held one out to her.

"There is no water, so Stephen doesn't get any."

The wine was whole. Maria put the cup on the floor. "Tell me what the rumor says."

"That Uncle Roger tried to murder you at the christening." His voice weakened on the word, and he licked his lips. He coiled himself down on his heels beside her. "Tell me the truth."

"That's the truth. It was a plot. They did not quarrel. Roger was kind as a mother to us, the night before."

Robert drank his wine in three long gulps. "Here, Stephen, get me some more, will you?" He handed his brother the cup. Stephen's shoulders hunched, but he said nothing, and he took Maria's wine with him. Robert said, "Where is Papa?"

"Halfway to Iste. I hope he comes back tonight, I have no wish to wait up for him.'"

"Is he really angry?"

"Now, what do you think?"

Stephen came back with a cup for each of them. He had mixed her wine with water. "Thank you," she said.

"So there will be a war," Robert said softly, excited. "We'll fight Uncle Roger."

"Papa thinks he will stand at Iste," Stephen said. "Papa will move up the valley, the Brotherhood will come down from the mountains. Duke Henry blocks him in the east."

"Oh, tactics. Leave that to Papa." Robert stood up. "Are you going with us, Stephen?"

Getting up behind him, Stephen held his long hauberk by the sleeves while Robert hauled it off over his head. The mail rang continually like little bells. Robert said, "It's not like training, you'll like it. Come with us."

He and Stephen laid the hauberk down across a chair. They touched it reverently. Robert put his swordbelt

484

down on top of it. Maria had never before noticed him to do anything carefully.

"Well," Stephen said, "there are other things to do, you know."

Robert whacked him on the arm. "No. Tell me, hakim."

Stephen flushed, his gaze pinned to the floor. Maria said nothing, curious to see how long he would let Robert tease him. He said, "Well, someone will have to . . . take care of Mama. And rule."

Robert roared with laughter. "Stephen, King of Marna."

Stephen chewed his lips. Maria got up. They had to let the servants back in. "Robert, come, let me find you a place to sleep. And Stephen has errands."

"Errands. Stephen the Serf King of Marna. I thought all he did was read books." Carrying his mail coat and his sword, he started to the door.

Maria rumpled Stephen's hair. She and Robert climbed the stairs to the top floor, where Stephen slept. "Will you kill each other if you stay here?" The girls had not yet cleaned this room, and it was awash with Stephen's clothes, books, and saddle gear.

"Mama." Robert touched her. "Can't we do something? Arrange for Papa and Uncle Roger to meet?"

Maria shook her head. For a moment they stared at each other. At last he looked away. She said, "Don't suggest it to your father, Robert." She went downstairs again.

Stephen was sprawled in his chair in the hall, eating off his fingernails and staring at the wall. The sun was going down. She took a long taper and lit it at the candle at the end of the hall so that she could light the lamps. A knight came in and spoke to Stephen, who answered him in a handful of words and sent him off.

"I suppose everything is well at Mana'a," she said, "or your brother would have told us."

Stephen did not answer. She came up to light the lamp in the bracket over his head. "I am accustomed to being listened to."

"Oh. I'm sorry, Mama."

She looked down at him. His hair was a darker brown than Richard's. "What did you do with that sword I gave you?"

"I've worked with it." Abruptly he sat up straight. "Did you put Robert in my room?"

"Yes. I—"

"My books." He bolted out the door, and she heard him racing up the stairs, calling to Robert.

THE DAWN WHITENED the sky. Maria dismounted in front of the church and gave her reins to a knight. Richard's men packed the road through the village and overflowed into the meadows along the river. The voices of the captains cracked in the still, cold air. Richard reined his horse in. The banner stirred heavily against its staff, and the big stallion shied from it.

Stephen came out of the church. Maria, waiting on the porch, stopped him and kissed him, and he went to his horse. He had no mail; he wore a leather tunic studded with iron. He mounted, stirrup to stirrup with his father. In his mail Richard looked twice heavier than Stephen. The boy spoke to him and he responded with a gesture.

Robert came out the door of the church, in his hand his sword wrapped in its belt.

"Mother." He hugged her hard. "Pray for me."

"I will. Serve God, Robert." She kissed him.

Turning back toward the open door, he genuflected and crossed himself. A horn blew. Robert went to his horse. The columns of armored men started off through the village. Richard backed his horse up. He raised his hand to her. His horse carried him into the middle of the army, and he reined it clear and galloped up toward the head of the road. The boys followed him. Maria stood on the porch watching them go. Robert turned twice to wave to her, but Stephen never looked back at all.

XLVI

JILLY SCREAMED, "MAMA, EVERYTHING IS COVERED WITH blood!"

Maria lifted her eyes across the walls of the cathedral. Her daughter's piercing voice rang in the dome over her head. On all the walls, there were red-smeared crosses, like grotesque stick figures. She followed the monk up the center aisle. Pools of red lay drying on the tile floor. The altar and the sanctuary were splashed with the stuff, and trails of red footprints ran all over the cathedral. She crossed herself. The damage turned her stomach, like spoiled food.

"Mama." Jilly ran after her, Henry and Jordan and their nurse galloping behind, noisy as a herd. "It's blood, Mama—isn't it? Mama, I'm afraid!" She caught hold of Maria's arm.

"It's paint," Maria said. "Stop screaming or go wait in the cart." She turned to the monk at her elbow. "Is there any other—is it just the paint?"

"They tried to break down the door into the vestibule." The monk led her on across the cathedral. Behind her the children shrieked again. Maria fisted her hands, her nerves milled ragged.

The monk showed her the splintered wooden door. A splash of red paint covered the chewed wood and the lock.

Maria started to touch it, but let her hand fall to her side. It was disgusting. It was frightening. "I will send to my brother William, it's his cathedral." The children clattered up to her. Their racket made her angry, and she chased them away from her. "Have the watch post a man here at night," she told the monk.

"My lady, if you will permit it, we should lock the place—"

"No. It's a church, you can't lock people out of a church. Whoever did this—" she took her eyes from the red ruined door. "A guard will scare them off."

"They are all swine," the monk said, in some heat.

Jilly took Maria's hand. "Mama. It's awful." She rubbed herself like a cat along Maria's side.

"Yes." She signed to the monk to open the broken door. They went into the vestibule. The raped cathedral pressed on her mind. "Who are all swine?"

"The Saracens, my lady." The monk looked surprised. "Who else did it? You'll pardon my boldness, but if we had not treated them like decent Christians—"

"Do you have any witnesses?"

"Someone saw them in the market place, afterward—"

The children raced out into the garden, and she followed them, grateful for the warmth of the sun. The monk padded along at her elbow.

"Talk to the three-armed beggar," Maria said. "He's always somewhere around, he must have seen something. Find out who did this and bring them to me."

In the garden, Jordan howled. Jilly screamed, "Give me that," and snatched for something in his hand. Maria separated them and spanked Jilly. "Jordan, go tell the groom I am coming."

The redheaded child ran off toward the garden gate. She lifted Henry in her arms. Turning to the monk, she said, "It should be easy to find out where the paint came from, too."

"My lady," the monk said, "you could choose any dozen of them off the street. They are all guilty, they all have done it in their minds."

Maria stared at him a moment. She knew he was right. She went down the brick path toward the gateway. "Find me the ones who did it with their hands."

Jordan strode importantly along the fence. The groom led up the cart, and the children scrambled over the wheel into it. They dragged the nurse groaning and complaining up after them. Maria mounted her horse.

488

There were still people in the market place, although it was early afternoon and the merchants had closed their stalls and gone home to eat dinner. When she rode around the corner into their view, the crowd cheered and hurried over and escorted her up the street, screaming to her in the Mana'an tongue she could not understand. It was easy to guess what they were saying: the Saracens who heard them were all running the other way. Silent, her eyes straight ahead of her, Maria rode up from the harbor toward the palace.

Jordan ran to get Rahman. Maria went to the little hall. A knight stood in the sunlight coming through the window, looking out at the garden. When she came in and he turned, she saw it was one of Richard's messengers.

"Michael," she said, "God's greeting. How is my husband?"

"He is well, my lady." He knelt down gracefully in front of her and kissed her hand. "He charged me to tell you that he is laying siege now to Iste itself."

"Are my sons still with him?"

"They are all at Iste, my lady—my lord Robert and Stephen Clerk and Ismael-Malik. They told me to bring you their greetings. The fighting has been heavy—" His face lit with enthusiasm. "It's been a great work, thus far, full of glory and mighty deeds on both sides."

She scratched her nose, thinking of the cathedral. This knight Michael was a handsome boy, tawny-haired, with a wide, elegant mouth. "What else did he say?" A page came in with a tray of drinks and food for the knight. "Eat."

The knight took the nearest cup. "He wants rope and mules, iron, cloth, carpenters—" He sipped the sherbet; a lemon moustache appeared on his upper lip. "Twenty thousand ricardi—"

Maria grunted. "This great work is dear." Rahman came in from the corridor, his perfume announcing him. Jordan trotted along beside him. "Michael, I will send for you later." She turned on Rahman. "Your people have defiled my cathedral."

The Saracen's thick eyebrows rose. He clasped his hands before him. "I can assure you, none of my tribe would soil himself by touching a place of Christian ritual."

489

"My lady," the young knight said, his voice taut, "what new wickedness is this?"

"Leave me, Michael." She frowned at him, and he went out of the room. She glared at Rahman. "It was a vile, stupid act."

His eyes closed, and he nodded. "Yes. Not all vile, stupid men are Christian."

"This is how you repay us for keeping faith with you," she said. She paced around him, her eyes on his face. "When we need you most, you stab us in the back."

Rahman's lips tightened. After a moment he looked away from her. "My lord's treacherous brother is a Christian. People think—"

"I am a Christian, too."

The Saracen moved away from her. The page brought him the tray of sweetmeats and cakes. "Yes, that has caused me no end of harm."

"Richard is a Christian."

Rahman swung back toward her. His eyes glistened with triumph. "It is widely known even among Christians that Richard of Marna in his heart accepts the truth of Islam." His lips curved into a nasty smile. "Do you deny it?"

"You know him little, Rahman. Richard believes in nothing."

Rahman's smile slipped a notch. "No soul is that pure." Taking a sweet he poked the page on the shoulder. "Serve this woman."

The page crossed the little space between them. Jordan lingered nearby, standing on one leg, his eyes unfocused in a daydream. Maria took a cup of the sherbet. "Leave us, both of you. Jordan, stay by the door." The two boys went out.

"The fighting goes well, one surmises?" Rahman asked.

"I suppose so. I don't understand those things."

"It's a grace in you. You should cultivate it."

"Tchah." She moved over into the sunlight. "If I weren't here, what chaos would you cause? We should double the watch in the city at night. Put guards in the Christian places."

Rahman bowed his head. "As you wish."

"I suppose we must watch the mosques, too," she said reluctantly.

"We cannot allow Christians in our sanctuaries."

"Then guard them with Saracens."

Rahman smiled at her. The sunlight from the window caught green on one of his rings. "I shall."

"But if you catch anyone, Christian or Saracen, I shall judge him." She walked up and down across the room. Jordan poked his head in the door and she sent for a messenger. The fair young knight Michael attracted her and she decided to keep him in her service. Rahman stood over his chessboard, a little onyx archer in his manicured hand.

"You've heard from Stephen." She knew they were playing chess by letter.

"That's my concern."

Maria sat down in the chair behind the white side of the game "This knight says Richard wants twenty thousand ricardi." The archers' long diagonal swoop across the board fascinated her, but she liked the little horses best, with their fiery leaps.

"Twenty thousand ricardi," Rahman said. "We'll have to guard it strongly through the mountains."

"He said something about sailing up the coast to a port in Santerois."

Rahman took the black archer off the board and put the white Vizier in its place. "It seems circuitous."

She said, "The Venetians owe us much. Talk to them about doing it."

Rahman bowed. "As you wish."

Henry rushed in the door, gave a glad cry, and hurried up to Rahman. The Saracen recoiled. "No, no. Not here." He shook his hands at the little boy; Maria laughed. She took the child in her arms. Jordan and a dark-haired knight came in.

"Rahman, you have errands?"

The Saracen sniffed at her and paced out of the room, his white robes folded like wings around him. Maria turned to the young knight. "Go to the cathedral, see what has been done there, and tell my lord William in Birnia." Henry squirmed impatiently in her arms. Putting him down, she went off to arrange Richard's supplies.

THE WATCH FOUND the half dozen Saracen boys who had attacked the cathedral. They were exposed in the market place for three days. Before the watch cut them down, at noon on the third day, the mob half-killed them; only one could walk away.

Maria picked up her reins. The watch captain was standing beside her horse. She said, "Get a cart to take them back to their homes." The six boys lay exhausted on the steps of the cathedral. Two women wept and hugged them: their mothers. In the market place the shifting Christian crowd called names and threw things at them.

William strode out of the cathedral and walked down to the foot of the steps. He had arrived only that morning. His enormous escort filled the side street beside the cathedral, by the garden gate. He came up to her and swung himself heavily into his saddle.

"They are ugly people, these Mana'ans."

"Can you fix the walls? What are you going to do?"

"What I have always meant to do: paint the inside. This makes no difference to me, only to God."

Maria rode forward. William's roan horse walked along beside her. Already many of the merchants were closing up their stalls. Over near the harbor a man stood on an empty booth and screamed and waved his arms. Many people were cheering him on. The boys in their cart rumbled away. William's knights poured out of the side street. An important voice shouted, and the knights ranged themselves around her and William.

The big knight was smiling at her. "Maria, where are you taking me?"

She looked innocently into his face. Ahead, the street climbed steeply toward the 'Aliqbet Mosque, like a round white stone above the groves of cypress on the hill. She led the train of knights up the right side of the street. Saracens before their houses stopped talking to watch them pass. The knights' commander rode up for orders.

"My lord, where are we going?"

"There." Maria pointed to the mosque.

William held one hand up to stop his men. "My sister, tell me what you are doing."

"Last night someone tried to break in there. Christians."

492

He pulled on his chin. "And the Saracens caught them and will not give them up?"

"Yes."

He nodded to the captain, and the other knight rode off toward the head of the column. They climbed the hillside, their horses at a walk. The cypress blocked the wind. Maria looked behind her: the full curve of the bay spread out below them, and half the city, veined in the green of its gardens and orchards.

They were coming to the mosque. Before they reached it, several men came out the front doors onto the court. Rahman was among them. Maria drew rein, and all the knights stopped. They gawked at the mosque and the sweeping view of Mana'a around them. Maria chewed her lip. Eight of the most important Saracens in the city were staring at her from before the mosque. Most of them were friends of Richard's.

"Maybe I should do this," William said.

"I wish you would." These men hated her.

William put up one hand to hold his knights where they were. He and Maria rode forward. The wind cooled her face and tugged at her coif. The eight Saracens stood before the mosque in a little group, their faces grim. Maria dismounted and walked forward into the lee of the mosque, out of the wind.

"Rahman," William said. "She says you have some prisoners of ours." He folded his hands on the pommel of his saddle.

Rahman clearly wished he were elsewhere. The old black man beside him was the chief Imam. He gave Maria a single poisonous look and turned his gaze away. Rahman said, "We have no prisoners, William. She is only trying to make trouble for me."

"He lies." Maria glanced up at the big knight on his horse beside her. "If nothing has happened, why is he here?"

William's colorless eyes flickered. The old Imam spoke to Rahman, who answered him, adding an oily bow.

"Rahman," Maria said, "you mark, if you do not give them up, I will take the Imam prisoner and hold him hostage until you do."

The Saracen directly behind the old man started, his

face coloring: clearly he understood French. The Imam did not. William said, nervously, "Now, Maria."

The old Imam spoke again. The other Saracens murmured in agreement. Rahman put one hand to his beard. His eyes stabbed at William.

"The Imam says he will discuss this matter after that unseemly woman has removed herself."

William hooted with laughter. He twisted his vast bulk in his saddle and lifted one arm to his men. The knights loped forward around them, spraying gravel against the wall of the mosque. The Saracens stood frozen in their places. One cried out indignantly. The knights' commander barked orders in his excellent voice.

"You forgot I speak Saracen, Rahman," William said. "Or perhaps I heard him better than you did?"

The Imam whirled and seized Rahman by the arm and shook it and shouted. Rahman looked around him at the knights. The other Saracens joined in scolding him. Suddenly he snarled at them, and they fell silent, abashed, even the Imam.

"Willliam," Rahman said, "you see what an embarrassment she is. If she does as she threatens, you will have as great a war in Mana'a as you do in Iste."

"All I want is those prisoners," William said. "Your friends are willing to give them up."

Rahman shrugged. He turned as if to view the wide bay spread out below them. Maria waited a moment; she had to admire his poise. She said, "William, someone will have to carry the Imam," and Rahman thrust out one hand.

"I will bring the prisoners to the palace."

William smiled. The wind tore at his clothes. "Then will take this old man there, until you do."

The Saracen who understood French leaned forward and whispered to the Imam. Gray-black, the old man's face turned toward Maria, stiff with hate. He spoke to Rahman again.

Rahman and William were staring at one another. William's eyes were half-closed. He looked amused by the game. Rahman said, "Do not risk this, William. When my lord hears of it, he will be displeased."

"Yes," Maria said, "with you."

Rahman shot her a murderous look. At last he walked

494

away toward the mosque. At a nod from William, the knights drew back to let him pass. The other Saracens relaxed. Their eyes went curiously to the knights around them. The Imam stood kneading his fingers together. Maria went to her horse and took the charter from her basket.

"William," she said; she went up to his stirrup again. "Tell him this must be translated and read three times a day for three days, in all the mosques, before prayers."

William spoke to him. The Imam's face turned acid, and he would not take the charter from her, he signed to the man behind him to take it. Rahman was coming back. Five of his Saracen soldiers followed, half-dragging the four Christians, bruised and wrapped in chains.

Maria mounted her horse. The wind brushed her cheek. She wiped her face with her fingers. She went back down the hillside, the Christians herded before them. William rode over beside her.

"That was the charter permitting errors?"

She nodded. "I thought it might make them happier."

He coughed, amused. "You are as bad as Richard sometimes. Have you heard that the old priest died in Rome? So I'm going to be a bishop after all. How did Richard talk me into this? Where is he?"

"They are all at Iste now."

William shook his head. They came to the foot of the hill. The street led them through the spice market. She saw that even here, deep inside the Saracen quarter, many of the vendors had not opened their little cupboard-sized shops. The city seemed quieter than usual. A score of people was already following her in the street.

They took the prisoners to the cathedral square and hung them up where the Saracen boys had been. The crowd that gathered hissed at her and William. The big knight scowled.

"Ugly people."

She had the charter permitting errors read in all the churches of Marna, except of course Iste. In Mana'a the Christians left the cathedral and went around the streets beating the Saracens and burning whatever they could set on fire. William's hundred knights and the city watch could not master them. Rahman brought in over a thousand Saracen footsoldiers. With the fires spreading through the Christian quarter, Maria was afraid to stop him. Twenty Christians were killed, but the Saracens cleared the streets. That night no fires burned, although the air still reeked of smoke.

The next day dragged by. Everybody loitered in the ward waiting for news from the city. Crowds milled before the gates into the palace. She fought with Rahman, Jilly, and the cook; everybody seemed intent on provoking her temper. But the city stayed calm, and the next day the city stayed calm, and slowly her household stopped cluttering the ward, and the crowds thinned to a scattering and drifted away. Richard sent requiring more money and more rope. Jilly and Jordan brought a pony into the hall, and it broke a vase of Rahman's. Maria went out alone again into Mana'a.

She went to see William, to ask his advice about a trial of law. His workmen were building scaffolding along the inside walls so they could paint over the damage. He walked up beside her when she came into the cathedral and took hold of her arm.

"Come into the garden."

She knew there was something wrong. She followed him out through the vestibule. The sky was cloudy, and she smelled rain coming. Two huge cats sprawled on the brick walk between the roses: William cultivated all the harbor cats. She looked up into the fat man's face.

"What's the matter?"

He turned away from her. "Roger has tried to make contact with me."

Maria's heart jumped. She could think of nothing to say. He had always loved Roger. He drew away from her. He stood idly rubbing his palms together. Around them lay the bright color-work of the flowers.

Eventually, she said, "Do you think they could mend it?"

"No." He shook his head. "Can they change the color of their eyes? This will end in a death."

He put his hands to his face. Maria trembled, wishing she could console him. The big knight before her made no sound. Eventually, composed again, he lowered his hands.

"Has he come to you yet?"

496

"I pray God he does not do me the insult," she said.

"Well, he did try to kill you. I can see your reasons." Suddenly he was easy again, hidden in his fat. "I have never been overfond of the men who tried to kill me. Except when I think that they failed." He erupted into laughter and strode away. Maria went slowly out through the cathedral.

She stopped in the market place to buy some cakes for the children. Half a dozen ships were in from Africa and Venice and Acre, and the vendors were hawking new goods. She lingered, enjoying the constant movement, the people arguing and bartering, the dhows and the surf and the sea gulls. Finally she went on.

"Mah-eee-yah!"

She waved.

THE CURVED STREET around the palace was packed so thick with folk she could not force a way through. No one seemed to be fighting. On the iron balconies above her, women were standing up to see whatever was going on. There was a sudden boisterous cheer, and she heard Stephen's name shouted.

She reined the mare around and wedged a way between a building and the people. A column of knights was riding toward her. In their midst Stephen was twisted in his saddle to shout to someone in the crowd. Maria ranged up before him, and his horse stopped.

"Mama." He leaned down from his horse to kiss her.

"Stephen," she said. "You are wearing mail." She put her hand on his metal shoulder.

"Yes. Isn't it beautiful?" His hand stroked down the chainlink shirt. "It's really Robert's," he said, his voice confidential. "I haven't won my own yet. Isn't it a beauty?"

Maria shook her head. She pulled him down again to hug him. Over his shoulder, she saw a litter coming along the street. Its red and blue curtains were drawn tight.

Stephen called out. The column started forward again. Maria held her horse beside his, screwed around in her saddle to watch the litter. Someone in the crowd shouted, and Stephen answered in Saracen.

497

"It's Anne, isn't it?" she said, when he faced her again.

"Yes."

"Why has he sent her to me? I have enemies here already to last me my life."

"We took all of Iste but the citadel—she was there. We had to do something with them."

She glanced once more at the litter. They rode through the park up toward the palace. The chain mail drew her eye again. "Did you fight?"

"Yes. Three times." He shook his head. "Mama, I was so afraid. Everything happened so fast—it was awful, Mama." He cast his eyes down. "Papa had to save me once."

Maria crossed herself, relieved.

"Robert goes right into the middle. He's always in the middle."

"I did not want to know that, Stephen."

They went up through the pine trees. Ahead, the towers stood like pillars of the sky. She said, "Why did he send you back? Did you capture her?"

"Oh." He puffed himself up. "I'm supposed to find out about the cathedral and the riot."

"Rahman must have told you."

"Yes, but Papa says it is a lie."

Maria laughed. They rode through the gatehouse. A shower of small stones rained down on them from the arch. Stephen turned to look up.

Jilly shrieked. "Stephen! Stephen!" She hurled herself down from the gate into his arms. Jordan climbed across the scrolled stone of the arch toward the rampart steps. Maria dismounted. The litter came up into the ward. She untied the curtain strings and held them back.

"Anne," she said. "Come out, you are here now."

The close litter smelled like a baby. A nurse got out, took the child, and stepped back. Maria held out her hand, but Anne struck it aside. She climbed out of the litter. Her clothes were crumpled and stained. She was fat; her chin and her cheekbones had disappeared beneath her flesh. When she looked at Maria, her mouth tightened to nothing.

"You are tempting me," Maria said. "I told you I am vindictive."

Anne turned away. Stephen was giving orders to his knights, sending them this way and that around the palace. Maria crossed the paved ward to a door, Anne and her maid behind her.

They went into the palace. Gold lamps lit the rooms. They walked through the spacious, carpeted rooms, past servants and petitioners, people waiting to see other people. Anne stared around them. Maria saw how she tried to straighten her clothes and smooth out her face.

Rahman was coming toward them, flanked by a Saracen scribe and one of the chancellors. He veered off to one side to pass them. His eyes studiously straight before him, he lifted one hand to Maria. She answered him with a gesture. They went down the stairs and around a corner to the room in the Tower of the Cross where the boys had once slept, where Roger had lived when he lived in Mana'a.

"Here," Maria said. "You will have this room." She stood aside to let Anne go by her. Anne stood just inside the door. Her eyes took in the room, its light-filled windows, and the low Saracen furniture.

"You see," Maria said. "We are good robbers. Better than you. I will give you three people to serve you. You will eat here, too. I don't know what Richard means for you and your baby, but if you make trouble for me—"

Anne walked forward two steps and turned to face her. Maria met her eyes. The hot impulse filled her to leap on Anne and scratch her face and rip off her clothes. She went hastily out into the corridor and pulled the door shut behind her.

XLVII

❦

THE TWO FIGHTING COCKS HURTLED TOGETHER ACROSS
the sand pit. With screams the Saracens around them
urged them on. Blood spurted from the whirling white
feathers. The birds screeched. Maria leaned forward to
see. The cocks' racket cut through the howls of the men.
Abruptly, the white cock flopped in the dust, spraying
blood across the dirt. The red cock's handler scooped up
his champion and paraded him at arm's length over his
head. All around the alleyway, voluble, the men turned to
paying off their bets.

Maria held out her hand, and Stephen gave her a ricardus. She tossed it to the beggar loitering nearby.

"I'm a good judge of a fighting cock," she said. "I
usually win. Bet on the next." She recognized the little
cock they were bringing up to fight; she had won with him
before.

"Mama, you will make me poor. Come back to the
palace."

She turned her mare out into the street. They rode at a
walk down the narrow sloping pavement. Behind them,
the ringkeeper called in his shrill voice for bets.

"Have you seen the messenger from Iste yet?" she said.

Stephen nodded. He reined his horse toward hers to
avoid a train of donkeys coming up the hillside toward
them. "Papa wants me to come back. He says I am the
only one who listens to his orders."

Maria watched him through the tail of her eye. His
eyes and the shape of his face were Richard's, his coloring, even his long hands. They passed the Saracen mon-
eyers' where Richard had all his money made.

"What is it like? Do you fight every day? I've always been told sieges are boring."

"Robert thinks they are. Uncle Roger attacks us every few days—something happens in one place, and we go to see, and in three other places Roger's men break out and fight. Papa calls it a Saracen defense." He smiled at her. "He says that's a trick that doesn't work."

Maria thought of Rahman and laughed. They were riding through a place where rich men lived. Some of the walled houses, above their sweeping parks, were as large as the palace.

"When are you leaving, then?"

"Tonight," he said. "It's too hot to ride in the day-time."

"You could stay another day," she said. "A few more days."

"Papa wants me back."

Maria looked away, angry; Richard had never wanted him around before. They rode out into the hot white street again, past one of the big public baths. Men in veils stood around the entrance, their eyes painted with kohl.

"Roger wants to fight," Stephen said. "He and Papa, hand to hand. Just the two of them. Papa will not. He's lame again, you know; when he rides his leg hurts."

She looked around at him. "Does he ride much?"

Stephen smiled. "Well, sometimes he sleeps on the ground."

"God's blood," she said. "He's cursed. He's driven."

"Robert offered to fight Uncle Roger, but Papa wouldn't let him, and they had an argument—just talk, but you should have heard them."

"Have they been fighting?" she said, alarmed.

Stephen shook his head. "No. Just that one time, they fought."

Maria braced her hands on her saddle. "Everything is coming apart." She lifted her head up. "What's going to happen when he takes him?"

Stephen said nothing. Their horses carried them up across the park.

"Does he talk about me? Does he miss me?"

"We all miss you, Mama."

"Good."

501

He shook his head, smiling. They went into the east ward, and she dismounted.

"I'll take your horse down." He bent and got her mare's reins and led it off. Maria went into the palace.

On her way through the Dragon Tower, Anne's page came to ask a hearing and Maria sent him back for her. The call to prayer sounded. The Saracens of her household assembled in the garden. Maria went to her hall. Rahman would be at his prayers; until he came she could not try the afternoon's cases.

Two women were spinning flax in the sunlight. She dismissed them, asking one to bring her the children. From the chest under the window she got her looking glass and fixed her coif. She thought of Robert, fighting with Richard; of course she fought with Richard constantly and little came of that. She would have to tell Stephen to tell Richard that she was pregnant again. She turned her head slightly, to see herself in the glass from her best angle. She liked her mouth, but her short nose was bony. She put the glass down.

Jilly and Henry rushed in, laughing, and danced around her. Maria hugged them. While they trod gleefully on her skirt and tried to trip her, she pulled the screen out from the wall. Jordan hurried in to help her. They put the matrah down on the floor beside the screen and Jilly brought over a cushion for Maria to sit on.

Panting, Henry's nurse arrived. Maria signed to her to wait by the wall. Jilly sat down cross-legged in front of her mother and lapsed into a daydream, while Henry carefully took off his shoes. Maria brushed Jilly's hair. Two lutenists and a fluteplayer came in, crossed to the alcove, and sat down behind the curtain to practice. She wanted one of the musicians to learn to play tambor, but they disdained it for a street instrument. Jordan leaned against her.

"Aunt, aren't you hungry yet?"

"Go find the Emir Rahman for me. He's probably somewhere with Stephen. When you've done that you can go to the kitchen and have them bring us all dinner."

He jumped up and ran out of the room, past Anne's page, who came up before Maria and bowed. "Madonna, my lady Anne is here."

"Tell her to come in." She smoothed down Jilly's hair over her shoulders. Fine as a web, it curled at the ends. "You have your father's hair, down to the root."

Anne in a yellow gown walked into the room; she clashed with the Saracen prayers on the walls. Her sullen maid carried the baby behind her. Anne settled herself in angles on the matrah opposite Maria.

"I will go at once to my petition, my lady, since we have no liking for one another. I want to go home to Santerois. My mother will pay a ransom for me and my son."

"You should have asked Richard. What did he say to you?"

Anne's face was white and slick as clay. She put her hand to her round throat. "He gave you no order?"

"No. Richard loves secrets, he never tells me anything. Did you speak to him?"

"I never saw him."

Maria raised her eyebrows. A thought ran into her mind, and she brushed Jilly's hair, musing. She did not care about the risk of Richard's temper if she could rid herself of Anne. "I might be able to arrange something— I have a messenger here now, from your cousin Duke Henry."

Anne's face brightened. She bent toward her. "My lady, if you would, Heaven have mercy on my lady."

"I will do what I can. I have not forgotten I am your son's godmother."

Rahman came into the room. Several of his pages brought him a matrah and spread it on the floor on the far side of the screen from Maria.

"Go," she said to Anne. "I'll talk to you later, after supper—no, you will sup with me."

Anne thanked her many times and left. Rahman sat on the other side of the screen, and Jilly went around to him, holding her hand across her face like a veil. Through the screen, Rahman said, "My lord will not like word of this, that you plot with the wife of his brother."

"Jilly, come here." Surely he had heard nothing. He was guessing. "I don't plot, Rahman."

"My lord will know of it."

Maria drew her daughter down against her. "You offend me when you bear lies to my husband."

503

"My lord will judge."

They sat in silence. Maria chewed the inside of her lip. The Duke's messenger was leaving in the morning. If Richard intercepted her, all the way from Iste, God wanted Anne to stay in Marna. Jordan ran in, breathless.

"Aunt, there's a messenger!"

"Bring him in."

WHILE SHE AND ANNE ate, they spoke seldom, of their children, or of the food. Anne had come alone. She looked curiously all around her at the star-covered ceiling, the furniture, the four servers who brought their food and gave them milk and sherbet. Maria held her hands out so that a maidservant could pour water over them, dried them, and nodded to the servants to go.

Anne's eyes turned up to the ceiling again. "It's beautiful, like an autumn night, all the stars twinkling."

"It's Saracen glass." Maria rose and went across the room to trim the lamps, to show off the ceiling at its best. "The Saracens think the stars show the future, they have names for all of them." Jordan came in. She stooped to listen to him.

"Aunt, Stephen is in the Tower of the Prophet. Someone is there reading."

Maria nodded. "Thank you. Stay in the antechamber. I left some cake for you." Rahman had given a farewell feast for Stephen, and they would be there all night, probably, talking, listening to poetry and music, and drinking. She went back to the table and sat down.

"The messenger leaves in the morning for Agato. A knight of mine will go with him to set the ransom. Give me a token that your mother will know."

Anne took a beryl ring from her hand. "I cannot find the proper thanks, my lady. You are most gracious to me, in truth I did not expect it."

Maria shook her head. "It is not done yet. If Richard catches us, we may both wish we were safely in the castle of Iste with Roger."

"Then why do you risk it?"

"To be rid of you."

The fair girl's puffy face hardened. "God's eyes. You are the only one of your whole clan who tells the truth."

Maria threw her head back. "Roger was light, when you met him, but he was no traitor."

"He betrayed me, too." Anne fisted her hands. "He left me in the street to be taken, like a—"

Whore, Maria thought, but did not say it. The other woman leaned toward her, her hands cupped before her.

"I want to go home. I'll do anything—I'll pay you anything."

Maria looked away. The stars twinkled in the ceiling overhead. She found Charles's Wain; as a child she had known some wish-poem on the star in its tail. She looked down at the beryl ring. "This is a pretty stone, so smooth." The clear yellow echoed the faint light of the lamps.

"It was my father's ring."

Maria laughed. "I knew him, a little—you know, he and Richard never got along either."

"My father was an upright man," Anne said sharply, "who got less than he deserved."

Maria shrugged. "I don't think we should talk of it. Are you comfortable where you are? Are you properly attended?"

"Yes, we are cared for."

They rose to their feet. Maria led the other woman toward the door. In the light from the lamps in the antechamber, they faced each other.

"Jordan," Maria said. She watched Anne's face. "Take my lady Anne to her chamber."

Roger's bastard came up beside her. She put her hand on the boy's shoulder. When she saw him, Anne started violently. At last she mumbled something and went out the door. Jordan followed her. Maria stood in the antechamber. The Saracen woman sat in one corner, Henry asleep in her lap.

"And that is al-Nasrani's wife."

"Don't call him that. The Christian in him did not sin."

"Perhaps not." The Saracen woman touched the little boy's hair. "But he will always be the Christian knight, to me."

Maria shook her head. She went out the door and

505

down the stairs, crossed the palace's ground floor to th
Dragon Tower, and let herself out through the poster
gate into the inner ward.

It was dark, although in the west, between the towers,
trace of red sky still showed. Maria walked along the edg
of the ward, where the vines perfumed the air. The firs
pip of the moon peeked above the shield of the moun
tains.

Someone came out of the Tower of the Prophet. Sh
turned her back to him. Gravel crunched under his feet
one of Rahman's guests come out to piss. The knight Mi
chael strode around the building before her, his silk sur
coat blue in the late light. He knelt.

"Madonna. Order me."

She gave him Anne's ring. "Tomorrow go to Santeroi
with the Duke's man." She glanced over her shoulder a
the Saracen squatting in the vines. He stood up, arranged
his robes, and went inside again. She turned to the knight.

"I expect the journey may take you through Iste, but i
you stay to yourself, no one there should recognize you."

The young knight gave her a slow smile. "Yes, Ma
donna. I understand."

"Michael. You are clever. From Agato go north to th
Castle of Becquis. Give the ring to the old Countess, anc
tell her I will take five thousand crowns in ransom for
Anne and the baby."

The young knight rattled off what she had said, word
for word. Carrying messages had taught him to memorize
Maria gave him a purse. "This will help you make your
way. Don't linger in Agato. If she thinks the ransom is
too much, ask her for four thousand."

Michael bowed over her hand again and went out of
the ward. In the Tower of the Prophet, quick music began
to a flutter of cymbals. She was forbidden to go in there,
although naturally she did, to show them they could not
keep her out. They did nothing worth spying on, for all
Rahman's secrecy. She turned back toward her own
tower, to go to her room and her empty bed. Suddenly,
thinking of Richard, she was so lonely she almost cried.

STEPHEN IN HIS GLISTENING MAIL made his horse dance. He circled Maria and came up on her right. "Mama, Rahman says it was you who threatened to seize the Imam, not William at all."

They rode down the path beneath the fir trees. A deer galloped away around the side of the hill. Maria said, "Rahman has a wonderful memory. It doesn't really matter now, anyway. Will you do what I said about the Jews in Iste?"

"Yes," he said impatiently. "I promise. Don't change the subject. Rahman says you and Anne are spinning up some plot together."

"Rahman, Rahman. Can't I hear anything else? You are leaving me alone and all you can do is talk about Rahman."

Stephen laughed at her. "You are in a guilty frame of mind." They rode on through the park. Suddenly he drew rein, and she stopped her mare and looked in the direction he was staring. Jilly and Jordan were crawling on their hands and knees playing horses in the sunlit park. Neighing, Jilly reared up and pawed at Jordan. Her long hair flew.

"You're going to have to do something about that," Stephen said.

"What do you mean?"

"Don't give me that stupid look, Mama."

She stared at him until he lowered his eyes, flushing. Down by the gate, his knights were drawn up in a double column. The porter was opening the other side of the gate so they could go through two abreast.

Stephen said, "Jordan's father betrayed us. I'm not going to treat him like my brother."

"Jordan is mine," Maria said.

Stephen looked away. His horse lowered its head and scratched the side of its face on its knee.

"Do you want to say something?" she asked.

"No." He gathered up his reins. Leaning forward, he kissed her cheek. "Good-bye, Mama."

"Stephen. Tell him I miss him."

"Mama, how can you say that—when you are plotting against him—"

507

"Stephen," she said, "go be virtuous." She drew her mare aside.

"Goody-bye, Mama."

He rode away down the last of the hillside, to join his men. Maria started toward the children in the park. Abruptly she reined in. He had said he wanted to leave at night—that it would be cooler to ride at night. She watched the knights trot out the gate, two by two. He had stayed for Rahman's party, naturally, but now here he was, riding off into the first heat of the morning.

She wheeled the mare again. Probably it was nothing. But she thought of the Saracen who had seen her in the ward with Michael, and her muscles tightened, as if at a shout of warning.

SHE WAS NOT SURPRISED, several days later, when Jordan said that Michael had returned, although he could not possibly have gotten to Santerois. Jordan had found her in the little hall, where she was working on her tapestry. She changed the color of the yarn before she nodded to the page to bring the knight in.

He walked into the room and knelt. "Madonna." Like them all now he wore his pale hair cropped close to his head. She turned back to her work.

"What happened?" She wove three rows of Aristotle's djellabah into the tapestry.

"Madonna, I did as you told me, I stayed out of Marna's way, but the Clerk came looking for me. I am to give this back to you." He took Anne's beryl ring out of his wallet.

The ring lay heavy in her palm. "That's not fortunate." She picked up the bobbin again. "Whom did you see there—only Stephen?"

"No—he took me to Marna."

"What did you tell him?"

"I didn't say anything. They found the ring in my purse." The knight shrugged one shoulder. "You know I am loyal to you, Madonna, but they never let me lie. They never asked me a question."

508

"What did he say?"

Michael looked uncomfortable. His eyes strayed away. "Madonna," he said, "I have forgotten."

"Oh. Then I can guess. Leave me."

Michael went out of the room. Maria turned the ring over in her hand. There were figures worked in the heavy gold around the beryl: probably some symbol of Fitz-Michael's had helped them recognize it. She remembered the look on Michael's face when she asked him what Richard had said, and she laughed.

"Jordan."

He came in, Roger-headed. She brushed off his velvet coat and kissed him. "Here." She put the ring in his hand. "Take this to my lady Anne. Tell her—"

"I don't like her," Jordan said. "I don't want to go there."

"Go anyway. God, you're getting spoiled, I'll spank you regularly henceforth. Tell Anne that I apologize and I seem to have made a mistake."

Jordan trotted sullenly off with the ring. Maria went to find Jilly and Henry. She missed Stephen. There was no one to talk to. In the corridor, passing Rahman, she gave him so hard a look that he laughed.

XLVIII

ALL DOWN THE RIDGE HIGHWAY FROM ISTE, RICHARD'S army was scattering home. The castle of Iste had fallen ten days before. Most of the men whom Maria passed were hauling sacks of plunder on their shoulders. One shouted rudely to her in Saracen. The three knights with her wheeled to chase him down the road.

Here the highway slithered along the spine of a sloping ridge; now and then, behind her, she could see between the brown flanks of the mountains to the plain of Mana'a and even the distant glitter where the sun struck the bay. Before her the road climbed into the heart of the mountains. She held her mare down to a walk, so that her escort could catch up with her.

Above her a pass notched the sheer blank face of the mountains. Riders and men on foot were swarming through it down toward her. The three knights took their places around her. They climbed up toward the pass. The air turned colder. In the shade, patches of snow lingered from the storm of the night before. A band of some dozen knights passed her. They yelled greetings back and forth to her men.

"Hey," one knight called. "Is that Dragon's wife? He is coming—he's just up beyond the pass, lady." He waved to her. With his friends he trotted away down the road, looking back over their shoulders at her.

Maria strained to see into the pass. She felt dizzy; she was fat with child and the height of the road unnerved her. In a few moments she would see Richard again. The mare broke into a canter. On her left the ground pitched off sheer down to the leafless trees below. All around her was only the blue sky. She leveled her eyes. The road snaked up the ridge into the pass. Groups of knights trotted by her.

A yoke of oxen lumbered down from the pass, pulling a flatbed cart. She had to rein her mare over to the side of the road to let it by. Her breath stopped in her throat. The cart rattled past her, almost within reach. Three men sat on it, back to back. They were half-naked in the cold, their bodies looped around with chains. The man facing her was Roger.

He saw her, he raised his head. She gave a low cry of pity. His face was discolored with bruises, one eye swollen shut, his hair matted with blood and dirt. Watching her, he broke into a smile, and he kissed at her. The cart ore him away. Anne's two brothers, gray with cold, lumped spiritless against him.

Maria gathered up her reins. The mare raced up into he pass. The road narrowed. The sun disappeared behind he shoulder of the mountain. Her mare fell to a trot. Three knights rode up over the crest of the pass. Just beind them was Richard.

He sat loose and graceless in his saddle, a white silk ljellabah open over his mail. Robert and Stephen flanked im, and a long double column of knights followed after im.

"Mother!" The two boys galloped past him and whirled around her. She did not take her eyes from her husband. She freed herself from the boys' embraces beore they could pull her apart. Richard's horse came up ead to tail with her mare.

"What are you doing up here?" A great yellowing bruise marked the side of his face. "You shouldn't ride when you are so great with child. You never listen to me. Rahman is right, I should put you in seclusion."

"You could try," she said. "I listen to you, didn't I keep Anne in Mana'a?" She reined her mare around to ride beside him. Their sons cantered up around them.

"Papa," Stephen said. "Tell her."

"Tell me what?" Her eyes flew up to Richard's face. His eyes were smoky with pain. He shifted in his saddle, easing his bad hip. "Tell me what?"

"Maria," he said. "Ismael is dead."

"Ismael!"

He turned to the boys. "Go do something."

They rode away. Richard started off again down the road, and Maria's horse followed of its own accord, shoulder to shoulder with him. Maria crossed herself. Ismael.

"What happened?"

"He took an arrow in the lung. He was all night dying. I held him all night."

Her throat lumped painfully. They rode down from the pass. In the distance the cart rolled along the mountain highway. She said, "O Ismael." She put her hand to her face.

511

When she turned toward Richard again, presently, he was watching her. She said, "Were you wounded? Stephen said that your leg bothers you."

"I fell. My horse fell."

"What happened to your face?"

"I just told you. My horse fell under me." He shifted his weight in his saddle, trying to find some way to sit that did not hurt. His voice rose in a whine. "Why did you plot with Anne? You'd have sent her back to Santerois where she'd have been like a knife aimed at me."

"What is she now?" She looked down at his hands, gashed and swollen, the knuckles split. "Did you fight with Roger?"

"I don't want to talk about it."

The baby rolled in her belly. She longed to lie down. Her eyes were raw and burning with tears. He twisted his body again, one hand on his hip. His head came around striking toward her. "Why didn't you come to Iste to see me? You go all over Mana'a, Stephen says, for all you're as big as a cow—why did you let those people burn half the Christian quarter?"

"Aren't you glad to see me, Richard?" She reached one hand out to him.

His horse veered toward her. He dragged her up off her mare and pulled her in front of him on his saddle. She closed her arms around his neck. His horse sidestepped nervously across the highway. His knights rode up all around them, laughing at them. There was a chorus of shrill lewd whistles. Richard's beard grazed her cheek. She turned her face into his shoulder and wept.

THE WHITE DRAGON streamed out above the Emir's Gate in the hard wind off the bay. Richard's men were riding their horses into a semicircle across the street. Maria reined her mare away from them. Behind her someone shouted an order. She trotted around the thick shifting press of horsemen. She wedged her mare up beside Stephen's horse; a knight made room for her. She looked past Stephen at Robert.

"Go to the palace and make sure everything is ready for us. I don't want any trouble when we come there."

512

Robert chewed on his fingers. He was thin; she had marked the night before that he hardly ate. "Go on," she said gently. "Stephen, you too."

Robert laid his rein against his horse's neck and circled away. Stephen sat motionless, his eyes on the cart in front of the gate. "I want to watch this."

Maria looked. Still wearing the fluttering white djellabah, Richard waited on his bay horse beside the cart, out before the crescent moon of knights. Every few seconds he glanced down at Roger an arm's length away from him. Anne's brothers huddled under the chains. Only Roger sat upright.

Two men walked toward them from the open gate. One swung a knotted cord in his hand. Maria wheeled toward Stephen.

"Do as I ask."

Robert's black horse was crabwalking toward the city. Stephen lowered his eyes. He turned and galloped around behind the knights, past Robert, and in through the gate. The people shouted and cheered him by name. Robert followed him.

Mana'ans fringed the top of the wall. They shrieked and waved handerchiefs. Richard pointed to one of Anne's brothers. The executioner and his boy went to the cart, opened a lock, and dragged the man off into the dirt. Beside the cart Richard was looking steadily at Roger. Anne's brother gave a single half-choked cry. The executioner lowered the body to the ground and stuffed the mouth with dust. They hung the dead man up by the feet against the arch over the gate, his face to the painted stone.

"Turn him around," Richard shouted. "Why should he see Mana'a?"

On the top of the gate, a man reached down with a staff to swing the body outward. Richard nodded to the other brother. He screamed and begged for life, but they strangled him in the same way and hung him up beside the first.

Roger stared straight ahead, his face serene, as if he did not care. Probably he did not. Maria crossed herself.

"God save him. He is the bravest man in Marna."

The knight beside her grunted in agreement. His eyes

513

on Richard, the executioner walked back toward the car
The garrotte dangled from his hand. Even the folk on th
wall were quiet. The executioner asked some question
Richard jerked his horse around.

"Take him up to the palace."

Breaking into talk, the knights rode up out of their for
mation, past Maria. She did not move. Suddenly sh
wished he had done it, that it was over. Lifting her rein
she started forward after the cart.

Richard loomed across her path. "Where are yo
going?" His horse shouldered into the mare, forcing i
aside. Blood stained the stallion's mouth. Its ears wer
flattened against its head. Richard was riding it into
frenzy. Maria backed away. He pressed the horse afte
her, its cupped nostrils red as blood. "I didn't tell you t
go."

The knights formed three columns before them, an
they rode under the gate into the city. Beggar childre
and vendors selling cakes and dukkah and sherbet race
agilely in among the knights. From the windows on eithe
side of the street, people cheered and waved their hands
Richard's horse tossed its head, trying to break his gri
on its mouth. Maria edged her mare away.

Up ahead, there was the sudden swelling yowl of
crowd. The front of the column was coming into a wid
square. Maria glanced at Richard. He was staring at hi
horse's withers.

"Al-Nasrani!" the crowd screamed. "Al-Nasrani!"

She lifted her reins and galloped up through the rank
of the knights, weaving the mare between them. A stallio
kicked at her. Behind her a man called, "Hold—hold—'
She broke through to the front of the column. The ox
cart rolled along before them all, naked to the howling
mob. Rocks showered it. She trotted her mare up into th
barrage.

Something struck her knee. The mare shied toward the
cart, snorting. The screams and the rocks stopped
abruptly. Maria pressed her heel to the bay mare's side
and swung her over, as close to Roger as she could ride.
The crowd drew back like a wave. Many of them even
dropped the stones in their hands.

Roger knelt in the loops of chains, his head bent to

514

protect his face. His shoulders were covered with bleeding cuts. Blood dribbled from his red hair. He straightened up, the chains in his hands.

"Sweetheart, you are spoiling the lesson. He won't like that."

Flies swarmed around him. The chains had rubbed his skin raw. The cart rolled from the crowded market place into an archway. The sound boomed in the narrow space. The drover called to his oxen.

"Where is my son?" Roger said.

"Here. And your wife. They're both well."

The cart turned a slow corner. Roger moved his cramped legs underneath him, until he was sitting under the chains, his arms across his knees.

"Maria," he said. "I would never have hurt you."

Astonished, she could not answer. She knew he meant it for an apology. Behind them in the market place, the crowd gave up a bellow, a trumpeting blast of voices.

"Rik! Rik! Rik!"

Roger jerked his head up. "Listen to them—they would cheer Judas if he won a battle—they would cheer a dog who gave them money—"

"If you want me here," she said, "say nothing against Richard."

He twisted toward her. "Go. I don't need you. I would rather they stone me to death than a woman shield me."

The street widened, and a mob surged toward them, all mouths and hands full of stones, fruit, and filth. A rock glanced off the cart. Maria raised her arm, and the knight directly behind her broke out of their rank and charged up past her and the cart. The mob ran away, shouting insults and obscenities at Roger.

"I have never lost before," he said. "Richard was always there to tell me what to do. I should have thought of that. Maria, my sister, promise me that I will have the Sacrament before I die."

"I swear." She crossed herself. They were moving up the street toward the palace. The gates stood open, showing the green quiet hillside beyond. The crowd thundered up another cheer for Richard. She made her mare stand still, so that the knights could pass her. Richard came up to her, and she joined him.

515

Together they went up the road through the park. All but a dozen of the knights swung off toward the towers on the wall. The cart disappeared. She did not mark where they took it. In the gatehouse, in a bright dress, Jilly was waiting, Henry beside her, and William just behind her.

Maria reined in on the pavement. The two children ran toward her, calling to her. Richard walked up to her stirrup. He lifted her down from her saddle. He held her a moment, between him and the horse.

"Thank you," he muttered. He could not look her in the eyes. Turning his back on her, he picked up Jilly in his arms and carried her in through the gate.

"Fox."

"Rocks."

Jilly gulped. "Locks! Locks."

Jordan said, "Ummm—" and the other children counted in a rush of numbers toward fifty. Maria, sitting beside the window in the light, was finishing her tapestry. She wove in the last of the cloud and broke the yarn in her fingers. Three strokes of lightning came from the cloud, to indicate Divine Wisdom. In the corner was the rayed sun she used as her device.

"Fifty," Jilly cried.

Jordan gave a pomegranate seed to each of the other children, even Henry, who was not playing. Henry's shirt was splattered with pomegranate juice. He headed for Rahman's chess table again, and the nurse patiently retrieved him.

"Lord," Jordan said; it was his favorite beginning.

"Board."

Something moved in the garden below the window. Maria lifted her head. Anne was walking out toward the park. Maria's hands with the yarn bobbin sank slowly into her lap. A man waited for Anne in the shelter of the wall. When he came forward, she saw that it was Robert.

She tore her eyes from her son. She picked a bit of fluff from the tapestry. The roller of the loom held the finished cloth up out of the way, exposing just the top of the tower

516

and Saint Augustine with his bishop's crook. Anne was supposed to be warded in her chamber. Only Robert could have gotten her released.

The door in the next room opened and shut. She heard Richard's uneven footsteps. She pulled the screen closed across the window. He came into the hall, talking over his shoulder to Rahman. The two men laughed. The children called to them. Richard answered, but Rahman as usual pretended not to see them. Maria thrust the yarn bobbins into her basket and went over to Richard, so that he would put his back to the window.

"Tell me what you are laughing at."

"Stay solemn." Richard patted her enormous belly. "You'll bounce him out."

Rahman was staring down his nose at her. Maria made an elaborate bow to him. "I'm sorry you do not sup with women, Master Grand Vizier, we would invite you to our Christmas feast."

"How is it a feast, if women be present?"

Richard laughed. "Depends on what you're eating." Henry rushed over to them, and his father stooped and lifted him up. Maria picked bits of pomegranate from the little boy's linen shirt front.

"This is a filthy child. He even gets dirty in bed."

"Mama," Henry said wisely. He pointed at her; he looked up at Richard. "My Mama."

"Is he going with us tonight?"

Maria shook her head. "Next year. He cries at church." At sundown the first Christmas Mass began.

"A sign of intelligence." Richard tickled the little boy into sobbing laughter. Maria glanced quickly out the unscreened window: Anne and Robert were gone.

"Where is Roger?" she asked.

Henry had hold of Richard by the beard. Maria went up beside him. He detached the little boy and put him down on the floor. "Rahman," he called. He gave her a piercing look.

Rahman came up before them. Richard said, "Show it to her." He folded his arms across his chest. Henry got to his feet.

517

The Saracen took a charter from his robes. Maria opened up the stiff greasy paper. There was Christian writing on it, but no seal.

"That's Roger's death warrant," Richard said. "When my chief men have put their seals on it, he'll die."

Maria folded the stiff wings of the paper and handed it back to Rahman. Henry said, "Mama." He held up a scrap of pomegranate meat he had picked from his shirt. Richard took the warrant. Stiffly he limped out of the room.

EVEN SO LATE in the year, the tower garden was bright with trumpet flowers. They had told her the Saracen name, but she could not pronounce it. She stood on the sloping lawn admiring the blossoms' gaping red mouths tongued in yellow. Behind her, one of the knights murmured, and Michael quickly silenced him.

"Madonna."

"I hear them."

Two people were coming up from the fir trees at the foot of the garden, hidden by the long swoop of the hedge. Anne's voice heralded them. Maria went down the green slope. Robert walked first around the corner, saw her, and stopped short. Anne, just behind him, nearly walked into him.

"Mother," Robert said. "Give me a chance to explain."

Maria went past him to Anne and slapped her as hard as she could swing her arm. Anne reeled. Maria's palm stung pleasantly.

"Michael."

The three knights came down to her and led Anne away. Robert stood staring at the ground. His ears were red as the trumpet flowers. Maria said, "Have you already forgotten Ismael?"

"She had nothing to do with Ismael. Mama—" he caught her hand. "It isn't right, what Papa is doing—it isn't fair, or Christian—no one even knows if Uncle Roger is still alive."

Maria freed her hand from his grip.

"It isn't right, Mother."

"Is that what she wanted—to know how Roger does? I don't believe it."

"Have you seen him? Where is Papa keeping him?"

"I don't know."

His thin face was bright as if some fever heated him. She touched his arm. "I won't tell him about this. Robert, please, don't let him know you've done this. Please."

"What are you going to do to Anne?"

"Now, you see?" She went up toward the palace, away from him. "How can I tell you anything any more?" She went between the banks of flowers to the door. Her Saracen maid was waiting on the step. Together they went into the palace.

MARIA HAD ASKED William to build a wooden stall into the sanctuary of the cathedral, opposite the pulpit, so that she and Richard could celebrate Mass without being stared at. She slid into the far side of the wooden seat, behind the carved screen. Jordan followed her with an armful of cushions. Leaning forward, she looked out across the cathedral, slowly filling up with people.

"Was this your idea?" Richard came in through the door from the vestibule. "Now I'll have to think of some other excuse not to come to Mass." He put his hand against her cheek.

"Isn't it beautiful?" Candles lit the altar as bright as afternoon. Angels and figures of saints covered the walls. The curve of the ceiling made them seem to bow toward the crucifix.

Richard sat down beside her. "It's a feast of fools." He shifted his weight on the hard wooden seat, and Jordan brought him a cushion. Richard settled himself, fussy as a broody hen. A tall monk went about the altar lighting the rest of the candles. Jordan climbed up on the seat to peep through the screen at the congregation.

"Bear it now," Richard said. He poked her belly. "I'll call him Jesus."

Maria pushed his hand away. "I know you don't blaspheme the Saracens' God." She pushed his hand away again. "Richard!"

519

"Why not—it's as good as a bed in here—no one would see us. Jordan, go away."

Jordan jumped down to the floor. Maria grabbed the tail of his coat. "God's love, Jordan. Stay here." She made the child sit down beside her, between her and Richard. Her stomach hurt. She had fasted all day, to make ready for the Body of Christ; the urge to eat was worse than an itch.

"I'm so hungry."

"Jordan." Richard shoved the little boy. "I'll give you a ricardus to leave us alone and stand watch outside."

The door from the vestibule opened into the stall. Robert came through it. His coat was black; Maria had embroidered blue flowers all over the sleeves. "Papa," he said, "I have something to ask you."

"What?"

"I want to see Uncle Roger."

Maria put her arm around Jordan's shoulders. The little boy leaned against her. Richard frowned up at his son.

"No."

"Papa, I fought for you. Doesn't that?—"

Richard said, "Do you think I'm a merchant—you pay me with one thing and get something else? What do you take me for?"

Robert glanced at Maria. Her heart was beating fast. She nodded her head at the door. "Leave us alone," she said.

The young man went out the door, and she shut it. "Jordan, go sit over there."

The page moved across the stall to the other bench. He watched them curiously. Richard looked down at his hands. The altar bells rang. Maria leaned forward and opened the screen halfway. In the front of the church, on the right, her household stood behind a row of standards. Stephen and Jilly among them. Stephen smiled at her. From the rear of the cathedral came the chant of the monks. A procession of candles came up through the darkness and the masses of folk gathered to celebrate the first Christmas Mass.

The monks sang their ancient prayers. The odor of incense peppered the air. The procession paced slowly toward her, the monks by twos, each with his tall white candle. The deliberate cadences soothed her. Her heart seemed to slow down to its quiet beat.

"What was that about?" Richard said. "That just now, with Robert."

"Anne. I've sent her to the Black Tower—Welf will be proof against her. Look at William."

Led by a monk with his gonfalon, William marched in the middle of the procession, his hands clasped before him. Even in the new pallium and his tonsure, he looked more like a Norman knight than an Archbishop. The monks circled the nave once and lined up facing the altar, and the Mass began.

William read from Saint Matthew's Gospel. Maria beckoned to Jordan, and when he came to her put her arm around him. "Here comes the trope. Watch." She glanced at Richard.

The choir sang an Alleluia. Three monks with shepherds' crooks paced across the apron of the altar, singing with their brothers. They had contrived it so that they turned their backs neither on Richard nor the congregation. Their faces shone with excitement. Striking the last note of the chant, the choir held it effortlessly, clear as a bell tone.

Suddenly, above the far side of the altar, a monk with a candle appeared from behind a drapery. He seemed posed in mid-air against the black curtain. The candle shone around his head and shoulders like a globe of hazy light. The congregation gasped, delighted.

"Aunt," Jordan cried. "Look!"

Maria sighed. She could just make out the scaffolding the angel stood on, draped in black velvet. The angel sang a question in Latin.

"What is he saying?" Jordan whispered.

"Whom are you searching for? he asks them."

The three shepherds chanted in answer, their strong voices jubilant. Maria lost track of the Latin. Jordan rose. His face was rapt.

The angel sang that Christ was born. The choir burst into the Gloria. Quietly, the angel blew out his candle and backed out of sight again behind the drape. The shepherds laid down their staffs to one side of the pulpit.

521

Many people among the congregation were singing a[s] well. Maria crossed herself. It had gone perfectly. Willia[m] was smiling in the pulpit. She glanced at Richard.

His face was hagridden. He sat hunched over, his eye[s] on the floor. Maria put her hand on Jordan's arm.

"Go wait outside."

"But—Aunt—"

"It's over, you will miss nothing."

The child left. Richard turned his face away from he[r.] He said, "You might as well pick up a knife and slas[h] yourself as love somebody."

Maria said nothing. She touched his arm, and he too[k] hold of her hand. He turned toward her, his eyes glisten[-] ing bright.

"What have I given you, ever? A ring, when we mar[-] ried, and another ring later—"

"Two horses and a looking glass. You don't shower m[e] with presents."

He held her hand tight. "I'm giving you something. [I] am giving you Roger. You can do what you want wit[h] him."

Maria started. She pulled her hand out of his grip[.] Through the rest of the Mass, she sat silent, Richard un[-] moving beside her. William raised the Host to be adored[.] The choir rang buoyantly of the Christ. Kneeling on th[e] steps before the altar, the monks one by one receive[d] Him.

The congregation marched up toward the altar, many singing with the choir. Stephen and Robert stood first i[n] the line, their palms together in an attitude of prayer. William signed to Maria to come forward to take the Sac[-] rament. She shook her head at him.

"I thought you were hungry," Richard said.

Maria did not answer him. He pushed her. "Let's go."

They went out to the vestibule. Jordan was waiting b[y] the door and dashed off for Maria's cloak and the basket with the boats. Stephen and Jilly raced in the far door.

"Mama, did you bring the candles?"

Jilly pulled on her dress. "Merry Christmas, Mama." She turned up her bright face to be kissed.

Stephen got the basket from Jordan and took out the boats. He had made them himself, broad-beamed to

522

withstand the waves. Jilly was dancing around Richard, trying to lure him into a game. Robert came into the vestibule and Richard turned abruptly away.

"There's one for each of us," Stephen said. "Even Bonaventura there." He nodded at Maria's belly.

Maria got the candles from the basket. Jilly and Robert crowded around Stephen, who explained how to fasten the butts of the candles to the flat boats.

"Only children do things like this," Robert said, but Maria marked that he took a boat and a candle. She went with Richard through the garden to the gate. Jordan ran ahead of them into the street.

Along the street beside the harbor, in the darkness, a thick skein of people moved. Some of them carried lit candles. The others swarmed around to light their own. The beads of fire spread from hand to hand, along the wharves, past the rows of anchored ships. Already many of the lights bobbed in the harbor, floating out across the dark water.

A groom led up their horses. Richard took hold of her to put her on her mare. She said, "I want to see him."

"He's in the treasurehouse."

She mounted her horse and gathered her reins. The cathedral bells began to ring. She turned toward the harbor. Across the broad sweep of the bay, a thousand bobbing candles floated, sailing out into the black water, until like stars they were drowned in the night.

XLIX

SHE OPENED THE PADLOCK AND STEPPED INTO THE ROOM. Roger stood in front of the window, his back to her, and his arms folded on the sill. An iron grate covered the window. The room was tiny, the only furniture a bed and a three-legged stool. Maria pushed the door shut. He ignored her.

"Roger."

He wheeled around. "Maria. I thought you were the man with my dinner. What are you doing here?"

"I came to see how you are."

She looked around the room again. He stood smiling before her, his hand on his hip. Her hands trembled. She sat down on the little stool. He went to the bed, sat, and picked up a ewer from the floor to pour wine into a cup.

"Here. You don't look well. I'm sorry, I have only the one cup."

Maria sipped the strong red wine. "Thank you." The bruises on his face had faded. He was freshly shaven, and his hair trimmed, although he still wore it slightly longer than the fashion. She could not settle herself. It amazed her to see him so calm while she trembled head to foot. She handed the cup back to him.

"How are you?" he said. "Other than—" he nodded at her belly. "What is this, the fifth?"

"The sixth."

He drank from the cup, filled it again, and passed it back to her. "I won't ask about the well-being of my blood kin." He sprawled across the bed, leaning on his elbow.

"Roger," she said. "Why did you do it?"

"Oh." His eyes slipped away from hers. His voice was thin. "I suppose there was nobody else worth fighting. You know me, sweet, I cannot bear to be next. Especially not to Richard."

He got up onto his feet. "Is that what he sent you here for? I would do it again. Tell him that. I would do it again this afternoon. But this time I'd take him, he couldn't hide behind a baby." He put his back to her and stared out the window. "You know what Richard is."

"Yes," Maria said.

"He was afraid to fight me man against man. He knew I would win."

"Yes." She grew calm, her hands steadying, and her voice smooth in her throat.

He stared out the window, his head turned to watch

omething in the park. She went up beside him to see
hat he was looking at. He made space for her. Half a
ile away, almost in the trees, Jilly and Jordan rode
areback on a pony. The boy's red head moved like a
eacon across the lawn.

"That's my son, isn't it?" Roger said.

"Yes." She put her back to the wall, her eyes on him.
He looks like you, very much." In the shape of Jordan's
ace, his nose, his expressive mouth. She said, "I used to
ink you were the handsomest thing in the world."

"Not any more?"

"No." She laughed. "No, I think it's Robert."

He put his hands on her. She backed away from him,
own the wall, and faced him, angry. He swung back to-
ard the window. The sunlight shone through the grate in
quares on his face.

"Go tell Richard to get it done."

She opened the door, reluctant to leave him alone in
he tiny barren room. At last she went out. She locked the
oor and holding onto the hand rail climbed slowly down
e narrow stone steps. The door at the foot of the stairs
was locked, and she rapped on it.

"Mama." Stephen opened the door for her. "I was get-
ng worried." He glanced keenly up the stairway. "You
hould have let me go with you."

The knight on guard outside the door fastened the lock.
tephen took the lamp. Maria followed him across the
toreroom and the antechamber, out of the treasurehouse.
hey walked along the path back toward the palace.

"Is he sorry, Mama?" Stephen strode up alongside her.
Papa isn't going to forgive him, is he?"

"Let me alone."

He wrapped his hand around her arm and jerked her to
stop. "Why are you angry with me?"

Maria pulled away from him. "I have something to do.
lease leave me alone." She went to the wooden postern
oor in the wall and let herself into the palace.

There was no one in the room of the star ceiling. From
he big chest at the foot of the bed, she took Roger's
eath warrant. While the wax melted, she found the R in
Richard's name and turned the charter right side up.
Richard had already forgiven him. Richard would forgive

him a dozen times, until finally Roger overturned Marr[
She spread the charter on top of the chest and used h[
Saracen ring to seal it. The charter she folded and put [
her sleeve, to give to Rahman. The ring she threw into t[
fire.

ALTHOUGH THE SHOPS and stalls were closed, as if for [
holy day, the cathedral market was packed with peop[
Mounted men kept the center of the square cleared. T[
wooden block stood on the paving stones. Under t[
draped scaffolding that covered the façade of the cath[
dral, Maria sat beside Richard, her children on the st[
below her. William was on her left. The new baby, n[
well, had stayed at home, with its nurse. She still had n[
agreed with Richard about its name. The bright sun w[
making her head throb. Directly before her, Robert to[
Henry on his knee. Jilly and Stephen sat on either side [
him. Maria fought down the impulse to touch Rober[
hair.

Three brass horns sounded. Through the crowd a mu[
mur of anticipation ran. They crushed forward to watch.

On foot, in a black coat, Roger came into the squar[
The sun turned his hair bright as copper. Many women [
the crowd called out softly. On the step at Richard's fe[
Jilly suddenly twisted to look up at him. Stephen reach[
behind Robert's back for her hand.

Roger stopped before the block. He faced Richar[
The three knights ranged themselves behind him. Ric[
ard's dark beard masked his face. His pale eyes did n[
blink. The two brothers stared at each other. Roger w[
utterly composed.

The priest and the executioner came out of the crow[
Roger knelt down. The priest anointed his forehead an[
his heart with oil, blessed him, and gave him a crucifix [
hold. When the priest stepped back, the executioner sa[
something, and Roger nodded, indifferent, half-turne[
away, and wheeled back and spoke.

"My lord," the executioner called. "He asks that h[
hands not be tied."

Richard nodded. The crowd sighed with a sensuou[

pleasure. The long, honed sword rang out of its sheath. Roger knelt down before the block, his hands on it. The strong wind off the bay caught his hair and tumbled the black ribbons on the lances of the knights. He laid his head down on the block, his cheek to the smooth wood, and the executioner stepped forward, raised the sword in both hands, and struck his head off.

The crowd shrieked. Richard was on his feet. Jilly wailed in terror. The executioner cried out, "God is just." Maria pulled her eyes away from the dripping head in his hands.

A wagon rolled up through the crowd to take the body. Jilly was screaming, her eyes white with horror, and Maria stopped to pick her up in her arms. Richard raked his hand across his face. Robert stood before her, his cheeks slimed with tears. He plunged down past Maria into the crowd and ran away. Henry still sat motionless on the step, his mouth open.

"Here," William said. He took Jilly from her. "Stephen—" He and Stephen collected the children and led them away. Richard was staring into the crowd before them. He had not moved except to stand. Maria went up beside him.

The crowd was packed like a feeding animal around the wooden block, struggling to dip their handkerchiefs in Roger's blood.

L

MARIA NAMED THE NEW BABY MABILLE. SHE LIVED ONLY a few days. They buried her under the altar in the cathedral, next to Roger. Robert did not come to witness it.

Maria felt it deep that he refused, although she said nothing to Richard about it. Later she heard them arguing. She went down the corridor in the direction of their voices.

"You're breaking your mother's heart," Richard shouted, beyond the closed door.

"Papa, leave me alone!"

She pushed open the door and went in. The room—Robert's room—was bare and monkish. The two men swiveled, their strained faces toward her. They glanced at her just long enough to see who she was and snapped at each other again.

"You could have come down there—"

"Papa, what good is it? What use is it?"

"If you don't know that—" Richard charged out of the room. The door crashed shut and rebounded open. Maria swallowed. Her hands were trembling. Robert turned away from her. He mumbled something at the far wall.

"I didn't hear you." Maria went up beside him.

"I'm sorry," he said, belligerently loud.

"Why?" She sat down on his bed, her eyes traveling the plain, neat room. All along one wall his weapons hung.

"He said I'm . . . something about breaking your heart. Something like that." He sat down beside her.

"Not my heart, Robert."

"Mama, why can't he ever admit when he's wrong? He likes being wicked." He thrust his hands out in front of him, palms up, the fingers like blades. "He's just a bad man."

Maria grunted. She saw how much he was like Roger. Everybody loved him and gave him whatever he wanted: he had no will of his own. She touched him, and he turned into her arms like a child and hugged her.

"I'm sorry, Mama."

"I know." She rubbed her cheek against his hair. He smelled pleasantly of horses and sweat. "Why don't you go to Iste? There's work there to be done."

"I've been thinking of taking the Cross."

She stiffened. One arm around his neck, she held him against her, but she made herself move away from him, her hands falling to her lap. "Well, in the meantime, go to Iste." Anywhere away from Richard. For some time there had been talk of a new Crusade to free Jerusalem. Perhaps it would never happen. She kissed him and went off through the palace.

SHE AND RICHARD hunted over the dry sand hills east of Mana'a. The winter had driven the deer down from the mountains into the steep cedar-choked gulleys along the coast. The sky was a brilliant blue, and the wind off the sea stung with salt. Maria rode hard, choosing the hard trails, and in the close terrain lost the dogs and Richard. She drew rein under a tall fir tree to let her mare rest. The dogs sounded far off. A dry barren valley stretched away from her, studded with thickets of aloes. Her mare lifted its head and neighed.

Maria rode down the slope in the direction of the dogs' distant barking. The air smelled acridly of dust. The quiet and the solitude lightened her spirit. Riding along a sandy slope, she came on a deep pit in the ground.

It was tremendous, hundreds of feet across. The gray-brown slopes ran down evenly to a pool of scummy water in the bottom. Nothing grew anywhere around it. The dogs were bugling in the distance. Maria tried to put her mare down the slope of the pit, but the horse refused. She dismounted. The ground crunched under her feet. Stooping, she picked up a bit of pumice stone, light as froth. The pit bewildered her: it was so evenly circular she suspected someone had dug it, but it had no obvious use. She went down the slope. The sunlight lay deep into the far side, but where she was the shadow was cold and dark. Her feet sank into the crumbling soil.

Nearby, there was a piercing whistle. Her mare neighed again, a ringing call. Above her, all around the edge of the pit, deerhounds appeared against the sky, and Richard rode up.

"What are you doing down there?"

She scrambled up to the rim, kicking the dirt in a cascade down the slope behind her. Richard dismounted and pulled her up by the hand onto the solid edge of the pit.

"What is this?"

"I don't know," he said. "There are two more up there." He gestured to the north. "The Saracens call them the Devil's pots."

She threw a stone into the pit; it fell halfway down the slope. "Why?"

"The water is poison."

"It's like a dead place," she said. "Did someone make it? The Saracens?"

He shrugged. He picked up another pumice stone and turned it over in his hand. Gray dust coated his palm. "They don't know." He threw the stone down. "It took me a while to see that in spite of all they have they don't know any more than I do."

That made her laugh, and she put her hand on his chest. "Nobody knows as much as you do, Richard." She leaned on him, to make him put his arm around her.

In the distance a horn called. He swung around and took his horn from his saddle. Maria picked up her mare's trailing reins. She looked into the pit. It was like a grave, like a dead world. At the blast of Richard's horn her mare leaped and shied across the sandy ground and the dogs all threw back their heads and howled.

They rode side by side toward the sound of the horn, in the direction of the sea. Birds hopped and crashed in the bush around them. The dogs ranged through the cedar wood.

"What happened to the deer you were running?" she asked.

Richard shrugged one shoulder. "In this country we'll be all day before we kill." He raised the horn and sounded again.

They rode out onto a broad open meadow, through brown grass rumpled in the sea wind. Stephen galloped toward them and drew rein.

"Father Yvet is coming, he will reach Mana'a by sundown."

Maria lifted her head. She saw a coincidence with Roger's death. Richard said, "I guess even a priest can move fast to get something he wants."

"Will you come to meet him?" Stephen asked.

The wind off the sea streamed in Maria's face. She was

530

loath to go back to Mana'a. Richard lifted his reins. "We haven't made a kill yet. You don't want to see him, do you?" he asked her.

She shook her head.

He turned back to Stephen. "You meet him. Put him up, feed him, see that he's comfortable. Make sure he doesn't go anywhere."

Stephen's head rose in alarm. "Mama—"

"Do as I say," Richard said curtly. "Maria, come." He galloped up over the hillside, trailing dogs. Maria followed him.

When they reined in, Stephen was riding away toward the distant glitter of the sea. She turned to face her husband.

"The Pope waited until Roger was dead."

"It looks like that, doesn't it?"

It was un-Christian; it made her angry. She nudged her mare forward. They were making use of what she had done to Roger. The dogs raced off ahead of them down the slope. They rode on. In the late afternoon they ran down a stag, and Richard gave it to the pack to eat. They went back to Mana'a along the beach. The swollen sun disappeared into the mist along the sea. The surf curled white against the beach in the dark.

"How do you think Stephen does with Father Yvet?"

Maria let her rein lie slack of the mare's neck. "I'm sure he's putting him up, feeding him, and making him comfortable." With a minimum of civility. The last thin edges of the sea rolled up the sand toward her mare's hoofs. She said, "What are you asking them for, Richard?"

"I'm not asking them for anything," he said. "I'm making a bargain. I'm getting what I deserve. They want soldiers, to free them from the Emperor. I want to be King of Marna."

She looked up ahead. At the end of the curve of the beach, Mana'a's lights sparkled on the plain. Overhead the stars were coming out. She drew the ripe sea wind into her lungs. She thought of the sand pit again, like a grave, like a dead world.

She stared up at him, thinking of Roger. She would

531

never free herself of Roger's death; the only thing left to do was to justify it. She said, "If you're to be the King I want to be Queen."

He shrugged, his eyes elsewhere. "Whatever you want. You can have your own coronation, two or three months after—"

"No. I want to rule equal with you. I want to be crowned together with you."

He laughed at her. She fought down her temper. There was no use in arguing with him. He would never give up of his own will.

He said, "Forget that idea. The Saracens would never accept it."

"I'm not arguing with you." She glanced at him, surprised. "If it weren't for me, the Christians would never accept you."

"Lord Jesus! You want too much."

She said nothing. They went inland three hundred yards to the road and entered the city by the Tower Gate. The streets were nearly empty. Twice on their way up to the palace the watch hailed them. Neither of them spoke all the way home. At the door into the stable, beneath the only torch, he lifted her down out of her saddle.

"You're my wife."

"That has nothing to do with it."

"It has everything to do with it." His hands on her arms, he gave her a hard shake. "Don't act stupid, Maria." He stepped back. The groom was coming to take their horses. Maria turned and went up to the palace.

FATHER YVET had brought a train of attendants with him, among them Brother Nicholas, who had come to talk about the monastery he was building in the valley of Iste. Maria went down into the rose garden, the big monk to leeward of her, and the Saracen woman coming after her with the shears and sacks. The monk sat down on the sloping grass. He cupped his paint-splattered hands on his knees. Maria glanced at him and saw him frowning.

"Have you spoken to the Pope's man?" she asked.

The monk shook his head. He scratched in his armpit, his face grooved. She turned to clipping off the blooms of

532

the winter roses. The Saracen woman went along behind her collecting them in the sack.

"What is it?" she said to Brother Nicholas. "Father Yvet?"

"Not just Father Yvet. The Holy See. They ought not to involve themselves in the world at all, but to go in harness with Dragon—they're had. They can't know what they're doing."

"I thought you liked my husband." She glanced at the Saracen woman, whom she knew spied for Richard. "Go, Lalla." The woman left.

"I know his methods," Brother Nicholas said. He threw his hands up in the air. "Besides, mark what they are doing, recognizing him—he has no claim to Marna but naked force. He wasn't even born here."

"I was."

"They are not crowning you King."

"They can have me crowned Queen."

The monk's broad, handsome face rotated toward her. She sat down beside him on the grass and took his hand, callused like Richard's. "You said yourself the Curia is walking the edge, when they deal with Richard."

"You are talking to the wrong man," he said stiffly. He tried to free his hand, but she held onto him. He looked across the garden. "You should be talking to Father Yvet."

"No," she said. Down the garden, elegantly gowned, Father Yvet was coming toward them. She looked at Brother Nicholas. "Will you help me?"

The marks of strain had left his face. He said, "Can you manage Dragon?"

"Can anyone else? Will you help me?"

"You know I'll do whatever I can for you."

Smiling, she rose to greet Father Yvet.

●   ●   ●

LENT HAD BEGUN. Rain drizzled down on Mana'a. She went to the cathedral, to see William. All the statues were covered in mourning cloth. She and the fat knight stood in the doorway looking out at the garden, gray in the steady rain.

"I wish I were in Birnia," he said. "I hate this place."

"What a remark." She put one hand on the chilly stone of the door frame. "Wait until the rain stops."

A monk came quietly into the vestibule behind them, a load of wood in a sling over his shoulder. Maria said, "William, I want to be Queen of Marna."

"So I'm told." William stared out into the garden. His head moved slightly from side to side. "I don't think he'll give it to you."

"I think he will."

"Maria, God's eyes, don't run against him now, over this." He swung toward her, massive in his bishop's robes, his cheeks pierced with short needles of beard. "He knows you are plotting something. He's just waiting for you to step once in the wrong place."

She leaned against the wall. Her gaze moved toward the monk building the fire in the vestibule hearth. Flames crackled under his hands.

"What are you plotting?" William said.

"Why should I tell you, so you can tell him?" She looked up at him, her hands behind her against the cold wall. She smiled at him. "There's no plot, William. Father Yvet owes me a favor, but you know he won't stand against Richard. I'm not plotting anything. Richard will do it all."

William grunted. He rubbed his nose vigorously with his finger. "There's more in this than I'm seeing. Tell me nothing else, Maria—I don't want any part in it."

"William," she said, "you are lazy."

He shook his head. "Just a coward." He laughed, his red gown shaking, and went off through the door. Two days later he left for Birnia.

RICHARD BENT OVER the enameled basin; with his cupped hands he scooped up water to wash his face. Maria shut the bedroom door. She crossed the room toward him and gave him a towel.

"Father Yvet brought me your message," he said.

Her stomach tightened; she sat down on the bed. He scrubbed his face with the towel. Maria groped her bare foot over the carpet, hunting for her shoes.

"Didn't I tell you to forget that?" He tramped away, pulling his clothes off. His belt went in one direction and his shirt in the other. "You have no sense of proportion at all, do you?—This is the most important thing I have ever tried and you'd wreck it for a whim."

She nudged her feet into her shoes and stood up.

"Do as you please, Richard."

He wheeled toward her. "Where are you going?" When she started toward the door he got in her way.

"To Castelmaria," she said. "Please move."

"Stop biting at me."

"I am not biting," she cried.

"What do you call it?" He took her by the arm. "Gentle feminine discourse? Be easy and let me talk to you."

"You've had days and days to talk to me, Richard. All I want to hear is the one thing you will not say."

His hand clenched on her arm. "You're not going anywhere."

"I'm going to Castelmaria if I have to climb over the wall and walk. Then see if you can do all this without me."

They stared at each other through a long silence. She braced herself on her wobbling legs and took a step toward the door, and he caught her by both arms and shook her.

"Maria—damn you, why do I have to bully you into everything?" He hugged her so tight she clenched her teeth. "Don't you trust me—haven't you any faith at all in me?"

She softened. Her arms went around his neck. She could fight with him in the morning. He kissed her. She put her hands on his shoulders and pushed herself away from him.

"Yes, I trust you. I trust you to do anything to get what you want."

He knocked her down. She fell on her side; he went off across the room, swearing at her in Saracen. Maria's head buzzed, and she sat up slowly.

"Go on," he said. "Get out, leave, if that's what you want."

She went out the door. In the antechamber, she woke up Jordan and sent him for her knight Michael. She hurried down through the dark palace. On the stairs, she heard Richard behind her calling for Stephen. She le herself out the door in the Dragon Tower and walke through the rose garden toward the stable.

It was a warm night, and the stable windows wer open. By the light that spilled into the barn she found he mare's bridle and went to take the horse out of her stall While she was bridling the mare, the stable door opene and several men with torches came in, dazzling her.

"Mama," Stephen said. "Come with me."

She put her hand on the mare's thick mane. "Where? Her heart began to beat fast.

He came up to the stall door and opened it. Mari went out past him. She hoped Michael would have th sense to stay clear. A groom came in, sleepy, his hea covered with a white cloth, and the knight with the torc sent him away.

Stephen took hold of her arm. Maria shook him vio lently off. She gave him a hard look, and he lowered hi eyes. They bustled her out of the stable and around th side of the palace, between the wall and the Tower of th Prophet.

Richard was waiting on the gravel walk to the trea surehouse. He said, "You can come out when you'r ready to accommmodate me."

Maria was too angry to talk. She walked away from hir toward the treasurehouse. Off to one side, she saw Mi chael, shy in the dark. Stephen caught up with her. H took her up to the little room in the top of the treasure house. Maria went over at once to the window. Stephe stood behind her in the doorway, solemn.

"Mother, I have to do this."

"Then do it, Stephen. I don't want the commentary."

He went out. She heard the lock snap shut on the othe side of the door. The cool night wind through the windov bathed her face. The side of her head began to ach where Richard had hit her. The room was bleak. The be was narrow as a trench. In the corner the three-legge stool lay on its side. She had meant to be farther away, i the mountains, at least, in the daylight, before he seize her. She had meant to make a great matter of it. Now sh would simply have disappeared. She had done it wrong

536

et it happen late at night, no one watching, no one nowing, a secret thing, Richard's competence. On the King's Road pay the King's toll. She sat down on the bed. Michael had seen. Perhaps it would still work. She would hink about it in the morning. She went to bed and slept.

N THE MORNING the room was already closing in around her. Sunlight poured in the window, striped by the gridled shadow of the bars. A knight brought her breakfast. She spent most of the day by the window, hoping to catch ome glimpse of her children.

Robert was in Iste, and without someone to tell him what to do, he probably would do nothing. William in Birnia would stay out of the issue. Stephen was Richard's, and Father Yvet would go with whoever seemed to be winning, probably Richard. Brother Nicholas and her other friends seemed of minor consequence now. She had underestimated Richard. She leaned on the sill of the window, her forehead against the iron grate. Below, the green park stretched, rimmed with trees. She could not see the palace at all. She could apologize to him, he would let her out, and she could try again. The thought made her laugh.

In the afternoon the tall knight who had brought her meals carried up a chest of clothes for her. Her basket of mending was thrown in on top of everything else. Woman's skills. The knight did not look her in the face and said nothing to her and she did not try to talk to him. He shut the door after him, and the lock clicked.

She paced around the room. On the wall near the head of the bed, there were thirty-eight short, deep scratches in the wall. She sat down and ran her fingertip over them. She wondered if Roger had made them, counting off the days. She lay down on her bed, her head in her arms, already bored. The afternoon crept along, dragging its shadow up the far wall.

A short knight brought her dinner; he came in without knocking first, and when he left she pulled the latch string inside the door, so that no one could get in without her will. She had no appetite for the meal he had brought her.

She sat picking over it. The light faded out of the room. She had no lamp; she went to bed, but she could no sleep. A night bird sang just outside the window. The jar ring uninflected ringing notes put her nerves on end. Fi nally, just before dawn, she dozed.

The knight woke her up, knocking on the door, but sh ignored it. She lay staring at the scratches on the wall. Thirty-eight days. This was her second day in the trea surehouse, and the twenty-third day of Lent. She woul not miss Easter Mass; either she or Richard would giv up by then.

She kept the latchstring tied inside the door. Whe noon came and the knock on her door signaled her lunc she ignored it again. She stood at the window, her arm folded on the sill. Deer grazed at the far end of the park She longed for sight of her children, but sundown cam without them. Morose, she let in the knight with her din ner.

That night she could not sleep again. She thought ove and over of the baby who had died: its feeble mewlin cry of hunger, while it vomited up everything it was fec Once, deep in the night, she wept. The next morning sh felt worse than ever before in her life. When the knigh came in with her tray of breakfast she nearly sent him t Richard.

She could not eat. She sat on the bed and faced th scratches on the wall. Throughout the day she longed fo death. She knew why Roger had gone so calmly out t die: the room was cursed.

In the evening, after she had forgotten to pull in th latchstring and they had brought her a supper she did nc want, she began to pass blood. She felt bloated and ex hausted, although she had done nothing for days. She fe the blood sign like a message: she should submit, she wa a woman. She lay down on the bed and put her face int the pillow and cried until she fell asleep.

Morning came. She felt no better. She dragged herse into her clothes and stared out the window. When the knocked with her breakfast she did not let them in. Th fallow deer grazed across the park. The little stag, darke than his does, strutted around wagging his tail. She misse

538

Richard. She wanted Richard. He was the only person who really knew what she was like; if her other friends had known all she had done, they would have hated her. She still had a ewer of wine left from the dinner they had given her the night before. She sat down and drank it, unwatered, until she was spinning drunk, and went to sleep. When she woke up sick to her stomach, deep night had come and she had missed her supper.

She went to the window. Moonlight painted the grass and the wind-curried trees. She put her cheek against the cold stone. In the sky, the tiny cold fires of the stars burned: homes of angels. She could die here. He could keep her here for the rest of her life. For her children's sake, she should surrender. She would, if Easter came. If she could not force him to come to her, she deserved no crown. That made her feel better, to think there was justice in it. She changed the blood-soaked rags between her legs and got back into bed.

The next day she took out her sewing basket and began to mend her clothes. Often she went to the window to watch the deer and the sky and to look for her children. There was no sign at all of the children and she realized Richard was keeping them away from her. At sundown the knight knocked, and she let him in.

He put the food he carried down on the stool, as he usually did, and knelt to put the dishes of the previous meal back on their tray. Maria sat down on the bed. His back to her, he said, "Are you warm enough at night?"

"Yes. I'd like a lamp."

"I'll have to ask," he said. He picked up the tray and left. She sat there savoring her first conversation in days. They did not bring her a lamp.

She began to lose her sense of time. When she had mended all of her clothes, she began to embroider them. At first she made flowers and birds but they bored her and she made up fantastic animals, dragons and basilisks, things with claws and wings and triple heads. When she ran out of thread she took apart the birds and flowers. She made up stories while she worked, about the beasts she stitched, the worlds they lived in, their remarkable qualities, and the heroes who fought them. Usually the beasts won. In the worlds where they lived there was no God.

SHE WOKE UP in the dark. Someone was beating on the door. She sat up, pulling the blanket around her.

"Yes?"

"Maria," Richard said, "let me in."

She got up. She was naked, and she wrapped the blanket around her. The full moon glared in through the window and cast the shadow of the iron grid across the door. She opened the latch, and the door swung in.

"Put on your clothes. We're going," Richard said. He stood in the bright barred light.

She sat down on the foot of her bed. "You know what I want."

He came into the darkness of the room, leaving the door half-open behind him. He went to the window, looked out, and turned around, his head and shoulders against the light. She watched him, wary, wishing she could see his face.

He said, querulous, "What's wrong with this place? That stinking monk has everybody convinced you're cooped into a barrel."

"I don't mind. It's very peaceful. How long have I been here?"

"Seventeen days."

She knew he was watching her. With the window behind him he was only a black shape to her. But he was here. Amazed, she realized that meant he was surrendering. She said, "When is Easter?"

"Tomorrow. If you and I don't go to Mass together—"

He broke off. She said, "What?"

"I don't know. I'm not ready to find out. Father Yve wants the Pope to crown me. I want to put my ow crown on my own head. You talk to him. Arrange tha and I'll crown you with me."

She drew a deep breath. "Yes." She could do it; she al ready knew what argument to use. "I will."

"Why are you doing this?"

She said, "If you could rule without me, you wouldn be here."

"Put on your clothes."

In the dark she pulled on a shift and a gown and groped around the floor for her shoes. They went down the steep steps and across the treasure room, and he knocked on the door. Torches burned around the treasure room. The chests and boxes were covered with dust and smeared with handprints. They went on into the ante-chamber. Three knights stood there, their faces yellowed in the lamplight. Richard went straight out the door.

Maria stopped on the threshold. Off across the half mile of grass lay the back wall of the palace and the round of the Dragon Tower. Richard was already halfway down the path. One of the knights behind her said loudly, "If she were mine, she'd never get out."

She turned around. The three men shuffled and looked away. "Roussel," she said to the tall knight. "Bring my chest back to the palace."

"Yes, Madonna."

She went out the door onto the sodden grass. The moon was sinking. Along the eastern edge of the sky, dawn light whitened. She admired him for having waited as long as he could: the Mass began at sunrise. She would hardly have time enough to change her clothes.

THE BEST OF BESTSELLERS
FROM WARNER BOOKS!

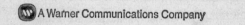